OUR
FATHERS'
WAR

Other books by JAMES BACQUE

FICTION

The Lonely Ones (paperback *Big Lonely)*

A Man of Talent

The Queen Comes to Minnicog

HISTORY

Other Losses

Crimes and Mercies

ESSAYS/ANTHOLOGIES

Creation (with Robert Kroetsch and Pierre Gravel)

Dear Enemy (with Richard Matthias Müller)

BIOGRAPHY

Just Raoul

Our FATHERS' WAR

A Novel

JAMES BACQUE

Toronto

Exile Editions
2006

First published in Canada in 2006 by
Exile Editions Ltd.
20 Dale Avenue
Toronto, Ontario, M4W 1K4
telephone: 416 485 9468
www.ExileEditions.com

The imaginary characters of this novel live among historical events, like
birds in the forest; the historical personages speak for themselves, mainly
in their own words. Here and there I have conflated minor events to suit
the narrative, as for instance in Lord Beaverbrook's mission to Moscow or
the Canadian army's attacks on the Scheldt estuary in 1944. I borrowed
part of the story of the actual bomb attack on Hitler in 1944 by Claus von
Stauffenberg, attributing this to the fictional Klaus von Zollerndorf.

Library and Archives Canada Cataloguing in Publication

Bacque, James, 1929-

   Our fathers' war : a novel / James Bacque.

ISBN 1-55096-635-9

   1. World War, 1939-1945--Fiction. I. Title.

PS8553.A28O87 2006   C813'.54   C2005-906927-9

General Editor: David Staines
Design and Composition: www.wakingtotheworld.com
Cover Painting: F.T.V. Savard
Printed and Bound in Canada

Sales Distribution:
McArthur & Company c/o Harper Collins
1995 Markham Road, Toronto, ON M1B 5M8
toll free: 1 800 387 0117   (fax) 1 800 668 5788

For our grandchildren,
Jessica, Rachel, Sarah, Lisa,
Ella, Andrew, Janet, Michael and Ian.
I wrote this book for you.
May you read, and understand.

Acknowledgements

This book, seven years in the making, owes much to many friends. Richard Matthias Müller made many corrections and valuable suggestions in draft. Paul Boytinck helped, as ever, for all those years and came with Elisabeth and me on a research trip to Königsberg.

David Staines, one evening in Toronto, astonished me by saying, "I'm your editor," though he had neither publishing house, nor I a complete manuscript. He surveyed the final manuscript twice, always to my advantage, and has never failed to encourage and give good advice.

Among publishers, Jack McClelland of happy memory, my publisher, editor, agent and friend, encouraged me to write the two histories from which this book has profited, and Barry Callaghan accepted the manuscript while still reading it, then did an admirable final edit. Michael Callaghan masterminded the book through design and production.

Marion Filipiuk, Bob Kroetsch, John Bemrose, Ernest F. Fisher Jr., Arthur Bishop, Gus Schickedanz, Karlheinz Wagner, Nikolai Tolstoy and Anthony Griffin all made helpful suggestions, and comments.

Special thanks to Col. Alan Earp and the Officers' Mess of the Argyll and Sutherland Highlanders Regiment of Canada for the rights to reproduce "Friesoythe Burning" by F.T.V. Savard.

Elisabeth, my best friend, my wife, has been just amazing. In 1997, as I was starting this book, we were short of money, so we had to leave Toronto to move to our old cottage. When I said I perhaps should write a potboiler, she said, "No, write that big book you've been talking about." So I did, and she has read and improved the manuscript many times, pencil and yellow stickers in hand, catching misspelled names, gaps, implausibilities, translating to and from German for me, making creative suggestions. Without her, I could not have done it. Thank you, thank you, thank you.

Contents

The selfless man is blinder and more brutal than others. —TOLSTOY.
From Kathryn B. Feuer, *Tolstoy and the Genesis of War And Peace*

I think that all this striving after greatness and domination is idiotic and I would like my country not to take part in it. —A.J.P. TAYLOR
The Origins of the Second World War

Ah, love, let us be true
To one another! for the world, which seems
To lie before us like a land of dreams,
So various, so beautiful, so new,
Hath really neither joy, nor love, nor light,
Nor certitude, nor peace, nor help for pain;
And we are here as on a darkling plain
Swept with confused alarms of struggle and flight,
Where ignorant armies clash by night. —MATTHEW ARNOLD
Dover Beach

LIST OF PRINCIPAL CHARACTERS

THE CANADIANS

Cameron Ogilvie Bannatyne (b.1876). Toronto. Wealthy manufacturer, owner of *Times-Loyalist* newspaper.

Sarah Blake née McLaren (b.1879), his wife.

Eleanor McLaren Bannatyne Giovanelli (b.1900), their daughter, married to Ferdinand Harold (Ferdie) Giovanelli (b.1895), publisher.

Grant Bannatyne Giovanelli (b.1919), James (Jack) McLaren Bannatyne Giovanelli (b.1920), and Gregory Stuart (Stinky) Giovanelli (b.1926), their sons.

Joseph Shearer (b.1919), friend and neighbour of Grant Giovanelli.

Yvette Vézina (b.1923), Laurentville, Québec.

Edward Burns (b.1911), professor at University of Toronto.

Bernie Hallett (b.1911), professor of History at Queen's University.

Alison de Pencier (b.1922), student of Art at University of Toronto.

Clara Dunsmuir (b.1915), daughter of Sir James Dunsmuir, Fredericton, New Brunswick.

Max Aitken, Lord Beaverbrook (b.1879, King, Ontario), Minister of Aircraft Production in His Majesty's Government (HMG) 1940-41, Lord Privy Seal.

THE ENGLISH

Sir Dudley Jeopard Treloar (b.1890), London. Cabinet Minister in His Majesty's Government.

Flavia, Lady Treloar (b.1893 in Frankfurt as Erika Frankfurter), his wife.

Victoria Catherine (Cat) Treloar (b.1920), their daughter.

Sir Winston Churchill (b.1874), Prime Minister of Great Britain 1940-45.

Diana, Lady Cooper (b.1892), friend of the Treloars and Max Aitken, Lord Beaverbrook.

THE FRENCH

Louise Abadie de Montauban (b.1920), nicknamed Marianne de la France Profonde by Jack Giovanelli.

Raoul Laporterie (b.1889), mayor of Grenade-sur-l'Adour, Landes, France.

THE GERMANS

Adolf Hitler (b.1889, Austria), Head of National Socialist Party, Chancellor of Germany 1933.

Joachim von Ribbentrop (b.1893), dilettante Foreign Minister of Germany.

Klaus, Graf von Zollerndorf (b.1912), scion of Swabian nobility, major in Wehrmacht.

Helmuth James von Zollerndorf (b.1940), son of Tati and Klaus.

Peter Maria, Graf von Metternich (b.1911), scion of Rhine branch (Catholic) of diplomatic nobility, major in Wehrmacht.

General Johannes Blaskowitz, commander of Army Group in southwest France, 1944.

Helmuth James, Graf von Blücher (b.1909), Assistant Deputy Minister in the Foreign Office, formally Helmuth James, but informally with friends, James or Helmuth.

Admiral Wilhelm Canaris (b.1887), head of Abwehr, Military Intelligence.

Hans Bernd Gisevius, former member, Gestapo, then Abwehr, became vice-consul in Zurich.

Albert Speer (b.1905), Hitler's architect, Minister for Armaments and Production 1942.

Wilhelm von Benzdorf (b.1910), doctor in Königsberg, nephew of Count Alexander Nikolai Miloslavsky.

Max Frankfurter (b.1868), businessman.

Cecile de la Morandière Frankfurter (b.1871), wife of Max.

THE RUSSIANS

Count Alexander Nikolai Miloslavsky (b.1876 on family estate near Tula, Russia), emigrated to Berlin in 1920 with Countess Anna (b.1894), his daughter.

Tatiana (Tati) Miloslavsky (b.1919 in Tula), his granddaughter, best friend of Clara Dunsmuir.

Josef Stalin (b.1879 as Joseph Dzhugashvili), Premier of Soviet Union.

Vyacheslav Molotov (b.1890 originally Skriabin), Foreign Minister of Soviet Union from 1939.

THE AMERICANS

Franklin Delano Roosevelt (b.1882), President of USA from 1933 to 1945.

Henry C. Morgenthau, Secretary of the Treasury.

Major Ernest Fiske, US army, Major of Schenkenberg during the occupation.

Harry S. Truman (b.1884), President of USA from 1945.

GLOSSARY OF PLACES AND TERMS IN THIS BOOK

Abwehr—German military intelligence organization.
Ack-ack—anti-aircraft fire (or guns).

Bomber's moon—a sliver of moon.
BSS—The Bishop Strachan School, for girls in Toronto.

Camp X—training camp for spies near Whitby, Ontario, east of
  Toronto.

Elsass-Lothringen—German names for Alsace-Lorraine.

FFI—Forces Françaises de l'Intérieur—French Resistance forces.
Flak—anti-aircraft guns.
FOO—Forward Observation Officer.

Gauleiter—National Socialist Party local leader.
Gestapo—Geheime Staatspolizei (State Secret Police).
Girton—college for women at Cambridge.
Greifer—German civilians searching for disguised Jews.

La Milice—French Police under Vichy government.
Ligne de Démarcation—between German-occupied and Free
  France.
LKW—German military truck.
Maginot Line—a line of forts facing Germany.

National Socialist Party—short form, Nazi.

OKW—German Army High Command.
Ossies—nickname of (fictional) Ontario Scottish Regiment.

RAF—Royal Air Force (Great Britain).
RCN—Royal Canadian Navy/VR Volunteer Reserve, (Wavy Navy).
RN—Royal Navy.

SA—Sturmabteilung, Nazi Party assault unit.
SHAEF—Supreme Headquarters Allied Expeditionary Force.
Signal—propaganda magazine issued by the German Foreign
  Ministry.
SOE—Special Operations Executive, for terrorist raids into Europe.
SS—Schutzstaffel, Defence Staff.
STO—Service du Travail Obligatoire, forced labour in Vichy
  France.
Stonk—artillery barrage.

U-boats—submarines. Also refugees in hiding in civilian population.
UCC—Upper Canada College, private school for boys in Toronto.
UTS—University of Toronto Schools, a high school for boys.

Vichy— capital of Unoccupied France.
Vimy Ridge—site of battle between Canadians and Germans in
  1917.
Volkssturm—militia raised in 1944-5 for last-ditch defence of
  Germany.
Wolfschanze—Hitler's HQ bunker near Rastenburg, Prussia.

N

200 Km

DENMARK

Aurich •   • Hamburg

(*Fassoythe*)   Bremen •

HOLLAND   Cloppenburg   WESER   • Hanover   ELBE

Amsterdam •

RHINE   Wesel   G E R M

(*Wescheren*)   Rheinberg •   • Essen   (*Schwandau*)

Antwerp   Düsseldorf   Leipzig •

BELGIUM   Cologne •

Brussels •   RHINE

MEUSE   Frankfurt

Luxembourg •   MAIN

• Nuremberg

FRANCE   RHINE   • Stuttgart   DANUBE

(*Schenkenberg*)

• Munich

Basle   AUSTRIA

• Bern

SWITZERLAND

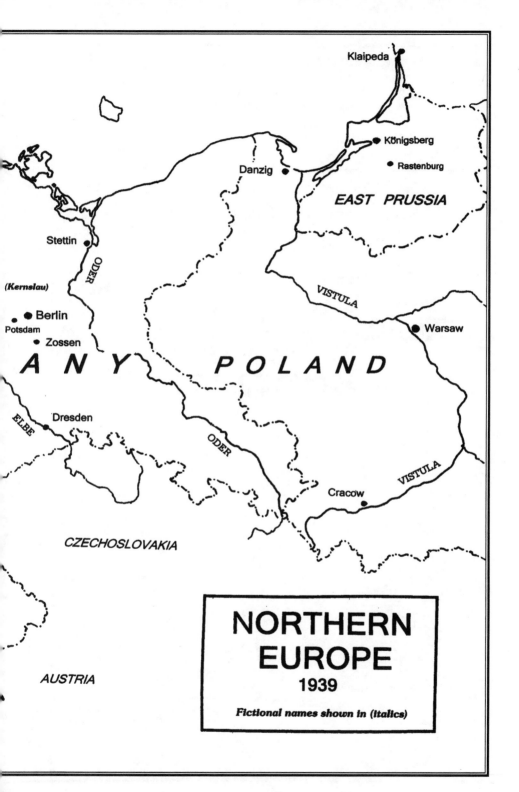

Klaipeda

Königsberg

Rastenburg

Danzig

EAST PRUSSIA

Stettin

ODER

VISTULA

(Kernslau)

Berlin

Potsdam

Zossen

Warsaw

A N Y

P O L A N D

ELBE

Dresden

ODER

VISTULA

Cracow

CZECHOSLOVAKIA

NORTHERN
EUROPE
1939

Fictional names shown in (italics)

AUSTRIA

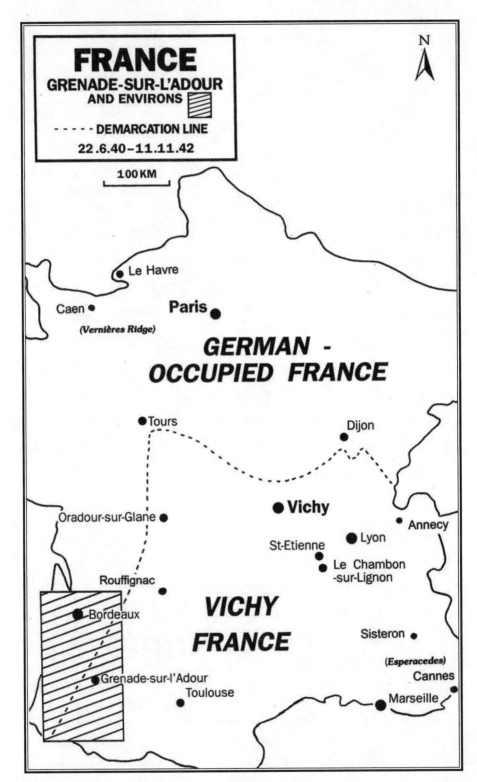

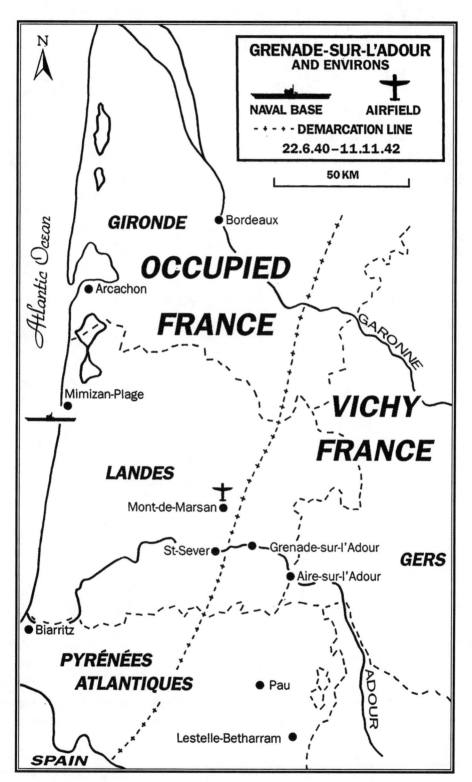

Our
FATHERS'
WAR

1939

Stone Cottage, Georgian Bay, Thursday, August 31, 1939

The children were playing on the lawn in the dark. Red and yellow northern lights spread like an eagle's wings above them 20 miles wide over Georgian Bay.

Inside Stone Cottage, a determined looking woman in an evening gown embroidered with a gold dragon was playing the rondo of the *Waldstein Sonata*, while her son Grant turned pages. Eleanor Giovanelli's right hand repeated the five-note theme while her left pounded bass counterpoint. 'It's like boots stomping ants,' Grant thought. The boots trudged on, ants running up the bare leg, and he smiled. His mother glanced up at him, feeling happy that he loved her.

Through the open French doors the shouts of the children came, "Look, it's an eagle." Eleanor Giovanelli finished the rondo and they ran out the door. "It looks just like the German imperial eagle," said her husband Ferdie. He stared up in awe, as he rubbed the thick scar on his neck where German shrapnel had entered, almost killing him at Ypres.

Around ten in the morning of the following day, the big red McLaren drew to a halt under the *porte cochère* of Stone Cottage. Standing to the right of the dusty car to welcome Dudley and Lady Treloar were Cameron Bannatyne and his wife, Sarah, their three children with their spouses, and five of their grandchildren.

Dudley straightened up with his joints popping, one foot on the running board and gazed over the car at the shining white head of his friend Cameron. Dudley said in a gentle voice, "Ah, there you are," as if he had been searching for Cameron for the three hours since Toronto. He took his friend's hand and smiled with his eyes averted downwards. "I'm so glad to see you my dear chap."

Dudley had forgotten his wife Flavia who was angrily trying to get out of the right rear door, while managing her wide-brimmed hat which she had just tied on with a lilac bow beneath her chin. Her hand went forth for Dudley's, whose tweed back was turned towards her, so their manservant O'Shea took her gloved hand.

Flustered at the lack of attention, which seemed to her a lack of welcome, she smiled a generalized queen's smile over the Bannatynes, then stepped down and said to Sarah Bannatyne, "You must be Sarah."

Sarah said, "I am glad to see you again, Flavia," politely reminding her that they had met in London two years before.

Dudley's daughter, Victoria Catherine Treloar, followed her mother out of the car, looking around at the huge woods. She noticed a tall brown-haired young man in blue blazer and white shirt open at the neck, gazing up past the trees. She straightened her grey silk travelling dress round her hips with a gesture that her watching mother thought verged on the seductive.

Victoria's travel ennui disappeared. She stopped thinking about her purpose in life, which had silenced her all the way from Toronto, and smiled at Grant. 'Oh, handsome,' she thought, and her resentment against her mother for dragging her onto this trip vanished.

She liked the dark brown hair curled by his tanned temple, his tall straight stance, but she was piqued that he was not interested when his mother introduced her.

She said to Grant, "My friends call me Cat."

Grant said, "I'm very glad to meet Victoria and her Cat." The unfamiliar pronunciation of her name shocked her and made her heart beat faster.

Alone in her room, Cat unpacked the tight two-piece pink bathing suit she had bought without telling her mother on board the *Empress of Canada*. She laid it on top of the navy-blue skirted bathing dress her mother had made her buy last week in Harrods. She shivered when she saw how small the pink suit was, and then hid it in the bottom drawer by the sachet of fresh lavender.

She hurried back downstairs so she could talk to Grant although on board ship she had already shrunk from the goose-honk Canadian accent with its swallowed 'Ayundeh' for 'And,' and 'Owetawa' for 'Ottawa.'

Dudley left his unpacking to O'Shea, and came down in a few minutes to talk with Cameron Bannatyne and his son-in-law, Ferdie Giovanelli. "Any news?" he said to Cameron as he came in, ignoring the women.

"It'll be another two hours to the BBC news," Cameron said, holding his hand amiably on his friend's back. "Shall we take a turn about, so you can see the place?"

His son-in-law Ferdie Giovanelli, a short, busy man handsome in blazer and white flannels, began discussing the European crisis as Bannatyne toured Dudley through the buildings and harbour. Dudley could not discuss the war crisis without fear, for his elder brother had died five feet from his trench leading his company towards the German lines at the Somme in The Great War. That had made Dudley the scion of the family, heir to a fortune, with an entree into the middle ranks of the Conservative Party. Now, in late middle life, having failed to prosper or rise to significance, he felt bewildered. Narrow-headed, beaky, long-legged, like a stork, he seemed even to his supporters an unlikely candidate for high office. Sometimes he thought that he had taken a wrong turn long before and lost his way, so that everything since seemed a mistake. He feared that his few successes were due to fortune, or to his family name, or to the help of others who took an inexplicable interest in him. Voters like honesty and a man not impressed by himself always seems honest.

Dudley had built nothing comparable to this broad estate hollowed into the woods that his friend was proudly displaying. He saw himself as a vine that clings to an old building, climbing high and spreading wide, unable to support itself. Cameron was like the forest protecting them now, treetops hissing in the wind while here on the path below the air was still. He felt sheltered beside this great oak of a man.

"You're not yourself," said CO Bannatyne. "What's gone wrong?"

"The young men don't want to fight. We have so little equipment, and we rely on the French, who are hopeless, without any will to resist." His skinny long hands drooped in despair.

"The Maginot Line is a farce," said Ferdie. "I was in France and Switzerland in spring, collecting our son Jack from school, and the French said Hitler can sweep round it, split our armies and feast on us." His aggressive manner was at odds with his fastidious dress.

Dudley sighed. "After all we went through in the last show, here it is again. It's what Max has been fighting all these years."

They went into Cameron's library and sat down. Cameron fizzed some soda into brandy, and Ferdie offered a cedar box of Cuban Panatelas to Dudley.

The Giovanellis were buoyant, handsome people: hard-drinking, intelligent, with a wild streak to them, in fruitful alliance with the well-organized, hard-working, austere Bannatynes. The Bannatyne wit was dry, they smiled appreciatively, made observations, where the Giovanellis laughed out loud and had startling insights. They lived for enjoyment; the Bannatynes to succeed. Cameron liked his son-in-law because of his cheerful nature and ability to size up people. After the war, he had set Ferdie up in a stock-broking firm which invested most of the profits of his companies. In 1934, after some observations Ferdie had made about Hitler during a trip to Germany to assess investment opportunities, he had also appointed him publisher of his newspaper, the *Times-Loyalist.*

Raised in genteel poverty in Montreal, Ferdie had been sucked into the army in 1914, promoted, wounded and discharged in 1918. Hospitalized in Toronto by clerical error, he lay in his bed in torpid pessimism. He was returned to life by Cameron's energetic daughter Eleanor, who had come among the beds in Christie Street Hospital bearing fruit, cigarettes, flowers and books. She had been struck right away by the captain with the friendly smile, sad eyes and charming humour.

At first he had felt out of place among Toronto gentry, most of whom claimed friends or relatives among the nobility of England. The men who ran the city aped British manners to such a degree that they dressed for dinner at their fishing camps. Ferdie followed their fashion with a correctness so extreme that Torontonians thought, not that he was showing that he had *gravitas* but rather, that because he needed to show it, he did not have it. Nevertheless, he was unobjectionable in every other respect, and married to one of the great families of society, so he was eligible for Toronto's boardrooms and clubs.

He had many friends and considerable money by 1929, when all was gaiety and profit. They had coasted, still wealthy, through the Great Depression.

Cameron rolled his cigar round as he lit it, then let a long blue puff drift up in the still air of the library. He said, "You know, we would be in no danger at all without Neville's damn stupid guarantee to Poland. It will turn us into allies of the Russians against Hitler."

Dudley straightened up. "But how could we be? Hitler has signed an alliance with the Russians against us."

Ferdie, who knew Cameron's argument, added, "He also signed an agreement with Neville in Munich, didn't he, and now where are we?"

Dudley said, "But does it follow that . . . ?" and trailed off.

Cameron said, "All that man says he wants is *lebensraum* for Germany in the east. Poland and Russia. First he takes Poland with

Russia's help. When Poland is gone, he falls on Russia. Then the sad sacks in England will demand we help the brave Russkies."

"What do you suggest we must do?" said Dudley mildly.

Cameron loved being asked for his opinion, which he gave while holding up his cigar like an index finger. "Let him take Poland, then let nature take its course. Avoid all continental entanglements. The bears will be tied back to back, ha ha. One will be destroyed, perhaps both. All we have to do is sit and watch." He sat back and made an arabesque with his cigar smoke.

Dudley sighed. "Perhaps Neville made a mistake, but there it is, we must make the best of it. We're all in this together."

Cameron said, "You know that this was what we did not want. A full scale European commitment without the least consultation with us."

Dudley was silent, aware of the gulf between the mother country and Canada but unable to cope with it. What he needed was unswerving loyalty in the crisis.

In their attachment to the British Empire, both Cameron and Ferdie were at odds with their family histories. During the *risorgimento*, Ferdie's father Cesare had emigrated from Italy to Edinburgh, taken an engineering degree, then come to Montreal to build railways. Cameron's grandfather had emigrated from Scotland after the English had pillaged his country in the eighteenth century. Yet in this young country old enmities were worn away, new loyalties grew up within the British tradition. Cameron admired the Empire, which he believed was the greatest force for civilization in the world, but he was determined that Canada should live independently. On his mantelpiece was a plaque saying Alter Caelum, Alter Mores in porcupine quills worked into birchbark.

He could not understand Dudley's pessimism because of the fundamental difference between the self-made man and the nobleman. Dudley had inherited his money, as his generation had inherited their Empire. He did not know how to spend money because he did not know how to earn it. Every penny spent he saw as capital lost. He often said to Flavia as he wrote out cheques for her enormous expenses, "A penny saved is a penny earned." But Cameron had made his money himself, just as his generation had built Canada. He spent as he liked, thinking, 'There's more where that came from' because it came from him.

They had met in a convalescent hospital on the estate of Lady Astor in 1917. Dudley, bewildered by the new responsibilities of his estates after the death of his brother, had been told he needed overseas investments in a country proof against Bolshevism, which he feared more than anything else. Cameron, wounded at Vimy Ridge, having already made a fortune in mining and manufacturing in Canada, lay in hospital planning new ventures. He and the canny financier from New Brunswick, Max Aitken, Lord Beaverbrook, joined their capital in a holding company which prospered so they trusted each other, depended on each other and viewed the world in much the same way.

At noon they all gathered in the living room to listen to the BBC news from London. The upper class voice of the announcer rose and fell like a ship on the waves of the ionosphere. If the single black upright telephone in the library rang at such a solemn time, it was ignored. They heard of the various manoeuvrings, demarches, predictions, announcements, explanations, proposals, denials and so on, all inconclusive.

As the news ended, everyone waited in case Cameron or Dudley spoke. Dudley said, "By the bye, Neville has gone to Scotland for the grouse, so it seems there's not much to this, let's hope."

"I don't trust that man for a moment," said Cameron.

"Oh I don't know. His heart's in the right place, even if he is an old woman."

"Not Neville, *Hitler*," Cameron said and smiled as he realized they were near to saying that Hitler was an old woman with her heart in the right place.

Paul Schmidt, a balding pudgy man radiating the stink of the quenched pipe in his tweed pocket, hurried through the crowd in the long Marble Gallery leading to Hitler's study in the Reichs Chancellery on Sunday morning, September 3, carrying his briefcase. Everyone stopped talking.

The dozens of ministers, generals, party officials, were of one mind about the crisis. If the British note in Schmidt's briefcase were an ultimatum, war was inevitable. If it was conciliatory, Germany would conquer Poland without war in the west. Everyone in the gallery felt the weight of empires pressing on him.

They pushed towards Schmidt, knowing he could not tell them anything, hoping to read the news in his expression, and careless of their rudeness in blocking his path toward Hitler's door. Schmidt edged his thick body towards the door. His genial face was frozen stiff.

"What's the news?" said several of the men.

"Class dismissed," he said. He tapped the briefcase. "Urgent for the Führer," knocked and then walked into Hitler's office.

Hitler in army uniform with the German eagle clutching the swastika emblazoned on his left sleeve, was seated behind his enormous desk in whose front were carved drawn swords. The Foreign Minister, Joachim von Ribbentrop, a narrow, foppish man, was standing by the French doors to the garden.

"Ambassador Henderson handed me this a few minutes ago," said Schmidt. "Then he asked for his passports." He offered the ultimatum to Ribbentrop. "It's in English."

Ribbentrop, who spoke English, nodded to him to translate. Hitler's nose twitched as he detected the smell of tobacco which he detested.

Schmidt stood at attention and translated in a steady voice: "More than 24 hours have elapsed since an immediate reply was requested to the warning of September first, and since then the attacks on Poland have been intensified. If His Majesty's Government has not received satisfactory assurances of the cessation of all aggressive action against Poland, and the withdrawal of German troops from that country, by 11 o'clock British Summer Time, from that time a state of war will exist between Great Britain and Germany."

Hitler stared ahead while Schmidt remained at attention, feeling his legs tingle. Hitler glared at Ribbentrop and said savagely, "Now what?"

Ribbentrop, conscious of his role in an historic event, was posing by the window, one hand on his hip, his back straight, as if waiting for the photographer to come in. He replied, "I expect the French will give us a similar ultimatum within the hour."

"It is a two-front war," Hitler said. "All your doing."

He gave Ribbentrop a look of contempt and hatred. There was a long silence. Hitler made a weary gesture, moving his hand across the desk as if to sweep the troubles away with the papers.

"Leave me," he said. The deep lines from his mouth and nose ran down to his jaw, his skin was pale and puffy. He was angry with Ribbentrop and astounded by the British ultimatum, but he could think of nothing except how to cope with the two-front war. He felt in his pocket for the pills which Dr. Morell had given him, to calm his anxieties.

Ribbentrop accosted Schmidt in the gallery. The officers and ministers nearby stopped talking and listened, so Ribbentrop took Schmidt by the arm and led him further down. He said, "You were translating when Bonnet and I talked in Paris in December. Why did you not tell the Führer what Bonnet said about Poland?"

"What did he say?"

"For God's sake, he said France had no interest in Poland."

"Excuse me Herr Reichsminister, but I translated nothing of the sort."

Exasperated, Ribbentrop hissed, "Bonnet told me to my face that France was interested only in her colonies and had no interest in eastern Europe." He stared at Schmidt as if daring him to defy his superior.

"Bonnet said France *had had* no interest in eastern Europe, but he was referring to the past. He said that in the future, France would take a keen interest in affairs in eastern Europe."

Ribbentrop stared at him aghast. "Why did you not tell me this? This is of the greatest importance."

"With the greatest respect, Herr Reichsminister, he told you that himself, in French, which of course you speak so well."

"But you translated," said Ribbentrop, who had forgotten most of the meeting which he now said was crucial.

"I was surprised when you told me to translate for you, but I thought that perhaps you did not want Bonnet to know how much you understood. In any case, that is what I did translate. Perhaps the mistake came because you were listening to Bonnet in French, not my translation in German."

Ribbentrop stared at him with a sick look.

"Now, if you will permit me," Schmidt said, turning with an attempt at military stiffness which his pudgy body could not execute. He went back to the dozen uniformed men waiting at the far end of the vast gallery and said, "The English have handed us an ultimatum. In two hours, a state of war will exist between England and Germany."

Ribbentrop, his face rigid, strode away without saying a word. Admiral Wilhelm Canaris, chief of Military Intelligence, said with tears in his eyes to his friend Hans Bernd Gisevius, "This means the end of Germany." Gisevius shuddered.

Schmidt, seeing Göbbels' ferrety face turn aside in aversion as Ribbentrop walked by, felt shivers of fear. 'How could Ribbentrop have misunderstood? The British have warned us over and over. Surely the Führer realized. But it seems that he did not.' He heard Hitler's snarl, 'Now what?' and saw Ribbentrop by the window, disaster with his hand on his hip.

'This is how we are governed,' Schmidt thought in amazement. 'By accident. We are governed by criminals and fools.' He took a pace after Ribbentrop to explain things to him, then turned back towards

Hitler's closed door and stopped. It was too late. The Führer would not back down now. He felt sick, he laughed, and when he said "*Auf wiedersehen*," to Hess, Göbbels, and the rest, his voice choked with despair.

Hitler rose from his desk, crossed the marble floor to the map table and looked down on Europe. He rested his left hand in the Atlantic, right hand beyond the Ural mountains. His armies were rolling deep into Poland; Britain and France were mobilizing, Dönitz's U-boats were already patrolling the sea off Ireland. He felt with a shiver the danger to the Rhineland on his left side, and to Prussia on his right. There was no way out. Ribbentrop had misjudged everything, so Germany must fight on two fronts. The generals milling outside the door, who had warned him of this, crowded into his head, repeating, 'We are lost.' Thinking of the burdens that he had to bear, he began to feel lonely as well as angry, and paced around the room, trying to imagine some way out.

He disliked being alone. Only before an audience did he feel perfect. In public, he was eloquent, he could persuade, bully, animate another human being, or millions, but when he was alone, he felt small. His writing was grandiose and confused. He was bored to read it through.

He rammed his right fist into his left palm, thinking, 'I must smash Poland in days, in hours, I must have 20 divisions in case the French attack. I will do it.' The mere determination cheered him up, and he repeated aloud, "I will do it," without having decided what he would do.

As he leaned forward, his uniform jacket as usual hung a little loose on him because of his curved spine, and his bowl haircut made him appear like a boy playing soldier. He knew that he sometimes gave the effect of a boy wearing a uniform too big for him so he stood extra-straight on parade, affected rigid military gestures, spoke harshly, threatened, and looked determined. He straightened up and crossed his arms. 'The Rhineland is ours because of me, Austria is ours because of me, the Sudetenland is ours because of me. It is by my will that all these things were done. My will be done.'

He started for the door to call in General von Brauchitsch, then stopped, remembering the voices of his cowardly generals. He would go beyond them, he would appeal over their heads to the German people in a dramatic radio address that would rally their spirits to fanatical house-to-house resistance should the French invade the Ruhr.

He called for von Below, his Luftwaffe adjutant, and walked into the winter garden through the French doors. The day was warm and mellow, people were strolling arm in arm along the Wilhelmstrasse, but he was indifferent to the weather except as a factor in military operations.

He paced up and down on the stone paths among the herbs and evergreens dictating to von Below. "Party members, our Jewish-democratic world-enemy has . . ." he began, but von Below interrupted him right away, asking if the appeal was to be directed to the party. Hitler stared at him for a moment, waking from the reverie of composition, and said, "Write, 'To the German people.'" He began to speak of how the British for centuries had sought domination of the continent by fighting the French, the Spanish, the Dutch and now the Germans. Then he noticed that von Below was having trouble keeping up since he had no shorthand, so he slowed down.

The British, he said, had lied during the Great War, saying the German nation was not their enemy, only Prussian militarism and the House of Hohenzollern. The British had said they had no designs on German colonies or merchant fleet, also a lie. Then the Treaty of Versailles imposed an unjust peace, threatening the death by starvation of 20 million Germans, as Clemenceau had said.

"I undertook to mobilize resistance against all this and in a unique and peaceful effort, to secure once again work and bread for the German people. Time and again I offered England and the English people understanding and the friendship of the German people. I was rejected time and time again. We know that the English people as a whole cannot be held responsible for all this. Rather it is the afore-said Jewish-plutocratic and democratic upper-class minority who want to enslave the world, and who hate our new Reich because we are a pioneer of reform which they fear might infect their countries as well."

He dismissed von Below, sat at his desk, and corrected by hand a public exhortation to members of the Nazi party, and orders to the army, Luftwaffe and navy. He ordered the army in the east to move with the utmost speed and violence; against the enemy in the west they were to do nothing unless attacked. The navy and Luftwaffe were ordered to attack the British. Finally, he wrote a long telegram to Benito Mussolini, the Duce of Italy, saying that after two days of fighting, the Polish northern Army was already surrounded and that in every area, the German advance had been far faster than predicted. He thanked Mussolini for his support, predicted an all-out war in the west, and asked Mussolini to continue in support.

All this destructive power moved and stopped at his command alone. In the afternoon of August 25, all the airplane and tank engines had started because he commanded it, the troops had begun to march, and parachutists had seized the Jablonka Pass. In the evening, he ordered them stopped, and they stopped, while he reconsidered. As he pondered, diplomats made their last pirouettes in the burning the-atre of Europe.

When he had finished writing to Mussolini, he buckled his Walther P38 pistol to his leather belt, went out to his bomb-proof Mercedes and was driven to his armoured train, *Amerika*.

The people who two days before had heard the Führer's confident voice over loudspeakers in the streets throughout Germany were shocked. They had been told over and over that the Führer had averted war by his great diplomacy. They had heard this after the re-occupa-tion of the Rhineland, again after the triumphal entry into Austria, after the reunion with the Sudetenland, the invasion of Czechoslovakia, the alliance with Russia. Until this moment, most Germans had been in awe of Hitler's successes. Now the worst was happening and they were stunned.

On this warm evening of September 3, 1939, the millions who had died during the Great War rose up like ghosts in everyone's mind. Most of them thought that this new war would finish Germany. And here their thoughts hesitated, for the men responsible for the catastrophe were the government.

Stone Cottage, Saturday, September 2,
Sunday, September 3, 1939

~∂⌐

The Bannatynes, Giovanellis and their guests sat down to dinner in the outer dining room, a screened verandah opening on lawns, flower beds and a grass tennis court. The lake was lying calm now, as if the wild winds of the night before had never occurred. Round the black reef the water undulated like an orange scarf.

"In my opinion, Britain will not act," said Dudley. He spoke with the uncertainty born of the conviction that when in danger one should hesitate.

Flavia, her voice charred by tobacco, cheeks rouged too much over the wrinkles which she did not know were caused by her constant smoking, broke in excitedly, "Dudley, tell them what Alex Cadogan said we should do after Munich."

"What was that, my dear?"

She turned towards Cameron, saying, "You remember, Alex is in the Foreign Office, and when Max asked him about what our policy should be after Munich, poor Alex said, 'We should go on being cowards up to our limit, but not beyond.'" Thinking they would all be exasperated, she was astonished that they all laughed. She said, "Hitler was right, he's a worm."

"Not poor Alex, dear, surely he meant Neville," said Dudley.

"Then poor Neville, they're both weaklings. Britain must act," she said with her chin up. She noticed with excitement that Dudley raised his eyebrows at her strong tone. "After the shame of Munich, she must, there is nothing else to do. Britain must save us." Saying 'us' she meant her mother and father in Frankfurt. Her father had refused to abandon his store to the Nazis, despite the government's anti-semitism, hoping that the Allies would humiliate Hitler so he would be forced to resign.

"My dear, we all deserve one chance," Dudley said.

He had been Imperial Postmaster in the Chamberlain cabinet, and had stayed on in cabinet after Munich because he believed in the possibility of a peaceful settlement. Alone, he had resigned in protest because Chamberlain had guaranteed the borders of Poland in spring, 1939.

"Yes," she said, "what you mean is, one *more* chance. Whenever will we tell that man he has run out of chances?" She gazed at him as if to say, 'There, you see, I don't fear him if you do.'

Dudley was distressed because he was sitting here in the empire's greatest dominion dining on first-class beef and a *premier cru* '29, while his mind was concentrated on the events he had once helped to decide, far away in London. Stiff and tall against the splendid view, the white wooden flagpole carried aloft the mixed red, white and blue crosses of the empire's banner that was also floating over Hong Kong, Bombay and the hedged fields of Kent.

"We should all just . . ." he began, but an angel had just walked into the room. He wished to say, 'We should cease quarrelling and love this beautiful world for the short time we have aboard it,' but it seemed simple-minded. His smile faded into a sad look.

Flavia sat rigid, which was her signal to him that he was in danger. Rigidity was what she used to discourage him in bed at night, but when this made him aloof she worried, because that was his shelter from her power.

"Well," he said coming out of his trance, "Duff said just before Munich that 'the honour and soul of England are at stake.' But why? I can't for the life of me see it. He appears to think that because we made a mistake in 1919, we should make the same mistake again in 1939."

"Which mistake?" said Cameron.

"Setting up Czechoslovakia."

"Not just Czechoslovakia," said Cameron. "The whole system is coming down."

That night, Victoria dreamed she was alone in the woods at the edge of the south lawn. Grant was under the *porte cochère* wearing a sword.

She wanted to leave the woods but hesitated to venture across the hot lawn because if she did, she must curtsy to him. She awoke near dawn feeling she had received good news without remembering what it was.

She yawned and stirred her legs, feeling warm and smooth, then looked at herself in the bureau mirror which she had tilted to see how she looked in bed. At times, she thought her hazel eyes, pale cheeks and abundant curling dark brown hair made her splendid, but she knew that the pale, willowy form was the most approved, and although she was tall enough, she was strong rather than willowy. She turned on her side and looked out the window, where sunrise was glistening in the tops of the huge maples while the forest below was damp and shadowy. Bird calls she did not recognize were echoing among the trees.

In her bath, with her bushy brown hair tied back, the window open looking into the bright sky, the pleasing smell of the woods drifting in, she thought about Rosey, Marquess of Roseneath, after the Oxford, Cambridge Boat Race dance. In a gazebo, chubby, laughing Rosey had tried to mount her, to her shock and wild laughter, butting away at her crotch several times having forgotten to remove her knickers. A few days later she heard that he had said he was very disappointed in sex, he and Cat had tried it once, and he could not understand why it was recommended.

She laughed and swirled the water round her legs. 'After all, what harm can come from it, Grant seems very innocent, he won't get his hooks into me.' As those words formed in her mind, she realized that she had just decided to let herself be as forward with Grant as she liked. 'In any case, I'll be on *Athenia* in a week, so nothing can come of it.'

She came downstairs for breakfast as he was standing in the front hall sorting the mail.

"Good morning," he said, "Here's one for you." He handed her an envelope with Rosey's handwriting on it.

"Oh thanks," she said and went in to breakfast with him.

After breakfast, Cat sauntered out through the door to the *porte cochère*, her head bent reading Rosey's letter. As she finished, she glanced up and there was the bright lawn ahead of her as in the dream, except that now she could feel the heat reflecting into her face.

Rosey wrote, in his usual disconnected fashion,

. . . things terribly jolly here, if only one could avoid reading about Herr Hitler. We were all at Annette's last weekend, dancing on the terrace to the victrola. American swing, very gay. How are things where you are? Where are you? I can't find Tonto on the map. You said it's in America but I don't see it.

Here the talk is one day all war and people rushing about with gas masks and shovels, then it is all peace again, until we don't understand anything. I expect it is the same at the top, I mean Herr Hitler and the rest. What does it all mean? I suppose they don't know themselves. And then suddenly we shall have to rush off and fight for the same sort of jolly butchers we had last time. And you will stay at home to count the corpses coming back. I do hope you will be back in time for the rest of the silly season. Now I think I'll leave you to stagger along to the club.

Grant followed her to the door, where he paused looking at her reading by the hydrangea blossoms that were shaking with burrowing bees.

He followed her across the hot hard lawn. Ahead of her the sandy road led into the spotted light of the woods beyond the rose garden.

She walked into the cool gloom of the woods, Grant after her, not worrying if he were welcome. She stopped by the stone wall at the end of the rose garden where white butterflies settling on the petals folded their wings like tiny dancers.

She was looking down as if she had seen something on the road. "What is it? Is it bad news?"

She said nothing. Her heart was beating quickly and she felt short of breath. The Chinese gong boomed through the still air.

"We have to go back," he said, "there's the picnic gong."

As they rounded the turn by the rose garden entrance, he saw Miss Ball, the housekeeper, leading her uniformed maids in caps towing wagons tinkling with china, cutlery, bottles, glasses, food, ice. Soon the families emerged into the bright sunlight, his Grandfather Cameron in a tweed cap, his father in yachting cap, blazer and white flannels, his youngest brother Greg, whom he called Stinky, and his young cousins in sailor suits and middy blouses.

Spindrift awaited them, 45 feet of gleaming white paint, shining mahogany, glittering brass and chromed steel, her engines idling. Keightley, who was boatman as well as chauffeur, handed aboard the ladies in their sundresses or yellow or pink slacks from Nassau, then they cast off.

Spindrift thrust smoothly through calm blue water that swelled into rolls then broke into foam tossed from her nickelled steel prow under three boys' faces. After much jostling for position, they now lay side by side, staring down into the transparent water, where sometimes a basking pike rolled and dove.

Keightley brought *Spindrift* alongside the natural stone dock on the south face of Sunset Island, 15 miles north of Stone Cottage. The boys leaped ashore, Grant among them, carrying the lines which they clove-hitched to pine trees. Young Stinky Giovanelli said, "Do you want to swim out to the old wreck?" which the three Giovanelli brothers always did on these picnics.

Today, their middle brother Jack was away on a canoe trip up north, so there were only the two of them, which Stinky regarded as a privilege. Grant, whom he adored and followed as much as he was allowed, said, "Yes," while looking round for Cat.

Deck chairs were set up under the pine trees facing west and the adults sat in the shade with drinks and cigarettes. The girls wound up the Victrola and played new favourites, "Siboney," "Amapola," "Begin the Beguine" plus some old favourites, including "A Wandering Minstrel I," from *The Mikado*.

Cat emerged from *Spindrift*, wrapped in a thick towel that covered her from armpits to thighs, smiling a little at Grant who was looking at her from shore holding out his hand towards her. She came down the gangplank holding the towel close round her chest. Forgetting his brother, he said in a husky strained voice, "Would you like to go for a swim?" his tone implying something momentous. "There's a nice beach round the far side." He did not add, 'Where we can be alone.'

He led her along a path between open pine woods and rocky ledges suspended over clear green pools in which dark fish were sculling.

Soon Flavia grew nervous about her daughter. She rose from her deck chair, which she called a *transatlantique* in the French manner, an effect which thrilled Eleanor who looked to her as a mentor of the latest fashion, and went back along the path to *Spindrift,* searching for Cat.

In the hot silent cabin, she found the tell-tale tissue and bill for the new bathing suit and guessed that Cat had bought something *risqué* in which she wished to appear before Grant but not before her own mother. To fear and disapproval were added stabs of jealousy.

"Now can you tell me?" Grant asked as they reached the beach at the end of the island. She sat on her towel in the shade facing the water horizon and he lay on his side looking across her.

"What would you like to ask?" she asked.

"In the woods, you were thinking something, then the gong rang."

She remembered feeling breathless at his nearness. She had wanted to break through his reserve, and then dance away. Now she had broken through but instead of feeling triumphant, she felt private with him.

She enacted a despairing tone, "It's just the bloody war." This was a lie but she had developed a devious turn of mind, to cope with her mother. "It's so stupid. All one's friends will have to go."

"But perhaps not. After all, they compromised at Munich."

She waved her hand. "How old are you?" she asked.

"Twenty."

"Then you'll go."

"If it lasts."

"It will," she said.

He tore off a wild rose from the bush by his side.

"Careful, you'll prick yourself."

"Never fear, Faint heart ne'er won fair lady."

"Do you write poetry?"

"How did you guess?"

"I thought you might. You have that look."

"What look is that?"

"The look of someone who writes poetry, of course."

"You mean Byronic."

"Perhaps more Ionic. You're tall, and you look quite capital."

"Oh, very good," he said.

"Would you let me read it?"

"I've been working on one."

Lying on his side on the sand, his head propped up on his hand, looking up at her, he recited three stanzas.

"That's . . ." Cat said, and stopped.

He waited.

"Short."

He burst out laughing, and she smiled.

He said, "You sound relieved."

"More intrigued. Can you make them up on the spur of the moment?"

"They're all spur of the moment except that of course one revises."

She looked around at the pine trees, the braided light of the ripples sliding underwater over the sand bottom before her. Something thickened the water horizon, then disappeared, and came back again. She watched it, thinking about the war on her horizon. Grant was still lying on his side on the beach looking up at her, her face shaded under a broad straw hat, thinking she was fun. He sifted sand through his fingers and then said, "Who are you?"

She treated it as a game. "Let's see, I'm Victoria Treloar, I'm good at languages . . . my ancestors have been at Ridderly since the time of good Queen Bess, they were all C. of E., then there were recusants in the family and now there is a Jew. I don't know, I'm the someone you see before you, wondering what to do with her life." She waved her hand distractedly, thinking of the war. "I've been accepted at Girton at Cambridge, to study moderns, but I'm not at all sure I want to do that, especially if war comes. And besides I'm, oh dear, I don't know, don't you know. Perhaps you can help me. Who am I?" She smiled at him invitingly.

"Well, to begin with you're charming."

He turned and looked out as definite smoke rose from a small smudge which was turning into a passenger liner. "Ah," he said. "I am becoming," he said. "Like that ship. Travelling towards you. Trying to find out more about you." She thought, 'You will, you handsome man,' and lay back, feeling a yielding lethargy. She looked at him and waited.

"What about your family?" she asked.

"Well, you've met them all now except my brother Jack."

"Where is he?"

"He's the adventurous one. On a canoe trip up north. He's always trying to prove himself. He has red hair and freckles so he resists authority, including mine. First team hockey, first team cricket, champion boxer."

"Maybe he's trying to keep up with his big brother." She bit her lip, as she narrowly averted saying, "handsome big brother."

"Or excel him. It's kind of ridiculous sometimes, because I don't care about any of those things. But at least he's funny. Come on, let's swim round the island." He got up with his back to her, embarrassed by the erection bulging his suit, brushed the sand from his thighs, then swam on his back out from the beach, and Cat abandoning her hat and towel swam after him with a good Australian crawl.

The others were finishing a song when Cat emerged from the water, and her father, looking pleased, said, "She rose like a Naiad from the seas," to which Grant, dripping wet, added, "Poseidon next her looking pleased."

Gleaming with water and blazing with the sunlight, Cat walked straight towards the adults on their deck chairs in the shade under the pine trees, asserting herself, as if to say to her mother, 'See, I am a woman.' Flavia with a moue threw her a towel as if to say, 'Cover yourself, you hussy.' But her face was more resigned than displeased.

Ferdie watched his son emerge dripping from the water, smiling, his back straight, muscles like a washboard on his flat belly, and touched the roll of flab round his own belly, once as flat as that, and coughed as he drew on his cigarette, which he smoked despite the damage to his lungs from the gas at Ypres. He foresaw that Grant would join up soon.

The girls wound up the Victrola again, more drinks were passed, the big white CPR boat charged towards them, pressing a white bow wave before her, decorative flags flying from her masts, and a cloud of white herring gulls circling the red ensign at her stern as passengers threw up bread for them.

At noon the next day, Sunday, family and guests gathered round the radio in the living room. "This is London calling. Here is the news. The Prime Minister has announced that His Majesty's government's ultimatum to the German Chancellor having expired without response from Herr Hitler, Britain considers itself to be in a state of war with Germany."

Everyone was silent. Several people glanced at Cameron but he was stunned. The Giovanelli brothers were thinking about joining up; the women about their men at war; the older men how to direct it all, and Cat about the U-boats threatening them on *Athenia*, and if this might mean that they would stay in Canada for a long time? She glanced at Grant, wondering what he was thinking. "At last," said Flavia with satisfaction, into a hubbub of voices, "We have at last done the right thing."

"Cameron, I must have a word," said Dudley. He got up, but Cameron was too shocked to move. He stared at his friend, remembering the horror of the Great War, thinking, 'Are we going to go through all that again?'

Dudley led his host into the library where few others were admitted. As they waited for O'Shea to bring down Dudley's despatch case, Cameron rested in his green leather wingback chair looking over the lawn to the whitecaps blowing in from the open, spraying over the reef that appeared and disappeared in the surge.

He had quit school at 14 to support his mother and sister. His mother would ride on the streetcar beside him, en route to church while he jogged beside to save the nickel. 'The royalty riding beside you does not know you have a hole in your boot,' he thought with a smile, wondering now what Dudley needed from him. 'Whatever it is, I will be generous,' he decided, as his mother had often admonished him.

Sarah was walking up and down the living room glancing in through the glass doors at them, worrying about Cameron. From the moment Dudley's telegram had come last week announcing his arrival, Cameron had been on the long-distance phone to his friends in Ottawa and Washington, or reading economic reports on Germany, Canada and the UK, or meeting manufacturers for anxious lunches in the Toronto Club, negotiating by cable through his agent in Switzerland for new Koenig-Bauer presses from Germany before the inevitable export restrictions were imposed.

For weeks now, Cameron had lived in a state of euphoric tension which Sarah was sure worsened his angina. He was also wakeful, rising before dawn to write editorials on international politics or summaries of Canada's manufacturing capacity. 'He is 65,' Sarah thought, 'never takes enough exercise, never ceases to think ahead, never rests.'

She had persuaded him to cut his cigars to one a day, after dinner, and the scotch to one before and one after dinner. She had put him on a restricted diet and made him walk every Sunday after church.

On these walks, they both felt again the camaraderie they had had before the Great War. In those days, when the *Times-Loyalist* was struggling, she had typed letters, named herself Ceres to write a gardening column, become Janet March for a cooking column and ennobled herself as The Duchess of Muddy York for a gossip column. The wildly popular gossip column boosted circulation so much that the *Times-Loyalist* turned the financial corner in 1908.

So she had been his friend, then his partner, lover and wife. Now she was in training to be his nurse. She wandered up and down the living room, occasionally glancing in through the closed glass doors, afraid Dudley was going to light a cigar though it was before noon. She did not know what she would do if he did light up—perhaps go into the room coughing and open a window. The main thing she wanted from life now was to go into old age with Cameron healthy beside her.

"For heaven's sake, Sarah, stop pacing about, will you," said Flavia. Sarah perched on the fender before the fireplace, then got up again.

"He's killing himself with this pace," she said, "and it hasn't even started."

"There's nothing else for it," said Flavia, and lit a cigarette. "Is the sun over the yardarm yet?"

It was a sign of the emergency that Sarah went to fetch the sherry herself, though Ball would soon be offering a tray of drinks.

Dudley glanced through the glass for O'Shea, who arrived with his briefcase. He took the briefcase, closed the door and opened it on the green baize table in the centre of the room. Cameron watched all this with affable curiosity, twirling his unlit Havana in the silver ashtray made from ore from his mine near Timmins. He had avoided lighting it because he had noticed Sarah fidgeting about the living room, and he did not want her coming in fanning herself and opening windows.

Embarrassed by all this ceremony, Dudley handed the envelope to his friend with a shy smile, saying "Max and Winston asked me to give this to you." He had been told to say ". . . give this to you in the event of war," but that seemed melodramatic and he could not do it.

The note asked Cameron to become the Canadian Co-chairman of the British Armaments Purchasing Commission of which Dudley Treloar was the British Co-chairman. It pointed out that his work would be easier if the full weight of his newspaper were thrown behind the production campaign. The letter was signed, "Max," and "Winston."

Bannatyne said, "On House letterhead, but from 'Max' and 'Winston.' So it is by no means official?"

"In view of today's events I am authorized to tell you that it was decided in August that Winston must be brought in on the first day. This is private, but Neville agreed before I left that Winston is to be First Lord." He sat back. "So it has become official."

Cameron's mind was working quickly, starting with the word Yes. 'Yes,' he thought, 'definitely yes,' excited by the prospect. He reached for the tall black telephone silhouetted against the shining water.

They talked to operators first in Mindemoya, the village nearby, then in Toronto, then in London, and finally, after half an hour, Dudley was connected to Beaverbrook at his house, Cherkley, near London. He came in from the tennis court to talk to Treloar.

"Dudley, how are you, where are you?" said Beaverbrook, his voice emerging intermittently in the uproar of what seemed to be Atlantic waves pounding the undersea cable. He told Treloar that "Neville has asked me to sound out the President. Will you meet me there in a week's time?"

"Yes, of course. Do you want any Canadian representation? I mean, from Canada, besides yourself?"

"Yes, of course. Have you got Bannatyne yet?"

"He's right here. Wait a moment." Holding the black upright receiver in his left hand, he whispered across it, "Washington, to see Roosevelt with Max, next week?" Bannatyne nodded.

"Then you'd better check with Mackenzie King," said Beaverbrook. "No. On second thought, leave that to me, I'll square it with him. Put Bannatyne on please."

"Hello Max," said Cameron bending down to the upright speaker, and holding the separate receiver to his ear.

"Are you there, Cameron?"

Bannatyne raised his voice. "Bannatyne here, Max."

"Good, glad you're one of us," Beaverbrook shouted. "By the way, Winston has just told me that it is official that he is back at the Admiralty. There's headline news for the *Times-Loyalist.*"

"There'll be U-boats out there looking for you, Max, so beware."

"Now don't print this yet, because I have not had it confirmed, but our man in Derry just telephoned the *Daily Mail* to say that *Athenia* was sunk an hour ago off Ireland."

"The *Athenia*. My God, isn't that the ship you're going back on Dudley?"

"Yes, what, is it sunk?"

Cameron nodded as Beaverbrook started speaking again, "Wait a minute Cameron, the editor is on the other line, hold on. Yes?" His voice faded a little as Cameron held on, but he could hear the questions, about the sinking two hours before, around 7 pm Greenwich Mean Time by an unknown U-boat presumed German. Berlin radio was disclaiming all knowledge of it so far. Many lives had been lost, but many saved.

"Cameron, you can print that ahead of the *Globe*. You see there are perks to this."

"Max, I'd expect nothing less from you."

"Well cheerio for now, I've got to write a leader about this. If my editors will let me. Cheerio."

"Cheerio, Max." He hung up.

"How many dead?"

"Not sure yet but quite a few, hundreds probably. A lot of Canadians."

Cameron immediately telephoned his editor at the *Times-Loyalist* in Toronto, reported what he knew and gave him Max's private number in London to call for further details. He laughed and winked at Dudley. "Max will hate that. If he complains to you, tell him that it's one of my perks."

He poured them a brandy and splash from the crystal decanter on the sterling silver tray, then lifted the glass. "To Max," he said, "mainstay of Empire, on whom the sun dare not set."

"To Max," said Dudley, and smiled. "Did you know Max has bought his own armoured car? Can't you see him arriving in front of Number Ten in an armoured car driven by a chauffeur." They both roared with laughter.

That night, Grant scratched into the paintwork of his bedroom door, *War! Down With Hitler.* His grandfather noticed it, and ordered that it be left "until that man is dead."

Schenkenberg, Germany, Friday, September 1, Sunday, September 3, 1939

⟶ ◌ ⟵

Tatiana Miloslavsky turned in her seat and smiled at Helmuth James beside her as the train halted in the small red-brick station at Schenkenberg south of Stuttgart. Tatiana was the popular daughter of the Countess Anna Miloslavsky, who with her father, the Count Alexander Nikolai Miloslavsky had settled in Berlin after the Red Army had murdered her husband, Tatiana's father, and seized the family estates.

The count, anticipating the revolution, had bought a big house in Charlottenburg in Berlin in 1912, and a film-processing company. The business barely survived under his fitful management during Germany's gigantic inflation, so the family scraped by on what the countess could earn dressmaking and the pittance the count brought in.

His granddaughter Tatiana was high-spirited, even giddy at times, but in repose, her shining face had a look of gentle melancholy in which some people saw thoughtfulness, and others, artistic reverie. Everyone saw much in her and thought she was wonderfully attractive. The young men, perhaps because they wished to have a reason other than young beauty, said that her dreamy reverie showed her poetic soul. That this was just the normal cast of features of her family did not occur to them. Young women admired her for her courage and her high spirits. None of them rivalled her in beauty, yet none of them was jealous of her, though some sighed when she danced elegantly past at a ball and felt that life had passed them by.

Tatiana had now been working for two years as secretary for Helmuth James von Blücher, the man sitting beside her. He was Assistant Deputy Minister in the Foreign Ministry and had introduced her to the man now standing feet firmly apart, scanning the carriage windows for her, Klaus von Zollerndorf. She had been invited for this weekend at Schenkenberg by Klaus' mother Countess von Zollerndorf, who agreed with her godson James that Klaus was too serious and needed someone "gay and charming and decorative to bring him out of himself." By this she was euphemizing her determination that he would marry before it was too late.

The countess was so proud of Klaus' good looks that she had sent photographs of him to an artist in Berlin who had been commissioned by the Minister of Propaganda, Dr. Joseph Göbbels, to do the portrait of a pioneer soldier of the Middle Ages, defending Magdeburg. The painter had accepted Klaus as his model, but changed his hair from light brown to Teutonic blond and his eyes from hazel-brown to Nordic blue.

The portrait pleased Hitler, who said that the face represented "the perfect image of the unshakable Nordic warrior." So now Klaus in stone stood six feet tall outside Magdeburg, resolute against all comers, and also in a sibling sketch in the national museum in Berlin. Göbbels reproduced the portrait in magazines and recruiting posters, so that the ideal became the typical.

When the countess heard that Klaus was interested in Tati, she was torn between a desire to reject the Slavic upstart and her fading hopes for grandchildren. After years of effort and hope, she was no further ahead in marrying him off. Indeed, she was now wondering if her handsome son seemed shopworn in the eyes of the mothers of the suitable families. She consulted Klaus' best friend Peter von Metternich and on his advice, with condescending bad grace, invited Tati for the weekend. Tati and James travelled coach class in the train, she with a wicker weekend case and wearing a hat which she and her mother had constructed from a trunk of clothing discovered in the cellar at Charlottenburg, and from the same trunk, a dress, suitably shortened, which her mother had worn to a ball in St. Petersburg in 1910.

Tati got down from the train feeling apprehensive but Klaus was there, handing her down, taking her wicker case from James, solicitous for her, so that she was at ease with him and looking forward to the weekend.

She sat beside Klaus in the front of the green Maybach and James beside their friend Peter Maria von Metternich with their long legs crimped in the rear seat as Klaus drove the narrow road up the hill from the village with the top down, the wind tossing his hair about, and his bare brown elbow on the doorframe. "What are you so determined about today?" she asked.

Klaus glanced at her, smiling. She was holding her hat down with her hand, looking at him under the brim, and he was charmed.

"I've been called up," he said, "In three days time."

"Poland?" she said into the wind.

"I shouldn't tell you," but he smiled and hammered the wooden wheel with his fist. "It's just so damned exciting, Tati."

"Yes," she said, remembering the story her mother had told, of disguising herself as a babushka, and hiding her baby under straw in the back of a farm-cart to drive out past the trucks full of Red Army soldiers come to shoot them.

Klaus' wife would be chatelaine of large estates in Germany, but money, land and title never entered her thoughts about Klaus. All she saw was a man with a strong-featured face and big jaw and something of the ascetic about him that reassured her. Exile had taught her that what most people spent their precious lives for was not worth it. Her family's estates had been confiscated, most of their money destroyed by inflation and their titles were worthless now in this land of National Socialist Revolution. But her work was interesting, she was popular, and she was enjoying life.

"Thank you, dear James," she said.

He said, "What have I done now?"

"Oh nothing, just introduced me to hundreds of interesting people, including one right here."

James had told her a little about Klaus' devotion to the strange visionary poet Stefan George, so she understood that Klaus had already abandoned regard for rank, land and money by espousing something he valued more, the culture and moral values of Germany. Secret Germany, they called it in the circle of young men round Stefan George.

Klaus was a captain in the family regiment so he was eager to tell her of the cavalry training they had been undergoing, and the magnificent discipline, abilities and conditioning of his men. "We have achieved such a high pitch, they are taking away our mounts and turning us into tankers. Now that, dear lady, is a military secret, so mum's the word. You too James, don't go trading that to your Oxford friends for naval secrets."

"Oh Klaus, stop here, would you?" she exclaimed, "I want to bring your mother some wildflowers." He drew up on the hill overlooking the deep green valley of the Guldenbach and she walked down through the tall grasses that dropped from the road to the rough pasture along the hedgerow, picking asters, goldenrod, daisies and sweet peas.

Klaus lifted his leg over the low door of the car without opening it, then twirled his body out like a dancer and leaned against the fender with James and Peter, smoking a cigarette and watching her.

"I should not have trusted her with the information about the conversion to tanks," he said, and Peter laughed.

"Oh, Klaus, when will you start to enjoy life more?"

"She's Russian, after all," said Klaus, unperturbed.

"Yes, one of our new allies."

Klaus observed with excitement how her skirt swayed as she stooped and gathered flowers into her hat. Her hair lifted and ruffled in the wind. He confined the pleasure he was feeling at the sight of her, thinking, 'Where will this lead?' He had never had an impulse in his adult life which he had not subjugated to his will. He made himself consider: war was coming; if he were not married, he could have no heir. He was more attracted by her than he had ever been by any woman. Now Klaus said, "I think it is my duty to marry her, so I can keep an eye on her."

"A wise move," said James. "If you don't, hundreds will."

When Tati turned, she was struck by the sight of the three young men, tall, shining with health, the breeze lifting their hair, flipping their jackets. She thought, 'There they are, all three good, James because he is Christian, Klaus because he is German, Peter because he is noble.'

Warmed by the sunlight with the breeze on her neck, she felt so in love with life that she wanted to fly. She twirled around, then ran up the hill towards them. Klaus looked impassively at her. She turned around arms apart embracing the green valley and said, "Oh it's all so wonderful." As she whirled, the flowers in her hand slapped his chest and he smiled. This love of life charmed him, making him think she was still just a girl.

That evening James, Peter and Klaus walked in the park while they smoked their after-dinner cigars, talking about the war situation. James stopped, flicking off ash and staring out over the dark valley where a rooster was calling near one of the village houses. From several, pale blue wood-smoke was still curling up from the stove that had cooked the evening meal.

"What do you think then?" said Peter to Helmuth James.

"We are doomed."

Klaus looked down. "I am going to resist this with all my heart and soul," he said. "After Order Number One, there is no going back for me any more. It is much simpler to run into a machine-gun burst."

James shook his head, unwilling to hear these words but Klaus would not stop. "I beg you to remain after my death the friends who knew how things were with me and what induced me to do things which others will perhaps never understand. One may say that I am a traitor to my country but I am not that. I regard myself as a better German than all those who run after Hitler. It is my plan and my duty to free Germany and thereby the world of this plague." His head was bowed because he felt torn by what he had just said, which he knew in his regiment would be regarded as treason but in his Stefan George circle would be loyalty to a higher Germany.

"I am not sure things are so bad," Peter said. "There is always hope."

"Hitler is mad," said Klaus, "there's no doubt. What reason do we have to go to war? Think of what he has said. Point by point."

Here, James was in his element, rational discourse based on arcane knowledge which he accumulated. "The whole Versailles argument is based on a bad outcome of an unnecessary war. They betrayed us at Versailles, but he himself has already undone all that harm."

"Except Danzig."

"Yes and that is a matter of pride, not of our self-interest."

"You speak as if pride were of no importance," said Peter.

"But he uses this pride on us like a bridle on a horse," James said. "Think of what he himself calls the root reasons. First, *Lebensraum*. It is the pride of empire. *Lebensraum* would be pure farce if it were not so deadly. The Foreign Office has been asked to provide names and addresses of all German farmers living abroad so that we can invite them home to take up the new lands. What new lands? The letters are already printed promising land to them and war has not even started. Worse," he said taking the pipe from his mouth and speaking rapidly, though normally he spoke in a slow and measured way, "is the talk of the stab-in-the-back theory, on which he bases his hatred of the betrayers of Germany—the Jews, communists and so on, and from which he got his mad theories of Aryan purity. I was in Tubingen last month and I talked to Professor Maier there who told me that it was the Kaiser and the High Command who stabbed us in the back."

"Even mad Hitler could not believe that," said Peter.

"Hear me out," said James which made Klaus smile, since he had heard James utter the phrase so many times at university. James tapped the dottle from his pipe onto the stone terrace near the balustrade on which Klaus was seated swinging his long cavalryman's legs

Klaus had been attracted to National Socialism's theories of race because they fitted with his picture of a proud Germany of Aryan descent and noble beliefs going back to prehistory. This also fitted with the notion which he hated to credit, that in 1918, the heroic Germans at the front had been betrayed by the mongrel-Germans in the rear—a rabble of communists, Jews, plutocrats. So he was skeptical

of the meticulous, academical James, wagging his pipe as he under-
mined Hitler's stab in the back theory.

"There wasn't any backstabbing," said James. "What happened
was the potato fungus, *phytophthora infestans*, which ruined our
stored potatoes. In 1914 the government was afraid of a food shortage,
so they took the potatoes out of the clamps in the fields and stored them
in schools all round the country. But the schools were too warm and the
potatoes spoiled. The smell was so bad they had to close the schools,
remember? Then the crops failed in 1915 and 1916 because the blight
was transferred to the fields by contaminated seed potatoes. Now the
High Command had to decide whether or not to manufacture copper
sulphate."

"What in blazes does copper sulphate have to do with anything?"
said Klaus, annoyed as people are when asked to think again about
something they have believed all their lives. He jumped down from
his perch and took a legs-apart stance, as if ready for physical argument.

"I'm sorry, I thought you knew—copper sulphate cures *phytophthora infestans*. So, they had a choice, use the copper for the potatoes,
or shells. They chose guns instead of potatoes—now it's guns or butter, according to Göring—and so 700,000 people starved to death.
That was the cause of the peace riots and the defeatism of 1917 and
1918."

"I never heard anything of this in cadet school," Klaus said. "It
was the British blockade that destroyed our imports, and the communists that wrecked the war effort at home. That's what we were
told."

"Nevertheless, this is the fact, according to Professor Maier who
is by the way both an epidemiologist and an agronomist."

"Is he Jewish?" said Klaus.

"Why? He is still there, so I assume he is pure Aryan."

"He doesn't have an axe to grind, then."

"Anyway, now we are being fed the lie that we did not lose the
war, we were betrayed, and therefore, if we stick together this time,

with utter devotion to the Führer, we are certain to conquer." As they went inside, James took Klaus by the arm and whispered, "Whatever you do, you can count on me to help."

Gathered round the radio in the library at Schenkenberg on Sunday night were the hosts, Count and Countess von Zollerndorf, parents of Klaus and of his young sister Caroline. Their guests were General Wilhelm von Frick, Tati, along with James, and Peter von Metternich with his fiancee, Clara Dunsmuir, of New Brunswick and London, with the chaperone, her aunt Edith Dunsmuir of Toronto. At five to nine, the announcer said that the Führer would speak in five minutes. The radio played several minutes of the *Baden-Weiler Marsch,* the normal introductory music for Hitler as chancellor. Then the announcer said, "Here is the Führer."

The count said, "He is not the Führer, he is the Chancellor, dammit."

Hitler read his speech in a level voice and when it was over, everyone waited for the old count to pronounce. He said, "War. Now we must sink our differences and all pull together for Germany." With a great effort, stooping, knees hurting, hands pressing hard on his chair arms, he forced himself up. "To Germany," he said, his glass uplifted.

Klaus, his face a mask of heroic rigidity, leaped to his feet with his glass and said, "To Germany." Everyone stood up, feeling they were doing something necessary but at the same time excessive. The war was still unreal, therefore emotion about it was unreal. People avoided one another's eyes for a moment.

Klaus put down his glass and said, "How can it be that Germany finds its strongest defender in this Austrian guttersnipe?"

"There is of course no connection whatsoever between Austrian and guttersnipe," Peter said haughtily. He laughed his gurgly deep chortle. Everyone thought this was tremendously funny. Peter leaned back languidly, smiling, hands locked behind his head. Clara felt a rush of love for him as Hitler's shadow fell over them.

She wondered what they should do now. She and Peter had been engaged only six weeks, and she still felt strange in Germany. They had met when they were studying at Cambridge in 1937. She took him canoeing on the Cam in "a Canadian," as the English call a canoe. He was amused that she kneeled to paddle, while the languid Englishmen he knew sat in their white flannels on the floorboards, shoulders against the thwarts level with the gunwales, lily-dipping their paddles in the muddy river. He had never met anyone like this tall strong Canadian girl, blue-eyed, long-boned, freckled, with bouncy red-blond curls, pale eyelashes and an eager look to her face that amused him. He bought her an ice-cream cone from a passing barge and they talked far into the night seated on the cold stone bench outside his stair, while the stars changed above the quad at Caius.

Early in life Peter had formed the idea that anything requiring strong conviction was probably false. Moderation was best, so he approached Clara cautiously, almost negligently, in the manner of the young English students around him. She startled him with stories of canoeing through the bush, and the bear she had seen standing in the river-shallows below Tatamagouche Falls, scooping out fish. He wanted to go there with her. Her mind interested him: she flashed to conclusions that he took longer to reach, so she was already on her way to another while he was still pondering the last. By the end of the evening they were fast friends; in six weeks they were in love, though not lovers.

The romantic, bookish little girl in Clara, who had been nurtured on romances she had read on misty summer evenings on the verandah at the fishing camp had for years fantasized that the man she would marry would be tall, handsome, brave, courteous, noble, probably French, a knight in a suit. Peter was a scholarship student in England, quiet, courteous, but seeming a little bit lost, in need of someone firm like herself. She began protecting him from the perplexities of being German in English society in 1937. But it did not satisfy her to dominate him: her need was more subtle and urgent. She wanted to submit to him, to lay down the burden of the love she felt for him, and feel him take it up. Sensing this, one day when they were lying on the grass after a winey lunch with friends on the lawn outside King's, he told her with a smile, "You can be sure I love you because I have submitted to your desire to submit to me." This made her feel so happy that her body convulsed and she spilled champagne on his chest. Feeling wildly erotic, she reached over him and kissed him heavily.

She decided to visit him in Germany in the summer of 1939, but she did not want to travel as a gaping tourist, nor as a rich playgirl. She was granted an interview by her father's friend Max Aitken, Lord Beaverbrook, owner of *The Daily Express* and the *Telegraph* in London, who accepted her offer to send home despatches about the youth of Germany. After several of these had been published, Helmuth James von Blücher hired her as a translator in the information department of the Foreign Ministry, where Tati worked as a supervising translator.

Clara's family was wealthier than the Metternichs, but not noble, and neither of them cared, although their parents were shocked. In August, having met Clara, the old count allowed himself to say yes, provided the wedding did not occur until December, by which time he half-expected to be dead of his liver cancer. The date was set for December 20. On the 12th, there would be a great ball at the Metternich Schloss near Idstein, then they would travel to Sir James' estate in Surrey and be married.

Clara, sitting beside Peter on the long Biedermeier sofa upholstered in a Jacobean cloth figured with books, took his hand during Hitler's speech, a thing she had never done in public before the war. When someone asked her, "And what will happen to you now, Clara?" she began, "Well, before the war . . ." and stopped with her mouth agape at the portent of the remark. Everyone in the room was still, as this phrase filled their future with tremendous mysterious menace.

"Everything has changed now," she said, then whispered in his ear, "Peter, I think we must get married right away." She squeezed his hand, and everyone saw in their open holding of hands, and the whispering, how much had already changed, and had already been accepted as changed. He whispered, "Right away."

In the dim hallway outside her bedroom, Clara spoke to her aunt Edith, who said, "If this is what you are sure you want, you must. But we must telegraph your mother." They had already tried to telephone and found all the international lines were blocked, "for the duration of hostilities."

Clara said, "And you must get to Switzerland right away."

"Yes." Edith stood for a moment, then hugged her niece and whispered, "I fear for you my dear, but I know you've got to do this. Now I must go."

"Are you leaving now? It's past midnight."

"Peter has arranged for a man from the village to drive me to Basle. He'll be here any minute. And Clara . . . ." she hesitated, then willed herself to go on, "Peter is such a dear good man, I am sure you will be happy. I could not leave you like this with anyone else."

On the following morning, after breakfast, Tati was down and waiting in the great hall to make sure Klaus would see her early in the day. She knew that if he were ever to ask her anything important he must do it now.

And in fact, Klaus did ask her to join him for lunch *à deux* on the tennis lawn. As Tati was leaving the hall, looking poised and elegant with her straw hat shading her perfect face, Clara whispered to her, "You look *magnifique*," kissed her and pushed her on her way.

They seated themselves on wooden spectator chairs beside the tennis lawn outside the west wing of Schenkenberg. Klaus poured apple juice for himself and handed her some of the estate's white wine, which she did not even taste.

They talked of tennis, and Clara and Peter, and then he picked up a pickle, bit off half and said out of the blue, "I have long been meaning to ask you if you would consent to be my wife."

'At last,' she thought, waiting for the rest. She had imagined this moment, how she would feel a rush of love for him, and say, 'Yes, with all my heart.' But he said no more. Now she felt nothing except that it was a very odd way to propose, with a pickle. In fact, all he had said was that he had been meaning to ask her. Had he asked her?

She sat silent for a moment watching the peasants in the field below manoeuvre a wagon loaded with sugar beets into the door at the gable end of the long brick barn. She could hear their voices faintly across the field that was buzzing with cicadas in the heat. Then, oddly, several motor cars drove quickly through the far gate towards the Schloss, puffing dust.

She looked up at him, waiting for more words, hoping to see some warmth or tenderness in his face. But he was sitting beside her, his head hanging, his eyes fixed on the grass, his big face expressionless and it seemed to her that he might be regretting what he had just said. So she took his hand and smiled warmly at him and said, "Yes," painfully aware that he had not actually asked her. With a tightness in her chest she realized that she had not said 'with all my heart,' and now she never would.

He raised her hand to his lips and brushed the back of her hand with his lips and said, "Then it is settled. We will be married in the spring. I shall apply for leave as soon as I get back to the regiment."

He sighed and got up and offered her his hand. She held his hand tightly as they walked back up the lawn to the house, but he soon took his away and said while looking at the ground before him, "By the way, between us, eh? Not a word to anyone? Agreed?"

'But why?' she thought, and did not dare to ask. It seemed to her that he had offered all that he was capable of.

But she managed to say, "But when? I must tell Mama."

"As soon as I have permission from the colonel. It is an officer's duty." He smiled broadly. "It is an officer's duty to marry." Then seeing the look of dismay on her face, he quickly added, "I have a strange sense of humour."

"Yes you do, at such a time. Oh Klaus." She looked at him in dismay and then, thinking she was risking her whole life but that now, if ever, she must be honest, she asked, "Do you want to do this?"

"If I did not, and if I did not think you are the dearest, kindest, most beautiful woman I have ever met, I would not have said a word." He laughed. "Duty or not."

He took her in his arms and kissed her firmly. She wanted to believe in him but did not quite. This made her feel guilty because she was not acting with a full heart. 'But then, there are always doubts,' she thought. 'I must go ahead and do what I know is right.'

As they walked up the gravel drive, he glanced at the window of the Rose room upstairs, imagining her seated up there in the pink-embroidered slipper chair nursing his son and smiling down at him from the open window as he rode Pegasus up the driveway after a campaign. "I am sure you will be happy," he suddenly blurted out, and pressed her arm, smiling down at her, and tears came to her eyes thinking of his goodness and simultaneously, 'I will be happy? What about you?' And then she reproached herself for criticizing him.

As they came up the steps towards the main door, Klaus' 13 year-old-sister Caroline burst out of the door saying, "They've sent for you, Peter and Clara are going to be married, they need you inside, hurry, they sent me to fetch you." She stopped in front of them breathless with excitement.

They stood there astonished at her behaviour and she suddenly stamped her foot and yelled, "Right now," then covered her mouth with her hand and apologized.

Klaus smiled a big-brother smile. "Yes, we know they're engaged," and she said, "No, today, now, they have to be married right now because of the war," and jumped up and down. "In the chapel because there's no time to do it properly, Father Gerstl has just come from the village."

The family, the weekend guests and all the staff had been called to the Schloss, his father the count from fishing in the trout pond, some from the park, some from reading or writing, some who had been listening to the radio in the library.

Peter and Clara were helping the butler to push the Bosendorfer grand piano out of the great hall. "Ah, there you are, Klaus," Peter said, "we'll be ready in a few minutes, where is your mother, here's the ring," speaking all in a rush. The piano blocked half the entry to the chapel, but there was no other place for it, and the organ had been broken since 1921. Six of the maids were inside dusting and mopping with their caps askew. "It hasn't been used for years," said Klaus looking inside.

"What is the confounded hurry, Peter?" Klaus said as he kneeled beside the piano to help old Egon block the casters.

"We've just heard that Canada is about to declare war on Germany."

Klaus started to laugh at this news but suppressed it because he saw Peter was in earnest. "And what the devil does that have to do with anything?"

"Clara is a Canadian."

"Oh, I thought she was English." Klaus stood up and brushed off his knees.

"Canada is an independent nation now, and has not yet declared war on us. The minute they do, Clara becomes an enemy alien. Then I am forbidden to marry her, and she will be deported or interned."

"Isn't she a German citizen now?"

"She has applied but it has not yet been approved."

"James said we must do it now, as the Canadian House of Commons is sitting today and the Prime Minister is going to introduce a motion in a few hours. Clara got a telegram from her father's agent in Switzerland a few minutes ago. Hundreds of Canadians died in the *Athenia* yesterday, so they are certain to declare war on us. So we have just an hour."

Peter laughed, his face red with the heat and excitement. "Isn't this bizarre? Thank God the banns were posted in time."

Tati tugged at Klaus' sleeve, pulling him into the great hall to talk in private. "Let's do it now, ourselves," she said.

"Do what?" he said annoyed at the way she was pulling him around.

"Get married. Right after them."

"Impossible," he said, trying to get away from her.

"But why is it impossible? They're doing it."

"For one thing, I haven't told Mother."

"But she will approve, you know that. In any case she's here, she will be at the wedding."

"For another, I haven't the right until I speak to my Colonel."

"But General von Frick could give you permission. He's just over there. He would be delighted, he likes us both, he told me last night at dinner."

"What's the hurry? Are you a secret Canadian?" he asked with a whinnying laugh.

Tati, catching the reference to Stefan George's Secret Germany circle, shook her head with a little smile. "Klaus, wake up, this is not dreamland."

"Excuse me," he said still smiling, "No, indeed it's not, but need we hurry because they must? That is the question."

Tati was shocked at his attitude, at the false smile, but she went on, "Klaus, we are at war, you have been called up, you have to leave tomorrow, you might never come back. Think of those poor people on the *Athenia*, not even at war with us, all dead now. That could happen to you. Klaus, I could not bear to lose you without . . . without . . . ," she wanted to say, "your child," but she was too embarrassed. He stared at her in amazement, beginning to understand.

"I tell you it is . . ." he was about to say ". . . impossible because I don't even have a ring," but his right forefinger encountered the little blue velvet box in his pocket containing the diamond engagement ring and the wedding band his grandmother had willed to him. He pulled out the box, and said, ". . . it is quite possible." He offered her a tight little smile, still annoyed at the haste being forced on him.

"Then it is settled," she said right away, consciously erasing the same phrase he had used on the tennis lawn to set the wedding date.

"But wait," he said with a devilish hard glint in his eye, "delay has a purpose, a chance to consider, do you want to do this, you know I am not a usual man, I have a big wolf note."

"Oh Klaus, yes, yes, yes, with all my heart I do." And she threw her arms around him and hugged him with such passion that he was staggered.

He went back to the piano, at which Helmuth was now seated, rehearsing the Mendelssohn wedding music.

Klaus, looking very odd, his mouth turned down, but his eyes sparkling alert, as if his emotions doubted what his will was commanding, took Peter by the elbow and they walked in earnest conversation back towards the main hall, where Tati was watching him as she talked to Father Gerstl.

Klaus said, "Tati has persuaded me that we must join you."

Peter clapped him on the shoulder, drew him close and said in his friend's ear, "Be glad, you'll never find another so precious. Some of us know that within that strange-duck presence of yours there is a poet-warrior, but how many young women have the patience to search you out? You'll be my witness and I'll be yours."

All that this speech did for Klaus was to remind him of his doubts. He was about to reply to Peter, when old Egon called them to the chapel.

With a feeling of dread in his heart, mixed with the beginnings of happiness which were taking him by surprise, he took Tati's hand and stood waiting for the priest to emerge from the sacristy. She glanced up at him hoping to see happiness, but saw a pale strained face.

They had searched the house and grounds for the Countess von Zollerndorf but she had gone walking and could not be found. Father Gerstl said that he could not wait any longer, as he was due to give the last rites to a man dying in the next village.

So the ceremony went ahead without her, Klaus standing for Peter, Tati for Clara Dunsmuir. The joyful music for the couple's departure was followed by the newlyweds hurrying back up the aisle to assist at the second wedding, a small comedy which caused tears of merriment, because everyone wanted distraction from war, and seized on any reason to laugh. Thus when Tati entered to the sound of Mendelssohn's music played for the second time, everyone smiled and she was smiling beside General von Frick with her head high, her heart pounding behind the bouquet of wildflowers and roses which Caroline had gathered for Clara, and which was now being used a second time.

Countess von Zollerndorf arrived at what she thought must be the wedding of Peter and Clara, just as Father Gerstl asked her son by name if he took Tatiana to his wedded wife. The countess thought her son had gone out of his mind. She sat down in grief on the last pew, seeing now that the wedding she had been imagining for him would never take place.

In her dream of this wedding, which she had cherished for years, after the ceremony, Klaus would play the principal cello in the Wedding Cantata, number 202, of Johannes Bach, which had been played at her own wedding. She was almost in tears, remembering the happiness of the duet between cello and soprano as she sang *"Phoebus eilt mit schnellen Pferden"* in joyful response to the deep rhythmic voice of her son's cello. 'And now it can never happen,' she whispered, watching them turn and kiss each other. In a flash, she knew: 'the girl is pregnant.'

After the ceremony, as they were standing talking in the great hall, Klaus embraced his mother, knowing she was disappointed, and patted her hair and whispered, "We are very happy, Mother, and it had to be. I'm ordered away so soon." This made his mother grieve more, for the wedding excitement had made her forget for the moment that he had been called up. Then she saw that he looked happy as he talked with Tati and told herself not to let her tears spoil his joy.

Klaus felt elated every time he looked at Tati, wondering how it was that he had ever feared anything about her, and laughed at himself for feeling so silly and happy. The laugh, a loud bark, startled Tati as it followed a moment's silence between them, so she glanced at him, and he said, "There, it's done, no going back now, and it's time to dance. Thank you, thank you, thank you, for all your kindness, and . . ." There he stopped, feeling he was leading up to something sententious, and said, "*Du bist mein echtes Berlinerinski,*" the first joke he had ever made for her. He bent down and kissed her. "Tonight we'll make love with our window open to the moonlight."

She felt faint with apprehension and wanting the night.

'And in two days he rides away,' he added in his mind.

The old count opened the first bottle of champagne handed to him by Egon Kreuzer, who was so old it was not certain that he could have done it himself. "Make sure everyone has some," he said.

"Very good, sir," said Kreuzer. "And where would you like the supper served, Countess?"

"Supper?" she said.

"Yes ma'am, the villagers have brought food, and they are awaiting your instructions now." A dozen or more village women as soon as they heard the news, had assembled fruit, black bread, *Spätzle*, and *Emmenthaler* cheese, hams, barrels of beer, *Wurst*, boiled potatoes sauteed in butter, tomatoes for the feast.

This was laid out according to the countess' instructions in the great hall on oak tables and sideboards as the Foresters' band struck up a march, Mayor Weissman blowing hard on the tuba. This too was a spontaneous gesture by the villagers, though the old count was perturbed lest they would play oom-pa-pa music and mazurkas, not waltzes.

"A waltz, we must have a waltz," said the old count, tapping his foot on the floor in three/four time. The countess gave him an apprehensive look, fearing he was going to try to waltz her about on his gouty old feet.

The little band led by an accordion started "Tales from the Vienna Woods," and Klaus took Tati in his arms as Peter also led Clara into the dance, only the four of them for the first waltz as the family and all the guests from the estate and the village stood round the room.

"How do you feel?" Tati asked him.

"Relieved."

In the middle of the dance, whirling her around faster and faster till she was breathless, something unspoken was bothering him, which he kept pushing out of his mind, and then he thought, 'What the hell, I might as well give in to it,' without quite knowing what 'it' was, and said, "You know, I'm feeling happy, I am. It's quite surprising. I'm not thinking about anything except how beautiful you are."

"Oh Klaus, I'm glad," she said breathless at the speed of his dancing.

"My god, we are being married by an accordion band," he said throwing his head back and laughing full out, which she had never seen him do before. "I do rather love you, my *bel canto*," and he leaned down and kissed her forehead still whirling her. She had never felt so light or so endangered on the dance floor, her skirt flying out from her left hand as they circled, bobbing and bowing to the villagers who passed by her like faces in a train window, around and around until she was dizzy.

When they stopped at last she was laughing and staggering holding on to him, unable to stand upright, and perspiring even into her hair. She took Peter's arm and he led her into the next waltz saying "I have never seen Klaus let go like this, it's amazing. He's in love."

Tati smiled and said "Good."

"And you're looking satisfied at last," he said.

"And Clara?" said Tati.

"She misses her family. But we'll go to Switzerland on our honeymoon."

"How can you? The regiment is called up."

"The war will be over by Christmas and we can go to Geneva."

When Klaus took a rest after an hour or so, standing outside on the terrace smoking a cigarette, Helmuth James von Blücher came out to stand beside him. He took Klaus by the elbow and led him across the terrace to the lawn, saying, "Now more than ever we have to stick together."

Klaus, heading off a serious discussion because he was still happy, said, "I'll be in Poland in a few days."

"Ah, good," said James, "You must come to Kernslau on your next leave, we can make some plans. Agreed?"

"Of course, Hitler is a monster, he must go, but how? We are at war."

"Yes, so we must be ready for the day the war is lost."

"It's a good thing you are not a soldier."

"And that you are not a diplomat, dear Klaus," said James.

"James, you must see my position. There is nothing I can do right now."

James nodded. He was in no hurry but he counted on Klaus to take action when it was necessary. James would not enter assassination plots because he refused to stoop to the level of Hitler, but he wanted to be informed of all progress towards a coup so he and the men around him would be ready to install a humane and sensible government.

Klaus went back inside thinking 'James, you want the consequence but you deplore the cause.'

Tati was coming out to the terrace by the east door as they went in the west. She stood by Clara who was smoking a cigarette and sniffing the scent of nicotiana blossoms in a pot on the stone balustrade.

Clara sipped her champagne. "What a wonderful night," she said.

Tati said "The last for a long time."

"Cheer up, have some champagne. Perhaps it will all come to nothing again, like Munich."

She offered her glass to Tati who shook her head and whispered, "I want to get pregnant tonight."

Georgian Bay, September 4, 1939

‑‑‑‑

As Flavia was wriggling into her girdle at Stone Cottage on Monday night, she said, "Dudley, have you noticed how Cat is whenever Grant is about?"

"He is good looking isn't he? I rely on you in that department, of course."

"Precisely."

"How so?"

"Must I spell it out for you?" She sighed, thinking, 'Men are so dense.'

"My dear, please do." He smiled at her. "You are so expert at it."

"He is not suitable." She emphasized the English pronunciation *syootable*, in contrast to the Canadian *sootable*. She clipped on a pearl dinner earring. "Mind you, I've nothing against Canadians but he is a Canadian."

"Yes, I had noticed. So was Bonar Law, our former Prime Minister, then there's Beaverbrook, and what's his name, Bennett, Sir Sam Cunard, Edward Blake, Beverly Baxter, that new young feller, Vincent Massey, his brother, the actor feller, Raymond Massey. Rather a lot of them knocking about, come to think of it."

"Cameron is not even a university man. Not to speak of her."

"But neither am I, my dear."

"But you had the war to cope with."

"And so did he. That's how we met, you remember, in hospital."

"Dudley, you force me to say it." He shrugged into his dinner jacket with a slithery sound of cool silk lining passing over fine Indian cotton.

She fastened the other pearl earring on with a clip, then turned and looked over her bare freckled shoulder set off by her black *crêpe de chine* dinner gown and said, "Dudley, he is common."

He said, knowing his opponent: "Of course, they are wealthy."

"Dudley, I am surprised at you. It's so common to be wealthy."

"Rather uncommon these days, I should think," he murmured, for he always spoke gently when contradicting. He stood at the pier glass, his hands fumbling with his black tie. "Yes, yes," he muttered, wondering how to begin and sure he must.

"Don't mumble," she said.

"You must understand," he said, "Cameron and I were both wounded in the same battle. He introduced me to Max who has preserved our fortune, and now I am here, as his guest, needing his help. I'd say he's a damned uncommon man." She turned and stared, unused to hearing him speak with feeling.

He hesitated, shocked at his tone.

She seized her chance. "And if anything were to come of it," she went on, anxious to head him off and excited by having provoked him, "he would want her to live here."

"Well, what's the matter with here?" he said, looking about at their huge room with a view over the bay, private bathroom, adjoining sitting room with a view of the woods, and good furniture everywhere, an Edward Seago on the wall. "Seems a damned fine place to me, you could play a chukker or two on the verandah, I dare say. I think she would be very happy, as far as the amenities go."

He looked down at his *boutonnière* as she fastened it to his lapel. "Would this have something to do with our own trouble, hmm?"

He had come down from Oxford with a double first in Mods and a rowing blue—'In a losing year' as he said—and met her at a garden party in June. A mild, observant man, Dudley had not at first approached her but watched her flamboyant, amusing behaviour attracting a crowd of blazered young men. She had noticed him because he hung back. So she went to him, her high heels dimpling the duke's lawn, flaring the skirt of her white dress, holding a champagne flute in her other hand, and said, "What . . . ," here she paused, as he gazed at her, "is so amyooozing?"

Flavia believed that because of her strong bony features, she had only a very few years of attractiveness—her mother had said, "You will be briefly pretty"—so she decided to marry, and settled on Dudley.

She knew she could make a harmonious marriage with him, since he was courteous and kind, had done well in the Oxford Union and was already being talked about in the Tory Party. She imagined herself controlling a powerful salon in London, advancing careers, dispensing favour. Soon she had his proposal. But when he tried to persuade his father, Sir Charles would have none of it. "Too Jewish," he said.

"But her mother's Christian. She's only half Jewish."

"And that's too Jewish by half," said Sir Charles. Flavia's father Max Frankfurter, member of a famous European banking family of Jews, operated a department store in Frankfurt, where Flavia had been born and raised. Her mother was a de la Morandière, baptized Cecile in Notre Dame Cathedral by an archbishop.

Dudley went ahead, with his mother's advice and permission, and married Flavia, in Grace Church in the Fields, near their estate in Essex. In a few years, his father had grown accustomed to Flavia and then fond of her. But her parents in Frankfurt had disowned her. In the 20 years since the wedding, Max and Cecile had never written a letter or sent any kind of message. It was as if she had died.

And now Dudley gave her the same fond smile his father had come to bestow upon her, as he said, "There's nothing to be done about such things my dear, we must resign ourselves to the inevitable."

She rose taking her train in her hand, adjusting her diamond shoulder clasp with the other, checking herself in the pier glass, and said, "Never."

"Never is rather a long time," he said starting for the door.

"How do I look?" she said, twirling before the mirror.

"Mm, I should say imperial. Almost tiara."

On the way downstairs, seeing herself reflected in the staircase window, she mouthed the word "never" at her reflection.

Camp Wanagami, September 3, 1939

Jack Giovanelli lay on his bunk staring out through the netting at the moonlight rippling towards shore. Classes started at the university next week, but he had no idea what he would do after graduation. He could take a graduate course, which was appealing since it would do no harm and would postpone the day when he would have to enter the business world of downtown Toronto.

The thought of a life in business made him feel sick. He would have to do the same thing over and over at set times in set ways until he was dead. The first day would be like the last. He wanted to become a writer but his brother Grant was already doing that, so he tried to imagine the life of a classical pianist, and practiced fitfully.

"You thinking about next year?" he said to his friend A.G. Douglas in the next bunk. A.G. was staring at the moonlit lake without loving it, thinking about his father who wanted him to join his insurance company. He too wanted to write, but he was afraid of readers. "No," said A.G., who never revealed anything intimate about himself.

Next day at sunrise, the few boys who were awake saw, far down the steep-walled lake, a few flashes like fireflies in the dark shadow floating from Dreamer's Rock Cliff. These were the girls from Camp Onawong in their white canoes, emerging from the cliff-shade, paddles dripping sunlight. Their yodels rebounded from the cliff over the flat water. A loon sang back, then scuttered across the lake with a noise like an outboard motor, wingtips slapping the surface in take off.

In the log house along the beach reserved for guests and parents, Alison de Pencier rose early and alone and walked down to the shore in the shade of the big pines. Her bare feet were cold in the soaking grass dotted with white dewdrops. When she reached the shore rock, she slid off her patched dressing-gown and stood with her toes in the water warming herself in the sun. She took a deep breath looking out over the calm water where a seagull floated high on the white pedestal of its reflection.

She swam the breast-stroke out to the deep water, turned and swam back in. As she walked to the guest-house, she sank to her knees, the skirt of her gown covering the wet grass, and snapped off a few gold-enrod and Michaelmas daisies growing by the path.

Alison was certain in herself, but uncertain in the world. Her reserve made people think she was holding back something interesting. This made them curious, and this questing after her made her shy, so now they thought she was deep. This was reinforced by her success at school: wanting to please her parents, she studied hard and stood first. So she also gained a reputation as a brain, whereas she thought of herself as a drudge.

Coming downstairs carrying her flowers, she paused at the foot looking across the room to a dozen people including her parents round the table. Her hair was held by a grosgrain ribbon that suited her golden skin colour, blue eyes and blond hair. She was wearing dark blue shorts over her tanned legs and a short-sleeved white shirt buttoned high because when she had been shopping with her mother to buy her first brassiere, the saleslady had said, "We're heavy for our age, aren't we," and Patience had said, "We're not proud of them."

'They're talking about me like two farmers round a cow,' she thought, 'I'll never shop for clothes with Mother again.'

She made up her mind and stepped off the bottom step. Seated at the breakfast table with his back to the stairs, her father Raphael noticed everyone looking past him. He turned and saw a beautiful woman who turned into Alison when she stopped at the foot of the table. She laughed and bobbed a curtsy as she had been trained to do on meeting important people. She said "Good morning," arranged the flowers in a water glass in the centre of the table, and bowed her head to the oatmeal porridge.

Her father, known to friends and family as Rafe, smiled at her, thinking, 'Bless your heart.' Her mother, seeing the approval round the table, was anxious. She had a vague feeling that whatever Alison had—beauty?—was dangerous, but Alison never gave occasion for her hovering anxieties to alight.

Rafe and Patience treated Alison with great kindness, to which she responded with utter loyalty. She was lackadaisical about herself, conscientious about others. In her family, in her society in those years, it was embarrassing to speak of such things, but they knew that Alison was both ordinary and extraordinary: her smile was perfect, not restricted by regret, bitterness, fear or supplication. She was natural, happy and hopeful.

After breakfast, 60 boys from Wanagami and 50 girls from Onawong gathered at the grandstand, five benches high and 50 feet wide, with ten touring British students in blazers, grey shorts and oxfords. They were accompanied by two red-faced masters in straw boaters, blazers striped blue and white, white ducks and shirts with ties. There were also three dozen assorted parents of the campers, who had arrived the night before on the old steamer *Majestic*, from Wanagami Station 50 miles down the lake. They sat on the old benches in their white flannels, blue blazers, flowered print dresses, sun-shawls, straw hats, parasols and dark glasses fanning themselves, to watch their children in the annual regatta.

The camp director, Bernie Hallett, peered round the crowd looking for a tall red-headed boy, found Jack and bustled up to him, clipboard at the ready. "Giovanelli, I have you down for the 200-yard alumni canoe race with Douglas," he said. He made a check-mark on his clipboard, and hurried away. A.G. burst out laughing. "Isn't he enjoying his little brief," he said.

"I have a great idea. You're in the bow, I stern it," Jack said. Each canoe, with a bow man and stern man, was to paddle to a buoy 200 yards away, paddle around it and return. The canoes started with a great flailing of paddles and splashing of water. At the far end, the canoes jammed as they all tried to turn round in the conventional manner, paddling the whole canoe bow-first round the buoy, but Jack and A.G. avoided the jam by turning, not the canoe, but themselves within it, so bow man became stern and vice versa. Thus they slipped round the buoy very close on, and took the lead. They finished two lengths ahead. "I saw that," said Bernie irritably from the dock. Beside him, his friend Red Ed Burns was smiling, which irritated Bernie more, because these boys had embarrassed him.

"And admired it no doubt," said A.G.

"That's not allowed, you know." Hallett waggled his clipboard. Beads of water speckled his glasses.

"I'm sorry, sir," Jack said, "I thought it was funny." A.G. and Burns laughed. Bernie, seeing he was being mocked, was furious and at the same time wished he had not taken it so seriously. "We'll refer it to the committee," he said. "Don't count on a ribbon," and he bustled away.

Alison laughed, Jack turned and saw a girl with a pleasant smile on her face and casually noted that she was good-looking but too young. Alison watched him with feeling of interest buzzing inside her like a fly in a bottle

A.G. said, "Great wheeze, Jack." He was more pleased with Bernie's offended pomposity than with the win. Jack regretted that he had upset Bernie so much because Bernie had helped him, one day years before, on the portage from Hall's to Hawk. Jack was thirteen years old, lying on his side under a heavy canoe. His padding had slipped, the paddles were cutting into his bleeding shoulders, the canoe pressing him back into the earth whenever he tried to get up. A pair of boots cut into the curve of daylight beside his head and he hoped two things,: that whoever it was would help him, and that he would not help him. He heard Bernie say, "You'll make it, Giovanelli, the landing's just ahead." Jack got the canoe up and made it to the landing by himself. Ever after, he had heard that voice giving him strength whenever things looked bad, and he felt he owed that faith in himself to Bernie.

Just before sunset that evening, as usual, everyone in camp gathered round the flagpole. Bernie Hallett joined his hands palm to palm and lowered his head awaiting silence, then nodded to Charlie Krebs, who lifted his dented bugle and played "Taps."

Hallett loved this moment every day. He dressed for it in a long white wool robe embroidered with Anglican symbols, mixed with symbols of the Ojibway people who lived on this lake. He lowered the flag, then held it to his chest, his eyes raised to heaven. He watched the black spruce spikes not moving on top of the black wall of the forest, he listened for the lake lying silent in its bed, he felt the air cool against his cheek.

He began to sing and the campers joined in,

> *Abide with me*
> *Fast falls the eventide*
> *The darkness deepens*
> *Lord with me abide.*

> *When other helpers*
> *Fail and comforts flee*
> *Help of the helpless*
> *O abide with me.*

They stood still as the singing echoed away. Black spruce speared the yellow sunset, the dry grass squeaked with crickets, the grey flagpole stretched up empty, the water lay like paint. During "Abide With Me," Ed Burns, balding head encased in a floppy raftsman's felt hat, was sitting on the dining room steps smoking a cigarette and singing, from the "Internationale,"

> *Arise, ye prisoners of starvation*
> *Arise, ye toilers of the earth*
> *For reason thunders new creation*
> *'Tis a better world in birth.*
> *Then comrades, come rally*
> *And the last fight let us face*
> *The Internationale*
> *Unites the human race.*

A Trotskyist who taught English literature at the University of Toronto, he had had no idea, when Bernie invited him here, that he was going to encounter this mix of woodsy Christianity and colonial patriotism.

Hallett held his head still like a moose listening. Clear but faint came the sound of a train whistle through the bush. "There, can you all hear that. I must explain to our guests that we are the only habitation for 20 miles, and the train engineers know this. There is no road and they know we are out of touch, so when there is a forest fire, they whistle to warn us. All trains in Canada whistle the letter Q, two long, one short, one long, approaching a crossing or station. But tonight they are blowing one short, two long, the Morse for W. It can only mean war. War has broken out."

Everyone stood still in amazement, many people glancing at each other, even smiling, because it seemed impossible that the tremendous news of a general European war could be conveyed by a steam-whistle in the wilderness. The whistle now sounded a little louder, and to Jack it was no longer the wild shriek of a lighted train rushing through the forest in the night, but their fate.

People began asking each other questions that no one could answer, and speculating on what might be happening, and doubting Bernie's news. They moved their hands as if searching for something they had lost, walked towards the dock, the dining hall, formed a small crowd around Bernie asking how to get more information.

The English guests were astounded. In three days, they were due to cross the Atlantic, where the U-boats might already be waiting for them. No one wanted to believe the news, but the more they assured each other it could not be true, the more they feared that it was true.

After about an hour, they heard an outboard coming up the still lake. Joe Killsbear from the Wanagami reserve down the lake cut the motor and stood up in the cedar strip boat he had built himself, gliding in to the dock. Bernie bent down to help as Joe said, "Evenin'. They're preaching war on the radio. Over to England."

Kroll Opera House, Berlin, October 6, 1939

Adolf Hitler, abstracted by thoughts about the speech he was coming to make, walked between urns filled with hothouse flowers on the steps of the Kroll Opera house. He paused at the ornate doors, thinking that Albert Speer would have done a much better job, then dropped his head and headed into the gloomy building between the guards of the *Leibstandarte Adolf Hitler* with their arms extended in the party salute.

On stage, in better lighting, gripping the lectern with one hand, he held up the other to calm the applause from the members of the Reichstag. Speaking in a moderate tone, he described the victory in Poland, mentioning the death and suffering along with the cowardice of Polish officers who deserted their posts at the crucial moment. He insisted on the moderation of German policy, and showed how the Poles had designed their own destiny by their cruelty towards the German minorities they controlled, so vicious that in some of the villages liberated by the German army, there was not a single man left alive.

He asked the members to rise while he read out the numbers of dead and wounded. He told the house that 10,572 Germans had been killed, 30,322 wounded and 3,404 were missing, although it was unlikely, given Polish brutality, that any of these would be discovered alive.

He turned to the war in the west. He mocked western journalists—"these miserable scribblers"—who, secure in countries that occupied 40,000,000 square kilometres, were afraid that Germany wanted to dominate the world, though she occupied only a few hundred thousand. Eighty million Germans must have room to live. Germany had shown over and over that despite the taunts of the hypocrite Roosevelt, she wanted to live at peace with her neighbours and that the Austrians had been overjoyed at the reunion with their brothers. The French themselves had solved the problem of the Saar after the Great War, and Germany had renounced her claims to Elsass-Lothringen.

He then asked, "Why should this war in the west be fought?" For restoration of Poland? Poland of the Versailles treaty would never rise again. This was guaranteed by two of the largest states in the world. What other reason existed for war in the west? "Has Germany made any demands of England which might threaten the British Empire or endanger its existence? On the contrary, Germany has made no such demands on either France or England. But if this war is to be fought in order to give Germany a new regime, that is to say, in order to destroy the present Reich once more and thus to create a new Treaty of Versailles, then millions of human lives will be sacrificed in vain, for neither will the German Reich go to pieces nor will a second Treaty of Versailles be made. And even should this come to pass after three, four or even eight years of war, then this second Versailles would once more become the source of fresh conflict in the future."

He sketched in the aims of the Reich government in Poland: First, the creation of a frontier in accordance with existing historical ethnographical and economic conditions; second, solution of minority problems, settlement of the Jewish problem, reconstruction and a guarantee of security in Poland. All this would be done by Germany, but not in any imperialistic way. Elsewhere, he went on, Germany needed her colonies back and access to raw materials and resources, just like the other great nations arrayed against her. Then there might be a revival of international economic life.

He suggested a peace conference, and named as the likely opposition to this, Winston Churchill: "Churchill may think I am weak or cowardly and that is why I make these proposals. If so, and if he and his kind prevail, this statement will have been my last."

He pointed out that "In the course of world history, there have never been two winners but very often two losers.

"May those peoples and their leaders who are of the same mind now make their reply. And let those who consider war to be a better solution reject my outstretched hand."

He ended with a prayer and with thanks to God.

This speech was very well-received in Germany but scarcely noticed in France or England. No one in the western press or in the *Chambre de Députés* or the House of Commons took up the vague suggestion for a peace conference. No more did they answer the taunts in the German press about the allied failure to live up to their obligations to Poland by attacking Germany while Germany was attacking Poland.

The indifference to his speech convinced him that he must now attack in the west. To encourage the generals, and to discourage opposition, he called the senior Wehrmacht staff to the conference room in the Chancellery. He stood before them at the lectern in his army uniform, to remind them of his status as a decorated hero of The Great War.

"For the first time since the foundation of the German Empire by Bismarck, we have no fear of a war on two fronts. Our treaty with the USSR assures that. Italy is our ally and our friend so long as the great Duce lives. Our people are united." He began to sweat as he anticipated what was coming next, the subject of his own greatness: "Everything depends on the fact that the moment is favourable now, and may not be favourable six months from now. As the last factor, I must in all modesty name my own person. I am irreplaceable."

There was an intensification of the attentive silence here as these uniformed bemedalled middle-aged men trained to service strained to hear what they could not believe.

"Neither a military nor a civil person could replace me, but assassination attempts may be repeated." At that moment, several persons sighed, perhaps hoping for an assassination, but Hitler, in love with what he was saying, soared over the obstacle, "I am convinced of my powers of intellect and decision. Time works for no single man, but must work for our enemies if they stay united. Now the relationship of forces is most propitious for us, and can never improve but only deteriorate."

He paused and gazed over the heads of the crowd to the dim far end of the room, and continued in reverence, for he was now speaking with a full heart about his divine mission, "Every hope of compromise is childish. This is our destiny, to which I am leading us. To victory or defeat. The question is no longer the fate of National Socialist Germany, but of who is to dominate Europe. No one has ever achieved what I have achieved. My life is of no importance in all this. I have led the German people to a great height, even if the world does hate us now. I am risking all this work so far achieved on one great gamble. I have to choose between victory and destruction.

"I choose victory.

"As long as I live I shall think only of the victory of my people. I shall shrink from nothing and shall destroy everyone opposed to me. I have decided to live my life so that I can stand unashamed at the end; if I have to die, I want to take the enemy with me. In these last years, I have experienced many examples of intuition which have led to success. I have heard the voice of prophecy and seen it realized. I shall stand or fall in this struggle. I shall never survive the defeat of my people. No capitulation of the forces outside, no revolution from within."

At the end he stopped without a conclusion, staring toward the end wall. He thought, 'I have done it,' remembering himself trembling in the streets of Vienna. 'Now I have assumed the role that I imagined in those days.' Everyone was silent. Most of them believed they had not just heard a speech, but had been subjected to an elemental force radiating from one person. Their concerns had been made to seem small, compared to this awful and enormous vision of a nation's life which for many had never been more than pageantry and promotion, but which now appeared to be bleak, awful, dark, terrifying, grand, and solemn beyond anything they had ever experienced.

A few of the officers were embarrassed for Germany and for their mesmerized brother officers, thinking the speech was ramshackle, incoherent self-aggrandizement, like his policy for the nation. Klaus von Zollerndorf looked around at the generals who had spent a lifetime in their vocation and remembered the economists, diplomats, engineers, architects, politicians, editors who believed this man was a genius, and thought, 'Only a dilettante can fool an expert.'

The next day, they renewed their planning for an immediate campaign against France. When the date came, the weather prevented the
attack. Again this happened, and again, as Europe entered the enchant-
ment, neither war nor peace, which people called The Phoney War. For
months, the heaviest missile dropped down on the front by German
bombers was poetry. A French *poilu,* Jean-Paul Sartre, who was a
weatherman at Morsbronn near Strasbourg, picked up one leaflet,
which was printed on a leaf-shaped piece of russet paper, veined like
leaves:

> *The leaves fall, we shall fall like them*
> *The leaves die because God wills it so*
> *But we, we shall die because the English will it so*
> *By next spring, no one will remember either dead leaves*
> *Or slain poilus, life will pass over our graves.*

1940

Kurfürstendamm, Berlin, April, 1940

Tati was walking along the Ku'damm carrying a two-kilo piece of salmon from Sweden for the dinner that Clara had promised to cook that night. She was happy, people nodded to her as they passed, 'and not just because I'm pregnant either,' she thought. 'Everyone seems in a good mood today.' She smiled at an old man shuffling towards her with a cane, waving his arms at the sky, muttering words about "Hitler," and "Jews." She sat down in the Café Bauer with the string bag at her feet and sighed looking up at the linden trees in pale green leaf.

'Berlin is sometimes beautiful after all,' she thought. 'If it weren't for the war, we would all be happy again.'

By "again" her mind was harking back to the time she remembered at the estate near Klaipeda in Lithuania before the Miloslavskys had sought refuge in Germany. That was where her grandfather Nikolai had been when they last heard from him three months ago. But now the Red Army had occupied Lithuania, and there was only silence from there.

Tati remembered summers at their tall red-brick house in the German style, the church with the round star of David window high in the east gable wall, and green hills beyond which she imagined the Red

Army like a bear ready to seize her. Here began her nightmares. Russia and Russians seemed to her enormous yet tiny, threatening yet intimate. She was whirling through dark space with a feeling of hugeness and tininess at the same time. She knew if she closed her eyes, her mind would go spinning out of control, whirling her outwards into vast galaxies, and inwards into tiny subatomic worlds and she would be sick.

A young woman's voice nearby said, "Norway has surrendered."

Clara sat down with an athlete's grace, her hand curving behind her to gather in her swaying skirt. She said, "Those poor people."

Tati said, "Now those thugs will be in power for many months more."

Clara sighed and said, "You look hungry."

"All the time. And I'm getting dizzy spells."

"Have you heard from Klaus?"

"No, but thank God, now he'll be safe."

Clara lit a cigarette, but Tati said, "No thanks, they make me feel sick."

She told Clara she had had a dream the night before. "Klaus and I were lying in the apple orchard at Schenkenberg, and when we looked up afterwards, there were two goats looking at us and chewing. They looked so thoughtful. And they had been watching us the whole time. We both laughed. So it will be a happy baby."

"Good, now go and see Doctor Steudel. You need special rations."

"How did you hear about Norway? Nobody's talking about it." They looked around the restaurant and at least one person was reading the back of a newspaper with a big headline, NORWAY SURRENDERS. "It's amazing. The British have been defeated. And nobody cares."

Clara said, "Come on, we have to go back to the office. I came out to find you." Tati got up and started away, but Clara had noticed her bag and picked it up. "Is this yours?" Tati said "Thanks," and took her arm.

Clara said with a big smile, "I've just heard, Peter's coming back from Zossen tonight." Blue-eyed, freckled, gold-red hair curling out round her face, Clara looked at her friend cutely from under her broad-brimmed hat and Tati burst out laughing, knowing exactly what that look meant.

After work, they walked back towards the Budapesterstrasse, buying odds and ends. Clara remarked how peaceful Berlin seemed despite the war, but Tati was feeling her bulk swaying in front of her. Once— it seemed forever ago—she had been lithe and bouncy, running down tennis balls, playing with the dog, dancing all night, putting up curtains at Charlottenburg. Now, it seemed to her, all that was past, she believed that her figure had been ruined and she would be heavy forever. She was lost in these musings so long that she arrived under the trees in front of the apartment house on Budapesterstrasse without realizing it.

Clara said as she unlocked the door, "Peter will be late as usual. He says, 'I have no sense of time,' but it really means, 'I've no sense of other people's time.' You know, he's never early."

She washed the salmon, slashed it side to side in two-centimetre wide strips, leaving it on the skin, then gave it a preliminary dressing of lemon juice, rock salt and minced dill.

"Wherever did you find fresh dill these days?" Tati said, marvelling at Clara's deftness. She felt inept in her role as a German wife.

"I grew it—see?" Clara pointed out the kitchen window where she had six herbs in a starter-tray, into the back courtyard garden where she had dill, tomato plants, parsley, spring onions all sprouting in neat rows.

"Aren't you a wonder. Now what?"

Clara made half the salmon into gravlax by covering it with a mixture of dill, lemon juice, coarse ground white pepper, and rock salt. She also made the sauce of minced dill, lemon juice, olive oil, vinegar of Modena, mild honey, and Kremser mustard mixed with Russian mustard and lemon juice. Then she weighted it down and put it in the refrigerator to marinate for two days. For the salmon that night, she mixed Worcestershire sauce, vinegar, lemon juice, and sherry. She stirred them, then applied some of the dressing to the salmon.

"Is this an old Canadian recipe?" Tati asked.

"I made this up," she said. "We went to a Japanese restaurant in Vancouver one summer where they had something they called miso sauce. They mixed up teriyaki and miso, but you can't get them here now, so I substitute these things. We'll heat the rest of the sauce while the salmon is cooking."

Tati went into the salon and lay back with her stockinged legs on the sofa, looking up at the Klimt print over the fireplace, which was faced with blue Delft tile. She put her hands behind her head and stretched out imagining angels' faces inside each square of the coffered ceiling three metres high as she talked to Clara through the open door. Peter's books were ranged behind glass doors on the far wall, bright cushions adorned the old chairs. Clara had sewed the curtains for the tall casement windows, and the pillow under her head was Clara's needlework. "How do you get time for all this?" she called out, and Clara came to the doorway with a mixing bowl in her hand saying, "For what?"

"All these things you do around here. I thought your family was rich."

"Yes, I suppose they are."

"Then why aren't you helpless, like me? All I can do is play the piano and sing a bit, and wear clothes, and ski and dance, but you can do anything."

"It's not hard. I just do them, most of them you can teach yourself."

"You know, I've decided to have him at Kernslau."

Clara, back in the kitchen, called, "Who?"

"The baby."

Clara came into the room and faced her—it was one of her gestures, to stand facing someone, often with a cigarette in her hand, then to command. She said, "You can't."

"Why ever not?"

"It's James' home, not yours. Besides, you don't know it's a boy."
She was bewildered by Tati's habit of stating as fact something that she
wished.

"But you know James invited Mother to stay there while he's in
Berlin. So it's my second home now. And it's out in the country. There
will be lots of milk in case I don't have any. Klaus of course wants
him to be born at Schenkenberg, but I put my foot down." Now she
adopted the whining tone that she used sometimes when Klaus was
being difficult, "It's so far, these days." At this, Clara began to laugh.
"It's just as far as it always was," she said.

"You know what I mean."

"No, I don't," said Clara, hoping for once to teach Tati reality.

"Distances are greater now," said Tati.

"That is stupid, distances are as they always were."

"But they take longer," said Tati, biting into a radish, "So that
must mean they are longer, *n'est-ce pas*?" She smiled the appealing
smile that Clara knew meant, 'I can't help being fun, forgive me.'

Clara gave up with a laugh. She poured out some mineral water and
handed a glass to Tati who sat up now, spreading her legs and her
skirt, and said, "I hate the awkwardness. I feel as if I've swallowed
a football. Anyway, they have a good midwife. Berthe Somebody."

Clara was puzzled. "Who do?"

"In the town hospital. That's why I want to go. You'll be there too."

"I'd love to, my dear, but I can't, I have too much work."

"It's settled. You have leave. Helmuth James said we can both go."

"You mean, you arranged for me to go with you while you have the
baby?" She sat down. "Tati, how could you? What will happen to my
annual leave now? You are such a meddler. You are getting more selfish every day, I swear, I'm sorry, I don't mean that, yes I do, Tati, damn,
how can you be so arrogant with your friend?" She emphasized the last
word, and sat back on the ottoman, thinking, 'No wonder her grandfather is so patient, these Miloslavsky women would make an angel
weep.'

"I did not think of that, it would be like a holiday, wouldn't it?"

"Not with Peter, you dolt," said Clara.

"Please, don't be a grouch, it's all for the best. Just think, you'll learn how it's done. She's the best midwife in Germany."

Clara moaned.

"I'll speak to Helmuth tomorrow, and arrange for you to have maternity leave. He's a little bit in love with you. It's the attraction of the exotic."

Clara laughed hearing plain New Brunswick called "exotic."

Tati looked forward to the birth without fear. She believed that pain in childbirth was caused by fear, which she had dispelled by accepting it as natural. She was recording the experience—her vital statistics, including weight, girth, sick days and so on, in photographs and writing. "I want you to be there because I want a record of what goes on," she told Clara, "so bring a notebook and write it all down."

"No photographs?" Clara said to tease her.

"Do you think they'll let us?" Clara, who had no desire to aim a camera between Tati's legs, groaned and diverted her with talk of names and clothes for the boy, who Tati refused to say was a child. The baby was a boy, nothing else.

The midwife, Berthe Hügel, was 81 years old, small, and much admired in the town of Kernslau, for she had delivered most of their citizens. She was beloved by the Catholics, the Protestants and the unchurched, and esteemed even by the doctors, who were all men, and glad to be relieved of the messy work at which she was expert. She led Tati to an empty four-bed ward, where Clara and Berthe spread the Kernslau sheets onto the bed. The loudspeaker in the corridor assaulted them with news—peace rumours from Berlin and Rome, arrivals of food shipments from Russia, the immense numbers of British and French soldiers captured at Dunkerque, interspersed with triumphant marching music.

Tati told Mrs Hügel that she was going to be awake and alert for the whole thing, so she could remember it, "and my friend will keep notes too."

As she was finishing, the next contraction hit her hard and she fell back clothed on the half-made bed saying, "oh, oh, oh, that was a big one."

Hügel helped her to sit up and after a few minutes, they undressed her and put her into a hospital gown tied down the back, and Tati lay back looking beautiful, her chestnut hair spread curling in a fluffy mass over the white pillow, her cheeks flushed. After the contractions had come down to about one per minute, Clara ran down the corridor to find Hügel. She came, her slippers whispering along the linoleum, looked at Tati, and said, "You're still smiling. Not time yet," and left. Tati shrugged.

Tati succumbed to a small dose of morphine when the contractions were continuous. So she was drowsy when the howling baby was lifted from between her legs and shown to her. Clara wiped her sweating face and said, "He's beautiful. He's wonderful. He's perfect"

Tati took him in her arms as soon as Hügel had cut the cord. She smiled on her scowling boy. "We will name him Helmuth James, that will please Klaus."

The loudspeaker announced that on this date, Friday June 14, history was being made: the Wehrmacht was parading through Paris.

*

Memel-land, Berlin, June, 1940

⮫⮬

While his granddaughter was giving birth to his great-grandson, Count Miloslavsky was seated on his horse watching puffs of dust rising from the valley road five kilometres east of his land. He knew immediately the dust came from Russians on the invisible road. He turned his horse and galloped to his forester's house. There Beissel hid him for a month, then fitted him out in the green uniform of a Lithuanian forester, with a shiny visored cap, which looked so funny on him that they both burst out laughing. Then he took the count in a cart to a farmer's track through the fields near a Russian guard-post at the border, set him down and told him to walk west just before noon. The Russians suspended the patrols for a few minutes when they changed the guards at noon, so for a few minutes no one was watching the strip of meadowland marking the border with East Prussia.

Beissel told him to walk, not run, while reading a newspaper because the guards had orders to shoot anyone who was running. He gave the count a salami, bread and cheese in a napkin, made the sign of the cross over him, and said goodbye. As he had been told, the old count took a copy of the *Königsberger Tageblatt,* cut two holes in it so he could see through it, and ambled along the sandy cart-road towards the meadowland just before noon. Nobody noticed.

Ignoring all the treasures of his estate, including three Dürers and one Rembrandt, he had saved a piece of green glass through which he liked to look at the sunlight. This he had cherished since boyhood, when he had retrieved it from the ruins of a burned house. He had spare socks and underwear in his pocket, and nothing else. He was happy to travel light. He stayed a week in Königsberg with his nephew, Wilhelm von Benzdorf, who was the chief of surgery in St. Paul's Hospital there. The count was happy to see Willy again, even though he was working 16 hours a day to make up for the doctors who had been drafted into the Wehrmacht. Willy diagnosed Nikolai's stomach pain as an incipient ulcer caused by a bacterium, and treated him with honey, herbs, boiled water and starvation. As he was leaving, he held Willy in his arms and wished him well. Then, thinking they might never see each other again, the count said unexpectedly, "You are like a son to me." Willy smiled and said, "Circumstances have made that easy." His father had been killed at Vimy Ridge in 1917. "I am sure we will meet again, Papa."

Three weeks after Helmuth was born, Tati went with her mother to Lehrter Bahnhof to meet grandfather Nikolai expecting what she remembered—tall distinction, reserved kindliness. She saw a weird green uniform, messy grey hair flying over a look of mild inquiry which she recognized with a thump in her heart. She called out, "Granpapa," and ran towards him with flowers in her hand. He was reaching out to her when the countess swept in to seize her father in a firm embrace. Then she towed him away towards the taxi, while Tati, still hoping to embrace him, started after. Then the countess remembered, and shrieked, "Papa, where are all your things?" He said, "This is all."

At that point Tati thrust the flowers at him and almost jumped into his arms. He patted her back and said, "There now, I've nothing else, all I need is here." He smiled and the countess said, "Do you mean you left all your clothes behind? You can't walk around Berlin like that." She looked scornfully at the uniform. "Do you know what the clothing ration is here. My God, what a feckless man, I should have come to fetch you."

The thought of the countess flapping through the Russian lines like a chicken, pecking anyone who got in her way, was so absurd that both Tati and her grandfather, now holding hands, laughed together. "When I think of the carriage-loads of stuff we used to take from Berlin for the summer, enough for one of Napoleon's divisions. And now here I am like this . . ." and he held out his empty hands.

"Oh Granpapa," said Tati, "We shall soon fit you out like a prince."

"He *is* a prince," said the countess.

"But no more, I like to be so free, I never knew what it was since I was a boy and I had my own little hut by the river, planted with sunflowers all about for privacy." He smiled at Tati. "You would have loved it."

"But tell us your adventure," Tati said. "Did you see Russians?"

"A cloud of dust in the distance, that was enough. Old Beissel hid me and then I got to Königsberg, now how did I do that? In any case, I met young Wilhelm my nephew in the hospital there, a remarkable young man."

"Oh, good," said Tati, "I have been wondering about him, I write him Dear Cousin letters every now and then, but he never replies."

"He's very busy," said the count. "He was curing infected wounds with maggots—all cured in a couple of days, and no bad scars. He also cured my stomach ulcer with some kind of antibacterial herb. Every doctor I had been to in Berlin and St. Petersburg had told me no more chocolate, no more alcohol, no more tobacco. It's never broccoli." He smiled at Tati. "But Willy cured me."

The old count was shown the new baby, which he admired in an abstracted sort of way, standing well away from the cradle as if the contents might be damaged by viewing. Tati laughed and picked up little Helmuth and held his face up. "Kiss him," she whispered, "he wants your blessing." And the count bent over and kissed the blond hairs on the square little head. He smelled the sweet skin with its faint odour of talcum powder, and smiled. Helmuth stared up at him and Tati sensed him resisting the familiarity.

It was decided that the count would visit for a few days before accompanying the countess back to Kernslau to help manage the von Blücher estate in lieu of Helmuth James, who had to live in Berlin for his diplomatic work. The Miloslavkys still owned the big, three-storey red brick house in Charlottenburg, which the old count had purchased in 1912, as a refuge from the Soviets but the count had been forced to let it to the Spanish ambassador to get enough income for his family to live.

His film studio was defunct because of the war so he had been reduced, through no fault of his own and despite his precautions, from inexhaustible wealth to the brink of poverty.

He bought a suit and went to a club for Russian emigrés, heard about possible work tutoring students and journalists in German and Russian, and within a month had moved into a flat with a friend in Berlin, while earning his keep. After the baby was weaned, Countess Miloslavsky took him to the von Blücher's estate at Kernslau, Tati and Clara continued at the Foreign Office, and Peter was assigned to temporary occupation duty near Bordeaux. Klaus was also on temporary duty at the army's western headquarters near Paris.

The old count often thought that the recent changes in the world were the greatest that had ever occurred, because all other changes had affected institutions that always evolved, such as religion, government or technology, whereas now, in the heart of human life, the family, an unprecedented freedom for women and children was displacing values that had endured, so far as anyone knew, beyond history.

He learned to cook and never missed his grand life as a seigneur, since everything around him was much more interesting than it had been on the estates, or in Petersburg. In six weeks he was elected to the emigré club, and in a year, he was president. He never allowed the loss of his country, estates or business to change his attitude to life. He said, "When bombs are falling on you out of the stratosphere, it is useless to worry about anything." According to Tati's Berlin friends, this was because of "his thousand-year-old Asiatic serenity," which he must have gotten from the Russian ancestry on his father's side.

He told her that he was an optimist "because I understand more than I know." And Tati replied, "And is a pessimist someone who knows more than he understands?" He laughed.

One day at his club, he was visited by the German partners who had taken over the film studio, and they offered him a part-time job as international agent and press representative for the news films and war-documentaries they were now making with the equipment which had once been half his. He accepted, and this salary, together with the teaching money, provided him and the countess with a living.

At dinner one evening he told them of one lady student who had asked him for advice after class. "She told me she had fallen in love with someone with grey sideburns, who rises above adversity. And she doesn't know what to do about it, he is so shy."

Tati, noticing that Clara was squirming with the effort not to laugh, egged him on, "And what did you tell her?"

"I said, 'But why are you confiding this to me, Madame, I am a Professor of language, not of the heart.'"

Tati collapsed on the ottoman with a shriek of laughter, "But Count Professor, don't you see, she is in love with you. You," and she pointed her finger at him, a gesture which, until this generation, had been thought to be far too rude for their family.

He was surprised by the thought and said no more but Tati loved to tease him, and often asked him how his star pupil was getting along. "You say she is learning English but she should be taking *le langage de l'amour*." She mooed the word *amour* so that it sounded like *Amoooooor* and waggled her head, so that he was more puzzled than ever.

His granddaughter's social freedom and her unconstrained character were part of the new way of life in the world, and he consoled himself by thinking that if this were true then the world had gained much and what it had lost was lost.

Berlin, July, 1940

On a warm evening, Clara stayed late in the Foreign Ministry office to type out some letters. She sat at Tati's desk because the typewriter was better than her own.

She was thinking of her father's bent arm, broken during the battle for Vimy Ridge, because she had just received a memorandum dictated by Hitler, following a visit to Paris and the war memorial at Vimy:

Propaganda destined for abroad must not in any way be based on that used for home consumption. Broadcasts to Britain, for example, must contain plenty of music of the kind popular among Britons. Thus, when their own stations fail them, they will start to listen to ours more and more. News bulletins should plainly state the facts without comment on their value or importance. News about British high finance, its interests in certain sections of the arms industry, in the leadership and conduct of the war, should be given without comment but couched in such a way that the listeners will themselves draw their own conclusions. For instance, in referring to British arms manufacturers, the writer should mention Shaw's play, Arms and the Man. *Little drops of water wear the stone away.*

The propaganda of the enemy must be ceaselessly shown to be false. For instance, I myself recently was informed that newspapers in Britain were complaining that the Germans were blowing up or defacing allied war memorials in France. I therefore took it upon myself to visit the memorial at Vimy Ridge, where I fought during the Great War. I saw no marks or defacements at all. On the contrary I was moved by the greatness of this memorial, and its concentration not upon the great victory won there but rather by the feelings of pity which it engenders. I had my photograph taken there and it will be published throughout the European press.

For our own people, we must broadcast not only the facts but also copious and precise commentaries on their importance and significance. Good propaganda must be stimulating. Our stations must talk about the drunkard Churchill and the criminal Roosevelt on every possible occasion.

There was in the art-room of *Signal* magazine next door a photograph of Hitler gazing at the tall towers of the Vimy memorial, which she put into the envelope, because she remembered her father talking about the battle, which until now had seemed to her remote as the Dark Ages.

She felt lonely for her father and mother. 'What would they think of what I am doing now, working for the Germans?' She had been evading this question until now, because the war had seemed unreal. The Phoney War, it had been called, because for so many months after the fall of Poland, nothing had happened. The work she was doing therefore was no harm to her country or the empire. But now, mighty Britain was shaken, her army shattered, her ships sinking all over the world, her cities collapsing under the Luftwaffe.

She gazed out the window feeling the warm air stirring the cotton sleeve of her dress and the papers on her desk. The tall windows opened on the Wilhelmstrasse, admitting the resiny smell of the poplars, lindens and flowers all in leaf along the broad boulevard.

A farm-cart loaded high with hay pulled by two old dobbins stopped and the driver got down, and placed two canvas nose-bags over their muzzles. He patted their necks, then climbed back up, reached into the hay behind him, and drew out a brown bottle, poured out a cup and sat gazing about, smoking his pipe. The trees showered shade down on him while the sparrows bounced around under the horses picking up seeds.

Clara thought, 'How peaceful it all is. Who could believe there is war anywhere.' She sighed watching the horses' heads bobbing together as they nosed into their feedbags, rubbing against each other like old friends. 'I must tell them in England how we feel here tonight.'

She started to type,

Dear Papa

    This letter will go uncensored, via a friend.

    It is so peaceful here it is hard to imagine that there is war anywhere. It reminds me of Fredericton on a summer afternoon when nothing is happening except the river running by and boys on bikes racing along the street.

    First news first: Peter and I are very happy together, when we see each other. He is a dear good man and so amusing, though like all German men, lazy about the house. He is well and sends you both his regards. He has warm memories of Charlton. We are both eager to see you as soon as this war is over.

    The mood in Berlin is not so much triumphant as relieved that it is all over, or nearly. But more important, for once the Party and the people are aligned for peace! Yes, it is true. No one here can see any reason now to prolong the war. Here is the big news: The Führer himself has said in private that he intends to put a stop to the war by offering to the English peace on generous terms, by which he means: Return of the German colonies taken by the Allies at Versailles; a free hand for Germany in Europe, and a free hand for the British Empire throughout the rest of the world where it already has interests. Furthermore, the French will be permitted to keep their country save for a few minor concessions in the east, and all their empire and fleet under the terms he will offer in future negotiations with Pétain. I know this is accurate because I had to type a Suggested Memorandum of Understanding With England on this subject for Helmuth James von Blücher, my boss (he is many levels higher, but a friend), and those were the terms (which I memorized) that were sent over to us on Chancellery stationery by von Below, the Führer's PPS, long before the negotiations began with the French government. So I know that this is what the Führer thinks, and von Blücher has advised him that in the circumstances these are reasonable terms, for the British.

My purpose in writing is to acquaint you with all this as soon as possible so that the English who must be in a dither now wondering which way to turn, will see that for once, this man is prepared to offer a reasonable settlement which will end the war! Tatiana von Zollerndorf, with whom I work, and whom you met at Schenkenberg in '38, the beautiful beautiful wife of Klaus von Zollerndorf, and I have become close friends. She is very funny and all the men are in tatters about her. She is a darling, knows le tout Berlin and makes my way easy at the Ministry. I am a senior translator now. People here know I "used to work for Lord Beaverbrook" and know him! As you can imagine, this being the propaganda section of the FM, I am looked on as something of an expert, both on newspapers and on England (and now of course Canada, which until this recent crisis had no importance, and has been magnified as the possible future home of the British government, after the invasion). Her husband, Count Klaus von Zollerndorf is colonel of a regiment that distinguished itself in France, and he is now promoted to the General Staff, which is a major coup.

So you can see I am well-connected and have reported to you not only the general mood but also the very specific thing I have seen, with source—thanks to dear Lord B's training, and I do hope this may make some difference as we all here believe there is no more need for this war. Never has this war seemed so unnecessary. Even futile. That is the general opinion high to low.

Please tell Mother that Tati has given birth to a happy healthy beautiful and intelligent little chap—I can hardly say baby, he seems to have been born as a little boy, not an infant. His name is Helmuth James, after guess whom. I have no plans (yet).

With all my love and hopes for peace now.
PS Please do not publish the photograph as people here might guess who sent it.

She kept a good copy, then on a separate folded sheet added a PS for her mother, *Besides, I hardly ever see Peter any more—only on leave, and the German Army pays no attention to my womanly 'schedule' so if I did get pregnant, it would be a shot in the dark.*

She opened the drawer of Tati's desk, withdrew the drawer, unrolled some adhesive tape, put the carbon copy of the letter into an envelope with her notes on Hitler's *aide-mémoire*, and stuck the envelope on the underside of the top of the desk, in the drawer-slot where it was concealed.

She was leaving for the von Blücher's estate at Kernslau for the weekend in half an hour, and she did not want to take the copy there. She would retrieve it next week and take it home, because it was not a good idea to leave it in the office, where the Gestapo had eyes and ears.

She addressed the letter to her father in London, wrote "Kindness of Freiherr von D." on the outside and put it in her purse with the hope that she was accomplishing something important for Germany and England.

As she walked home in the warm evening, greeting people with smiles all the way, she realized, 'It is not enough.' The words made her stop walking and say aloud, "What is not enough?" A dog on a leash passing by looked up at the sound of her voice, and she nodded to the owner, a woman in a tweed hat with a pheasant feather angled across the temple, and knew right away she had been evading her conscience. The letter was not enough to salve her conscience. She could no longer help the Germans in this war. She must leave the Foreign Ministry.

Five days later, in London, Sir James Dunsmuir was seated at his bacon and eggs in Portland Place reading Clara's letter which had just arrived from Spain with the morning post. He rose from the table, called for his car and took the letter round to his friend Beaverbrook at the Air Ministry.

Beaverbrook read it right away, said, "I'm off to see the PM in a moment, I'll take it with me." He tucked the letter into his pocket.

The day was bright and warm, but the coastal radar had shown large enemy formations approaching the Channel coast. There was at least half an hour till they would be over Kent. Beaverbrook suggested to Churchill that they walk to the Cabinet War Room through the park. So far in the war, no bombs had been dropped on London, although the RAF had several times bombed Berlin and Hamburg. Hitler was still appealing to the factions in England that opposed the war.

"But we shall take no chances, after all the bombs are random and might fall on Halifax as readily as elsewhere," Churchill joked.

Beaverbrook laughed. Guarded by two secret service men in dark suits, they were crossing the park on their way to the New Public Offices in the Strand, where the Cabinet War Room was located deep underground.

Churchill sat on a bench to light a cigar. Beaverbrook patted his pockets for a match and found the letter. He read it to the Prime Minister as they sat under the lime trees, puffing his cigar into blue circles.

"Doubtless she means well," said Churchill. "What is that photograph?"

Beaverbrook handed it to him, and Churchill gazed for a long time at Hitler standing before the Vimy memorial. "Are you going to publish this thing?"

"She asks me not to."

"It would be a coup for you."

"Yes. And perhaps a coup against you."

"Indeed?"

"Well, clearly he feels the power of that monument. Have you seen it?"

"No."

"It is most moving. A tremendous sermon against war. All pity, sorrow and waste. Not a square inch of glory in the whole huge thing."

"Then it's not for me."

Churchill winked. Beaverbrook stuck the photograph in his pocket.

"You'll notice that she knew days ahead the terms he offered to Pétain," said Beaverbrook.

"Did she now," said the Prime Minister, "Thanks Max, I missed that. So she has very good sources. Might we make use of her in the future?"

Beaverbrook was surprised. "But what do you think of the information?"

"The supposed offer to us? Well, we've already had intimations along this line. I should imagine Hitler's offer will be presented, if at all, under the guise of a generous settlement, which will include a few tempting morsels, but not the *raison de guerre*, and we shall have to negotiate, and the longer we negotiate the more the tempting morsels will be withdrawn, until none is left, and we are being urged from all sides to compromise, compromise, compromise in the interests of peace. How I hate that word."

Beaverbrook was about to ask which word he hated, compromise or peace, when Churchill rumbled on, "It was what happened every time we dickered with him after the *Anschluss*." He made an abrupt gesture and cigar-ash landed on his lapel, which Clemmie hated. "You can't trust a man who has no bad habits."

"On that ground, you and I have nothing to fear."

Beaverbrook looked glum. Churchill stuck out his jaw. "I do not believe for a moment he is sincere. His method has always been to divide our counsels and weaken our resolve. And he has been successful. No, we shall not negotiate, now or in the future. I have not become His Majesty's First Minister in order to negotiate away the birthright of the British people. I am the wrong Minister for that." He lifted his chin smiling down his nose and said, "Max, you are my best friend in the world, and wisest counsel, what would you advise?"

"You are a great fraud—you pretend to ask for a navigator when all you want is a pilot."

Churchill smiled. "How well you know me," he said.

"And my answer is, yes, I will help you to the maximum of my strength, regardless of what you choose to do." He held up his hand to stay his friend's thanks. "But since you ask for advice, I would pay attention to this,"—he flourished Clara's letter—"and find out if she is right, and if so, let it be known to them by the back door, that compromise is possible. After all, there are elements in Cabinet which favour negotiation."

"Name the traitors," Churchill said. "Surely you don't mean yourself?"

"You know how I feel about the Empire, you know my campaigns against indifference and foreign influence."

"What are you leading up to?"

"Even if we beat Hitler, it is clear now that it will cost us the Empire. We must consider that. It is only common sense. We are nearly bankrupt now."

"Common sense leads to common results," Churchill growled, and got up, ignoring the advice he had requested.

Berlin, July, 1940

Coming home from France, Peter sent Clara a telegram from Reims, so he was looking for her in the crowd on the platform at Berlin Zoo. He saw the paper of flowers she was waving, then heard her voice calling "Peter, over here," as she pushed through the happy women and older men welcoming the soldiers home. She hugged him close and kissed him on the lips despite the smell of two days sweaty travelling and his scrubby beard. He hugged her close and called her *meine Kanudierin*, which he did when he was pleased with her. They held hands in the taxi, while she told him her news. He was thinking, 'What a great girl I married,' while she thought, 'Dear good Peter, I shall stir him up a bit.' She ran a bath for him in the big cast-iron tub, and led him to it. Then she took off her clothes, said, "Move over," and climbed in.

That evening, Clara went to Tati's flat to help prepare the dinner party she was giving to celebrate Peter's return. She found the place so dusty she could not believe it. "Don't you have a charwoman?"

"I did, but she's gone home to help her mother," said Tati, knocking over a Meissen figurine with a duster then catching it with her free hand. The apartment was like their marriage. Tati had brightened the serious things—flowers stood on the dark oak mantelpiece, paintings hung on the somber brown walls, china figurines danced in front of Klaus' many books on the overpopulated shelves that rose to the lofty ceiling. In the centre of the dining table of dark mahogany, which lent a solemn rigour to the act of eating that Klaus approved, Tati set flowers, the napkins were pink or baby-blue, and at dinner parties she floated red rose petals at random on the dark wood

At first Klaus had disapproved of her passion for tiny pieces, especially on the bookshelves, but he loved her for accompanying him sensitively in Schubert and Mozart duets for cello and piano.

A knock sounded at Tati's door and she went to answer it, saying over her shoulder to Clara with a happy smile, "Here's Peter."

It was Peter with a sly smile and flowers in his hands, saying, "Close your eyes, I have a surprise."

Tati closed her eyes and heard heavy footsteps, a rustle of clothing, then big arms went round her and lips pressed her lips, and she opened her eyes and saw Klaus' hazel-brown eyes altogether too big and close. He picked her up and said, "I must see him, where is he?" They went to the nursery where Helmuth was asleep, on his back, his squarish head pink and hot-looking. Klaus set her down and said, "He's marvellous. So mature. Like a little bald man."

Tati whispered, "He has curly blond fuzz coming in now. You'll see in the morning. And he drinks and sleeps and looks around. He knows all about me already and he is dying to talk to me. We have little conversations. I croon and make eyes at him and he laughs and gurgles and points already. He points and his eyes follow people across the room."

"What colour?"

"Blue. And I am sure now they will stay blue. He is the most marvellous little boy already."

They tiptoed out into the corridor and she left the door ajar, and Klaus took her hand.

"I got four weeks leave yesterday," he said, twirling around the salon, "what a campaign, what a victory, France was ours in three weeks," he kept on twirling until she began to feel dizzy, "we have only 50 casualties in the whole regiment, I have four weeks leave and I have earned the Iron Cross."

"Oh my god," Tati kept saying over and over, thinking of all the fears she had had.

"And champagne. I liberated this in Reims, day before yesterday, and saved it for us."

Count Miloslavsky came in from his club and saw his granddaughter's husband for the first time. He clicked his heels and bowed from the waist, like a Prussian officer, then they embraced. Klaus like all proud Germans condescended to people from Eastern Europe without thinking about it, but he liked the serene look of this man, and sat him on the sofa to hear about the escape, and what the count had seen of Russian armour and discipline.

Klaus said, "It's all wonderful. What more can happen now? Hurray for all of us, especially you, Tati, the most beautiful woman in Europe." He raised his glass of champagne.

Klaus settled beside Tati on the sofa and talked on about the French campaign. His regiment had penetrated deep into southern Belgium in the first fortnight of the attack, with no difficulty at all, then turned south towards Reims. Most of the French divisions they met surrendered after a short struggle, or none at all. Soon they had so many prisoners all they could do was disarm them and send them to the rear under their own officers. In three weeks, they had arrived beyond the farthest point of penetration of the army in the Great War and the fighting was virtually over.

"After that we were *en touriste* going wherever we liked, it was magnificent. There were millions of refugees, but nothing else in our way. We just shooed them home and went on with flowers on our tanks. It was a picnic, I tell you, just the way war should be—tremendous preparation, decisive victory, and a just peace after. War is for the making of heroes."

"What just peace?" Clara said.

"They say in the Bendlerstrasse that Hitler is going to offer England peace."

"And Churchill will turn it down, I expect," said Peter.

"Then he is a fool. The English have lost the *casus belli* now and their strongest ally. Peace is inevitable, and now people say that the Führer's offer is very generous. We see that he is not mad, as we thought. That man's father is war."

Peter was surprised. "This is not what you were saying in September."

"I'm a soldier. Victory changes everything," said Klaus. "But let's not talk about that. Don't look gloomy, Clara, he has no plans for your empire."

Clara looked at him. 'My empire? Does he see me as an enemy now?'

"Klaus, you seem too happy," she said.

"It is over and so few have died."

"It's not over," she said. She disliked asserting herself against this big, strong, aristocratic war-hero, thinking she ought to hold her tongue. She felt very constrained these days, for she knew she occupied an inferior position, as a woman in this male-oriented society and as a beaten Briton, and yet she did not feel in the least inferior.

But Klaus ignored her. He said to Tati, "How is Berlin taking it?"

Tati said, "Well, people are glad, but they're somehow reluctant."

Clara said, "In the office we were disappointed because we had been praying for France to hold out." Klaus looked grim though before the victory he would have approved. 'What has happened to Klaus?' Clara thought. Was victory going to turn him into just another arrogant German? Not since she had known Peter had she felt her own difference from Germans so much. If a German detected an accent in her voice, he thought she was English, so she said, "No, I am a Canadian." Thereafter they called her an American. For Germans, there was no such nation as Canada. This had at first made her feel very odd, as if she was from Nowhere, without history. But to be placeless in the minds of others made it easy to fit in. After a year she passed as a tall red-haired north German even in north Germany. Coming into the Foreign Office married to a Metternich, under the aegis of Helmuth James had helped, for she was accorded a status that might have taken years to achieve. By the spring of 1940, she was thinking like the open-minded Germans she knew.

Klaus stroked his chin, thinking. Something was wrong. People here did not feel as he did. Victory had not united them. He was upset because his friends seemed to be not much moved by the stunning victory in France.

'It is bound to be different for soldiers,' he thought. 'We risked our lives and it is over at last, and we are alive. They can not feel as we do.' But Peter had been through as much of the campaign as he had, and there was no exultation in Peter's manner. He turned to his friend and asked him point blank, "What do you think now?"

Peter sighed. "I have to admit that I was hoping that if the French held out, then there would have to be negotiations, and Hitler would be out. And now . . . I don't know."

"Don't know what?" Klaus said.

"You see, the problem is, such a huge victory discourages the opposition here and confirms those thugs in power."

Klaus was shocked to hear the word thug, which he had used himself two months ago. Doubt returned to his mind: if victory did not satisfy the people, what was the use of it? He was embarrassed because he saw how far the joy of victory had lured him toward Hitler.

"Aren't we blockheads," said Peter, ever the peacemaker, "Two weeks ago, we were all anxious because we were in a life and death struggle, and we thought, 'If we can just get past this hurdle, then everything will be all right.' But now we are past the hurdle and worrying again. Let's for once, just sit down and enjoy ourselves. Here's to your baby."

Clara thought, 'This is why I love you,' and lifted her glass of Piper Heidseick.

As they were completing the toast, Klaus proposed another, to show he was with them in spirit. "A toast to France," he said, "may her civilizing mission survive this passing drama." They drank without enthusiasm, thinking this was a very forced sentiment.

'Klaus always brings something uncomfortable into the occasion, some high strong principle, some maudlin statement,' Clara thought. 'If only he would relax.' She wondered if in six months, Klaus would be toasting the survival of the British civilizing mission after another German conquest.

She glanced at Klaus' book shelves—Bismarck's social reforms, Tolstoy's *The Law of Love and the Law of Violence,* Proudhon's early socialist writings, most of them concerned with bettering mankind. Peter brought out the brandy, Tati went to bed, and the others stayed up late, drinking and talking. They went for a walk arm-in-arm in the balmy darkness, and although there seemed to be an unusual number of people on the sidewalks in a good mood, Berlin was not in ecstasy.

Clara, who had intended to resign from the Foreign Ministry weeks before, had postponed writing the letter to Helmuth James because the war did not seem serious—people were calling it "the sitzkrieg"—and then because he was called to Paris to deal with problems of the new occupation forces, and she did not want to leave a letter for him without any explanation face to face. He had only just now returned, and she was determined to go in the morning and do it. She met Helmuth in his office in the Adlon and laid the letter before him with the warning, "I must go, James, I am most grateful to you for your help, but you must understand my position now."

"But what will you do, my dear Clara?" He could not help condescending to her, although he admired her forthrightness and her energy.

"I shall be teaching English part-time with Count Miloslavsky. I'll miss you and Tati and everyone in the office so much."

"Perhaps we can find non-sensitive work for you."

"No," she said, "nothing for the government."

He pointed to the ceiling and mouthed in English, 'Walls have ears.'

He picked up his grey gloves and said, "Shall we go for a walk?"

They went into the Tiergarten, where people were walking slowly because of the heat. The air was like grey jelly, and wraiths of mist hovered over the Neuersee beside the path. She was feeling almost faint with the heat, her face was flushed and rivulets of perspiration dampened her hairline, so he found a bench and sat her down on it.

He told her she had made a wise decision because he had heard that morning that Heinrich Himmler, in charge of the SS, was looking for people like her who understood English and American jargon. Expressions such as "nigger in the woodpile," "boffin," "gremlin," "Kilroy was here," "Bob's your uncle," "gimme a break," "wooden nickel," "buffaloed," baffled scholars who had been to Oxford.

"But surely they send their messages in code?"

"It's incredible, but the Americans and English—even Roosevelt and Churchill—are talking on a radio-telephone link that was scrambled by a machine built by Siemens. Himmler could scarcely believe his good luck, but then his listeners were mystified by what was said. The memo came round this morning asking for personnel who might help the SS."

Clara shuddered.

"I said we had no one. But we will backdate your resignation by three months, and say we think you have left the country. But we still need you."

"Not for the government."

"No, not for the government," and he leaned across the bench and embarrassed her by putting his mouth close to her sweaty head and whispering in her ear, "We are rescuing U-boats, taking them by train out through Vienna to Hungary and then Turkey. Right under the nose of the SS and SA and Gestapo and the whole damn works."

"All right," she whispered, "I can do that."

Hyde Park, New York, July, 1940

❦

Cameron Bannatyne, Lord Beaverbrook and Dudley Treloar were driven by Bannatyne's chauffeur Keightley in the dark red McLaren from Toronto through vineyards and apple orchards on the long hillsides of the Finger Lakes to Hyde Park in the Hudson River Valley where President Roosevelt was waiting to meet them, far from reporters.

They spent the night at a hotel on Lake Skaneateles, then started at dawn for Hyde Park. The chauffeur parked the car at the end of the railway station where President Roosevelt was sitting in the shade at the wheel of his Ford. The top was down, he was smoking a cigarette in an ivory holder, wearing a seersucker suit and white panama hat. Two big men in dark suits wearing dark glasses and fedoras walked straight up to them and blocked their way. "Identify yourself please, sir," said one, standing between them and the President's car.

"It's all right, Mr. Daniel," the President called out, "I've known Dudley for years." Daniel paid no attention. He said, "Excuse me, sir," and patted them all down, then asked them to open their briefcases. They opened their cases while FDR was calling out, "Sorry about this, they won't do a thing I tell them." Then the security men stepped aside and let them pass.

They got into the Ford, Beaverbrook beside the President in front and Dudley holding his bowler on his head beside Cameron, his white hair flying in the windy rear. A small black car pulled out of the station after them and kept pace, ten lengths behind on the narrow winding road roofed by elms and overlooking the Hudson river.

The President parked in front of a tall verandahed house set at the top of a lawn that sloped to the river 100 metres away. The secret service men lifted the President into a wheelchair. The effort was plain in Roosevelt's face as he dragged his dangling legs over the car seat into the wheelchair. Beaverbrook helped to wheel him up onto the veran-dah. Roosevelt said, "Thanks Max." Beaverbrook's round gnomish face broke into a wide smile, which emphasized even further the great width of his mouth.

They sat at a round table overlooking the lawn. "Well, what do you think?" the President said, gesturing down to the river. Tall elms beside the garden threw long shadows from the morning sun over the bordering roses and peonies. A wooden dinghy with a gaff-rigged sail slanted across the river, heading up against the slow current. The far bank was a wall of green, striped black with shadow where creeks fell in from the steep hills above.

Dudley said, "It's hard to believe the world is at war. Most of it."

A tall young woman with a diffident air, and eyes for the President, came onto the verandah with a tray. She set out three teacups and a cof-fee mug, and the President introduced her with an affectionate smile. "Cameron, Dudley, Max, allow me to introduce Missy Lehand with-out whom nothing worth doing gets done around here." They all rose, and she said, "Good morning, gentlemen, I hope you are not too tired after your long trip."

"It was marvellous coming down the Hudson," said Cameron.

"Dudley," the President said with a smile, "I remember you pre-fer tea."

"I must say," Dudley said, "I am impressed by your memory. Or your staff work." They both laughed as the President said simulta-neously, "Staff work," with a happy smile up to Missy Lehand. She said, "I'll leave you gentlemen. If you need me later, Mr. President, I'll be in the library. You're lunching with Mr. Justice Frankfurter and Secretary Morgenthau."

"I shall join you in coffee, thanks Mr. President," said Dudley.

"No, it was Dudley and Franklin last year, so let's keep it that way."

"Fine, Franklin," said Dudley.

"What can I do for you gentlemen?" Roosevelt said, pouring the coffee.

Dudley opened, as they had agreed. "I am sure, Franklin, that you are fully informed as to the nature of the tragedy in France." At this, Roosevelt's face turned sad and he looked away. "A terrible business," he said, "simply awful. I wish we had been able to find some way to help."

"You can help to avert a similar tragedy occurring in Great Britain."

"You have the greatest fleet in the world. Hitler has nothing to compare."

"A modern ship however strong is indefensible against air attack."

"I am surprised to hear that from a naval officer of your experience."

"We should be up against U-boats as well as air power, and that air power is now based on aerodromes in the Low Countries and France only ten minutes from Portsmouth and our whole south coast."

"You make it seem as if England itself is indefensible, in your opinion."

"If the Luftwaffe is as strong as we think it is, and if Hitler throws his whole navy into the attack and launches a full-scale invasion before the last full moon in September, it is the opinion of our Imperial General Staff that he will have a better than even chance of success, no matter how well we fight. We have rather fewer than 300 tanks in the whole island, and no artillery to speak of. We lost practically all our modern equipment in France. Our army has disappeared. What we have now are some defeated regulars, a lot of willing volunteers who can't shoot and are armed with the oldest rifles in the world."

"I have heard that Hitler has made an . . ." Roosevelt hesitated. "An offer to settle out of court, as it were." He smiled, and then his face suddenly grew very stern. "Will you accept it? Will you even consider it?"

"We do not negotiate on our knees."

"Oh dear," said the President, but Dudley went on. "Not that we are on our knees, but Herr Hitler seems to think we are."

Roosevelt had not been informed of any peace offer by Hitler; his statement to Dudley had been disingenuous, probing for information he suspected but did not have. And now he knew: Hitler had made an offer and the British were negotiating, for if they were not, he thought, Winston would have told him already that he had refused. The President had to decide if the British would quit or if they would fight on in hopes that the Americans would come to their rescue. If that were the case, he would help, for a price. He would demand the abolition of the Empire preferential tariff protecting markets which Roosevelt's supporters coveted. The President would also tell the British they would have to sell their interests in the US to pay for arms. And they would have to listen to his advice on how to manage the Empire, notably the movement for independence in India.

He asked Beaverbrook, who he knew was Churchill's best friend, "And if all else fails, if the Germans get ashore, what will you do with the fleet?"

"I am sure you know as well as we that we are not planning on giving up."

"But you have not given up on planning," Roosevelt said with his famous sunny smile. He stuck his jaw out, pushing his cigarette holder up at a jaunty angle. They all laughed. The easy camaraderie he had just created was his greatest political asset. It was said that even his enemies liked him.

Max said, "In the last resort, the Navy will bring the Royal family, the House of Commons, the Bank of England and as many army personnel as possible to Canada, and we shall fight on from there."

"Bully," said the President.

Cameron said, "The essence of this war is air power. We need planes now." Roosevelt said nothing. "We are producing Hurricane fighters right now and are setting up to produce bombers in Canada. The new Rolls-Royce Merlin engines will also be produced here."

Beaverbrook said, "We have bombers coming along which can carry ten tons from Yorkshire to Berlin. And fight their way through if necessary with three electrical turrets mounting twin .50 calibre machine guns. We shall soon be producing six per day. Loaded with incendiaries, these planes will be able to destroy a city in one night."

"Something that Göring was unable to do in Rotterdam even though he had total air supremacy," the President said.

"They have nothing like these planes, and nothing like the quantities we are about to produce. We shall destroy Germany from the air."

"And what do you need from us?"

"Right now, ships and fighter planes."

"The Congress has tied my hands with this blessed Neutrality Act. Ham Fish, Congressman, who lives just down from here, thinks he has made it impossible for us to help you no matter how threatening the Germans become. But I tell you in private, there's more than one way to catch a fish even if he is really Ham." He laughed at this joke, which he had made many times before.

Cameron was deadly serious. "You are forbidden to sell us arms. But the law says nothing about junk. You have 400 P40 Tomahawk fighters at Leavenworth. You fly 200 of them to the US border-side of the 290, the highway leading north into Saskatchewan. You close the road for repairs, land the planes on your side, mechanics disable the aircraft by removing the distributor, so the planes are unflyable. The pilots are bussed out. The planes just sit there. That night, our trucks arrive and tow the planes over the border, we repair them, and *voilà* we have saved 200 fighters from the junk pile."

The President laughed and slapped the table making the cups rock. "Grand, grand, I love it. I'll have to check this with the flyboys and the legal beagles but already I like it. Wait till Fish gets wind of this one. Oh boy." He chortled. Then he straightened up and said, "Now what's all this about McLaren cars, the Currie company and Packard?"

"McLaren builds cars. Currie builds the engines. That was a McLaren car we came in. We'd like to present it to you if you will accept it."

"No thank you, far too dangerous," Roosevelt said. "Not automotively, I'm sure it's a grand car. No, politically. But thank you all the same."

He rummaged in his briefcase as Cameron said, "Packard wants to buy Currie, but we can't sell because we need Currie to produce engines for our Hurricane and Mosquito fighters. But we need more than we can make there. We are willing to licence our new Rolls-Royce Merlins to you. These are the most powerful engines in the world. Over 1,700 horsepower. They drive the new Mark IV Spitfire at over 400 mph."

"Very impressive," said the President, who had in his briefcase a secret assessment of the new British engines which he had forgotten.

"McLaren and Currie are controlled by my wife's brother, Sam McLaren. On the advice of our government, Sam has refused the Packard offer because we can't afford to let the control pass out of our hands in wartime. However, we have discussed this with Winston and Prime Minister King, and here's the idea: Sam accepts the offer, Ottawa authorizes the sale of 50 per cent of McLaren and Currie to Packard, forming Packard-McLaren, which then gets the exclusive licence to build the Rolls-Royce Merlin in Canada, and Packard USA gets the right to build the engines in the USA."

Roosevelt lit a cigarette in his holder. "It sounds complicated."

"Believe me, it will work, I have done a dozen deals like this with Max. But here's the best part—Packard in Detroit can send the almost-completed engines over the border, on an intra-company transfer to Packard-McLaren, which is hard for your Ham Fishes to detect and to prove."

"Well, you boys seem to have it all worked out. I am impressed. Did you bring along any paperwork on this?"

Cameron handed him the shopping list. Roosevelt began reading it as the others waited in tense silence.

Beaverbrook lit a cigarette as Roosevelt scanned the list. When he saw the President's gaze lift from the page, he said, "There is one matter we did not want to put on paper. The Germans are privy to some of our best-guarded secrets about hydrogenation of oil in the coal-to-oil process that Standard Oil and Royal Dutch Shell have invented. The Germans have secret agreements with some of your oil companies to share technical knowledge on increasing aviation fuel octane, which increases performance. As you know, they have no oil of their own."

The President said, "But you know Stalin is giving it to Hitler. I don't understand that arrangement he has made, do you?"

"Stalin is desperate. He has done everything he could to sic Hitler onto us. In any case, the understanding between the oil companies, yours and theirs, is so close that the German government is guaranteed a royalty on every drop of aviation fuel refined in this country and sold to the RAF."

"Impossible," said the President.

"I assure you, patented processes for manufacturing synthetic rubber have already been sent to Germany. Standard Oil has been shipping high-octane aviation gasoline to Germany, which has been used against us during the Battle of France. We want this stopped."

Roosevelt looked very disturbed by this. "I shall look into this and have it stopped." He sat back and looked from Beaverbrook to Bannatyne to Treloar. "Isn't it curious that you know all this?" he said. This was the critical point Beaverbrook had been coming to. Now the President had to be told in such a way that he could pretend that he had not been told, that the Canadians were spying on them and broadcasting propaganda to Americans through radio stations purchased under fictitious names.

No one spoke. Silence was Beaverbrook's way of telling Roosevelt that they were doing things which Roosevelt should not know.

Roosevelt said, "I see. Well, I respect that. But I need a hint."

Beaverbrook glanced at Treloar, who nodded, and said, "It begins with an R." And Roosevelt nodded, thinking, 'Rockefeller.'

"Well, boys, that's all right then," he said.

Bannatyne said, "And the planes?"

"It won't be easy, but we can manage somehow." In a different tone of voice, quiet, measured, he said, "I am for him, I am all for him. He is a great man. If anyone can save you, he can." He did not need to say he meant Churchill.

He watched the river, remembering. How far he had come from the days of his youth here, when he could run and sail and swim. And yet he was still here by this river, under these trees, in the same sunny weather he remembered and loved. And pinned to this chair, he still held the power of life and death over the British Empire and perhaps over Germany as well.

He sighed and returned to them. "Tell Winston this, from Long-fellow,

> *Thou too sail on O Ship of State*
> *Sail on O Union proud and great*
> *Humanity with all its fears*
> *With all the hope of future years*
> *Is hanging breathless on thy fate."*

Three weeks later, Bannatyne received by government courier a copy of a letter written by the President on White House letterhead to John D. Rockefeller asking Rockefeller to help Bannatyne in whatever way he could.

Berlin, July 19, 1940

Albert Speer, handsome and well-dressed in a tweed hacking jacket, grey flannels and tie of red French silk, showed his pass to the usher at the door of the distinguished visitors box in the Kroll Opera House and was waved through to the stair, together with his wife Margarete. As they emerged just above the stage where Hitler would speak to the members of the Reichstag and guests, several women noticed him and whispered, "There he is, isn't he handsome, they say he is the Führer's darling now. He is redesigning Berlin for us."

There was in the rustling and whispering of many hundreds of people echoing from the high ceiling the intense satisfaction of being present at a great moment in human history. Victorious Germany speaking through the amazing chancellor who had rescued her from humiliation, was, rumour said, going to offer a magnanimous peace to the British Empire.

Hitler stopped before the closed door to the stage to straighten his tie and brush back the lock of hair falling over his left forehead. Then he stepped forth into the light and as the applause began, walked up the steps to the rostrum. He gripped the sides of the lectern, listening to the applause, thinking not of the war, or even of the peace treaty to be signed with Britain, but of building a new greater Germany.

Fat Hermann Göring, President of the Reichstag, resplendent in a white uniform, held up his hands applauding as he looked with adoration at his leader. Everyone rose clapping. The noise was tremendous, for they knew that their applause was making history. Hitler listened to the surging sound like waves on the shore going on for minutes, his chest swelling with satisfaction. This was what he had wanted ever since the days when he had starved in a dirty suit in Vienna. Once Great Britain signed the peace treaty that he would outline here today, he could begin to beautify Berlin.

He glanced up at the box to his right and saw his architect Albert Speer where he wanted him to be, exposed to this mass adulation in the highest assembly of the nation. 'One day, I will be known as the greatest artist of all time. For no artist before me has worked on a canvas as vast as Berlin, as Germany, as the whole of Europe,' he thought. He held on to the lectern because dizzying waves of feeling accompanied the vision that was elevating him above the clapping audience. The walls of the building fell away and he could see thousands of miles over Europe. Timeless destiny fused with this dazzling moment in his brain. The people before him were applauding a long shining autobahn leading from Berlin through green farmlands to the palm trees beside the Black Sea. He imagined the moment when the army would present Russia to him, in the shape of the golden keys to the Kremlin. 'But you have not even decided on the invasion of Russia yet!' he thought. He smiled, holding up his hands, then grew solemn. The applause died.

He wanted to persuade the English to end the war, so he spoke gently, never with the hoarse urgency that seized him when he was soliciting votes, or bullying the leader of a small country. Now he was silky, his hands describing graceful curves that wooed sympathy. He addressed the British leaders: "I can see no reason for this war to go on. You have lost your reason for war. Poland is administered under German control, as part of the Greater German Reich which now stretches from the North Cape to Spain, from the south of France to Russia. We invite you to join with us in administering a peaceful world. No harm can befall the British Empire while she is allied with us, and Germany guarantees, as we are willing to do, the integrity of the Empire against all comers." Speer was flattered when Hitler looked at him while saying, "Let the reconstruction of the world begin now with the help of the British Empire."

Hitler had asked Speer and Margarete to come to dinner in the chancellery, so Speer took a double whiskey at the Adlon on the way, thinking that dinner would be the steamed vegetables and rice mush that Hitler subsisted on.

Hitler greeted them at the door to the private dining room, kissing Margarete Speer's hand. "But my dear Speer, why have you been hiding this treasure from our eyes?" And then with the elaborate southern deference he thought was due to women, "My dear, please feel free to join us in our little *tête à tête,* whenever you wish. We need youth and beauty about us all the time, isn't that right Speer? You as an artist must realize this, for you have demonstrated it in your choice of a life companion."

He smiled at Margarete, who said, "Thank you, mein Führer."

Speer said nothing, for Hitler loved to run on without interruption. He looked for the drinks tray, fearing soda water, and was surprised when he discovered that Hitler had ordered a delicious ragout of beef, with all the burgundy he and Margarete wanted. "After all, it is time for some of us to enjoy the fruits of conquest," said Hitler. He poured a glass of water. "This is Vichy water."

Speer said, "*Veni, vidi, Vichy,*" and Hitler looked puzzled until Speer explained the joke. Hitler grimaced, hating his triumphalist philistinism to be noticed.

Hitler was still feeling pleased about his visit to Paris that week with Speer, when they had walked down the Champs-Elysées, and then visited the Paris Opera, where he had corrected the French tour guide on a point of structural detail about the building. He said, "Wasn't Paris beautiful? I often wondered if we would have to destroy Paris. But now it is your job, Speer, to make Berlin ten times more beautiful."

Speer, who had been astonished at Hitler's exact knowledge of the Opera building's dimensions, had also thought it was typical of his banal mind, so he replied, "Beauty is in the eye of the beholder, mein Führer, it can not be quantified."

Hitler glared at him, hating to be corrected like this in front of Margarete. He checked her expression, but her eyes were cast down.

He had an ineradicable feeling of inferiority to Speer and all successful artists because in his student days he had twice sent his drawings and architectural renderings to the Arts Academy in Vienna, and had been refused admission. He had exposed his soul to the professors, thinking it was beautiful, and they had said, "Insufficient."

Because Hitler saw Speer as one of the elite which he wanted to join, he felt contradictory before the young architect: he was a hopeful dilettante craving creative artistic power, and a world-conquering dictator, commanding everything except what he wanted most. Genius. *Speer*.

"When I was young I was poor but I lived in palaces of imagination," Hitler said. "When Hanisch asked my occupation, I said 'I am a painter,' and he said, 'Well, it's not hard to make money doing that. I see lots of house-painters working these days.' And I told the poor dolt, 'I am not a painter of houses, except through the imagination. I am an academician and an artist. I am also a writer.' What do you think of that, eh?"

"You have always been noted for your daring," said Speer.

"Bah," said Hitler, "it is all rot anyway. I mean, what the academics say. When this is all finished, there will be terror in the universities and art academies of Germany, believe me, we have already rid them of the Jews and communists, and now the time-wasters and super-aesthetes will have to go too. Maybe to the front. Picture that, eh Speer? A battalion of professors advancing on the enemy with their fountain pens uncapped. Wouldn't that strike terror in the hearts of the commissars."

Margarete laughed but Speer said nothing. Hitler for years had hated the Viennese academics, but now he could have his revenge by mocking them in front of the artist he had made the most eminent of all.

As dessert was served, Hitler began to expound his ideas for the future. "The plans we have been making for rebuilding Berlin, my dear Mrs. Speer, I can not in all fairness to the German people, begin to implement until I have ended the war in the west."

"But mein Führer, whatever can you mean, there is no war anywhere else." Hitler laughed for a long time, until Speer glanced at Margarete.

Hitler stopped and wiped his eyes with his napkin. "Oh Mrs. Speer, you have read my mind, it's true, my work is not finished, I shall have to invade Russia soon but they will collapse in a few weeks. Then we may invade England. But I hope it will be unnecessary, because they will give up as soon as Russia collapses. Their only hope now is that the Russians will pull their chestnuts from the fire."

He saw that both Speer and Margarete looked appalled at the prospect of this new war, so he said, "They have already seized the Baltic principalities, they scheme in Bulgaria and Rumania, and they will seize our oil there as soon as they lose their fear of the Wehrmacht. It may not be possible to keep the army in such perfection as it now is. It is time to crush them. Then the British will collapse."

Hitler waited but Speer said nothing. Hitler went on, "Back to architecture. You and I can begin after we have dealt with the British. But you have sealed your fate, you may never leave Germany again, for I have declared you a national treasure. You can not leave without my permission."

Speer was angry. He had always looked down on Hitler as a talented amateur architect, without any originality, whose taste was for the decadent neo-Baroque. It was intolerable to be treated as a possession.

Speer said, "I hope this mark of your favour does not become public because it would make your friends jealous, and your enemies will say it is proof that even your friends must be kept by force."

Hitler saw that he had offended a genius who he wished would accept him as an equal. He said, "My dear Speer, don't be offended, you know I wish the best for you, your dear wife and for Germany. Forget I said anything—you are free to come and go as you wish. I beg you, do be careful where you set foot, for my enemies would love to strike at me through you. Together we have great works to accomplish, fit for a great nation destined to endure a thousand years." He stood up and walked around the room, "This will remain our little secret. Now, let us have some fun."

He jingled keys in his hand as he led the way down the tunnel to the Arnim Palace, talking as he went. He opened the door and flipped on the lights. Margarete gasped. She was used to her husband's models, but this one was amazing, 50 metres long, depicting the boulevard that would lead five kilometres through central Berlin past the Great Dome to the Triumphal Arch. Hitler put on his gold-rimmed spectacles and giggled. He had calculated that the volume of the dome of the Hall of the People at the end of the boulevard would be three times Saint Peter's in Rome. The boulevard would be much wider than the Champs-Elysées. "These are the designs I made when I was in Landsberg prison 16 years ago. My buildings will convey my spirit and time to far posterity."

Speer said, "Then we must build to be ruined," and sketched how the Great Dome and the Triumphal Arch would look a thousand years hence, making them resemble Roman ruins. In silence, Hitler watched Speer sketch, envying the quick sure strokes. "You have understood me," Hitler said with a whinny of laughter. "Your husband is a genius, Mrs. Speer."

"Yes," she said.

Hitler kneeled before the model to bring his eye to the view of the pedestrian, then began changing the lights to produce noon, dusk, night. As the stars came out and the tiny lights inside the model buildings shone, Margarete Speer sighed. Hitler smiled. Speer, leaning over the table, gazing at his handiwork, as Hitler made suggestions, which always tended to the gigantic, mumbled "yes" over and over, while discarding the ideas in favour of improvements of his own.

Speer and Margarete left the Chancellery late, excited by visions of buildings vast and beautiful stretching all round the capital city of the greatest nation on earth. They walked slowly, so he could sense the bulky darkness of the buildings along the Wilhelmstrasse shifting shape and think about the proportions of long boulevards, and how to enliven the massive orderly structures so they would not be boring.

Margarete, seeing that he was in the brooding mood which always came on him after a meeting with Hitler, said, "The client is being difficult."

"He is a derivative dilettante in love with the neo-Baroque."

"I am amazed at how you speak to him. You ignore him, you speak your mind, he defers to you. You are his unrequited love."

Speer burst out, "He is the only man in the world who could commission on such a vast scale. The man's like the devil, he has a hundred guises—soldier, statesman, diplomat, politician, writer, but thank god, not artist. No, not that." He stopped on the sidewalk, fingering the smooth expensive silk cuff of his shirt, thinking, 'That makes me Faust, selling my soul to Mephistopheles,' and at that moment, air-raid sirens moaned and searchlights snapped erect all round him, poking high into the dark air as he had made them do for the Nuremberg rallies, a palisade of light to protect civilization from the howling barbarians outside.

He said, "This is how Britain answers our peace proposal." He took her hand and they ran back toward the Chancellery air-raid shelter.

Berlin, November 12, 1940

Adolf Hitler could not make up his mind what to do next. He considered the whole world, seeking opportunity. He kept asking himself, 'Where is the weak point?' because he conceived the world as a battleground. The Americans he disregarded because they were too remote, had no culture and their Anglo-Saxon blood had been weakened by yids and niggers. To invade Britain, to take over Spain and Gibraltar, to roll through Turkey to the oil of the middle east, were possibilities. But if he invaded Turkey, his northern flank would be exposed to Russian attack. 'Stalin will always have 200 divisions ready to attack me through Bessarabia. He can march on Ploesti and even with that ramshackle army of his, get there in a week. It is no good. Something must be settled with that man.' He told von Below to call Ribbentrop. He would invite Molotov to Berlin.

At the door of the Chancellery, Hitler greeted Molotov, a blunt little man in a fedora and mauve suit favoured by the *nomenklatura* of Moscow.

Hitler shook his hand and escorted him to the four-metre high main door to his study. Ribbentrop stood by the window, as he liked to do, so he could glance out while trying to think up something to say. Molotov, imperturbable, sat down on a straight wood chair before the gigantic desk. Hitler walked up and down, gesturing. "The British are finished. I have offered them a generous peace, like the peace we have given to France." He paused for the interpreter. "They have refused because they are led by a bungling dilettante, Winston Churchill, who has failed in every crisis of his long undistinguished career. He is so in the hands of the Jews that they call him behind his back Weinstein Churchill." He laughed. Molotov sat looking glum with his square small hands planted forward on his knees.

"It is the Jews who keep England fighting," Hitler insisted, forgetting that many of the senior communists around Molotov were Jewish.

"Is the Führer informed about American supplies to Churchill?"

"The interest of Roosevelt is to pick up pieces of the British Empire. They bought Newfoundland for 30 old ships. Who knows what they will pay for Canada? Maybe a hundred. The US has no interests in Europe. The British are ridiculous, trying to force their antiquated policies on Europe, without a single ally." He smiled towards Molotov, who did not budge.

Molotov said in his monotonous voice, "If it is Germany's intention to manage Europe, why is Japan included in the Tripartite Pact?"

Hitler, agitated, controlled himself. "This is not aimed at you," he said, aiming his forefinger at Molotov, who did not wince. "You were invited to join. Germany and Italy will regulate Western Europe, and the Tripartite members will adjudicate the affairs of the British Empire, when the time comes for division, as it will soon. There is no reason for Russia not to share in the booty. You could have a warm-water port on the Indian Ocean, whenever you wish. But we must first settle the question of the Balkans."

"What question is that?" Molotov did not betray any special interest here, but he was wary, for in June 1940, Stalin had judged that Hitler would be locked in a wasting struggle with the French for years so he had ignored the secret protocols of the two Soviet-German agreements of 1939 and occupied the three Baltic countries, plus Bukovina and Bessarabia. Now Hitler, triumphant, was turning his eyes on territories Stalin could neither defend nor return without a frightening loss of face, which might bring the traitors to his bedside with a revolver one night.

Hitler said, "We were forbearing after you arrived without warning in Bukovina. We asked our friends in Hungary and Rumania to confer these territories on you in the Vienna Awards. In this you see our far-sighted restraint, which will continue after the British are done for. Especially will this be so if in our present life-and-death struggle we can count on the help of our great ally, Marshal Stalin." He finished this mouthful, disliking the mealy-mouthed quality of it, and stared hard at Molotov to cow him.

Molotov, who often sat unflinching as Stalin pronounced terrible threats in his grim, hissing voice, said, "We will cooperate in this great enterprise. We wish to know the date and scale of the invasion of England."

"That, of course, is classified information," Hitler said. "But I can assure you that if you will advise your wise and stern leader and your other colleagues in Moscow to expect great events, world-changing events, which are right now being planned here in Berlin, they will not be disappointed either at the scale, the timing or the results." He lost control and said, "We will crush them like bugs," smacking his right hand in the palm of his left as he walked, grinding his heel in the carpet.

Molotov noticed that the people he had mentioned just before, saying he would crush them like bugs, were the Russians, not the British. Who were the bugs? "I am not sure I heard correctly. Are we being invited to join in the Führer's life-and-death struggle with England on the understanding that England is already dead?"

Hitler stared at him, then went to his desk, sat down and began to read documents. Everyone was silent. After a moment, Ribbentrop said, "I am sure you understand that the Führer is preoccupied with grave matters. He will continue the discussion tomorrow." Molotov got up, inclined his head to Hitler who did not look up from his desk, and they went out.

The meeting with Hitler, scheduled for the following day, was cancelled. Instead, Molotov and Ribbentrop met in the Foreign Ministry building in the Wilhelmstrasse, where they had lunch and then talked all afternoon. Molotov told Ribbentrop that he hoped Hitler had not been offended and Ribbentrop replied that the Führer never allowed his personal feelings to influence his responsibilities to the German people and the Greater Reich.

They broke for dinner, then continued over coffee. Ribbentrop kept trying to raise the subject of Bukovina, which Molotov kept avoiding because he had to consult Stalin. The air-raid sirens went off and Ribbentrop ushered his guest into an elevator that descended 15 metres to the shelter, which was bright and well-furnished.

"It is protected by six metres of concrete which will withstand direct hits by the largest bombs and last a hundred years, the engineers tell me," Ribbentrop said. They talked until nearly 11, occasionally interrupted by the room shaking under the impact of the bombs. After the all clear had sounded, they went back upstairs and Ribbentrop escorted Molotov to the door of the Ministry, where the Russian Embassy car was waiting.

"In confidence I can tell you, my friend," he said, putting his arm round Molotov's shoulder, "that it is the Führer's irrevocable will that the British be crushed and the Empire divided among the victors."

"And when will this invasion take place?" Molotov said, wondering if this foolish man would drop the crucial hint that Hitler was too canny to betray.

"It is impossible to tell this early, of course, but let me assure you that the British are already strangling in our U-boat net and bleeding to death under our bombing raids. They are finished. *Kaput.*" He drew his hand across his throat.

"In that case," said Molotov, "whose were the bombs that were falling just now, and what were we doing in your wonderful shelter designed to withstand a dozen direct hits and last a hundred years?"

Ribbentrop shrugged, as if to say, 'There is no teaching this dull little man,' and bade him goodnight.

Molotov told his chauffeur to drive round Berlin for a while as he noted in a pad evidence of bomb damage.

1941

Toronto, February 12, 1941

On the afternoon of his 22nd birthday, Joe Shearer, who played left defence on the Trinity College hockey team, was lacing up his skates in the locker room and listening to Brian Mackie in the next alley talking about the advantages of joining the navy.

Mackie was wearing a naval officer's uniform under a dark blue greatcoat, with bright brass buttons and a big collar, turned up to frame his well-combed hair and his alert little face. He was one of those men who succeed in life without any conspicuous merit. He sided with authority, took control of people with small ambitions, and displayed confidence of success to his superiors, whether he had any basis for it or not. He never told the whole truth and never a complete lie. He was nicknamed Smoother.

He said, "You know, lads, we've got to win this war, so sooner or later you'll have to join up. I've heard it on the grapevine that conscription is coming soon, and anyone who joins now gets to pick his service. This way, you won't have to go over the top into machine gun fire."

"I heard that too," said one of the players.

"It's true," said Mackie. "And your university fees will be paid too, after the war. When I get back, I'll go straight back into university, any course I want, no exams."

Joe had always been a little in awe and a little suspicious of Mackie because of his effortless successes; seeing him so glamorously dressed with all the first team gazing at him, Joe was entranced. He played hockey to get glamour because he was convinced that he was unattractive to girls, so the sight of Smoother Mackie made him yearn for just that handsome greatcoat, just that important uniform, just that air of quiet authority the clothing seemed to confer. If he were dressed like that, his luck would change, he thought. He might even get a good date for the college dance. Maybe even Margot Cochrane. At that moment, he decided to join the navy.

That night, he went next door to Grant Giovanelli's house and walked in the unlocked front door. Mrs. Giovanelli disapproved of this freedom, but Grant was Joe's best friend, so he pooh-poohed her, reminding her that he had the freedom of the Shearer's house next door. He knew his mother would think this was an unequal trade since she thought the Giovanellis were very important people in Toronto and the Shearers were not significant.

Grant came down the stairs two at a time, saying, "Hi Joe, what's the word?" And they went out onto the front verandah, where Joe told him what Smoother Mackie had said.

Grant laughed, "You mean you're going to join the navy to get your fees after the war? Come off it, Joe."

"Well, the uniform looks pretty good too," said Joe. "Maybe I can get a date with Margot Cochrane before I drown. Anyway, I'm going down to HMCS York now, do you want to come?"

"And join up, just like that?"

Grant had been considering what to do about the war for over a year. Classes would end in eight weeks. His father, wounded in the Great War, approved every time the subject came up. Grant's mother was keen for him to go, as it was his duty to King and country, she believed, but she was not pressing him. He sat beside Joe on the front steps, smoking and thinking, then said, "Have you got a couple of streetcar tickets?" So they went together and joined the navy; Joe thinking of the uniform and Margot, Grant thinking of the sea, England, and Victoria Treloar.

Toronto, April, 1941

On a warm afternoon in spring, Ed Burns was lecturing his Modern History class in Falconer House at the University of Toronto.

Jack Giovanelli gazed past Burns' halo of fading curls, born auburn but greyed by a night of fascist shellfire in Spain, out the leaded casement window to the swollen buds in the topmost branches of a maple tree and beyond, the blue sky covering the city with drowsy warmth. A hand lawnmower whirring through the new grass played under Burns' voice like continuo.

Most of the students on campus finishing their lectures that day were half-asleep, attending in case the professor hinted what would be on the coming exam. But in Burns' class, they listened in excitement. It amused him to perplex the favoured young men from Little Big Four schools and the women from the Bishop Strachan School and Havergal College seated before him. This was why he was nicknamed "Red Ed."

He loved opening these sealed minds to the realities of life in Depression-years Canada, showing them how their wealthy families maintained a lofty indifference while millions of farmers and labourers and their families suffered to the point of starvation. Talking of the greed of the rich easterners, he gestured, and the leather patch on the left elbow of his Harris tweed jacket, which had cost him all the money from an article sold to *Saturday Night* magazine, dangled by the last thread. Jack Giovanelli watched it in fascination, hoping it would fall off. He would pick it up and give it back to him and then Burns would ask him to go for a beer. Near the end of the lecture, Burns said, "Struggle is the condition of life. It is both history and destiny according to Marx, Darwin and Hitler. Darwin discovered the struggle for survival and the resulting adaptation of species. Hitler says that the superior Germanic Aryan race must cleanse itself of polluting elements to win living space. But Trotsky says that communism is the struggle for justice carried on by class warfare until the dictatorship of the proletariat results in the withering away of the state. When that happens, social justice will prevail. So mankind's hope is that Trotskyism emerges intact from this war." He put his fist in the air and said, "Up the revolution, papers tomorrow for Giovanelli and Jackson." He slapped his raftsman's hat on his head like an exclamation point.

The students streamed out and Jack Giovanelli waited with A.G. Douglas until Burns was ready. They walked down the broad curving oak stairs together and out into the cool air and hot sunshine on Queen's Park Crescent.

Burns said, "Any comments from our distinguished visitor from Maths and Sciences?" A.G., who had a high reputation on campus as the freshman with the highest matriculation marks ever achieved, was still in a twisted position as he walked, spine curved out to the right, head thrust forward. Although he had audited only one of Burns' lectures, he was certain of his opinion. "The discussion is pointless because no one can predict human behaviour, therefore you cannot provide for it, except negatively. If you don't know the variables of behaviour, how can you provide for them?"

"What's your solution then?"

"Solution to what?"

"To the inherent problems of capitalism."

"The problem is not the problem, it's believing that life is a problem to be solved."

Jack, eager to prolong the moment, said, "How about a coffee?" and Burns said, "We can do better than that. We'll go to the KCR." This was the student's tavern on Bloor Street.

He led them up Philosopher's Walk past Trinity College.

"Why aren't you guys in uniform?" he asked. A.G just shrugged, but Jack said, "My brother's in the navy and I'm thinking of the air force this summer,"

Burns said, "Don't. You'll just get your brains blown out in this capitalist fandango, they're doomed to destroy each other anyway."

"But you're a Trot," said Jack, hurt but eager, "you fought in Spain. Now you Trots are at war with the Stalinists."

Burns ignored him and looked at A.G. with wary interest.

"And what about Hitler?" he asked A.G.

"I'd say Hitler is doing everything right."

Burns barked, "You're saying Hitler is right?"

"I said he has done everything right. As an English professor, you surely know the difference between being right and doing things right."

Burns was amused by the arrogance of this young student, correcting an English professor's English. A.G. reminded him of himself as a student at the University of British Columbia.

Burns said, "Are you going to join up?"

"No," said A.G. "The rational thing to do is to enjoy it." Burns bellowed, "Enjoy it! Thousands of people dying, women and children bombed in their beds, Fascism and Stalinism triumphant, and you're going to enjoy it. God, man, it's not a spectacle."

"Well, of course it is a spectacle, but if there were no deaths there would be no significance. It's the element of deadly risk that makes it serious."

"You are a sardonic little prick, aren't you?" said Burns. Jack was appalled and delighted at the insult, but A.G. said, "I see the world the way it is, not as you imagine in your jejune analysis."

"Good," said Burns unoffended, "I like that. You're very young to have realized the meaning of jejune."

Jack was happy. He was wearing a new red sports coat, he had good marks this year, money in his pocket and he was walking up Philosopher's Walk with his brilliant best friend and his brilliant professor.

Burns ordered beers and began talking about his new collection of poems, just published, about "the stupid comedy of mankind." He drank his first beer straight down, then ordered another, still talking about his collection and at the same time watching a pale girl. He was wondering if her pallor signified leukemia or something else fatal, when a line popped into his head, 'Even death has its drawbacks.' He jotted it down and A.G. seeing he was finished talking about the book, asked, "What do you think of the war situation now?"

Burns replied, still staring at the death-white girl, "It doesn't matter who is winning. This is the end of capitalism. After, Marxism takes over."

Jack said, "I think it's a titanic struggle between good and evil."

"Good lad," said Burns.

On the way home, Jack asked A.G., "Did you mean what you just said to Burns?"

"I said a lot of things to Burns."

"That you're just going to enjoy the war?"

"Of course."

"Don't you have any principles?"

"It's fatal to have principles. The war is about principles."

"What do you believe in?"

"Opportunity." He laughed.

"I don't believe that," Jack said in astonishment, but A.G. laughed harder.

Toronto June 22, 1941

The chief steward at the Varsity Club was standing in the sun on the stone front steps looking up and down empty University Avenue, remembering how it had looked just last year, crowded with cars and pedestrians. He had a hopeful look on his face as he saw a tall man approach with his tweed jacket slung over his shoulder, held by an upraised thumb, and whistling "La Marseillaise." The steward stepped aside, opened the door with a flourish that said he was glad to have someone to serve at last and said, "Good morning, Professor Burns." Burns said, "I suppose the president is late again?"

"Profound apologies, and will you have a drink?" He ushered Burns to his seat at the damask-loaded table in the empty dining room. President Simmonds, his old friend from the University of British Columbia, had summoned him for this meeting to discuss complaints about Burns' teaching which he had received from a number of benefactors and parents of students.

The windows were open and warm air drifting in carried the scent of roses from nearby gardens, and a hint of traffic fumes. The place seemed hollow to him because most of the members were off overseas.

He reread the letter which Tom Simmonds had sent him. He was being warned for the last time that he could not preach Marxism to his students, who were supposed to be "taking" Chaucer, Shakespeare and Milton. Although they had been friends for years, Simmonds had rolled out his full complement of initials, T.T.R. Simmonds, to sign the letter. Seeing that, Ed wondered if Tom knew that he had started the joke that the initials meant Time To Retire, a phrase that all the faculty now used.

He sauntered into the hot hall for a copy of the *Times-Loyalist,* then sat down again in the dining room to wait. He shoved away the desolate little plate of canned black olives and limp celery sticks, and the dish of melba toast and pats of stale butter that constituted hors d'oeuvres in Toronto clubs.

He was reading about Rommel's defeat of a huge British tank force in the desert when the president came in, leaning back as he walked with a paltry swagger. His little smile opened over small yellow cat's teeth.

The president came straight to the point, "We want you to stop talking about Trotskyism, communism and so forth, during your lectures. No politics. That's not so hard is it?"

"Tom, I'm teaching History as well as English, at your request."

"That is not a license for political agitprop. You do it even in English classes, I have been told."

"Shakespeare is full of veiled allusions to the politics of his time, safe old Milton delivered the Areopagitica in defence of the very liberty I require from you, Wordsworth propagandized for the French revolution, Dickens was a social reformer . . . ."

"I am informed that you sometimes end your lectures with your fist in the air shouting 'Up the revolution.' Now, Ed, you can't expect the bourgeoisie who pay you to teach their sons and daughters to be grateful to you for advising their children to rise up and slaughter them in their beds, now can you?"

Burns was laughing. "There is a way out for them."

"What is that?"

"Join the party. Here, I have a card waiting for you, with your name on it." He reached into his pocket and drew out a party membership card, but the president held up his hands in rejection. Then he put his head in his hands and said to the tablecloth, "Ed, Ed, I hired you because I was a fervent admirer of your poetry—and I still am—I've admired you a long time, I've put up with your awful cigars and your mad politics, and the way you treated the Dunbars, I've defended you against the myriad philistines of Toronto but if you don't give up this hectoring lecturing I must conclude that you are a suicidal maniac."

"You've thought that since high school."

"Can't you compromise, just a little?"

"How can I compromise? Everything political that I teach has been developed and tested over years by brilliant men. It is a certain truth. It's like science, it's so demonstrated."

"To you, to you. Just as Catholic dogma is to the Pope."

"I'll debate our model for mankind with the Pope in Rome or anyone here, just give me the forum."

"I've already given you a forum, Ed. And you abuse it. Now that's enough," he said with a hand in the air as Ed tried to protest. "I must tell you that the board requires you to be silent on politics in class as a condition of your continuing employment at this university. Requires," he repeated. Ed had been denied tenure, so he could be dismissed at any moment without recourse.

"But if I'm fired, I'll have to join up. Wouldn't you want to keep me out of the army, Tom? Think of the damage I might do to our war effort."

The president shook his head. "Oh Ed, will you be serious? You're embarrassing me. You're going to lose your job. Don't you want to be an academic?"

"Cacademics," said Burns

"What?"

"We eat caca, we teach caca."

Simmonds had resolved not to lose his temper and not to march from the table no matter what Ed said, but he was aghast. He was aware of a number of other professors who had just come in and had seated themselves as far as possible from his own table.

"How long am I to be censored in this outrageous way? Is it for as long as I am at the university, as long as the war lasts, what is it?"

"It will be at the pleasure of the board. But I do not think they are being unreasonable, you are being treasonable. " He sat back satisfied with this thunderbolt, already looking forward to reporting this to his board.

"Treasonable. That's a laugh. Can't you dolts get it through your heads that I am not an ally of Hitler's? I am a Trotskyite, so I am at war with the Soviet Union, it was Stalin who murdered our leader, a man I admired very much when I saw him in Norway a couple of years ago."

"You went to Norway to meet Trotsky?" The president was appalled.

"Yes, I made no secret of it."

"Oh this is worse than I thought."

"He condemned your enemy Stalin and predicted the alliance with Hitler."

"Nevertheless he stands for violent overthrow of this society, permanent class struggle, dictatorial control of the economy by the central political power, and so on."

"But totalitarianism is what we are implementing right now in this country, and no one in the university is objecting."

"It is a wartime necessity."

"Just as communism is a peacetime necessity. But you won't even guarantee that silencing me will end with the war, except at the pleasure of the board. You are instituting here the totalitarianism you are fighting."

The president was angry because Burns was not giving in as he ought. "If you can't see the difference between Hitler and ourselves, then . . . ."

"Not Hitler. Stalin," said Burns, hissing the word.

"We are not fighting Stalin . . ." the president stopped, confused, and Burns interrupted, "But we *are* fighting Stalin. Right now. He's Hitler's ally for God's sake, he attacked Poland too, he is supplying Hitler. God, what dolts." He slapped his head in dismay.

"Yes, yes, it was a slip of the tongue, we are aware of all that."

At that moment, heads were lifted all round the dining room as a steward came in, speaking to each table in turn then hurrying on to the next. People were standing up and leaving, looking excited.

The steward leaned over the table fluttering with his important news. "Excuse me, sir, we were sure you would need to know, the hall porter was listening to the radio just now, and Germany has invaded Russia."

"Are you sure?" The president stood up, wiping his lips decisively with his napkin, with a serious look. This was a crisis that he would have to deal with right away, by calling a meeting. Then remembering that there was nothing the university could do about this battle between alien powers 7,000 miles away, he looked at Burns who was smiling.

President Simmonds realized that the whole issue with Ed was moot now—communism was no longer the enemy, even Burns' Trotskyism would be tolerated. He was grateful to this odd red duck who had brought such important issues to his table. He leaned down, offered his hand to Burns. "Well that does it. You're off the hook. You're on our side now, Ed. I'll speak to my board right away. Excuse me," and he walked away with his portly frame swaying side to side, though he had drunk nothing.

Placentia Bay, Newfoundland, August, 1941

In his cabin aboard HMS *Prince of Wales*, Prime Minister Churchill stared at the reports on his desk. 'There has not been a significant victory for us in this war so far,' he thought. He had been in office for 15 months and rumours against his leadership were alive in the smoking rooms and among the backbenchers. 'Not one victory for which we could ring out the bells of England. And now this . . .' he finished, staring at the cable that reported another disaster in the Mediterranean.

Under that report lay another like a snake under a rock, the warning rattle of the Japanese takeover in French Indo-China, and under that, reports of the tremendous defeats of the Red Army, driven back 600 miles in a few weeks, unable to make a stand anywhere. A line from Shakespeare came into his head, 'But if the while I think on thee dear friend, All losses are restored and sorrows end.' He let his reading glasses fall onto his cheeks and rubbed his eyes, wondering who was the friend who would restore his losses and realized that it was Roosevelt.

He unlocked the door, stepped over the water-tight sill and went up to the bridge. The officers saluted, and the captain came forward. "Sorry sir, we've run into a patch of fog which will delay us some hours, I'm afraid."

"Can we not grope our way along depending on the magic of radar?"

"It's only useful for the larger objects, I'm afraid, sir."

"In such a ship, it is only the very largest objects that would provoke our concern, captain."

"But the low growlers are even more dangerous. The RCN weather report predicts a clearing trend in about three hours."

Frustrated, Churchill drew a cigar from the pocket of his "zip" as he called it—the zippered one-piece suit which he wore for comfort and because it was so easy to put on. He put the cigar in his mouth and was about to light it when he decided to defer to the captain, who disapproved of smoking.

He saw the captain watching him, so he shot his jaw forward, then grunted and walked off the bridge, the unlit cigar still in his fingers. He said over his shoulder, "I shall go for a toddle," waddled backwards down the companionway ladder to the open deck and paced forward into the blankness, judging his way by the lines in the teak.

He heard the next shriek of the ship's siren as if far away, when he was at A turret 90 feet ahead. From the thick fog nearby, came the shrieking of the sirens on his escort vessels. He walked forward on the wet teak deck to the foc'sle, concentrating his mind on Roosevelt. 'He is the solution to our problems,' he thought. 'I must bring him to our side. English civilization now depends on our relations.' Contemplating the huge events of which he was master, and victim, he lit the cigar and stared ahead into the fog.

The fog, shifting in shreds of grey and pale grey, and layers of cold and warm, dense and light, changed the sound and sight of everything until he imagined that time had disappeared and he was in the tenth century. There was a Viking ship ahead, tall curved prow appearing from the cloudy mists.

He began composing a new section in his book about the English-speaking peoples.

In the ninth century after Christ, when King Alfred was entering upon his desperate inheritance, Vikings in their horned helmets who had already conquered northern France, and parts of Britain and Ireland, set forth in their beautiful long-ships in search of new lands to the west, which had been rumoured to them by the sagas of the Irish explorers. After a perilous voyage their dragon prows grounded on the wooded shores of a new world, where the captains raised the banners of European civilization before the startled gaze of painted savages.

How we do not know, the colonies faltered, perchance under the attacks of feathered warriors emerging from the primeval forest that stretched thousands of miles to the west. Certain it is that the hearth-fires of these pioneering Europeans guttered out after a generation or two.

No man braved these stormy seas for another five hundred years, when from Bristol and other ports on the rough western coast of Britain there set forth a new band of English-speaking seamen, searching the north Atlantic for whale and cod. And here on the lifted coasts of the new-found-land there arose at first humble huts, which were soon augmented by stone churches and substantial houses of European design and modest comfort. Here were planted, never to be cut down, the red, blue and gold standards of Britain's first colony beyond the seas.

He was interrupted by the loud blast of the siren from the bridge as dense cold air above reflected the sound onto his head. He added to his composition a last fancy, that the Vikings, rowing their ships through these waters with their sodden sails hanging limp on the yardarm, bugled to each other with curving rams horns.

He turned back toward the stern, losing the vision of the Vikings under their flaxen sails. He gazed past A turret, its huge muzzles lashed tight into canvas snoods, in "swelling pride," as he had himself written of these new King George V class ships, to the bridge where the watch officers were scanning the shredding mist with binoculars to their eyes.

The sun broke through, blue-grey sea shone to port and starboard, and a blue watery sky shone down on them. Again the clouds closed, and re-opened, until the ship were at last clear and steaming full ahead for Newfoundland and the President of the United States of America.

"Where did you go, sir?" said Hemming, the officer of the watch, a brown-bearded lieutenant. "We were worried about you."

"On this mighty ship we have nothing to fear," said the PM. "I have been alone with the Vikings." He climbed the companionway stairs with much puffing, holding hard to each rail to help lift his weight.

The air in his cabin was scented with roses from the garden at Chequers, sent by Clemmie as a parting solace. A signalman knocked and stepped in with a paper in his hand. Churchill began patting his jumper for his glasses, and the aide offered to read it. The PM said, "Go ahead then," and the aide read out, "Hush, Immediate, Admiralty to Moonlight, Sunrise, repeat C-in-C CNA FONF. Five U-boats estimated to be in your general vicinity Period Aircraft and ships investigating Period."

"Has the President's convoy been informed?" the PM asked.

"Yes sir, they have been repeated in the signal."

"Pray ask the captain if he could spare a word with me."

In a few minutes Captain Leach appeared and saluted. "Prime Minister, you sent for me. Which of these approaching American ships would you like me to sink first?"

"All those that pose a danger to us. Now, I am concerned for the *Augusta,* as she is now in our waters. Can you reassure me?"

"I can indeed, Prime Minister. There are already dozens of ASW aircraft in our airspace, British, Canadian and US. *Augusta* has a strong flotilla of destroyers screening her, and they will be supported by the RCN. By the way, sir, you may not have heard, on our way back next week, we shall be escorted as far as Iceland by six American destroyers."

USS *Augusta* and her escort destroyers were already at anchor off Argentia when the British ships appeared low on the south horizon under a picket of Canso aircraft wearing red white and blue roundels. The day was sunny, the wind kicking up a few whitecaps in the broad bay. Clouds braided purple and white like rope stretched above the warm land to the east, kittiwakes, herring gulls and murres flew about the grey warships, some at anchor, and six others hedging the horizon on picket duty.

The *Prince of Wales* anchored and soon Churchill, wearing a dark blue high-buttoned sailor's coat, holding with one hand to a brass stanchion amidships in the Admiral's barge, came spraying over the sea, and touched the fenders alongside the *Augusta*. He mounted the swaying mahogany ladder as the band played "God Save the King." He saluted and stood puffing on the deck holding himself up on his cane, to which there was fixed a flashlight for navigating in blackouts. Roosevelt, supported by his son Elliott, stood under the awning stretched over the quarterdeck, smiling broadly.

Roosevelt said, "At last we get together."

"Yes, we have." Churchill took Roosevelt's strong hand, smiling up at him.

They sat down and Churchill beamed round him as various American officers were introduced, and he also introduced his own staff, including Beaverbrook, incongruous in a business suit. Coffee was served and they began to discuss the war, as British stenographers took notes.

Beaverbrook, Cameron Bannatyne and Harry Hopkins, Roosevelt's friend and advisor, waited in chairs nearby, able to hear the conversation, ready to advise the President and Prime Minister on the crucial supply aspects of the war, especially supplies to England. Roosevelt mentioned payment for these supplies, referring to the large supplies of gold the British government had in South Africa and in Canada.

Beaverbrook stirred in his chair at this because the British were fighting while the Americans were doing business. He had arrived feeling pessimistic about the mission, because he had had harsh experience of the American attitude towards the British Empire.

When Churchill asked him to talk about Stalin, Beaverbrook said, in a strong voice, "Yes, but first, apropos what we were saying earlier, do you remember, Franklin, that we were told that if we agreed to the 12-mile limit off your coast, all would be well between us? We did agree. But all was not well." The President was looking at him in surprise. Beaverbrook went on relentlessly, "We were told that if we stopped the export of drink from the Empire to the United States, there would be a wonderful improvement in our relations with America. There was not.

"If we made peace with Ireland, we were to enjoy forever and ever the favour of America. We did as we were told. But it brought us no comfort in Ireland and little credit in America. If we settled our war debt, even at five cents in the dollar, we should have the complete approval of the United States. We settled, and earned ruin in England and abuse in America."

At this, Churchill growled, thinking the President would be very angry for he was responsible for some of these problems.

"We were incited by you to break the alliance with Japan. We did so. And look where it has taken us! The Japanese are our relentless enemies. And the Americans are our unrelenting creditors. Now we are told by you and Willkie that if only we stand up to Germany, all will be well. We are doing so. But we would stand up better if we knew that there would be something left to provide sustenance for our people in the day of hardship which will come with victory."

The President had drawn his head back looking amazed. All the other Americans were looking to him for a tip on how to react.

"A speech, if I may say so," said Churchill, "unsurpassed in its shocking rudeness." He glared at Beaverbrook. And then—he couldn't help himself—he giggled.

The President smiled and leaned forward and touched Beaverbrook's hand. "Easy, Max, you'll bring on the asthma."

There was a roar of laughter at this, the tension was defused and all the embarrassing truths Beaverbrook had expressed were left undiscussed, but tacitly accepted. From then on, there was no more mention of gold in South Africa. The formal cordiality was replaced by comradeship.

The President consulted his watch as a rating set a cocktail tray on the low table before him. He said, "The sun is over the yardarm in Scotland, I deem it to have passed the yardarm here as well." He mixed the Old-Fashioned cocktails and handed one to Churchill. "I have just authorized a partial ban on supplies of gasoline to the Japanese. Only the high octane airplane gas initially. Both my Henrys wanted me to ban all oil to the Japanese, but I like to keep the noose loose round their neck and just give it a tug to remind them now and then." He smiled.

Churchill beamed. He said, "Now we must discuss what must be our proper course should they decide to lay hands on the Dutch oil fields." He tasted his cocktail and barely suppressed a grimace of disgust.

Roosevelt said, "The question is simple: how do we manoeuvre them into attacking us without exposing ourselves to too much danger."

Churchill was astonished at the boldness of this. Roosevelt grinned and stuck out his jaw. "I think we'll have plenty of warning. I shouldn't tell you this, Winston, but between ourselves, we have broken the top Japanese code. We are reading all their most important dispatches within a few hours of their being sent."

"Thank you for entrusting this very good news to me," said Churchill. He chortled. "Now I shouldn't tell you this, Franklin, but between ourselves, we have deciphered the German Enigma machine codes and we are reading some of their most important naval dispatches within a few hours of transmission."

"Then I shall pour us another to celebrate," said Roosevelt. He reached to the silver cocktail shaker on the mahogany table beside him as Churchill went on, "We relied on this deciphering—we call it Ultra—during the hunt for the *Bismarck*. We weren't sure we had found her, but then we decrypted a message from Naval HQ in Berlin addressed to an officer in Athens, whose son was on the ship, telling him his son was on his way to Brest. And this made assurance doubly sure."

"And sealed the poor boy's fate, I bet," said Roosevelt.

Churchill looked at him in surprise, thinking of his son Randolph, and of Elliott Roosevelt. "I confess, I had not thought of that before," he said, his voice a low rumble, as it usually was when he was expressing something serious. "It is the pity of war."

Roosevelt handed him another cocktail, and Churchill took it with a grimace. "We must share our secrets," Roosevelt said.

"Indeed, we must," Churchill growled.

"Let me begin with the secret of these wonderful cocktails," said the President.

During their *tête-à-tête* lunch in the captain's cabin, Churchill said solemnly, "Franklin, I put it to you plainly. I do not believe that alone as we may be, and even with your great help, we can beat Hitler. By that I mean I expect the Russian front to be static within a year, if not to have retreated behind the Urals. And where will we be then? He will turn his attentions to us. And there is no telling what will happen then, but I fear the situation is of the utmost gravity." He lit a cigar with a wooden match. Roosevelt noticed that his hand was trembling slightly.

He fitted a new cigarette into his long holder and lit up himself. "Winston, you must realize my position. Both the House and the Senate are dead set against war. If I asked them for a declaration, they would argue for three months and vote no. I may make war but I may not declare it."

"You know that we have asked our Canadian friends in New York and Washington to express directly to your people the gravity of the world crisis, and they have reported to me that 50 per cent of the Congress is now for war, with another 20 per cent expected as probables."

"Yes yes, I've heard about this, but it is not true, in the sense that these opinions are strong on Monday, weak on Wednesday and gone by Friday. The following week, they say the opposite."

"Then we must tack to the wind."

"By all means," Roosevelt said, and Churchill went on with a list of supply problems, each of which Roosevelt solved with a wave of his hand and a note to a staff member. Churchill could scarcely credit how lightly Roosevelt regarded these problems, and wondered for a moment if the President were trifling with him. But there was no doubt left in his mind after the President told him that from now on, the US Navy would contribute escorts to convoys from the North American shores to Iceland.

They rejoined the others under the canopy on the quarterdeck. Churchill, feeling like a child at Christmas with a hamperful of presents—P40 Tomahawk fighter planes, destroyers, Sherman tanks, aero engines, freighters, long-range reconnaissance aircraft—turned to Beaverbrook, who was doubling aircraft production in the UK every six weeks, and said, "Now Max, you've done such a wonderful job with the fighters, can you give me the bombers I need to reduce Germany to rubble?"

Beaverbrook proved, with a mass of figures accurately quoted from memory, what was the maximum possible, and then said he would provide 20 per cent more. Roosevelt looked on in amusement. He liked Beaverbrook—they shared a common love of New Brunswick and, to both of them, everything was possible that was good.

"That still leaves a shortfall in the supply of Lancasters," said Churchill. He looked at Cameron Bannatyne. "Can you build them in Canada for me?"

"How many do you need?" said Bannatyne, leaning forward with interest. It was the first time he had spoken at the conference.

"Four hundred," said Churchill, doubling the figure he had had in mind, because he liked the look of Bannatyne. He stuck his chin out, forcing his cigar up in the air defiantly, posing the challenge.

"When?"

"In one year, if possible."

"You shall have them in ten months."

Churchill grunted with satisfaction, turning away with the words, "I shall hold you to that Max."

As they were going in to dinner that evening, Cameron said to Beaverbrook, "What exactly is a Lancaster?"

Beaverbrook laughed and punched his arm, and said, "Good man."

Roosevelt was being wheeled in to the dinner talking up to Churchill, when Churchill was interrupted by first the captain, then Beaverbrook and several others who had been waiting all afternoon with urgent messages from Hong Kong, Ottawa, London, Cairo, Athens.

Roosevelt felt left out as this business of war and empire passed him by. Winston alone was defending democracy, the world was changing day by day, and he was paralyzed by Washington politics.

At dinner Churchill said to Roosevelt, seated at his left, "It has been brought to my attention via our agents in Germany that Hitler is attempting to succour his armies with infusions of young volunteers from many countries in Europe, to join his campaign in Russia. To this end, he has begun to wage a propaganda campaign throughout the rest of the world, to convince us that he is leading a defence of civilized values against the threat of godless communism. We must be careful, Franklin, lest it come to be believed among the broad masses of our two peoples that this new campaign of Hitler's is anything but the extension of his ambition to rule first Europe and then the whole world."

Harry Hopkins noticed every word so that he could write them down later and inform Stalin about the western attitude.

Churchill asked what was the supply situation as Roosevelt had found it out from his ambassador. Hopkins replied, "They have lost or have transferred behind the Urals hundreds of factories in the Dneiper basin and Ukraine, they've lost the Krivoi Rog iron mines, two aluminum smelters, half a dozen aircraft and aero engine factories. And of course all that food production. The government will soon be in flight to Kuibyshev. The situation is very grave. They predict the final crisis in about six weeks."

As Roosevelt foresaw the collapse of Russia looming in the phrases "grave situation," "flight of the government," "final crisis," he remembered the same phrases coming across the Atlantic to him during the Battle of France. He had been forbidden by America's neutrality laws to help France.

He had vowed then he would never let that happen again. During the Battle of Britain, he dared to help with munitions, risking the loss of the next election, because most Americans thought they should stay out of the war. But now he had made a change. He would not say this to anyone else, but he told Churchill, "I shall court war in order to get war."

"And this is your settled policy, in the Pacific as well as here?"
"It is. But I say nothing about it."
"The world is for war. You shall have war in these seas as well."

That evening, after dinner, elegantly dressed as an Air Commodore of the RAF, Churchill presented his plan for a propaganda coup against the Axis. Hoping to push Roosevelt to a quasi-alliance with Britain against Germany and Italy, he proposed a joint statement of the high principles supposedly governing the aims of the two countries. On the way over, he had drafted a proposal, which he now handed to Roosevelt suggesting with a display of uncharacteristic diffidence that it might be of interest.

Roosevelt adjusted his pince-nez and looked down at the paper, noticing cigarette ash on the lapel of his dark blue suit. He brushed it away as he quickly read Churchill's draft. 'The only man in the world who writes stentorian prose,' he thought, and vigorously crossed out some orotund phrases.

They wrestled with some of the clauses, and agreed a document which sounded just the right note, Churchill thought. The Atlantic Charter, which Roosevelt and the Prime Minister signed together for the photographers, expressed their hopes for a better future for the world. They supported the right to self-determination for all peoples, after a "peace which will not only cast down for ever the Nazi tyranny," but by "effective international organization will afford to all States and peoples the means of dwelling in security within their own bounds and of traversing the seas and oceans without fear of lawless assaults or the need of maintaining burdensome armaments."

On Sunday morning, warm and calm, church parade was held on the quarterdeck of the *Prince of Wales*. Roosevelt, accompanied by Elliott, his Chiefs of Staff and Harry Hopkins, came across the water to Churchill's battleship and was carried up the ship's ladder by two seamen. With a grim look on his face, Roosevelt slowly swung himself along the deck half the length of the ship to the quarterdeck where Churchill awaited him with an anxious look on his face. He yearned to help, at the same time admiring Roosevelt's determination. 'This man will never let us down,' he thought.

The sailors of the two fleets stood side by side without regard for rank or nation, sharing hymn books, and sang out hymns they all knew from childhood. Beaverbrook, a son of the manse, knew all these old Anglican hymns, and some Presbyterian ones beside. They were singing "For Those in Peril on the Sea," when a humpback whale broached 50 yards off, its barnacled flukes shining in the sun before they crashed back into the water again in a great fountain of water that went unheard in the music.

As the hymns sang out over the blue-green sea, Beaverbrook was wondering why Winston was bothering about the Charter. The clause about traversing the seas and oceans was only a cover for Roosevelt's plan to send war goods in American ships to Great Britain. The grand phrase about self-determination for peoples meant nothing, for Churchill had already refused self-determination for the people of India, and Roosevelt would not allow self-determination for the peoples in the Philippines, or Hawaii, or any of the Indian tribes taken over by the US. There was not a chance that the Russians would give up their conquests in eastern Europe. Millions of the Poles they had conquered in 1939 had been deported, enslaved or murdered. All this the Prime Minister and President knew. 'Why is the preaching of high principles so often married to low deeds? Why do we preach high and act low? Why do we preach at all, since preaching has no effect? Why does it have no effect, since we preach so well?' He wondered if the answer might be that the purpose of preaching is to mask evildoing.

At lunch, Harry Hopkins pointed out that Stalin "can never agree to the right to self-determination since he has ancient Tsarist claims on Finland, Poland, Latvia, Lithuania, Estonia, Bukovina and Bessarabia." Churchill looked thoughtful. "Then we must find ways of accommodating our allies who are fighting so bravely in defence of their homeland. *Inter arma silent leges.*"

Hopkins thought with satisfaction, 'Aha, he does not mention the Poles, who also are our allies and fought for their homeland. Then it is settled in his mind. I must tell Molotov this right away. Self-determination does not apply to the Poles.'

Toronto, Brandon, October, 1941

Jack Giovanelli was dreaming on a wood bench in the hall of the History building on a hazy, warm fall afternoon, about banking his Spitfire over Kent. He had changed his mind about music because it seemed such a precarious way to make a living, so he was taking an arts degree while practicing piano two hours per day, and taking a musical theory course at the Royal Conservatory.

Both his brother Grant and Grant's good friend from next door, Joe Shearer, had joined up, half the young men in his graduating class had gone, and soon the others would go too. His father and mother expected him to go because it was his duty. For Ferdie Giovanelli, the Great War had been two and a half years of horror; his best friend had been killed, he had come home wounded and shell-shocked, but he was satisfied that he had done his duty for King and country.

Jack was thinking, 'Why am I here studying Elizabethan feudal structure while half our leaving class has joined up?'

He had not finished his essay on Queen Elizabeth's foreign policy and scarcely prepared the topic they were supposed to discuss today. He watched the young men and women coming down the stairs from the class just ended. Two of the men were in uniform, finishing their term while beginning basic training. He was about to trudge up to class when he saw a young woman coming down.

She was carrying her books in front of her chest and smiling as if she had just remembered something pleasant. As she walked by, he followed her with his eyes, and then, unwilling to lose sight of her again—already she seemed familiar to him—he got up to go after her.

At that moment, he saw Gillian Armour in the crowd and ran up to her. She gave him a big smile, was ready to kiss him if he wanted, because she was so in love with him. He said, "Moo-moo, who is that absolutely beautiful girl up there?" Ahead were at least ten young women.

"Which one?" said Gillian, her voice very deep and strong.

"Moo-moo, don't be that way, I think I'm in love, in green."

"She's my cousin, Alison."

"Introduce us right away, please." He hurried Gillian along to keep the girl in sight.

"Hello, Alison," said Gillian, "this too-handsome young man wants to meet you. Alison de Pencier, Jack Giovanelli." Gillian was painfully learning the patient generosity that intelligent plain girls had to acquire in youth.

Alison, who was studying art history, remembered meeting Jack at Wanagami in the summer of 1939 because she had been struck by how much he looked like *The Portrait of a Young Man* by Raphael.

"What are you taking?" he asked.

"Art and archaeology."

"On a scholarship," Gillian added. "Careful, Jack, she's way over your head. Ten firsts and the Edward Blake scholarship."

Alison blushed and gave Gillian an irritated look.

Gillian said, "Ta-ta, Alison. Jack, see you at the *thé dansant* tomorrow? Remember? We have a date?" She left with a yearning glance at Jack.

"Yeah, sure," said Jack, and then, "Oh my god, I've missed my class."

"Hadn't you better hurry?"

"History can wait. Would you like a milkshake?"

"I've got to go home and wash my hair."

"It looks fine to me."

"And I have to study."

They had arrived at the bus stop in front of Trinity. "That's where I pretend to study," he said.

"Why pretend?"

"I don't know. This whole place feels like dreamland to me."

"Young people are supposed to dream." She smiled.

"Not in wartime. Tonight maybe?"

The bus arrived.

"Where do you live?" he said, by way of goodbye.

She got on the bus. He looked up at the window and she mouthed one word through the window. "Roxborough." The bus started away.

At dinner that night, he was very distracted, but he would not tell anyone what was bothering him. Young Greg guessed. "You met some girl. Dad, isn't he reaching the horny age too soon?"

"Boys," said Mrs Giovanelli warningly. "Not at the table."

They were in the big dining room, Ferdie, Eleanor, Jack and Greg. Lying by Jack's feet, their Irish setter Hoover was looking up hopefully to Jack's hand, which occasionally sneaked a bit of food down to him. They were lacking Grant, who was in naval officer's training school at Esquimault in British Columbia, four days and nights by train away. Although he was still safely in Canada, the unfilled place at the table made Ferdie Giovanelli pessimistic about the war. Royal Canadian Mounted Police had come to his office with a subpoena for all his documents, and interrogated him rudely for three hours. They said that they were investigating all Italian-Canadians. Many had been interned already as suspected enemy aliens. He had had to telephone the Minister of Supply in Ottawa, a friend of his, and then produce his birth certificate and that of his father, showing that the Giovanelli family had been Canadians for 70 years, documents showing that he had served as an army officer for 30 months in 1915-1918, that he had been wounded and promoted, then served for six years as a Governor of the University, and that now he was on a government board supervising prices and trade. The Mounties' visit had depressed him—the war was spreading, hatred was growing, Hitler was winning.

After dinner, Jack looked up de Pencier. He phoned and proposed a coffee break from studying, but she said she had to work right through.

Three times in the next few weeks he called and twice she agreed to meet him— once after school for tea, another time for lunch. He was surprised at his own behaviour, but he could not make up his mind if she were too young and innocent for him or perhaps hiding thoughts she judged were too deep for him. He imagined that she was looking down on him, which made him eager for her good opinion. One cool night in late fall, he decided to give her a hard push. He phoned her, said he was coming down right away and was going to take her to see a painting. He borrowed his father's red Buick, pulled up in front of her small house, and they drove down to lower Yonge street, where he ushered her into a Honey Dew restaurant as if it were an art gallery, to show her a picture that he loved.

"Yes," she said, "I like it too."

"Oh. You've seen it?"

"Yes, the original is over at the art gallery."

"It is?" He gaped at her. He had been so pleased by the picture, of a northern Ontario lake, that it never occurred to him it was only a print.

"You mean I dragged you all the way down here to show you a print?"

"It's all right." She smiled. "I like it."

"Can we go see the original now?"

"The gallery is closed."

They sat down with coffee.

He said, "At school that day, with Gillian? . . . You seemed familiar, did we meet somewhere else, last year. Or is it because beauty always seems familiar?"

"Wasn't it at Wanagami?" She was put off by "beauty," because it entered a claim to her that she refused to honour.

He thought of saying, 'I love you, marry me before I go away and get killed,' but he was sure she would just smile and say nothing and conclude he was an idiot. He said, "You don't laugh much, but you smile a lot."

She said, "I don't know if that's a criticism or a witticism," and he laughed and applauded. She was so annoyed she wanted to leave and began to look around. He said, "I like the rhyme, that's all, no fun intended."

He realized while chatting on about university and the course, which was starting to bore him, that he was launched on a sentence that could only end with ". . . so I'm quitting school and joining up." He uttered the words with alarm because he had not consciously decided this, and had spoken mainly because he wanted to open his heart to her.

"What branch?" she said.

"The Air Force," he said, "next week. I'm going to fly Spitfires."

"Isn't that awfully sudden?"

"Everything is speeded up these days, isn't it?" he said. And before she could ask what he meant, he was annoyed with himself for trying to inveigle her into this decision, which he suddenly realized was exactly what he wanted to do, regardless of everything else.

"I'd better get you home, it's time to wash your hair again, I just saw some dust settling in it."

She smiled. He wanted to tell her he loved her for her smile. He drove her home and said, "Maybe I'll write to you," at the bottom of her steps, his breath a puff of light in the cool air, while red and yellow leaves came pirouetting around their shoulders. He waited. She said nothing. Then hating to part so indecisively, he added, "Will you write back?"

She slightly nodded.

He said, feeling reckless, "I'll miss you," and walked away, hoping she would think he was heartbroken and wondering if he was.

She was relieved and disturbed by this parting. He was touching because he was now among the very young who were going to war.

He drove home in regret, convinced that he loved her because she was so beautiful and made him feel beautiful, but that she would never want to see him again because he had made such a fool of himself.

But he was glad that at last he had faced the fact that he was sick of school and could not continue, at least while this war went on. There was nothing left to do but join up. He felt terribly lonely—his life was on the line for her and she did not even know it.

He lay awake looking out at the streetlight glowing like the moon in clouds. Why did she affect him so deeply? Was it just because she was beautiful?

He got up and sketched out a poem to her because he knew Grant was writing poetry to Victoria, so he thought it was the right thing to do, but it was absurd. So he tried to tell her his feelings in a letter, which he soon crumpled up. Then he wrote in his journal, *What a fool. Told her I've decided to quit school and join up. Incredible. Hardly thought about it till that moment. So now I have to. And why? Only because standing in front of her, so gentle and harmless, the lies in me evaporated. I don't want to be at school studying Elizabethan history and political structure while the Germans rampage through Europe destroying places I want to see. So like an idiot I lay my life down before her as if I were a knight taking her colours before the joust. And she handles it all with such cool aplomb. Most demeaning. Why am I such an idiot with her? What is it she makes me feel? I hardly know her, yet I have strong feelings about her. She's beautiful. What is beauty? The bloody word has me by the throat and I don't even know what it means. Truth, yes, as Keats says,—Beauty is truth, truth beauty, that is all, Ye know on earth And all ye need to know—but Keats was talking to a jug, for God's sake.*

When he awoke he dressed quickly, wondering if he had made a big mistake. There was no conscription, he did not have to fight. But he had told Alison he was going. He leaned over his walnut desk with his tie dangling onto the journal, and saw that he had reached the last page of the bound book and wrote on the inside back cover, *FINIS. Appropriate to end this and my youth with a doomed love affair.* He closed it and put it in the desk drawer.

At noon that day, he was in the history department office asking for Professor Burns. Burns came out wearing a brown uniform with the insignia of a captain in the Ontario Scottish, the regiment Bernie Hallett commanded.

Jack said, "Sir, you're in uniform."

"You have a keen eye, Giovanelli."

"But you told A.G. Douglas and me last summer not to join in this capitalist foofaraw."

"I did not. I said not to join in this capitalist fandango."

"But here you are."

"I advised you on *your* course. I said nothing about me, did I?"

"No sir, but . . ."

Burns was carrying a suitcase of books, a paper bag and a child's leather schoolbag on a strap over his shoulder. He handed the paper bag of documents and the schoolbag to Jack as they walked out into the cold drizzle.

"In the first place, do as I say, not as I do. In the second place, you have no convictions or ambitions so far as I can see, which is probably a good thing, because you don't have much in the way of equipment to achieve any goal significant enough to satisfy your fairly well-developed ego. And finally, it would play hell with your love life, *n'est-ce pas?*"

"Well, you're a sardonic sort of a prick, aren't you?" said Jack, to his own amazement.

Burns laughed so hard he had to stop walking. "Did I say that?" he asked. "I called Douglas that, didn't I?"

"Yes sir, and he is."

"Well, and doubtless so am I. Look, I'm sorry, you got me at a bad time. I have to get up to Camp Borden right away or I'll overstay my leave, and you know how Hallett would hate that. Come with me and we'll talk it over on the train, and if you don't like it, just get on the next train back."

He was walking very quickly up towards Bloor Street, Jack hurrying to keep up.

Burns said, "I can take you in the Ossies, as a first step, officer training, nothing serious, nothing you can't handle."

"Ossies, sir?"

"Ontario Scottish regiment. Infantry. But you won't make a good infantryman."

"Excuse me, sir, I think I'd prefer the air force."

"Ah the glamorous role of the fighter pilot with the white silk scarf around his vulnerable neck. But what they want now is bomber crew, and you know what that means—hundreds of hours in the air in a slow-moving plane loaded with tons of explosives over heavily defended targets dropping bombs onto women and children."

"What else could I do?"

"You speak perfect French, you don't take discipline well, they're looking for recruits to parachute into Europe on special missions. Come on, here's the streetcar." The wooden doors swung open. Burns got up and turned around. Jack gazed up at him and jumped aboard.

The parachute trainees went by train to Camp Shilo on the prairies where they got off into trucks floating like boats on the hot mirage of the tarmac.

The land seemed flattened by the tremendous sky that stretched low to the rim of the world. The wheat had gone in, the black fields shimmered under a pale dust in the sun.

They arrived at a bleak collection of wooden huts built in the depression by unemployed factory workers and bankrupt farmers who had been forced to work for their dole. Dinner was dried roast pork with apple-sauce which they ate at long trestle tables. After the food, everyone scraped the residue into empty oil barrels by the swing doors into the steamy kitchen. Jack walked out into the cool night thinking of Toronto, his mother, and Alison. Mother would be making phone calls, organizing food, wine and music for the St. Andrew's Ball, which was due in a month. The course would be finished in three weeks. He realized with a jump of joy—he actually jumped in the air and twirled around—he could take Alison to the ball.

He sat on the edge of his bunk and wrote,

Dear Alison

*Here we are on the very edge of the world, or so it seems—
we did not see a hill for the last six hours of the trip. All day we
do calisthenics and tomorrow we start practice jumping from a
tower 90 feet high. A very motley crew we are, prairie farm
boys, cod fishermen from Nova Scotia, miners from northern
Ontario, factory workers from Oshawa, a school teacher from
Regina, and the odd wandering troubadour like yours truly. I
played boogie-woogie for the mess tonight, after dinner, on an
upright as old as Manitoba. There is one mysterious French girl
training here with us who was exhausted by all the unfamiliar
dances they were asking her to do, and the men flocked round
her like birds to a feeder—there was only one other purported
female, an enormous jolly cook with arms like hams.*

*I am hoping to swing you about in a waltz or two at the St.
Andrew's Ball on December 9th—it is late this year because of
the war. Mother is the chief organizer this year—our name
used to be MacGiovanelli—and I shall turn up in our family
tartan at your door about six pm to whisk you away to the dinner
before the ball in the Royal York.*

I hope you are well and shampooing every day.

In the dining hall the next night, he was introduced to his jump instructor, who told them they would all be training for the First Canadian Parachute Regiment, all but one, the young French woman named Marie, who was on special assignment from the Free French in Britain.

After dismissal from dinner, he stood next to her as they were scraping their plates into the oil drum. Other men were crowding round her, but Jack sensed she was uncomfortable in English, so he said, "*Je me permets de vous adresser dans le langage de Molière.*"

"*Ah, m'sieur, c'est si gentille.*"

"*Vous vous rangez du côté du general de Gaulle?*" he said.

"*En principe, M. Giovanelli, mais plutôt du côté britannique. Et
vous êtes Canadien?*"

"Oui, mam'selle. Mais j'ai fait mes études pendant deux ans en Suisse et j'ai beaucoup voyagé en France."

"C'est vrai? Où ça?"

"Paris, Vézelay, Marseille, Toulon, Cannes, un peu partout dans le sud de la France." He was mimicking the bing-bong accent of southern France, which made her laugh.

"And you profited from your education very well. You speak French *comme un vrai Français.*"

"Thank you. Would you like to go to a movie in Brandon on Saturday night? We all have midnight leave."

"Thank you very much. Will it be *tenue de soirée?*"

He smiled, pleased that she had a sense of humour. "Long uniform, I believe. By the way, what is your last name?"

She hesitated before saying it, as if trying to decide something. "Laporte."

"Really?"

"Should I not know my own name?"

"I don't know, you just seemed unsure of it."

"I'm not used to this. I can't tell you my name."

"Why not? We're all in this together."

"That's why I can't. Suppose one of us is captured."

"But we're only going to Brandon." She laughed.

He waited for her near the bus stop at the camp gate in a cold dusty wind. They had been climbing up and parachute-jumping off the 30-metre tower in harness all day, practicing rolls and doing calisthenics, and he was sore but also exhilarated.

At dinner in the hotel next to the railway station, she asked Jack to order a bottle of wine but the waitress said "Wine?" in astonishment.

"It's illegal to drink here," he said to Marie.

"Why aren't they all dead of thirst then? God, what a depressing country."

She lit a cigarette without offering him one, drew in a great lungful of smoke and blew it out steadily looking around the high-ceilinged room. She seemed exasperated.

"What's the matter?"

"I wish I were anywhere but Canada."

He was shocked. He had never thought of his homeland in any way except as a friendly sort of a place, with great geography.

"I brought a mickey of rye," he said. "We can have rye and ginger if you like."

"What is that? Whiskey and ginger ale?"

"It's quite popular here. Not bad."

He ordered two ginger ales and poured a slug of rye into each, holding the mickey under the table. She tasted it and set down her glass. "That is the most disgusting drink I have ever tasted."

"But it makes you drunk," he said cheerfully, and she started to laugh. She laughed until he thought she was putting it on. Finally she slowed down and put her hand on his arm and dabbed at her eyes with a handkerchief she had trouble finding in her uniform.

"Thank you," she said, and held her nose while sipping some more rye and ginger.

He watched her, wondering what was wrong with this one, and decided to get away from her soon.

"What's your real name?" he asked.

"I told you, Marie."

"Obviously a fake."

"Why say that?"

"I'm sorry, it's just that you don't respond to it. There's always a hesitation."

She said nothing.

"Tell me your last name?"

"Marie will do."

"What, was there a name shortage when you were born?"

She smiled. I had another name, but for now it is Marie and only Marie and please do not ask me again. It's nothing personal, it is the same for all of us who escaped and will go back," she said waving her hand vaguely to include people she seemed to see, invisible to him. He glanced round the crowded room, where officers dining at big tables were also drinking brown drinks and smoking cigarettes. "Don't you see, if they know who we are out here, they can take reprisals on our families."

"OK then, where are you from?"

"That also I can not tell you."

He threw up his hands in exasperation.

"Jacques, it's the war, believe me. If it weren't for that, I would tell you everything." He smiled, amused to hear his name in French again.

He sat silent for a while, as the beef arrived, cooked brown, with gelatinous gravy rigid beside mashed potatoes containing hard white lumps, and a gluey-looking pile of yellow green slime. Marie asked the waitress what the yellow-green stuff was and the waitress bent down, peered at it and said, "I think it was cabbage."

"I am amazed at the way Canadians eat," she said, stirring her food about with a look of distaste. "How do you ever get nourished?"

Jack thought, 'Twice we go to war to save you guys, and you nag us about our cuisine.' But politely he said, "It's wartime, remember?" Then he smiled and added behind his hand, "In peacetime, it's just as bad."

She sipped at her drink and set it down. "You are always so cheerful and joking, even now, when things are so bad."

"Maybe it's the company," he said, and immediately thought, 'Liar.'

"In Europe we are always imagining how wonderful things used to be. Because when we look at things today, we see how terrible they really are."

"Which of course means they always were."

"Voilà."

"People out here call this tomorrow country."

"But in Canada you do not seem to believe you have a great future as a nation, the way Americans do."

"Perhaps not. We're not nationalistic."

"What do you believe in?"

"Who, me?"

"I meant, Canadians as a nation. Why are you fighting?"

"Well, Canada is not a nation so there is no 'we' to believe in anything. Most of the older ones believe in the British Empire but most of the young like me don't any more. And of course the Québeckers don't. Canada is really just a government in search of a country."

Marie was amazed. "You say that so lightly, as if it is true."

"Well, it is true."

"Un peuple heureux n'a pas d'histoire," she said.

"True. But all of us believe in peace, order and good government, that's in the constitution, I mean the British North America Act, that's our constitution." 'What a weird date,' he thought, 'talking about the BNA Act.'

"In France, as you know we believe in *la Gloire, la mission civilisatrice*, the sanctity of French culture, eldest daughter of the church and so on, *la patrie, la nation.*"

"And where did it get you? Waterloo. And Sedan. Verdun. And Compiègne. Twice."

"But the art, the writing, the wine, the music." She laughed, and touched his hand lightly. "The cooking."

"Yes, the cooking, the true religion of France. The revolution disestablished the church in order to establish the restaurant in its place. Think of it, the candles, the bread, the wine, the long black aprons like soutanes . . . ."

"The order of service, the reverential attitude, the expense."

As they left, she took his hand and said, "Thank you for the very protestant dinner."

They went to see a new movie called *The Wizard of Oz*, and she was charmed. Innocent Dorothy was still dancing in his head as they came out. The wind had calmed, the night was mellow, and Marie took his arm familiarly, something no woman had ever done to him before. "It's too bad we have to go back," she said. "I'd like to go dancing."

"So would I." They walked along in silence. So many topics had been forbidden to him that he gave up talking and enjoyed the mellow air that smelled sweetly of grass and prairie loam, of the river winding below them, and woodsmoke coming from many chimneys far-spaced round them.

She broke away from him and began to sing, a French song he had never heard, Piaf probably, then held out her arms to him as she sang down the deserted street. He took her in his arms and danced to her singing. Then she switched to "Over the Rainbow" from the movie, which she pronounced 'Ovair zee renbeau . . . bairds fly ovair zee renbeau,' and he started to get into it with her, and to sing and dance and twirl her round as best he could on the gritty pavement.

When their four-week course was over, they were paraded in the enormous main hangar and each one given a brass parachute pin, which they were entitled to wear like a medal. As well, they each got their cloth insignia of a 'chute to sew on their uniform.

In the train on the way back to Toronto, he gave her South African brandy from his flask. "I've done some research and I know that you are the illegitimate child of the Duc de Bris, who when he was a handsome young knight, was riding one day and, feeling thirsty, knelt at the brim of a green pool in the woods, and saw when he looked down, instead of his own face, a beautiful young woman. He looked up and there, across the pool looking at him, was the same young woman. He plunged into the pool and swam to her side, but by the time he got there, she was gone. But as he emerged from the pool, looking for her, or a towel, a strange bird with a long red tail swept down, landed on his head and gave him a piece of paper from its beak. On the paper was written Beaulieu 2904. The bird shat on his shoulder and flew away. But when he emptied his pockets at the dry cleaners, the piece of paper was gone and he could not remember the number exactly. He tried—Beaubien 2099, Beautemps, Beaumont—and got nowhere. After two years, his mother said, '*Alors, ça suffit*,' and sent him to a ball where he met the girl from the pool who although she was beautiful had no husband, because she was in a wheelchair. She said 'What took you so long?' and married him right there because she could see he had all the characteristics of a good husband—he was obsessed by her, he wasn't very bright and he could swim. She was a mermaid, which made it hard to have kids, so they adopted you. You are the daughter of a mermaid."

She was laughing, "Not the Duchesse de Bris."

"Now you choose your name. You will be either Marianne de la France Profonde or La Duchesse de Bris." She smiled and pressed his hand, and then held it, saying, *"D'accord. Je m'appelle Marianne."*

They went up to the dining car for dinner. In the roaring cold space swaying between cars, stinking of coal smoke, she stopped and looked up at him. He refrained for a moment, wary, so she stood on tiptoes, put her arms round his neck and kissed him. Nothing like this had ever happened to him before. Girls were supposed to wait, so he was alarmed. The train motion knocked them back and forth between steel walls, but he braced his shoulder to take the brunt and they went on kissing.

'What next,' he thought in a panic. 'Don't give your life away to a stranger, don't be a fool,' but could not help himself. He slid his hands under her shirt and rubbed her bare back. She drew away and said, "Not here."

"Where?" he said eagerly, at the same time wondering, 'What?'

"When things are right, there is always a bed." She pressed her forefinger against his lips and smiled, and pried open the door lever.

More excited by a woman than he had ever been in his life, barely able to keep his hands and lips and eyes off her, he followed her swaying greatcoat down the aisle, glimpsing lisle stocking on her narrow calf, thinking she was marvellous and frightening.

They ate hot roast pork sandwiches on soggy bread beside the cold window watching the forest unreeling while he told her about canoe trips. As the train passed along a high cutbank, a sign flashed past. "Sheean," he exclaimed, sitting up, and pointed out the Spanish

Rapids flashing in the moonlight, which he and A.G. had shot on their canoe trip, two summers ago. "We saw moose just downriver from here," he said.

She wanted to tell him about growing up in Les Landes, where the wild boars were hunted in the oak forests, and on cold wet mornings in November she could smell the Atlantic salt in the dripping woods. Her father's house sat on a hill overlooking the valley of the Adour where she and her father caught trout, and they went out for Sunday dinner at noon, *en famille*, six courses with three generations and then walked the woods until dark. She pressed his hand and said, "There was a river near our house and I loved to go in swimming in the summer there, under the oak trees by an old camp ground, and it was so peaceful. I would like to take you there after the war, but . . ."

He waited with his breath held. This was the most she had ever told him, and he was touched. It was like an engagement offering.

She got up and they swayed back down the aisle toward their car. In the space between the cars where they had kissed, he hesitated behind her, wondering if she were going to embrace him again, but she went on down the aisle while the heads of the soldiers turned and watched her, and then seeing him close behind, went back to their books and magazines.

"Tell me how to write to you."

"Write to 7568905, Camp X, Army Post Office Five. That will reach me."

He laughed.

"What is Camp X?"

"A training camp. For special services."

"What's special about them?"

"Would you like to find out?"

"You are mysterious tonight, sevenfivesix. Is it OK if I call you by your first name?"

She smiled. "I like Marianne de la France Profonde." She leaned forward from her seat and kissed his cheek and whispered, "You're sweet."

They slept, her head on his shoulder. She snored once or twice. The whole car was dimly lit and men all round were collapsed on their seats, their heads back, and snoring.

Night like a tunnel fell back as they roared toward the glitter of a lake from which the sun was boiling up furious red.

He said, "Why don't you come and spend your leave with us?"

"Wouldn't your mother be shocked at your bringing home this strange French woman when you already have a girlfriend?"

"Why do you say I have a girlfriend?"

"I saw you writing and looking eagerly for a letter when there was none."

"Well, you are already a good spy, aren't you? Anyway, she does not answer my letters, so I guess I'm not missing much."

Later, as they rolled slowly down the Don Valley into central Toronto, she said, "Would you like to volunteer for a dangerous kind of work?"

"This isn't enough, eh? Three guys got hurt just training at Shilo, they'll probably never jump again."

"This is also interesting and important."

"Of course, or 7568905 would not be doing it."

"Right. I'll mention your name to the commandant, if you like. You would be very good at it."

"What commandant?"

"The camp you're going to, Camp X, at Whitby."

"How do you know where I'm going? Jesus, you're strange."

"One of the things I was told to do at Shilo was to look out for prospects."

"For what?"

"Special services. Inside Europe."

"You'll be at this camp?"

She nodded.

"I'll think about it."

They got off the streetcar at the turning circle on St. Clair. He looked up with a shiver. The clear blue sky was being invaded by dark clouds racing in from the west. In a few minutes, they were walking under the opening flurries of a snowstorm.

Two horses covered with blankets white with snow were hauling a coal wagon up the street while the driver and helper sat smoking and chatting under the roof of the driver's compartment. They waved as they went by and she read the gold and red sign, ELIAS ROGERS. The harness was jingling with bells and the hooves left a trail of dark holes in the snow between the lines of the wheels. All was muffled in echoless quiet.

He told her about growing up here, the Saturday night skating in the park, snowball fights between Catholic and Protestant boys, tobogganing down the slopes of the ravine, being hit by a truck on his bike at this corner, the girls who came on Saturday night to dance cheek to cheek to swing band records in hot basement playrooms with the lights turned down.

When they reached the bottom of his street he stopped and pointed to the great dark rise of the house 50 metres ahead, partly obscured by the maples he used to climb, and now by the falling snow streaking in front of each of the many lighted windows, yellow in the snowing blue-dark.

"This is my favourite time to come home," he said, "It all looks so safe, doesn't it? We live in such safety here, nothing can ever harm us, eh? Even now, I feel this."

"May it be so," she said.

Hearing his voice, Hoover, their Irish setter, began barking wildly and lunging at the end of his cord by the front door of the house. The dog was frantic with love jumping up to lick his face, and lifting her skirt with his nose as they mounted the snowy steps to the lighted verandah.

His mother was at the door, in her evening silk, smiling. "Mother, I'd like you to meet Marianne de la France Profonde. Hi Mum." He gave her a kiss and a hug as Marianne took off her gloves composedly, looking round the big hall, and keeping her knees together against the sniffing dog. His father in his customary blue pinstripe suit came out of the living room with a smile, and greeted Marie warmly.

"J'étais soldat en France pendant la guerre," he said, to make her feel at home, and she said, "So it is a family tradition, to defend France?"

"You might say."

"Jack, you said her name much too quickly," said Mrs Giovanelli, and he said "Marianne de la France Profonde, nicknamed Marie l'Obscure"

Marianne covered her lips with her hand, astonished that a son could treat his mother in such a cavalier way. 'Surely she will rebuke him,' she thought, but Mrs Giovanelli, who saw that something was up, could not guess what it was since she did not know the term *La France Profonde*.

Jack had been embarrassed his first day at school at Châteauroux in Switzerland because the French pronunciation he had learned from his mother had been mocked by the teacher. Thereafter he saw his mother as faintly ridiculous. To speak French correctly was the first step in his liberation from her.

To maintain the proprieties, his mother had placed Marie in Jack's old room on the second floor and sent Jack up to a third-floor bedroom he had used as a child.

That night, after everyone had gone to bed, lying breathless on his bed, he heard a creak on the back stairs and ran barefoot down the hall to find her. As she came to the top step he bent to kiss her in a fever of anticipation. He had never been in bed with a woman before.

She gently pushed him back, took his hand and led him down the hall to the door he had left open, backlit by the softly falling snow like sparks streaking in front of the streetlights. She took off her dressing gown and lay down beside him. He thought he loved her more than his heart could bear.

He was amazed that there was no struggle; all the other girls he knew, though eager enough, made love in a fearful turmoil of shamed excitement before they finally refused.

The snow was a thick silent mantle of glowing whiteness over roofs, lawns, filling the street from door to door. He stood in bare feet where he had stood as a boy, when this top floor had been a nursery, on the cold wood floor before the window, his face pressed against the cedar bars fastened there to prevent his young self from falling to death 30 feet below. He tasted again the chewed cedar and fingered the tooth-marks he had made long ago. He puffed his breath out the casement watching the thin clouds trailing over the white moon, the light on the snow-thickened branches. Two boys were walking home with skates over their shoulders. He could feel the sting in their red cheeks, the thin pain of the skate laces tightening across his fingers, the melt of snow on his eyelashes. He let out a little whimper for time completely gone.

Stranraer, Moscow, October, 1941

The note from the Prime Minister read, "My dear Max. I wish you to go to Moscow with Mr. Harriman to arrange to succour the Russian armies so far as may be possible from our own supplies and those of the United States."

Beaverbrook met Harriman and Bannatyne at the airbase at Stranraer in Scotland and walked down the slippery concrete ramp to their seaplane, a Canso which would take them to HMS *London* in Scapa Flow.

The wing, perched on struts low above their heads, sheltered them from the cold drizzle as they walked under it towards the floating hull. At the tip of each wing was a bulbous tank for extra fuel.

"This is an unlikely contrivance," Beaverbrook said, "I'm not sure I want to get in this."

"You own half the plant that built it," said Bannatyne.

"Then all aboard for Moscow," said Beaverbrook.

At Archangel, a DC3 was waiting to fly them to Moscow. As they took off, Harriman handed a mimeographed sheet to Beaverbrook. "This was handed to me in Washington just before I left. Take a look."

INFORMATION FOR AMERICAN TRAVELLERS TO MOSCOW, VALID TO END 1941. ORIGIN: AMEMB, MOSCOW, JULY, 1941.

American visitors will encounter difficulties in Russia that originate in collectivization difficulties now exacerbated by wartime shortages.

1) The hot water in Moscow, supplied by communal steam systems running through big pipes in the streets, is turned off on May 15 and on again on October 15.

2) Rationing for civilians is graded according to status in the Soviet system. It is considered impolite and even anti-Soviet to point out that in Britain and Canada, and even in Germany, rationing is equal.

3) If you are housed in an hotel or private apartment, Russians of every kind including maids will appear in your room unexpectedly, even if you are *en deshabille* in the bathroom. No shame or provocation is intended.

4) Microphones are everywhere, even in the trees in the parks, and along the eaves of some houses in the Arbat.

5) The official line on the 1939 Soviet pact with the Germans is now a) In August, 1939, Britain and France, out of blind and perverse hatred of the world's first socialist state, refused to conclude an alliance with the USSR in time to deter Hitler from war, thus leaving the USSR without allies in case of a Hitlerite attack; and b) the pact was intended to gain time to rebuild Soviet defences. This line is now being taught by political commissars attached to Red Army units, is appearing in the papers now, and doubtless will soon be taught in all the schools.

"Microphones in the trees," said Cameron. "What kind of country is this?"

Harriman leaned close to Cameron's ear and whispered. "A very weird one. Look, have you noticed?" He pointed up at the air-nozzle that was supposed to deliver them fresh air from overhead. He twisted it. No air came out. He whispered, "When we sent these planes over here, they were checked thoroughly for every working part, including things like that. It's not working now because they've put a bug in it."

After a four hour flight, they descended towards the airport from the west. Bannatyne saw acres of wreckage all over the terrain west of Moscow. "Looks like the Germans were here already," he said to Harriman beside him, who said, "Those are dachas, little country cottages, for Moscow people."

"But they look tumble-down."

"They are."

In air so cold that it hurt their cheeks, they stood in the melt from new snow at the airport as a band played the national anthems, then paraded past stern young soldiers holding rifles at the present. The chauffeur drove them in a black Zil via the ring road around Moscow to Stalin's country house, called the Nearby Dacha, in wooded hills off the Smolensk road where 16 dachas for visitors surrounded Stalin's own. Eager for fresh air, Bannatyne rolled down his window and discovered that they were almost two inches thick. "They're bullet-proof," he said to Harriman. "Do you know the first thing Max did in the war? Bought an armoured car for himself." Beaverbrook grinned with boyish delight at the amazed look on Harriman's long, sly face.

In Beaverbrook's dacha there was a large reception hall, where all kinds of food and drink awaited them on a long table. Then Bannatyne and Harriman were escorted under pine trees sparkling with dripping snow along gravel paths to their own dachas.

Bannatyne found in his dacha a salon and a bedroom almost as big as the reception hall, with ceilings four metres high, walls painted strong red, doors painted black, tall curtains masking every window, dim electric lights, and a gigantic bathroom, at least 20 by 20 feet, with a tile stove at one end, and a tiled bathtub three metres long and deep enough to drown him. Into it water was slowly dripping. He looked up to the dim tiled ceiling and could not decide if the roof were leaking, or if it was a shower. He took off his clothes and laid them on the bed. He was completely naked when a young woman walked in without knocking, said something in Russian and began opening curtains without regard for his nakedness.

After he had changed, he went back to Beaverbrook's dacha. His Lordship was bustling round the laden table, picking here and there, obviously impatient to get to the great man whose dacha was darkly silhouetted through the trees. "We're expected over there for dinner at seven," he said. "Maybe we'd better line our stomachs with oil, if we're going to keep up with their toasts." He swallowed some caviar and tossed back a vodka. "I'm starting to rather enjoy myself," he said.

Stalin, a short, still man wearing a loosely-belted grey army tunic, sat at his desk in the dacha an hour before his guests were due, talking on the telephone to General Zhukov who was in charge of the defence of Moscow. His hair like grey turf, his face expressionless as usual, he was puffing on his pipe, trying to grasp the complicated situation, in which the enemy, supply, weather, civil defence, air power, army morale and troop movements all overlapped and affected each other.

Zhukov was explaining the situation to him for the third time. Stalin could not think clearly because he was more concerned about losing control to Zhukov than with improving the situation. Zhukov explained once more his plans to cope with the German attack but Stalin still did not understand. He ordered Zhukov to come to the dacha so they could confer with maps.

Stalin was reputed wise among those who did not know him. Those who did, feared him. He was made of cunning contradictions. He knew Hitler planned to destroy communism, yet he allied himself with Hitler. He despised intellectuals, and pretended to their achievements. Most of his supporters he arrested and shot. He said that mass violence was the means to utopia. He played the role of father to his people, while driving his daughter crazy and refusing to liberate his son from German captivity.

Russia was made in his image, a country at war with itself, held together only by his violent will: one Russia was bureaucrats, camp guards, soldiers and secret police. The other was frightened workers, sullen, half-starved, drunken, short-lived, and ignorant of the outside world. His country was two because he was two Stalins, and one hated the other.

His character and his regime had been largely formed by Lenin, who used him because he was vicious and despised him because he was vulgar. Humiliated, Stalin vowed to excel his mentor and tormentor. He demanded strict adherence to Leninist orthodoxy, which he enforced by Leninist terror. He did not see, and no one dared point out, the absurdity of parading the orthodoxy of a leader who was an opportunist.

As a boy in the Tiflis Theological Seminary in Georgia, he had learned to mask his feelings behind an expressionless face, which puzzled people and frightened the weak. To be strong, strongest of all, the man of steel, whom nothing could affect, was his goal in life—everything else was subjugated to that ambition which had only one source—his suspicious ego.

Hitler's invasion of Russia had stunned Stalin. In communist theory, fascism represented the final stage of the evolution of capitalism which would self-destruct in imperialist conflict. Stalin had signed the alliance with Hitler in 1939 to assure Hitler that he was safe in the east and could therefore attack France. He believed the capitalists would tear each other to pieces. In the end, Soviet Russia, weak, chaotic and terrorized as it was, would pick up the pieces of empire cheaply.

Through the spring of 1941, he had refused to believe the reports from all sides that the Germans were preparing to invade Russia because he was afraid that if they did, the Red Army would collapse. In the first four weeks after the German attack in June, he had cowered in his dacha, scanning the reports by telex, telegraph, telephone and courier that told only one story—collapse after Red Army collapse, huge surrenders of demoralized Russian soldiers, crowds of Ukrainians throwing flowers on German tanks.

The Germans were skillfully carrying out the greatest encirclements in the history of warfare, capturing more soldiers in a few weeks than had ever been captured before in a whole war. The Red Army was shrivelling like a leech in salt. Nowhere did the Red officers who for years Stalin had been terrorizing with faked charges of treason, make a determined stand against the enemy. Stalin thought, 'They were afraid of me before, now they fear the Germans more. There is no way out of this, because a greater fear has come over them.' Having learned from Lenin that only terror could make men obey, he did not know what to do.

As his western visitors arrived, Stalin stood up and regarded them without interest, his left eyebrow raised, his mouth invisible under his huge moustache. He was about Beaverbrook's height. They sat in up-right hard armchairs in a tight circle with the interpreter. Harriman took out a steno pad and crossed his long legs, in their elegant Brooks Brothers pinstripe trousers, showing shiny black oxfords, and began to take notes in shorthand. To his left sat Bannatyne, then Molotov, the Foreign Minister, and Maxim Litvinov, a former ambassador to England, both in Moscow mauve. Neither of them spoke a word of greeting.

Beaverbrook began to describe the voyage but Stalin cut him short impatiently. "I'm not interested in that," he said. "Tell me about your great friend Churchill." So Beaverbrook described Churchill's war work, in general terms, and his recent speech to the House of Commons promising aid to Russia. Stalin was suspicious, as if Beaverbrook might have come all the way here to tell a few pointless lies about Churchill. He knew that Beaverbrook in 1919 had been the friend of Churchill, who had sent soldiers to fight the Red Army so he had no reason to believe the English were now his friends. However, they were offering help that he needed. He was forced to see them. He resented them.

He rudely interrupted Beaverbrook's encomiums of Churchill with, "What is his attitude towards invasion now that the German armies are fully committed in the east against us?"

"We do not believe Hitler will attempt an invasion now."

"I meant your invasion of France."

"I am very much in favour of it."

"Aha, then you will do it." Stalin was suddenly very interested.

"It is a very difficult thing to do."

Stalin snorted. "The English did not find it too difficult to send an expedition all the way to Archangel to help Denikin in 1918. Nor did they think it was too difficult to invade the Crimea in 1854, which is much farther away. So why not now? Against Germany?"

Irritated, Beaverbrook said, "It is not so easy to cross the Channel. Ask yourself Marshal, why did Hitler not invade England last year while our army had no weapons? We were so badly equipped in 1940 that Churchill asked me to make him some pikes. I said, 'Do you want bows and arrows as well, though there is a shortage of string.'"

The translator had difficulty with the word pike, so Beaverbrook quickly drew a picture of one. Stalin looked at it and contemptuously threw it aside.

"The answer is sea power," said Beaverbrook, "and its twin brother, air power. When we were most threatened last summer, he asked me to make sure we had enough aircraft to defeat the invasion. Thank God we made them in time, and Hitler never arrived."

"So if you have enough planes to defeat him on the English side of the channel, you have enough to defeat him on the French side."

"Right now, it is impossible. We don't have the ships."

"Right now is the best time, when his armies are far away from you."

"I can only repeat Marshal, that we are not ready."

"If you do not intend to invade Europe while Hitler is fighting here, then you do not intend to invade at all. Therefore you intend to leave the Soviets and Germans to fight to the bitter end. Then you think you will be strongest. But you will be wrong."

Beaverbrook said, "I opposed our intervention in your revolution in 1919. I have been defending the Soviet Union to the British since you were attacked. I have recommended all possible aid to your country. But I find your attitude incomprehensible in view of our dangerous mission here to offer you help. Ask yourself, Marshal, what was the policy of the Soviet Union when Hitler was attacking us?"

"It is all right," said Stalin airily, studying Beaverbrook with interest. He was thinking, 'Well at least there is some fire in his belly. We can use him.' He said, "When you fight the Devil, you must fight like the devil." He smiled, his huge moustache lifting to reveal his mouth for the first time, filled with tobacco teeth. Beaverbrook shuddered, for it was as if he had opened his mouth to swallow the prey.

Harriman wrote Stalin's words in shorthand as translated, then added his own comment for Roosevelt, 'if we fight Hitler, we become Hitler?'

Molotov said, "We think you are negotiating with Hitler through your prisoner Rudolf Hess."

At this Beaverbrook, thinking 'Damn you both,' put his hands on the arms of his chair and started to rise. Stalin let out a bellow, eyes crinkled up, yellow mouth open again.

Stalin said, indicating Molotov, "You see what you are up against? He is inhuman, you will never get the better of him. He never stops thinking but he has no imagination, that is why he is useful to me. He is a clockwork mouse. I wind him up and set him down and he goes exactly where I point him." Beaverbrook looked at Molotov, thinking there must be some reaction to such contempt. Molotov sat rigid as if his mauve serge suit were a straitjacket.

Molotov said, "Did Hess bring documents? Conditions for peace?"

"He brought a copy of Hitler's speech to the Reichstag, offering peace to England." He handed Molotov a copy.

Stalin said, "Why don't you execute him?"

"That would mean a trial."

"Shoot him first, have a trial later."

All three of the westerners were silent, thinking, 'We'd better leave,' when Stalin went on, "Why have you come here?"

Beaverbrook blinked. "Why, to offer you help."

"What help?"

"Arms."

"What arms?"

Bannatyne said, "Tanks, airplanes, rifles, whatever you need. Trucks, railway track, machine tools, wheat, boots, raw aluminium." As the list went on, Maxim Litvinov's eyebrows went up. Stalin glanced at Harriman, who said, "We also can supply all those things except aluminum."

"And your President has decided he will do this?"

"We are already supplying the British, so there should be no difficulty to supply another country opposed to fascism."

"And in what quantities?"

Bannatyne and Harriman named the quantities they were prepared to supply. Stalin was interested until Harriman began naming the gigantic American production figures and then his mask slipped for a moment betraying incredulity. As Harriman finished, Litvinov jumped to his feet and shouted, *"Molodets Oora,* now we will win the war."

Stalin offered many toasts at dinner. Beaverbrook, seated next to him, was curious about the red wine Stalin was drinking from a small glass, which he refilled himself from a decanter set before him. Wondering if the wine were better than the wine for the guests, he poured himself some. It was the same. Stalin also inverted a small shot glass over an open bottle of Georgian champagne. Beaverbrook asked him why he did this.

"To keep in the bubbles. You know, you are a very inquisitive man, but I like that. If you are not inquisitive, you learn nothing. These two here"—he waved at Litvinov and Molotov—"they're hopeless, no fun in them at all. I like your spirit. But what a queer name you have, why did you pick such a weird name?" Bannatyne burst out laughing. "Beavers are industrious, and Max is an industrialist."

"I am from Canada," said Beaverbrook, "and to us it is not a queer name. In any case, there was a brook near my father's house and in it lived beavers, and when I was a boy I used to go there and watch them working away. They never stopped, not even in winter, always building their dam and their runways and repairing their house and training their kits."

"Like Germans," said Stalin. "All the same, a queer name." He stared at Beaverbrook who thought, 'What big teeth you have, grandmother.'

Walking to their dacha afterwards in the cold clear night, Bannatyne said, "We're going to have trouble with him. All he understands is fear."

Harriman said, "He is a very unnatural man."

Beaverbrook was silent. For years, he had admired the Soviet attempts to better the lot of mankind but now he was filled with doubt.

Off Iceland, November, 1941

Grant Giovanelli stood on the bridge of *Sheguiandah* looking out over a calm grey sea southeast of Iceland. The winter sun was low and misty in the southern sky but he could see the black dot of a big plane, possibly a Focke-Wulf *Kondor* coming in from the east, so he rang the hooter for action stations, and the anti-aircraft crews came running up to strip off the covers, twirling the guns on their platforms and aiming up towards the plane, which was now heading towards Reykjavik.

Grant kept his binoculars on it. The plane slowly grew into the high-winged shape of a *Canso*, so he ordered the crews to stand down and watched the plane as it flew to the northwest past them, close enough so that he could see the wheels tucked up into the hull. The pilot waggled his wings at them as he flew by, so Grant ordered a star-shell sent up. It exploded a hundred yards ahead of the ship, the whiteness of the magnesium flare turning into a red light that fell slowly into the sea.

Bannatyne saw the flare while he was looking down onto the convoy as it scored the sea with a brief vee of white heading towards Iceland, and the safety of Reykjavik. He knew that his grandson might be out here somewhere. The steward brought him tea and left him with his papers strewn over the seat beside him and the folding table. He wrote in his diary, *Arrived Reykjavik noon Thursday the 22 easy flight from Stranraer. Convoy below heading west. GG in it?*

After the evening watch, Grant Giovanelli went down to his cabin where he set his typewriter on the desk and began to write. He worked on his novel for a little while, then switched to letters, as the ship was due into Reykjavik the next day.

Dear Lady Cat, thanks for your lovely letter. You can't imagine how much it means to hear a friendly voice out here

*on the stormy edge of the world. I take your letters to sea
with me and read them over and over, as I've just done. My
last letter to you having been returned to me after 19 days
because of censoring problems—I revealed too much of my
whereabouts—this one will be more circumspect. Here I
am in a little un-nameable belonging to the Royal Unknown
Navy about one hundred miles south of the island of Censoria,
hunting for German inconnus, with my little typewriter on the
wardroom table. It is pulled against the near fiddle and
jammed with a length of wood against the far fiddle, so it
can't go bounding about the table as the ship rolls with my
fingers racing after it like a mouse after cheese.*

*I am writing my long-winded and very funny novel,
entitled <u>Suds</u>, about a Methodist brewing tycoon who can't
stand the taste of his own beer. And some poems and letters to
Jack, Mum and Dad and my commanding officer asking for a
posting which will get me nearer to a certain noble feline.
There is a better than even chance of this as there has been an
unforeseen change of our duties. In which case I shall bring
you a jar of the precious fluid distilled from trees at Stone
Cottage. God how writing that name brings back memories
of that long weekend with you—those few days that seem like
a whole summer now. The last before the deluge. But now I
say to you, après le deluge, moi.*

*Frère Jacques has fallen in love simultaneously with two
women, both French, at least one is French from our defeated
ally, and the other is a family domesticated in Canada. Maybe
it's inevitable—he went to school in French-Switzerland for
two years. The former is mysterious, quite good-looking in that
gaunt French way, bright and brave, with no name, or at least
none that she will tell us, having escaped from Nowhere and
intending to . . . this would be censored so I shan't say it.*

*Anyway, here is an effusion on the subject of young love,
in my best Shakespearean mannerism:*

Short Sonnet for a man who can not make up his mind

Love's Double

He has two loves, one like a day in spring
Chanting with promises that ripen not;
One like a summer day which is so hot
That everything is ripe, and no birds sing.

Because his love is true, but born a twin
He cannot choose, till one has chosen him
I'm like him, but my love's twin goal
Resolves in you, whom I love heart and soul.

I was glad to hear that you are happy at—what is the word, Guy's?—I can't read your writing—is that the name of the hospital?—and even getting to know some more Canadians, at the felicitously named Number 24 Canadian General Military Hospital. Dad told me that a friend of his is in the administration there. His name is Captain Jack Ewing, and he is a very nice chap with access to a car (auto) and gasoline (petrol) who can get you lovely (loverly) things should you want them, the next time you are down there on one of your exchange training visits.

Adieu, au revoir with all the love that's welcome from . . . Grant G.

PS Please send me a picture of yourself, preferably two.

Wolfschanze, Rastenburg, December, 1941

In early December, Hitler received a report from the army Quartermaster General, Wagner, describing the materiel situation on the eastern front as "a catastrophe." He handed it to Jodl and said, "What do you make of this?"

Jodl, who had seen the report in draft, scanned it briefly to make sure it had not been altered, and said sadly, "And the manpower shortage is a crisis."

Hitler snarled, "Exactly. The war can no longer be won."

"Yes," said Jodl gently. He handed it to the impassive Halder who said, "We have reached the end of our human and material resources."

"Nonsense," said Hitler abruptly. He squeezed the paper into a ball and hurled it into the corner.

Halder watched it bounce. He said bleakly, "Nevertheless . . . ."

"Nevertheless what," Hitler shouted. "And whose fault is it? That goddamned idiot Höppner and that fool Brauchitsch, if we had stuck to the original plan we would have the whole Ukraine now, never mind mucking around in Moscow. Nevertheless nothing."

He stamped his foot and left the map room and hurried through the drizzle 20 metres to the Führer bunker, SS guards snapping to attention and saluting as he passed in the dark, his brow furrowed, muttering angrily as he went.

"Reached the end of nothing," he said aloud and burst into the sitting room, where the secretaries were having tea. They jumped to their feet and smiled, greeting him warmly, for he was popular with them all. He sat by himself in the corner drinking his tea with his hands wrapped round the cup to keep his fingers warm. He was angry with Jodl for having agreed that the war was lost. He must retrieve the situation somehow, although it was impossible. Now he had the long war on two fronts that Germany could not win. 'Then why go on?' he thought, and the answer was as always: because life is struggle.

General Heinz Guderian arrived by train in the snowy forest at Rasten-burg in East Prussia the next day. He was wearing the leather great-coat that he had been wearing when he accompanied Hitler in the happy parade down the Champs-Elysées in Paris 17 months before. But now he was not smiling. His face was grim, and he carried his briefcase with the bad news tight under his arm, nodding to the various salutes he encountered on his way through the SS guards posted out-side the newly constructed Führer-bunker.

He was admitted into the map room which still smelled of newly-poured wet cement. Around the great table were 16 generals and *aides-de-camp*, all standing, all in uniform. They greeted him formally, in loud voices because most of them had been deafened while serving in the artillery during the Great War.

Brauchitsch stood at attention, ignoring the pain in his heart. Stiff with duty, he was bound to Hitler by financial favours and fear of black-mail. Formal, slow-witted Keitel, known as Lackeitel, was Hitler's reluctant toady; clever von Kluge saw through the Führer's ploys, yet could not outwit him; sickly von Rundstedt was too weak to fight either the enemy or Hitler; Halder worried about the enormous risks Hitler took, fearing disaster every day; sceptical Jodl, who shared Hitler's south German background, foresaw defeat and obeyed the orders that led there.

These and the rest had gathered now for a major conference be-cause the Wehrmacht's major goal, destruction of the Red Army, had not been achieved. New Russian divisions whose existence had been unknown to Hitler in June, were driving back the freezing German troops.

Guderian, his grim face twisted into a scowl, clicked his heels and shot out his arm in the party salute, which Hitler returned. Then he shook hands with Guderian, staring up intently at the general, whom he had not seen since the great victories in France.

"We meet again and we shall triumph again, you will see."

Guderian said, "It is very difficult for our men. We have asked too much and we must make changes."

"What is the problem, what has stopped you?" Hitler was already irritated, sensing what Guderian was up to. He leaned over the 1/1,000,000 map with his arms spread wide encompassing the enormous distance between Warsaw and Moscow. His thumbprint covered an area 25 kilometres wide but he was personally attempting to control units as small as 300 men.

Guderian looked down confused by the huge scale of the map, thinking, 'It is impossible to display our problems on a map this size.' He said, "We need a detailed map of the area west of Tula."

Hitler said, "This is the scale of our war, general."

"This is the scale of a six month advance by millions of men," said Guderian hotly. "In case you have forgotten why you won the Iron Cross, mein Führer, let me remind you that we fight day by day, hour by hour, and drop by drop of blood and gasoline. You order me to take Moscow as if it is only a dot on the map, and I have neither the men nor the supplies."

One of the generals gasped. Hitler glared at him. The general covered his mouth as if coughing.

"Your theories do not interest me," said Hitler. He rapped the map on the word Moscow. "I expected you, here, in the Kremlin by now."

"We have outrun our supplies. There is not a decent road from here to Tula . . ." he indicated a distance of over 300 kilometres, occupying only a few centimetres on the map ". . . except what we build. We have no gasoline, not enough food, and no winter clothing. There are casualties because of the lack of clothing. The wounded are freezing to death in hospital." Halder and several others nodded and moved around because this was all true, although the Führer refused to credit their reports. Guderian lowered his voice. "There was panic on our front, mein Führer."

"It must be stopped," Hitler said.

"There is no alternative to withdrawal."

Hitler paced up and down, his right arm chopping the air hard before him, making sweeping gestures. "If that is why you have come all this way, to tell me this, then you have wasted your time."

He glared at the silent generals. "There will be no withdrawal, every man will stand to his post with fanatical resistance, regardless of any breakthroughs to his left or his right, or even if he is surrounded. The order must be given, resist, resist, resist," he shouted. The generals bowed their heads and stared down at the maps in silence.

"But this will mean enormous losses," said Guderian.

Hitler stared at him. "Do you think that Frederick the Great's grenadiers died gladly for him? Do you? Do you not know that even the ignorant Slavs died gladly for the Tsar at Austerlitz? You stand too close to the events."

Guderian tried to speak. Hitler silenced him with a glare. "You have too much pity for the soldiers. You ought to disengage yourself more. You must be hard, hard, hard." He hit his fist in his cupped left hand and his hoarse voice rose again as it did in his speeches at Nuremberg. He shouted at his generals, "And that goes for all of you."

That evening in Europe, that afternoon in Washington, that morning in Hawaii, that night in Japan, for the first time in history, all the leaders of the world were acting on the same event on the day it was happening—the Japanese attack on Pearl Harbor.

Steaming away from Hawaii on his aircraft carrier, Admiral Chuichi Nagumi, a burly, gruff, painstaking man, was relieved as he watched the last of his returning pilots land safely on his carrier's deck. The pilots were reporting with glee that the attack had been a tremendous success. They had sunk eight American battleships or cruisers and destroyed many airplanes on the ground. Carefully maintaining radio silence to keep his fleet hidden from the Americans who would be sure to send out their carriers against him, he turned west and steamed for Tokyo.

But a single low-powered radio transmission from one of the returning pilots—one word, *Tora Tora Tora*, reporting complete success —had been picked up 4,000 miles west by the Japanese Home Fleet under Admiral Yamamoto. As he heard the news from his chief signals officer, Yamamoto looked at the two fingers and thumb of his right hand remembering the terrible moment in 1905 when the Russian naval shell had crashed into his bridge. He saw clearly in his imagination the brave young pilots landing on the dangerous decks. He remembered the young American officers he had known in Boston and Washington, who might have been killed. 'And now the others will come,' he thought gloomily, for his studies in the US made him understand better than any other Japanese the strength of the country Japan had just attacked.

He had told Prime Minister Tojo, 'We can run wild for a few months, perhaps a year, but then vengeance will come. I hope you will avoid war with America.' The Americans could replace all the ships lost at Pearl Harbor in a year or two, and Japan could never match them. Still, if war had to come, this was the best possible beginning.

Tojo had also been extremely reluctant to go to war with the United States, Britain and Holland all at once, but he was cornered. Roosevelt had already frozen all Japanese assets in the United States, cut off shipments of oil, gasoline and steel and suspended diplomatic relations with Japan's allies. The Imperial Navy used 400 tons of oil per hour in peacetime, and if the nation were not to be strangled by the encircling powers then they must attack while the time was right.

Yamamoto dictated a message to Prime Minister Tojo, who was asleep at his home in Tokyo when the telephone rang. He heard the news of the great success and gave thanks to Heaven. Then he dressed formally in shirt and tie, black coat, polished black oxfords, striped trousers, grey gloves and top hat to go to the Imperial Palace to inform the Emperor.

In England, on the evening of December 7, Winston Churchill, drinking brandy at his country home, Chequers, was informed by his butler that an American news broadcast had said that the Japanese Navy had bombed American battleships, sinking several. He was glad. Now he was certain Britain would be on the winning side. He went to the emergency telephone.

Franklin Roosevelt was seated in his wheelchair at his desk in the White House, on the telephone to Admiral Husband Kimmel in Hawaii about the damage, while the ammunition was still exploding in the bombed ships. As soon as he hung up, he received Churchill's call. He turned his chair to look out at the noon sun shining on the green lawn, as Churchill said from the darkness, "What's all this about Japan?"

Roosevelt replied, "It's quite true, they have attacked us at Pearl Harbor. We are all in the same boat now."

At midnight a few minutes later, Josef Stalin, half-asleep watching a movie in the Nearby Dacha, was disturbed by an aide with the news that Japan had attacked the United States. He went with Molotov to the planning table to discover where Pearl Harbor was. When he asked Molotov what the attack meant, Molotov replied that Russia was saved, and so were they.

Hitler was drinking herbal tea and talking history with the secretaries and their visitors in the sitting room when von Below handed him the telex report from Tokyo. Hitler read it over, slapped his thigh, said, "This is the turning point," and ran outside to find Keitel and Jodl. He burst in on them in the map room of the Führer bunker waving the report, and said, "The Japanese have attacked the United States. This is the turning point, this is the decisive moment of the war."

All three of them thought the same thing: 'What does it decide?' Hitler, seeing their expressions of incomprehension, said impatiently, "I must discuss this with Ribbentrop," turned and went back outside.

Jodl said, "Ribbentrop!" and burst out laughing. Keitel was worried to see Hitler so excited because that usually meant some bold new venture, and Germany was already stretched far beyond her capacity.

Four days later, with apparently no purpose unless to gratify Japan, or perhaps to risk everything on his own *Gotterdämmerung*, Hitler declared war on the United States.

Roosevelt was determined. Stalin could scarcely believe his good luck. Churchill was happy. Tojo was relieved.

Toronto, December, 1941

Eleanor Giovanelli told Jack that she wanted him to wear his grand-father's kilt to the 1941 St. Andrew's Ball which she was organizing. Jack said, "I'd prefer to wear the Giovanelli tartan, you know, Mum, basil green and tomato red on a field of spaghetti." She looked at him with an exasperation compounded of awareness of his faults, and her never-failing ambition for him.

He had to wear the kilt because moths had holed his evening clothes. In any case, he knew Marianne would not laugh at him because she had to wear something borrowed herself. Mrs. Giovanelli gave her a dress she had worn herself some years before, which was "still in style because it was made in good taste."

Marianne tried on the dress with help from Eleanor thinking, 'How odd this is to be putting on a gown to go to a ball in Canada while *Maman* is probably in the kitchen and Papa is doing what?' She imagined her elegant father chopping wood in the cobbled courtyard of the château wearing suspenders like a German.

She glanced at herself in the mirror and was surprised at how thin she looked. She turned to see how the pale green trim of the bodice off-set her pale shoulders, and decided it went well with her brown hair and brown eyes. She thought, *'Que je suis belle ce soir! Enfin, après ces mois de militaire, c'est un plaisir d'être chic.'*

Eleanor Giovanelli was known in her club set as The Duchess, for her airs and graces. Seeing that Marianne was French, educated and self-possessed, she immediately imagined her to be noble if not royal. Thus she put on her best *grande dame* manner with Marianne, who re-sponded with decent simplicity.

Marianne like an aristocrat, praised Mrs. Giovanelli's taste in Coal-port and Crown Derby, her paintings, furniture, the grandfather clock of carved oak, because she remembered what her mother taught, that people get on better if they praise and thus encourage each other, that this is like sun in a garden; without it, plants like people droop and never come to bloom.

On her first evening there, after dinner, Marianne played a piece by Rameau. At the end, she said, "It sounds better on a harpsichord." Eleanor, who had never even seen a harpsichord, except at the Conservatory, was thrilled by this casual familiarity. She asked Marianne about her early life, but all she would say was that she was educated in a convent. Mrs. Giovanelli implied that she thought Marianne was of noble lineage. "Perhaps you are a countess."

"Never that," says Marianne, "although there were kings in my family."

Eleanor was awed, but Marianne laughed and said, "There were kings all over France, in the old days."

Jack, in his borrowed kilt, escorted Marianne into the vast ballroom of the hotel, following his mother and father, who in turn followed his grandfather and grandmother. All were led by a piper in kilt and sporran from the Ontario Scottish Regiment playing "The Road to the Isles." Entering the room behind the Colonel, Bernie Hallett, were also the Prime Minister of Canada, William Lyon Mackenzie King, a cautious little man of rebellious Scottish lineage, and several cabinet ministers. There was a warm round of applause as they were piped in and seated at the head table beside Mrs. Giovanelli.

She had made sure that despite the wartime shortages, everything was as it had always been in peacetime: there was a pipe band and all would dance the Schottische, the Eightsome Reel, and the Dashing White Sergeant, followed by Viennese waltzes, foxtrots and some Charlestons. There was good roast beef at the dinner, and Mumm's champagne and Johnnie Walker Black Label.

Standing in her gold Worth gown beside her handsome husband she watched the swirling scene with satisfaction, alert for emergencies to extinguish. But Bannatyne, watching his grandson in a kilt, about to go off and fight the Heinies, was also seeing with the eyes of the Great War. The gas was swirling in, the French on the right were running. His best friend Edwin Currie was falling dead ten feet from the parapet during the counter attack at First Ypres. He thought of Edwin and the words in the Bible, *For those we love and see no more.* The words made him sigh, and he turned away from his daughter who seemed so satisfied with it all.

Jack held Marianne's chair as she settled down for dinner, and she whispered up to him with a smile, "It's all seems so ancient and barbaric, very much like home. Do they roast sheep over there?" She glanced at the huge stone fireplace. She looked so droll with her eyebrows lifted and dark eyes wide with amusement that he burst out laughing.

He patted her gloved hand and took his place beside her.

Bishop McLeod rose to say the grace, in Gaelic and Latin, ending with a prayer for victory. "Is he speaking or coughing?" Marianne whispered as the bishop horked out the Gaelic and Jack laughed. "It's Gaelic."

Colonel Bernie Hallett stood and led them in the ritual of passing the whiskey glasses over the water glasses in memory of Bonnie Prince Charlie, then proposed the king's health, which Ed Burns, now a captain, drank with his water glass, to signal his disapproval of British imperialism. The women, young and old, were bare-shouldered, their hands and forearms clothed in white kid gloves. Their chests were powdered and adorned with family jewellery. The men except for the kilted few like Jack and many in uniform were stiff in white tie. The talk was of Pearl Harbor and Hitler's declaration of war on the US, during a bitter mocking speech in the Reichstag. He had said that Roosevelt was a cowardly war-mongering plutocrat, surrounded by Jews and serving their money-grubbing interests.

The men round the table were busy observing the obvious. With satisfaction, they were all saying, "Now we are all in it together," as if the Americans had only been a little slow in accepting their duty, when in fact the American people *en masse* were strongly against this war.

But nothing mattered to the men now except to "get on with it," and "finish the job." Many of them believed that the outcome of the war was now decided. None of them remembered that it had been only a few months before when they had faced an overwhelming enemy, as the Germans did now, and none of them had in those days thought of surrender.

Alison saw Jack a few yards away near the punch table and thought he looked tall, tanned and happy in his kilt and formal black jacket with white ruffled shirt. She heard his voice once through the music and loud talk, and looked towards him often.

Later, at the punch table in the main ballroom, she was alone for a moment and he came up and asked her to waltz. She opened her dance card, and as she was reading it she pressed familiarly against him, unaware of what she was doing. It was as if her body independently of her mind had done what it wanted. She glanced up at him and smiled, "I do have an opening, second from now," but he could think of nothing but her, her eyes looking up at him with a friendly expression, the warmth of her breast on his arm, and he took her in his arms and stepped onto the floor with her regardless of the cards.

The admiration he had felt for her at the university returned, and he smiled down at her, thinking she was very young and happy, and he said, "I'm very glad you decided to dance with me."

"Why?" she said, meaning 'Why would you think I might not?'

"Because I wrote to you and you did not write back."

"But I did."

"When?"

"Weeks ago."

"Where did you send it?"

"Some funny name like, Shilo. Manitoba."

"I left there a week ago."

"That must be it."

"What did you say?"

"Oh, nothing much, our cat died. My bicycle was stolen. I might go into postgraduate work." She said all this with a happy smile which had nothing to do with her words, but only with how she was feeling towards him.

"I asked you to come to this dance with me."

"I didn't get that letter, did you write two?"

"Would you have accepted?"

"That depends."

"On what?"

"If I had been free, I would have," she said with a laugh.

"Well, at least I have succeeded in eliciting a reaction from dear distant immovable Miss de Pencier."

She lowered her eyes, because she recognized the quote, from Dickens, and knew that it conveyed romantic pain.

"Excuse me," he said, "that was uncalled for."

"That's all right," she said very softly, "I'm sure you did not mean . . ." she trailed off.

"Mean what?" he asked, leaning a little back from her.

"Must we?" she said sharply

"I think we must. Time is short."

She nodded. "There is nothing I can do about that."

"Why not?"

"These things take time." The moment she had said that she was flustered because she knew he would take it as encouragement, which she had not intended.

"What things?"

"I knew you'd say that," she said quickly. "Nothing special."

"What happened today, dear Miss de Pencier? 'Nothing special. The house burned down. Someone proposed to me. Nothing special.'"

"Now that would depend on who did the proposing, wouldn't it?" she said, challenging him. Suddenly leaning back in his arms and smiling at him confidently and flirtatiously, she knew she was happy. He had broken through into territory long forbidden to her and she was excited. She could see from the lift of his eyebrows, his stiffened back, that there was much more than banter now in his attitude to her, and she did not mind.

Surprised at her sudden forthrightness, he said, "That day I left, I thought you were so darn standoffish. I was scarcely able to bring myself to send you a letter from Shilo. Now I'm wondering if you've changed?"

"I know, people say that," she said regretfully. "It's something I can't help. I don't mean to be, not so much as people seem to think."

She looked up at him with a smile that seemed to say, 'You see, this is how I am.' And this made him love her.

She was astonished at herself, doing something she had always imagined, opening up to a very handsome and interesting and charming man. She felt complicit with him, as she never had with a man before.

He was feeling light-headed, because his usual flirtatious banter had turned real; intense feeling was being created by the light words. He had so little time, he wanted to know if she would wait for him to come home. But the waltz was almost over, the ball would soon end, he would probably be posted overseas soon, so he plunged on, feeling very reckless now, and said what he wanted, "I said I was glad to see you because I admire you beyond all reason, because you are so incredibly beautiful not to mention good natured and smart and you have such a lovely pensive smile that I noticed that first day at school when I fell in love with you despite the fact that you are obsessed by shampoo. So there, now you have me at your mercy, my hoping heart is laid bare for you to tramp on." He said this with an insouciant and desperate smile that made it impossible for her to know if he was serious.

'Why would you imagine I want to trample on your heart?' she was thinking in amazement. She said nothing but looked up at him with a smile, for to her, words were no longer necessary.

When the music was over he continued to hold her hand so she could not leave without speaking. She looked up at him, no longer coy, and said, "Why would you imagine I want to trample on your heart?"

"It just felt that way," he said. "Wrecked. Maybe you didn't mean to."

She withdrew her hand and he walked her back to the punch table, and she saw Don Wright, her escort of the evening, standing talking to her mother. He looked peeved. Alison said, "I'm so sorry, I got carried away."

Jack slightly bowed to Mrs. de Pencier, who said, "I believe I knew your mother at BSS, Eleanor, isn't it? She plays the piano marvellously?"

And he said "How do you do?" to Don Wright and Mr. de Pencier but he heard nothing of what they said, feeling only Alison's presence standing close beside him, until she lifted her white gloved hand and arm and laid her hand gently on Don's shoulder just as she had with him and danced away.

He was amazed that she could do that so lightly after the passionate feelings which had just begun to grow between them. Mrs. de Pencier saw how her daughter looked and how Jack was watching Alison on the floor, and she thought, 'Oh dear, this is the one.'

Jack stood unwilling to move, until a bothersome feeling of duty, like homework undone, distracted him from Alison, and he realized with dismay that this duty was Marianne. She would be feeling lonely and neglected, knowing so few people here.

He walked around the floor towards her, aware of where Alison was dancing at every moment, feeling depressed by the thought of Marianne. 'But how can this be,' he thought, stopping at the main door where people were crowding in and out, laughing and holding each other by the arm, and occasionally glancing at him with a questioning look, 'How could I have yearned for her yesterday and yet feel depressed at having to go and dance with her now.'

He forced his way forward, holding champagne in his hand for her, and seeing her long, rather pretty face, which was looking anxious, concentrate on him, he felt again towards her as he had earlier that evening. She continued to talk animatedly with the young officers who had clustered round her, while making sure she kept him in sight. 'So she wasn't lonely after all,' he thought, 'And I might have stayed longer with Alison.'

Camp X, December, 1941

The day after Jack reported back to his base in Toronto, he received written orders to report to Camp X at Whitby 50 miles east of Toronto. He would be picked up in the evening by a bus.

At Manning Depot number two, he was joined by six other men. They were taken out of the city in darkness through farmland to a country road where the bus stopped. A car in a lane blinked its lights, and they were transferred to it and another just behind, then driven by a route designed to confuse them, to a barred gate at the end of a farm track.

They humped their duffel bags into a barracks decorated with signs reading THE ENEMY IS LISTENING, and KILL OR BE KILLED. They were ordered by a burly, bristling sergeant major to take the beds assigned by little slips of paper on the rough brown blankets, and to have their feet on the floor within five seconds of the whistle in the morning or miss breakfast.

After a solid and filling breakfast of oranges, oatmeal porridge, bacon, milk and coffee, he was ordered to report "On the double" to a newly constructed clapboard building half a mile away over the rough turf. As he trotted, a Tiger Moth biplane zoomed down over the end of the field where some men were running around in the gloom. From the plane fell dark round objects like bombs among the men, and he paused for a moment, watching for the explosion, but saw only puffs of white, then the men running away from it.

He passed a squad of men marching with exaggerated precision, commanded by an officer who was yelling out the pace, not by the conventional left right, left right, but Bang Bang, Bang Bang.

Inside another white clapboard bungalow smelling of new-cut pine, he reported to Major General Kertin, who was seated behind a desk in a small crowded office. He did not see, until he had turned round to

178

close the door, that Marianne was sitting to one side of the office obscured by the standing door. She gave no hint of hello or even of recognition, but sat staring ahead, her warmth hidden like her dark brown curls under her officer's cap. It was as if he had done something wrong and was about to be disciplined by the headmaster, but Kertin simply told him to sit down. He made no reference to Marianne.

"Now," said Kertin, shoving a sheet of paper towards him, "sign this."

Jack read it over. It said that everything that passed between them in this room was top secret. If he was judged later on to have revealed anything at all, he would be court-martialled.

He signed.

The major general leaned back in his squeaking wooden chair, wondering about this boy before him. Why had Marie chosen him? Were they lovers? He sat up straighter and began the routine warning statements.

"If you sign up for this course, you will train here for two months and then for about a year in England. You will then be parachuted into France where the whole purpose of your existence will be to damage Germans. Is that understood?"

Jack felt a tremendous thrill run through him. For a moment he could scarcely breathe.

"At the end of the course, which will be entirely in French, you will be able to run a mile over rough country with an 80-pound pack on your back in eight minutes, kill a sentry in silence with your bare hands, fasten a bomb to a bridge, set a time fuse and be far away when the fuse goes off. You will be able to parachute from an aircraft at 600 feet at night and land alone without injuring yourself, find your way through strange countryside to a destination you've never seen. You will be able to set up a portable radio system, encode a 200-word message in five minutes and send it by Morse while the Gestapo detector trucks are closing in on you, then pack up the equipment and make your escape. You will swear that if you are captured, you will withstand torture in silence for the sake of your comrades, and to kill yourself with a cyanide pill if you are unable to hold out. You will do this for king and country. Are there any questions?"

Jack could not speak for fear of laughing, the whole interview seemed a melodramatic joke.

"Is this the whole, what is it, invitation?"

"Rather."

"Isn't there any sort of physical and so on?"

The general smiled a little. "We know all about you."

"How?"

"We know that you are sound morally, mentally and physically. We know your IQ. We know that you resist institutional discipline, but have your own." He leaned forward as if confidentially and said in a friendlier tone, "Listen, laddy, we are not asking you to make your will ours; that's what the army does. Can you make our will yours?"

The general stared fiercely at him and Jack stared fiercely back at him. The general nodded and said, "We're very proud of our recruiting teams. So far, no one who has gotten this far has said no."

Jack smiled. "Damnit, I just want to say, I've been 200 miles with one friend down the Missanaibi to Hudson's Bay through a blizzard in September and this sounds like a lark." As he was finishing, he was embarrassed for being so flippant.

"I assure you most humbly," said the general, who had never been humble in his life, "I have done some of this myself, and having climbed in the Alps in October alone, and lost three toes, I recommend you not to take this lightly. There will be absolutely no repercussions if you say no now."

"I agree."

"Then jolly good, welcome aboard young fellow-me-lad, you'll do, I'll warrant," he said, and took out a cigar. Jack glanced at Marianne.

"Meet your group leader. Captain Marie whom we call Quiconque." She smiled, stood up, shook his hand and said, *"Félicitations. Soyez le bienvenu."*

There were forms to fill out and he wanted to call his father in Toronto to inform him of his whereabouts, but he was told the call had already been made. And he did not need any personal equipment, it would all be supplied new. Marianne-Marie took him to the supply building down a path of Lombardy poplars still crowned with a few yellow leaves wagging in the bright sun and told him to report to her office in building Q7 as soon as he was ready.

On his first training morning at the camp, the instructor said, "You are going to learn close combat. By this we mean, how to get near the enemy and kill him, silently if possible. Here is the syllabus." He passed out limp sheets of soft white legal size paper with the syllabus fuzzily printed on it.

CLOSE COMBAT *Syllabus*
1st PERIOD
a. Introduction to CC—*Objects and Explanation of the system.*
b. Blows with the side of the hand—*Practise with dummies.*
2nd PERIOD
Other Blows
a. How to kick
b. Boxing blows
c. The open-hand chin jab
d. The use of the knee
e. Use of head and elbows
f. Fingertip jabs
3rd PERIOD
Release from holds
a. Wrist
b. Throat—*With one or both hands*
c. Body holds
d. Having released, show subsequent attack
4th PERIOD
Crowd Fighting
a. Technique
b. Practise with dummies
c. "Mad" half-minute

5th PERIOD
Knife fighting
a. Practise with dummy
6th PERIOD
Special Occasions—Killing a sentry
a. If you are armed with a knife
b. If unarmed
c. Spinal dislocator (Note Special care when practising)
Disarming the enemy—Searching a prisoner; escorting a prisoner; securing a prisoner; defence against downwards or sideways blow; gagging a prisoner.

Jack read the syllabus, imagining himself on a dark road in France by a fallen sentry who was looking up at him in fear as Hughie Macleod used to do in the boxing ring at school. But instead of "Break, box on," he heard "Kill him," echoing from this moment in this snowgirt room, so he kicked the dummy in the head, then reached down and stabbed him through the Wehrmacht uniform—already slashed to ribbons on the chest—into the straw heart. And then there was nothing but himself alone with his boot on a corpse. There would not be another round. There was no elation. No seconds would congratulate him. He was appalled.

Jack soon learned from British commandos what to do once he had safely landed from his parachute jump. He knew how to blow up a bridge with a suitcase bomb, send Morse code on a portable radio, and how to knock out a sentry. He was excellent at orienteering at night by a small compass and stars and he had memorized the names and locations of 50 villages and towns round Mont-de-Marsan in the southwest, where his new persona had been born.

He had replaced his impeccable north of France literary accent with a very good Landais accent. And Marianne had instructed him in various arcana of the region—why the farmers sometimes wore stilts in the fields, the name of the British general who had terrorized the Landais during the Hundred Years' War, why the fields in the valley of the Adour were so small, the number of grams of bread in the current ration card.

In May, he received notice of his overseas posting, and left a note on Marianne's desk, inviting her to dinner. Her pool-secretary came in and told him that Marianne had left for England that morning, by air.

"Did she leave a note for me?"

"Nothing, sir," said the uniformed young woman. "Except to say that you will meet over there."

Washington, Christmas, 1941

On the evening of Wednesday, December 17, 1941, President Roosevelt, wearing his suit but no topcoat, sat outdoors in his wheelchair at the airport watching the landing lights of the DC3 bringing Prime Minister Churchill and Lord Beaverbrook. Rarely did the President go to the airport or railway station to welcome a visitor, but this was their first meeting of wartime.

"Well, Winston," he said, as the Prime Minister advanced across the tarmac in his dark blue Royal Navy uniform, "we are at last in this together."

"Everything has changed but you and I are the same. Firm friends."

"That's exactly how I feel."

The President asked after Beaverbrook's asthma.

"I expect it will be much better in this balmy climate," Beaverbrook said, noticing the bags of fatigue under the President's sad kind eyes.

They rolled slowly in the President's Packard, windows open, the motorcycle escort well away from them. Men and women walked arm in arm, old people strolled along walking their dogs.

"It was very strange flying to your lighted city," said Churchill. "London has been dark for ages."

The President touched his knee. "Nothing can defeat us now."

"The first part of our problem," said Harry Hopkins in the President's bedroom the next morning, "is to keep the Russians in the game till we can get our boys over there to give them a hand."

"Whoa, hold on there," said the President. "I think we must decide our priorities with the Prime Minister. Will it be Japan first, or Germany?"

Harry Hopkins looked at him in dismay. He had thought that the President had already decided the major enemy was Germany and therefore the first task was to help Russia. But Roosevelt's Chief of Staff,

General George C. Marshall, a grave man, much respected by everyone, nodded in agreement with the President. This was decisive. Marshall rarely spoke, and then usually when the President asked his opinion.

"Let us go and see the Prime Minister," said Roosevelt. "He said to call on him in his bedroom as soon as we were ready."

He rolled his wheelchair down the hallway two doors, where he knocked, said, "Winston?" and heard the reply, "Come in, Franklin." All of them walked in after the President. There stood Churchill, completely naked, his pink bulky body glowing fresh from his bath. Jane Goodwin, his secretary, was standing nearby blushing. Beaverbrook burst out laughing and Churchill said, "The Prime Minister of Great Britain has nothing to conceal from his good friend the President of the United States." He wrapped a silk kimono round his body, then sat down with his cigar at a table strewn with papers, orange juice glasses, and his spectacles, which he now placed on the bridge of his nose. He grinned owlishly round the room. "I was just sending a rocket to Auchinleck to spur him on against Rommel," said Churchill. Goodwin made notes as Churchill finished dictating.

"Now then, gentlemen, to business," he said, and climbed into bed.

Beaverbrook took his place in a chair by the head of the bed. The President rolled up beside him, and the others clustered round in chairs.

"Priorities," said Churchill.

"That, and the question of payments," said the President. He did not want to discuss payments today because he knew the British were bankrupt. But he had promised Treasury Secretary Henry Morgenthau that he would. "Right, then priorities it is," said Churchill. Roosevelt was silent, humouring Churchill, who always liked to get in the first and last words. Churchill glanced at Hopkins, aware that he had something to say about Russia.

Hopkins said, "The Russians are in desperate straits right now, worse than when you were there, Max. They have thrown the Germans back from Moscow, but now their spies in the east are saying that the Japanese are about to attack them as well, so they don't know whether or not they can safely withdraw any more soldiers from Amur and Vladivostok."

Beaverbrook added, "If Vladivostok goes, then all of the wheat that is actually on its way from Vancouver right now will not get there, and there is serious danger of famine in Russia this winter. Also, their production figures have fallen drastically below projections. The relocation behind the Urals is far behind schedule and many factories have been lost."

"How do we know their figures" said Churchill, "when the Russians themselves tell us nothing?"

"Ambassador Davies has very good sources in Russia," said Roosevelt. "They have been completely reliable up till now."

"I think our Russian friends may be embarrassed at their small production compared with our countries," said Hopkins. He was always careful to soothe Churchill on the subject of Russia because of the ancient enmity between Churchill and Stalin.

Churchill grunted, "It is most likely that they don't want us to know how weak they really are, so they will be the more easily able to bluff us." There was a slightly embarrassed pause after that. Churchill went on regardless, "My sources in Russia tell me that some of their soldiers are still wearing footcloths in the snow, because they have no proper boots. Most of their artillery is drawn by horses, or even by the soldiers themselves."

"The German Army moved mainly by horses when they attacked Russia," said Beaverbrook.

"They're eating them now, I'll warrant," said Churchill.

Hopkins said, "We have heard from some of our missions to England that the supply situation there is pretty precarious. Goods sometimes lie rusting on the docks in Glasgow and Liverpool for months. Orders from the highest levels are often ignored, and nothing gets done or very little on the factory floor. I wonder what truth there is in these allegations?"

Beaverbrook said in a very determined way, "I am a Canadian. I have often criticized the English. But today they are showing themselves so strong in adversity, so determined, so capable of such brilliant acts of heroism and self-sacrifice that I count it one of the greatest privileges of my life to be allowed to serve under their banner . . ."

Beaverbrook continued, "There are only two kinds of people in the world, those who get things done, and those who get things right. That's why it's so hard to get things done right." This got nods of approval and smiles all round, and Beaverbrook, gratified, went on, "But we have tripled aircraft production in three months and will triple it again this next quarter, so something is being done. We are producing at the rate of 18,000 per year now and expect to add to that substantially very soon."

"Well said, Max," said Churchill. "You deserve glory for this."

"Good for you, Max," said the President, "I want you to talk to our Donald Nelson and ginger him up a bit, I'm sure you can do it. Now, gentlemen, the whole purpose of this little exercise that we call the Second World War is to prepare a better world. Much of the shape and atmosphere of the world after the war will be determined by what we do now. Later on I'll want to discuss our plans for world food relief after victory, and our plan for the United Nations. In the meantime, Missy will give you a paper I have done on the subject."

"Very good, Franklin," said Churchill. "I fully agree."

"But just for now, may I say for the record, my belief is that we must devote much of our new production right now to Uncle Joe. We must get along with him because we can not get along without him. I know he is ruthless when the country's interests are at stake, but I am told that he is always reasonable. I'm quite confident that we can do business with Uncle Joe now and after the war. Especially will that be so if we treat him with consideration and generosity now."

Churchill said, "Max has referred to his origins and you know that I have frequently boasted of my American mother. However, I was not aware that Joe Stalin is your uncle, Franklin. Surely this information should be classified Most Secret and not be disclosed until after the next presidential elections." There was loud laughter at this.

The discussion of major priorities was over very quickly. Everyone round the bed realized that the most dangerous opponent was Germany. If they concentrated on defeating Japan first, Germany alone might conquer Russia and then be able to invade Britain, but Japan alone could not possibly conquer any one of the allies. The question was, where to bring their weight to bear on Germany.

After long argument, with Beaverbrook and Hopkins urging an immediate invasion of Europe, Churchill and Roosevelt decided they were not strong enough. Instead, they would drive the Germans out of Africa with a double assault in 1942. The British would attack from Egypt, and the Royal Navy would land a combined British-American force along the north African coast from Morocco to Algeria.

"Are you satisfied?" said Roosevelt on Christmas Eve, as they went outside on the south lawn to light the Christmas tree, an immense dark spruce.

"Very much so," said Churchill. "It has been a most gratifying experience to see the generals and admirals and air marshals all conferring and agreeing so readily and harmoniously. It augurs well indeed."

"We have more hard times ahead of us," said Roosevelt, thinking of the catastrophic defeats the Americans had suffered at Pearl Harbor and the Philippines, the Canadians at Hong Kong and the British in Malaya. "And I am sure there are many more ahead. But with this Africa business, we will surely turn the corner."

"We shall," said Churchill definitely.

They pushed the switch together. Thousands of coloured lights sprang to life, right to the top 60 feet high. Hundreds of spectators standing waiting on the lawn cheered and clapped. The President made a few good-humoured remarks, then introduced his great and good friend and ally, the Prime Minister of Great Britain.

Churchill began, "My friends, I may even say, in the presidential manner, my fellow Americans, for I have American blood coursing in my veins. On this hallowed eve, our thoughts naturally turn to our beloved sons and daughters whose lives are at risk every moment in defence of the liberties shared by our two great democracies. Let us pray for peace and goodwill for all in this war-weary world tonight, and let us so bear ourselves that with God's help we may bring this dreadful conflict to a successful conclusion, restoring peace and prosperity to all mankind. Merry Christmas."

Inside, they sat or stood around the piano and sang "Silent Night," "Jingle Bells," and "The First Noel." Then Roosevelt and Churchill sat alone in the south verandah.

"It's the first time we have been alone together," said Churchill.

"Yes it is," said the President.

"To think, that an Oriental fleet in the remotest ocean of the world, the middle of the Pacific—it was of the Pacific that Coleridge wrote, *Alone, alone, all all alone, alone on the wide wide sea*— should change our common destiny in this sudden but momentous manner, and should disappear again in silence to the east, like a deadly serpent recoiling for another strike. Why, it's simply unprecedented in the whole history of human endeavour."

Roosevelt considered this and said, "They disappeared to the west."

"Yes, quite, and it has been given to us to change all these patterns, and create history ourselves. I sometimes go into the map room alone, and think about the awesome nature of these events, but . . ." he stopped, momentarily silenced and then gave a little laugh. "You know, I told Violet Asquith during the first show that a curse should rest upon me, because I love this war. I know it's smashing and shattering the lives of thousands every moment—and yet—I *can't* help it—I enjoy every second of it." And he added with a smile, "And you will too, I can tell."

Roosevelt gave him a wicked grin. "I know it already, Winston, I know it already." They laughed.

"Now I do hope we can get down to business with this League of Nations thing," Roosevelt said.

"What League of Nations thing?" said Churchill. "I thought they had gone bust."

"Oh dear, I need a holiday," said Roosevelt. "I mean, United Nations."

"Let us hope that this slip is not a bad omen for our pet project," said Churchill.

"Yes indeed. At any rate, we want to conclude with a bang here. And I think this should do it. Missy forgot to give this to you the other day in your bedroom." He handed Churchill a sheet of paper with his thoughts on how to set up the United Nations and its constitution. Churchill looked at it and made a few notes and handed it back. "It is always best to speak large and look wise, if at all possible," he said waggishly, doing his best to charm the President, who loved his humour.

"Now, I'm serious about this one," said Roosevelt.

"But so am I," said Churchill. "If I weren't, I couldn't make fun of it."

Churchill gave a rousing speech to the Congress, and then travelled by overnight train with Beaverbrook up the Hudson River valley to Ottawa. As their dining car swayed through the night, gently rattling the cutlery on the damask tablecloth, they discussed the question of payments. "There, that's the menace, out there, Morgenthau's place," said Beaverbrook, gesturing towards Hyde Park station, which was near Morgenthau's country estate. "He put Franklin up to it."

"Up to what?" said Churchill, tucking his napkin under his jowls.

"That first morning, in your bedroom, remember? Franklin said we had to discuss priorities and payments. But he never brought up payments, did he?"

"For which I am profoundly thankful," said the Prime Minister.

"So far, we have made all the war effort and they have made all the money. And it will be so for some time to come. They demanded the South African gold, they have been pressing the Canadians for gold. In short our financial relations with the Americans have been so loosely handled that it is necessary now to take up a firm policy and to pursue it even at the risk of serious disagreement."

"Oh come now, this is impossible."

But Beaverbrook was relentless. "I have been in business, Winston, you have not. Our present position is, they have conceded nothing. They have exacted payment to the uttermost for all they have done for us. They have taken our bases without valuable consideration. They have taken our gold. They have been given our secrets and offered us a thoroughly inadequate service. We are told over and over again that we get such wonderful results from the Purvis Mission, but in fact he has nothing to his credit except a kindly disposition on the part of Mr. Morgenthau and that is easily bought at such a price. The American government is asking for the moon and won't pay sixpence. We are bankrupt. After the war, the Empire will be gone and the Americans will rule the world."

Churchill lifted his glass of champagne and stared out at cheerful windows spreading welcome mats of light on the snow round dark farmhouses. Above them stretched dark hills under a clear midnight sky.

"Bankrupt?" he said finally. "What does the word mean?"

"It means you can't pay your bills and the debt collectors take your property. Which is already happening. Newfoundland, Bermuda, the Bahamas, Jamaica, and no doubt soon they will require bases in the Far East. And you know that Franklin wants to abolish Empire preference and drive us out of India."

"I'm not moved by the power of money," said Churchill. "You know they said in '36 I'd sold out to the Jews, Weinstein Churchill they called me . . ."

"I forbade the *Express* to print that," said Beaverbrook "But would you have voted and written as you did without their money?"

"I don't know. I praised Hitler in the twenties in several articles, for nothing. Journalists are like fruit flies, all in a swarm about something one minute and defunct the next. I was no different, except I resorted to politics." He bobbed his champagne glass in front of his nose, looking waggishly at Beaverbrook. "Would you say you never sold your opinion?"

The next day, Churchill addressed the Parliament of Canada. He praised the immense contributions of Canadians to the war effort—the planes, ships, aircraft, munitions, tanks, trucks, now pouring off the assembly lines, and "your magnificent fighting men, supported by large contingents of volunteer women in uniform." Then he touched defiantly on the defeats recently suffered by the allies, which he vowed soon to avenge. With the North African invasion in mind, and also remembering the large French-Canadian population of Canada, he described the situation in France in 1940, when he had tried to persuade Premier Reynaud to move the government from Bordeaux to North Africa.

"It was their duty as it was their interest to go to North Africa, where they would have been at the head of the French Empire. In Africa, with our aid, they would have had overwhelming sea power. They would have had the recognition of the United States, and the use of all the gold they had lodged beyond the seas. If they had done this, Italy might have been driven out of the war before the end of 1940, and France would have held her place as a nation in the councils of the Allies at the conference table of the victors. But their generals misled them. When I warned them that Britain would fight on alone whatever they did, their generals told their Prime Minister and his divided Cabinet, 'In three weeks England will have her neck wrung like a chicken.'" He paused, then said, "Some chicken. Some neck."

The members erupted in laughter and cheers. Beaverbrook and Bannatyne in the Visitors' Gallery stood up laughing and applauding, each seeing the headlines the next day in their papers, DEFIANT CHURCHILL SCORES DIRECT HIT.

Roosevelt called him and said, "Bully for you. It's fun to be in the same decade with you."

1942

North Atlantic, February, 1942

Grant Giovanelli was on the bridge of the corvette HMCS *Sheguian-dah*, watching the captain con her through the narrow entrance leading into St. John's harbour. His eyes were streaming tears from the cold wind as he watched the ships in the crowded harbour, thinking of a hot bath and a warm clean bed in the Hotel Newfoundland, a grey squared bulk he could see in the centre of the city. The captain stood beside him, his greatcoat turned up over a thick wool muffler.

"Take her alongside, Giovanelli," he said. Grant was amazed, for going alongside was an almost holy ritual always conducted by the captain on every ship in the navy, but he picked up the speaking tube and said, "Port 20, slow astern," to avoid a trawler emerging through mist. Now he knew that the captain was going to resign as soon as he got ashore. He had been drinking alone in his cabin for over a week, unable to speak coherently except in the mornings.

Once they were alongside, Grant checked the wire hawsers on the bollards to make sure she was secure, then went to headquarters in HMS *Avalon* where he received a signal in an envelope from the secretary to Commodore Leonard Murray, FONF, or Flag Officer, Newfoundland Force. He tore it open eagerly, because it was unprecedented for a junior officer to get a signal from such a high-ranking officer.

He read in astonishment that "You are required to attend this day at 1400 at this office." Murray as FONF had operational command of all the escort forces based in St. John's, under the overall commander in Halifax. 'What could he possibly want me for?'

He carried his seabag into the hotel, checked in, lay in a hot bath for ten minutes, then dressed in his best uniform and took a taxi to Murray's office.

Murray waved him to a seat in his office overlooking the harbour and said, "How is morale on *Sheguiandah*, Giovanelli?"

Grant thought it was very strange to be questioned this way. Why was the captain not here doing this? But he answered eagerly, "Sir, we are all keen to get going and have some battle experience."

Murray lifted his eyebrows at that, and smiled slightly.

"I am very sorry that you have had two commanding officers in the last month. I need not tell you, Giovanelli, that we are short of suitable officers. I am glad to hear that that has not damaged morale."

"Not at all, sir. But I had no idea, sir. Has the captain left?"

Murray nodded sadly. "He just left here. Resigned. I had no choice but to accept it," he said. "The man is sea-weary. You'll be alongside for probably a couple of weeks while we search about for someone to take her over. It won't be easy, as you know. There are prodigious difficulties in finding suitable officers to command these days."

Grant felt sorry for the captain, who seemed a very good sort, although he drank too much. There was a long silence while Murray stared out the window over the harbour where the afternoon sun and shadows were passing over the freighters, destroyers and one aircraft carrier moored there.

'It's now or never,' Grant thought, and said, "Sir, let me have her."

Murray swung his swivel chair around and looked at him for a long time, then said very quietly, "By Jove, I will."

"Thank you, sir." said Grant.

"Mind you, I'm taking a big chance on you and you must not let me down."

"Sir, I will do my best," he said passionately.

"Good man," said Murray, and got up as they shook hands warmly.

Grant was so happy walking down Water Street he could not take a taxi. He wanted to skip as he went. People turned and smiled at him as he himself smiled at strangers and said, "Good morning."

'I've got my ship,' he thought. 'Oh will we do things together.'

He decided to evade the regulations for once, so he could tell Cat his good news, unimpeded by the busy scissors of Navy censors. So he wrote to his mother, enclosing a letter to Cat, which would be delivered by hand in Toronto by a friend returning the next day. He told his mother briefly his good news and asked her to send the enclosed letter to Cat with his grandfather the next time he went over.

Dear Cat

This is a happy day in my life. I am writing to you from the Captain's cabin on board HMCS Can'ttellyou, alongside in the port of Inconnu. I have just been given this ship, which makes me one of the youngest captains in the Navy. It's amazing—I am terribly inexperienced, though on entry I took all the short courses—gunnery, navigation, signals, Asdic etc., but I know nothing of command except what our poor unfortunate captain (now on shore appointment) did and which I will never do, I hope.

For instance, once at sea, we had to pass a secret message to another ship, which required us to come very close alongside steaming parallel. This is tricky because when ships draw close, there is an extra pull like gravity pulling them together. The captain saw the distance narrowing and instead of giving two very minor helm orders, called down "Hard astarboard," corrected immediately by "Hard aport." It was too late, there was a collision—a minor one, the sterns kissed, making a hell of a row but doing only cosmetic damage. One hates to come into port looking like that—you pusser Brits call us the Royal Collision Navy."

The captain was determined to report the warrant engineer to the Flag Officer with a view to court martial for disobedience of an order. The engineer got very angry and said he did exactly as he was told, and of course, he has an engine room log showing all commands received from the wheelhouse, written down as they are received. I intervened and begged the captain to forget it, especially as he would have no chance to prove disobedience. At first he seemed very angry, but at whom? And then he kind of relented and sighed and put his head in his hands and said, "God I hate this job." And the whole matter was dropped except that the captain's morale, never high, slumped after that. He never liked the Navy—he had been in the merchant marine, and he was getting on. And this is the same guy who aborted the attack on the U-boat. We had one in our Asdic and he simply called off the attack at the last moment. The depth charges were actually primed to go and we were two seconds from a sure kill, when suddenly he ordered the wheel hard aport and full ahead both, and never gave the order to drop the charges. And the captain never explained why. Anyway, he just walked off the ship in St. John's and resigned, and so here I am. It's a weird way to get a ship, BUT morale is good and I am high as a kite and running around poking my nose into everything."

He signed it *Lonely for you—Grant* and then added a PS: *I've just been told more good news—oh, I can't tell you. But look at the map I sent you of Georgian Bay, to the top of the Bruce Peninsula, find a town and then look at the map of Scotland. Now use your imagination. LFY Grant.*

PPS As you've no doubt guessed by now, this letter comes to you via my dad and Lord B.

St. Lawrence River, March, 1942

⌒⊙⌒

Able Seaman Joe Shearer bent his six-foot-four-inch body to go through the companionway from the galley to the deck of HMCS *Hudson* half-shoving, half-carrying a heavy steel garbage bucket ahead of him to dump it over the side. On deck, he stopped, seeing a black puff of smoke coming up from the funnel of HMCS *Memagog* half a mile away in the Gulf of St. Lawrence. At that moment he heard a distant boom, and saw the *Memagog* slowly roll sideways towards him. The white streak of a torpedo headed towards his own ship, and he shouted, "Torpedo to port," and sat down, thinking it was safer.

On the bridge, Captain "Smoother" Mackie, heard the shout and rang action stations, then shouted "Full ahead both." The *Hudson* surged ahead and the torpedo passed close astern. Now the captain ordered the engines stopped because the U-boat was using Gnat acoustic torpedoes that were homing on the noise of the screws.

The ship's PA, which had been playing a radio broadcast by Kate Aitken on cooking recipes, gave way to Captain Mackie saying, "Away lifeboat crew, pick up survivors." The crew ran to the whaler slung on davits near Shearer, climbed aboard and the chief bosun's mate supervised the lowering. At the order "Out pins-slip," the boat disengaged from the falls at the top of a wave and the crew pulled towards dark heads in the water. Mackie ordered full ahead along the torpedo's line of bearing trying to make an Asdic contact. Kate Aitken described the new short skirts for this season, which would save cloth for the war effort.

Captain Mackie on the bridge heard a shout from the Asdic room saying that they had contact with a U-boat 100 yards astern. Although the ship was now stopped, Mackie instructed the depth charge officer beside him, "Shallow setting," and then, "Drop charges." The command crackled into Leading Seaman McMichaels' headphones who was in charge of dropping the depth charges from the aft station.

"Sir, we're stopped," he said into the mike. "There's men in the water."

The order came, "Drop the fucking cans." McMichaels with a scream pulled the pin allowing three depth charges to roll off the stern.

"Run," McMichaels shouted to Joe and they both ran forward.

One tremendous explosion followed by another, sent mountains of water into the air that drenched the ship for 100 feet with dead fish, bits of metal, lifting the whole stern section of the ship, slamming the three-ton rudder against the hull and forcing the steel plates inwards over the ribs like the skin on a dead man's chest, for 50 feet ahead of the transom.

"Oh my God," came Mackie's voice over the PA.

McMichaels was lying on the deck. "They're all dead now, you stupid ass." He wept and screamed and slammed his fist on the steel deck.

Joe got up and stared at dead fish on the deck, splinters of shredded metal, bodies of the *Memagog*'s men in the sea face down. Kate Aitken's comforting voice came back on the loudspeaker telling them to bake their banana bread in a 350 oven.

Joe had no idea what to do, so he emptied garbage cans over the side.

Half an hour later, the crew of the whaler, drunk from the store of rum aboard, were rowing back towards them singing "Roll Along Wavy Navy Roll Along." A body lay face down in the bow. Joe helped the drunk seamen haul the body in a cargo net up the side of the stopped ship. The body slithered like fish onto the wet deck so covered with oil his hair was like a helmet.

Joe stared at Lieutenant Robarts, who was ordering him to clean off the dead body in a harsh, frightened tone of voice.

Thinking, 'What's got into you, it's only a dead body,' Joe kneeled down and began to empty the pockets. He had never seen a dead body, but he was not repelled. The dead man's eyes were still open reflecting the bright sky to which they were apparently looking. The face was pale and unbearded under the oily film, the hands open and unhurt. He seemed so alive that Joe began to say "Sorry," as he fished out his ID from his inside pocket. The young man had been Able Seaman J.R. Vézina of Laurentville, Québec.

Robarts said "Well done, Shearer," and marched away.

After a party of seamen under an officer carried the body away, Joe found lying on the deck where Vézina had lain, a shiny steel whistle. The pea inside it had been flattened. 'I'm sorry,' Joe thought. Now Kate Aitken said, "That's all for today, I hoped you enjoyed our program, we'll be back tomorrow, same time, same station. Goodbye, and God bless."

At that moment, the warrant engineer in charge of the damage control party reported to Captain Mackie that the aft bulkhead had been shored up, but he doubted it would hold in a rough sea. Mackie, his smooth face unaffected by any concern over the damage he had caused, told the signalman on the bridge to make a signal to Halifax, "Am badly damaged astern, am out of command and require immediate assistance." Now the engineer officer reported that both boilers were dangerously damaged and were shut down. He reported three men dead, two from steam burns and one from flying metal, all caused by the depth charges.

A pump crew kept the after compartment clear while the *Hudson* was towed to Sydney. Mackie rewrote the log in order not to describe what had happened.

Joe was posted on shore assignment to Halifax. Drinking one night in a bar, he heard that HMCS *Toronto* was the ship to be in because they had a great canteen and an electric gramophone, and the citizens of Toronto kept sending them good food. HMCS *Hudson* was still in drydock, so he applied for a transfer, and was told to report one morning to HMCS *Stadacona*, the notional ship that was the navy's headquarters in Halifax.

On the morning Shearer reported to the rating seated behind the postings desk, Lieutenant Ivan Westwood was standing supervising proceedings, distracted by thoughts of women. This morning, she was Francine Bourgeois with crossed arms lifting up her pale green sweater beside the bed in his hotel room after the dance at HMCS *Stadacona* last night. He stared at the white papers on the oak desk outside the drill hall where the dance had been held, thinking of her white bottom emerging as she undressed in the half-light. In a reverie he saw her standing by the bed saying in a soft voice,"You can do anything you like, Eve-Anne, I don't care how dirty it is."

He had done what he liked and now he was appalled to think of what he had done, hoping to do it again as soon as possible.

Suddenly, seeing Shearer standing before the desk, he had an inspiration. He took over the questioning.

"You want a transfer to HMCS *Toronto,* sailor? Any specialty?"

"No sir, I'm just a bare-assed seaman, sir." Westwood looked at him in shock wondering if this man were mocking him for dreaming of Francine's bare bottom. But all he saw was a tall dark-haired sailor with a long face.

"What happened to your ship?" he said, opening Shearer's paybook, in which he now saw there was a substantial cash bribe.

"We were depth-charged, sir."

"Depth-charged, sailor? How could you be depth-charged? We don't have any U-boats." Westwood put the money in his pocket.

"It was a frigate, sir."

Westwood smiled. "And just who depth-charged your frigate, Shearer?"

"We did, sir."

Westwood stared at him speechless.

"Our captain dropped the cans while we were stopped."

Westwood said, "I heard about that, I couldn't believe it. You mean it actually happened?" He laughed and shoved the paybook back at Shearer, "I'll see what I can do for you."

Joe was drinking in the bar car of the train on the way to leave in Toronto when Westwood appeared beside him, a little drunk. "Hello

Simpson," he said and sat down. Joe said hello and continued to stare out the window at the St. Lawrence. "It was just a few miles downstream from here," he said.

"What?" said Westwood.

"The *Memagog* went down. She's still down there with 20 guys in her."

"I've been thinking, Simpson. How would you like to be an officer?"

Joe looked puzzled. "Officer? I'm a bare-assed seaman, sir"

"I think you'll do, you know."

"Do for what?"

"Where are you headed?"

"Toronto, sir."

"So am I," said Westwood. "Look, this is a pretty amateur navy we've got . . ."

"I'll say."

"And we need good men in charge. Officers."

"You mean me?" Joe was appalled.

"Where did you go to school?"

"UTS, sir."

"There you are, best school in the country, and here you are, bare-assed seaman with probably twice the IQ of your CO, who was by the way, a pusser captain who kept the brass gleaming and couldn't find Brazil if he was in the Amazon."

Joe twirled his drink slowly staring at the rushing river.

"Report to HMCS *York* when you get back. Ask for me. I'll make sure you get in the officer's training course, and ask for you on my new ship."

"What ship, sir?"

"HMCS *Toronto,* 31 knots max. I expect they'll offer me the command next week." He smiled modestly, expecting congratulations.

Joe could not congratulate him because he did not believe the navy would promote such a sly one.

"Thank you very much, sir."

A crooked little smile appeared on Westwood's pink and white, rather pretty face, his lips curving cynically. "I wonder if you would return the favour, Simpson. I have a commission to do on the way back."

When Westwood had heard of Vézina's death, he had wangled the assignment to return the effects of the dead seaman to the family in Laurentville near Québec City. He had done this in order to get the necessary leave, hoping he could fob off the job on someone else and then hurry up to Toronto. "Would you do that for me?"

"Sure," he said, "I could do that. Nobody's waiting for me." He took a drink. "It's funny. I pulled Vézina out of the water."

"Don't tell them that."

"Yes sir."

Westwood took a letter from his pocket. "Your captain gave this to my orderly officer. It's just a matter of dropping by, to have a drink and a little chat. They've already had the funeral. Oh, and give them his effects." He handed Joe a small bag, and Joe felt guilty remembering the whistle, which was in his own seabag. He wondered if he ought to hand it to them. Could they possibly want such a grisly thing?

"Thanks very much. Can I buy you a drink, Simpson?"

"Yes sir. Thank you very much, sir." Joe was so embarrassed by Westwood's smug fraudulence that he almost wanted to apologize for not being taken in by it. He fell into confusion, not knowing quite how to correct him. As he accepted the drink from Westwood's silver flask, he said, "Sir, thanks for the offer to transfer me to your ship, but you'd better change the name on the posting to Shearer."

"Why is that?" said Westwood.

"Well, it's my name, sir."

The silvery spire of a Catholic church rose above the train, surrounded by two-storey houses, their roofs huddled close together as if in conversation, the trees puffed out round them like protection. The village seemed settled, content and peaceful. Joe was thinking that it might be interesting to meet some French Canadians, walk one of those pretty little streets under the tall old elm trees, and hear the church bells ringing.

"By the way," Westwood said, "don't mention this to a soul."

As Joe walked along the street under the elms that he had imagined, carrying Vézina's bag, people greeted him as if he belonged. Even the young women smiled at him and wished him *"Bonjour, m'sieur."* He felt they were turning round to look at him after he passed.

Ahead of him at the foot of rue du Traversier, the river shone grey and smooth, innocent of shipping. He found the house easily, numero 24 rue du Traversier. It was two storeys like the others, faced in thin slices of coloured fake-stone stacked up like sandwiches, with a concrete front stoop and wrought iron railings. Dreading to see Vézina's mother dressed in black and weeping, he knocked on the door. A tall woman in a red-striped apron with her brown hair piled up very high in tight little curls looked up at him. *"Oui?"*

"Bonjooer madame," he said, agonizing over his French. *"Je sweeze easy to . . ."* and he trailed off. *"Poor votre feese. Je m'appelle Joe Shearer."*

"Entrez, entrez, soyez le bienvenu," she said, turning aside and leading him into the kitchen, where in a flurry of French that he could not understand she dismissed another woman, whose hair she had evidently been setting.

As Madame cleared away the hair dryer, Monsieur Vézina entered, a short man with his steely hair cut *en brosse.* "Sit down m'sieur," said Vézina. "What is it you wish?" They began to talk in a mixture of English and French.

"I'm very sorry about *votre fils, m'sieur.*" He held out the seabag. *"Qu'est-ce que c'est ça?"*

"His effects, sir. His things are in it."

Madame was now weeping and drying her eyes with a handkerchief.

"Did you know him?"

"My captain asked me to bring these things to you. I'm sorry." He glanced helplessly at Madame, wishing he could say something correctly in French to show goodwill.

A little boy ran into the room and whispered in French to his mother, "She won't come down because her teeth haven't arrived yet." He sat down and began studying Joe.

"Did you see him . . . die?" Madame Vézina asked in French, and Vézina translated.

"No, madame, he was in the water when there was an explosion."

"He drowned?"

"Well, we were attacking a U-boat, and the depth charges went off and he was knocked out and he drowned, I guess, I didn't see it, we were being torpedoed at the time. Ships were blowing up. His ship sank."

"Oh, *mon Dieu*, all the brave young men in the river." She put her face in her hands.

Joe heard action at the front door, and then a young woman with light brown curly hair and a calm sweet expression entered the room, evidently a daughter. Joe stood up, a full head taller than she, feeling clumsily big.

"Ma fille, Yvette," said Madame Vézina, sourly because she did not approve that Yvette had changed into her best red velvet dress with a Peter Pan lace collar, and put in her new teeth and come straight into the room to see the tall handsome Anglo dressed up in his sailor suit like a little boy.

"Enchantée, m'sieur," said Yvette and sat down quickly facing Joe. She smiled full at him.

Everyone was silent.

"It's a hard life," said Vézina.

Thinking he meant the navy, and glancing at the brush cut hair like his own, Joe said, "Are you in the military?"

Madame crossed herself and said, *"Mon Dieu, non."*

"Look at that, *m'sieur*," said Vézina. Yvette handed her father an envelope, looking all the while at Joe. Vézina took out the letter and handed it to Joe.

He read, under a Government of Canada embossed letterhead, "Dear Mr. and Mrs. Vézina. I regret to inform you that your son Joseph Legace Vézina was killed in action while pursuing a U-boat." Joe glanced up at Vézina a little puzzled, and Yvette whispered, *"Vous voyez, c'est en anglais."*

"I'm sorry about that, sir. Maybe I can see about it."

"Oh mon pauvre," said Madame Vézina, through her husband, and sat down at the table, dabbing her eyes. "He was only 19, and it was just out there in the river, I used to dream of drowning in that river, but now, it is my son who sleeps there."

Vézina patted her shoulder, "Remember, *maman*, we buried him last week, in the cemetery by the church, with his ancestors."

"Of course, of course, but it was the river killed him."

"It was the Heinies killed him."

Joe was about to say "No, it was Smoother Mackie . . ." but stopped in time.

Madame Vézina sighed and turned to the stove. *"Excusez moi, m'sieur. Voulez vous du café?"*

"Thank you very much," said Joe, but Vézina silently pushed a bottle of rye across the oilcloth with an empty tumbler. He had already half-filled his own glass. Yvette sat shining at him. She was distractingly pretty, he found, so nice to look at that he had trouble to look anywhere else.

Having studied him for a minute, Yvette made up her mind. "Thank you for coming *m'sieur*. It was very kind," she said in French. Joe was easily able to understand. He looked at her gratefully, then felt shy and looked down saying, *"Merci beaucoup,"* quite well.

"Are you from Toronto?" she asked in English.

"Yes."

Now she returned to French, and Joe heard, *"Nous l'avons visité l'année passée . . . l'Exposition . . . belle ville . . . énormément d'arbres.*

Et le beau lac si vaste." Joe understood what she had said. He smiled gratefully.

"Why are you in the navy, eh?" said Vézina, "Is there conscription in Ontario?"

"No, I volunteered. *Je suis . . . volontaire.*"

"Why?" Vézina looked mystified.

"Well, to tell you the truth, all my friends were joining up," said Joe, glancing boldly at Yvette, and smiling. "Some liked the uniform." She laughed. "And because I would get free university tuition. But now, I don't know, it looks like the Germans and Japs want to take over the world."

"Joseph, he did not have to join, I forbade him to, the curé told him not to, but he went anyway, and now see what has happened."

Vézina went on, his fist hitting the table hard enough to make the glasses jump a little, "It is all for the generals and politicians, for the bankers and Jews." Madame drew herself up tall in stiff approval of these sentiments.

Joe was astonished. He had never heard anything like this in his life.

"And who is by our side?" Vézina went on. "To whom do we send wheat and tanks and airplanes? To atheist, anti-Christ communists. The enemies of the church, every church, even yours." He poked his short finger out at Joe. He got up, went to the cupboard, drew down a bottle of cognac, poured out two glasses and handed Joe one. "*Santé, m'sieur,*" he said and his face broke into a broad smile.

When he said *"au revoir,"* Yvette said only, "*A la prochaine fois, j'espère.*" But if he had not understood the words, he would have known what she meant from the sympathetic expression in her brown eyes.

He left the house in chagrin, sorrowing over the death of the young man whom they had plainly loved so much. He wanted to say to all the people he met on the street and at the hotel, "I am sorry, so sorry that he died."

His was the only armed forces uniform seen since 1918 in Laurentville.

London, Spring, 1942

The letter that Grant had written to Cat off Iceland arrived at Cadogan Square in early February. Cat walked home from the underground station with her legs aching from standing all day at Guy's Hospital, wishing for a hot bath and a long sleep. His letter was lying on the table in the front hall, but she was too tired to read it. She took it upstairs with her, turned out the light over her bed and fell asleep on the counterpane fully clothed.

Early in the morning, she awakened to moonlight flooding into her room and thought, 'I forgot the blackout curtains.' She turned on the light, turned it off again, padded over to the window in her patched white lisle stockings, fastened the curtains and sat in bed with her portable leather writing desk in her lap, still in uniform, reading the letter and thinking what to say.

It is so kind of you to write so often when it is so difficult to get the time to reply in kind. (Oh dear, so many "sos" now you will tell me that this is a so-so letter) There is so little to tell you that it is not even worth censoring. I have been informed that I shall be allowed to read at Girton next term, but I shan't go. The news from Girton was rather surprising, as one had not expected it. But Guy's seems so much more appropriate at the present time. Perhaps later I shall train my brain better and keep up with you in the witticism department. At Guy's one sees things that are perhaps not taught at Girton—for instance, we had to do a brain surgery for some poor airman who had been shot down with a severe concussion and haematomas, all over his face and upper body, with a dangerously elevated intra-cranial pressure which we had to reduce immediately as it could lead to permanent brain damage. He was under GA of course, but I watched the doctor with a hammer and chisel hammer a hole into the man's skull. Je te le jure. A surgeon said later that we have all the most advanced surgical and medical techniques and apparatus in the world today, including the sulfas and all the penicillin we need.

Father is deliriously busy, dashing about the island with Goma (that's short for Godfather Max, IE, the Beaver) improving the production of you-know-whats to present to Herr Hitler, so we hardly see him. Mother WAS running what is left of the London social season, along with the superb Lady Braggart, (real name Brockhart) which means entertaining Empire soldiery such as yourself, if you can ever come.

Until lately, that is. Now mother has suddenly grown very mysterious. I think she has come upon some new kind of war-work. Whatever it (hush-hush) is, she has stopped hovering over one so.

Here, Cat hesitated. She had used up the main space, and now had left only the final flap, at most five or six crammed lines. A paragraph of thought loosely formed in her head:

I suspect you have fallen in love with me. You want to know how I feel. I don't know how I feel. And I won't know until I see you again.

She actually wrote,

I send you my picture separately as you asked in your last. And with this I send you all good wishes. With fond love to your mother and father and renewed thanks for an idyllic week in your beautiful Georgian Bay. It lives in my memory like a dream of the peace for which we all yearn.
Miaow.

She read this over, not noticing that she had addressed him with the French intimate *tu* and mailed it.

Toronto, Laurentville, Spring, 1942

Joe Shearer stood at a semblance of attention before Ivan Westwood's oak desk at HMCS *York* in Toronto. Westwood's pink skin glowed but his puffy bloodshot eyes evinced the penalty of last night's drinking and dancing.

"What do you want?" said Westwood, wondering what time it was, and if he had time to bathe before going out with Anne. "Oh yes, you did Vézina, the boy in the river. And you're coming to my ship."

"Yes sir. Thank you, sir."

"Well, you got to the family all right?"

"Yes sir, but there was one problem. The regrets letter went out in English."

"So? What did they expect? Greek?" Westwood sat back in his wooden bucket chair, which creaked and began to spin slowly, making him sit upright abruptly feeling sick. He rattled a yellow pencil between his teeth.

"Sir, they are French. A very nice family."

"Vézina. Thought it was Greek. Got a zed in it. Tell you what, Shearer, if it is such a tragedy for them, I'll have it issued again, in Greek." He groaned. "French." He rubbed his fair hair.

"I'll take it to them, sir. I can explain now, in French."

Now Westwood smiled knowingly. "Aha. You've been studying French."

"Yes sir." Joe smiled sheepishly.

"I see, I see. And does, did Vézina have a sister?"

"Sir. I don't see what that has to do with it. They're a very nice family."

"And the sister too, no doubt. Ah Shearer, I sense that you are a man in need of a word of advice about women?"

"I could certainly use some, sir."

Westwood rested his chin on his hand and said nothing, thinking about Diana last night in the back seat of the car with the heater going and the policeman coming up, saying, "Are you all right, Miss?" his flashlight playing hungrily down her bare front as she covered up hastily.

Joe stirred his feet. "Yes," said Westwood, rubbing his eyes, "yes, women. Too much of a good thing. Tell you what, there are two main sorts, is she beautiful or is she good-natured?"

Joe grinned. "Both, so far as I can tell."

"Then you're in love. Pick up your letter here tomorrow, so that you can rectify His Majesty's mistake."

"Bonjour," Joe said at the door of the Vézina house, taking off his cap.

"Entrez, entrez, soyez le bienvenu," she said, as if she had been expecting him for hours, although he had not informed them he was coming.

He walked into the kitchen which smelled of woodsmoke and baking bread. Having studied French every day for his whole leave, he was no further ahead with pronunciation, but Yvette, standing by the woodstove with her hair lit like a halo from the window behind her, seemed able to understand him regardless. And although he did not at first understand her sentence—*"Nous sommes seules parce que mes parents et mon frère sont partis rendre visite aux cousins à la campagne,"* he heard *"parents,"* and *"visite,"* and realized that he and Yvette were alone in the house.

He had never been alone in a house with a young woman before. Her smile told him she was now expecting something dramatic and very pleasant to happen. And he was somehow the cause of this. He was not sure what she was expecting and he had no idea what to do about it. He knew he was staring at her impolitely but he could not help himself: by her smile, by the way she leaned slightly towards him sometimes, and her evident pleasure in seeing him, she was making him feel warmly towards her, and at the same time, she was giving him permission to feel warmly towards her.

"Have you a profession?" she asked in French but he did not understand.

"Vous n'êtes pas curé. Alors, êtes-vous avocat?" He did not understand, so she stood up, said *"Avocat,"* put her father's grey fedora on her head, blew a loud whistle by putting her fingers between her lips, said to him, *"Non non non,"* put his hands in imaginary manacles, led him round the table, sat him down again, then sat herself on the other side of the table, rapped the table with a wooden spoon, and said, *"Oyez, oyez, oyez."*

She looked absurd with the fedora on her springy hair. She winked and laughed. Joe was enchanted.

"Oui, lawyer," he said agreeably.

"Are you sad to go back? To the war?" she asked.

He understood *"triste,"* and guessed the rest.

"Ah, yes," he said. "But I am glad to see you again." He blushed and looked down at his tunic. She was silent, thinking of something, her eyes wincing. She said in English, "Hi 'ave joined the hair force? They will send me to England. You must give me your haddress in England," she said, handing him a piece of paper.

"But I don't live in England."

"But it is in England that one makes the war."

"But we fight over here, at least out there." He gestured towards the river.

"Mon Dieu, but I will be in England."

"But I would like to see you anyway. Here is my address in Canada."

He wrote it down, pressing on the thin worn oilcloth, then handed it to her. "You understand, this is just my navy post office box in Halifax." She folded it and slipped it onto the pocket of her skirt.

"Allyfax?" she said. "Where is that?"

He explained, drawing her a little map of Canada.

"Et me voici," she said, handing him her address on a piece of paper. Her eyes concentrated on his face and she looked wistful when she handed him the paper. "Now you write to me in the air force."

"I will write to you," he said fervently.

"And now you must go," she said glancing at the window, by which Joe understood that he had been too long alone in the house with her, because the neighbours were certainly watching. "But just a moment, first," she said. "To help you with the war effort."

She folded down before the stove and drew out three loaves of hot bread.

"You must take one with you to the war," she said. She wrapped it in brown paper, and handed it to him. As he was leaving, pink-faced, in love, covering her with thanks, she touched him lightly on the sleeve, and said "Please write to me."

"Yes, of course," he said looking down at her. He was yearning to lean down and kiss her face turned up so willingly towards him.

The scent of bread all round her and the welcome in her face made him dizzy. He backed awkwardly into the closed door, and she reached around him and opened it, still smiling up at him, and he felt he was being embraced. As he walked down the street, frequently turning to look back, she stood in the open doorway waving, and sometimes waving to the side to the watching windows.

In the train looking out the window at the woods of the mountainous south shore, he leaned back, pulled out the address to memorize it, and discovered the letter of condolence in French that he had forgotten to hand to her.

Berlin, Summer, 1942

Clara sat by the open window of her hot apartment in Berlin feeling homesick and melancholy. Peter had not had leave for over six months, and his regiment was fighting savagely near Rostov. She had a new job teaching English with Count Miloslavsky at his private school. She was also helping Helmuth James smuggle refugees out of Germany. This work was horribly frustrating. They knew from Canaris at the Abwehr that the Foreign Ministry phones were tapped, their mail inspected, their home phones bugged, their courier boys suborned and all their top officials followed day and night. Time and again they had arranged passage for U-boats—refugees in hiding—to get to Turkey, Switzerland, Spain, Sweden, and then found that the police had come the day before. Within a few weeks, the next of kin would receive an urn and a death certificate stating that he or she had died of heart disease.

Just now, she had finished four hours of typing, wearing white cotton gloves so her fingerprints would not appear on the keys. Every time she closed the typewriter, she had to burn the draft papers in the fireplace: on hot days, when even a wisp of smoke would excite suspicion among the neighbours, she had to burn drafts bit by bit in the toilet bowl, then wipe it out and flush it. She had to save and hide the precious carbon paper and the ribbons, because either could betray what she had been typing.

A few weeks later, Helmuth James telephoned to ask if he might come by that evening. After a dinner of turnips, potatoes and fresh green peas Clara had grown, he muffled her telephone under two pillows and said, "I've just received a letter from a friend in Stockholm who wants us to take care of an old couple in Frankfurt. Named Max and Cecile Frankfurter."

"What do I do?"

"Wait a moment, I haven't told you how difficult this will be." This was his euphemism for dangerous. "She is diabetic, he is a cranky old man, and you will have to cross the border to get them to Le Chambon-sur-Lignon, where we have friends."

"It's always difficult."

"All right," he said. He gave her detailed instructions and the papers. He wished her good luck, kissed her cheek and was out the door. She was on her own, with his mission. She packed, not knowing how long she would be gone, mailed a letter to Peter at the front, left a copy for him on the mantelpiece and set the alarm.

She got up while the sky and the city were dark and silent, dressed herself in the cold room by the light of one candle. The only sounds she heard were her clothes slithering over her cold skin, and her bare feet sticking to the wood. Standing up in the kitchen in her overcoat, she ate one hardboiled egg, drank ersatz coffee, then walked through the cold streets to the Zoo station carrying her bag. On the train to Frankfurt she sat with her bag containing her own passport held hard in her lap. The fake passports for the Frankfurters were hooked over her brassiere strap at the back, so she could feel them every time she leaned back against the dirty velour of the seat. If the train police found the fake passports while inspecting her own ID, she would be sent to a concentration camp.

Max Frankfurter had been arrested in 1940 and sent to the Jews' House, where Jews married to Christians were interned while the Nazis made up their minds what to do with them. He had written by a friend in Turkey to his brother Fritz, head of a bank in London, demanding help. Fritz had promised that he could arrange a *passeur* for them if they could get to unoccupied France, and had also written to Helmuth James von Blücher via a friend in Sweden.

She knocked on the door of the Jews' House and was greeted by the face of a middle-aged woman with starvation rings round her worried eyes. Clara gave the code-name, Bernadette, and Cecile Frankfurter reached inside the door, pulling out a bag. She brought out two bags, closed the door behind her and, looking all around her warily, led

Clara into the street, carrying both bags herself. Clara took one of the bags from her and Cecile Frankfurter said, "What's your name?"

"Clara von Metternich. I think you've been told what we're . . ."

"Yes, I've been told, we have to go to the station, he's there, in the washroom, they came for him yesterday . . ."

"Who came for him?"

"The police. They left a notice. He's to report today. They may be following us now—" she looked around "—the attendant there said he could hide overnight, thank God you've come, so young for this, aren't you?"

At the station, the attendant in his dark blue uniform was sweeping the tile floor near the men's washroom. "We're here . . . is he all right?" Cecile said anxiously, and the attendant said, "He'll be all right, I gave him a sweet bun and some coffee for breakfast, but he wanted tea so I guess he is thirsty."

Max Frankfurter came out, a short angry man, wearing a suit too big for him with the sleeves clumsily cut back. His face was gaunt, his belly protruding with incipient hunger oedema and he fastened on Clara, ignoring Cecile. He said abruptly, "Are you the one from Berlin?"

"I'm taking you to France, yes," she said, and showed him the passports.

"They told me a man was coming," he said angrily.

"Let's go," she said.

They were passed by the guards on the platform who were examining all travel documents, on the watch for spies, saboteurs, and escaped prisoners. There were also civilians employed by the Gestapo, called *Greifer*, who hunted through crowds for people who looked or sounded or acted Jewish. They were paid for each arrest. Clara found them their seats in a compartment with three others, so they could not talk freely.

Just after Karlsruhe, Cecile, her face sweating and her eyes worried, said to Clara, "Would you help me, please?" She led the way to the lavatory.

"I must have water, I'm going into shock," she said. Clara knocked on the door calling that they needed water. After a few minutes, a skinny, worried looking woman came out, apologizing, and hurried away.

Cecile explained hastily, as she sat down on the closed toilet, lifted her skirt and rolled down her stocking, "Would you fill this for me please? I can't do it while I am so shaky—please hurry."

She sat back against the wall while Clara plunged the hypodermic through the rubber seal into the capsule of insulin, withdrew the opaque fluid, and handed it back to Cecile. She was swaying around, there was a hammering on the door and a shout and Cecile forced the tip of the needle into her thigh, where Clara saw many dark marks, the tracks of previous injections. The hammering started again, and Clara threw back the door and shouted, "Stop the damned noise."

"It is not permitted for two to enter," said the uniformed conductor.

"The woman is sick, she's diabetic, she needs help, please leave us alone."

She tried to slam the door, but the conductor had his foot in it. "If you're sick, we will find you a doctor, but you must not be in here the two of you with the door closed."

Clara hissed at him while thrusting the insulin syringe and emptied capsule in his face, "is it forbidden to take medicine in the train?" and tried to elbow him out of the way, then turned around to help Cecile who was getting unsteadily to her feet, trying to obey. He said, "Passports," holding out his hand. Clara refused and he said, "If you do not show me your passports, I shall put you off the train."

Clara saw the sweat starting on Cecile's face and closed her eyes in self-reproach for losing her temper. "Of course," she said, "You will find they are in perfect order." She led the way back to their compartment, found the passports in her shoulder bag and started to hand them over. Max reached up and grabbed them all away from Clara saying, "Don't let go of them."

He turned the open first page of each towards the conductor, who again tried to take them. Now Max stood up and balled his fist and said, "Take the numbers not the passport." The conductor said, "I shall call the police," and left the compartment. Clara seized the passports from Max and ran down the corridor after him, and handed them to him.

He wrote down the numbers, the compartment number, and handed the passports back to Clara. When she sat down again, she showed the passports to Max, who turned his face to the window and said nothing.

For an hour before Basle, they had the compartment to themselves, so Cecile asked Clara, "Have you been married long?"

"Since September, 1939," she said.

"You seem so young." Then she added wistfully, "We have a daughter."

Max looking out the window said without turning around, "We had."

Cecile looked significantly at Clara and shrugged.

Cecile waited until Max fell asleep, snoring with his mouth open, then spilled out the story as fast as she could, in an urgent whisper, constantly looking at him to see if he were wakening. She was a Christian with a Jewish great grandmother, which had not mollified Max' family when he asked permission to marry her. This permission was granted only after she became pregnant, which Max' father thought was blackmail. Their daughter was born, which disappointed Max, for he had wanted a son, who would have been named Frederic, after his best friend, killed in the war. He named the girl Frederica and waited for the son who never came. Max devoted himself to the store.

The child who had locked them together and driven them apart had her father's bullying self-aggrandizing character, which at first amused Max. As she grew older, he admired and indulged her. He treated her like a boy and began to have fantasies about bringing her into the business, but the state of the country after 1918 and the deep conservatism of businessmen and of his family, made this impossible.

In 1919, Frederica, seeing how things stood for women in Germany, begged to go to England to study, so Cecile took her to her uncle

Fritz in London, and she attended London University. "It was so difficult," Cecile whispered, glancing at Max to make sure he was still asleep. "She came back alone, didn't tell us a word beforehand, sat down in the salon and *told* us she was getting married. To an Englishman. Named Treloar. Of course not Jewish. She had cut her hair, such beautiful dark-red hair she had, cut it short like a boy, she was wearing makeup and one of those flapper dresses, and drinking martinis and smoking—the polite young woman we had sent to London had been turned into this flapper who treated us like friends. There was a terrible row, Max told her to leave and she went by herself to the Steigenberger Frankfurter Hof. She never even went up to her old room which I had kept for her as it was." Cecile wiped her eyes. "And from that day to this, we have never seen her."

The station at Basle, a huge hall crowded with thousands of people packed close together and swaying and dodging in time with each other as they passed, was guarded by armed German police on one side of the customs barrier that ran down the middle of the building and by French *Milice* in their black uniforms on the other side.

They had only a few minutes to get to the Lyon train once they were through customs, so Max put his elbows up in front of him and began elbowing people aside as he shouted, "Get out of my way." Clara could see ahead a furrow opening in the dense crowd with outraged people on either side shouting at Max, while making way for Clara and Cecile. Cecile looking panicky, said to Clara, "We'd better keep up."

They got through the crowds in time to catch the last train to Lyon.

Max attracted attention to them all the time—by turns defiant, combative and despairing, querulous and apathetic, usually bitter, sometimes humorous, and always demeaning and demanding of Cecile, who deferred to him hoping to manage him. Clara had twice seen people staring at them and she was afraid that one of these might have been a *Greifer*. When she got down from the little train that had slowly climbed from St-Etienne under clear blue skies to the high plateau, she had decided she must do something about him. She helped Cecile step down and waited as Max came, carrying only his briefcase, leaving his bag. Cecile had her own bag in her hand, she turned her back on the train and said with a sigh, "It's so beautiful," looking to where where the grey streets of Le Chambon-sur-Lignon frayed out beyond the Evangelical Temple and the football field. Max stared around for a porter, but there was none. He jerked a forefinger towards Clara, ordering Cecile with the gesture to send Clara over. When he realized that no one was going to help, he went back up the steps, took the heavy bag they had brought in addition to their personal cases and briefcase and tugged it along. A *Milice* policeman in black uniform watched him without a word, as the bag simply tumbled down the steel steps, Max after it. He picked up the bag and hurried past the policeman. As the bag hit the policeman's knee, sending him staggering, Max kept on. The policeman shouted but Cecile came over saying, "I'm so sorry, he's half-blind you know."

A tall man with broad forehead and declining hair, hurried towards them pulling a child's wagon, his wife beside him. Pastor André Trocmé introduced himself and his wife Magda, who was beautiful with clear skin, oval face, peaceful expression, and a thick brown braid round her head like a crown. She helped André put the Frankfurters' bags in the wagon and they descended the curving street past the front of the Evangelical Temple, to his house a few metres farther along. As they walked, they were joined by a pudgy smiling prelate in black, who introduced himself, Abbé Abraham Glasberg.

He held out his hands to welcome them both, and said, "Abbé Glasberg, call me Abbé Abey." He loved this joke: he had been born Jewish, converted to Catholicism and now was principal secretary to the Archbishop of Lyon, who had sent him here to arrange with Trocmé to accept refugees. Max, who hated show-business people, at first looked sourly at him, thinking, 'Another stage-Jew,' but soon was won over by Abey's humorous outlook on life, even here, in conquered France.

Abbé Abey took Cecile and Max for a walk after dinner in the yellow light just before sunset, when the birds were singing their evening songs, the people of the village were promenading and the few tourists were looking for a café where they might get a glass of wine, which was why Max had agreed to come out with Cecile. "Why do people round here think that life must be lived without wine?" he asked Glasberg querulously, and the priest said, "Look," and pointed up to the lintel of the main door to the temple.

Max stared up into the dimness under the roof and saw nothing at first, until his eyes grew used to the shadows and he slowly made out words engraved in stone, '*Aimez-vous les uns les autres.*'

"So," he said, "I've seen lots of religious slogans before; they don't mean a thing."

Glasberg said, "Ah, quit whining, we're risking our lives for you." Max stared up at the lintel, lost in thought, and Cecile realized that what Glasberg had said was registering with him. Max, beginning to think he might be safe among friends for the first time in years, allowed Cecile to mention Frederica without objection, because of the freedom he was feeling. The loss of his former life had liberated him from the conditions of that life, which included ostracizing his daughter. Hearing her name aroused in him a curiosity he had been suppressing since 1920. He was going to London only under duress, so she was not entitled to think that he was running to her. Now, without admitting any error, he would see her. When he went to sleep that night, he heard Glasberg's words, 'We are risking our lives for you,' and saw the awesome words written in the shadows under the deep roof.

The next evening in the kitchen after dinner, Cecile talked to Madame Magda, saying she was amazed that they risked so much to help the refugees who came here by the thousand. Magda was washing dishes one by one in a huge sink of solid stone from which the water ran in a groove cut into the stone. She removed the rag stopper from the hole and looked out the window as she said, "There is nothing surprising about it."

"Oh but there is. It is extraordinary. We've just come from Germany where so few people would help us, and so many were ready to rob us or take us off to the camps. You are most extraordinary people."

"We are not unusual at all and you must not think of us this way," Magda said severely, spreading her hands down her apron. "You needed help and we are helping you. What's so extraordinary about that?"

Timidly she said, "I'm just grateful, that is all."

"Thank you, believe me you are most welcome, but there is nothing to praise. We are acting normally, it is the Nazis who are abnormal." She snapped open the tea towel, hung it on a wooden rod by the window open to the evening air scented with grasses and shrilling with crickets and blew out the oil lamp.

⤫⤬

Lady Treloar was in her room, writing her farewell letter to Dudley, with her bags already packed beside her on the floor. She reread the letter, which her friend Lady Diana Cooper had promised to put in his hands in two days, when Flavia expected to be in France. The letter read,

Dearest

By the time you read this I shall be in France, in the Free Zone. Cecile and Max are en route to Grenade-sur-l'-Adour near Mont-de-Marsan, remember? and I have found a passeur who will bring them on to Pau, where we can escape to Spain.

I have kept your name entirely out of this, except that Diana did mention your name to Dicky in Lisbon to help swing the tickets to Lisbon.

If I had told you, it would have endangered your career, in which you know I have believed since I first saw you. I can only ask you to trust me entirely. Every precaution has been taken, and I am sure we shall succeed. I promise I shall return to you soon. I know how you felt about their behaviour when we were engaged, feelings which I shared equally with you. Nothing can ever excuse or explain their cruelty to us both, but if ever there was a time for forgiveness, it is now. I know you will understand when I say that I could not stay still any longer while my own flesh and blood were in such danger. Please believe in my sincere and complete devotion. I love you with all my heart.

Ever, F

She checked the new girdle, heavy with the sewn-in gold bars, the thick wad of Spanish *pesetas*, the second passport in the name of Huguette de la Morandière born in Toulouse, the precious visas through Ireland to Spanish Morocco to Spain, the tickets from London to Dublin, Morocco, Cadiz, and the train ticket to Madrid. There she would be met by a Spanish *passeur*, Francisco Bosca who had been hired by the Jewish Agency representative in England to accompany her to the border northwest of Barcelona. They would cross over the border at L'Estelle-Betharram and then she would travel on her own to Mont-de-Marsan, where she would meet Raoul Laporterie, who would arrange to bring her parents out from Le Chambon-sur-Lignon where they had been hiding for weeks, waiting for her.

The bus rolled across the hump-backed bridge over the Adour river into Grenade-sur-l'Adour, and halted on the place Montesquieu in front of le Bar-Tabac de l'Adour. Feeling nervous but looking nonchalant, she got down with her portmanteau, and looked across the square, ablaze in white light, through oak and chestnut trees whose leaves were brittle brown from drought, to the peeling sign: *HÔTEL DE LA POSTE*. Beside it was a sign reading *LA PETITE MAISON* in blue on a cream background, over a modest clothing store with one large window. She crossed the square, the sun warming her shoulders through her thin dress and sat on a bench, noticing who entered and who left the store, the door ringing with a little bell each time.

After half an hour, wishing not to be conspicuous, she got up and walked to the door of the store and entered. Immediately a short young woman with a sharp face came up to her, smiled pleasantly and said, "*Comment puis-je vous aider, madame?*"

Flavia said in perfect French with the accent of Toulouse, where her family had spent their summers, "I wish to see M. Laporterie."

"Who is it who is inquiring?" asked the young woman. Two other women in the store stared covertly at her.

Flavia, not used to being questioned by shopgirls, said haughtily, "I am Madame Bonnafoux from the *parfumeur* at Toulouse."

"It is concerning what?" Madame Laporterie, a heavy figure in dandruffed black had emerged from the back of the store. She had been trained to ask many questions so as to give her husband time to get away if necessary.

Flavia stood on her dignity. "Perfume, of course."

"We are already well-stocked."

"I am here to see M. Laporterie, not you."

"Would you like to go round the side? You will see a door there with a brass knocker like a horse."

Lady Teloar said good-day stiffly and went out.

The young woman in the store, Laporterie's daughter, immediately ran through the hallway into the house and whispered, *"Papa, une Anglaise splendide."*

Flavia went around the corner and knocked.

As the door opened, Flavia saw before her a young-looking man, who she knew was in fact middle aged, dressed in a dark blue suit, with a kindly expression, blue eyes, and an elegant pearl-grey fedora on his head, as if he were about to leave the house. He was altogether handsome.

"Bonjour, madame, comment-allez vous?"

"Très bien, m'sieur, et vous-même?"

"Je suis très content de vous assurer que tout va bien chez Laporterie. Comment puis-je vous aider?"

"I come from the *parfumeur.* The shipment of *muguet de bois* has arrived at the factory." This was the code given her by Yvonne de Rothschild to inform Laporterie that she had arrived safely in England.

"I am glad for the *parfumeur*, of course, but I do not see what that has to do with us at *La Petite Maison.*" He smiled politely.

She was startled. "That was the message that . . ." she paused, having almost said Mme de Rothschild. She had expected recognition, a smile, warmth. "The message given by the *parfumeur* . . ." she hesitated ". . . who also makes wine."

"Again this information is pleasant but useless to me. If you will permit me?" He started to push the door closed.

She said, "But monsieur, I am helpless without you."

"Good day, madame." He closed the heavy wood door. She picked up her cloth bag and turned to go. A policeman was barring her way.

Feeling sick, she started to lean against the doorframe, but he took her arm very firmly. "Come with me, madame," he said.

The police station was in the *Mairie,* on the square's far side, next to the bar. She was paraded across the square and all the people there, farmers in wooden clogs, farm wives in bare feet wearing leather sandals, farmers on horse-drawn wagons slowly passing by, idlers smoking in the open air terrace under the palm trees, watched her go in silence.

After she had been locked in the cell, the policeman, André Tachon, sat down on a bench outside the door, opened her handbag and read her passport, which showed her to be Bonnafoux, Vivienne Gentilly, of Toulouse. "Why am I here?" she demanded, "I've done nothing wrong."

"Quiet, madame," he said calmly. Then he remembered her portmanteau, opened the cell door in silence, took the portmanteau, locked the door again, and took the portmanteau into the outer office. He came back, sat down, closed her passport and now told her to sing *"La Toulousaine."*

In her summers at Le Mas near Toulouse, she had heard this song but could not now remember it. "A caged bird does not sing," she said.

"Repeat some lines," he said.

She was silent, furiously thinking. Nothing came back.

"Then give me a recipe for *cassoulet.*"

"Beans," she said.

"But madame, according to this piece of paper, you are from Toulouse. I have never known a woman from Toulouse who could not sing that song nor give the recipe for *cassoulet.* I do not believe that you are from Toulouse. Therefore, I believe nothing else in this *carte d'identité.*"

She closed her eyes. 'Why did I ever think I could get away with this, when I can not answer these simple questions. This is the end of me now.'

After about an hour, a middle-aged woman wearing ordinary civilian dress opened the cell door and ordered Flavia to take off her clothes.

"All of them, without exception." The policeman left the room which looked into the cell. Very reluctantly Flavia disrobed in front of a stranger for the first time in her life. The woman felt the girdle, found the gold bars, cut them out of the girdle and told her to put her clothes back on. The woman left the cell, the policeman, André Tachon returned and sat down, saying nothing. In a few minutes, Laporterie arrived.

He bowed slightly to her saying, "Madame," and sat on the bench outside the cell. Now Tachon began to question her through the bars.

"Why are you here?"

"To see M. Laporterie."

"M. Laporterie does not wish to see you."

"Is that true?" She appealed to him with her eyes. He made no response.

"I ask the questions," said the policeman. "Why do you wish to see M. Laporterie?"

"I wish to ask him for help."

"What kind of help?"

"The last shipment of perfume you sent out arrived safely and my friend wishes for more."

"Is that why you brought so much gold with you? To buy perfume? Five kilos of gold?"

"My friend needs three times as much perfume next time."

M. Laporterie blinked at that and said nothing. He sat there watching her, then left with André Tachon. They went over to the hotel terrace overlooking the hot Place and sat down with a pastis and cigarette, their normal noonday routine.

"What do you think?" said Tachon.

"I can't make her out yet. Her accent is perfect, she says she is from Toulouse, so does her *carte d'identité* but she does not know '*La Toulousaine.*'"

"Maybe she is not musical."

"Neither is '*La Toulousaine.*'" They both laughed. "And she can not give a recipe for *cassoulet.*"

"Ah, you are a sly one, Tachon," said Laporterie, much amused.

"And she does not walk like *une vrai Toulousaine*." He waggled his meaty hips, and Laporterie laughed.

"We'll take her to *Obersturmbannführer* Haberfellner at Mont-de-Marsan. He'd pay a pretty price for her, wouldn't he?"

In her cell, Flavia sat on the wooden bench listening to the sounds of the village coming through the big open barred window from which she could see over a small field where a tethered goat was grazing, to the wide stream bed of the Adour River, now shrunk to a few pools joined by wandering threads of brown water.

Now and then the goat brayed, sometimes a heavy truck slammed the road and shook the air as it thundered through heading for Pau. The warm air breathing through the bars smelled of grass, roses, peace. She lay on the bench, trying to still the nervous twitching in her foot. She fell asleep, dreaming of being twisted in a sheet for burial, then wakened with a frightened cry to see Laporterie watching her through the bars. She sat up shivering with fear, thinking, 'He wanted to hear what language I talk in my sleep.'

She sat up and said angrily, "*Quoi alors?*"

"You see," Laporterie said, "we are all humble *Landais* here, not used to such gilded persons as yourself. Therefore, we must get advice on what to do from *Obersturmbannführer* Haberfellner of the Gestapo in Mont-de-Marsan. Across the line. In the occupied zone."

His blue eyes observed her acutely as he pronounced the German names, pronouncing every syllable of the full name of the Gestapo. Her foot jumped involuntarily; she tried to suppress this sign of her fear by swiftly crossing her legs.

"And what has that got to do with my simple request to see you, M. Laporterie?" she asked.

Tachon said, "If as you have clumsily implied, you had been sent to M. Laporterie by someone who knew him, you would not have brought gold, because everyone who knows M. Laporterie understands that he is completely honest and has never dealt in the black market of any kind. Especially not in gold. You have endangered his life."

Her hope disappeared. Yvonne had told her that Laporterie had done everything out of the goodness of his heart, accepting no payment, not even for expenses, but she had not credited this. 'What can I tell the Gestapo, they will surely see right away I am a fraud, will they torture me, what will I say to them, I must not betray anyone.'

Tachon opened the cell door. She was feeling faint and off-balance on her high-heeled shoes, so she stumbled coming out, and leaned against him for support. Laporterie, looking concerned, came in as well and together they escorted her outside into the front seat of Laporterie's Juvaquatre. She got in beside him and Tachon remained in town.

Laporterie roared out of the square at high speed, the little car bucking at first, because it was fuelled on high octane aviation gas stolen from the German air base at Mont-de-Marsan. She started to speak, "We are alone. I must speak frankly . . ." but she was interrupted as Laporterie, lighting a cigarette with one hand, steering with the other, spied a pigeon on the road and swerved to hit it. He sped on, staring intently into the rear view mirror to see if he had hit it.

Now she believed she would die at the hands of this idiot even before reaching the Gestapo. She burst out recklessly, "If you turn me over to the Gestapo, I will be killed. I came from England, I know Yvonne Rothschild, whom you helped, she told me you do it for nothing, but I did not believe her, I thought I would need gold, I need you to save my parents, refugees, you have done it before, please do it again. For God's sake, don't turn me over to the Gestapo."

"Enough, madame," he said harshly. "Save it for Haberfellner."

He stopped at the bottom of a shallow valley beside a guard house under the Vichy flag, in front of a wide steel barrier blocking the whole road. He said curtly, "Wait here. Do not run, if you run in those shoes you will be caught immediately. Then you will be shot."

She could see 100 metres away across the shallow valley a similar guard house and barrier, under the German flag. All the trees as far as she could see in either direction had been cut to stumps, and from the tops of the guard posts, a machine gun emplacement looked out. One guard was walking back and forth carrying a rifle. This was the terrifying *Ligne de Démarcation* where Yvonne had almost died. It looked peaceful, even normal, like any other peacetime border-crossing in a village in Europe. As she watched, the barrier far away on the German side lifted to allow a big blue bus to crawl across No Man's Land in between. It came to a halt before the Vichy barrier, and all the 40 or so passengers dismounted and lined up to go into the guard-house to show their papers. The bus was now blocking the line of sight between the guard-house and the Juvaquatre. She thought, 'Now's my chance. Do it, do it.'

She opened the door quietly, got her portmanteau and purse from the back seat and started to run across the road keeping the bus and passengers between herself and the guardhouse. Then she forced herself to walk casually to the rear of the bus, and wait, still hidden from the guardhouse. As the first passengers came back out of the guard-house, she joined them casually and got on the bus unchallenged. Her heart beating heavily, she walked down the aisle, and the first person she saw was a Vichy policeman, reading *La Gironde*. She hung on a leather strap to keep from fainting, then swung on down the bus feeling the sweat pouring down her chest.

She passed the policeman, found a frayed wicker seat with a single-sheet newspaper published in Bordeaux lying on it, and sat down, bending her head to read the paper. She read and reread a single advertisement showing a Frenchwoman sweeping her yard as a pair of German soldiers passed by her with smiling approval. Under the young woman was the legend, *Français, Françaises, Balayez Vos Cours*. She prayed for the bus to move. On and on the driver chatted, smoking with passengers by the road. Finally he got back on and started away. Laporterie had not emerged from the guardhouse as the bus pulled out. She sighed with relief and tried to read her paper which was vibrating visibly in her hands.

All the way to Grenade, the bus stopped here or there to let off a woman with a shopping bag or let one climb on. One had a blind-folded baby pig in her arms, one a wicker basket of eggs. In Grenade, the driver got down and shut off the engine. He stared back into the passenger compartment and said cheerfully, "End of the line, madame."

'God it's the end of me,' she thought, getting down, holding her head turned away from the bright square, as she followed the driver into the bar, planning to ask for the time of the next bus to Pau. The Juvaquatre pulled up beside her and Tachon jumped out and stood in front of her as Laporterie hurried up.

"Oh my God," she said, and dropped the portmanteau. She was feeling so faint she thought she would fall down. Each of them took one arm, Tachon picking up the portmanteau, and Laporterie said, "Please, you are not under arrest, we simply want to talk to you." They politely walked her to a metal table under an umbrella.

"I am glad you tried to escape," said Laporterie. "If you had not, you would be in a Gestapo jail right now." He pulled out a Gitane and offered her one.

"But what are you doing to me?" she said, accepting a light.

"I can not trust everyone who comes to my door, you see, no matter even if they know the code. That is not enough. Clearly you were not *Toulousaine*, as my daughter suspected in the first moment, and as André found in a few minutes. You are carrying an enormous amount of gold. Why? No one told us you were coming. So, what are you? We do not know. How did you get the code? We do not know. To threaten you with the Gestapo was my only course. To see if you were afraid. Because only a German spy would not be afraid to go back."

"I don't understand."

"If you really were a German spy, you would simply have gone with me to the Gestapo, and we would all have had a little laugh, and that would be the end of it." He drew on his Gitane. "Only an innocent person would try to escape at the risk of her life."

She began shivering with nerves, thinking of the risk she had run.

"Madame, I admire your courage, but not your brains. *Et la voilà,*" he said and laughed, putting his warm hand on hers, which was still shaky. "Madame, please forgive me, but these things are necessary sometimes. Now, here we are, what would you like?"

"My parents are hiding in Le Chambon. I want you to help me get them out of France."

"No," he said. "You don't understand, you are my guest, you are my guest in *les Landes*, you must get accustomed to us. First, the aperitif, then the lunch, and later, perhaps, some business." He smiled, full of charm, and added, "Never perspire."

"It's too late," she said, mopping her brow with a gesture that was quite unladylike, but she didn't give a damn. For a few minutes, it was all she could do not to weep. And then suddenly, with the aperitif before her and a cigarette in her hand, the song came unbidden into her head. She began to sing *"La Toulousaine."* They all laughed and joined in. Soon the whole terrace was singing the song with them. When she had finished she was weeping and laughing together, staring through her tears at Laporterie thinking he was wonderful.

Berghof, October, 1942

Adolf Hitler was sitting in the enormous main salon of the Berghof in front of the great window staring at a dark dot which might be a *chamois* on the Obersalzberg. Looking on these cliffs hung with eagles, raked by avalanches, confirmed his sense of his own power. He saw his empire stretching from the Atlantic to the Urals, all controlled by him here in the Berghof which he had designed at his own drafting table. The most dangerous enemies had always been among the Germans, in the church, on the General Staff, in the communist party. He hated them for threatening Germany with disunity when he must have perfect obedience to win the war.

"The man must be mad," Hitler said, scanning the report which Göbbels had set beside him on the 20-foot long table in front of the window. "Doesn't he realize what we can do to him?"

"Perhaps he thinks his popularity in Münster will save him," said Göbbels.

"He must be made to realize how dangerous this is, mixing religion with affairs of state, what does he know about it? It is lies, all lies, and none of his business anyway. I'll throw him in a camp and see how he likes that."

Göbbels said, "You must meet him and calm him down because if you don't, we will lose Münster, and probably all Westphalia."

Joseph Cardinal Schraum got into the Mercedes which had been sent to the station for him, staring in awe as the car started into the mountains rising towards the Berghof. "It is 2,200 metres," said Bishop Thuring beside him, guidebook in hand. The bishop loved to be informed, and insisted on informing his cardinal. He whispered, "Charlemagne sleeps in legend above the valley of the Unterberg where one day he will arise and recreate the German Empire that was lost with his death." He closed the book and sighed with satisfaction.

The cardinal wondered why Thuring would think this pagan legend was relevant at such a moment.

The car passed through the first check-point in the outer perimeter fence, "Fifteen kilometres round," Bishop Thuring whispered. They passed through the inner fence, "Four kilometres round," Thuring whispered. The cardinal sat in heavy gloom, thinking the whole place was like a wild-animal park.

To meet the man who was known throughout the church as The Antichrist, Schraum had clothed himself in his cardinal's vestments, black cassock closed with 24 red buttons down the front, red cingulum around his waist, red skull cap, and large gold cross round his neck. When he was ushered into the room he was so apprehensive on seeing Hitler scowling at him, that he lifted his cross to kiss it to protect himself from the devil, then realizing the insult, dropped it hastily. It swung heavily around for a moment, and he had to still it with his hand. He glanced nervously at Göbbels as they were introduced, wondering if his gaffe had been noticed. Göbbels, delighted at this terrible insult, feared that Hitler, raised a Catholic, would throw him out, but Hitler ignored it. He kept to his plan to lull the old man with fine words, then strike later.

The cardinal protested against the government's euthanasia policy, threatening to denounce the German government formally to the Vatican.

Hitler listened in silence. He said abruptly, "I didn't know about this. I will have it investigated." He assured the cardinal of his support, shook his hand saying goodbye, and looked intently into the cardinal's eyes. The moment the cardinal had left, he shouted, "How many euthanasia trucks are there?"

"Twelve," said Bormann.

"Get 20 more and work round the clock on the essential job of ridding the Reich of this vermin. As for that filthy old hypocrite in skirts, I'll have him on a meathook, no, better, he will go to the Eastern front. They are insane, all of them, all they think of is controlling their flock, no wonder they call them a flock, since they are all sheep to be sheared by any pretentious old nincompoop in skirts, which is after all what they should wear, since they are so interested in their choir boys. Bah. Disgusting. I happen to know that that old bishop who just left here has been chasing choir boys all his life. And one of those poor boys committed suicide."

Hitler walked round the room in front of the huge window overlooking the deep valley. "How dare they speak that way to me, I who have given my life to Germany, I who am married to Germany. He chopped the air with his open right hand while punching rhythmically up and down with his left fist. "How did these idiots get their power over an intelligent race? They're worse than the Jews who are the source of their influence. The naive trust of the good-hearted German people is mocked by the cynicism of these half-Jews with their sickening doctrine of submission, and submission to whom? To them of course, hiding behind their candles and altars and skirts and their immense hypocrisies. He spends his life pandering to the money-grubbers of Westphalia with his Jewish heresy. God how I hate religion. It is my task to make this people great as fate has made me great. And Wagner."

He paused, and one of the aides, Percy Schramm, who was surreptitiously writing his words down, said, "Wagner? I don't understand."

Hitler leaned back in his chair watching a small cloud forming, blowing away and reforming over the Obersalzberg, and said, "As fate made Wagner great, so he made me see greatness. To see it is to become it. I have built up my religion out of *Parsifal* because one can serve God only in the role of hero without pretense of humility. I first heard *Gotterdämmerung* in Vienna and I still remember how wonderfully excited I was going home, until I passed a gang of yammering Yids. Called Goldsomething, no doubt. All they do is drag the people down into the muck of their gold-worship. Hah. There is a good name for a Yid family, Goldverehrung to go along with Goldberg and Goldwasser. I'll smash them after the war, they'll see what it is to be heretics."

Göbbels pleaded, "Mein Führer, the people are not so advanced as you in these matters. We must prepare them, many of our villages are still in the dark ages or the Yids and priests would not have such power."

Hitler made an impatient gesture. "Oh, all right. Bormann, cancel it. We will finish the job after the war. But when that day comes, they will regret having written their names in my black book. The worst influences on the German people are the pastors and the priests of both confessions. I can not give the whole answer now, but everything is being entered in my black book, don't worry. The time will come when I will settle with them permanently, without any ceremony. That is my irrevocable decision."

Now Göbbels, who knew him very well, gave him the reward for his good behaviour with Schraum. "Did you hear about the people at the FO who were trying to decide on what to give our champagne salesman for his birthday?"

Hitler said, "I wish you would not call Ribbentrop a champagne salesman, he is after all a Minister of the Reich."

"They decided to give him an inlaid box containing a beautifully handwritten copy of every treaty he has negotiated on behalf of the Reich since he became Minister. And when they got the typed copies all together to give to the calligrapher, someone pointed out that we have broken every one of them."

Hitler stared at him, then broke into a smile, and started to laugh. He laughed so long he was still wiping his eyes and chortling when lunch was announced.

Grenade, November, 1942

As Max and Cecile Frankfurter stood in the front hall of Pastor Trocmé's house saying goodbye, André Trocmé said to Max, in French, "Don't speak German on the train. Or anywhere public. French only."

Clara had asked Trocmé to warn him, thinking Max would take it better from a man than from her. She knew that Max disliked her because she was a woman and in charge. Max glared at her, suspecting that this was her way of shutting him up, because his French was rudimentary. He said towards her, "Why is that?"

Trocmé said, "Germans are rare here. You do not want to attract attention."

"German is the language of their masters," said Max.

Now Clara stepped in. "Herr Frankfurter, I must warn you, if you do speak German in public I shall have to leave you. I do not want to risk my life because you have no common sense."

Max gave her a look of hatred. *"D'accord."*

Clara stepped down first from the train, shading her eyes against the sun shining low across the stubbled fields around the station at Grenade-sur-l'Adour. Cecile followed and then Max. Flavia was standing beside Raoul Laporterie in the shade of trees feeling nervous about this meeting with her father, the first in 21 years, the first since her marriage, the first since she had rebelled against him, had married against his will and had changed her name from Frederica to Flavia.

But when she actually saw him, short, suspicious, obstinately holding onto the handles in the stairway despite the passengers pushing from behind, she felt such a strong impetus to embrace him that it was as if a hand in her back shoved her forward, and she ran to him and embraced him, saying, *"Papa, papa, je suis si heureuse de te revoir,"* with tears in her eyes. She seized him round the shoulders and Max, blinded by the sun, felt himself enveloped by a strange perfumed woman half a head taller than he, and struggled to free himself.

"Papa, it's me, Flavia," she said, "Frederica, Erica, I'm so happy you are here safe and sound."

Max said, "What is this, you don't know your own name?"

Cecile standing anxiously beside them hoping Max would not shove Erica away, whispered, "She changed her name."

Max allowed her to kiss him on the cheek.

Mother and daughter both took this for reconciliation. Flavia picked up his bag and he followed her like a child after the teacher, still looking suspiciously around and wondering who among these people was making notes to report to the police. Ever since crossing the border into Vichy France, he had feared that this whole escape was a monstrous illusion which would end in a disaster worse than he had evaded.

As he thought this, he growled, "Let's get out of here," just as they came to Raoul Laporterie, standing waiting for the reunion to end, smiling on them, dressed in an impeccable pale grey suit, wearing his *melon*, his face so pink with health that it seemed to be powdered.

Max, Cecile and Flavia slept in one room on the second floor of the Laporterie house on the main street of Grenade. At dawn, Max awoke, hearing the roosters. The church bell boomed out six o'clock and he was about to go back to sleep when he noticed a rumble from outside. He peered out through the shutters and saw a grey military truck grinding along the cobbled street, and then another. He opened the shutter a crack and then saw the black crosses of the Wehrmacht. He began to tremble.

'They knew about us all along, they're everywhere, they can get me anywhere,' he was thinking. He was so frantic, he thought of jumping out the window to kill himself. He was putting on his shoes to run downstairs to jump in front of a truck when Cecile awoke, hearing him crashing about.

She said, "What are you doing?" in a whisper, and he said, "They're here, they know we're here, they're here," pointing out the window. She stared down at the grey trucks rolling by and turned back to him, knowing instantly what he was thinking about and ran to him and threw her arms around him, pushing him onto the bed, covering him with her weight and putting her hand over his mouth. Laporterie came to the door in a nightgown and said, "The Germans have taken over the zone. Quick, no time to lose, we must get to Pau before they change the border guards."

Clara embraced Flavia and Cecile. Flavia said, "I'll remember your courage all my life" with tears in her eyes. Cecile said, "Thank you from the bottom of my heart," in French and German and then tried it in English, "From my bottom heart," so they parted laughing. Max shook her hand and said, "*Hertzlichen Danke.*"

Laporterie drove them with their bags in the Juvaquatre to Pau and parked in front of the Hôtel Vinet, where his old friend Henri Vinet was standing to welcome them. He said as they were getting out, "Quick, here they are," as a Citroen of the Wehrmacht entered the street. "Get inside, we'll have lunch." Laporterie noticing *Vive de Gaulle* written in the dust on the trunk lid of his car, wiped it off with his handkerchief.

Vinet said, "Into the dining room, it's full of Germans, they'll never think of looking for you here." He knew that the police were looking for Laporterie—they would not imagine it was him dining with German officers.

Cecile took Max's arm as they waited at the doorway for Vinet to make the arrangements, for every table was taken with German officers having lunch. The room was loud with their talk and blue with cigarette smoke. Max said in horror, "I can't go in there." She hissed, "Speak French, we are from Elsass-Lothringen."

"They speak German there now," said Max as Vinet ushered them to a table where two German officers were finishing their lunch. Vinet said, "Excuse me gentlemen, we are very crowded today owing to the unexpectedly early tourist season this year, permit me," bringing up a chair in each hand to set them round the table.

The Germans nodded, and the captain with close-set grey eyes who normally had a cold, inspector's expression, allowed himself to smile as he made room for the others. 'After all,' he thought, 'you catch more flies with honey than with gall.'

Vinet said, "The menu is *épuisé* but we can give you omelettes, with one *steak-frites* to share, and of course a salad."

He went away, curving easily among the close-set chairs. The captain lit a cigarette and asked, "Are you from this region?"

Cecile said, "We thank you for liberating us, we are from Elsass-Lothringen," just as Flavia said, "We are from Toulouse."

The captain studied each one separately as Flavia stared at him in shock, thinking he had heard the fatal contradiction but he simply said, "You are welcome, it is our duty and our pleasure."

Laporterie said that he was from the region, and he would be pleased to advise them about the white wines of the Jurançon. He knew a man with a vineyard nearby who had had an exceptionally good year in 1940. They were fortunate because it was still in good supply and especially suited to the German taste, resembling a Sylvaner d'Elsass. He gave them his card, and the captain was busy writing down the coordinates of the vineyard owner when the *Miliciens* came to the door of the dining room, looking for Laporterie but saw only German officers and their French friends. Vinet edged past the police in the doorway with the omelettes. The captain rose and thanked Laporterie.

Vinet said, *"Bon appétit,"* and Flavia glanced at her father, thankful that he had not said a word. Max said, "I have no appetite."

Laporterie thought that it would be too dangerous for them to take the Juvaquatre, so they borrowed Vinet's little Renault for the trip up to L'Estelle-Betharram.

When they got there, Bosca was sitting as agreed, in the terrace of the Café Marechal by the cobbled square overlooking the steep valley. He was smoking a yellow Spanish cigarette and drinking pastis.

He threw up his hands when he saw Laporterie getting the bags from the Renault and said, "No bags."

"You said you would have a mule," said Laporterie. "Where is it?"

Bosca shrugged. "Not possible," he said. "Come on, it's getting late." He snapped his fingers, Laporterie opened his wallet and paid him 10,000 francs. Bosca snapped his fingers again. "Three," he said, "not two." Laporterie added 5,000. Bosca said, "Follow me."

"But what about our bags?" Max said, "We can't go without them."

"I'll take care of them," Laporterie said. "We'll see you after the war."

Cecile embraced him, Max stood aside, thinking they had just been robbed and were now about to be delivered to the Gestapo. Flavia embraced Laporterie with tears rimming her eyes.

They started up the steep street towards the high pass with the sun on their shoulder. Max said, "Did Laporterie pay for us? Did you already pay him?"

"He won't take a *sou*. He does it out of the goodness of his heart."

"You think we'll get our bags back? You're dreaming."

"I'm not worried, papa. If he'd been planning to betray us, I would be in jail. He has ten kilos of my gold in his car."

Max stared at her. "Ten kilos? Is that true?"

"Of course," Flavia said, still walking, so he had to run to catch up to her.

Rastenburg, December, 1942

~~∽◯𝒢~~

Adolf Hitler leaned over the map table in the Führer bunker, trying to plan how to get reinforcements to General Paulus' Sixth Army surrounded at Stalingrad. The Sixth Army had never been defeated but now it was trapped inside a circle of Russian armies attacking from every direction.

Göring had assured Hitler he could supply Paulus by air, but the supplies that did get through were inadequate. German soldiers who had entered France as happy conquerors were starving to death in the freezing cellars of the city. They had no winter clothing. Their guns and engines refused to work in temperatures that sometimes went down to minus 40 Celsius. The Russians attacking them were clothed in furs and thick wool, their guns worked in the coldest weather, each Russian killed was immediately replaced by another. The only warmth the German soldier got was from warming his hands on the barrel of his machine gun through the socks he was using as mitts.

All the generals were advising retreat; Hitler ordered the soldiers to stand fast. After a bitter argument with the Wehrmacht top staff, Hitler once again purged his staff of anyone who opposed him, terming them defeatists. These were most of the generals who had led the army to victory in Czechoslovakia, Poland, Norway, Belgium, Holland, France, Yugoslavia, Greece and Russia. Soon the new men too lost confidence in him and only obeyed his orders from their sense of duty or from fear. Hitler could barely bring himself to speak to any of them except to demand information and issue orders. He ordered the army to fight to the last man, to remember Frederick the Great and never quit. Now Hitler was like his soldiers of the Sixth Army, isolated among his enemies.

He worked all day in a hostile atmosphere in the map room, then in the evening retired to his personal bunker with the secretaries and a few party officials or visitors, rarely or never with an army officer. There it was that he was handed a message from the Premier of

Japan, Hideki Tojo, in the evening of Sunday December 13. He stared at it incredulously,

Today, when the knowledge is gaining ground among all right-thinking people that a better world can only be achieved by the complete victory of the three Axis nations, I should like again to proclaim to the whole world that our three nations have the unalterable will as well as the power jointly to achieve victory.

He took off his gold-rimmed reading glasses and stared around wearily, wondering if this could be a joke. He asked von Below who had given him the telex, and was told it had come in from Ribbentrop's office. 'That idiot,' Hitler thought. 'He doesn't have the imagination to make such a joke. It must be real.'

He passed the telex around the room to the secretaries who were drinking tea, and several of them glanced up uneasily. Something was bothering the Führer.

He sat down, shook his head and said, "To think that I am helping this little yellow menace to bring down the British Empire, which I have always admired. How strange life is."

1943

Germany, February, 1943

Starving and freezing, the German Sixth Army surrendered to the Russians at Stalingrad in February 1943, the first German defeat since September 1939. Hundreds of thousands of men had already died fighting in ruined streets during blizzards and cold so deep that exposed skin was frozen in a few seconds. A hundred thousand more of the dying survivors entered Russian captivity.

Hitler ordered six days of national mourning in memory of the Sixth Army. Every radio station in the country played Beethoven's *Fifth Symphony* that day.

All over Germany people who had been blindly faithful to the Führer now began to doubt him. In Munich, heartland of the party, university students posted signs and distributed leaflets that said:

> *Fellow students! The nation is deeply shaken by*
> *the defeat of our troops at Stalingrad. Three hundred*
> *and thirty thousand Germans have been senselessly*
> *and irresponsibly led to death and destruction*
> *through the cunning strategy of a corporal from*
> *World War One. Our Führer, we thank you.*

Fellow students! The German people look to us!
As in 1813 the people looked to us to destroy the
Napoleonic terror, so today in 1943 they look to us
to destroy the terror of National Socialism.

Sophie Scholl stood, early in the morning of February 18, in the atrium of Munich University, floating these leaflets into the courtyard below. She was seen by a janitor. She and many others were arrested and executed. Her brother Hans died saying *"Es lebe die Freiheit."*

Iceland, Ireland, February, 1943

His Majesty's Canadian ship *Sheguiandah* slammed down on the trough of the wave so hard the lights went out and the coxswain had to turn on the emergency lights.

"I thought we'd hit something sure," said First Lieutenant Orle Larsen. "Water's like cement in here."

"See about that would you, Number One?'

"Aye aye, sir," said Larsen, and went down to the lower decks to find the coxswain.

Grant was standing on the bridge with his knees flexed to take the shocks as the little ship, only 205 feet long, crashed through heavy seas towards Hvalfjord on the southwest coast of Iceland, where they were due to take on supplies from HMS *Hecla.* He called down to the wheelhouse to reduce speed, and they approached the island under its meringue of cloud.

By dusk, they were in calm waters 15 miles off the mouth of Havalfjord. Ahead rose dark eroded hills, black in the shadows, mauve in the fading light, and limned with green along the streams that cut the slopes. The approach was east north-east between two capes miles apart. The radar operator shouted, "U-boat, bearing 248 degrees, range 2,000 yards."

Grant immediately rang action stations, both engines full ahead and port 40. He trained his night glasses on the U-boat which was making no effort to dive, travelling west very slowly. Within a minute the crews were at the guns, rotating the turrets to bear on the U-boat.

He ordered his gunnery officer to fire at will, then focused his glasses on the U-boat, which was screened by the water erupting around it from the *Sheguiandah*'s four inch shells. The U-boat turned towards them slowly, presumably to fire torpedoes. Figures on her foredeck swivelled her gun round to aim at the *Sheguiandah*, and he saw the red wink of burning cordite as the shell left the muzzle. The U-boat's first shell hit the *Sheguiandah* on her port bow, sending shrapnel and splinters clanging into the bridge, making two of the men on A gun below him scream in pain.

Grant ducked instinctively banging his head on a stanchion, then stuck his head up again immediately to search for torpedoes. Two white tracks were coming at him, lit by the moon which had just sliced through a cloud.

He called for port ten to bring his ship parallel to the enemy course. Fire and smoke erupted from B gun below him. The ship had been hit but A turret was still firing. He lifted the glasses from the torpedoes, praying they were not Gnats, and saw flame spout up from the U-boat. He hung over the bridge-railing and saw the torpedoes run past. Screams were still coming from the wounded lying on the deck by A gun but the rest of the gun crew were cheering the fire and smoke from the U-boat.

They were now only a few hundred yards from the U-boat and he could see without his glasses men falling from the conning tower into the sea as the U-boat slowly rolled on her side towards the *Sheguiandah*. The light of the fires inside the U-boat silhouetted the men clambering out. If the fire spread to the ammunition and diesel fuel, the U-boat would blow up damaging the *Sheguiandah*. He rang full astern, backing the ship off to 200 yards, then ordered ship's boats away to pick up survivors.

Six prisoners were taken to sick bay in manacles, for the surgeon to treat, two for wounds and all for nausea from swallowing sea water and oil. Grant went down to the sick bay to interrogate one who could speak some English. He wanted to know if the U-boat had been alone and why it had stayed on the surface. The wind had picked up so the *Sheguiandah* was rolling a little as he made his way aft, but the air smelled of land, and he could hear a seagull overhead.

He pushed open the sickbay door and stopped. Four men in underwear sat manacled and dripping on the only bunk, two more stood against the wall in oily underwear, all their faces black, hair matted, their expressions afraid, sullen, defiant, dazed. The room stank of sweat, oil, sea water, vomit; the two overhead bulbs encased in steel mesh glared down. He could barely speak for revulsion. Aware that he was standing in a door that blasted light into the dark sea where more U-boats lay, he slammed the door closed, greeted the surgeon, and looked at one young man—only a boy—with blond hair and staring blue eyes and an expression both frightened and defiant.

Grant said, "Who speaks English?"

The boy said, *"Ich kann, ein little, bischen, bitte."*

"What is your name?"

"Josef Salmen."

"Why were you on the surface?"

Salmen looked at one of the standing men, apparently an officer, and spoke German. The officer nodded and Salmen replied, "Because of holes in *unserem Boot*, water-holes."

"Are there any other U-boats in the vicinity?"

Salmen looked helpless, and the surgeon, who had taken a year of medical German while studying at university, said, "He doesn't understand vicinity, sir," and translated. Salmen checked with his officer, who shook his head vigorously, and Salmen said, "No."

"No boats?"

"I think he means no answer," said the surgeon. Grant thought, 'I couldn't believe him anyway.'

He was struck by the young man's demeanour now—he was dignified, though young and in a difficult position, but there was in his eyes something appealing, as if he were amused by the whole thing. Grant wanted to ask "Why did you join such a dangerous service?" and knew it was impossible. He thanked the surgeon and got out into the sweet salty air, wanting to know why Salmen was fighting.

Making the approach to Hvalfjord, he rang down for "half ahead, steady as she goes," then focused his glasses on something mysterious beyond *Hecla* in the narrow inner harbour. At first the thing was so huge that he thought he was fantasizing it out of shore rocks in the dim light, but then he realized this was the *King George Fifth*, one of the huge new King George Fifth class battleships.

He signalled to the *Hecla* that he had sunk a U-boat off the island and was bringing in prisoners. A few minutes later, the signal winked back, "Well done. Proceed to mooring 22." They passed the *Hecla* on their way to the mooring and a line of seamen on her deck cheered.

At dawn, they saw on the high signals staff of the KGV a signal from the admiral aboard, congratulating him and inviting him to dinner at 1900.

"WMP," Grant signalled back, for "With Much Pleasure," and ordered an extra tot of rum for the crew at noon.

Admiral Tim Fletcher, only five feet tall and known as Tiny Tim, with preposterously hairy eyebrows, looked up at him with a tight smile, congratulating him on the kill. "We came in here yesterday with six escort ships and no one spotted that U-boat. But you did. Why?"

"Well, sir, perhaps he wasn't on the surface yesterday."

"Perhaps. In any case, you have prisoners who must be properly interrogated. And the Western Approaches Escort has just lost a corvette and destroyer to enemy action, so I want you to join them as they take over your eastbound convoy." Grant obeyed eagerly for now he would have shore leave in London.

"Thank you, sir."

"Oh, and Giovanelli, don't enter anything in your ship's log about prisoners, or why that U-boat was on the surface."

"Yes sir."

"In case you're captured yourself, do you see? Not that you would permit such a thing to occur," he said and waggled his comical eyebrows.

That night, Grant braced his knee on the side of his bunk as he always did to steady himself in case the ship rolled in the night. He was relieved for himself and the ship, but he could not stop seeing the black silhouettes in the burning U-boat trying to escape.

The kill brought back his terrors. Around and around in his head images danced, starshells bursting in the dark over burning ships, the faces in the fire-filled sea of men screaming, the orders to break off rescue duty to chase a U-boat, leaving men in the sea, the enormous explosion as the *Manitoulin* went up, then legs and arms and burst torsos of human beings slammed down on the bloodied decks along with the steel plates, stanchions, hot metal debris of the exploded freighter.

He put his head in his hands concentrating on Cat in the rose garden, a blue summer day at the bay, the bees forcing entry into the sweet william. He drank, walked on deck, saw the moon travelling the sea to the south, and simultaneously the long sunset streaking the sky to the north, the shining wakes of the dark-hulled freighters tugging black coal-smoke, then went below to work on his new poem.

The *Sheguiandah* joined the British units and together they sailed for Belfast, where Harland and Wolff were to repair a crack in their boiler, while the crew took two weeks leave.

Grant and his friend, Lovesick Lee, dressed in civvies, sat in the train to Dublin en route to Galway, where Grant wanted to visit Yeats' tower and the Blake castle at Tuum, where his mother's ancestors had lived a thousand years before. Then they would return to Dublin, to buy Barr and Stroud binoculars, far better than the type supplied by the RCN. They would go the Abbey Theatre, sight-see in Dublin, then take the ferry for Holyhead.

After they crossed the border into the Irish Free State, he felt almost as if he were back in Ontario again. The countryside was Holstein cattle grazing on deep green grass in fields between hedgerows, narrow dusty roads, tree-shaded streams. The names were all from home— Newcastle, Fermanagh, Cookstown, Tory Hill, Bainbridge, Cavan.

They took an old black Ford taxi from Tuum out to the fields surrounding Feartagar, the ancient Blake family castle, four storeys high, built in the style of a Norman keep, with one narrow entry and high crenellated battlements. A narrow slit ten feet above the entry opened onto a pouring lip to direct hot oil "onto magazine salesmen," said Lee.

Grant ducked through the doorway and started up the stairway whose steps, walls and banisters were all of stone. Halfway up, the stairway ended abruptly then started again six feet higher up. Narrow slots in the sidewalls showed where there must have been wooden beams supporting a wooden insert that would have been raised when enemies attacked. He stared at this with his hand on the curve of stone handrail, polished to black glass by a thousand years of human hands resting where his now rested.

He stuck the toes of his boots into the slots, and crabbed up to the next floor like a mountain climber up a chimney, emerging on the roof to view through the arrow slits of the crenellations, the fields, wet and green on this still November day. Walling in the field all round stretched the forest of hardwood, now turned grey-green and dull brown in the hazy light. He thought of the faces and hands of his ancestors who had been here and whose names had been forgotten by their descendants. Nothing was left of them, unless this stone ruin. He vowed to tell the Blake cousins about the decay of the ancestral home, so they could rebuild it after the war.

Lee was outside leaning against the wall, smoking and drinking Irish whiskey from the flask he carried. He held out the flask to Grant, who shook his head, feeling that this was a magical moment he did not want to degrade. Lee pointed to a plaque in the wall beside him, lettered in Irish and English. The English side, holed by bullets, said this was a keep dating from 1060AD, and was maintained by the state as an historical relic. Lee laughed. "Target practice for IRA kids," he said. "I heard they recruit a lot of them round here."

The sheep watched them as they stepped from hillock to hillock to avoid the watery hollows on the way to the black taxi waiting in the laneway.

Yeats' tower rose from a brown brook running over the kind of granite used to build the walls. The sound of the water drowned out the noise of civilization, Grant said, thinking it was a good place to write. The black mood like despair that had hit him off Iceland and which he had sublimated into poetry, took him unawares as he looked at Yeats' peace.

'What am I doing with my life?' he thought. 'I am not doing what I want to do, and I am doing what I don't want to do. I have no doubts about the justice of the war, so why do I feel like this?' No answer came to him, except, illogically, 'Yes you do have doubts,' which he suppressed immediately saying to himself, 'That's ridiculous, it's a good war.'

No one in this neutral country was urgent with the war—as they returned east on the main highway, they were blocked for ten minutes while a flock of sheep crossed the road behind the shepherd and scurrying dog.

In Dublin, he and Lee bought the binoculars, visited Trinity College Library, and then had lunch in a pub in Grafton street. Grant was talking about the Blake castle and the invasions of the Normans. One of the men at the next table spoke out, "Would ye be talking about t'Blakes of Galway?"

"Yes," said Grant. "Sam Blake was my great-grandfather. He came from Galway in 1832."

"Ahh, the Blakes, I know them well, horse t'ieves and renegades all," the Irishman said softly. Lee, who had been bored by Grant's preoccupation with his Blake ancestors, laughed and invited the Irishman and his friend to pull their table over. The other man followed, hunching his chair over the floor, and their tables joined like two ships at sea. The first Irishman, round-bodied, round faced, with a cap of pale blond hair, his sagging trousers held up by a rope, told stories of the Blakes while the other dark-haired, square-headed man listened in amusement.

The Irishman, Benedict Ryan, spoke in a low breathless voice, almost a whisper, and sometimes put the back of his hand to the side of his mouth, Dublin style, to show that he was not saying what he was saying.

The other man seldom spoke. His accent was odd, as if he had learned English as a second language. Grant decided that the pronounced glottals probably derived from the Gaelic of west Ireland and he instantly constructed a romantic history for the man—educated by a hedge-teacher fleeing the Black and Tans, now a poet in Dublin.

Lee was getting drunk. Raised an Irish Catholic in Toronto, he made friends with anyone who interested him—Anglo-Tories like Grant, Jews, blacks, Americans. He was interested in Louis Armstrong, Proust, Lena Horne, New Orleans jazz, Faulkner, all the richly rare and the strange, especially the "damned and the doomed," in the Scott Fitzgerald sense.

Ben Ryan was describing some Blake history that Grant had never heard. "The Ryans and Blakes were deadliest enemies for generations. Did you hear of Kate O'Neill and her happy history in the great house at Oughterard? This was not the castle, you may imagine, but a wonderful great stone house set upon a hill such as might have delighted the eye of a painter. One day, when old Thomas Blake lay dying in the bed to which he had often taken his maidservant Kate, the priest came to him and said, 'Now Thomas, you know you'll soon be gone, so it's time for you to marry the lass on whom you made a child, so you can leave the place to them, or else the state will take it all, for you've no legitimate heir. So I'll marry you now, and then administer the rites.'

"And that was what happened, and the boy grew up in the great house with his mother but never went near a school. So he came into his millions, and one day, driving through Dublin in his Rolls Royce, he went the wrong way up a one-way street because he could not read the sign, and he was killed by a lorry driven by a navvy who could. Leaving a child and heir who was brought up to read before he could drive, and made many benefactions in the village, so now it is a wonderful place to live not a good place to leave, as it was for 300 years. So the Ryans brought peace to the Ryans and Blakes, and the Blakes brought wealth to the village of Tuum. For you see, the wonderful thing about it was, the priest was a Ryan, Benedict Ryan, the same as I am."

He smiled vaguely and said, "That has a nice ring to it, doesn't it, 'Benedict Ryan, the same as I am.' He reached into his pocket and took out a short stub of pencil and wrote *Benedict Ryan, the same as I am,* on a thick mass of folded paper, which he stuffed away again in his inside pocket. As he did this, there was a bemused silence for the poet at work, and then Lee said with a sardonic chuckle, "And was he your grandfather?"

"Who, the priest?" said Ben. "Indeed, the very man, how did you guess? But it's not to be whispered in the family, not to be talked about at all. But he was, all the same, and his son, my father, raised in an orphanage, then sent out to school in Westport. Well, blessed are the peacemakers, for they shall inherit the earth." He raised his glass and they drank to the peacemakers.

Grant returned from the washroom feeling that rush of affection for humanity which is natural to a man drinking with good company in a warm pub on a rainy afternoon. He liked these people all laughing and talking animatedly, and the girls who looked at him with interest, not furtively like the girls at home. He felt that he was becoming a well-travelled man, wise in the ways of the world, and accepted by the eyes of women in this famous old place.

The square-headed man with the strong accent said abruptly to Grant, "Why did you buy these?" indicating the binoculars, which Lee had opened and had been using to peer round the room searching for a waiter. "Surely they give you the best in your very royal navy?"

"The better to see you with," said Lee.

"Soon you won't" said the man. "With our new schnorkel U-boats, we can stay underwater for the whole Atlantic, only come up to fart."

"You're a German," said Grant in astonishment. Lee, Ryan and the German laughed.

"*Jawohl,* the name's Müller," said the German and stuck his hand out towards Grant, who ignored it. He realized with horror that the name he had heard as Miller, was in fact, Müller. Müller withdrew his hand and said, "But you're not allowed to shoot me here."

"What are you doing here?" said Grant.

"I might ask you the same," said Müller. "But I've already seen the answer." He glanced at the package of binoculars.

The waiter in a long black apron like a half-soutane came with a tray of full glasses, and Müller paid. Grant said no, but Müller had already given the waiter the money. The waiter said, "If the gentleman insists, I'll take it twice," and then went away.

Grant put his money away thinking, 'Well, I won't say thanks.'

Müller said, "To answer your question, I'm with the Embassy."

"How did you get here?"

Müller held out his sleeve towards Grant's face, and said, "How do you think? There's the famous *Unterseebootgestank.*"

Grant drew his head back stiffly and said, "Lee, time to go."

"You haven't touched your glass," said Ben, eyeing it thirstily.

"You can finish it." He got up. Lee did not move.

Ben stood up and put his arm round Grant's shoulder and said, "We're in a neutral country, we're both poets you and I. Why not sit down and enjoy yourself? Reinhard has studied Goethe at Göttingen. He's been to Yeats' castle."

"For God's sake, Ben, I can't drink with him, he's the enemy," Grant said, feeling his tongue skid around on the sibilants. But the moment he said that, he remembered the question he had wanted to ask of the blue-eyed young prisoner in his oily underwear in the sick bay.

"And so the Blakes were my enemy, and I'm happy to take a drop with you, clap you on the back and call you friend. 'Romantic Ireland's dead and gone, it's with O'Leary in the grave.'"

"I don't see what that's got to do with it," Grant said grudgingly, knowing he was being priggish, trying to ignore the naval authorities in his mind. Lee refused to get up, and Grant found his excuse, "Well, I'll have to stay, to make sure Lovesick doesn't let out any naval secrets." He sat down and began to drink again.

They sat in the pub for two hours, and Müller told stories of mountain climbing in Banff where he had been an instructor before the war. Grant heard about their expedition to Dublin in a U-boat, fascinated.'What would he say if I told him I had sunk one of their U-boats a week ago? He probably knew some of the men on board.'

Müller said, "Do you like riddles? I'll give you a riddle I made up myself. A man sets out on Monday morning to climb Mount Norquay. It takes him ten hours. He sleeps at the top. Next morning he sets out on the descent. Same route. It takes him three hours. Is there any point on the way down where he is at the same place he was the day before *at the same time?*"

Lee looked at him, sucked on his cigarette and gazed up at the smoked beamed ceiling. Grant wanted to say yes, but could not think of the reason. Then he thought maybe Müller would not ask the reason, so he impulsively said, "Yes."

"Good," said Müller, "that's right. How did you figure it out so fast?"

Grant stared at him nonplussed, and the answer came in a flash, "Because if another man had set out to descend on the day the climber started up, they must have met somewhere. So they would have been at the same point at the same time." He shrugged and Müller reached over and clapped him on the shoulder. "Very good, very good young man, you will go far in life, you will indeed go far."

Grant smiled in relief. 'Müller is not such a bad chap after all,' he thought. After a few more drinks, he stopped worrying and asked the question, "What are you fighting for?"

"So I can go home," said Müller, slurring his words.

Grant felt quite drunk. "Self-contradictory. Must be something more. What everyone is fighting for. You see."

"We lost last time, and we were very poor. Ate turnips. Ugh. You got rich."

"But then we were poorer, and you got richer."

"You must admit, very strange."

"Very strange."

"Can't be it then."

"What?"

"Why we're fighting."

"We're not fighting."

They looked at each other and everyone laughed.

Lee and Grant got back to the hotel late and tipsy. In the morning, Grant realized that he had left the binoculars behind. He went back to the pub, where they told him the German gentleman had taken them for safekeeping to the Embassy. So they went to the German Embassy, an elegant old Georgian house flaunting the red, white and black Nazi swastika, where Müller came downstairs to greet them with the package under his arm. He offered them the guest book to sign. They signed, Grant thanked him stiffly, feeling very weird, to be thanking a sworn enemy for guarding his weaponry, and Lee was smiling at the strangeness of it all, converting it into an anecdote for his shipmates.

Berlin, February, 1943

As Clara got down from the streetcar in Pariser Platz on a cold, grey morning, she hesitated, looking across the platz, thinking she must be at the wrong stop. The Hotel Adlon was gone. Where the grand entrance had been, a prisoner of war with a big red G painted on the back of his coat was wheeling a barrow of mortar towards a new, slovenly-looking wall of dull red brick. She looked above and saw the Adlon's familiar six storeys of elegant casement windows, topped with the rounded dormers in the penthouse. Prisoners were bricking in the whole ground floor of the undamaged hotel, except for a narrow entrance, to guard against bomb blasts.

As she edged past the prisoners, her foot slipped off the duckboard into the muck. One of the men bent down to clean off her shoe with his bare hand and addressed her in German, then in French, "*Nous sommes prisonniers de guerre depuis trois ans, aidez-nous.*" He looked up at her with tears in his eyes, then bent his head and kissed the shoe he had just cleaned. "*Merci,*" she said, "*je vous aidera si je peux.*"

Everyone in the foyer was silent, or spoke in whispers. She could hear Beethoven's *Fifth Symphony* playing on a radio in the manager's office. Two people got off the elevator as she stood there, neither of them greeting her. She greeted the elevator boy, whom she knew, and he whispered, "*Guten Morgen.*" He reached out with a grubby white glove and drew the latticed brass gates closed.

Helmuth James von Blücher, wearing the elegant pale-grey uniform of the Foreign Ministry, rose and helped her take off her coat then offered her coffee. She refused and he walked round his desk looking grim.

"Sad days," he said.

"Indeed."

"And I'm afraid I must make them sadder. Peter's been wounded."

Clara had long feared this: she clenched her hands at her sides and froze her face waiting for the worst.

"This came in." He handed her a telegram addressed to herself. It was the standard typed form saying that her husband had been wounded, to which Helmuth James had added in pencil, "Returning home by hospital train this AM."

Clara felt her nerves fire up and a shot of adrenaline hit her stomach as she thought, 'This is it, this is what I feared all along.' She imagined the scream, the groan, the blood in the dressing, and she said, "Where?" Then she sat down thinking she was about to faint. She was thinking, 'Peter, kind, thoughtful Peter, please no, let it not be true.'

"In the leg, left leg; shrapnel entered the thigh and the calf, the muscles are damaged." She wanted to say, "Not *the* leg, not *the* thigh, *his* leg, *his* thigh."

"He needs an operation, that's why he is coming back. I'm sorry on such a day as this to give you more bad news. I did not want this telegram to arrive unannounced."

She looked up searching for some way to make this a mistake, and said, "But why was it sent to you?"

"You see, it is addressed to you here in this office, I imagine the army records show you still working here."

'Then he must have been in about six o'clock,' she thought, because he had telephoned her at six-thirty. 'How kind of him.'

"It's very kind of you." The thought of what caused his kindness overcame her determination not to weep. She saw Peter lying unconscious in a field somewhere unable to walk while snow covered him. She drew out a handkerchief from her purse, thinking, 'I must pull myself together and not weep like a weak sister.'

She sniffed. "But how did you know all this? It's not here." She tapped the telegram.

"A friend of his, also wounded, called me looking for you."

"How will I know where to go to meet him?"

Helmuth wrote the address of the *Reservelazarette* on a memo pad, ripped it off and handed it to her. He clipped his own card to the telegram. "This may help."

"I'll go there now. Is that all?"

He seemed about to say something more, then pointed to the ceiling above, crossed his lips with his forefinger and shook his head.

He said, "Goodbye," then leaned forward and whispered in her hair, "See you tomorrow night."

She had already left the office when she remembered the prisoners down below, so she went back in, and said, "Helmuth, those men who are working on the hotel, are they French?"

"Yes," he said.

"But I thought we had an armistice under which they went home."

"We do."

"One of them asked me for help."

He said, "They surrendered, they are being correctly treated. Why should they go home and sit by the fire when our men are being wounded at the front fighting to save Europe from Bolshevism?"

She opened her mouth to protest, and then realized he had been speaking for the microphone.

She walked out of the lobby feeling that life was a fantastic melodrama that was also as real as pavement. Peter's wound, Helmuth's strange behaviour, the tremendous defeat at Stalingrad, the hundreds of thousands of dead young men lying in the snow like garbage, terrible visions whirled around in her mind like a gathering tornado which she was unable to escape. She walked all the way with tears in her eyes from smoke and sorrow, to St. Hedwig's Hospital in Grosse Hamburgerstrasse.

In the street hundreds of women with bleak expressions were lined up, many carrying little parcels of food as if they expected to see their men right away inside the red brick building. She had to line up for more than an hour in the vicious cold, while the women talked, blowing on their hands, about the cut that week in the butter ration, the difficulty of finding fish or meat.

Inside, it was so cold the soldiers behind the counters were wearing balaclavas and thick boots, their breath visible as they talked over the cards and files. The PA announced that a train carrying wounded from the east had come in that morning, and visitors might be able to see their relatives the next morning in the hospital, but she must show her marriage certificate.

When she was allowed into the hospital the next morning, having waited outside for three hours, the corridors were loud with the radio broadcasting Beethoven's *Romance in G* into every ward. From time to time, the announcer came on to give the latest from "The Front," where "our glorious troops" had made "tremendous gains" against the enemy, who was "still fighting with his back to the wall." He finished by saying that "the crucial decision in this hour of supreme crisis was going to favour our magnificent soldiers, who were fighting with the courage of lions against a barbaric foe. Heil Hitler."

Then the horns of Wagner shouted down at the end of the ward, as she went along row after row of men on temporary stretcher-beds in corridors, on stair-landings, in the entrance hall, in empty offices. Human eyes looked at her from ovals of white bandage; faces pleading, wary, watchful, despairing, sorrowful, stared over rough beards from hairy heads wrapped in bandages, men were moaning, some were talking in voices they had to force over the music—it seemed as if they were all looking at her in hopes of release.

In the ward, at the bed number where he ought to be lying, she stared in horror at a grey blanket smooth over an empty bed, and turned and ran back to the nursing station to ask what had happened, certain he had died. Then she heard his voice calling "Clara, Clara," and turned to see him with a desperate smile, standing up on crutches leaning towards her in uniform, with the left trouser cut off revealing an enormous bandage. She burst into tears and ran to him and embraced him almost knocking him over as she wept onto his dirty lapel. "Oh God, Peter, when I saw the bed, it was empty, oh God, empty, oh God, thank God you're here . . . oh oh oh."

He held her as close as he could with one arm, tears in his eyes. The war, which had come home with him with its teeth still in his leg, vanished and he thought, 'I'll never go back.'

There was no room in the hospital for ambulatory cases so Peter was sent home with her, after she had been given a small paper package of sulfa powder, and instructed in how to change his bandages. Helmuth James was coming to dinner that night in the flat which Clara and Peter were renting from friends of the von Blüchers, so she went shopping with her string bag in the afternoon while Peter slept.

Helmuth James was in a despairing mood when he came to the flat at eight that evening. Clara handed him a glass of schnapps, telling him to drink it down to warm himself. As always, the first thing he did was to cover up the telephone. Then he asked Peter to describe what was happening in Russia. "This is a complete disaster. The army can not recover from this for at least three years. There was panic. We would cut down wave after wave of Russians running towards us in broad daylight and falling dead under our guns. We fired until the barrels warped and still the Russians came, and the recruits said, 'They'll never stop, it doesn't matter how many we kill, they keep coming.'"

The flat was cold, but she had lighted a fire of wooden sticks collected from bombed buildings to help keep Peter warm. He was seated in front of the fire in the grey and rose Jacobean wingback chair which was a wedding present from Nikolai Miloslavsky. His leg stiff in bandages rested on a small ottoman, crutches propped against it.

On the gas stove, she had a ragout of beef bones, carrots, potatoes, her own fresh pot-parsley and tomatoes she had preserved herself in August. She held a bottle of Valpolicella towards Peter for him to open. When he did not reach out his hand, she bent down and saw he had fallen asleep again. She glanced at Helmuth James with a fond smile, as if to say, 'You see, he belongs here safe at home, not at the front,' but he was launched on the war situation. She did not want to hear about the war any more, but he went on, "Every German will be made to realize that now we must make a supreme effort. Racial purity will count for everything now, that is going to be the new party line.

They'll demand total war, war to the extremes, such as no one has ever seen before. We must eliminate all undesirable foreign elements from our society for the maximum effort. The Jews and communists are nearly gone from Berlin, and soon all Germany will be cleansed. Then there will be no possibility of a second betrayal on the home front. That's what is starting to happen."

Clara shuddered thinking of her fate being linked to the Jews because of what she was doing. He got up and started to walk around on the carpet. "Canaris has warned us, the Gestapo is already watching us, you know we have been sending out messages discussing peace terms, quite illegally, if we are caught we are doomed. You must be more careful than ever. We have decided to suspend the U-boat shipments for the time being, unless we are certain of all the precautions." He looked rather sick, because he was feeling ashamed of his treachery, which did not sit well with his upright character.

"Another thing, they may be preparing a propaganda coup at your expense. One of the top ministers in Churchill's cabinet, Leo Amery, Secretary of State for India, has a son, John, who is a fascist, writing propaganda for Göbbels out at Babelsberg. Göbbels has only just discovered this and now he's planning to crow about it in the world press. It will be embarrassing for Churchill. And they may be planning the same thing for you.

"But how could they? I left the FO in '40."

"My dear Clara, how long have you lived here, without knowing these people? They might just use your photo and quote something you translated or wrote for me in '39. They might just arrest you and refuse to feed you until you sign something and pose for some pictures for them. If they find out you are here."

"But if they haven't so far, why would they now?"

"Because as I say, they are getting desperate, the war is going to get serious now, they are already pulling out all the stops. And when the allies get here . . . well."

"James, I've known the consequences from the beginning. All I have to do after the war is tell them what we've been doing. I'll be fine."

"God, you have such trust. We haven't had that in this country for generations. But I know from what my friends in Sweden tell me, that the allies are not going to negotiate with Hitler or any other German. There is no hope, they are going to smash us to bits this time."

Peter recovered slowly until, after three months he was able to walk, with a limp, but without pain. He was given a staff position in the Replacement Army, under Klaus, with temporary headquarters in the Bendlerstrasse, a kilometre from their flat.

At the Bendlerstrasse, in control of over a hundred thousand trained and well-armed men of the Replacement Army stationed throughout Germany, Klaus began to plan the assassination of Hitler, to be followed by a coup which he would engineer with Axel, Hans Bernd Gisevius, Peter, Helmuth James, and dozens of others. Clara volunteered to type the most important memos for Klaus, Peter and Helmuth James.

Once, during an air raid on a winter night when the neighbours were in the local shelter, she was in the garden, retrieving an oilskin pouch of documents from the compost heap, when the sirens started and she looked up at the Lancaster bombers crossing the moon, holding the papers in her hands warm from the compost, thinking, 'Down here we are doing our best, if you only knew what we are doing.'

London, March, 1943

Grant and Lovesick Lee crossed the Irish Sea by ferry in a storm that threw the ship around like *Sheguiandah* in a gale. Lee became known as Seasick Lee. They came down the gangplank in Holyhead far apart in spirit, for Lovesick was looking forward to sleeping with the first available girl in London, and Grant was so concentrated on Cat that he went into the first phone booth he could find while Lovesick stood, feet at odds with the rest of his body, smoking and grinning at the many girls who were at the quay welcoming friends.

The "trunk lines" were busy said the operator, so there would be a two-hour delay. Grant sent her a telegram, then they walked to the train station and bought tickets to London.

"Have you made up your mind where you're going to stay?" said Lovesick. He said he had an aunt in London who had invited them both.

"Thanks for the invite, but no, I'm going to Claridge's," said Grant, "you know, just in case." 'Just in case,' of course meant Cat.

Lee smirked revealing his rotted brown teeth and Grant regretted taking him even that far into his confidence. Lee amused him and repelled him. He felt uneasy, thinking that he was exploiting Lee for his humour while feeling disgusted by him. Travelling with him had been a bad idea, he decided. Lee's teeth were such a depressing sight that Grant winced whenever Lee smiled.

"You've got to do something about your teeth," he said. "The women will avoid you like the plague when they get a glimpse of those decaying chompers of yours. If you want to get laid, take my advice, go to a dentist when you get to London."

"Can you get laid at the dentist's here? I say, jolly good, up the Empire."

As soon as Grant got to his room at Claridge's, he called to Cat's house in Cadogan Square, but there was no answer, so he took a taxi.

He thought he heard air-raid sirens far away as they passed Hyde Park corner but he said nothing, hoping the driver would not notice. They pulled up in front of 52 Cadogan Square. Darkness was rising around them in the streets and the windows of the house were dark.

"'Ere we are then, guv," said the driver.

Grant looked out the car window at a tall narrow house with no front garden, and high steps leading up past a light-well, the sort of house that in Toronto said to him, 'poverty lives here.' He said, "This can't be it."

"Something wrong then?"

"The people I'm going to see are rich, so this can't be the house."

"Ware you from then, guv?" said the driver turning to look at him.

"Canada. In Toronto, this would be a poor man's house."

"Well, over 'ere, it's a rich man's 'ouse."

"Just wait here a mo' till I check, right?"

The maid who answered the door said, "Lady Treloar is in the country, but Miss Victoria will receive you in the drawing room." She curtsied and said, "Can you see your way?" He said, "Yes, fine," over his shoulder and took the stairs two at a time, turned along the darkened landing and went in the doorway of the drawing room, which was lit by several candles.

She was seated on the chesterfield beside a young man in civilian clothes, whose arm was around her. The young man took his arm away from Cat and stood up.

"Oh, Grant, we've just heard, Rosey is dead," she said and burst into tears. "Fell out of an aeroplane. You remember, I told you all about him in Canada. He was 23, it's so dreadful, so sweet and so young to die. And here you are, and I'm so . . . ." She put her face in her hands. The young man drew the handkerchief from his sleeve and offered it to her.

"Oh, that's terrible," Grant said, trying to remember who Rosey was. "Is there anything I can do?"

"Grant, I'm so sorry, may I present you to my friend, Viscount Ardagh. Scatters, my friend from Canada, Grant Giovanelli."

"I'm so glad to meet you," said Scatters in a low voice.

"How do you do," said Grant, fearing he had interrupted a love scene.

Scatters said, "Should I call your mother?"

"Oh, would you? Have you the number? She's in the country."

"Abingdon 280," said Grant, hoping she would not hold it against him that he had remembered it from four years before. But when she got through, she was told that Lady Treloar would not be back for a fortnight.

"Mother gone a fortnight?" said Cat. "She didn't say anything to me. Do sit down. Have some whiskey. I'm so sorry about this. How was your . . ." she hesitated, then smiled. "I was going to say trip, should I say 'How was your convoy?'"

She looked around as if for help and his heart went out to her.

"It was fine," he said.

"You're in the navy, I take it?" said Scatters.

"Yes."

"Canadian?"

"Yes."

"I see. Well done."

"Thank you."

"Thinking of joining up myself. Papa was in a cavalry regiment, but now it's all tanks and I'm a fearful driver so I'm rather thinking RAF. Nothing to crash into up there." He touched his finger to his chin and made the little musing murmur that the English utter to call attention to a witticism.

"Poor Rosey was in a bomber over Essen," said Cat. "They were hit and he just fell out through a hole in the floor."

"The plane got home?"

"Yes, but they didn't see a parachute."

He lifted his glass. "Here's to Rosey." As he said that, the air-raid sirens went off close by, the long low moan rising to a probing shriek. They all lifted their glasses and sipped.

Scatters said, "Let's all go to the Bagatelle before it gets bad."

"Oh no, should we?" she said, her face brightening. "Yes, let's, but we'll never get a taxi now."

"Oh my God," said Grant, "I told my driver to wait." He dashed downstairs and gave the patient driver a huge tip. Then Cat and Scatters and he piled in, and got to the Bagatelle, off Piccadilly Circus, a *boîte* with Irish waiters got up in the tight striped shirts and berets that Englishmen thought all true Frenchmen wore. The crowd was singing "Lili Marlene" in English as they entered and found a table. Scatters snapped open a gold cigarette case and offered Gold Flakes. Grant took one, Cat tried to light hers and then laid it aside with a frown.

The band began playing, drowning out the sound of air-raid sirens. She stood up and opened her arms to him making him almost dizzy with excitement, then danced close to him and whispered in his ear, "You rescued me, thanks. Scatters is so maudlin, and too in love. Don't you think love ought to make you feel better, not worse? He says I make him feel worse, he certainly does me. I think he thought my defences would be down because of poor Rosey, but there you are you see, nothing works as expected, you can't plan at all, can you? Not in wartime, I mean, unless for war, of course. But then he's only a child."

He moved his hand feeling her dress slip over her warm back. This was what he had dreamed of all across the Atlantic. "God, it's so good to see you Cat."

"All my admirers tell me how beautiful I am, straight off. Not you."

'Now why did I say that?' she thought, 'it sounds so boastful, but he makes me feel so wild, I can't help it.'

"I don't play by your rules."

"Have you written me anything?"

"I'm trying, in a desultory way. I don't get much time."

"The ones you sent me were wonderful."

"One was all right. The other was only a start on a poem."

She gazed at him, Rosey forgotten. "I hope you're not making notes about me."

"You should hope I am."

"Why?"

"Because then your quality will outlast yourself."

"I've thought of writing things too."

"Don't."

"Why not?"

"You think subjunctives are those little signal boxes beside railway tracks."

"Aren't they?" She laughed and pulled him closer.

"And you can't spell."

"Cad. How dare you notice. I'll never write to you again."

She leaned back in his arms. "Oh dear, I can't keep that promise, you write me such amusing letters. Some of my admirers have to wait months. Yours are the only ones I answer right away."

"You can't imagine what they mean to me at sea. Alone in that cabin. There are two things keeping me going, your letters and the crew. A wonderful bunch of men."

"And how do they get those letters to you at sea? Does a little plane fly over and drop them in your funnel?"

"I get them in port and take them with me and I reread them, dopey. Over and over." He kissed her on the cheek. "They make me love you."

"Oh dear, serious again, if I marry you will I have to stop writing to all those other poor dears who are just hoping and hoping for a misspelled letter from Cat to get them through a hot desert night?"

"You can write all you like, if it will help the war effort."

The music stopped and they went back to the table, where Scatters was seated staring across the room.

"Ah, there you are," he said, and slumped down.

The waiter popped the cork on a bottle of Krug and poured it out. Grant said, holding up his glass, "This is like New Year's Eve. I'm amazed, I thought London would be buttoned down."

"Perish the thought, never been to so many parties in my life," Scatters leaned forward through the haze of tobacco smoke and shouted over the music, "It's the dance of death." He laughed and leaned back looking around, cigarette at his fingertips. Scatters was the right name, Grant thought.

The band was playing "Moonlight Becomes You." Grant asked her to dance. She opened her arms to him again and held her forehead against his cheek.

"I missed you all this time," he said. "Every moment for years, I've missed you."

'How nice,' she thought and leaned back and smiled at him. She was feeling tipsy from the mixture of wine and sorrow. "It seems so odd," she said, "to be dancing when there is such bad news all around one. It all seems to come and go so fast, people are young one moment, and then they're dead."

"I know," he said, "We haven't much time, so I'll tell you, I love you."

Her arm jerked. 'That's the third time this month,' she thought.

"Say something," he whispered in her hair, his eyes closed.

"Can't say anything right now." She pressed her cheek against his as if in answer.

"Because of someone else?" He glanced around the room. Scatters was laughing and talking to the two girls at the adjoining table.

"No, no, because of the war, everything."

"I won't go back without something definite from you."

She said, "Then I'm glad, because you won't go back." She smiled, and he loved her more.

"I love you."

She hiccupped. "Oh dear."

"I've loved you for years, I love you now, I'll love you all my life. I love saying this."

"Sh," she said, thinking he should never have said such a thing while she was grieving, and then agreeing with him that none of them had enough time. She whispered, "Don't tempt fate," and touched her finger to his lips. She led him back to Scatters, who was now looking cross-eyed. She held out her bare pale arm and hand to him.

"Cheer up Scatters," she said, "have a dance with me. I've got the hiccups."

Grant sat smoking.

He stared at the dancers, trying to see her as she came in and out of sight, her green skirt twirling.

He ground out the cigarette and saw a poster on the wall of a sailor and a shiny young girl leaning close to him. The caption read, 'Tell NOBODY not even HER.' He bent over the table writing in his notebook, *See you after the war, PS Look at the poster,* and got up, feeling that he was endangering the best part of his life, went over to her, pushed the note in the hand she was holding on Scatters' shoulder, and left the room.

She could not read the note on the dim smoky dance floor, so when the music stopped, she took it to the table and uncrumpled it under the table light and read it. Then she got up and ran to the entrance and looked out into the street, but the night was misty and the streetlights were out. She could not see past ten yards. An old man was sweeping off his steps next door.

She stood bareshouldered in the cold air hiccupping, wanting to hear more of the wonderful daft words Grant had been saying, words that had made her laugh and shiver with delight and longing.

The next morning, she went to Claridge's and was told that he had checked out, leaving a forwarding address in Toronto. Hoping that he might come back for mail or something, she sat down in the dim Palm Court, where she had often sipped tea with her mother while listening to the string quartet that played each afternoon, and wondered what to do.

In came Lady Diana Cooper, a famous beauty, a wit and dear friend of the family. During the abdication crisis in 1936, she had made all England laugh by calling the King's mistress, "That American uptart." The room was dim because the tall windows had been blacked out and taped against air raids, and the lighting was low, but people noticed her, waved to her, smiled at her. She acknowledged them all with a slight bow and turn of her head as she sat down beside Cat and said in her hoarse, cigarette-raked voice, "Are you moping my dear? You look as if you're moping."

Cat gave a little wail.

Diana had often heard such tremulous wails from women before, every one elicited by what she called an *affaire de coeur*. She considered Victoria, remembering her own suite of admirers, all of them still her friends—"except the one I married, of course"—and decided that it was inconceivable that any man would have rejected Victoria. "Ah," said Diana. "A man. And you have rejected him."

Cat nodded.

"And now you're afraid you've lost him."

"Rather," she said.

"They always come back, my dear, they always come back. The poor dears, they can't help themselves. You're not to worry. Today you think you're bereft, but he will come back, you'll be much sought after, as I was," she said, pushing a cigarette into a long ivory holder. "Bear in mind one cardinal principle."

She smiled, teasing, waiting to be asked, but Victoria was still wondering how to find Grant and did not think to ask. Diana leaned forward and said, "Many will save you from one."

Victoria cocked her head. "I know you already have a coterie my dear. You must receive dozens of proposals and not a few propositions. Make the least of them, I say."

Cat looked at her. Diana shrugged and said, "Be light as the morning breeze, after all you are young young young, and to be young is very heaven. Do not make up your mind, your mind will be made up for you by events and feelings you can not control. By which I mean, those which you no longer wish to control."

She sat back, puffed on her cigarette held between forefinger and thumb, her elbow raised, ordered tea and smiled at Cat, who was thinking that she was rouged too much, perhaps because she was becoming wrinkled.

"Your mother is worried about *un beau Canadien* who troubles your dreams, I understand. If he's anything like Max, I say snap him up. But make him wait a bit first, men are like game you know, always better if they're kept hanging about in the cold for a bit before consumption."

"I think I've made him wait too long already."

"Nonsense. They never go bad. They're bad already. Now, come along with me to Max tonight, at Cherkley."

"No, thank you, dear Diana, you're such fun, you did cheer me up, I've so much to do. I'm on duty tonight, I'm a nurse now, you know, at Guy's."

"My dear, I was there in 1917. How wonderful. Take care of your feet. I must be off," and she left in a cloud of cigarette smoke and perfume saying goodbye to friends around the room, who waved and smiled at her.

Diana walked out feeling like a traitor. Flavia had taken her into her confidence on the subject of the unsuitable Canadian, and now she was advising Cat to take him.

Lord Beaverbrook liked to entertain young Empire soldiers, sailors and airmen at his great house at Cherkley, just outside London. It was part of his love of the British Empire, to give these young men and women, all far from home and risking their lives for a cause he loved, happy times, and a good dinner. This evening was Canada Night, and he had invited both the Giovanellis, and three of their friends—Red Ed Burns, Bernie Hallett and Lovesick Lee.

Jack had met Lord Beaverbrook several times in Toronto, and always found him funny and charming, so he came to Cherkley expecting a good time, not realizing that his brother would be there, along with Lovesick Lee, Ed Burns and Professor Hallett. He was delighted to see them getting down from one of Lord Beaverbrook's motors, having been driven down from London.

"Where were you, how are you, when did you get here, how long have you got," they were saying as they brought out their cases, dunnage bags, gifts of food and whiskey from home, all smiles and questions and high enthusiasm, except for Lee, looking sardonic as usual. Ed Burns, favouring a strained back from heaving a jeep out of the muck at Aldershot, was making fun of the great wealth of their host. They saw Beaverbrook standing with Lady Diana Cooper framed in the doorway at the top of the stone steps, grinning his gnome-grin and saying, "Welcome home, tonight this is Canadian territory."

Beaverbrook led them into the great hall, two storeys high, flanked by ornate staircases, introducing them on the fly to Lady Cooper.

In the elegant drawing room, where the British guests were standing drinking cocktails or whiskey, Diana saw a tall handsome young naval officer and thought, 'Something is different about him.' Grant greeted his kid brother Jack with a big smile, putting his arm round Jack's shoulder, and she did not wonder he troubled Cat's dreams.

Diana drew Max aside and asked him to arrange the table so that she might sit beside Grant, and he said with an impish look, "It's already done, but I'm afraid you will not find him fit for your consumption."

"Why not?"

"I'm afraid he's an Avey." This was a code word between them for Another Very Earnest Youth. They were making the world uninhabitable for Aveys by excessive fun.

"Oh dear. I had hopes for him."

She took her seat beside Grant with not much hope. She had once told Max that, "I used to think that Canadians are just Scotchmen who have sobered up, until I met you." But she had not changed her opinion of Canadians—only of Max.

Grant said very little and drank too much. Diana left him alone for most of the dinner and directed her light across Grant to Max at the head of the table.

Then with the shape she made her first effort. Having talked a great deal herself, she whispered to him, "Would you like to get a word in edgewise?" and smiled. His thoughts had shifted from regrets over the way he had left Cat, and wondering how he might recoup before leaving next morning, to distaste for these people who were living in ease and luxury supplied by the men who fought the U-boats and storms of the north Atlantic.

"Tell me, what do you think of our little island? Are we worth risking your life for?"

"Mmm," he said, satirizing the evasive hum with which upper-class English dismiss a comment without commenting.

"Dear boy, do tell, I suspect you're concealing something delicious."

She amused him, so he decided to talk. "It was very peculiar. I arrived at Claridge's yesterday, in uniform, with my seabag. As I was starting to get out of the taxi, a man in a cockatoo suit leaned over me with a comic opera hat on and said, 'This is Claridge's, sir.' I said, 'I'm sure it is,' and started to get out, but he blocked my way. He said, 'Are you sure it is Claridge's you wanted, sir?' and I said 'It is, and you're in my way.' I surged past him and several other cockatoos surrounded me as I went to the desk . . . ."

A very old general across the table said, "There are no cockatoos in Claridge's, young man. A cockatoo is a kind of parrot, I believe." He glared at Grant.

"Yes sir," said Grant, "I think they were afraid other guests might be contaminated by the sight of a scruffy seabag. At any rate, the desk clerk said, 'Have you a reservation, sir?' and I said, 'Yes, one was made in my name, Grant Giovanelli, by the Lord Privy Seal, Lord Beaverbrook.' 'Oh, I see, sir, Lord Beaverbrook, of course, sir,' said the clerk in that officious sycophancy that oils the wheels of Empire. And now transformed into a young rajah by the magic of class snobbery, I was escorted to my chamber by two cockatoos, vying for favour, and a tip."

This delighted Diana. Lord Beaverbrook was looking at Grant, his broad mouth stretched wide in an approving smile. The general glared.

Diana took him into the drawing room and sat him down beside her on the sofa, allowing her red silk skirt to flare wide over his near knee taking possession of him.

Lord Beaverbrook told an anecdote. "It is no secret that we are short of aluminium, and yesterday I remembered that my old friend Cameron Bannatyne, grandfather of young Grant here, had bought a warehouse full of aluminium bars in the first week of the war, so I cabled him asking if he still had them in his warehouse and here is his reply as transcribed in my office."

He reached into his pocket for the cable, settled his spectacles on his wide flat nose and read, "REURS I HAVE TEN THOUSAND BARS IN MY WHOREHOUSE IN SUDBURY. YOU ARE WELCOME TO THEM ALL CO BANNATYNE

All the guests roared with laughter and Beaverbrook peered over his spectacles round the room enjoying the fun.

Grant laughed despite himself, but he was feeling very uncomfortable in this room filled with women in evening gowns and men in black tie enjoying themselves so much. Lady Cooper patted his knee. "Cheer up, dear boy."

"You see, I was thinking," he said, "of this dinner and everyone so nice, and how the food we ate tonight was brought across the Atlantic by men who are quite likely to die on fire in the ocean."

Lady Cooper stared at him, deciding that perhaps he was not right for Cat after all, and Beaverbrook said, "Now now, young fellow me lad, I assure you the fowl was not so old as you imply, and the brandy is not from the New World."

"All the same," said Lady Cooper, "he has a point. We must listen to these young men. After all for whom are we fighting this war, if not for youth?"

"All you fight is the battle of the dinner table," Ed Burns said. "The young fight the war. And I assure you that we shall clean up this mess that your generation made, and make damn sure there is not another."

Everyone in the room was silent. Grant stared at his knees feeling embarrassed at having provoked Ed's outburst. Lovesick sniggered and stored this away for future use. Bernie Hallett, normally in awe of Ed, was angered by this unparalleled rudeness, and said,

"If you want to teach history, Ed you must first let history teach you."

"What's that supposed to mean?" Ed so often looked down on Bernie that he usually scoffed when his friend made a point.

"You keep saying that after the war, the Marxists take over, but just look at Russia, what a mess communism has made there."

"The wrong people are in charge," Ed said. But Jack, familiar with this argument, said, "It's communism all the same. Blaming the leaders doesn't wash. There's something wrong with the system, not the leaders." He felt very daring for stepping out against his professor. Ed started to explain the difference between the systems, but people kept interrupting him, and he could not finish.

In a moment's quiet, Beaverbrook said, "The professor is right, it is a mess, but I doubt that the propagation of Trotskyite class warfare will change anything but the names of the gangs at war."

"Russia is a hate-filled mess," said Bernie, who sympathized with the Christians, who had been persecuted there since 1919. "And yet look at the way they are fighting." This vague admission of some faint merit in the communist rulers was just the sort of fair-minded nonsequitur that made Ed sigh over Bernie.

Grant smiled at his kid brother, thinking he was looking very fit, and sat back, getting himself drunk so he would not think about Cat. Diana decided that even if Grant was an Avey sometimes, he was also amusing and handsome. She said, "I understand you are a friend of Cat Treloar?"

"Yes, or I was, till last night. Do you know her?"

"Very well indeed, since a child. What happened last night?"

"I appear to be in a very grumpy mood these days. I offended her. That is, I did if she cares enough to be offended by me."

"Dear boy, she cares a great deal."

"How do you know?"

"I saw her in Claridge's today. She was looking for you."

Grant sat up. "Really?"

"Yes, she was most eager to see you. And sorry about last night."

"Oh my God, can I call her from here?"

"She's on duty tonight at Guy's or she'd be here."

He frowned. "If I went up to London now?"

"You couldn't see her at Guy's, and you could never get past the dragon at the gates in Cadogan Square." Grant knew she meant Flavia, and forgot that Flavia was away.

"You must write to her right away. Care of my London house. I shouldn't tell you this, but Flavia so disapproves of you that she has told the butler from now on to stop all your letters. So you must write via me. Here," and she gave him her card. "And, dear boy? May I say something?"

"Thank you, thank you for this. Yes, of course." He looked at her and she looked at his eyes, and over his face, touched by the eager youth being turned bitter by the war. "Don't be quite so hard on us, we're all doing our best in our different ways," she said and patted his hand.

He was at his omelette and oatmeal in the morning room with the *Times* open before him, reading about the Eighth Army pursuing Rommel through Tunisia when he heard tires on the gravel, then the front door opening and the butler's voice at the door answered by a young woman who sounded like Victoria.

The truth of what Lady Cooper had said the night before was coming in the door towards him. Cat was looking tired and anxious. He got up and said, "Good morning. What brings you here," as she said, "Grant," and held out her hand towards him so it seemed to him for a moment a stage gesture. But the anxious smile on her face made him so happy that he lost the wariness he had felt on seeing her, and embraced her, bending down so as not to force her head back and kissed her. She shuddered. She had never been kissed with such tenderness before, and her body leaped against him.

He whispered in her hair, "Can we get married, I love you so much."

"Yes, if you want to."

"Of course I want to, more than anything in the world. But do you?"

"Well, yes."

"You sound doubtful."

"It's just Mother."

"Bother your mother, it's not her I'm marrying."

"She'll bother us."

"Not when we're married." She smelled the porridge on his breath.

"When?"

"Oh God, I only have two more hours."

"Oh no, can't we ring up someone?"

"For what?"

"For more leave?" She was looking at him with such appeal that he hated saying, "It's my ship. I'm the captain now. The men are all returning there now, I can't let them down."

From the side of his eye, he saw someone move in the doorway. Lady Diana Cooper was standing there with Lord Beaverbrook. He wondered how much they had seen and then decided they were already part of the wedding party.

All the way back to Derry he thought about her, but when he got to the ship he thought only of what he had to do. By the time he had walked up the gangplank, saluted, and gone to his sea-cabin behind the wheel-house, he was as remote from her as he had been off Iceland, except that now he felt a warm banked memory of good news awaiting him like the smell of new-baked bread.

The next day he reported to the vice-admiral in charge of the Canadian ships in port, and handed him a typed report of the conversation he had had in Dublin with the German about the new schnorkel U-boats. Then he was ordered out to sea again, escorting a convoy south to Gibraltar.

Zossen, near Berlin, March, 1943

Klaus was summoned to Army Headquarters at Zossen in March. He got down from the train at the little station at Münsdorf south of Berlin, then walked past army truck-traffic to the enormous pine wood plantation concealing the buildings. He had last been here in July, 1939, to convert his regiment from cavalry to tanks, but all he recognized now was the road from Münsdorf and the forest.

Throughout the woods were gigantic grey concrete towers shaped like the heads of half-buried rockets pointing up from the pine-needled earth. These were emergency exits from the acres of air-raid shelters lying ten metres under his feet. They were part of the smoky, noisy, dusty construction going on all round him, of buildings, roads, flak towers, radar assemblies.

The Afrika Korps Section was housed in a building like a nineteenth-century Schloss, with casement windows, an elegant fanlight over the broad wooden door. It made him think of the time when war was cavalry and infantry. He paused there, remembering the years of training he had had on horseback, now all pointless.

A tall grey-haired colonel with a swastika armband came to the duty officer's desk, thrust out his hand and said, "Heil Hitler." Colonel Felsen took him to the map room and began to speak, picking his way from word to word. He said, "The strategic situation is very encouraging. Our aim is to reinforce here, here and here, with units of the 21st Panzer, including 88 millimetre flak-anti tank guns. Then we shall land a parachute and glider force behind the British at Mareth, followed by shelling from Italian ships off Zarat, here. Then the Führer will force Franco to help us take Gibraltar. A small force will suffice, the British will panic and retreat from Mareth, and there you have it, Americans and British surrounded, cut off, disorganized. Then we roll the Americans back into the sea. They have no taste for battle. Any questions?"

"Sir, have the supplies arrived, or are they on the way?"

"Your job is not to worry about supplies."

"What is my job, sir?"

"You will emplane at Rangsdorf to fly to a high-level meeting. Do you understand?" A ghastly expression wriggled onto his face, and Klaus thought he was sick. Felsen said, "You are to have the supreme honour." He saluted again and walked out of the room.

Klaus realized that Felsen had been smiling because he was to see Hitler. He walked along the path under the tall old pines. 'That fool. We'll roll them back into the sea, eh? Why didn't We do it back when it might have been possible, in November. And who are We? Vichy? The Italians? So this is what we have come to, relying on defeated armies to pull our chestnuts out of the fire. This must stop. But how?' He decided to memorize every detail of every guard unit, check-point and ID requirement at every stage on the way to Rastenburg until he could touch Hitler's chest. The next time he went, he would carry a bomb.

At the entrance gate to Rangsdorf he was checked by Luftwaffe personnel, who were very perfunctory, no doubt because he was in an OKW staff car.

Brandenburg, then Lower Pomerania and finally Prussia lay out sparkling white. Tree shadows angled from the roads like fish bones from the spine. Tiny trains tugged their own shadows along the snow. Here and there, a dark blue river clotted with ice meandered north to the Baltic. As they came closer to eastern Prussia, the pine woods spread like dark fur round the white shoulders of the lakes.

From the airfield, cleared of snow and shining in the bright sun, he was chauffeured through the pines to the complex of buildings round the Führer Bunker, a low flat-roofed grey building stippled with the shadows of the pines. A group of officers was seated in the sun on deck chairs outside the Führer-mess, smoking and drinking. Beside them a table lay spread with canapes and drinks under an oak tree still covered with brown leaves.

He was introduced to several of the generals who welcomed him, and offered beer and smoked salmon.

At 12:15, as arranged, he was taken into the Führer bunker, which still smelled of the pine-wood drying in the walls, checked again by SS guards, then ushered to the door of the map room, over which was printed the motto, *Wer Kampft Hat Recht.*

The Führer, in an unbelted field grey tunic, standing five inches shorter than Klaus, shook his hand, and with an inquiring look on his face, glanced from the Ritter Kreuz medal at Klaus' neck, upward into Klaus' face, while he held on to his hand. The Führer's grip was strong, his eyes blue and very concentrated on Klaus, who had to will himself to keep his gaze unflinching.

Hitler was seeking something in the face before him. He boasted about his ability to read character, but he looked in faces to find what he could use—hesitation betraying weakness, confidence displaying strength. Nothing else concerned him. Only he was of interest to him. He believed that everything happened because of his irresistible will and for no other reason. Yet he also said, "I do not want war, war has been forced upon me." He complained of the traitors around him, who frustrated his irresistible will.

He let go of Klaus' hand, having decided that here was an intelligent Nordic type, strong-willed but obedient. This man was familiar, but he did not know why.

Hitler turned and began speaking, as he led Klaus with one hand on his arm to the huge map table. His left hand capturing Gibraltar, rapping Tunis with his right, Hitler told Klaus he needed a trustworthy man to convey his orders to Rommel, Kesselring and von Arnim in Africa, and to report on the situation. Klaus understood that he had to report to Hitler what he wanted to hear and nothing else, regardless of what he saw in Africa.

"You will carry my orders to Rommel. He will have all the reinforcements he needs, 200 tanks have left the Stuttgart tank park for Naples, they will arrive in two days, plus 30 of our new high-velocity 88s and all the gasoline he needs."

He analyzed the North African situation, giving many details of the impending attack, code-named Zebra.

"I will attack first the British, who will retreat as they did at Dunkerque, Narvik, Dakar, Greece, Crete, Singapore, Hong Kong, Tobruk. I will send in gliders, parachute troops and panzers." As he was finishing, the urgent telephone rang, and Schmundt handed it to Hitler. "Most urgent, *mein Führer,* your report on the American situation."

Hitler took the phone, said, *"Ja"* and listened for several minutes as the assembled Wehrmacht generals standing round the table whispered among themselves. They seemed tense and upset, their faces grey and unhealthy looking. Nobody smiled, nobody spoke aloud until first addressed by Hitler.

Hitler snapped a few questions into the phone, then hung up, pointing to the Kasserine Pass, and said, "The situation has changed to my advantage. The Americans and French have failed to link up, they are both out of gasoline and I shall take advantage of this new situation by Plan Elephant," and he went on to identify the units, commanders, targets and timing of Plan Elephant.

"Rommel must bring back the new panzers from Mareth and send them through the Kasserine Pass, between the American and French armies, exploiting the complete disorganization behind the American lines. Attack to begin in two days. That is my irrevocable decision."

"But *mein Führer,*" said Schmundt, as the generals round the table began to whisper more audibly, looking distressed or angry. "What is it?" said Hitler, studying the map.

"The tank transporters have just arrived back in Tunis, half of them need major repairs. Their transmissions are damaged by the sand. It is not possible."

"To a National Socialist, all things are possible."

"Then let us order the transmissions to join the Party," said a voice.

Hitler glanced up, surveying the faces that were all impassive on rigid bodies. "It is not a bad idea, they are more use than any ten of my lily-livered generals around this table."

He recited to Klaus the number of new 88s, tanks, long-barrelled Panthers, ME 109s and so forth, available to von Arnim in the north and to Rommel in the south. Allowing one extra day to repair the transporters, he showed how Rommel's tanks could be transferred in one night without the Allies noticing, assembled east of Kasserine and then sent into battle after a brief artillery bombardment. He sketched in the development of the battle to the point where the Americans retreated confused to the seacoast, asking for a cease-fire. Then he glanced at Klaus and said, "Now, recite that to me as you will to von Arnim and to Rommel."

Klaus recited it all, at which Hitler said, "Good. You'll do. Now here is the hard part." He outlined the morale situation in the theatre. Troop morale remained high, he said, despite the many retreats and the lack of supplies, because the men had tremendous faith in Rommel, whom they regarded as a saint of battle. But the Field Marshal was losing faith in himself, said Hitler. Von Arnim was hostile to Rommel, for this reason and because he judged Rommel to have given up against Montgomery.

"It will be your mission to restore his self-confidence and to make sure that he and von Arnim understand with perfect clarity that they are to follow my orders. If these orders are followed, success will follow as the day the night."

He urged Klaus to carry all this out with National Socialist faith and vigour. "It is this faith that will carry us through difficult times as it has before," he said staring up into Klaus' face. As a goodbye, he said, "No papers, take it all in your head. It is the best way."

Schmundt leaned close to Hitler and said, "*Mein Führer*, Plan Elephant takes nearly all the units you assigned earlier to Plan Zebra."

"What do you mean?" said Hitler.

"Plan Zebra must be cancelled."

"Yes, no, what is it? But of course it is cancelled." He was starting to ask, "Didn't I say that?" and covered up with a diversion. He stepped back, said "Enough," waved his hand at the table, and said, "Army Group south," at which two aides glided aside the Tunisian map and floated in the map of southern Russia.

Klaus went back outside, dazzled by the sunlight, amazed by the hostility around the table. He was depressed by Hitler's confusion and indecision, and at the same time impressed by Hitler's grasp of detail. The silent side of him was advising, 'Detail, yes, but the Americans, who came from 4,000 miles away, can not be disorganized, will not run into the sea. How can Rommel give von Arnim reinforcements, while facing the British who have just driven him back a thousand kilometres? This is another Stalingrad in the making. This man's idea of war is to reinforce failure.'

He flew back to Berlin making cryptic notes as he went, of all the points he would have to deal with when he returned here one day soon with a bomb.

That night, after the usual film, Hitler asked Schmundt about von Zollerndorf, and as Schmundt started to read from the file, Hitler remembered that six years before, Klaus had posed for the painting in a famous recruiting poster idealizing the handsome, blue-eyed, blond young Aryan type. "Yes," said Hitler, "that's it. But Zollerndorf has brown hair and brown eyes." He frowned and then laughed. "Well, even a loyal National Socialist painter deserves his artistic freedom."

Klaus was flown in Hitler's personal Focke-Wulf Kondor to Naples, where he changed to a JU 52 transport for the long flight over the sea to Tunis. They had to fly at night, because British aircraft carriers were patrolling the area, so he landed just before dawn.

At the airfield, he saw Admiral Canaris, head of the Abwehr, getting out of his plane, which had just landed. He exchanged salutes, and Canaris introduced himself. "I just flew in from Greece to interview some French officers we caught down south last week. May I offer you a lift? I appear to have the only car on the field."

Klaus looked round the field, where there was no transport waiting for him. He knew Canaris was under surveillance by the Gestapo, so it would be dangerous to befriend him. But there was no other car in sight, and no message waiting for him. "No car, no message, and I'm in a big rush," he said. "Damn fools."

"Where are you going?" Canaris asked, although he had been informed by his own agents about Zollerndorf's mission to Rommel. "South, towards Sfax," said Klaus.

Canaris was thinking that Klaus was an arrogant fellow, and might therefore be indiscreet. He decided to test him. "I would have thought that someone travelling on Emil's orders would have at least a Mercedes waiting for him," said Canaris, using the name Emil for Hitler, a code-name known only to conspirators.

"It makes no difference even if the orders come straight from Rastenburg, the army still screws up . . ." Klaus said, then realized he had been trapped into admitting to a stranger that he knew the significance of the name Emil. He shut his mouth. 'Damn,' he thought, 'this sly devil has caught me out in ten seconds. I must be more careful.'

The dusty streets of Tunis were turning russet and pink with the light from the sun dawning over their left shoulders as they drove.

Canaris said, "There's a wonderful Roman Colosseum at Touga not far to the west of here which we might visit. Much bigger than the Colosseum in Rome. Would that interest you?"

"It would," said Klaus, shocked at such a trivial suggestion. "But I'm afraid I haven't time. I am on a Führer mission. As you divined." He pressed his lips together and sat silent.

Canaris sat for a while, a little disappointed, not by the seriousness of the young man, but that it was wasted on such a worthless end. They rode for a few miles in silence and then Canaris lit a cigarette, offering Klaus one, and said, "What do you think of our situation?"

"We may have to put the top up," said Klaus, glancing up at the hot sky.

Canaris laughed and went on, "In the war, I was thinking."

"Ah yes, the war," said Klaus as if it had just occurred to him. Then he decided Canaris was testing him. He had heard this handsome, charming, witty man, who had lots of girlfriends, was passing top-level military information over secret telephone lines built by the Wehrmacht Signal Corps, to allied agents in Switzerland. Klaus scarcely could believe this, and now that he was talking to Canaris for the first time, he saw a foppish dilettante with too shrewd a wit, and no overt sign of the courage or high moral purpose necessary for such dangerous work. Could he be spying for the Gestapo?

"I think we must not do anything to prolong this war by even one day," said Klaus.

"Yes, my thoughts exactly," said Canaris, and turned away looking over the side of the car. "I said that to our beloved leader, and the day afterwards he declared war on the USA. Did you meet him?"

"Yes."

"Did he stare you in the eye for a long time as if he was searching for something?"

"Yes."

"Did you decide what he was looking for?"

"I don't know. Fear?"

"No."

"Admiration?"

"Obedience. And what did he find?"

"I'm here," Klaus said. He motioned towards the driver's uniformed back, and gave Canaris a look which conveyed his uneasiness at the way the conversation was going. Canaris said, "Never mind, he's stone deaf. Artillery."

Soon they were hot, they had their dark glasses on, and their shirt collars open as they curved along the verdant valleys under the brown mountains, laced here and there with silvery-green olive tree terraces.

As they emerged from one dusty flat-roofed village, where the Arab boys stood with their *osselets* in their hands gaping at them, they saw ahead a flock of sheep crossing the road. As they slowed to let the sheep pass, Canaris stood up, gave the Nazi salute, then sat down. Klaus stared at him. "When did you start saluting sheep, Admiral?" he asked.

"You never know where you'll see a party bigwig." He turned and smiled at Klaus, who decided that after all, he must be genuine. 'No National Socialist could make a joke like that,' and so, quite late, he laughed, which made Canaris think, 'Well, it doesn't take much to get a reputation for genius in the Wehrmacht now.'

He said, "What are you reading these days, Colonel?"

"Memos, reports, statistics, you know." He sighed, thinking of his days at Göttingen when he had gobbled up Göthe, Catullus, Ovid, and Shakespeare in English.

"No, I meant for your mind," Canaris said, turning to smile at him.

"In the army, it is best if it is not known that you have a mind."

Canaris laughed, and Klaus went on about the book he was reading, Robert Musil's banned novel, *The Man Without Qualities*. "I don't know why it was proscribed."

"Exactly," said Canaris. "It is a book without qualities."

"Indeed, my opinion. The man is a fool, maybe a dangerous fool."

"Why so?" asked Canaris with extreme interest, now pulling his peaked cap down to shade his eyes so he could see Klaus better.

"Well, because all the characters and the writing itself, are enervated, their behaviour is dilatory, energy as a human characteristic is mocked, intelligence is made to seem like a matter of endless hair-splitting . . . ."

"Surely that is his point, that the fetid drawing rooms of the *fin-de-siècle* Austro-Hungarians bred a fungus that infected the whole empire."

"Yes, but Musil is a dolt, so he is himself spreading anomie to his readers in Germany."

"Ah, you are a moralist, then?"

Klaus had never thought of himself that way. "I would have said so, in the days when I was . . ." he stopped. He had been about to say, "when I was attracted to Hitler," but this seemed too dangerous, so he finished by saying, "when I was naive," and wondered if this too-bright little man would guess what he meant.

"And now?"

"Now, I don't know—I see what is happening on the eastern front, and all morality seems to collapse under the impact of those irreplaceable losses."

"I don't follow, what do you mean?"

Canaris' quick little blue eyes, emphasized by his white-blond eyebrows, were firm on his face, and he was holding on to the strap on the door to keep himself still in the bouncing car. Klaus decided to trust Canaris. He said in a low voice, "I mean, we are losing the war, and that moralizing idiot at Rastenburg is the cause of it all."

"It seems that we agree on more than literature," said Canaris. He let go of the strap and sat back with a sigh, thinking that Klaus was bleak. And that he would do.

Klaus parted from Canaris with a warm handshake and promises to meet again soon in Berlin.

As Klaus walked away, Canaris thought, 'Von Zollerndorf has the smell of death on him.'

Klaus walked across the road to Rommel's trailer, hidden under a shadowy canopy of camouflage netting strewn with olive branches. As he walked up to the door of the trailer, a soldier in a strange uniform but with a kepi came running out the door, down the three wooden steps almost at Klaus' feet. A German officer with red hair and wearing a grey cape stood in the door aiming his revolver at the soldier. He pulled the trigger, the soldier was punched in the spine and fell forward. He lay without moving.

The officer replaced the revolver in his holster and walked back into the trailer. Two sergeants came rushing out and as Klaus walked in bewildered, the red-haired officer called out, "Get him out of here before he starts to stink even more. And you, Gruber, search him and take away his weapon."

He turned to Klaus. "What do you want?" he said irritably.

Klaus said, "I have been ordered to report to General Rommel."

"He has gone to the front."

The sergeant came to the door behind him and the red-haired officer, ignoring Klaus, said to the sergeant, "Now what?"

"Here are his things, sir. There was no weapon."

The officer said, "Are you doubting the word of a German officer?"

"No sir."

"Then do not contradict me. Of course there was a weapon. If there isn't one, find one."

"Sir, I was just reporting what I found."

"Then report finding a weapon."

"Yes sir. What weapon shall I report?"

"Are you a dolt? Are you trying to ridicule me? Eh?" He smacked his gloves on his hand.

"No sir."

"Then see to it. Report a dagger."

"Yes sir," said the sergeant in relief. "Shall I buy a dagger, sir?"

"Why in hell would you buy a dagger, you ass-faced cretin?"

"Sir, to put in the bag with his ID and his rings and his money, for the report."

"Put it in the report, not in the bag. Now get out of here before I put you in a bag."

"Yes sir." Sergeant Gruber saluted and left.

Klaus who had been about to remonstrate with the officer, thought, 'If I say anything, it will cause an incident, and I am already in deep enough. Better let this pass and go after the bigger prey.' But then he could not help himself. He said, "I shall report this incident as soon as I return."

The captain looked at him without expression. He said nothing. Klaus waited.

"Papers," said the captain, and now Klaus noticed the name plate on the desk. Major Peter Garstang. He offered his *soldbuch* and the orders Schmundt had given him.

Garstang tossed them back so Klaus had to make a grab for them before they fell on the floor.

"You'll ride on our convoy. We're moving up in about 20 minutes. Try not to be an asshole if you see somebody shoot a Brit. The man was a German political refugee, which means Jew, captured while serving with the so-called Free French Army, and all such are to be shot on sight." He smiled, his crooked buck teeth protruding between his very red lips. "According to the orders of the man who sent you here."

"I want to see the order," said Klaus.

Garstang handed him the order entitled, "Most Secret, Most Important, Officers Only, OKW/WFSt/Qu an Panzer Armee Afrika 9.6.1942." The message read:

According to reports to hand there are said to be numerous German political refugees with the Free French units in Africa. The Führer has ordered that the severest measures are to be taken against those concerned. They are therefore to be mercilessly wiped out in battle, and in cases where they escape being killed in battle, a military sentence is to be pronounced immediately by the nearest German officer and they are to be shot out of hand, unless they have to be temporarily retained for Intelligence purposes. Commanding officers are to be told orally. This order must not be forwarded in writing.

Captain Raabke, one of Rommel's supply officers, led Klaus out of the trailer towards the waiting convoy of trucks, each armed with a machine gun on the cab-roof. Raabke said, "Please don't think we are all like him," with a slight motion of his head backwards to indicate Garstang, who was following them. "The General himself does not know what that man is doing."

"He showed me the Führer order," said Klaus. He felt betrayed: never before had he seen documentary evidence of Nazi racist policy.

"Garstang is the only one who obeys it," Raabke whispered, "talk to me later about this."

They set off in a convoy of four trucks. About a mile south of the town, three dark dots over the western hills developed into Hurricanes with rockets bulging under their wings. The planes circled behind them and flew straight up toward them.

The drivers stopped and the machine gunners crouched and began to fire. Garstang stepped down from the cab of his truck and ran over to the olive grove that bordered the road, machine gun bullets whacking the road behind him. The gunner in Klaus' truck was hit, and fell over the side of the truck and slammed onto the gravel where he lay still. Klaus jumped to replace him as the Hurricanes climbed, turned and roared back from the rear for a second strafe.

Klaus was on the gun, firing at the planes. For a moment, it was like tennis—the ball was suspended in the air before him, and he hit it hard. He got the last Hurricane in the engine, smoke erupted, the plane cartwheeled and crashed.

Klaus stood up to cheer, but his hand was stuck to the gun. He pulled and saw a bloody mess stuck on the handle of the gun, and bits of bone and skin hanging from the end of his sleeve where his right hand had been. There was something wrong with his head—he could see only one hemisphere, to his left. He tried to get down from the gun mounting, and fell onto the road, feeling part of his hand tearing off.

The remaining Hurricanes disappeared over the hills to the south, men were rushing around the trucks, some screaming. Klaus was lying on his back on the road thinking he was falling down a tunnel under the truck wondering how badly he was wounded, deciding that it was very bad.

"Careful, old chap, we'll soon have you right," a voice whispered, lifting his head to give him a drink. Beyond the kindly man he saw Garstang standing, looking down at him. Garstang said from far away, "Is the truck all right?"

His right arm ended in a stump at the wrist, he had lost his left little finger, two other fingers were broken and cut and his right eye was blind, under a black patch. He lay in bed in hospital, thinking 'I shall climb out of this hole, I will not let this beat me. I shall climb out of this hole, I will not let this beat me.'

The pain was relentless but he refused the morphine, even the codeine that was offered, thinking he would recover more quickly without drugs debilitating his body. Doctor Hans Garms, the best neurosurgeon in Germany, was flown over from Naples to operate on 'The Führer's patient,' who had just been awarded Oak Leaves to his Iron Cross. When Garms, a slight, sallow man with narrow dark eyes described the operation to reconnect the nerves in his remaining fingers, which were now splinted useless, Klaus agreed, but stipulated that he would not be given anaesthetic.

The doctor tried to persuade him. "The pain will be inconceivable. I will be operating on the most sensitive part of your body, fingers and fingernails, the palm. We can not have you wriggling about."

"I will not wriggle. Clamp me down if you wish."

"All right then, if you will not have a general, you will have a local. That's for sure."

"Don't you see? No anaesthetic. None at all."

His method of dealing with pain he had learned long before, as a boy in school. The schoolmaster beat the boys. The first time Klaus was called in—for breaking a window with a ball—he told the master he had not thrown the ball. But he refused to say who had done it. The master beat him bloody, but Klaus would not tell. He vowed to himself, 'I'll die rather than give in to this injustice.'

From then on, Klaus regarded these beatings as a contest: he would not give in to the master regardless of the pain. He practiced an evasion technique he invented during one of the beatings. He stared at a bright coin lying on the study floor and said to himself, 'I am not here, I have gone through that round window to the clouds.' The boy left behind in the study sent him messages but he refused to answer. He was another boy in another place, filled with light and loud music.

After that, he practiced absenting himself from difficulties, argument, boredom, delays in trains, by first concentrating on a bright light—in the sky, off a belt-buckle, in a window, or at night, a star. He then repeated to himself, 'I have gone there.' From the first day on, Klaus knew the master could never make him do anything against his own will. By the age of 11, he had graduated from fear of his master, without any help from his father.

In his 16th year, when he was writing romantic poetry in the style of Göthe, he had met Stefan George through his poetry, and then as one of the circle of devotees. He came to believe that the bright light that had been his refuge, was his soul. It was time for him to cease the selfish use of it to protect himself from pain, or to insulate himself from others. On the poet's advice, he dedicated the light and all that his eternal soul meant to him, to the service of mankind. But he could not understand what this required him to do next, so he decided that the first step must be to dedicate his life to the people and the land around him, Germans in Germany. When that was achieved, he would know how to serve all mankind.

He lay in his bed on his side near the window, looking out over flat roofs edged with white-painted concrete blocks from which little shrubs of green stuck up like the straggling hairs round a bald man's head. In the narrow cavern of the street below, whining music like a balalaika twanged. Farther away, the dark arabesques of date palms spread black against the burning sky, and he thought, 'Why?'

'I have lost my youth, my hand, my eye because of the maniac in Rastenburg. And I am not alone.' He saw the grey ghosts on the Russian front who fell in the forest, in fields, in snow, in wheat, thousands upon thousands of them, all grey ghosts awaiting a leader to make their sacrifice worthwhile, a real leader, not the fake Messiah with the intent eyes and the square moustache. A real leader, one to sanctify their deaths by saving the lives of the men now headed for death. Himself. At the head of the crowd of grey ghosts, saving the young men from madness.

When the pain of the operation mounted to such a height it was threatening to drag him back from non-where, he repeated to himself, sometimes even aloud, to drown out everything else in his mind. 'This is for Germany, I will endure, this is for Germany, I will endure, I will, I will, I will . . .' He was saying this through his clenched teeth when he fainted.

The nurses at first thought he was shell-shocked, and then they vied to see who would take care of the handsome brave officer.

Klaus remained in hospital in Tunis for three more days until British shells began exploding in the western suburbs. The last of the top staff officers were starting to be evacuated. On a hot evening near the end of April, Garms told him he would be placed on board an HQ staff plane that night to fly to Naples. "And from there you will have to go to my friend Richter in Regensburg. He is the only one who can do the next stage of your hand." The doctor looked round to see if anyone was listening and said sotto voce, "Goodbye, I shall not see you again."

"Won't you be on the plane too?"

The doctor said, "I must thank you for being the cause of my presence here. I will not go. I have chosen captivity."

He looked out the window and sighed. "I can not bear the waste of life any longer." His sallow face relaxed into a look that seemed to appeal to Klaus for understanding. "Please, don't repeat that, or my family may suffer."

Klaus was driven in an ambulance after dusk with 11 other staff officers to the same airfield where he had arrived ten weeks before.

With his left arm in a sling and his right stump bandaged, he walked up the aluminum ladder, thinking at first he was shaking, until he realized the motors were making the plane throb. He took a bench seat with his back to the corrugated metal side of the cabin. Unable to do up his safety belt, he asked the officer next him to do it.

"Raabke," said the officer. "We met at Sfax."

"Ah yes," said Klaus. "A lot has happened since then." Raabke offered his left hand and they touched forearms.

Major Garstang, in a grey cape with a monocle on his right eye, clambered aboard last. No one greeted him. When he sat down, on the end of the bench, the officer next to him got up and moved away.

The JU 52 transport roared up into the darkness. Through bullet holes in the fuselage, caused by Allied fighters on the inbound run, Klaus could see the flames streaming back from the engine exhaust. Concentrating on these to forget the pain in his hand, he fell asleep.

Half an hour after takeoff, when they were well out to sea, the co-pilot came back to Klaus and leaned over him and shouted in his ear, "The captain would like you to come forward." He stood back, and Raabke, who seemed to know that something odd was happening, undid his seatbelt for him, and Klaus, crouching under the low metal roof, went past the partition to sit beside the captain. The pilot took off his headset and said in Klaus' ear, "The men have some business to do back there. Do not look around, do not leave here until you are told."

Klaus felt cold air on his neck, and a roar. He started to turn round, but the pilot put his hand on Klaus' knee and shouted. "Don't move."

A few minutes later, the co-pilot came back. Klaus went to the cabin. Everyone looked at him, except Garstang, who was not there.

Raabke leaned forward and shouted, "You will find out in Naples."

At the base in Naples, Raabke and the pilot walked close on each side of him like guards, to a staff car waiting for them at the edge of the field. In the baking hot mess, Raabke opened a window and offered Klaus a Lucky Strike. He had bought schnapps and coffee, and brought them to a corner between two windows where they could be private.

"You have witnessed something disgusting and tragic which I never believed could have happened in the Wehrmacht. What happened out there . . ." he faltered. "We have no faith any longer in justice under this regime. We have seen crimes committed with official sanction. It is in the name of the victims of injustice that we ask you to remain silent."

Klaus said, "How dare you place me in this incredible situation?"

"Please," said Raabke. "Save your moral outrage for those who deserve it. Garstang knew that the Hitler order was being disobeyed by most of the officers in the Afrika Corps. Then we discovered evidence that he was going to denounce them in person at the highest level when he returned. And you know the penalty for disobeying a Führer order."

Klaus looked at Raabke, and saw a typical young officer, well-trained, obedient, well-turned out, educated, decent, who had risked his life against the order.

"But it is not honourable to . . ." he was about to say "withhold my evidence," when he realized he was not sure of the path of honour now.

"I don't know," he said. He took temporary refuge in a technicality: "If Garstang already had the Führer order, why did he bother to pretend to find a weapon on the prisoner?"

"Covering his flanks, that's all. Not relying solely on the Führer order, because he was the only officer obeying it. So he camouflaged it."

"But everyone would know."

"Everyone does know and no one does anything," Raabke burst out. "That's the point. We decided we had to do something. We couldn't let this go on any longer."

Klaus sighed and Raabke went on, "When you came, we were worried about you, because you came direct from Rastenburg, on Führer orders. But then we saw how you reacted in Garstang's office. We took a chance because after he shot that prisoner, you said you would report him."

"Yes." Klaus sighed and passed his bandaged hand over his forehead. The pain was always worst when he was tense.

"There was a priest in Poland in '39," said Raabke, "a friend of Lucie Rommel, whom the general and his wife went to see in Danzig after the victory. They were told by a Pole that the priest had disappeared. Into a concentration camp. Then, one of our staff officers, a wonderful man, was arrested for treason. Garstang testified that this man and the priest had been sending out information to the *Times* about the SS atrocities in Poland. In fact, all that the officer had done was correct, to send a memo up the line to Blaskowitz saying what he had witnessed."

"But why didn't the general stop him?"

"Why indeed?"

"And then?"

"Did you ever think it odd that the Lion of Warsaw, General Blaskowitz, was removed from his command and sent home in disgrace?"

"I did, and I heard something about it."

"What?"

"That he protested an order to relocate Polish civilians."

"He protested the murder of scores of thousands of Jews, priests, gypsies, the usual victims. That's why he was sent home. And Garstang arranged that too."

"But he was only a major. How could he get such power?"

"You have never felt the hand of the Gestapo have you?" Raabke said. The SS, relying on Gestapo informers, was policing the army in the east by reading Enigma messages, tapping phones, even of the highest generals.

"When I saw your name on the flight manifest, I had to decide whether to let you stay behind, or bring you. Prison camp would kill you. So I took a chance. Now, you're to sign this."

He handed Klaus a typed paper, which read, "I witnessed the suicide of Major Peter Garstang on a flight from Tunis to Naples last night. He opened the emergency escape door and jumped out. He did not say a word or leave a note." Below this was typed *Klaus von Zollerndorf.* Below his name, 11 other names had already signed in as witnesses. Klaus sat for a few moments, smoking a cigarette from a holder taped to his bandage, and staring out the window at taxiing planes, wanting more time.

His duty was to the Army, which could not condone such an execution. But was he not already committed to a higher duty, to Holy

Germany, and to all mankind? Had he not sworn himself to the high morality of Stefan George? Words came into his mind, 'Duty, honour, courage . . .' but he did not know where they led him any more. Raabke had brought him from Tunis because a prison camp would kill him. They had risked their lives to save his own. They were counting on his honour. 'How much more will *we* have to do to kill Emil, and take over the government. If I do not sign, they may think they have to kill me too, but they have already tried to save my life by bringing me.'

"It is best that you sign," Raabke said.

Klaus decided, 'If I am willing to kill Emil, then I must be willing to sign.'

He asked Raabke for a pen, which dripped ink on his hand, and some on the paper. 'What will I not do now?' he thought. He signed, a shaky signature because he was still clumsy writing with his left hand.

He was taken north by hospital train with hundreds of wounded men, in wheelchairs, on crutches, blinded behind bandages, lying groaning on stretchers with unimaginable wounds in their chests, abdomens, backs, with no arms, one arm, or no limbs at all, heads lolling in their chairs, with burns to their faces so their shrunken cheeks glistened red round their puckered eye sockets. These ones looked like animals trapped in a cage of shrunken flesh, their eyes searching round in panic for release, or rolling eerily disconnected from each other and the brain within. Some of them complained, some of them moaned, one of them shrieked as he was moved, but most of them bore their horror in silence. He kept silent himself.

He sat by his window staring out at the hills as the darkness floated the sunlight up the sides of the mountains, practicing the yoga exercise that helped him to absent himself from his body so he could get through the operations. 'Much better two hours of pain than six months of recovery,' he repeated to himself. 'There is a duty ahead of me which I must fulfill no matter how much the pain may be. I want the pain. It is mine. I will bear it. I will bear it. There is nothing I can not bear.'

Late in the afternoon, the train stopped in a huge station which he knew must be Munich, although all signs had been removed, and he was looking out the window as a locomotive slowly rolled past them, bearing the sign *RÄDER ROLLEN FÜR DEN SIEG*. A car stopped three metres away and he saw through the lighted window a dining table set with white linen, cutlery, glasses.

An orderly leaned over his seat and said, "That is *Amerika*."

Klaus started and turned round. The orderly explained, "The Führer's train. *Amerika*. He can not be on it, or they would close the curtains—oh, no, there, he is there, you see? It is him."

The Führer in a grey belted tunic stood by the table waiting while a steward in white jacket closed the curtains. "You see," said the orderly, "he knows we are a hospital train. He can not bear the sight of the wounded, so he always has the curtains drawn." He smiled, proud of the Führer's sensitivity.

The word spread through the car that they were standing next to the Führer's train. One soldier began singing,

Underneath the lantern
By the barrack gate
Darling I remember
How you used to wait
T'was there that you whispered tenderly
That you loved me
You'd always be
My Lili of the lamplight
My own Lili Marlene.

The orderly went to his seat and said, "Stop!" The soldier, whose arm was in a cast ending at the stump of his wrist, smiled up at him and went on singing. The orderly shouted that the song was forbidden in Germany, but another soldier called back, "This is Afrika."

Soon the whole car and then the whole train was singing. All the lights were turned off and they completed the rest of the journey to Regensburg in darkness.

Hirschberg, May, 1943

Klaus wondered how to arrange his reunion with Tati. She would not behave like a German wife. She would turn Slav, weep and feel sorry for him. It would be best to meet somewhere public and impersonal. He sent a telegram to Helmuth James saying he would meet him and Tati at the Adlon for lunch on Tuesday, May 4.

The day was warm, and the elevators were not working, so he climbed four flights to Helmuth's office in the Adlon, and there, in the dim hallway he saw a figure like hers. She was standing by Helmuth's door, having been listening for his rapid hard step on the stair. She peered to see who it was, for she was short-sighted, then she ran down the hall, embraced him, looking into his eyes, and drawing him close to her chest. "I'm so glad you're back," she said, and he sighed with relief, thinking, 'That's the way, good girl.'

That afternoon, going into the flat, he saw that she had put his cello case away, but had forgotten to remove the music stand from its place beside the piano, where he had sat to play duets with her. He felt the self-pity beginning and said, "It's nothing." He stood there for a moment, hardening himself, then went into the bathroom to wash his face.

When he came out, he saw she was weeping as she moved around the dining room table, setting the table. She wiped a splash of tears from the dark mahogany and said in a strident voice, "You can sing."

Klaus sat at his desk in the Bendlerstrasse fingering the medal with the three fingers and thumb of his left hand, wondering why, if medals signified reputation, reputation itself was not enough. 'It is for old age,' he thought. 'When one is forgotten, one wears this as proof that one was young once and a hero. Which is to say, that wearing it proves that one is no longer young, nor heroic.' He laughed aloud.

A secretary, new to the Bendlerstrasse, came in to his office, heard Klaus snort with laughter and eyed the enormous photograph of the

Führer over his desk, and looked surprised, for it was well-known in the Bendlerstrasse what Klaus thought of Hitler. To the unspoken question in the young secretary's eyes, Klaus said, "It hangs there to show everyone that the man is mad." The officer stared in shock at him and backed out of the office as if it were Klaus who was mad.

Klaus' latest plan was to give Hitler one more chance before he acted. He wanted to persuade him to share the leadership with senior generals who knew how to lead the army. If Hitler acceded, he would soon be in the power of his generals, instead of the other way round. Then, at the proper moment, this slow coup would become the final coup: Hitler would be pushed into resigning for the good of the nation, or he would meet with a fatal accident at the front. The new men would conduct the war while the Foreign Ministry negotiated for peace.

He slit open the sealed envelope the young secretary had left for him, and saw that he had been appointed to give a course of lectures on organizing staff at Corps level at the Army War Academy in Hirschberg.

In the barracks at Hirschberg the following week, he dressed with difficulty, tugging at his boots with the tines of his metal right hand time and again until he thought he would have to call for help. Finally, he got the boots on, and slipped into his uniform with the bright yellow epaulettes bearing the number 8. On his posting to the general staff, he had been honoured by his regiment, the 8th cavalry, with the right to wear his regimental uniform in perpetuity. He recognized this honour by wearing the yellow epaulettes of the 8th instead of the red epaulettes of the general staff, an insignia no other officer had ever refused. This had raised some eyebrows round the Bendlerstrasse, where he was regarded as a holy fool. Here at Hirschberg, surrounded by "poodles" as he called them—lapdogs of the general staff—he expected the epaulettes to shake a few heads. He brushed them clean and marched out to breakfast.

After breakfast, near eight o'clock of a warm summer morning, he confronted a roomful of poodles, many of them generals with poor eyesight, as the flashing spectacles and monocles evinced, and most of them suspicious of his youth, fame and oddity.

Klaus thought of the immense power these men had, or were supposed to have, over manpower, transport, artillery, tanks, horses, trains, food. 'Here is my chance to change the fate of the nation, to convince these old poodles that we must do something right away or the nation will be delivered to catastrophe.'

From experience, Klaus knew that senior officers being lectured in a closed room soon drowse off, so he told the orderly to open the windows. As he arranged his papers, waiting for the wood-framed wall-clock to tick to eight, he smelled the warm air coming into the room full of the scent of the pine woods nearby, mixed with the scent of grass being cut. He wondered if opening the windows was a mistake—everyone could hear the soporific sound of a hand-mower, like cicadas. As the minute hand touched eight, he got up from his desk, greeted the officers, then turned to the blackboard where he had written the words Command Structure, with several large boxes and arrows pointing from one to another. He began with the army's complicated command structure.

"I have been told to explain something I do not myself understand. I begin in confusion because to my mind, the mere fact that we are studying it in the midst of crisis at the front indicates that there is something terribly wrong here at home. The command structure overlaps, duplicates and at the same time neglects many important things," he said, making new lines on the board representing the various lines of responsibility and authority. "The underlying principle seems to be to assign responsibility without authority and authority without responsibility. The system contradicts, confuses, amends, terminates and reinstates all at the same time. Nobody understands it. I have studied it for years now, and I have experienced it, and I do not know how it works."

He gazed over the audience, thinking that so far as he earned their attention, so far he would lose their trust.

"Yet now, when every mind is precious and every soldier is essential, we sit, hundreds of us, studying this hopeless mess. I tell you, if we had all spent a month here trying to design a command structure that was as absurd as possible, we could not have succeeded as well as we have by our inadvertence, incompetence, skulduggery, slovenliness, carelessness, and empire-building. Gentlemen, we have enshrined chaos."

Several of the monocles in the room fell into cupped hands, two of the generals stood up ready to expostulate, or to leave ostentatiously, but Klaus went on in a very hard voice, speaking at them, "If you think I exaggerate, let me quote to you from the Quartermaster General's report for May, 1942."

He held the bound pamphlet in the air, grey-green cover outwards, and recited from memory, "'At the end of March, 1942 only eight of our 162 divisions on the eastern front were ready for action. We had only 140 tanks for our 16 armoured divisions.'"

Several of the officers gasped.

Klaus paused. "We had 50 per cent more casualties by April 1942 than Napoleon had men in his entire army. These amounted to one third of the strike force we commanded in June 1941. That's the overall picture. Here is a detail in a letter I received from a friend."

He lowered the pamphlet and tried to extract the letter from his pocket, but his partly-restored finger and thumb kept slipping on the paper. The tension in the room mounted because everyone knew how badly he had been wounded. His thumb gripped the paper against his remaining finger, he pulled out the envelope, and then had to struggle again to hold the envelope with his prosthesis while he extracted the single flimsy sheet of paper.

At the end of the long process, someone in the room sighed, and there was a slight movement as of suppressed laughter, the laughter of sympathetic relief.

Klaus said, with a slight smile, "Thank you for your patience. My friend writes, dated May, 1943: *'One armoured division which had been mauled in Ukraine was assigned as reinforcements an infantry battalion on foot, with no motorized transport at all. This armoured division in 1941 had been the fastest formation in the army, with the greatest striking power any division has ever had in the history of warfare. And why were foot-soldiers assigned to this fast force? Because all its own remaining and well-trained cadres had been broken up and dispersed to other units.* "' The restless generals had by now sat down and were listening.

"Gentleman, some of the artillery of these poor bloody foot soldiers was mounted on sleds that were drawn by horses, when they were available, otherwise they were dragged through the snows or mud of Russia by soldiers. This is what we have come to.

"There is another example of the fatal errors which have been made. This war is not just a struggle of arms against arms, of factories against factories, but of the will of the people versus the will of the people, a factor which the staff work neglected to such an amazing degree that we were in fact startled in the autumn of 1941 to find that the Russian army had the will to fight. After all, it was the prevalent opinion of the staff in June 1941 and I quote, that 'We have only to kick in the door and the whole rotten structure will come tumbling down.'" This well-known remark made by the Führer, he had thought would cause resentment, or even laughter, but there was not a sound in the room. Klaus saw how far he was going now towards outright rebellion, which made him hesitate for a moment. But then he thought, 'Courage, *mon brave,*' and went on.

"Once again, too late, the party has tried to compensate for grievous errors, by taking important measures to assure strong morale among both the soldiery and citizenry of the nation. As soldiers, we appreciate the Führer's far-sighted wisdom in attending to this grave matter at such a critical moment in our decisive struggle for our supremely glorious national existence." Several of the generals looking exasperated by this thick irony, he relented. "That is why I have been studying the Russian campaigns waged in the past, and also the Russian spirit as evinced by their literature. I found this a strange experience. One might conclude that Russian fiction reads like history because

Russian history reads like fiction." At this quip there was an uneasy stir among the older generals, who disapproved of young smart-alecs joking when they ought to be attending to serious business. "That is not an idle quip. It bears on this campaign in which we have been hampered by the partisans, who believe in Russia, a fact well-known to anyone familiar with their literature. Our staff work has ignored this major factor to our great cost. Trying to deal with the partisans has cost us dearly. It is not too much to say that without this guerilla force behind our lines, the enemy could not have recovered and recoiled as fast as he has. This was a foreseeable difficulty, for anyone familiar with the literature and history of the country.

"Reinforcing this ancient patriotism is a new factor, terror. The only thing Russians fear more than a threat to their state, is their state. Stalin gives his soldiers a simple choice: refuse to attack and be shot, or attack and possibly live. In the interest of expanding our general knowledge of our enemy, I would like you to hear what a great Russian writer said of Napoleon and his winter campaign in Russia in 1813."

He opened his copy of *War and Peace* to the second volume, and began, "In *War and Peace*, Leo Tolstoy writes: '*The cause of the destruction of the French Army in 1812 is clear to us now. No one will deny that that cause was, on the one hand its advance into the heart of Russia late in the season without any preparation for a winter campaign*'"—here Klaus paused for a long moment, while the generals were still, because they all knew that the Wehrmacht had suffered terribly from lack of winter clothing in the winter of 1941—"'*and on the other the burning of Russian towns and the hatred of the foe this aroused among the Russian people.*'"

Here he paused even longer, for many in the room knew and hated the murderous policies of the SS behind the lines, which had alienated even the friendly Ukrainians, who had at first welcomed the Germans as liberators.

Now Klaus felt he might earn their trust. He went on reading from *War and Peace*:

" 'But no one at the time foresaw what now seems so evident, that this was the only way an army of eight hundred thousand men—the best in the world and led by the best general—could be destroyed in conflict with a raw army of half its numerical strength and led by inexperienced commanders as the Russian army was. Not only did no one see this but on the Russian side every effort was made to hinder the only thing that could save Russia, while on the French side, despite Napoleon's experience and so-called military genius, every effort was directed to pushing on to Moscow at the end of the summer, that is, to doing the very thing that was bound to lead to destruction.' "

He closed the book. The room was silent. He said, "And we know whose strategy has brought our army to its present predicament."

Still, no one had reacted with any sign of anger. He stared at them willing them to protest, but no one did. A few got up, glancing at their wrists as if to show that time was forcing them to depart. He hoped that at least one person would approach him to congratulate him for saying what all were thinking, but it seemed that all condemned him for it. He heard the briefcases being clicked and snapped shut, and thought that this was the sound of minds closing. Then the clack of boots on the tiled floor, then silence.

He walked outside.

Several of the generals looked at him oddly. The sunlight rouged the bald spots on their grey old heads, they walked looking neither to left nor right, all stiff unreflecting people doing everything as it had always been done. No one spoke to him until one man, bulky in his major-general's tunic, his thick neck bristling with short red hairs sticking out over his collar, his hair shorn almost to the scalp, and a choleric redness to his bloated cheeks, came up to him and said, in a voice charred with the smoke from the thick cigar in his hand, "Young man, I heard the scandalous Jandl speak at his graduation last week, and I thought, 'If we do not shoot this traitor before he spreads his poison any further, then we can not win this war, and do not deserve to. And now I have heard you spreading the same defeatism, and I think the same thing of you. If I thought your life were worth it, I would challenge you." He turned and walked away.

No one else spoke to Klaus, to agree or disagree, to praise or censure. He was like someone who has been caught in an embarrassing intimate act in public. He walked back to the barracks alone.

Dubno, Ukraine, October, 1943

Axel, Baron von dem Bussche, a captain in the No 9 Potsdam Infantry Regiment, wearing three ribbons for bravery, was walking towards his plane on the airfield at Dubno in Ukraine near Tarnopol, just before noon on Tuesday, 5 October 1943, on his way back to Berlin. He heard bursts of Schmeisser fire coming from a field beyond a line of trucks. He ran forward at a crouch, drawing his sidearm as he went, expecting an attack by partisans, who often used captured German weapons.

He sheltered behind the lead truck and looked out on a file of SS men lined up behind a crowd of men, women and children, many of them naked. The SS men were in the firing position, right leg braced behind, left leg forward, head inclined to the sight, gun barrel pointing out past the left shoulder. Ahead of them about ten metres away, the people were arranged in ragged ranks, some milling around getting undressed. The front rank stood still before a long pit. The women were weeping and wailing, the men shouting, the children crying. They were supposed to take off all their clothes and pile them, and most were already naked, but the young officer in charge could not restrain himself from giving the order because he thought that it was unseemly to make them undress to be shot.

The young officer shouted "Fire," and the SS men opened fire on them, their muzzles moving from left to right in unison. Axel felt protest start in his chest as the relentless hammering went on and on, each bullet a death. He shouted "Stop," but his voice was blown away by the firing. Each volley took about five seconds until all had fallen. As the SS men reloaded their guns, the next rank of civilians was ordered forward. But they hesitated seeing their companions dead on the ground, and some among them writhing and moaning and calling "Help." Again the young officer could not wait, and shouted "Fire" while the second rank was still not in position, so they fell all over the place. Several of them, unhit, tried to run away and were cut down many metres from the grave.

Axel hurried up to an older SS Obersturmbannführer who was standing by smoking a cigarette. "What is going on here?" Axel asked.

"Executing commissars, Jews, partisans—the usual."

"What do you mean, usual? These are civilians. Including women."

"Children too. We're following orders to clean this place up and make it fit for German farmers. These people support partisans at night."

"But there aren't any partisans in this area."

"And this is the reason why."

It was on his lips to say, "I order you to stop this," but the SS man was under a separate command and would refuse the order, then report him to the Gestapo for discipline.

He walked back to the plane, still hearing the shooting.

That night in bed in his barracks at Zossen, he felt the agonizing firing again, heard the screams among the bullets, he heard the children crying, he saw the people fall forward, he saw their bodies twitching in the heaps, people running away naked, falling, soldiers ordering the next line of victims to drag bodies back to the pit, he could not sleep. He saw them falling forward all the time, he felt that he was falling forward. Some of them were moving, some falling onto others, the women screaming, the children holding their parents' hands, the SS men holding their guns up and aiming and firing, aiming and firing their moving muzzles over the backs and heads of people.

When he closed his eyes, he was in the pit, looking up at the blade of the bulldozer coming over him, earth falling into his face, but he could not raise his arms. The regimental doctor gave him sleeping pills, which blurred his mind the next day. The doctor then recommended sick leave, and his friend Major von Weizsacker signed his service book for an indefinite leave with no destination. He went to see his friend Peter von Metternich at his flat in the Budapesterstrasse in Berlin.

Clara came to the door and ushered him into the salon, where Peter was standing with his cane before the fireplace.

"Just a little birthday present from the Russians," Peter said, meaning his leg. "I'll be better in a few weeks." He put his finger to his lips and shook his head indicating that Axel was not to talk. At the same time, he kept up a one-sided conversation on the glories of the Wehrmacht and their new attack in the Crimea. Then he swung himself to the dining room table and wrote a note to Axel. *Mike in the phone. Write.* Peter handed pencil and paper to Axel.

Axel wrote *I saw SS murdering civilians in Russia. Thousands,* and got the reply *See von Zollerndorf at the Bendlerstrasse.* All this time they were talking disconnectedly of the problems of von Manstein in the Crimea.

Klaus von Zollerndorf noticed Axel von dem Bussche's panda-eyes wandering to the border of swastikas inlaid in the perimeter of the parquet floor of his office. Klaus laughed and said, "When I pace around, it is that path I follow." He smiled. "I need some fresh air, let's go for a walk and then have lunch at the Adlon, agreed?"

Their boot-clatter echoed over the curved stone staircase going down to the ground floor, the steel door squealed shut over trapped grit, and the immense cobbled courtyard echoed with talk from the officers strolling in the sunshine. Klaus paused to arrange a meeting with two of them standing watching workmen digging into a pile of reddish dirt on the north wall, caused by a small bomb which had caved in part of the stone wall. As they went out, the guard at the iron gate gave him the army salute and said, "Good day, sir."

Von dem Bussche was very impressed by this tall young officer with the black eye-patch and gloved hand who had earned the Iron Cross, and the confidence of the General Staff. He thought, 'This is the man I want to tell.'

Klaus lit a little Dutch cigar as they sat down on a bench under the golden leaves of a birch tree by the *Neuersee* in the Tiergarten.

After von dem Bussche had told him what he had witnessed at Dubno, Klaus said, "Did you try to stop them?"

"I spoke to a Luftwaffe officer who was there and he said there was nothing we could do. I got the impression that the orders came straight from the highest levels."

"Indeed, they do."

"What can we do?"

"We are still considering how best to proceed."

"Are you considering assassination?"

"You see, it is not so easy. First there are the difficulties of spirit."

"Of spirit?"

"What is the spiritual effect of an assassination? How can it be good for Germany?"

"Hitler himself has recommended it, for the good of the people."

"What do you mean?"

"In *Mein Kampf*, he says himself," and Axel found himself reciting the Führer's words which he had memorized, "'If by the instrument of governmental power, a nationality is led towards its destruction, then rebellion is not only the right of every member of such a people—it is his duty. And the question—when is this justified?—is decided not by theoretical dissertations but by force—and results.'"

Klaus was astounded. He stared at Axel, thinking, 'This is what I needed, and from what a source.'

He realized—for the third time—that his mind was made up. He would do it. He began to consider the decision, wondering if he had taken everything into account. Perhaps he should postpone action again, as he had before, but this time, there was a difference, he felt his mind moving away from such havering, and towards what the Führer had himself recommended as the decisive qualities—"force, and results."

He started to slap one hand into another, until he remembered, and instead made a fist of the remainder of his left hand and shook it in the air, saying, "Are you sure? This is amazing."

Axel nodding said, "Nobody reads that goddamned book. All too snobbish to hobnob with the guttersnipe. Yes of course I'm sure."

"And if Bormann takes over? Or Göbbels? Then there is the question of the morality of the act. Is tyrannicide permitted to the Lutheran conscience? To the Catholic conscience? I suspect that it is easier for me as a Catholic than for you as a Lutheran."

"Lutheranism condones the killing of a mad tyrant, and in any case I have long since transcended these considerations." Axel wondered if his last statement was arrogant, so he added, "My dear Zollerndorf, I have the greatest respect for you, so I beg you not to interpret what I have just said as in any way condescending to you. I condescend to myself now, my former self. I have changed."

"What you can not change, changes you," said Klaus, sitting down.

"But I can change it. I intend to."

"What do you intend?"

"To kill him."

"How?"

"Ahh."

Axel leaned forward excitedly as if to contain his churning stomach, clasped his hands tight and said in a low urgent voice, "In four weeks time, he is due to inspect the new field equipment for the army, including a new type of greatcoat. I can arrange to be one of the officers presenting the equipment, in fact, I helped to design some of it. I shall wear one of the coats. Under it I shall have the grenades."

"And?"

"I shall throw myself on Hitler and cling to him till it goes off."

Klaus drew on his cigar, staring at him. He said, "Good."

"All I need is the bomb."

"And the fuses," Klaus murmured. "They are the hardest. However, we are expecting some from the British."

"I am prepared to kill him as soon as I can. I only need the opportunity."

"We will provide it." They began to walk round the park, Klaus scanning the branches and lamp-posts for Gestapo microphones. He told von dem Bussche that Hitler had ordered 100 captured Allied bomber pilots to be shot in retaliation for each raid on German cities. He was not deterred by the fact that the Allies held hundreds of thousands of German prisoners, and that they might retaliate. "We must do something about this right away, or the shootings will start, on both sides. I will have you seconded to my office at the Replacement Army and your first job will be to get the name of every Allied flyer who has already died in captivity, then our friends in the *OKW* will present that list to Hitler when he asks for the names of the executed prisoners."

"Thank you," said von dem Bussche. His heart was pounding as it did before he went into action, because he knew he would die in four weeks.

Klaus said, "We have a code for where we meet, usually here in the Tiergarten. This bench is Weimar, that one is Potsdam, the one down there is Cleve. And so on. Shall we have lunch?" He got up.

"I don't understand, how will I know which is which?"

"I'm sorry, I thought you knew. Each of these light standards was donated to the park by a town in Germany. This one came from Weimar, so the bench nearest it is the Weimar bench. That bench over there is Bad Kreuznach, because the lamp just beyond came from Bad Kreuznach. And so on. They're all on the Grosser Weg."

"Is there a map somewhere?"

"I'll draw you one at lunch." and he took the young man's arm and walked him away. "You'll memorize it and burn it."

Normandy, London, October, 1943

⁓୧⅁⁓

Jack kneeled down beside the boy's body on the grass, unbuttoned the uniform half-expecting him to protest, reached inside feeling the smooth hairless chest and snapped off half the aluminum identity disk that was still warm, then walked away, crouching, from the burning house covered by Carlos and Johnny at the cliff-edge. At the edge he turned round and hurled himself out of the red glare into the darkness down the path to the rubber boat on the stony beach. They heaved it in, Carlos started the engine and they banged away. A mile out, he stopped the engine to listen for sounds of any boat pursuing. Johnny said, "What happened? Did you shoot him?"

"I knocked, he came to the door, I threw a smoke flash through the window, I heard a shot inside and he fell over dead. He never knew what hit him. Then you guys stormed in the back way."

"It must have been the other guy shot him, the one we got inside."

"Well, anyway, we got the set, that's the main thing," Carlos said.

"He was just a kid," Jack said. His fingers curled over the smooth aluminum. He kept telling himself, 'Better him than me,' but something hard in him remained unsaid.

He took the light bit of metal from his shirt pocket and set it on Curran's desk with the illusion that the warmth disappearing as it lay on the desk was the last bit of life evaporating from the boy's body. Curran said, "Good show, that was their latest centimetric radar. The only one we've got."

"Thanks."

"I heard you've stopped eating."

"No sir."

"You're worrying about killing a German soldier."

"No sir, I did not kill him. He was shot in the back by one of his own men who thought he was me coming in."

"Listen, it's war, millions have died, millions more are going to die. Now forget about it."

"Yes sir."

"You have a week's leave."

"Thank you, sir."

"Remember, you did it for king and country."

"Sir, I did not kill anyone."

"Then stop worrying and start eating."

"Yes sir."

He waited for Marianne in the crowded lobby of the Savoy. Six months had passed since they had seen each other. She had been twice to France, and he had raided the coast by rubber boat twice, then had flown back to Canada to train recruits at Camp X for three months. He saw her coming through the doors into the huge lobby, crowded with soldiers.

He stood up, so she would see him right away. She came in looking tanned and healthy, her head high, looking round, a curl of her hair escaping from her cap. She slowed down on her way through the crowd to the inquiries desk, to respond to two young American officers, who both turned, talked to her and smiled. One took her arm as Jack started forward. She turned and saw him.

He held out his arms and she put down her bag but avoided kissing him on the lips, offering him her left cheek, then the right. He kissed her cheeks, then tried to draw her close and kiss her on the lips. She turned her face away. He let her go.

"What's the matter?"

"Nothing," she said. "How are you?"

"Boy, have I missed you. Let's put this in our room." He swung up her bag, but she put her hand on his arm. "Let's have a drink first."

He looked at her with a question in his face, 'What's wrong?'

She avoided answering by taking his free hand as he worked his way through the crowd into the narrow long bar. He knew the bartender, an old Scotchman, Jock Bertinelli, and signalled to him over the heads of two men drinking with two women in slanted blue RCAF caps. Jock handed him two scotches between ducking heads at the bar, and Jack returned to her. She had found one chair at a table occupied by a grey-haired British major and a young woman in nurse's uniform.

"So," he said, sitting on her bag beside her. "You were in Scotland? Do you realize it's been six months since we saw each other."

"You were in Canada?"

"And France. Snatching a radar set. Here, I got you this in Paris." He handed her a gift-wrapped bottle. She opened it and saw the label, Chanel 69. She said, "Where . . . ." and realized the joke. She smiled, shook her head. "You're always joking."

"It settles the grief. You were in Paris too?"

Glancing at the British officer, she whispered, "Keep your voice down. Yes, I helped set up a *reseau.*"

"How was it?" He turned his back on the grey-haired officer.

"If you can believe it, boring. Endless meetings. Even now, people argue over their rights and privileges."

"Did the Germans leave you alone?"

"Oh yes, I had good papers, they've improved everything a lot since '41. How was Canada?"

"Felt sort of empty. Everything is over here. I saw Mum and Dad and A.G."

"And?"

"And what?"

"Did you see Alison?"

"We played some tennis."

This was a *double entendre* which he did not intend: for him and Marianne, tennis was code for making love, to get past the censors on the phone and the mail.

"Is that what you call it?"

"For Christ's sake, Marianne, look at what I just gave you, what does it mean?"

"I'm sorry, Jack."

"You bloody well should be."

"But it would be quite natural," she said with a gentleness that he did not comprehend.

"What's not natural is six months apart and not glad to see each other." He glanced up at the middle-aged officer who seemed to be trying to persuade the young nurse of something. Tufts of grey hair were growing out of his nose and his ears. Her ear curved pink between two curls of brown hair.

"I'm glad."

"I was waiting for you, you came in and I thought, 'Aren't you looking *belle, ce soir*,' and you looked right past me at those two Americans."

"Because they were . . ."

"And you let him take your arm."

"What was I supposed to do? Deck him?"

"Yeah."

"Well, I didn't."

"No you didn't, but I killed a guy."

"Curran told me you're blaming yourself." She lit a cigarette, leaned back and said through the smoke, "Is that why you're so belligerent?"

"When did you see Curran?"

"Yesterday."

"You were at Aldershot yesterday?"

"Yes, is that so bad?"

"Why didn't you find me?"

"I thought you were already here. Besides, I didn't get in till ten last night. Jack, what is it, why are you like this?"

"Marianne, you don't even see me in the lobby, you flirt with two guys, you don't want to kiss me, you don't want to go up to the room—you know how hard it is to get a room now."

"I say, do you mind," said the grey-haired officer. He steadied the table, which Jack had knocked as he gestured.

"And right away, you suspect me of tennis with Alison."

"That would be normal. Jack, don't be cruel, it's not like you."

"For Christ's sake Alison, the guy was dead and I leaned over him and felt around inside his uniform to take his ID."

Marianne had heard the name Alison, but she felt the desperate sadness in his voice, and she could not criticize him.

"And now I have this catastrophic dream every night when he looks . . . oh never mind, you know."

She caressed his head and whispered, "I know. You had to go there, you had to do that."

"I don't believe that, not any more." He covered his face with his hands and said, "I was the intruder, he was already there, I know, I know, why was he there in the first place."

"Exactly."

"But you declared war on him."

"But they invaded us."

"Jesus, this is what I didn't want to start. Because it never ends."

"Curran said you haven't eaten for days. Let's have dinner now." She got up.

The grey-haired officer said, "I say, would you mind awfully if we borrowed your room while you're at dinner? Be glad to stand you to a spot of Woolton pie."

Kernslau, October, 1943

The chief conspirators met at the von Blücher estate at Kernslau on Sunday October 17, a day so warm that Tati decided they would sit on the lawn overlooking the lake. Hans Oster was there, Admiral Canaris, Hans von Dohnanyi, Alex von dem Bussche, Peter, Helmuth James, Adam von Trott, General Ludwig Beck and Klaus. Helmuth James would summarize the war situation, placing their own actions in an historical context and making recommendations for the future, especially contact with the British.

As Tati walked out carrying a briefcase, she glanced up. The sky was bomberless, a few clouds drifted down from Denmark, a breeze turned the lake to blue tweed. Helmuth watched Klaus come over the lawn, black patch on his eye, black glove covering the prosthesis, half a glove on his left hand holding a briefcase. The awkward turn of his head gave Helmuth a rush of sympathy so strong it was like panic. He rose and embraced his old friend, certain that his presence proved that their purpose was good. Nothing to which Klaus attached himself could be wrong.

Klaus sat down in the deck chair, aware of its frailty under his big frame, and opened a copy of Stefan George's selected poems. As the others began arriving from the house, he read one of the poems he thought was apt to the day. He wondered if later on he might read it out, to inspire them all:

> *When once this generation has cleansed its shame*
> *Has thrown from its neck the villein's yoke*
> *In its entrails feels but hunger for honour*
> *Then from the battlefield covered with endless graves*
> *Will flash the bloody gleam . . . then through the clouds*
> *Will rush roaring armies, then through the fields*
> *Will rage the horror of horrors the third storm*
> *The return of the dead!*

If ever this nation from her cowardly slackness
Remembers her election, her mission:
She will receive the divine explanation
Of unspeakable dread . . . then hands will be raised
And mouths will sound in praise of her worth
Then in the morning breeze a true emblem will flutter
The royal standard and bow itself in greeting
To the Noble, the Heroes!

As he finished reading, he looked around at them all, thinking, 'These are the Noble, the Heroes.' Clara poured out the chicory-coffee and Helmuth said, "I'm sorry that Gisevius is not here yet, but I will start anyway, because I have discussed this with him, and I believe he has seen the paper?" He glanced at Clara, who nodded, for she was in charge of distributing papers.

Klaus sat back in the deck chair, thinking Helmuth was decent and intelligent, and therefore an impediment to action. Helmuth was now in his element, speaking on a moral issue with far-ranging consequences. He read slowly and Klaus added 'ineffectual,' to the list of his friend's qualities. This made him feel disloyal and he remembered Tati admonishing him on this subject, 'We love our friends for their qualities and with their limitations, and you have never not loved Helmuth.'

"We have decided the conditions for ending the war," Helmuth began. "They include the form of government of Germany after the war, the punishment of the Nazi criminals, the relations of family, parish, Land and Reich, preservation of the nobility, freedom of belief and conscience, the franchise, the fundamental role of Christianity in the new Germany. But others remain unresolved—the questions of church and state, national territory, foreign policy, reparations, punishment of Allied war criminals, and so on. And assassination. All of these derive from the war itself, or from the underlying causes of the war, which leads me to think that in order to understand our future role we must first understand the war itself. What is the reason and what is the moral point of all this destruction? And what should we understand by studying it? And once it is understood, what can we do? To understand the phenomenon we must understand its causes." And here he began a long, reasoned and well-informed history of the events leading up to the crisis at Sarajevo in 1914, and the injustices of the Treaty of Trianon. Everyone there was feeling the same thing as he went on, 'this is a perfect history lesson, but we already know it, please get on with it.'

"We Germans were the first to suffer from Hitler, and continue to suffer along with others. The SA, the Jews, the cripples, gypsies, people in mental homes, were first. Generals and economics experts predicted in the thirties that war would be a disaster. Most including Hitler said that Germany could not win a long war. Yet that is what we have, because of Hitler."

Klaus, stretched out in the warm light, eyed the bright-leaved trees beyond the fields, imagining how he would position his tanks here for a defence of the Schloss, in order to draw the enemy into enfilading fire, then counterattack. He stretched, and the chair collapsed under him.

"Damn," he said, "I'm sorry, Helmuth, stupid of me."

"Never mind," said Tati, who along with Clara was acting as hostess. She ran barefoot over the grass to the house and returned dragging a wood chair by the back, like a recalcitrant child, its heels bouncing on the new grass, leaving streaks where the last of the dew was still glittering.

Helmuth continued, "By any standards, the war was lost last summer. Yet it continues, because of Hitler. The war he had started with little purpose and great risk was lost, and could be continued only by his will, and was continued by his will, against the will of all his military advisers. We are now into a crescendo of destruction whose end no one can see, except that it will exceed everything known in the world before. Yet the real danger to Germans—Hitler—has been hidden from Germans behind a barrier of German ideology, German propaganda, German education, all reinforced by terror camps, corrupt courts, police raids, massacres, whereas the USSR, UK and USA are described by Germans as the only threat to Germany. It is noble to fight the Soviets, evil to fight Hitler."

At this, Tati glanced at Clara and squirmed, for each felt queasy about her own part, however necessary, in misleading not only foreign countries and the world press, but also the German people.

Canaris lay back with his eyes closed relaxing. He had been to many long meetings in his life and had learned to empty his mind of all ennui, but he heard with dismay the shuffle of the papers in Helmuth's hands, and peeped from under his eyelid to see how many pages were left to go.

Helmuth went on, "So far I have talked of the physical damage to Germany and other countries. But there is a greater cost, which we are already paying and which future generations will pay, for hundreds of years. This is the spiritual cost. Unborn generations of Germans will feel the shame and pay the cost of what we are doing now, because it is of the realm of the spirit, which outlasts us all. The cultured, progressive, pacific Germany of the 18th and 19th centuries—our nation of dreamers and philosophers—has been submerged by a wave of the most destructive barbarism." Oster and von Dohnanyi exchanged glances, for it seemed that at last he was coming to the reason for the meeting.

"It is true that we have already discussed much of this among ourselves in this group but I have put this down on paper as a summary of what has impelled us all up to this point, and which will, pray God, move us to a conclusion. For that reason, to make it part of the record, so that the world may later know, I would like to include here a German translation of part of a letter I wrote in English to a friend at Cambridge.

Hitler has told Field Marshal von Manstein commanding on the southern front, that 'The German general and soldier must never feel secure, otherwise he wants to rest; he must always know that there are enemies in front and at his back and that there is one thing to be done and that is to fight.'

No one in Germany outside Hitler's immediate entourage knows that the Führer thinks and talks this way, that there are 'enemies at the soldier's back,' supplied gratis by der Führer himself. But even in Germany, people do not know what is happening all around them.

I believe that at least nine-tenths of the population do not know that we have killed hundreds of thousands of Jews. They go on believing that the Jews have just been segregated and lead an existence pretty much like the one they used to lead, only farther to the east, where they originated. Perhaps with a little more squalor but without air raids. If you told normal Germans what has really happened they would answer, 'remember what ridiculous things they said about our behaviour in Belgium in 1914/18.'

Another fact: German people are very anxious about their men reported missing in Russia. The Russians have allowed our men to write home, which is a very shrewd thing for the Russians to do.

Tati, who had typed most of this during three nights before, now began to drift off like Klaus, thinking, 'And what will all this high-level discussion mean when the Mongol soldiers are climbing over us?'

Helmuth kept on, "Well, these cards are on their arrival in Germany, locked up or destroyed but not allowed to reach the families."

There was a stir of outrage round the circle at this.

These facts about the mail from Russia are neither known, nor when you tell them, believed. And where the facts become known, as with officials dealing with the cards or the relatives, there is a widespread belief that the cards are faked and that the Führer in his magnanimity wants to prevent the raising of hopes by the beastly Russians which are unfounded and must give way to still deeper despair once the facts become known. But the cruel fact is that he wants to sharpen our hatred so we will fight like maniacs.

About 1000 of these cards somehow passed the censor through some technical error. The recipients who tried to answer in the normal way through the ordinary channels were arrested, questioned and kept in confinement until they realized what it would mean to them if they ever talked about the fact that they had received news from their men. Things like that go on all round us for months and perhaps years.

General Beck sat up even straighter, outraged at this insult to the army. As Helmuth James went on, outlining some of the social policies which they hoped would be implemented by the new government, Beck thought, 'This is not resistance, it is revolution.' Klaus had asked him to take over the provisional government that would follow the assassination, but he wanted no part of the socialist revolution that he feared von Zollerndorf and the admirers of Stefan George wanted. He had accepted the provisional leadership in the name of the moderate conservatives of Germany who, he believed were the vast majority.

Helmuth James went on, "We now have 19 guillotines at work without most people even knowing this, and nobody knows how many are beheaded per day." There was a stir of incredulity in the crowd.

"If you don't believe me, go to the SS HQ on the Münchner Platz in Dresden and you will see a guillotine, where they have been executing so many people that they now raise the blade by an electric winch.

"In my estimation there are about 50 daily, not counting those who die in concentration camps. Nobody knows the exact number of concentration camps or of their inhabitants, but we do know that of the thousands of Jews who lived in Dresden before the war, only about 40 are left. All the rest committed suicide, or were sent to concentration camps, where they last on average about six days. Then the ashes are returned along with a death certificate, stating, 'Shot while trying to escape.' There is a concentration camp only a few miles from this estate, and my district-commissioner told me that he only learnt of the fact when he was asked to issue orders to stop an epidemic of typhoid spreading from the camp to the village. By that time the camp had been in existence for months. Calculations on the number of KZ inmates vary between 150,000 and 350,000. Nobody knows how many die per day. By chance I have discovered that in one single month 160 persons died at Dachau. We further know that there are 16 concentration camps with their own cremation apparatus. I was told last year that a big KZ was being built in Upper Silesia to accommodate 40 to 50,000 men of whom 3,000 to 4,000 were to be killed per month. But all this information comes to me, even to me, who is on the lookout for facts of this nature, in a vague form. We know that many hundreds of Germans are killed daily by the various methods and that these people die not a glorious death, as those in occupied countries do, knowing that they go as heroes, but an ignominious death among robbers and murderers.

"All these dreadful facts illustrate one central point: we have fallen into a moral stupor caused in part by Nazi terror, but also magnified by our own indifference. And the awful thing is that if we 'win' this war by these cruel means, we will have confirmed to ourselves and confirmed ourselves in, the belief that sectarian hatred is of the essence of Germany." Canaris sat up and opened his eyes, about to speak, because he believed that Helmuth had just expressed the main point. Helmuth glanced at him, slowing his words; Canaris waved to him to continue.

"Because a German victory would mean that hatred will have triumphed over our enemies, who are the only people who can end this regime right now, seeing that we ourselves have failed. Our duty is not just to Germany, not just to German honour but to the whole world."

"Yes," said young von dem Bussche. "And then?"

"Hitler is the enemy of Germany."

Klaus sat up hoping that this meant Helmuth approved assassination. "Does this mean you now approve of shooting Hitler?"

Axel said, "Not shoot. He wears a bulletproof vest. We'll bomb him."

Helmuth smiled at him, thinking, 'Brave Axel,' and went on, "The Allies and Hitler have in common a determination to fight to the extreme end regardless of the cost. There is in existence right now a

Führer order to destroy all important factories, dams, bridges, generating stations, and major buildings in Germany that come under threat of occupation by the enemy. This policy will be the greatest possible tragedy for the German people."

There was a stir of indignation here because none of them had heard of this order. He looked up, realizing that this sensational news had been until now completely unknown to the others.

Klaus said, "This is very sad news, which would be unbelievable if it did not come from you. And it confirms us in our determination to act. But can we get to the point, which is the act?"

Helmuth said, "I'm sorry, I'm trying to be complete, to show you why I have prepared this plan . . ." He paused and spoke in a strange low voice, strained with emotion, which made them all alert, for he rarely showed his emotions, ". . . because I believe we shall never meet again. This is the last time we shall see each other alive."

Tati thought with amazement, 'That is right,' and everyone on the lawn was silent for a moment, thinking of the preciousness of life and this moment under the shining sky among the trees hissing with the wind.

Helmuth went on, "It is our job, I suggest, to be prepared for the crucial moment."

"Prepared to do what?" Clara burst out. Everyone looked at her in surprise at this challenge to a man's authority. Tati made a strange sound, a bark like a laugh, amazement with a tincture of delight.

"We must decide the end before we choose the means," Helmuth said.

She refused to be infuriated. "I asked a simple question."

His face seized up with patience. "The 'what' will be decided by what we think is best for Germany in the comity of nations," he said.

"What a romantic notion," she said, sure that the stiffening in him showed he was uncertain. "The Allies see no difference among us, we are all bad Germans."

Peter said mildly, "I think we must decide if we are going to act, and how."

Klaus said in an urgent tone, "We are faced with a choice of evils, acting, and doing nothing. All our intellectualism is a form of evasion." He now switched to English and quoted, "Thus conscience doth make cowards of us all." Peter smiled, shaking his head, and Helmuth James looked sad. He understood Hamlet's conscience very well.

Klaus went on, "For German honour alone we must strike."

On the stone terrace a man was waving at them. Hans Gisevius, tall, smiling, very well-dressed in a grey suit he had just bought in Switzerland, came across the lawn bearing packages of chocolate, bags of coffee from Turkey, and cigars for Klaus and Helmuth. He sat down, accepting some of the muddy ersatz coffee, and said, "I'm sorry I'm so late, I was in Zurich and, Clara, I went to see your father's agent, as you asked, and a letter was waiting. Here."

He handed her the letter. As Helmuth continued to read aloud from his long memo, Clara read her father's letter. *My darling Clara, I hope you are well and surviving as well as possible. I have been beavering away here at producing things, as you know, and we have had little success. Little Winifred Spencer got your present some time ago, but I'm sorry to say that as soon as she tried to wind it up, it broke. I think it was too old a toy for her. Too bad. Perhaps after the war something can be done to mend it.* He went on with news of her mother, who was back in Fredericton, and ended with love to her and saying he was asking the agent to send along a box of Ganong chocolates from home.

When Helmuth paused to sip at his coffee, Clara said to Helmuth, "Do you remember you asked me to find out what happened to the letter to your friend in Cambridge that you just read out?"

"Yes?"

"I sent a copy via Hans who handed it to Allen Dulles in Zurich. Well, the reply has come. My father writes that the present—that's the letter—arrived and was given by Beaverbrook—that's from beavering away—to little Winifred Spencer—that's Churchill—but that when she tried to play with it, it broke. That means he discussed it in Cabinet and they are not interested."

"And that is the British reply to all our sacrifices?" Axel exclaimed. "This childish nonsense? My God. Incredible."

"What about the fuses?" said Klaus.

"What fuses?" said Axel, scenting action.

Hans said, "For our gift to the Führer. Dulles told me the British want nothing to do with us. But he will have the fuses dropped into France and delivered to us in Annecy."

Helmuth looked from face to face as if seeking some new hope, and then sank down into his chair looking tired.

With a feeling of excitement mixed with dread, Klaus foresaw the fuses for his bomb silently swinging down into a field in France at night. But he wanted to hear from Helmuth why it was that he was risking his life, before he risked his own. "Helmuth, you are the only man here who does not accept that it would be better to succeed in a violent coup, than to do nothing against this regime. Yet you risk your life to help us."

Helmuth bowed his head. "We must be stoical, but I can not help hoping."

Everyone was silent. Each of them had hoped, but for a moment they shared the despair of this serious man. Peter said, "If God had meant us to be stoical, he would not have given us Jesus Christ."

"Christ condemned violence," said Helmuth.

Klaus waited. In a little while he said, "Helmuth, we have heard a lot of fine sentiments from you and we expect nothing less from such a great mind. But still we don't know what you envisage for postwar Germany. Or should I say, Germany after the coup d'état. We have discussed this; I am sure we all agree that we should put an end to the discussion today, so that we can act. Is that agreed?"

Helmuth said, "I am not sure that we should act."

Axel hissed, "Kerensky," and Klaus looked up at him, then at Helmuth, ready to side with him if he took offense at this insult. Helmuth, who liked the impetuous Axel, smiled and said nothing.

Adam said, "Then why are we here, Helmuth? Is this just another Heidelberg talking-shop?"

"Not at all," Helmuth said. "But we must face reality. Nothing can be done now to affect the war, not even assassination. We must suffer the consequences. We have fallen and it is our fate to suffer the fall. However if some are determined to go ahead, they will rescue Germany's soul, and her honour."

"Best kill him," Canaris said, lifting one white-blond eyebrow in emphasis.

"There is no other way," Axel said.

"That is the rule of violence, I am talking about the laws of love. The way to end violence is not to participate in it and to persuade others to stop."

Klaus said, "This is futile. We wish to act, you do not, it's as simple as that. Helmuth, you are a philosopher and a dreamer."

"I am sorry you say that in a spirit of contempt."

"My apologies," Klaus said, then added, "to you and to the whole circle." There was an embarrassed silence which he waited out, then said, "Nevertheless, the generals have failed to act, now it is time for the colonels. Who is with me?"

Axel said, "I am. I am fed up with waiting, I insist that we make a plan now for the seizure of power, and I shall volunteer to kill him myself."

Helmuth looked at him with a sick expression, fearing already the loss of Axel, to whom he felt like a protective big brother.

Axel explained, "There is a meeting in three weeks to show him the new personal equipment, uniform, sidearms, rocket launcher. I am to demonstrate the greatcoat. I shall strap grenades under it and then throw myself on him and hold him till it goes off."

Everyone thought, 'I could never say such a thing.'

Tati was looking at brave Axel, wanting him to live, and he saw in her face what she was thinking. He said, "But you must be ready with a plan to take over after he is gone. That is what I ask in return."

Klaus looked at Helmuth. "Do you approve?" he asked.

Helmuth was silent.

"Do you object?" he said.

Helmuth was silent.

"All right," said Klaus. "Here is my plan."

In bed that night in the gun-room, whose walls were hung with rifles, over-and-unders, double-barrelled shotguns, needle-guns, target pistols, bird-guns, Peter said mildly, "You rather amazed us all when you jumped on Helmuth James today."

"Why shouldn't I have my say?"

"No reason, except that that is not the way it has been in Germany."

"*Moins ça change, plus il faut le changer.*"

That night, Klaus had a terrible vision of Germany as a dark tribe dominated by men in black uniforms banded together by oaths and scars and wild ideals of courage, blood and death, which made him hate Germany, and drew him to love and save it.

Teheran, November, 1943

"Never before in human history has so much worldly power been gathered in a single room," said Churchill. He paused. The translators worked this into Russian, and Stalin nodded his approval. As Churchill continued his opening statement at Teheran, Stalin talked to Molotov beside him at the huge round table, tapping a small black Russian cigarette into a brass ashtray, and doodled wolves' heads on a piece of paper.

Churchill, aware that the British were the weakest of the Allies, brought out a stereopticon with slides of the destruction of Hamburg. He handed this to Stalin. "These are photographs of Hamburg after the RAF raid of last July. Over 80 per cent of the houses have been destroyed. At least 40,000 people died in the firestorm. We are planning a larger campaign against Berlin starting tomorrow. The Germans can not long stand this onslaught."

Stalin peered into the machine. "Good. How long can you keep it up?"

"We shall smite them with ever-increasing force," said Churchill, "Germany will be a smoking ruin when we break into it."

"With such air power, you should find it easy to land in France." This was the theme of their talks for the rest of the day. Stalin and Voroshilov mocked the difficulties of a sea-borne landing, saying that the Germans and Russians both crossed wide rivers all the time. General Marshall, resplendent in full uniform with all ribbons blazing, said, "I have been a soldier all my life, and I never heard the expression landing craft until a few months ago. Now I think about little else."

"Good, if you think about it, you will do it," said Stalin, who admired Marshall. It was decided that the Americans and British would land in France in May, 1944.

They went on to discuss the shuttle bombing of the Ploesti oil fields, the invasion of Italy and the resumption of the Arctic convoys, on which Stalin was very insistent. "The Allies have not lived up to their contractual obligations to the Soviet government," he said. "These arms are very important to us. Without them, we can not win the war. If my generals see no prospect of victory, they will advise me to make peace."

This threat, which Stalin thought was the most menacing of all, had no effect on Churchill or Roosevelt, who had already decided that the hatred between Stalin and Hitler was now so intense that they would never negotiate with each other.

Roosevelt glanced at Churchill, who was responsible for the air and naval power to escort the convoys to Archangel. "We listen to your reproaches with regret in our hearts but calm minds," Churchill began, "because we know that we have made every effort against appalling odds to send supplies to you, and because we remember that in the dark days of 1939, 1940 and 1941, while we alone were fighting Hitler, the Soviet Union, Hitler's ally, was indifferent to our fate, and that upon Hitler's betrayal of your alliance with him, we offered to you all that was in our power to give, a policy initiated by Lord Beaverbrook and myself, approved by the British public and carried out by ourselves and later by the President despite terrible losses and the ingratitude and even hostility displayed both at Archangel and around this table by the representatives of the Soviet Union." Hopkins and Roosevelt looked appalled.

Stalin listened to the translation, and on the western faces there was some relief as they noted the calm tone of his reply. The translator said, "The Prime Minister has a good memory. The Head of the Soviet government also has a good memory. He remembers for instance that after Hitler attacked Russia, the Prime Minister said in response to a question as to what the British policy would now be, 'If Hitler invaded Hell, I would at least make a favourable reference to the Devil.'" Stalin smiled mischievously and added in English, "Stalin is devil."

The tension round the table collapsed, and people who had been holding their breath relaxed and began to smile at each other. Roosevelt smiled and thought, 'This is a man I can talk to, he is get-atable.'

"But what is this about Archangel?" Stalin went on.

Churchill explained that British sailors stationed there to service their incoming ships had been denied visas to return to England on leave. They were prisoners if not hostages of the Russians. Several had been arrested and imprisoned after a brawl in a bar with Russian sailors. As he was speaking for the translator, Stalin was whispering with Molotov, who was nodding. He did not admit it, but he understood some English.

Stalin nodded and replied, "I was not aware of these problems. I assure you that the sailors who wish to go home on leave after heroic service in the mutual cause, will be given visas right away. Furthermore, the case of the British sailors will be investigated right away with a view to their early release. No such minor incidents should be permitted to impede the workings of the grand councils of the mightiest powers in the world."

There was general satisfaction at this result.

At the dinner table the next night in the Russian legation, Stalin said to Churchill, "We were impressed by your photographs of Hamburg, and hope you will have further success with your bombing. You said that 'Germany will be a smoking ruin when we break in.' We would like to know what you expect to do with the Germans in that smoking ruin?"

"We have scarcely discussed that," said Roosevelt. "I dislike making plans for occupying a country before we are there. You never know what you might find." His son Elliott, in the uniform of a colonel in the United States Army, whispered in his ear, "Well done, dad."

Stalin went on, "I am glad you have joined in," he said. "We have not discussed your unilateral statement that the Allies will accept nothing less than unconditional surrender."

"Bilateral, surely," said Churchill, although he too had been miffed by Roosevelt's high-handedness.

"It is our opinion that the terms as announced by you without our consent or foreknowledge, will make the Germans fight harder, because they will be afraid of the unknown. If you don't know what the police have in store for you, you fear them all the more." Here he smiled the yellow-toothed smile that had repelled Beaverbrook in Moscow.

Roosevelt, who had been the first to demand unconditional sur-render, listened, but did not change his mind. He wanted a free hand to deal with Germany. He said this, and Stalin said, "Yes, but it is not necessary to say so in advance."

"What are your ideas, Marshal?" said Churchill, deferring to the rank that he knew made Stalin proud. He himself was wearing the ele-gant blue of a commodore of the Royal Air Force, Roosevelt as usual was in a suit, a summer-weight cloth because Teheran was warm.

"We should break up the country into pieces, eliminate the Junkers and shoot the whole German General Staff and at least 50,000 more." He raised his glass. "They are the core of the army. To the deaths of 50,000 Germans."

Churchill said, "The British Parliament and public will never tol-erate mass executions. Even if in war-passion they allowed them to begin, they would turn violently against those responsible after the first butchery had taken place." He touched his fist to the table as he waited for the translator to finish, and ended with, "The Soviet gov-ernment must be under no delusion on this point."

Stalin raised his glass again and said, "50,000 must be shot."

Churchill stuck out his jaw. "I would rather be taken out into the garden here and now and be shot myself than sully my own and my country's honour by such infamy."

Everyone was silent, fearing what might happen next. Roosevelt raised his glass. "A compromise. Not 50,000, but 49,000."

Churchill winced. Eden was making signals begging him to desist. The President's son Elliott got up woozy with champagne and said that he cordially agreed with Stalin and that the United States Army would support the shooting of many hundreds of thousands more Germans. Churchill, so angry that his bald head was red, got up from the table in silence and pounded out of the room towards the garden.

Roosevelt shook his head, thinking, 'Winston, you've done it this time,' but Stalin got up with a worried half-smile on his face and followed by the translator and Molotov, hurried out of the room.

Stalin placed his hands on Churchill's shoulders and said, "It was a joke, please come back." He was smiling, which Churchill in the half light could barely see, though he could smell the tobacco smoke on Stalin's breath. He nodded, looking down, and thought, 'Nobody but this unnatural man would pretend that murdering 50,000 prisoners could be a joke.'

He returned to the table and sat down, then growled, "Who in the world will not have his laugh amid the skulls?"

Stalin was not finished with the Germans. He wanted Churchill and Roosevelt to go much further. "I have no faith in the possibility of reforming the Germans. When I was in Leipzig in 1907 for a conference, 200 German workers failed to appear at an important meeting. They would not leave the station until their tickets had been punched, and there was no station-master at the station. By the time a station-master was found, the rally was over. This mentality can not be changed. They will always be obedient to whomever takes power over them."

Roosevelt said, "Hitler is mentally unstable, and this disease has spread to the whole German mentality. We must control them."

There was general agreement around the table when they broke for lunch. Roosevelt had refused a private meeting with Churchill, but had asked Stalin for one. He judged that it was more important for mankind's hopes for peace to charm and cajole Stalin, than to placate Churchill, who was loyal to him and would, he was sure, forgive him. Churchill, however, was not one to take an insult at face value: he demanded, and got his own private meeting with Stalin.

Churchill opened the meeting by saying, "I wish to discuss the fate of the Polish people, for whose defence the British government went to war." This was a sore point for them both because Stalin had been Hitler's ally and had attacked Poland in 1939.

Stalin had been alerted to this by Hopkins, so his answer was ready. "The fate of Poland will be decided by the Polish people."

"It is also about the borders of Poland that we must talk, because they can not settle that question alone," said Churchill.

"But it was your own Lord Curzon who settled the matter for all time by drawing the eastern border where we will fix it after we have driven out the Germans."

"And the Poles?" said Churchill. "There are millions of Poles on the Russian side of that line. What will happen to them?"

"They will have new lands to the west," said Stalin. Churchill was mystified. "What new lands?" he asked, thinking of Canada.

"In Schlesia, Prussia, Brandenburg," said Stalin, pushing his thick short forefinger over the map. Churchill loved maps. He drew himself closer to the table, took out three wooden matches and laid them parallel to each other on eastern Poland, central Poland, and western Poland.

"I see," he said, then he smiled and moved the matches one by one to the west. "You take from Poland, Poland takes from Germany."

"It is best not to express it so," said Stalin in a soft voice. "I expect that the Germans will flee as we advance into Germany and the Poles will flow into the empty lands the Germans leave behind."

Churchill looked grave, then shrugged and said, "And if a few German toes get stepped on, it is too bad."

Stalin began his meeting with Roosevelt by picking up where they had left off at lunch. He said, "I do not agree that Hitler is unstable. I admire him very much. He is a clever man doing daring things, who has gone too far and thrown away the fruits of his first victories by trying for one more."

He was asserting himself because he felt strengthened by the competition for his attention between Churchill and Roosevelt. Harry Hopkins had told him that Roosevelt respected strong men and regarded Stalin as among the strongest in the world. Also, Stalin's armies had begun winning consecutive victories against the Germans, despite the disasters caused by his own bungling. He was sure now that Hitler could never beat him, though he also believed that Russia alone could never beat Germany.

Roosevelt said in a mollifying tone, "I thought it would be grand if you and I could settle this instead of leaving it up to the boys in pin-striped suits."

Stalin looked puzzled, as this was translated, because he thought "pinstriped-suits" meant prisoners in the gulag.

"Settle what?" he asked.

"This business in the Baltic."

"What is that?" Stalin looked rock-hard.

"Many of us want to know if the Baltic peoples will have a free democratic vote after the war."

"All the peoples of the Soviet Union are free." Thus he was claiming to Roosevelt's face that the Baltic people were Soviet citizens without having to state it directly. Roosevelt then asked him point blank for the guarantee. Stalin replied that all the peoples of the Soviet Union were already well-represented both in the Party and in the government. Annoyed, Roosevelt said that it appeared that Stalin did not understand what was meant by democracy. He pointed out that in the United States, there were many people descended from Polish or Baltic ancestors, and that these millions of people all voted, and many were demanding that the United States guarantee the freedom of their homelands, "by which I mean the right to their property and the right to elect their own government."

At this, Stalin's voice grew very soft and he replied, "It is the settled policy of my government that we make no territorial or political demands upon our great and courageous allies. This means avoiding the profound mistake of trying to understand or advise upon the difficulties that the ally, whether it be Great Britain or the United States, faces in its various conquered territories, including India, the Philippines, Hawaii, South Africa and so on. However, since the President has been so good as to inquire, let him be assured that we will make every effort as soon as possible after the destruction of the last vestiges of Hitlerism in Poland and elsewhere, to afford the various peoples concerned the means to express their will in the formation of their new governments."

When he had finished, there was a long silence. Stalin filled his pipe, which was difficult for him because of his withered left arm. Then he lit it, blew out the match, and puffed a cloud of strong smoke.

Roosevelt's face looked haggard and puffy. He was thinking, 'Don't let him see he offended you. Take it easy. He has shown his teeth by mentioning the Philippines and India, be content with what he just said.'

He moved on to the idea for the United Nations. Stalin, regarding all this as blue-sky planning with no relation to the realities of bombs and guns, was glad to oblige the President with courteous agreements, which cost him nothing, to all the UN proposals, vague as they were.

The President saw that Stalin regarded these proposals as trivial. So, although he had the agreement in principle, the animating spirit was missing, which discouraged him.

Harry Hopkins, waiting outside the meeting room door, looked at his chief's face with dismay but Roosevelt said nothing. He wheeled himself past Hopkins with his mouth set firm. 'At least I did not blow up at him,' he thought. He had gone in there vowing that no matter what happened he would not say anything angry or cutting to the man. He was beginning to wish that he had.

Berlin, December, 1943

～⤙⤚～

Clara tried to get up but her leg was pinned by a wood beam. She was freezing cold, frightened, shivering, on her back under heavy floorboards. Cold wind full of smoke was pouring down the cellar stair at her face. She pulled and tried to turn her leg, feeling the stocking tear while dust and bits of mortar fell on her face. The cellar stairs had collapsed, dust blowing in on her on the cold smoky wind. She found her flashlight by her hand, shone it on the joist and realized that she could pull her leg inch by inch towards her at the proper angle and it would come free.

She pulled her bleeding leg clear, struggled up, and found the emergency saw and crowbar. But when she started to remove rubble, more began to topple towards her, and she could not see how to prop it up. She decided to try the outside stairwell, but something seemed strange. 'I'm already beside the outside stairwell. I must have been blown right across the cellar,' she thought. 'Didn't I start out by the laundry tubs on the far side, by the stone wall?' Now she felt panic: what if the inside stairwell were blocked too? If no one missed her till Monday morning at the office? If the house were on fire and the firemen drowned her with the water? If the gas mains were open and suffocated her?

Voices sounded faintly above. Men were digging. She called out and they shouted back to her, and in a few minutes they opened a hole big enough for her. They pulled her up to the light. She stood up, covered with dust, thinking how bedraggled she must look.

"Why is it so light?" she said

"It's nine o'clock in the morning, Miss. What is your name please? And which house was this?"

"I thought the raid was just over."

"Was there anyone else in the house, Miss?"

"No, I was alone."

She clambered back, despite the pain in her left leg, toward the house over the rubble towards the remnant of the doorway, while one of the workers urged her to come away. But she went back in, found the stairwell and limped up, holding her hand against the soft bulge of the papered wall. At the top, the paper was ripping open, pressed from be-hind by loose bits of mortar and plaster. It tore, and soft broken plaster sifted past her onto the stairs like pus from a wound. She found the bandages she was looking for and bound the scratches and deep cuts on her thigh and calf.

Their bedroom was a shambles, but she could see that it was intact except for a hole in the ceiling which might be fixed. The bathtub was full of water, her normal precaution. In it were floating bits of lath and torn scraps of charred paper. She looked up in fear of fire, then real-ized that the paper was not burned—it was blackout paper blown in from the windows. She worked in the house for the rest of the morning, tidying up, covering the hole in the ceiling, and then took a sponge-bath from the water in the tub.

When she went out to find Tati, the air-raid workers were still pull-ing debris away from doorways, tapping on foundation walls to see if anyone answered. She left them and started to pick her way through the loose bricks, glass and boards blown into the street.

The time was past noon, but Budapesterstrasse was in twilight, under the smoke. Snow mantled the ruins, making them seem a natural part of the landscape. The air-raid shelter in the Langbehn's garden looked like an igloo. At the corner, the anti-aircraft gun barrels were horizontal, with canvas caps over their muzzles, snow decorating their upper edges.

People walked by with worried eyes above the scarves over their faces against the smoke. All the way to the Cornelius Brucke at the canal end of Budapesterstrasse, she could not see a single familiar sight. Height was gone. Tall buildings had disappeared taking with them their echoes. Trees lay on their sides, heaps of rubble replaced houses where she had danced, dined, drunk tea, embraced friends. Where walls of apartment buildings had once stood, ruins of neighbourhoods smoked on the hill all the way to Charlottenburg.

At the Wittenberg Platz, she looked around for the tall red brick apartment building on the corner. Hearing a roar, she turned round and saw a six-storey building starting to collapse. It seemed to give up and slump down, with a roar worse than a train in a tunnel. Graceful arabesques of dust rose round the disappearing building. A fireman dragging a hose did not even turn round to watch.

She said to the fireman, "Where is Wichmannstrasse, please?"

"Gone, madame."

"Where was it?"

He gestured towards some heaps of smoking rubble decorated with snow and ice. "I'm sorry ma'am, the street is worse than this." She looked round thinking, 'What could be worse than this?'

She deduced where it had been by orienting herself to the fountain in the centre of the square, which was undamaged, and started along. Two grey-haired firemen holding the brass nozzle of their rigid hose fired water upwards on a fiery lump until the hose ran dry. They dropped it limp on the ground and half-walked, half-crawled over the slithering, steaming rubble to the doorframe, still standing alone, with no door in it, calling out, "Where are you?"

In and around the platz, streetcars shawled in snow lay on their sides, upside down, broken in half, flat-tired busses kneeled with their roofs smashed in, smoke rising from the engine compartments. Most landmarks had disappeared. 'Oh Tati, where are you?' she thought, praying that she had gone to the air-raid shelter at the far end of the street. She started down the shallow central chaos of bricks, stones, crippled furniture and spears of timber, between the smoking heaps on each side.

She counted the taller piles of rubble along the sides, allowing one to a house. Beside one pile, a girl of about 16 in a jumper picked up a brick, dusted off the snow, set it down, picked up another, dusted it off, set it down. A woman in a sable coat was standing on an unharmed piece of the sidewalk, trying to talk to her. As Clara came up, the woman in the coat said, "Her whole family is dead in there, she won't talk."

Passing an undamaged phone kiosk, she thought, 'Might as well' and dialled Tati's number.

Tati said, "But where are you?"

"I'm in a kiosk in Wichmannstrasse, but I can't find you."

"I know, you're across the street, wait there, I'll come out."

As Clara watched, Tati's head emerged from a hole in a heap of rubble across the street, she scrambled up on top of the heap, and then picked her way down, and came across the street, saying loudly, "How good to see you, Frau Bemberg, come along in."

Clara wondered if she had been bombed out of her mind, and then realized that Tati was afraid of the neighbours, who belonged to the Party.

She followed Tati, who was wearing a ski jacket and dark slacks spotted with dust, up a trail over the heap and down a tunnel into a basement strewn with bricks and sticks. Radiators torn from the wall hung loose on their twisted dripping pipes.

"This is my woodpile," said Tati, pointing at broken furniture. "I found a wonderful little wood stove at the porter's lodge and it keeps me warm."

"But when were you bombed?"

"When not? This house was first hit three days ago, I've been cleaning up ever since. And now again last night." She was hectic, even hysterical. "What do they think they're doing, bombing ruins, it's crazy crazy crazy."

She sat down on a crate and covered her face with her hands and wept. Clara kneeled down beside her and put her arm around her shoulder, kissed her wet cheek and said, "It's all right, we will get through this somehow, just hold on darling, a little while longer, we can do it, you've already done so much." At this, something crashed down on the floor above them, the ceiling quivered and dust pulsed in the air.

Tati sat up and started to laugh, looking wild. "It will get worse before it gets better." She looked around. "Come," she said, then said, "Oh, wait." She gathered up an armload of broken bits of wood, gave them to Clara and they carried the loads to the inner courtyard. Then she led the way through a hole in the wall of the next house, up a long stairway to the remains of the flat. As they went she explained that the stairs of her house had been destroyed, so they had to go the long way round, through the Schmidts next door, to reach her own, through a hole blasted in the common wall.

She swept aside a curtain. "*La voilà.*" Clara stared around, amazed at the mess, and Tati noticed her face. "The first time Klaus saw this, I was afraid he would think it was my housekeeping." She collapsed on the sofa, then sat up, wiping her eyes. "Oh, it's so good to see you, and have a good laugh. I'm scared stiff of air raids, aren't you, but somehow it seems safer here, not so much left to fall down on one. Do you remember, this was our bedroom, we sleep in the spare room now, if he's here, which is seldom, and this is the remains of the kitchen, which I am repairing by myself. I've grown quite handy now, and the salon as you see is unimpaired, amazing what does and does not happen, oh and don't open that door, or you'll fall straight into the basement, that's the stairwell. I heard you went to Kernslau last week. How is Helmuth, I miss him so much, but I'm stuck here at the office and it's so much safer there for him. Oh . . . I'm so glad to see you," and began to weep again, saying "I'm sorry, I'm sorry, I'll get over it, I will." She straightened her shoulders and said, "What about tea?"

"But why don't you go to your grandfather's house in Charlottenburg?"

"Nikky leased it to the Spanish Ambassador after the Embassy was burned out. You see? It doesn't matter where the Miloslavskys settle, Tula, Klaipeda, Charlottenburg, Wichmannstrasse, they all go up in smoke."

"But Charlottenburg hasn't been hit?"

"Might as well. I can't go there, can I?"

She began to get out the cups and saucers, dipped water from the bucket into the kettle and talked. "I am so alone these days, even when Klaus is here, he's never here, he is always at Bendlerstrasse." She stuck another table leg into the stove, they drank tea and ate some sweet biscuits from France that Klaus had been given and Tati said, "When we've finished here, we'll go back to your place and straighten up."

She bathed the wounds in Clara's leg with boiled water and iodine, then stuck on a better bandage. They worked the rest of the day, part of the night, and by noon the next day, they had restored much of Clara's apartment. The water came back on, the plumbing worked, and there was even brown-out electricity for two hours in the late afternoon. Clouds rolled over Berlin, and there was no visit from the RAF.

"Our place is such a mess, I don't even want to go back there, and Klaus is always criticizing me for the housekeeping."

"What do you say?"

"Well, I soon realized he doesn't care about housekeeping at all."

She wiped a finger through some dust they had overlooked on Clara's dining room table. "What he cares about is the rules of housekeeping. He wants the laundry done on Monday, if there is water, the ironing on Tuesday, if there is electricity, the shopping on Wednesday, if there is anything in the shops, the bed made before breakfast, if there is anything for breakfast, but he has no idea if the corners are clean, or if we have mice, or why doors squeak, but he will moan if he sees a book open face down, because it shows an untidy habit of mind, best expunged right away, in case it spreads to other things, like I don't know, maybe sleeping face down."

She laughed. "But he is such a dear, and so brave and correct, and even romantic, we play music together, or we did before the accident, he reads me poetry, and brings me flowers and then complains the vase is cracked, so I tell him he's testy because he's hungry, and feed him, if there is something and everything starts glowing again, and he tells me his thoughts. Quite poetic and also practical. Is Peter like that? I mean, so various?"

This speech made Clara laugh, but also made her feel left out. Beautiful romantic Tati brought out the beauty and romance in others—but just now, she was making Clara feel smelly, tired, unwashed, a tall, gangly, new-world girl with long bones, hard flanks, minor bosom and flat practical views.

They slept together in Clara's bed, and shared one egg, chicory coffee and three slices of grey bread in the morning.

"We need cheering up," said Tati. "I know, I have a hair appointment this morning. Why don't you come along and we'll get our hair done."

"But what for?"

"Something nice might happen, you never know."

Charlotte the hairdresser was glad to see Tati, having heard of the damage around the Wichmannstrasse.

"I'll have a wash and set." Clara sat back and stretched her legs out in front.

"And Your Highness?" said Charlotte in Tati's ear, taking her head in her hands and turning it this way and that in front of the mirror.

"Something suitable for air raids," Tati said. "Close to the head."

While she was in her usual stupor under the dryer, she remembered she had an appointment as well to try on a new hat at Zabet's in the Friedrichstrasse, so they walked to the shop across the Pariser Platz from the Adlon. Zabet welcomed her with a warm smile and said, "I was afraid you had forgotten."

"No, I was just blown up."

"Here it is," said Zabet, producing a pale blue felt cloche. "And here is something new." She pulled out two small grosgrain ribbons. "You can tie it under your chin in case of an air raid." The two women started to laugh, and Zabet looked shocked. "But you see, the concussion could blow it off."

Tati gave her the Aryan clothing cards for the felt in the hat, and they started across the Pariser Platz laughing as Tati described her own concussed head sailing away by itself with the cloche still attached by grosgrain ribbons. They stopped when they saw the big grey Horch staff car parked in front of the Adlon, and the big man in the back seat filling out the car requisition.

Hans Bernd Gisevius handed the requisition to his driver. He had just returned from France on leave, he had 100 oysters at his feet on ice in two steel buckets marked Feuer, he had no money, and no idea which of his friends was in town. The Adlon was the place to start. The driver was following him into the hotel when he heard Tati shout his name. He exclaimed, "Just the ones I want to see. Guess what I have? Oysters. Who's in town? I want some champagne."

The doorman carried the two buckets while Hans took them by the arm into the American Bar where he accosted the chief steward, demanding a case of champagne for heroes just back from the front.

"Well now," he said, with his foot on the rail and his elbow on the mahogany bar, looking around. "I was in Paris seeing Stulpnagel about the western solution," he said in a whisper.

"And?" Tati said.

"He is for it."

"Wonderful."

"I was also collecting material for my book on these louts—every mistake, every crime, every lunatic impulse—it's all there. Five hundred pages."

"It's too dangerous," said Tati smiling at him in admiration.

"I don't keep it here," he said. "It's in Berne. But we must stop whispering, or at least pretend we are arranging an assignation."

He waved his cigarette holder in the air. Tati, who had always admired his height, lean frame and elegant clothes, sighed. He was so neat and everyone round the room looked grubby. They smelled of smoke, their eyes were red from lack of sleep. Even their haircuts were disorderly, since most people were cutting hair for each other.

Clara exclaimed, "Look, over there in the corner, by himself, reading, the tall man with blond hair? Who is that? He looks very familiar."

Tati said, "It's some English writer who's working for the propaganda ministry. Somebody Wodehouse."

"I know. P.G. Wodehouse," said Clara. "I've read his books, very funny. He's famous. What's he doing here?"

"Captured in France. He's done broadcasts for Göbbels."

"Dear old Adlon," said Hans, "you never know who's going to fall down drunk at your feet."

Clara was distracted, watching Wodehouse sip his cocktail and gently turn the page of the book before him, puffing on a cigarette in a long holder. She wanted to talk to him about England, home, literature, anything but dusty bombed Berlin and the bad news from the front.

Hans Bernd said, "I've rented us a suite."

"But Hans, it's so expensive. How can you?"

"What do I care? What good is money in a war anyway? Besides, I don't have any, so that's all right. I've always wanted to give a huge party at the Adlon, but my stuffy old family always said 'too expensive, too expensive,' so tonight's the night, and you're my hostesses."

He had a four-room suite and walked through without remarking on anything as if accustomed to such peacetime splendour. Tati exclaimed, "It's just like 1939." Although both she and Clara had been brought up to the taste of the rich, they were so accustomed now to the dust, wreckage and confusion of their homes, that they were both silenced at first by the carved and painted Louis Quinze furniture, the bathtub set in a mahogany box, the ornate fixtures that seemed to be of solid gold, the Adlon-blue leather letter-case on the rosewood escritoire, the lemonwood end tables on elegantly curved legs poised on the pale wool carpet.

Clara tried the bathtub taps, which worked. She eyed the towels, then started the water. She called Tati who gazed in relief at the gushing hot water, and said, "So this is how we used to live."

They bathed and then dried themselves on the thick long clean towels with a feeling of pre-war luxury.

Hans was on the phone, beginning with his office and Helmut James von Blücher who promised to bring two Swedish diplomats. In the little pantry-bar, Clara set to work on the oysters with wood-handled knives sent up with the champagne from the kitchen.

Tati said with a sigh, "I feel so stupid watching you. Why aren't you helpless like me?" Clara worked with one hand flat on top of the oyster, the other gently inserting the tip of the springy blade into the thin flat end of the oyster, then giving a slight twist so the shell parted.

"I used to do dozens of Malpeques every September at the garden party my parents gave at Dunnsford."

"Didn't you have servants?"

"Oh yes, lots but mother and father insisted we all learn how to do things. I can portage a canoe, I can recanvas it, I can chop wood and lay fires. I once shingled a roof, I planted and hoed vegetables, I can stook wheat, I can mow hay in the barn, and I can sew and knit and drive a car and play the piano and I can play hockey if I have to." She laughed.

The outer doors opened and closed, the phone rang, the voices and the smoke from the main salon grew stronger.

"We'd better hurry, they'll be ravenous. Perhaps you could show me how to do it," said Tati. Clara instructed her but Tati stabbed her palm. She wrapped her hand in a handkerchief and went on working. "Isn't it odd that a Russian countess and a Canadian are serving oysters to German officers and Swedish diplomats during a British air raid on Berlin?"

"Maybe we'll be lucky tonight."

There were cheers in the salon, and calls of "Peter," and Clara rushed out to see Peter just back from a therapy session, leaning on a cane in one hand, holding a live goose up in the air with the other, its wings flapping, its head in a bag, its feet tied together. He started towards her, nearly fell and then took her in his arms while he dropped the goose to the floor and hugged her close and said, "I love you, Merry Christmas," and she closed her eyes on the smell of him, disinfectant and smoke.

Tati brought oysters, Hans passed champagne, and Peter, leaning on his cane in the middle of the salon, raised his glass and said, "Here's to 1943 when we got good news from every front. We enticed the enemy ashore into Italy where we are now demolishing their armies as we did in North Africa and Sicily, we ordered Italy to join the Allies, so now the Americans are being dragged down by the Italians instead of us. Our troops in the east are advancing towards Berlin, our wonder weapons are now being produced in greater numbers than ever before—the jet-propelled propaganda missile, the high-velocity anti-tank poster, the armour-piercing Party salute, the radio-controlled concentration camp, and so forth. To our beloved Führer who has brought us all this good news. Soon may he hang . . ." he raised his glass ". . . over every German hearth from Spain to Vladivostok."

There was a cheer, glasses were raised, though two of the officers there gave each other what Berliners were now calling "the German glance," signifying fear of someone eavesdropping. Hans, inspired by his friend, advertised the oysters. "Here they are ladies and gentlemen, get your fill, Belon oysters from Brittany, and I'll tell you we had the devil of a time capturing them. Our men had to advance on their bellies over murderous defences—razor-sharp moules concealed in the rocks. Once they were surrounded, the oysters surrendered like Italians, but then our courageous supply teams had to get the trainloads back through British bombing to Berlin where we got the necessary certificate of racial purity, which I have here." He held up a copy of the *Volkischer Beobachter*. "These oysters are racially sound, so slurp them down."

Towards midnight, someone began singing "Oh Tannenbaum," and the loud talk changed to sentimental singing. Tati noticed through the crowd Walter Guderian, the nephew of the general, with a very sweet expression on his young face, singing the carol, as if he were remembering happy times with his family round the tree at home. Tears rimmed her eyes. She remembered the old Count sitting beside her at the piano as she learned the carol. She thought of little Helmuth and her mother at Kernslau and was eager to get there for the holiday. Clara said, "Let's all go together. Tonight."

Helmuth James von Blücher was going there with his Swedish friends, leaving that night in a lorry loaded with furniture to go back to Stockholm.

The Swedes dropped them in the small station at Angermunde, where they were told the Stettin train was delayed. Peter, Clara and Tati sat on the wood floor in the station with their backs to the wall half asleep, while civilians and soldiers patiently waited on benches, or lay full length on newspapers on the floor, resting their heads on dunnage bags. One old woman gnawed sausage from a roll she kept concealed in the blanket over her knees, casting wary eyes around.

Clara watched dawn outside the dusty window turn the eastern clouds green, then yellow over the low, wide-spread hills until there was red light all along the horizon turning the inner wall of the station bright pink.

The train arrived and they helped Peter up, saying, "Make way for a wounded soldier," at which people turned to help him. But all the seats were taken, so the women sat on the floor of the corridor, with the goose, now tied up in an Adlon pillowcase, and the last few bottles of champagne, while Peter stood because there was no room to lie down, and he could not sit on the floor, because his leg could not bend.

Some of the windows had been blasted away, then the spaces filled with cardboard which was leaking cold air mixed with coal smoke.

Peter unplugged champagne and offered it to their neighbours, two sailors of the Kriegsmarine U-boat fleet.

"What is the news from the North Atlantic?" Peter asked. "We used to hear of nothing but victories, and now we hear nothing."

"We've been ordered home, too many losses," said one, with a weary face. He took a swig of champagne and passed the bottle to his friend who wiped the neck and drank. "There hasn't been a U-boat out there since June," said the other, a red-bearded man freckled to the edges of his eyes.

"May," said the tired young man. "We were ordered back from Newfoundland in May and in Lorient they told us we were the last boat in. We lost 16 of the 20 boats of the Canadian patrol in one month. Everyone I knew in the service except three on my last boat is dead." He handed the bottle back to Peter. "What happened to you?"

"Eastern front. Shrapnel. Near Vinnitsa."

"Well, you've got damned fine medicine for it anyway." He stared at Peter, thinking, 'At least I can go back to Anne-Liese a whole man.' "Here," he said, "why don't you lie down, I can move over."

The red-bearded sailor got up and Peter said, "Thank you very much" and, with Tati's help, got himself down with his leg stretched out. Spoon-fashion, from behind, Peter curled round Clara's long body as she curled round Tati from behind. Tati went to sleep thinking about seeing little Helmuth and her grandfather and her mother again, wondering if the goose would fit in the old wood-stove in the summer kitchen.

Clara fell asleep smiling with her face in Tati's air-raid hairdo.

1944

A Wehrmacht tank-park near Berlin, January, 1944

Axel von dem Bussche strapped the grenades round his waist inside the new greatcoat he was to model for Hitler, arrived at the parade ground an hour early and waited out the demonstration of the new Super Tiger tank grinding through mud and ditches while he was standing five metres from the Führer. He looked at his watch. Three minutes left before he was due to stand close in front of the Führer, two minutes until he must set the fuse. He looked around at the silver-edged grey clouds, the black trees at the far end of the parade ground, thinking, 'Goodbye everything.'

Hitler turned leaving the officers who had accompanied him, and strode to the staff car while two generals ran after him. Once again he had changed his itinerary as he often did to foil anyone planning to assassinate him.

Axel was shaking and so pale that the officer next him said, "Are you all right old man?" Axel could not speak. He nodded and pressed his right elbow into the bulge in his greatcoat against the bomb thinking he could never go through this again, while the friendly officer looked at him thinking, 'Incredible the effect that the Führer still has on us.'

At the meeting that night when Axel explained what had happened, Klaus thought, 'I must do it myself, or it will not be done.' He met many times with Helmuth James von Blücher and the others, irregularly, secretly, briefly and only after great difficulty in arranging time, place, agenda, personnel, all of which had to be worked out and encrypted, then transmitted, seldom by phone, and if on paper, only by Tati and Clara. Even when arranged, such a meeting might be interrupted or cancelled by an air raid, or an unforeseen shift in normal duties.

Now the feeling among the conspirators was that the top leaders of the party should be killed at the same time. Once Hitler, Bormann, Göring, Göbbels, and Himmler were removed, the coup d'état could begin. In the chaos after the assassinations, the Replacement Army, well-armed reserves guarding the homeland, would lead the rising. Their men would seize Government ministries, arrest party leaders, occupy radio and TV studios, newspaper offices, and announce that the army was restoring order.

By 1944 it was believed by nearly everyone in the world except the Germans that Germany was already beaten, that it was only a matter of time, and therefore death, until the war ended. So many people died in the catastrophic British firestorm raid on Hamburg in July that they could not be counted. Rumour said that fifty or a hundred and fifty thousand had died in a few hours. The loaded trains rolled day after day into the deadly concentration camps of Germany and Poland, a thousand prisoners at a time, the guillotines pounced on the necks of people every day and every night throughout Germany.

The Nazi leaders, fearing the war was lost, and with it their lives, denied what fear made them believe. They said that their new "miracle weapons" would soon create a decisive German victory. They said that history favoured Germany. They said that the stars favoured Germany and fabricated horoscopes for the newspapers predicting favourable events soon to come. They magnified the atrocities of the enemy to increase the hatred of their soldiers. They demanded

'*Totaler Krieg*' and increased production of weapons of every kind. They made movies proving that Germany was bound to win. They prophesied many unlikely events that would save Germany, except the only one that lay in their power, their own removal.

Berlin, February, 1944

Clara received a limp grey-green postcard ordering her to report next day for a medical examination to determine her fitness for "Compulsory service in the Women's Voluntary Labour Force." The paper gave her a sudden frisson of hope. That the government was reduced to such a mean card on official business was a sign of the final weakness. The end of the war and the Party tyranny must come soon.

That night Peter came in the door with frostbitten ears complaining, even as he took off his leather greatcoat fringed with dripping icicles. "God, it's cold out," he said. "Can we get some heat in here? I suppose we're out of fuel again?" She said nothing but filled the stove with wood she had scavenged and sawn herself, ignoring his insinuation that they lacked wood because she used so much during the day.

Peter thought, 'You clod, she is risking her life to help U-boats, she slaves alone here all day in a freezing cold flat and never complains. Stop complaining.' He sat down hugging himself while she draped a woollen shawl round his shoulders. He avoided her eyes, feeling ashamed of himself and therefore resentful of her.

Peter was at war with himself because he could not provide for her. A proud Metternich, he was ashamed of this cold flat, the terrible food, the clothing shortage, the lack of transportation. When he was depressed, he blamed her for staying in Germany. 'After all,' he thought, 'if you had not insisted on getting married, you would be safe in Canada. We could marry after the war, if I survive. If I don't, you're better off single than my widow.' At the same time he admired her for her courage. She always supported him and never questioned him. Some shortages she ignored, for the others she contrived solutions, the danger they never discussed.

Clara drew tight the canvas shroud over the door-hole into the dining room, where she worked on her non-teaching days. She had loosened it earlier so she could go in and out of their dining room where, despite the dust and cold, she worked at the translations and editing for *Signal* sent to her by Helmuth James and Tati. As she pulled, the rod fastening it above the doorway came loose from the cracked plaster, the curtain sagged down, and plaster dust puffed into the room. Peter exploded. "God in heaven woman, could you do something properly for once?"

"I'm sorry," she said.

"That's all I hear, all day. Sorry, sorry, sorry, we don't have this, you can't have that. There was a staff meeting at Rastenburg yesterday and von Richthofen was on the phone from the front to Keitel and he said, 'If you doubt what we are doing, get up here and take over this shambles yourself.' and hung up. The Führer saw Keitel's face so he asked what Richthofen had said, and Keitel—*Lackeitel*—told him."

"My God. What did he do?"

"He shrugged, said it was time to give Richthofen some leave. Is there any tea? Schnapps? I've been cold all day; Army HQ is trying to set a good example to the nation by freezing the senior officers to death."

Relieved that he was no longer criticizing her, she gave him a glass of schnapps, pushed another section of rafter into the fireplace and put a blanket over his lap as he sat by the fire trying to control himself. He regretted his outburst and could not tell her so. He put his hands to his face and wiped them around as if to take off the fatigue and then felt her hands creeping round his neck from behind, loosening his stiff high collar, reaching down to his chest, rubbing his shoulder, neck and head. He sighed, fell back in the chair, said, "Sorry," and fell asleep.

She took the subway to the Medical Examiner's building the next morning, where she received a cursory medical exam. As she put on her clothes, the doctor handed her a card telling her to report to a factory in Tempelhof-Mariendorf in the east end.

She arrived in the early afternoon in front of a concrete block building in inferior Bauhaus style, on which a blue water tower perched, incongruous as a bright beret on a grey old woman. She stood before the building enjoying the warmth of the sun on her cheek and side of her neck, savouring her last hour of freedom. At the barbed wire gate she was accosted by an old man in field-grey with a Replacement Army badge and a rifle who asked her for her papers. Then she was admitted into a narrow dark hallway.

A voice issuing from the concrete-block wall beside her elbow made her look down and there she saw a barred hole with half a face looking up and demanding her papers again. She showed them again and was told to go through the door. Ahead of her a steel door squeaked open and she saw a low-ceilinged room with bright lights hanging over tables before which sat women with their hair done up in bandannas and white snoods. A roar of exhaust machinery dampened all talk. No one looked up at her, but she noticed some of the men carrying wooden trays wore dark ragged clothing with G painted on the back in white. Prisoners of war.

Everyone wore brown paper identification tags pinned to their work-smocks and felt slippers instead of shoes, to avoid sparks from the concrete floor.

The foreman, in a dirty white lab coat whose left cheek had been smashed in and then stitched back together with gleaming red scars bordered by dead white stitch marks, took her to an empty place at a long table rimmed by women with their heads bent before balance scales. She sat on a stool beside a woman who neither spoke nor glanced at her, while the foreman told her to fill each black silk bag with the prescribed measure of the black powder which was cordite. She had to make sure that the balance needle on the scale was exactly in place, or else the shell would fall short, or overshoot the target.

Beside the balance-scale lay two wooden spoons, a wooden tray piled high with the black grains of cordite from which she was to dip each measure to place into a bag drawn from the pile beside her forearm on the table. The bags went inside mortar shells to be fired against the enemies of Germany. She glanced at one of the prisoners, and wondered if he was secretly shorting the bags.

The next morning, in darkness, she picked her way down the street towards the Emma stop, the start of her long journey by subway, street-car and bus. Behind many houses the winter coal, which in autumn had been piled up in the open for lack of storage space, had caught fire from incendiaries and was seeping stinging smoke into the air. There was not water enough in the hoses to extinguish these fires so on still days the streets were covered in coal smoke, sometimes so thick that dawn lasted all day.

Day after day, she went with her eyes weeping through smoking streets, where firemen were digging for people buried alive, to Tempel-hof/Mariendorf to make shells. Every day at noon, the whistle on top of the blue water-tower shrieked, beginning the half-hour lunch break, when she would sit in silence with the other prisoners—she had started to think of herself as a prisoner of the system—and ate half a hard-boiled egg and a cucumber, or a bit of cheese and bread from a paper bag which she saved and used until it was worn to shreds, when she used it as firelighter. She was now so skinny that her pre-war underwear bagged on her.

She often looked at the expressionless silent faces of the prisoners of war who carried the heavy boxes in and out of the factory floor, but they avoided her eye. At the end of every work day, when the whistle blew, everyone stopped, pushed back his chair and walked to the room where they changed back into their shoes. The woman beside her never said anything to her despite Clara's overtures, so, after a few tries, there was silence between them as there was amongst all the others. Once in a while the foreman with the smashed face issued an order in a loud voice; the rest of the time the whole place was without a human sound.

One Sunday morning in March, she woke to sunlight. Peter was out at army headquarters in Zossen, so she cleaned up the flat and then went out to call on Tati. She was out, so Clara came back into the street and looked around. The day was warm, the sky was blue and she gazed up, wondering if the Americans were coming. All at once, she was de-pressed, thinking, 'In weather like this at home, we would go fishing, Mother would garden, my whole life was like springtime, and now a beautiful day makes me afraid of bombers.' She looked up at her half-wrecked house, thinking of the mess within, the hopelessness of their lives and said aloud, "I don't want to live in this dump."

She sat on a stone which had fallen by her front gate with her face in her hands trying not to weep. Up and down the street women were hammering mortar off bricks with a tinkling sound. Clara felt a rush of pity for these women and hatred for the war.

Her neighbour across the street, Frau Braun, was holding a wrapped broom, watching a yellow canary, which kept flying to the mirror on a dressing table blown from the house in the raid two nights before. The bird would peck at the mirror then fly back to the cage set up nearby. It would perch on the cage, singing, then fly back to the mirror, peck, and return to the cage, singing. Frau Braun looked over and called, "Good morning."

Clara got up and crossed over to her to ask about the bird.

"Poor thing," said Frau Braun. "Its mate was killed and she thinks she sees him in the mirror, and tries to get him to come back to the cage."

When the lindens were finishing their blossoming, the daffodils had drooped, and lilac branches heavy with blossom were leaning over the burst boards of fallen roofs, the German foreman at the bomb factory came up to Clara at her bench. He held up a paper and said in a loud voice, "You, out," and gestured with his thumb towards the changing room.

"Why, what's the matter?"

"You failed the medical test. It's official, here, from the Ministry. Out."

"But there's nothing wrong with me," Clara said.

"Shut up," said her seat-mate, with her head bent over the workbench.

"You failed. You have to leave now," said the foreman. Clara got up and started to follow him protesting, but several people as she passed said, "Shut up, get out of here, go, stop arguing," and so on. None of them had ever spoken to her before.

He handed her a sheet of paper headed Ministry of Labour Services, with a boilerplate printed paragraph, which left a space for Reason, in which had been typed TB. She went into the dirty changing room, thinking of the bright spring morning awaiting her outside if she stopped arguing. She got her shoes and worn old wool coat and went out the door past the guard and along the street, feeling as if she had been sent home from school, but free like the sparrows bobbing over the new grass beside the smashed sidewalk. Loud birdsongs came from above. She looked up. What had once been a brick wall was now a cliff pierced with the rough outlines of window-holes like a mud-cliff she had once seen on a canoe trip, where flocks of swallows had been flying in and out. 'I'm sure I'm all right,' she thought, 'but I'll get an X-ray.'

A bus was waiting, as if for her alone, at the foot of the street and she was taken right away to the subway, which was working. She was back to the Budapesterstrasse in less time than she had ever taken. Daisies were blooming among bricks in the ruined gardens, women with kerchiefs on their heads were out again cleaning off bricks and piling them up as if getting ready to rebuild their houses that morning.

She got to the track over the rubble heap that led to the scarred door of their building, thinking of the dusty damaged interior she would enter. Working at the factory, she had been warm enough in winter, part of a system. She had not had to choose. Now that she was at home in the middle of the morning, alone, she felt free and useless. In her diary she entered the events of the day, and then added, Bizarre. Feeling useless because I am no longer contributing to the effort for a war I hate.

The following day, she went to see Dr. Wettlaufer for a chest X-ray, but he had moved on account of bomb damage. A note on the shattered door told her to "report"—'even our language is military now,' she thought—to St. Luke's hospital nearby. She went there and, after waiting for ten hours, until almost the time she would have been leaving work, she was admitted. A tired technician placed her chin on the bar and shot her picture.

"Who is your doctor?" the technician asked, and Clara replied, "Wettlaufer."

"But he's in A Block, Emergency Admissions," the technician said. "Well then, I'll give them to him tomorrow, or next day."

"Could you tell me what you saw?" Clara begged, and as she saw the technician's face close down ready to say a firm 'No,' she said, "Please, you know, just in case of a raid or something, just so I know?"

"I saw no evidence of TB. But I did not say that. Now go along with you."

The next morning, she went back to see Helmuth James at the Foreign Ministry in the Adlon, who had asked her to come in.

He picked up his grey gloves although the day was warm, and took her for a walk in the Tiergarten to talk. He said, "We need you right away. We have three people all ready to go to Istanbul and no one to escort them. But you must be on staff, so we can issue you the papers." Twisting his gloves together nervously, he added, "The final days are coming," and she realized that soon they would make the attempt on Hitler.

"But Helmuth James, what has changed?" she asked.

In fact, what had happened was that Helmuth James had decided to accept the consequences, which he approved, of an action he disapproved. His conscience would not be so troubled because Klaus had taken the responsibility. But what he said to Clara was, "It is time, that's all. I can not approve but I will not oppose."

Seeing her puzzlement, he thought she was wondering what he planned for her to do. "When you left, I put it around the office that you had been sent on special assignment to translate for the Embassy in Paris. Now your assignment is up. It's very simple. We want you to take these three people . . ." —he slipped an envelope into her handbag— ". . . to Turkey on Monday."

She wanted to deserve the confidence he had shown in her by bringing the envelope. She thought about what the Allies might do to her if she rejoined the Foreign Ministry, and about what would happen to the U-boats if she did not.

"I have prepared a new passport for you to give to the occupying forces. That will get you out of Germany and into safe territory."

That afternoon, she resumed her old desk beside Tati.

Tati assigned her to write a news release for the foreign papers accusing the Allies of war crimes, for example, bombing holy sites in Rome. She handed Clara a brief report from the Italia wire service, which was being maintained by the German government now that Mussolini had lost control of most of his country.

"In an act of unparalleled barbarity, British and American terrorists destroyed and damaged historical monuments precious to the history of civilization, to which these air pirates are indifferent."

Tati said, "Make it a news story."

Clara remembered that on the day she had started here in 1939, she had protested against being told to write something untrue, "But it's not true."

Tati's superior had said, "Where do you think you are? The Ministry of Truth?"

"But no one will believe it," she had said.

"Of course they will; they have nothing else to believe."

She wrote a story saying that the bombers hit an ancient and holy railway marshalling yard and destroyed mediaeval relics, including two diesel locomotives dating from the thirteenth century. Then she wrote the real one and submitted it, while passing the other around the office for a laugh.

Lyon, May, 1944

Heinrich Overmanns, nicknamed "Henke," took off his uniform, lifted his lame leg into the hot water in the tall zinc tub and sat upright. He was thinking about what to wear, and where in Lyon to go tonight. He gazed down at his scarred, bent right leg, an inch shorter than his left following the wound he received from a personnel mine near Tula. Henke shuddered in his bath and put the memory of Russia out of his mind. Here in Lyon, smelling the spring air blowing through the window above his head, he felt lucky to be alive. As a crippled soldier, he had been offered occupation duty in France. A Francophile and aesthete in love with French literature, art and cooking, he had always wanted to live here, and now he had an office, a shared car, staff, easy work and plenty of leave. He was happy, as sentimental Germans said, to live *comme le Seigneur en France.*

As a boy he had gone with his father to a parade of the Imperial Dragoons on the Kurfürstendamm in Berlin. Germany was epitomized in that stirring sight. He felt in himself the erect, tense pride of all those young males in tight gold and scarlet uniforms, shakos tossing, controlling their huge glowing horses by hand and thigh, and tightened his own thighs like theirs. He was fascinated by the weapons shining at the ready. Male pride filled him, he wanted the army, he wanted the pride, he wanted the men.

On his evening escapades, as he called them in his diary, he liked to put on civilian clothes, go to a public place, and befriend a young man. There were very few, since most were prisoners of war in Germany or had been drafted there for hard labour in the STO. Henke favoured the railway station where the *Milice* conducted random roundups, trolling for an escaped prisoner, a young man evading the STO, or a resistance fighter. He would wait until he saw a comely young man in trouble, then "save" him from the French. The chivalrous saviour would then offer the young man a drink, a meal, a ride in the car, and try to capitalize on his gratitude. Henke knew his game was suicidal, since he was disobeying Paragraph 175 forbidding homo-sexuality, the army's strongest taboo. He was also risking blackmail or murder if the young Frenchman turned violent in the room. Thus the thrill of danger pulsed inside his pleasure, as it had on that day when he was young on the Ku'damm. Perhaps tonight, *le beau idéal*—young, agile, beautiful, intelligent—would step down from the Paris train with a smile on his curved lips.

He looked around the Gare de Perrache at the crowd coming off the Paris express, all carrying bags and looking tired. The hall was loud with the clicking of their wooden-soled shoes on the cement. And there stepping down from the train, much as he had imagined him, was a magnificent young man, tall, muscular, straight-backed, with bronzy-red hair, an alert expression on his fresh young face, aware of everything round him. Jack Giovanelli was carrying a cheap blue card-board suitcase containing clothing made in France in which were packed ten British silent fuses for an agent in Annecy. Although the clothing and suitcase were apt, he looked radically different from the furtive, skinny young Frenchmen of 1944, who scurried by hoping not to be noticed by police.

Overmanns noticed that his shoes had thick leather soles, which were very scarce in France.

"Are you lost?" Overmanns said.

"No." Jack smiled and Henke was thrilled. "But I do need a taxi."

"I'm afraid there are none. May I offer you a lift? I came here to meet a friend but I don't see him. Let's have a *coup de rouge* while we're waiting."

Jack was suspicious since the stranger was not looking through the crowd for his friend. He started towards the taxi-phones, Henke beside him. "Are you French?" Henke asked.

"Of course," said Jack, with a sensation of fear chasing across his chest like a wind-squall. He reacted as Marianne would have; he smiled and shrugged. "What else would I be?"

"Permit me. I must see your papers."

"And why should I show them to you?"

"Let me tell you, your papers say you were born in Amiens." Jack felt panic, but kept his face impassive. Black-uniformed *miliciens* with grim faces shouted as they herded the crowd into the centre of the echoing hall. Each young *milicien* believed it was his imperative duty to search out enemies of the state, because a state must have enemies, because there was a war on, and they must protect it. None of them could say what the state was or what it did, except by parroting a formula about the Head of State, Petain, *Le Maréchal*, the Hero of Verdun. They said they believed in the patrimony of France, a state which no longer existed. These young Frenchmen lived in anger because of the contradiction between their present servitude and their deep feelings.

This was the danger that Henke counted on.

Jack, seeing them coming, drew out his papers. Henke compared the clothing in the photo with the clothing Jack wore at that moment, and said, "Just as I said, Amiens, and here is more proof. You are wearing now the clothes in the photo." He leaned forward so close that Jack smelled his cologne. He hissed, "It is a dead giveaway, it never happens in real life."

Jack shrugged. *"Ça arrive parfois.* Clothing is not so easy today."

"You were born in Amiens because the records were destroyed in June '40. Hmmm?" Overmanns smirked. Jack's heart thumped. The west doors opened, admitting more policeman in black, their arms spread and shouting, "Stand still, form a queue." The people, who had been looking tired and anxious, now, as if by agreement, looked down in resignation. Each one, thinking only of himself, felt overpowered. The civilians outnumbered the *miliciens* ten to one—if one had led a charge to the doors, the *miliciens* would have been powerless to stop them. No one broke. Several officers began examining papers.

"Come on," said Henke, picking up Jack's bag. Jack wrenched it away from him with such force that he almost knocked Henke over. Henke said, "Don't do that, I'm helping you." Captain Fougères, in charge of the *miliciens*, spotted Overmanns in the crowd and saluted.

"My brother, just arrived, " said Overmanns, and they passed the control.

As they stood outside Jack said, "Thank you but my papers are in order. You know yourself it is impossible to get new clothes these days."

"Listen to me, it doesn't matter, they pull you in for anything or nothing, then you're off to the Ruhr and British bombs, understand? You don't look stupid but you don't seem to know anything, that's why I asked if you are French." He paused. "I am trying to help you, *mon frère.*"

"Why?"

Henke hissed, "Because you're beautiful." Jack laughed. *"Oui, et vous êtes mignon, vous même."*

He picked up his bag and walked along the sidewalk. "Stop," said Henke, "stop, please," starting to limp after him and putting one hand on his revolver. Words came into his mind, 'Too beautiful to shoot.'

Jack ran as hard as he could for the streetcar, the bag banging against his knees, expecting the shot, the impact on his back, his head thrown under the wheels. He grabbed the handle by the door, and swung up onto the platform as Henke watched his bottom with a groan of regret.

Jack got off the train at the station in Annecy, set the bag down and lit a cigarette. He looked around. There had been time for the French to have sent out a warning to all station police to look for him, and he did not want to endanger the contact, a young German woman who was to wear a green hat with a pheasant feather. The platform seemed clear, so he walked across the street to the *Café du Gare*, and saw her right away, wearing a suit. She was seated alone, behind a hedge of low evergreen in boxes but there was a German sergeant at the next table leaning close, talking to her.

This was unexpected. Jack stayed outside the hedge a few metres away, looking around as if for a friend. He rehearsed their lines: "Good afternoon, Madame, is this place free?" If she thought someone was following her, she would say, "I am expecting a friend." If she thought it was safe, she would say, "Yes, it is," and Jack would place a string bag containing the fuses hidden by potatoes under the table.

Jack came over and stood by her table ignoring the German, and said in French, "Good afternoon, is this place free?"

Tati said, "I forget," jumped up, threw her arms round him and kissed him on his lips and said, "I am so glad to see you." The sergeant got up and walked away looking disgusted. Tati whispered, "He was bothering me. And you are so late."

"I was spotted in Lyon, they may be after me."

"What will we do?" she said.

"Keep your eyes open—what about him?"

"He was just trying his luck. The dangerous ones are not in uniform."

"I'd better get away from you. They're under the potatoes, ten of them." He set the string bag by her feet, leaned over and kissed her.

Tati said, "Wait. They're after you, I can help. I have diplomatic immunity."

Jack hesitated, then said, "I'm sorry, I can't stay with you. Orders." He left, thinking that if she called him back, he would stay.

Tati paid her bill, and finished her coffee. She picked up his bag, sure she had not been spotted. As she walked out, Hans Bernd Gisevius left his table and followed her towards the station.

Jack walked out into the street, feeling the shock of her kisses, and looked back. Her chair was empty.

The weather was warm and sunny at first, and he made 35 kilometres the first day until his feet began to bleed. He stayed four nights in a safe house owned by a farmer near Sisteron, who told him the maquis were gathering in the high plateau called Le Vercors, to the west. The farmer asked Jack to tell his contacts in Grasse to request air drops of machine guns, dried food, cigarettes, anti-tank Piat rockets and radios.

When his feet were better, he started again. The first few kilometres lay over rocky meadowland that rose up a steep hill to the east. He slept that night under a blanket in the open, shivering with cold and vowed to make it the next day to the safe house 20 kilometres further along.

He inhaled the clear air and watched the blue-green edges of the hills shrivel in the smoke of forming clouds, then burst through again into soft blue light. He saw German convoys in the valley far below, before he could hear them. He would hide behind a rock or a tree or a goatshed, and spy on them as they came up towards him, probably going to fight the maquis.

South of Digne, there was an option—to go down into a curving valley, where he would meet more traffic, or to strike off on a paved *Route Nationale* higher up. He chose the high road because it was shorter.

High up on this road, he sat on a red and white stone that said 44 KM to Saint-Vallier and lit a cigarette. The air was still. A vulture floated on the air far below him, a speck moving over the curving green river.

The road disappeared round a spur ahead, holding tight to the rock face. The drop from the edge of the road was so steep, he could not figure out how they had built it. In places, there seemed to be nothing beneath the road but air. It was so narrow that in places two cars could not pass.

He heard something not like wind or birds. An engine. On a piece of the road, far below and behind in the shade of the mountain, a truck moved towards him. It would be here in a few minutes. The rock above the road was too steep to climb. He ran ahead and looked round the curve. To the right, the big drop; to the left, cliffs as steep as before. He ran back and started to climb the steep cliff. Two metres up, the rotten ledge under his foot broke off and tumbled onto the road with a crash. He slithered down with it, landing on his knee. As soon as he stood up, he knew he had hurt the knee. But he had to shove the rock over the edge, so the truck would not have to stop. On his hands and knees he shoved at the rock, till it was at the edge, then tilted it over. It slithered for a couple of metres, then bounced out and fell without a sound. The engine-sound lifted on the wind. He could wait and be caught, or go over the edge, or try to go up again. He flung himself at the rock face, clutching with bare hands and elbows, boots and knees, reckless of blood. He crawled over a slithering scree that spurted gravel down onto the road, and curled into a shallow saddle on top of the spur, four metres above the road. He was visible to the oncoming truck.

The truck came in sight, and moved towards him. He kept his cheek pressed hard against the rock, looking straight down into the driver's face. The driver was looking ahead, not upwards. Beside the driver, another face looked out the window over the side, down into the drop. The truck disappeared underneath him. The engine stopped. He heard a door slam and a voice, in German.

He heard another engine but he could not see another truck. The second engine stopped. A door slammed. Germans shouted and talked. He realized that a second truck had been coming the other way. Now they were blocked, head on, unable to pass.

The Germans talked, shouted, and argued. His knee ached and stabbed with pain. He could feel it swelling against the cloth of his pants.

The first truck backed into view. Now they could see him. The driver's head was out the window. He was looking backwards, the assistant walking behind the truck, motioning him to come on. For minutes it ground backwards. It bent round a corner and it was gone.

Now the hood of the other truck began to emerge round the bend, and the truck made it round the corner, guided by a man in front bending over to see the wheels and the edge.

Then that truck drove down the hill after the other.

They must have passed each other beyond the farthest curve because, in a little while, the truck which had reversed away came back, the same driver looking ahead and the other soldier walking in front, bending to check the wheels. They would see him if they looked up.

The back of the truck disappeared under him.

He watched a long cloud float from a distant peak, dissolving. He tried to move, but his body was clinging, unable to let go. He felt the mountain moving under him. He told himself this was because he had watched the moving cloud too long. The motion of the cloud made the mountain seem to move. He was afraid that if he let go of the rock he would fall into the valley. He lay there trying to get rid of the fear. He lifted one finger up and put it down, and said to himself, "There, you didn't slide." He did this with another finger, until he could raise his whole hand for a moment, then his head. He stopped because he was dizzy. He was sure that if he tried to move, he would dislodge this rock and fall down into the final air. He made himself move by repeating, "If you don't move, you will die here."

At last he got his legs over the edge of the saddle and moved backwards down the cliff, unable to see below. When he went into the final slide, his eyes were closed. He ended up lying on his side on the road. The pain rose in him like a drug filling his body. He vomited. He lay on the road not caring if he lived or died.

He remembered the portage. He was 12 years old. Bernie Hallett had said, "The landing's just ahead." He got up and fainted.

The sun came up on him asleep in the middle of the road. He heard sheep bells. He tried to sit up. The shepherd held out his crook and stopped the flock. The dog circled round him, barking every time he moved.

For three days he stayed in the shepherd's high hut. The shepherd, named Becker, made him cold poultices with water from the stream and applied a mixture of herbs to the knee. Jack was lucky, he said, in a bing-bong Haute Savoie accent. He came this way twice a year, taking the sheep to the high meadows, bringing them back in autumn. He said more Germans were coming. There was fighting in the Vercors.

After three days, the knee had improved. He set out alone on the road to Saint-Vallier. He turned to wave goodbye, but the shepherd was walking up the hill with the crook in his hand and the sheep tinkling ahead of him and the small black and white dog dancing round them. He vowed to come back here after the war and buy Becker a drink.

In the village at the foot of the mountain, where the Petit-Siagne turns right to run into the main river, he went into a bar and leaned against the zinc, asking for brandy. He discussed the war for a few minutes with the bartender, and then asked about the buses. Georges closed the bar and took him to the bus stop and said, "He will drop you in Saint-Vallier, there is no charge for the ticket," shook him by the hand and left.

He was the only man in a crowd of stooped old women in black with string shopping bags in their hands. They were short, their grey hair pulled into buns under their black kerchiefs, their faces were brown and wrinkled, they glanced at him, they said, "*Bonjour, m'sieur,*" with their eyes averted when he greeted them in their own Italianate accent. They asked nothing but their eyes told him they knew, and that he was safe. In their string bags were potatoes, a plucked chicken, eggs in paper, to barter.

From Saint-Vallier, he walked south until he could see over the olive valley to the sea. Below him a few lights among the stubby olive trees went out like fireflies. He slept on the ground under a low oak tree to avoid the sky-frost, and before dawn sat with his back against the trunk eating cheese and bread, then drank the last water from his canteen. The sun came up behind him walking down the cobbled street of Esperacedes, casting his shadow up a wall. He passed through the smell of bread baking, down to the *calvaire* as he had been instructed. She was in her field, a fat grey figure picking jasmine flowers which she put into a black belly-bag.

"Aha," she said, with her head cocked to one side, pleased. "I heard you were coming. Help me fill the bags. The flowers have to be picked before the sun gets on them. Then we'll have a drink."

Normandy, June, 1944

Field Marshal Erwin Rommel, commander of Army Group B in France, checked the weather reports on the afternoon of the fourth of June, decided that the enemy could not risk a landing in such seas and left Paris to go to his wife Lucie's birthday party at Herrlingen, 400 miles east.

In the car, he checked and re-checked the maps showing the disposition of the Fifteenth Army near Calais, and the roads from there to Normandy. He was trying to decide how to change the disposition of forces made by Hitler. The Führer had ordered three SS Panzer divisions, the strongest in the world, to sit tight in the Pas de Calais area. They were far from Normandy, where Rommel believed the attack would come.

In Normandy, he had about 100,000 men to face an enemy he was sure could land 100,000 first-class troops in 24 hours. Half his troops were first-class German units, the rest were weary and wounded veterans from the east, plus a few thousand disaffected Russians, mainly Ukrainians, who had deserted the Red Army en masse and had no interest in fighting.

Rommel and Hitler had agreed that they must defeat the landings on the beaches in the first few days, because Allied planes would destroy all the bridges over the Seine, preventing supplies and reinforcements from reaching the front, except in the short summer night. Therefore the panzers must stay close to the beaches. But Hitler had just ordered them to be withdrawn to the east, hidden away like a miser's hoard. 'How can he do this? It is a recipe for disaster,' Rommel wondered as they came within sight of Trier. He looked north along the long plateau above Trier, remembering the scene near here a year ago, in Reichsmarschall Göring's train when the chief of the Luftwaffe's fighter force, General Galland, had told Göring that American P51 fighter planes had been shot down here, far beyond their normal range. If true, this was a disaster for the Luftwaffe and all Germany, because it would mean that Allied bombers would have fighter protection and, therefore, air superiority over the whole Reich.

Göring said it was impossible for fighters to have flown so far, and Galland said he had seen the plane. Göring said, "I am issuing an order that they were not there, do you understand? That is an order, and I shall report it to the Führer." Galland had saluted and said, "An order is an order," then left. Göring had looked at Rommel. "You see?" with a smile. 'See what?' thought Rommel, 'How can he report giving an order stating that something did not happen?'

'Perhaps if I go to the Berghof,' Rommel thought, 'I could convince the Führer face to face. If he is being misinformed even by Göring, maybe others are fooling him too. No one likes to be the bearer of bad tidings.' But then he remembered the shoes he had bought for Lucie in Paris, and that Manfred would be at the house. He also remembered a meeting with Hitler, who had accused the whole general staff of cowardice and threatened to turn the SS on them.

He stopped at Herrlingen, 150 miles short of Hitler.

Seated at sunset before the great window in the Berghof watching the shadows like a tide-line rise up the tinted peaks, Hitler thought the whole scene resembled the inevitable ending of his regime. In the east, the armies were in retreat for the second year, outnumbered and outfought on every front. Speer, now the Minister for Armaments and Production, said that after the Balkans were lost, there would be no more chromium and not enough oil. Arms production would end. In the south, the army had been in retreat for two years. At sea, the U-boat campaign had failed and the surface fleet was paralyzed. Air raids had destroyed Hamburg, Essen, Düsseldorf, Cologne, and had cut production of oil and rubber so much that troops at the front were already rationed to less than their needs. And now, reports were coming in that the landings in the west were imminent.

He had originally prepared for landings in Normandy, but now had withdrawn the panzers eastwards, ostensibly to defend the Pas de Calais, east of the Seine. None of his generals dared to ask why the Allies would land east of the Seine if their air power could isolate the Germans west of the Seine.

The war had changed Hitler's strategy, which was no longer based on daring and confidence in German superiority, but on scarcity, fear and blame. He would assign a general enough troops for a mission, then as they went into battle, move essential supplies to another front. When the attack failed, Hitler fired the general. He had assumed command of units as small as a battalion on every front, but he did not know how many soldiers could be carried in a standard LKW. He restricted the freedom of command of all his generals, he demanded reports on the results of minor artillery barrages by six guns, he issued orders which he superseded without cancelling the earlier orders; to punish Göring for his deceitful optimism, he cancelled all fighter production just as it was peaking, demanded that engine factories start producing flak guns, then retracted the earlier orders.

Everyone around him was his lackey, or feared him. Many were both. Those he trusted most deceived him. Those who spoke the truth he mistrusted, so that the reality at the front was never known to the higher command. Everyone around Hitler lived by illusions that reflected each other as in a hall of mirrors.

At 2300 hours on the windy night of June 5, 1944, the minesweeper HMCS *Aurora,* commanded by Lieutenant Graeme Frederic Evan Price, set out from Portsmouth, making ten knots towards the French coast, 90 miles away. A few minutes out of port, Price activated the degaussing belt, then opened the sealed envelope handed him at dockside, and read that he was to steer east by south at 12 knots to latitude 50deg 30min., longitude 5deg west. There he was to stream his paravanes, bangers, foxer gear and sweep towards the French coast, beginning to mark the cleared channel with buoys when he was in ten fathoms of water. The little ship rolled as the seas built up from the west, but Price rolled with it, accustomed to worse than this. He stepped into the captain's cabin for a minute to smoke his pipe, then returned to the bridge, picked up his binoculars, and swept the horizon.

"This is it," he said to Sub-Lieutenant Clark, his number two officer.

Clark nodded. "I hope they're asleep."

"Not bloody likely."

To each side he could see, whenever they crested a wave, HMCS *Lily* and HMS *Scarborough*, each with a bone in her teeth as she mounted a wave, ran down the far side, slammed into the trough, quivered, rose and slammed again. Price hated this work. At any moment a mine—pressure, acoustic, contact or magnetic—might kill them all in a flash. There was nothing to do now but steer straight through on course or there would be no clear path for the invasion fleet.

As the Allied ships were approaching the French coast on the night of June 5, 1944, Hitler slept.

On the night of June 5, the Commander in Chief of the German forces in the west, Field Marshal Gerd von Rundstedt slept.

Field Marshal Rommel slept.

Along the darkened scoop of sandy coast, the German local commanders went to bed thankful that on such a stormy night there could be no landings.

While the clouds were turning grey in the east of the Baie de la Seine, there appeared on German radar screens along the coast so many green dots that they soon coalesced into a solid phalanx pulsing toward the coast.

The first broadside from USS *Arkansas* produced a concussion so powerful that it blew out the lighting system on the Canadian minesweeper *Penetanguishene.* As her emergency lighting system flickered into life, the *Arkansas'* shells exploded in the sand among the bunkers on Omaha Beach, setting the dry grasses on fire.

The German commanders stared in amazement through the observation slits at 6,000 ships and thousands of aircraft coming in from the storm. Dots of lights winked along the fleet, and ten seconds later whistling shells blasted into the sand below them, blowing rock, sand and trees 100 feet in the air, bringing down their own barbed wire on their own paths and doorways. As a result some of the German personnel mines along the beach blew up from the pressure.

"Fire," the German officers said. The guns rocked back and their sound boomed for miles around as huge shells trailling spikes of flame 40 feet long shot towards the enemy. People abed in England awoke with the sound of the aircraft engines in their heads, and knew that the invasion had begun.

Brigadier General Daniel Fox, deputy commander of the Canadian Third Corps, paced around outside his tent in the south of England, having just come from the latest briefing in General Eisenhower's command post. He stuffed his pipe full, lit it, and closed the steel spark-lid in the lee of the radio van. Then he looked up at the grey clouds just becoming visible in the dawning light. The general imagined them blowing in from the Atlantic over long rolling waves eight feet high that broke over the bows of the landing craft and soaked his men. He knew and admired dozens of the men he was sending over, including Bernie Hallett and Ed Burns of the Ontario Scottish regiment. He kept his fingers crossed for them as he checked his chronometer. One hour to go.

Jack Giovanelli's uncle, Ducky McKay, was riding in towards the beach peering over the gunwale of the DukW with Bernie Hallett and Ed Burns, regardless of the enemy fire coming at them and banging off the armoured doors. Hallett roared the command, "One minute to target," readying the crew to open the bow doors. The noise was stunning. Shells exploded beside them, bullets clanged on the steel hull, airplane, tank, bulldozer engines roared, men's little voices screaming went unheard a few yards away. Hallett noticed McKay with his helmeted head above the gunwale peering in towards shore and shouted, "Get down."

McKay, thinking he was being ordered ashore, scrambled over the gunwale while Burns shouted at him to stop. McKay leaped into the surf, too soon, and sank out of sight. The captain threw the DukW's engine in reverse and they bobbed in the waves, an easy target, trying to retrieve McKay, while more bullets rang on the hull. Burns threw a life-ring down to him and McKay emerged next to the ring, seized it, and waded ashore.

He was on the beach ahead of the rest of them and stepped on a personnel mine. It did not go off, because it was designed to explode on the second impact, which came when the jeep emerged carrying Hallett and Burns, and drove straight onto it. The wheel blew off, and the car lurched over onto its side, spilling them all onto the sand. Machine gun bullets spurted up sand around them and slammed onto the chassis as they took cover, and then ran for the grassy dunes higher up the beach.

Private Joe Killsbear followed his officer, Bernie Hallett, through the open doors onto the banging steel plate, then leaped out onto the sand, seeing ahead of him the dark caves he had first seen in his dream-quest on Dreamer's Rock Cliff in Wanagami years ago, the bears with their red eyes and flashing teeth roaring towards him. Two jaws clamped tight on his right leg and felled him on the edge of the water where he lay bleeding into his khaki trousers, the blood leaking out very fast into sand and water.

He pulled himself higher on the sand, then curled round on his side to inspect the damage, and saw a lot of blood. At that moment, a medical officer kneeled beside him and began to clean and bind the wound. Then two orderlies carried him back onto the landing craft. The whole of Bernie Hallett's command unit was dispersed within a minute of landing.

Hallett ran up the beach and threw himself down onto the grass behind a sand dune panting with the effort, then rolled on his side to look back down the beach. He shouted, "Joe? Joe Killsbear?"

Ships with gaping bows were stuck into the surf at strange angles, dark dots all down the beach were men wallowing in the water, sand in the strong wind rose from the beach and pricked his cheeks. The explosions were continuous, obliterating the boom of the surf that was flinging white spray gleaming in the sunny air over drowned tanks.

McKay walked up erect, tripped over Hallett's foot and looked down as Hallett shouted, "Get down you idiot." McKay saluted, then sat down beside him, pulled out a silver cigarette case, lit one, passed it to Hallett, and then offered him a pull on his silver flask. Hallett, who had never tasted alcohol or tobacco smoke before the war, pulled on his cigarette, swigged at the flask and crouched again. The radio operator arrived carrying his heavy pack and set it up. Three more men ran up beside the radio man and prostrated themselves. The noise of exploding shells, machine gun fire and bombs was so great that Hallett had to shout into McKay's ear, "Did you see where Burns got to?"

"No," said McKay, "I'll take a look." He unsnapped his field glasses, stood up and swept the beach to the west, towards the American sector.

"I think I see Major Burns down there." He handed the glasses down to Hallett who kneeled on one knee scanning the beach.

He said, "Get over there and tell him there's a change of plans, we're going to rendezvous right up there by the church, do you see?" He pointed uphill past a small pillbox now canted at a strange angle as if fighting off incoming aircraft. "And mind you take cover as you go, there's lots of cover if you run from dune to dune."

McKay saluted again, then started down the beach, marching in the soft sand with a sort of stiff wade, arms swinging back and forth in regulation form, but his legs wallowing around out of rhythm. As he neared Ed Burns, machine-gun bullets from a dugout 100 yards above singed the air around him and blasted fragments of rock up into the rim of his helmet. He could smell the smoke of the burnt rock and his eyes went foggy from the dust, then he was blown onto his back by a mortar shell.

He got to his hands and knees, swinging his head around, wondering if he was hurt. He started along the beach trying to keep the sea on his right, but it kept swinging up in front of him.

Red Ed Burns with six men crouched in the shelter of a tank whose tread was blown off. The turret was lopsided but the engine was still running, making the drive-wheels churn in the sand. Every now and then they caught on a part of the track and the tank convulsed like a wounded animal.

McKay saluted and Burns said, "Where'd you come from?"

"Sir, uh, down there . . ." He turned and pointed back to where he had started. "I have a message for you." He stopped.

"Well, what is it?" said Burns.

"Sir, I can't remember."

Burns said, "McKay, I have a big job for you." He glanced round. "B platoon has lost its lieutenant. I want you and Sergeant Boon here to take these men up over that dune"—he gestured over his head towards the manufacturer's marker on the tank—"and take out the machine gun up there. It's bothering me."

Wriggling through the dry grass, where white daisies were blooming, McKay crawled with Boon and the ten others round the back side of the nest and looked in on the bloody bodies of two young Germans. As they were lying there speculating on what had happened, more machine gun fire erupted from higher in the dunes, and young Armstrong rolled over coughing and dying. They jumped down into the machine-gun dugout beside the dead young men. McKay sent Corporal Barton back for a stretcher party, then wriggled away uphill with the rest of his platoon to find the gun that had killed Armstrong.

McKay and nine men crawled on their bellies for half an hour up the track among the grassy dunes. They found no nest but, beside the smoking wall of a wrecked house, they came on abandoned cartridge belts and spent cartridges. From here, a farm-track led inland to a narrow road through the *bocage*. For two hours, growing hotter and sweatier in the strong sun, they worked inland through fields and laneways, and up narrow roads like corridors running between walls of trunks and branches impossible to enter. Far ahead on a white road, they saw a few Germans walking away.

About ten o'clock, finding no one around them, the nine remaining men of the platoon sat down in the shade of an elm, facing away from the narrow road and began to eat. Then they lay back in the grass and fell asleep. McKay got up, drank the last of his rye and decided to walk ahead for a reconnaissance.

Turning a curve of the *bocage* he looked down on the grey roofs of a village leaning close together. He marched down into the village, which seemed deserted, found a glass-fronted bar with *Bar-Tabac* on it, and started for it. Two soldiers talking came out together and saluted him. He returned the salute and walked in. He stood at the mahogany counter and said in English, "One cognac, please, make it a double."

The bartender stared at him in amazement, saying nothing but his eyes switched to the door that was opening, letting in a man who came up behind McKay with something in his hand. The German said, *"Hände hoch."* McKay put his hands up with a cigarette between his fingers.

Wolfschanze and Berlin, July, 1944

※

Bowing his head into the plane at Rangsdorf, Klaus von Zollerndorf held his briefcase with his live hand because his prosthesis-hand was so clumsy and he did not want always to be looking down at the case to be sure he still had it. The fuses and bombs were in that case. He had trouble mounting the ladder to the plane because his prosthesis could not grip the metal handrail of the ladder.

As they flew at 2500 metres over West Prussia, an officer watching him read documents with his head resting on his gloved prosthesis whispered to his companion, "The great man is posing for Rodin."

The view of the earth from the air which normally made Klaus feel serene, passed through his vision without meaning. He was concentrating on the problem of crushing the glass protector on top of the wires, to force contact and start the reaction that ended in a small explosion triggering the main bomb. He had to insert pliers inside a narrow opening in the aluminum case, then twist the wires together while crushing the glass vial. He had to do this while holding the case with his claw-like prosthesis. The manoeuvre required practice, since he could not control the prosthesis as finely as he wished.

He reached into his side pocket to extract the pliers, which reminded him of the moment at Schenkenberg in September 1939, when he had told Tati they couldn't get married right away because he had no ring, and his right forefinger had encountered the blue ring-box in his pocket. Distracted by the memory, he dropped the pliers on the metal floor with a clang. A well-groomed officer with shining pink cheeks across the aisle, whom he had already greeted because they had been at cavalry school in Bad Kreuznach together, picked them up and handed them back, saying, "What's that?"

Klaus said, "For the cello, to help me tune it." The officer said, "I didn't know you played."

"Oh yes, and I'm hoping I can do it again." He held up the claw in its black leather sheath, feeling the weight of the heavy steel claw dragging at his aching shoulder, vowing once again to get an aluminum version built.

"Hard luck," said the well-groomed officer and yawned and turned and looked out the window, and did not ask how it had happened, because he disliked front-line stories. Before the start of the war, he had already made himself an expert in communications and codes so he would never be sent to the front line. So far, the shots he had heard fired in the war were the bangs of anti-aircraft guns in the distance.

Klaus rebuked himself, thinking, 'What a stupid mistake. If he is wondering how I could think of playing the cello with a hook like this, then once the coup begins, he'll remember the twisted pliers.' He glanced across at the expression on the man's face to see if he could read anything there but it was closed in self-satisfaction. He had the look of a man who has arranged his life to suit himself and no other.

He glanced down through the window as they passed over a great estate, its grey-roofed *Schloss* reminding him of Schenkenberg and the wedding. Tati would soon be waiting by the phone at the Foreign Ministry, ready to do whatever Helmuth James told her.

He fell asleep. He dreamed he was playing his cello for the satisfied man across the aisle, but the bow would not touch the string. No matter how hard he pressed, the bow remained just above the strings. He awakened with his heart pounding, his face and armpits beginning to sweat at the effort of trying to bow the cello.

He forced his mind onto getting his briefcase past the SS guards into the bunker, going to the washroom, opening the fuses, fusing the two plastic bombs, getting to the map table beside Hitler, describing the deployments of the Replacement Army against any North Sea or airborne landing while at the same time the fused bombs at his feet neared the moment of explosion, and von Häften had to come to the door to call him away for an urgent phone call before the briefcase exploded.

He had already tested two of the fuses which Tati had collected from the agent in Annecy. Each had worked after he had twisted the wires together with the special pliers; there was no sound for ten minutes, then it had exploded with the small bang necessary to ignite the main bomb. But there were many other contingencies to consider. It was normal for Hitler to order constant changes in his security to confuse assassins. Already, six attempts had been made, and none had come close. He rehearsed the contingencies: *'What if there is a new inspection team at say, Restricted Area Number One outside the bunker, demanding I open my briefcase?'*

'I will pretend I left something on the plane and return to the airfield.'

'What if I place the bomb near Hitler, then leave but it does not go off?'

'Then before emplaning, I will remember the briefcase and retrieve it.'

'What if it is discovered unexploded?'

'I will be warned by Geber, then go underground in Berlin.'

He passed through the gate at the airfield without incident, carrying his bag himself. One SS guard offered to help him, but he clutched the bag and said, "I can do it myself, thank you," and got into the car.

As the Opel rounded the last turn, he saw with shock, immense activity round the main Führer bunker. 'Why was this not reported to me,' he demanded in his head. Scores of *Organization Todt* workers were swarming round the bunker, mixing cement. He panicked for a moment, thinking the Führer must be absent because no one could work in such an uproar. Then he remembered that he had been warned that headquarters had shifted to temporary quarters in the Speer barracks, just 100 metres away.

He took a deep breath and held it for 12 seconds, then released it, thinking, 'Calm, calm, calm as a lake at dawn.'

He was half an hour early, which gave him time to rehearse what he had to do, and what he had to say to the Führer during the conference. He felt for the angled pliers in his pocket. Five minutes before the appointed hour, he was walking up and down outside the door to the map room, smoking a cigarette, when an aide told him the conference was running on time for once, and that the Führer would see him in about four minutes.

Klaus went into the men's room, sat down on a toilet in a cubicle and drew out the fuse. He dropped the pliers on the tiled floor, bumped his head bending to retrieve them, and for a moment felt hysteria starting at the picture of the clumsy assassin blowing himself up in a toilet while the fate of the world turned on a pair of pliers. He fumbled with them, holding the aluminum tube with his prosthesis, applied the pincers to the narrow neck containing the fatal wire, crimped it in tight with his left hand, put the pliers back in his pocket and rose, sweating now, flushed the toilet and was about to wash his hand when the aide opened the outside door, and said, "Please hurry up, the Führer is ready."

He wiped his perspiring brow on his right sleeve and carried the briefcase past the SS guard into the room, where Hitler was standing with his arms crossed on his chest.

"Ah, my dear Zollerndorf, how are you?" the Führer said.

"My apologies *mein Führer*, better thank you." Many of the officers bowed in deference to his terrible wounds, and remarkable courage.

"Good, we will get to you in a few minutes. Meanwhile, we will finish with Army Group Centre." Hitler went on about the situation in the east which they had already been discussing for three hours.

Klaus placed his briefcase on the floor under the huge heavy oak table, right next to Hitler's foot. He glanced at his watch: eight minutes to go. As arranged, Lieutenant von Häften came to the door and said that there was an urgent phone call for Colonel Count von Zollerndorf. Klaus excused himself and walked into the hall where von Häften was waiting. They hurried out into the roaring air filled with the stink of diesels and cement dust to the HQ Opel waiting for them.

As they were getting in, there was a tremendous explosion behind them that rammed the car door into Klaus' leg. Most of the roof of the Speer barracks was blown off, bits of debris fell among the trees, one small lump landing on the roof of the Opel in front of them and people began running in and out of the smoke.

The driver stood staring in amazement. Klaus said, "Another damn mine going off. Speer should have that checked. Hurry up, I must get to the airport right away, I must warn Berlin."

"But look, sir," said the driver, "is it the Führer?"

He pointed to a stretcher team carrying a stretcher with a body lying on it under the cloak that Hitler had been wearing, left arm dangling over the side. Klaus slammed the door and the driver sped away to the airport.

They were passed through the gate and out onto the field, where Klaus told the pilot, "Berlin, Rangsdorf, right away, and watch out for enemy aircraft. That may have been a bomb."

Two hours later, he was taxiing on the field at Rangsdorf, looking out the window for the staff car that was supposed to meet him. He ran down the stairway from the plane towards the small terminal. There was no sign of car or adjutant. He went into the office of Captain Höffer the administrator and dialled the commandant of the tank regiment that was supposed to be on its way into Berlin.

He was astounded when the colonel himself answered.

"Where have you been?" asked Klaus. "What've you been doing?"

Aware of the interested look on Captain Höffer's face, he pretended he was anxious about the car. "It was to be here now, where is it? Yes, the conference is over, complete success, we won all our points."

This was the code to signal that Hitler was dead. That code which should have gone out two hours ago, was to signal one section of the *Grossdeutschland* Motorized Infantry Replacement Training Brigade to seize the radio station at Königs-Wusterhausen, and the other section to proceed to the Valkyrie assembly point south of Berlin, with 24 tanks. He was wondering how to cope with this emergency when he saw von Häften staring at him anxiously, and realized that Höffer had just spoken to him. With an effort he recollected the words and said, "Yes, thank you very much," to Höffer's offer of his own car and driver to go to Berlin.

He arrived at the army's Headquarters in the Bendlerstrasse half an hour later and went straight to General Fromm's office, expecting to find him busy with the arrangements for seizing radio stations, Gestapo headquarters, and the arrest of Himmler. He was relieved to see the skinny figure of General Beck, standing very erect in the office next to Fromm's, as he made a phone call. He was the most important element of the whole coup because he was loyal to the highest principles of German life, had sacrificed his career rather than serve Hitler and had agreed to head the provisional government.

Klaus found Fromm pacing his office. Without stopping, Fromm said, "What is Beck doing here? This looks like treason. What is going on?"

Klaus looked at him in amazement, then into contempt. Fromm had agreed to this and now was frightened as danger approached.

"I didn't get the call from Rastenburg that you promised," Fromm said, unaware that he was contradicting the innocent pose he had just adopted.

Beck in the next office was talking to Stulpnagel in Paris, ordering him to arrest every SS officer he could find, and to inform Rommel. Klaus called out, "Rommel's in hospital, tell him to tell Speidel and Kluge."

Klaus saw that Fromm was hesitating because he was afraid. Keeping very calm he replied, "The lines were cut by the explosion, it was enormous, excuse me," and he rounded Fromm's desk to take an incoming call on Fromm's phone.

Hours went by like that, Klaus and Beck making and taking phone calls, checking up on people, ordering units into action, demanding to know why something had not been done as arranged, asking the Valkyrie plotters in Paris, Vienna and Prague what was happening, and giving them orders.

Outside Berlin, the plan was unfolding as it should: Gestapo, SS and party officers were being arrested wholesale all over Europe. In

Berlin, nearly all the army units that were supposed to be on the road towards the bridges, radio stations, telephone exchanges, ministries, SS and Gestapo headquarters, were still in their barracks. Only the reliable Ninth Replacement Training Battalion was active, on its way to reinforce Count von Helldorf, chief of Berlin police. Most of the people Klaus called were bewildered, telephoning one another, hesitating, wondering which way to jump, or if to jump at all. Dozens of officers came to see Klaus, and Fromm paced around, then disappeared down the hall, leaving his office to Klaus.

The phone rang about 6.00 pm and Axel von dem Bussche's voice said, *"Klaus, something terrible has happened. The Führer is alive."*

"Impossible," said Klaus, "I saw his body myself."

"Radio Deutschland has just announced that he survived an assassination attempt and will speak in two hours."

"It's a fake," said Klaus, "Keitel will say anything. They keep a record of Hitler's voice with pre-recorded announcements for just this sort of thing. Pay no attention."

Fromm came back into his office, having heard the radio announcement, his face sweating and said, "Count Zollerndorf, you are under arrest for high treason. The penalty for this is death." He stood there with his mouth open, having no idea why he had added the last gratuitous remark.

"On the contrary, General Fromm, you are under arrest. Take him." Von Häften and two other officers with drawn pistols aimed at the floor took Fromm by the shoulder and led him to a secretary's office next door. Klaus called out, "Give him cognac and a cigarette. It will calm his nerves," and laughed for the first time that day.

Fromm sat down shivering, but thinking, 'This is good as long as they don't shoot me, it will mean I am exonerated.' He began to prepare a statement for the SS who he was sure would soon be here. He decided not to try to escape, as he might be shot. It would be best to be found under arrest. He wondered if he should suggest that they put handcuffs on him.

Beck came in looking very serious and told Klaus that although the plan was working in Paris and Vienna, nothing was going right in Berlin.

General von Witzleben, who had come out of retirement to help Beck, came up the curved staircase shouting, "Where is Zollerndorf?" He came into the office saying, "This whole thing has been one magnificent bungle. We're all going to be shot."

Klaus, his voice hoarse from shouting and cigarettes and lack of food and water, attempted to convince Witzleben to hold the faith, but Witzleben interrupted, "The troops have been ordered back to barracks by direct orders from Hitler in Rastenburg, and they have obeyed. This whole thing is finished." Klaus stared at him with his mouth gaping.

Fromm's special missions officer, Captain Bastien, appeared in the door, saluted and requested permission to see his chief. Klaus asked why. Bastien held out a telex from Rastenburg announcing that the Führer had taken personal charge of the investigation, that new photographs of the Führer taken in front of the blasted building would be distributed within six hours, and that he would broadcast at 10 pm, referring to the events of the day.

Six more officers with drawn guns entered the office, followed by Fromm. He glared at Klaus and said, "You have been caught in the act of committing high treason, you are under arrest. Give me your weapon."

With a sad expression on his face Klaus said, "They've all let me down."

General Beck stood up and requested permission to keep his revolver because he wished to kill himself. Fromm inclined his head and one of the young officers took Beck into the corridor. A loud shot sounded through the building. There was a thump followed by a groan. Klaus drew his gun, fired towards one of Fromm's men then ran into the corridor. Fromm shot Klaus in the back. Klaus, bleeding from the wound in his shoulder turned into his old office and slammed the door. Then hearing the pounding of boots outside as Fromm's guards arrived, he stood aside, opened the door and dropped his gun on the swastika pattern.

"You have been tried and convicted and you and these four others will be shot. Downstairs," said Fromm, with his gun pointed at Klaus' chest.

They walked past Beck's body, still twitching and jerking, blood gurgling out with his breaths. Klaus saw the blood leaking from the distinguished old head lying on the floor, and thought, 'In a few minutes, this is me.'

Fromm said, "Finish him off," and as they clattered down the curving stone steps towards the steel door, another shot banged in the hall above.

Klaus, von Häften and three others were led to the wall just outside the door, and Klaus was told to stand with his back to the wall. He said, "Goodbye Werner," and von Häften said, "Goodbye Klaus."

Ten non-commissioned officers of the Guard Battalion lifted their rifles, aiming at Klaus. As the countdown began, he felt his heart beating so hard that it could burst. He shouted, "Long live Holy Germany."

They fired.

At about 2 pm Clara answered the phone in her office and heard a voice that did not identify itself but sounded like Axel saying, "Your book *Simplicius Simplicissimus* has come in and you can pick it up today." The phone clicked and she turned to Clara and whispered in an awed voice, "It is done and Klaus is safe."

"Oh, is it really?"

"Yes, and he is safe. Oh thank God," and she put her hands together as in prayer. Clara hugged her hard and they danced while the other girls in the office stared at them. Clara led Tati into the hall to get away from the others. "I can't believe that it's over," Clara said. "Oh, it is so wonderful, at last. But it's true. He is gone, gone, gone."

Tati pirouetted in the hallway, then ran back inside to her desk, grabbed her handbag and started for the door pulling Clara with her, calling back over her shoulder, "We're gone on official business." They ran down the hall together, Tati skipping and out onto the Wilhelmstrasse. As they walked quickly to her flat, where Frau Roser was taking care of Helmuth for the day, she said aloud, "Oh, isn't this terrible, to be so glad that someone is dead." She thanked Frau Roser at the door and swept up Helmuth into her arms and kissed him rapturously, thinking with pride that all his life he would remember this day when his father had saved the whole country from the tyrant.

On the train to Potsdam, she was babbling with joy, sometimes in English, to the amazement of the people in the car staring at them. Then she walked so fast along the Hegelallee towards Axel's house that little Helmuth had to run to keep up; she was full of plans as to what they must do now that peace was imminent. The new regime would open the western front to admit their troops throughout Germany.

Clara and Tati were collating, sorting and stapling copies of the new constitution when Axel looking withered came into the room and whispered, "I have terrible news."

"What could be bad today?" said Tati.

"I'm so sorry, Klaus has been shot."

"Shot? Why? No, no, who would do such a thing?"

"He went back to the Bendlerstrasse, they were waiting for him."

"Who was waiting? What are you saying? Please, Axel, explain."

"The bomb went off but Hitler escaped. Now they are arresting all suspects. Klaus was already at the Bendlerstrasse, directing operations of the Replacement Army when General Fromm walked into his office and arrested him. He was shot a few hours ago, in the courtyard. He shouted 'Long live Holy Germany.'"

"Shot. At the Bendlerstrasse? His own office? Impossible. Hitler is dead."

"The information was not correct. Others died, but not him."

"Oh my God. Shot, Klaus is dead but not Hitler?"

Axel nodded.

"Oh my God, they killed the wrong man."

"The Führer has scheduled a broadcast for midnight."

"Oh oh oh," Tati moaned, turning round. She started to fall down. Clara and Axel caught her and sat her down in the salon. She was murmuring, "Oh please God, not my Klaus, let him be, let this be wrong news too."

Clara turned on the radio and the "Badenweiler Marsch" began. Once the introduction to a Hitler speech, it had been not played for years to avoid boring the listeners. Now it had been chosen as the unmistakable Führer-anthem to reinforce the authenticity of the broadcast. The harsh voice of the Führer came on the air, sounding normal. He spoke of the assassination plot hatched by a small clique of criminals and then of his survival. "I regard this as a fresh confirmation of the mission given to me by Providence to continue towards my goal."

'My mother, the count,' Tati thought, and went to the phone to warn her grandfather and mother, who were at Kernslau, to come to Axel's house. But all the lines through Berlin were blocked.

"The documents," Clara exclaimed. "They will come for us, here, we must burn them." Tati did not react but stared out the window at the darkness among the trees. Clara got up and went into the salon where Axel was pacing up and down talking on the phone.

"Axel, we have to get rid of the papers."

"Oh my God, of course. I forgot. Excuse me . . ." and he hung up and came into the hallway with Clara and said, "Where are they?"

"But this is your house."

"Tati hid them, I don't know where." They went to Tati who was sitting by the window staring out, moaning and rocking herself. Tati turned her head and stared at them. It was as if she had died. Her shoulders bagged down, her eyes seemed shrunken, her whole face lifeless.

Clara kneeled beside her. "Tati where are the papers?"

Tati got up and took them to the cellar. Behind the washtubs was a bricked-up fireplace once used to heat wash water. She knelt down and pulled out bricks revealing the suitcase. Clara knelt, drew out the suitcase loaded with all the files they had brought from their own flats. She said, "Where can we burn them?"

"No," said Tati, "they must be saved."

"Yes. But I must stay here, in case," Axel said. "Take a shovel from the shed and go into the Cecilienhof Park, far down at the other end by the Jungfernsee. The ground there will be soft. Mind you put it deep, and cover it over with grass when you are done, and throw the excess earth away into the lake. Oh, and here, wrap it in these." He brought sheets of bright yellow oilcloth from the hall cupboard and found them a wheelbarrow in the garden shed.

Clara put the suitcase in the barrow, covered it with the cloth and they started out along Am Neuen Garten towards the Jungfernsee, Tati dragging her feet and gazing at the ground with no animation in her face. The moon lighted them as they turned the corner of the high brick wall on the west side of the Cecilienhof, casting long shadows ahead. Several people walked by without remark, although the steel-wheeled barrow was squealing on the cinder path. Bombed-out refugees on foot with their belongings in a barrow were common in the streets these days.

Clara led the way along the winding walk, through a small copse of oaks and lindens lit sideways by the moon, and up over the slight rise in the woods at the northwest end, then down a winding cinder path towards the Jungfernsee. Clara looked up at the enormous oak above them, sited herself in relation to the lake, a cement bench nearby and the great curved bay-window of the north room of the Cecilienhof itself, then started to dig. Tati sat motionless on the bench as Clara dug knee-deep into the sandy earth, then deeper still. She wrapped the suit-case in the oilcloth, then tipped it in and filled the hole. Then she replaced the sod, picked up the extra earth in the shovel and flung it all around. The groundskeepers had been called up for labour service so there were many dead leaves lying around. She gathered up armfuls, which she scattered over the earth. Panting with her shirt wet she col-lapsed on the bench with her legs out before her.

Tati sat with her head bowed. She said, "I feel as if I am burying my whole life here." Clara thought, 'If we take the barrow and shovel back to the house, and they are waiting for us, they'll know what we were doing.' She got up and pushed the barrow to the far end of the park where the bushes were thickest and shoved it out of sight. Then she went to the shore and flung the shovel as far out into the lake as she could. It spun in the air and splashed, and she imagined she could see it glinting under water. Then she went back and sat down on the bench beside Tati. The moonlight shivered on the water ahead of them and she felt a shiver of apprehension herself.

"Now Helmuth is Count von Zollerndorf," said Tati in a sad voice. "Not that it matters any more. And now you have the wreck of me on your shoulders." Her eyes began to stream in a passionless way but she did not sob, as if there were no point in her tears.

Clara said, "We go straightaway to Schenkenberg."

"We can't get away from them, they're everywhere. It doesn't matter where we go, we will be arrested too."

"From Schenkenberg we can get away to Switzerland."

"They know everything. We're helpless."

The tears stopped. She was staring with no expression out over the lake. "When I was young I believed in everything good and beautiful and now there is nothing left. They have smashed it all, and me too."

"No, no, no, even this will end one day, and Helmuth will grow up and be brave and good and strong."

"Don't give me hope, I hate it."

"Tati, this is not you."

"I am not me. Tati died."

"Now don't be ridiculous, you're as alive as I am here, and you will pick yourself up and go on."

"No."

"You will because of Helmuth. Because of your crazy mother. Because of your grandfather. Because of . . ." she hesitated. She was going to say "the memory of Klaus," but she couldn't; to say it so soon was like killing him. "Because of Klaus. Because the Nazis don't matter, all they can do is kill. But you and I are alive and we can give life."

"There's no point living."

"There is no point except what you give it."

Tati shrugged.

"It's what Klaus did. It was enough for him. He knew what he was risking. And he died with a blessing on his lips."

Tati snorted. "Yes, he blessed dreadful Germany." But Clara's words remained in her mind. 'He died with a blessing on his lips.' She thought, 'Now that is something worth living for.' But when she looked up she thought, 'The moon is circling me like a vulture.'

Berlin, July, 1944

Early in the morning of 21 July, Clara and Tati were packing in Clara's flat, while Peter was lying on the sofa with little Helmuth half-asleep beside him. Peter turned the shortwave radio to the BBC. The announcer described in accurate detail the events of the previous day and finished with the statement that a number of prominent members of the officer class and high-ranking civilians had been shot or were about to be arrested. He named Axel Freiherr von dem Bussche, Helmuth James Graf von Blücher, Admiral Wilhelm Canaris, Klaus Graf von Zollerndorf, his brother Carl, Adam von Trippe zu Solz, Karl Heinrich Stulpnagel, General von Beck, Werner von Häften, General von Witzleben and many others. The announcer read the names of their friends to all Germany, each name a bullet to the head. Clara listened with her breath held as the list went on, but it did not include Peter Maria von Metternich.

"This is a death sentence on them all," said Peter.

He struggled off the sofa, pulling up his trousers. Then the unimpassioned BBC voice also announced the "Kith and Kin" decision of the Führer—each close relative of the plotters was to be arrested immediately.

Tati said, "I warned Axel that this would happen. The English don't care about us. We might as well be lice for all they care."

"Churchill is gloating that Germans are killing Germans. He does not care why; it just makes his job a little easier," said Clara from the bedroom, packing clothes into a knapsack.

"There are no *people* left in this world," said Tati. "Everyone is just a murderer." She spat out the word with hatred.

"Sh, dear, you'll wake the neighbours."

Peter carried the sleepy boy down to the car. He woke up when the doors slammed, and said, "Where are we going, Mummy?"

"To a beautiful village called Schwandau in the Harz mountains."

"I know, because daddy tried to kill the Führer and now he's dead."

"Yes, it is too bad. And now we must run away."

"Can Daddy ever come home again, a long long time away?"

Tears burst from her eyes, and she hung her head.

"I'm sorry, Mummy," he said and stroked her hand. Tati spoke a formula she had rehearsed for Helmuth: "We must remember he did it for all of us because Hitler is a very bad man. Of course you must never say that."

"Did he kill Daddy?"

"Yes. Daddy promised me to teach me skiing."

"He was a great man, Helmuth. Never forget that."

"This makes me very sad. I liked Daddy."

Peter had in his briefcase false papers prepared by Helmuth James von Blücher in case the coup misfired. But as the investigation went on, even these might become dangerous. If they were stopped by a zealous officer, he might check with the Foreign Ministry and discover that the originating officer was the wanted von Blücher. Peter had informed Hans Bernd Gisevius in Berne where he would go if he had to flee Berlin and that he would soon need papers for all of them. They drove out Zeppelinstrasse heading west and south to Schwandau where Peter's family had friends.

In a blacked-out village about 20 miles out of Potsdam, Peter's car broke down. They left it in the station parking lot and continued by train. After many delays, the train arrived in Schwandau a little after two in the morning. Peter limped alone into the dark village while Clara sat in the station with Tati holding Helmuth's head on her lap as he slept.

The steel-shod heels of Peter's boots clacked loudly on the cobblestones but he could not tiptoe. Many windows were open to the hot night, and he wanted no one to notice their arrival. But the dew made the stones slippery so he had to shuffle very slowly. It was almost four am when he tapped on the black front door of Herr Vogelstein's half-timbered house.

Vogelstein's family had been for many years gamekeepers to Peter's mother's family, von und zu Stolberg, on the estate near the village. During the prosperous years of Bismarck's Germany, they had liberated themselves from service while retaining a great respect for the von Stolbergs. Vogelstein prospered as a butcher in town and was elected mayor in 1929, an office he still held. Peter had helped Vogelstein to raise money for a local hydro project.

He had sent the mayor a letter by a friend months earlier to warn him that he might soon need refuge and asked him not to reply, as his incoming mail was watched. Vogelstein regarded this letter as a compliment, from a Metternich noble to a servant. The letter did however irritate his wife, who heard Peter's knock, and came down in her night dress. Annoyed at having been awakened, she said, "The mayor is not here," and started to close the door.

Peter said, "Don't you recognize me, Frau Vogelstein? Peter Maria von Metternich." He gave her the courtesy of a slight bow, to flatter her.

"That does not change the fact that Herr Vogelstein is away."

Peter presumed on hundreds of years of tradition when he said, "I have no doubt of his welcome when he returns. When will that be, please?"

This reminded Frau Vogelstein of her husband's respect for the Stolbergs. "How many are you? Are they out there? I can't see anything."

Peter said, "Thank you. We are four. I shall return in a few minutes."

He came back to the station looking glum and said, "Let's go."

"What's the matter?" Clara asked.

"It doesn't bother me that I am begging from my mother's gamekeeper, but that all our devotion, all our betrayals, all our risks are for nothing, all because that guttersnipe . . ." he stopped. "Look at me, trudging along here like a gypsy. What a fool, a fugitive in my own country, thinking that we can save Germany's honour. Nobody gives a damn about honour any more, what a quaint conceit. Just over that hill in Nordhausen, there's a cave filled with slaves dying by the hundreds every week, living like trolls inside the mountain to build rockets for that maniac in Berlin. What madness, and we think we are salvaging something for Germany. What we can expect now is to be bombed to dust."

Clara looked at him, appalled. Urbane, smiling Peter had never said anything so bitter before. She said, "Up," and Tati got up, setting the sleepy boy on his feet. He walked along holding her hand, eyes closed, head nodding against her hip.

Frau Vogelstein was at the door, this time barring it. She was a momentary person, who did and said things as they came into her head, and abandoned them as soon as a new thought came along. The thought in her head now was of her husband's reaction when he came back to find his house filled with refugees, never mind if their name was von Metternich.

"You did not say there was a child," she said. "We can't have children here." This was an echo of what she had been telling herself since the age of 40 when she realized she could not have a child. For 20 years she had devoted herself to keeping her household a hell of tidiness because 'we can't have children here.'

Peter exploded, "Oh for God's sakes, woman, can't you see we are hungry and tired and need a place to rest!"

Tati began to cough.

"Yes, that's what I see," Vogelstein said. Now she imagined herself in the important role of nurse-doctor to this sick woman, who she had decided was a countess. But then she thought of all the extra work. "And who is to do all the work and clean up after that one"—she glanced at Helmuth who was staring up at her yawning— "which you did not tell me about, and how am I to feed all these hungry mouths?" She crossed her arms on her chest. "You'll have to come back in the morning. We can't see a thing inside, all the candles are gone, and the fuses are burned out." She made as if to close the door when she noticed little Helmuth offering small round white objects to his mother.

"What are these? Fuses?" she said. "Where did you get these?"

"They're ours, I brought them from our house," he said up to his mother.

Frau Vogelstein, who was now beginning to fear that discourtesy to this Metternich would upset her husband, saw her way out. She seized on the fuses as her excuse to back down. "Well, that's all right, we'll be able to see." And then she added, "Thank you very much."

"How did you get those fuses?" Tati asked him, as she tucked him in under a goosedown comforter which he threw back as the night was warm.

"That's Daddy's sweater," said Helmuth, indicating the sweater she had been wearing round her neck ever since they left Berlin.

"Yes," she said, nestling her cheek down into it.

"Daddy showed me about fuses. They're important. They make the light go on and off. There are 20s and 40s. I got them from our house."

"Did you go to other houses? I thought I saw more in your knap-sack."

Helmuth turned over and said nothing. He had been forbidden to go into bombed houses, but he had not realized that the piles of rubble along Wichmanstrasse were houses. He and Jürgen had found fuses, wine, vegetables and a bicycle, which they had stored in their own "fort" in a rubbled courtyard.

Tati guessed, but was too tired to scold him. She fell asleep with her clothes on, and her head pillowed on Klaus' sweater. When she woke she had a headache and a high temperature, the onset of what people in Berlin called *"Bombenfluenza,"* a flu caused by dust and stress.

Herr Vogelstein was delighted to see Peter on his return the next day. His wife, seeing the honour in which her husband held the Metternichs, now made a great fuss over them. When Clara reported that Tati was sick, Frau Vogelstein did not complain but whisked up the favourite village cure for every sickness—red wine, raw eggs and sugar, a concoction which soon made Tati feel a little better.

Tati read in the paper that her mother had been sent to the concentration camp at Ravensbrück. The Gestapo was searching for Peter, Clara, the old count, herself, and Helmuth. Tati retreated into torpor. The more she avoided doing, the harder it was to do anything. After a few days, Clara sat down beside her and began to massage her head.

Tati said with no expression in her voice, "My anguish is like a metal band round my head squeezing tighter and tighter. No matter which way I turn it is always there. No matter what I think, it always comes back to the same thing. We are refugees and am I to bring up another boy to be murdered by the next lot of gangsters?" She began to weep again, and Clara stroked her head and said, "We have to get through this, so Helmuth can grow up and be happy. After all, his father left a blessing for the children."

Berlin, July, 1944

After the bomb, Hitler ordered Germany to a new level of dedication. His method was to intensify what was already failing. Terror. Hitler ordered that all the families of the suspects in the assassination be rounded up. Trials were to be summary and swift. The convicts were to be hanged and photographs taken of each execution and sent to Hitler, so he could be sure his orders had been carried out. The Allies were notified that the next time a mass terror raid occurred, 100 Allied airmen in German prison camps would be executed.

In France, the police would shoot without trial any terrorist caught in the act. In accordance with the European *Landkriegsabkommen* convention of October 18, 1907, ten Frenchmen would be shot for every German soldier murdered. If there were not enough captives, then hostages must be taken among the civilian population, and executed. All names of those shot must be reported to the Führer. Every British commando captured was to be shot. Any German officer disobeying these orders would be court-martialled and might be shot himself.

These orders were encrypted on Enigma machines and sent by radio to every front. The radio intercepts were made at Bletchley Park in England and decrypted almost as soon as in General-Oberst Blaskowitz' headquarters, Army Group G in Rouffignac in the south of France.

Rouffignac, July, 1944

The sun was rising over the hills as General Johannes Blaskowitz walked up the main street of the cock-crowing village. He stopped at his gate. Bees were invading the tallest flowers warming in the sun. He bent to sniff the peonies and felt the dew cupped in the flower wet his nose. He marched inside and sat at the piano in the drawing room. The piano was why he had requisitioned this house. He began to play the soft, wandering adagio of Beethoven's sonata, marked *Lebewohl*.

At the end of the allegro, he closed the piano with a sigh and went across the hall to his office, where he sat at his desk, erect, the sun shining through the leaded windows warming his back, thinking about the situation. He had been dismissed and recalled now twice, while Germany lost her honour along with the war. He remembered writing something about this in his diary. He unlocked the 1940 volume that was in the drawer, and read,

Oct. 25, 1940: Today, Schlange-Schöningen and I discussed why such atrocious crimes are witnessed silently—with disapproval certainly, but still in silence. No general has summoned up courage to prevent the honour of the German army and of the German people from being besmeared in this way. The old army protected Germany; it looks as though she will perish of the new.

His adjutant, fat, sweating Willy Stumpf, in the former dining room of the house which was now the message centre, heard his chief playing the piano and waited until the movement was over before he entered Blaskowitz' office, bearing a wire basket of messages. Blaskowitz closed the diary as Stumpf came in.

"Good morning, Herr General. Here are the night messages and one that just came in from OKW marked urgent."

Blaskowitz opened the OKW message and read Hitler's latest edict. 'So now we are to murder prisoners,' he thought, 'while the madman in Rastenburg is plotting new ways to . . .' His mind stopped on the edge of that precipice. Then he realized that Stumpf was still standing before him, looking at him.

He said, "The times ahead will be very hard. Do you want a transfer?" This was so unexpected that Stumpf did not know what to say. Was this some new way that Blaskowitz had to show his displeasure? "No, *mein General*, of course not."

"Good, then we stay together, at least for a while. Sorrow and hardship are easier to get by with a friend who shares them."

He read the messages from *Das Reich*, the panzer division on its way north to Normandy from Toulouse. They had encountered guerilla resistance in a village called Oradour-sur-Glan, but had fought their way through. They expected to reach the Loire tomorrow. The message was for information only, as a courtesy to him, because the division was commanded by Hitler. The telephone rang. The *préfet du departement* was on the line.

Blaskowitz had some French and the *préfet* had learned some German, so they were able to converse by switching back and forth. The *préfet*'s voice was shrill with grief as he said that the whole village of Oradour had been murdered by *Das Reich*. The men had been shot, the women and children had been herded into a church, which had been set on fire. No one had survived the flames. Over 600 people had died. The *préfet* begged Blaskowitz "in the name of Europe, in the name of humanity, to stop these horrors."

Blaskowitz promised to look into it, then dictated a severe message to OKW demanding an investigation. As he was dictating it, he felt weary—the whole thing was futile, because OKW would pay no attention to the incident. Instead, he wrote a new message saying that he had already started an investigation and was determined to bring the culprits to justice.

He looked out the window, framed in climbing roses, towards the hills of the Dordogne in the east, and thought, 'This is the end, this war must be stopped. But how?'

Grenade, July, 1944

On July 23, while the battle in France was intense, Marianne was called into her CO's office at the base on the west coast of Scotland.

"At ease, Montauban," Colonel Curran said. She planted her boots wide apart on the curling red lino of his floor. "We have a little job for you." Curran was a Francophile who had lived in Bordeaux for seven years, selling British cloth to tailors. His daughters had grown up there, and he took an intense interest in Marianne.

As she stood in front of his desk in her uniform, at ease, he saw her as she must have been just a few years before, in her light blue jumper at the *Lycée des Jeunes Filles* in Bordeaux, regulated, educated, isolated from boys and sport. The life of the street was unknown to her, yet here she was, fit as an athlete, trained to kill a man with a blow of her hardened hand.

He looked down at his papers as he talked, moved by her patriotism, and said, "I just want to say before we begin," and he got up, moved by strong feelings which he had been trained not to feel. "I just want to say, ahem, you have done well."

Marianne was wary. She was afraid that he was about to declare a primitive passion for her. She had been aware for months that his eyes followed her round the mess hall, that he spoke to her more often than necessary, that it was he who censored the small mail she got. Then she noticed that the paper he had been working on was a crossword puzzle and she was relieved.

"You know that we like our team leaders to choose their own men."

"Yes sir."

"Who will you pick?"

"What is the mission, sir?"

"Excuse me, yes. The German airbase at Mont-de-Marsan. That's why we need you. Local knowledge. You'll have about two dozen men of the local resistance to help you, organized by the mayor of Grenade-sur-l'Adour. I believe you know that town?"

"Yes sir, I was born in Château de Lalanne, near Saint-Séverin."

"That could be helpful. You jump on the eleventh, depending on weather. The moon will be one quarter. You have two weeks to prepare here, then you'll go to our airdrome north of Bournemouth. You'll take a York from there and drop at around 11 pm."

"I'll take Dominic," she said, "Johnny, James and Carlos."

"I see." He tapped his pencil on his teeth. "Good, then, I'll assign them."

Marianne found out all she could about her local contact, Raoul Laporterie, the mayor of Grenade-sur-l'Adour, near the German base. She even knew the clothes he would wear that night, a suit, and a soft homburg. He would be driving a *Juvaquatre* and would say to Marianne, "We are expecting rain from the north later on."

Their target was 12 Focke-Wulf *Kondor*s, four-engine reconnaissance planes which could fly to Newfoundland and back. Once they were destroyed, Marianne was to lead the men away. Above all, they were to avoid capture. It would be better to destroy half the planes and retire intact, than to go for the rest at the risk of capture.

There was no Catholic church near the base, so Marianne went into the Church of England St-James-by-the-Sea on the last afternoon. It was the first time she had been in a church since she had left France in 1940. She genuflected, then crossed herself, which shocked an old woman in the pew across the aisle, then sank to her knees and prayed to the "One God of all the Christians," for her family, her people and her country.

She walked back to the base. She was due to take off at 10 pm. Dinner was served in the mess at 6 pm. She drank two cups of coffee, then went to her hut to write. She sat at the scarred old school-desk, taken from the town school for the duration, and began to write her letters and her will.

She wrote *Cher Jack* and stopped. Ahead of her was the adventure she had been planning for years. It was hard to cast her mind far ahead to an imaginary moment when she might no longer exist, and he would be reading this. She began, *You have come back when you had been missing for months, so perhaps I will too, and this will all be a false alarm.* When she had finished, she wrote on the envelope, *In Case of My Death*, signed the sealed envelope, and addressed it to Jack.

Then she went for the final inspection in the briefing hut beside the tarmac. She was wearing the prescribed French civilian clothes, some of them her own, the rest supplied to her by the SOE. Her brassiere, lipstick, the perfume in her bag, the bag itself, all were made in France.

They flew with the sunset to their starboard behind slashes of red cloud over the black Channel towards the Atlantic, avoiding the German air defences around the U-boat pens in Brittany. The jump-master lit her cigarette for her and shouted "Bomber's moon," indicating the thin sliver of moon emerging from the clouds to the east, casting a wan light over the Garonne coming up ahead of the York's port wing. Bordeaux was dark stick-docks fingering the silvery water.

She was nervous about going home—how had France changed? Were the people depressed? After the mission would she risk a visit to her parents' house? Were they even there?

The jump-master flicked his cigarette butt out the side door in a flare of sparks and shouted, "Right then, who's first?" Marianne shouted, "I am," and stepped forward as he hooked her on, then hooked each one on to the jump-line above the door.

He said to Marianne, "I'll count down from three, laddy, and whack you and over you go. Give my regards to 'Itler." She opened her mouth to say she was Lady not Laddy, but he whacked her bottom and she stepped out, legs bent, felt the harness tighten between her legs, felt herself swing upright, and silence swell up.

She swung back and forth, trying to orient herself over the Adour, but she had forgotten it was droughted out because of the heat, so there was no water to shine. As usual, the descent seemed interminable and then the field grew huge. She saw the flashlights winking below, the trees rushed up beside her and she was coiled for impact. She hit with knees bent, toes pointed and was up and running with the chute, tripped and got the chute down. There were two men with lights around her speaking rapid French, and then they were all together on the edge of the wood.

The York banked round once and she looked up, cursing the noise and wanted him gone. The plane dropped the supply chutes. The canisters hit with such a loud bang on the hard earth that she looked around to see if the Germans had noticed, then helped Johnny and Carlos drag the canisters into the woods.

One of the Frenchmen identified himself with the code-phrase which she had forgotten to ask for because they were in the right place, at the right time. If he had not been the right man—he was a boy of about 16—she would have been dead already.

They walked through the woods and out into a field of wheat, past a 12-foot-high menhir 2,000 years old, and casting a moon-shadow where she had picked wildflowers when she was young.

At the road, there was Laporterie standing by his Juvaquatre, smoking a cigarette. He was a jaunty little man with a courteous and authoritative air. He offered her Bas-Armagnac from a bottle in his hand, and the bottle passed round the group. They were a cocktail party on the road in the dark. She asked if there was any danger of a patrol.

"The Germans have their hands full now," he said. "The French and the Americans have just landed at Saint-Raphael and Cannes."

"Wonderful," she said. "They didn't tell us. Now we won't have to escape."

"Also, they've left Mont-de-Marsan airport."

"How do you know?"

"I was there, today. I saw them go, in trucks."

"All of them?"

"I went into the airport. There were no guards."

"And the *Kondors*?"

"They all flew away yesterday."

"Well then, what the hell was the point in letting us come, risking our lives for nothing? Eh?" She paced up and down. "Why the hell didn't you tell us this before we left? Goddamnit." The news was like a blow to her head, she was dizzy with it. She had trained for this for years and it was taken away from her. Her war was over. She had done nothing.

"Madame, you do not understand. The Boche are very negligent about telling me their plans. The planes left yesterday, but it meant nothing; they leave, and they come back, but it was only today I understood—when the guards left. Then I knew the planes would not come back, but it was too late to radio to London. Our radio moves around of course, right now it is 60 kilometres away. I could not be there, and also here."

She sighed. She was convinced. She looked at James, wondering what to do. Their war was over. All their lives were already saved.

Laporterie offered her a cigarette and the bottle. "I hope you are not disappointed," he said. "It is after all what we want."

"What is?"

"For the Boche to go home, *n'est-ce pas?*"

Faint over the rooftops of the town silhouetted against the moonlit sky to the south, rifle fire sounded.

"What is that?" she demanded.

He said, "I told the boys not to go, now they are for it. What will become of the village? *Oh les pauvres*, listen to that."

Machine gun fire hammered hard. The sky brightened behind the church steeple. Laporterie counted, then they heard a slight whump.

"Molotov cocktail," he said. "About two kilometres."

"Or gas-tank exploding," said Marianne. "What is happening?"

"Oh the poor little fools. I ordered them not to."

"Not to what?"

He took a swig of the armagnac and offered the bottle to her, but she waved it aside. "Go on," she said. He was reluctant. "They are just boys, proud of their armbands," he said. "That's all."

"Listen," said James. Because of a slight shift in the air they now heard the rapid sequence of an MP40.

Laporterie said, "They heard that the 117th division would be coming up from Pau. They said they would attack it. I ordered them not to."

"Why?"

"20 half-armed kids, just children of 15, 16. They will be massacred. And then think of the reprisal. At Oradour, they massacred the whole town, burned them alive in the church. Think of it, this is my town."

She puffed on her cigarette, then took the bottle from him. "But you were willing to attack the airport."

"That was before I heard about Oradour. Don't you know? They murdered 600 people there. I can not expose my town to that. The Germans are leaving, why should we impede them?"

A flare of red light backlit the steeple of the church, and Laporterie counted again till the sound arrived. "Two, three kilometres," he said, "Just the other side of the village. At the old château."

He was smoking a cigarette, his *melon* on his head, wearing a suit, his shoes polished, and drinking armagnac. He was ridiculous. "You knew," she said.

"Of course I knew, knew what?" he said.

"That the Germans were coming. Up this road. And you did not tell us."

"I did not know. The boys said they knew, but they are just children. They have poor sources of information, whereas I am in touch with people in the *Mairie* at Pau, who tell me everything. And they said nothing."

"We have to help them. Up, we're going." They all got to their feet and started down the road towards the village.

"Stop, I order you," shouted Laporterie. She kept on marching. Dominic, James, Johnny, and Carlos followed her. Laporterie stood in the middle of the highway with a revolver in his hand. "I beg you, do not do this," he called after her. "You will be killed, the town will be burned, and the Germans are going home anyway. That is what we want, the Germans to go home, and they are going home."

When they got near the *Mairie*, she said, "There is a bridge over the river to our right, but the river is almost dry. We will march up the river till we reach the château, then will follow the wall out to the highway. That is where we will see them."

She began to trot along the main street which was also the highway to Pau, past Laporterie's store, through the main square where the palm trees and *platanes* shaded the pavement and benches from the pale moonlight.

She ran through the shade to the entry to the bridge and then slid down the muddy bank, which reeked of urine from the men who drank in the bistro nearby, and out onto the gravel of the empty river. The others strung out behind her, looking up the bank, sometimes high over their heads, knee-high in the marshy areas. The sound of gunfire ahead was loud now, she could hear voices shouting. Muzzle-flashes sparkled in the woods. She heard a scream, gunfire, silence.

She came to the crumbled edge of the château's garden wall where it stuck out over the eroded bank of the river. She whispered, "Wait here." She rappelled up by vines that fell from the top of the wall, then crouched down as she hurried forward. The firing was now coming from her left, about 100 metres away. She saw a flash of a gun muzzle and the sound of firing at once, turned her head to see it but something slammed her sideways. She hit face down into the earth, smelled earth and saw stars going out.

The German convoy commander, Lieutenant Richard Weigel, a tall fair-haired Saxon with blue eyes, had been nodding off on the front seat of the command car beside his driver, his cap on his head, his steel helmet on the floor beside his feet. When the first shots came, he jumped from the car, forgetting his helmet, pulling out his revolver and running towards the gunfire, back bent, head low. As he ran under a tree, a branch swept off his cap and the moonlight glinted on his fair hair, Georges Dubosc from the village shot him and was, in turn, shot as he stood firing, by Germans aiming at the flashes of his gun muzzle.

The Germans found Marianne's body and carried it to an LKW where they dumped it in beside Weigel's body. They rode beside each other, bouncing with the motion of the truck, to the *Mairie* where the Germans threw Marianne's bloody body on the front steps.

They set up their guards and tents in the abandoned airbase at Mont-de-Marsan and slept for three hours. The sun came up like a bayonet. Red light bled into the clouds and turned the steam pink over the mobile kitchens. Sleepy men were straightening up outside their tents in the grass by the tarmac when the second convoy with the rest of the battalion arrived from Pau.

The new commander radioed to Rouffignac to report that they were taking immediate reprisals on the village. Then they turned the convoys around and rode back to Grenade, all guns loaded. In the main square in front of the *Mairie* at nine in the morning, they drew up, and the commander, Hartmut Nordmann, shouted at the open door of the *Mairie* for the mayor to come out.

Laporterie closed his eyes, put on his jacket and, thinking this was the last thing he would ever do, appeared in the doorway, expecting to be shot. He stood on the stone step above the black stain of Marianne's blood. Nordmann ordered him to approach his car. Laporterie, who had learned German in captivity during the Great War, walked towards the car and stopped five metres away. Nordmann told him to round up 30 young men or be executed himself, along with 100 more.

"You have one hour," said Nordmann. He was nervous: this was the first time he had commanded in action, and he was sure of one thing—he must maintain authority over his own men and the French. Having watched his father smoke, he identified smoking with authority, so he lit a cigarette, blew out smoke in a long stream and held the cigarette to his face frequently. He began to pace back and forth in the square. After a few minutes, a sergeant from the radio truck came over to him with a message.

NO REPRISALS TO BE TAKEN WITHOUT SPECIFIC AUTHORIZATION THIS HQ STOP TAKE HOSTAGES 20 TO

ONE FOR TRANSPORTATION STOP NO ONE IS TO BE SHOT WITHOUT PERMISSION THIS HQ. STOP MESSAGE ENDS STOP BLASKOWITZ

In one hour, there were 23 boys, one young man in a wicker wheelchair, and six girls who had volunteered to take the place of young men. Nordmann stood up as Laporterie approached. "They are here, *mon capitaine*," he said.

"March them over there," said Nordmann, indicating the long stone wall of a house across the square from the *Mairie*. Then he shouted orders to his officers to move the trucks out of the way. Laporterie stared at him, thinking, '*Mon Dieu*, don't do this, please, do not let this happen.'

The trucks started, the air was blue with their exhaust which hung over the square. The young people walked over to the wall in a clump as if seeking protection. The captain ordered them to disperse along the wall. They spread along the wall, glancing at each other as if to say goodbye. One joined hands with another, until they all had joined hands and faced the Germans with their backs to the wall, holding hands.

Nordmann stood 20 metres in front of them and raised his revolver and fired six times. He fired just over their heads. Bits of stone fell down and the bullets ricocheted away with a whizzing sound. One of the boys fainted, falling while still held half-erect by the boys on either side, who let him slide down. One of the boys then fell on his knees beside his friend, thinking he had been shot, and kissed his forehead.

Nordmann shouted, "You are all cowards. You attack in the night, after your country has surrendered. Cowards die many times before their deaths. You will go to Germany to work for the Fatherland. Into the trucks."

The boys and girls, shocked to be alive, ran for the trucks.

Then Nordmann shouted in French, "Your town will be burned, starting with the *Mairie*. Mayor, you have ten minutes to warn your people."

Laporterie ran into the *Mairie* and soon all who remained of the small town, including six people who had been hidden in the attic of Laporterie's house, assembled in the square, hundreds of people, as soldiers with flame-throwers went through the town setting fire to every other building. Smoke filled the air over the town, bits of ash floated down on their heads and shoulders, the crackling of old timbers and the crash of falling tiles sounded over the hundreds of voices screaming and weeping in the square.

Nordmann watched the men starting the fires and said to Laporterie, "You lost the war, signed the armistice, you must abide by the peace treaty." It did not occur to him that his own country had broken the terms of the armistice.

One grey-haired soldier with a canteen of schnapps at his waist offered it to an old Frenchman standing beside him, as if they were at a reception, and said, "*La guerre, nicht gut.*" The Frenchman took a swig as he watched the black smoke billow up from the *quartier* where his house had stood.

Women ran up to the trucks as the engines were starting, to hand in the few little bits of clothing and food they had been able to find, and the prisoners blew back kisses and the mothers waved and wept and called out words of love and courage.

As Nordmann got into his car, ready to leave, he noticed Laporterie still standing on the steps of the *Mairie*. He gestured to him to come over, and Laporterie crossed the square, knowing what was about to happen. The commander said, "*Vous aussi, macht schnell,*" pointing to the trucks loaded with boys and girls. Laporterie turned to see his wife running across the cobbled square towards him screaming, "*Non non.*" Laporterie took the hand of one of the boys who leaned over to help him and got up as the truck started to drive away, and his wife fell to her knees on the cobbles weeping and praying.

That night, when his convoy bivouacked on the tarmac of the abandoned airfield at Mont-de-Marsan, Nordmann saw again the fallen boy and the friend who leaned down to kiss him goodbye. The red flames of the burning town were rising and fading into black. He turned over in bed and tried to obliterate the scene by imagining a walk through the forest near his village but, when he came out of a certain favourite passage in the trees to a view over the valley, he saw that his village was clothed in red flames, white steam and black smoke.

Esperacedes, London, August, 1944

Jack Giovanelli was told by the FFI agent in Cabris that Curran had ordered him to stay with Nancy Cusack until further word. He helped her to pick the jasmine early in the morning before the sun destroyed the scent, then drank wine all day and played chess and listened to her play Brahms and Elgar on her cello.

She told him of her friend, a writer named Jean Bruller who often visited her. His new book, *Le Silence de la mer*, had been published the year before under the nom de plume Vercors, by the clandestine *Editions Minuit* in Paris, and she gave him a signed copy. He sat in the sun eating peaches, reading the book and listening to Nancy practice.

One day in early August, they heard gunfire to the west and saw the planes with the red, white and blue roundels flying inland, turning above the village, and then diving intently down at the beaches where the landing craft were coming in with the French and the American soldiers.

The Germans left Cannes the next day in trucks and trains going west, and that afternoon the town was free. He reported to an American commander on the beach at Saint Raphael, who told him he might get a plane out in a week. When Jack told him what he had been doing, and that he could report on the strength of the resistance in the Vercors and the valley of the Rhone, the American colonel picked up the phone, got him a seat on a plane to Sicily, and sat him down in his villa to debrief him.

The following night, he was back in England. Marianne was not on the base and the duty sergeant could not find her name on any of the papers before him. Nor was she on the duty roster posted inside the hut door. He asked to see the duty officer, Major Deckman.

The major was behind a desk. He got up and shook Jack's hand.

"Welcome back," he said. "Bloody good show, I heard."

"Thank you, sir. What about Marianne? Where is she?"

"I'm sorry, Jack. We lost her."

"What do you mean we lost her? Is she captured? Dead?"

"Dead, I'm afraid."

"How do you know?"

"It was in France, near Mont-de-Marsan. She led a group of, we think, FFI against a German convoy. She was shot right away."

"Are you sure? Who told you?"

He handed Jack the letter she had left. "I'm dreadfully sorry, but there was no doubt. The mayor of the village sent a radio message. He saw her body."

The word took his breath away. He thought, 'her body.'

He walked out feeling the loss in his eyes, hating to know that her beautiful body was now 'a body.'

'I've lost her, she's gone, she can't come back.' He saw her in Brandon, laughing at Canada, stepping from the open door of the plane into the wind ahead of him, shouting "Yippee.'"

"Let's get married."

"*Pas pour l'instant.*"

"I'm serious, for once."

"*Cela suffit. Faut pas être si sérieux.*"

That was when he had guessed: every time he got serious with her, or proposed marriage, she spoke French to him. Marriage made her think of France, ergo, in France she had been married.

He clutched his head and walked out onto the airstrip where the Welly transports were lined up with nowhere to go today.

He limped along the grass verge of the tarmac. 'We had nothing in common except each other. And the war. And now the goddamned war has taken her away. Where will I go, what will I do, whom will I love? I am lost.' He kept walking and wanting to shout, tears sprouting in his eyes and wetting his cheeks.

He rubbed his head thinking, 'I have lost a brave honourable person whom I loved and scarcely knew.'

He stuffed his hands in his pocket, found the letter, and tore it open.

Dear Jack,

You have come back when you had been missing for weeks, so perhaps I will too, and this will all be a false alarm. In any case, dear Jack, I must give you this so you will have knowledge of me no matter what.

I was born in 1920. Does that surprise you? It surprises me how young I am to be doing this, having lived so little, having such responsibility, but it also surprises me how old I am compared to you.

I went to the school in my village Saint Sever, for two years, because I refused to leave Maman and Papa, but then because the school was so bad, I agreed to go to Bordeaux and then to the nuns in Paris. Where of course I fell in love, this time with the city and then more slowly with France, I guess you might say, with the culture and historical mission of France. It was not so much love as recognizing my fate. No wonder it was a Frenchman Malraux who wrote La Condition humaine *which equates culture and fate. That is what I mean. I am glad you read it for that book is my belief system, if you like.*

I was married once. He and I were engaged, 1940, the attack came, he was called up on May 9, 1940, we were married at noon in the Mairie, his train left at 1400. It was the moment of the Marne again. I never saw him after that. He was captured soon after, and I have never heard a word from him. I escaped in a Bantry Bay boat from Brittany. You can see why I could tell you nothing—the reprisals against him would have been too easy, in a prison camp.

I am in this war for ourselves, for France, for civilization. I am out of time, I hear the plane. I love France, I love you, I am glad we knew each other, I hope we shall meet again and this letter will be a relic we shall wonder at in times to come when we are at peace in a café in the sun telling war stories to children.

Now I must check my gear and seal this. Hard to do.
With all my heart, ta toute dévouée,
Marianne de la France Profonde
Louise Abadie de Montauban

Normandy, July-August, 1944

Bernie Hallett and Ed Burns were asleep in the shade of trees outside the hot command tent in the early morning when the order to take Vernières Ridge came through; first on the phone, then repeated by telex. They agreed that it was out of the question to send the men in daylight against the SS division who were dug in on the crest of the ridge, and had Tiger tanks, many 88s, plus mortars trained on the hay field fronting the ridge. Bernie asked for clarification, which General Fox always permitted, even though such requests emanating from other officers were a way of evading or delaying orders. This time, Fox paid no attention to the problems, but repeated the order, with the subscript: From highest levels.

Bernie Hallett at forward HQ watched the first attack go in, saw the SS guns cut down his men by the dozens. Then American fighter-bombers swept in from the west and attacked the Canadians with bombs, rockets, and cannon fire. One of his officers in the lead stood up exposed to German fire and was cut down screaming in incoherent rage at the pilots.

Within a few seconds, dozens of men were wounded and lying down in the hay calling out for help. Bernie wanted to run out to them and could not bring himself to do it—he was crippled by fear for the first time in the war. He had been on Juno Beach and had gone all the way to Bayeux on D-Day, then attacked Caen, but he had never seen butchery like this. Five minutes into the attack, it had been routed and his men were lying wounded or dead, or running bent over back to the woods on the north edge of the field.

In the forward command tent, under trees 200 metres behind the start line, Bernie phoned Fox and told him what had happened. Fox said, "I ordered the air strike myself; they had the right coordinates," and read them off to Bernie, who checked them on the map on his knee. "Pilot error," said the general, "I'll send a rocket up."

And then Bernie uttered the first blasphemy of his life, "Jesus fucking Henry Christ, it's just murder up here, get your fucking plans right."

He slammed down the phone, amazed at himself, then went to pick up the phone again to apologize, and Ed put his hand on the receiver and said, "He'll call you, don't worry."

Bernie put his head down on the table, trying not to weep.

In ten minutes, the general called back to apologize. Measures had been taken to make sure it would never happen again. Then he ordered them to take the ridge before nightfall.

Bernie called Ed into the tent and said, "Ed, this is murder. We can't do this wrong again. Any ideas?"

This was a singular moment for both of them, a plea from the helpless colonel of the regiment to a company commander, spontaneous, heartfelt, and necessary. Bernie was thinking three things: 'They are all brave men; we can't do anything like this again,' and 'The band done it, that's what done it.' This was a phrase, famous at his school. It was uttered by a British Army sergeant major at the moment when the school cadet corps, parading before him, made conflicting moves because the band played the wrong music and the boys fell into disorder, some marching one way round the football field, others crisscrossing them, and some falling about, laughing and joking. The moment had remained vivid in Bernie's mind because he had been the battalion commander, responsible for the embarrassing shambles, which he realized had been correctly diagnosed by the sergeant major. At that moment, he had realized something important about himself and human life: he was fit only to live within the order of an established institution and, secondly, that in battle, unity is the unifying and victorious principle.

When the Canadians at Vernières had begun to sense the disorder in their own lines advancing, the attack faltered and then it was destroyed by the planes. Every man exposing himself to instant death, seeing such horrible disorganization, felt the binding sense of unity that leads to victory disintegrating within him. Each one began thinking the same thought, how to save himself from the mess. The Canadians had been defeated by the reckless disorder in their allies more than by the Germans.

Ed was what Bernie needed. He was independent, needing the support of no institution because he was his own guiding principle. His strength came from within him. He was the tree, Bernie the vine clinging to it.

Ed suggested three improvements. He also asked permission to address the men before the next assault. Bernie listened in admiration as Burns sat on the gun-turret of a Sherman facing all the surviving infantry of the regiment with a megaphone and said, "Right lads, the colonel's asked me to say a few words before the next go-round. We've had one bad go, but now we're going to do things a little differently. The Germans are scared and ready to run. We've already hurt 'em bad. Now we're going to put in a full Victor—the FOOs are up there now calculating the yardage—so the Germans will be dead or paralyzed or running away when we get there. Then three squadrons of Tiffies plaster them not us with rockets and lastly, the Wasps go in with smoke and fire, and we follow them.

"Now in a moment you'll go back to the canteens, you're going to get a hot dinner and that's when the guns go in. So while you're eating, they're dying. And when half of them are dead and the rest are scared to death and they are burning in their trenches, blinded with the sun in their eyes and our smoke, then we're going in over the blue line to score the winning goal."

Inside two hours, the immense barrage had been calculated, orders issued, shells taken from their packing and stacked, new gun barrels installed, trajectories computed. The men saw all this organizing activity, and thought, 'They are helping us to the maximum, now we shall succeed.' Their confidence rose when they saw hundreds of four-inch, Bofors and 25-pounder shells burst in the German lines, throwing black smoke and dust upwards shot through with orange flames. The artillery barrage was followed by the promised Typhoons blasting the German lines with rockets and cannon, then the Wasps waddled up masking the Ossies' tanks and men with smoke, and spouting flame 100 feet ahead of them through the bitter dust.

Ed had timed it so the setting sun was in the eyes of the Germans as they tried to see through the smoke from the Wasps and the burning hedgerows. He dropped his arm, blew his whistle, whistles up and down the start line shrilled, and Ed charged with his gun up. The frightened young men yelled and ran after him so that the gun-stunned Germans, who had hoped the Canadians were defeated and would not attack again, saw hundreds of screaming shadows pouring bright flames and firing sizzling bullets that smacked into them out of the blinding glare of the sunset shining through white, orange and black smoke.

Bernie did not join the charge because Fox would disapprove of him leaving his command post during the action, although many of the senior Canadian officers did just that, and were not reprimanded. He began wondering if his reputation with his own men was on the line, and he decided he had to try it.

He took an HQ rifle as soon as the stonk lifted and started towards the field where some of the wounded were still lying, being tended by the stretcher-bearers. At the edge of the bush, he hesitated, afraid to expose himself directly to the fire. 'Far enough,' he said to himself. 'You've proved your courage now, stop being a fool, go back.' Bullets sizzled through the leaves beside him. It was forward or back. He ran forward. The men were masked by smoke, so the first wave was not sure where the German trenches lay. But then a breeze blew the smoke away, and the Germans in the second line began cutting them down as they came nearer, some running crouched, others wriggling through the hay past bodies cut down in the first assault.

Bernie felt the bullets whizzing by his ear, and ran to the hedgerow. He hunkered down into a shallow foxhole trying to keep his head and shoulders below the grass. He started to pray. 'I can't get up there again,' he thought, imagining the moment when the bullet would hit, tearing through cloth, ripping open his skin, penetrating cartilage, bone, causing blood to spurt into his lungs, drowning him in his own blood. The fear was so strong that it seemed he had already been hit, he was breathing hard, short breaths, his heart was pounding, his vision stained yellow, and tunnelled straight ahead. Everything he saw confused him.

He had his head down, his whole body curled into a fetal crouch, fearing that his side was above the grass exposed to bullets. 'Nobody knows I'm here,' he was thinking. 'If I can just stay down here till dark, I can crawl back then.' Something hard on his right side kept butting him when he moved. He reached round to get rid of it and found a flask full of the Calvados he had liberated. Now, regardless of the bullets, he squirmed round to get the bottle to his lips and started drinking. He knew he should get up and run at the Germans but he could not get himself to stick his head out. A Sherman tank engine roared towards him. He squirmed round to look. The tank was coming straight towards him

In a moment, the treads would crush him. He jumped out of the hole thinking, 'Now I'm going to die for sure,' and ran towards the German trenches, screaming and firing his rifle as he went. He jumped one ditch in which he saw, as he hurtled over, men lying dead or wounded below his flying feet. Then in the next trench he found six Germans staring up at him with their hands up, shouting, "Surrender, surrender."

"Christ, you better," he shouted, and jumped down into the trench because machine-gun bullets were now shooting past him, one hitting something metal with a terrible clang. He grabbed the rifle from the nearest German and ordered him to lie down. He squatted down and they all understood and lay down in the trench.

Ed Burns was screaming, his rifle in the air, as more Ossies jumped into the trench, and others jumped right over it, four feet wide, in full packs, and went on running towards the next German trenches. Ed said to Bernie, "Jesus, it was you, I wondered. That was a crazy thing to do," and Bernie said, "I've shit my pants," and began to shake.

Late that afternoon, Ed Burns stood on the top of Vernières Ridge, his red hair grey with dust, and looked down into the broad valley, chimneyed with black smoke and speckled by fighters firing rockets and machine guns into the masses of tiny trucks, horses, tanks and infantrymen under swirling dust and smoke trying to escape and said, "That's for Spain, you shits."

Québec, September, 1944

Aware that Roosevelt was planning to meet Churchill and Mackenzie King at Québec in a couple of weeks, Secretary of the Treasury Henry C. Morgenthau went to the White House to report on his recent fact-finding mission to England. Morgenthau liked to tell Roosevelt that he was "the President's conscience," which the President tolerated because he knew that Morgenthau controlled many thousands of voters in New York City. For the same reason, he had allowed Morgenthau to fly to England to consult with Eisenhower and Anthony Eden on what they were going to do with Germany after the war, although the Treasury Department had nothing to do with foreign policy.

At a meeting in SHAEF headquarters at Widewing in the south of England, Eisenhower said that he wanted to "treat 'em rough." Morgenthau egged him on and Eisenhower ended by saying, "I hate Germans, they're just beasts. Too bad we didn't kill more of them in Africa." He promised that if no one else would do it, he would go to the President himself and recommend rough treatment.

Morgenthau reported this to Roosevelt in his study at the White House on a hot day in August. The air conditioning had broken down again, so the windows were open to the lawn and the Potomac in the hope of a breeze. The President was seated behind his desk in his shirt-sleeves, and Morgenthau took off his seersucker jacket and sat down.

"No one is planning how to treat the Germans roughly, but that's what you wanted, Mr. President," Morgenthau began. He said that the existing plans included the rapid restoration of the German economy. The President looked grim at this news. "Give me 30 minutes with Churchill and I can correct that," he said. "We have to be tough on Germany and I mean the German people, not just the Nazis. You've either got to castrate the German people or you have got to treat them in such a manner that they can't go on reproducing people who want to continue the way they have in the past."

"It is important that the Germans be stopped permanently," Morgenthau said, his pince-nez glittering on his nose. "You have the power, and therefore the duty to rid the world of this evil, not just Hitler, but the Germans as a whole."

"Kill 'em all, Henry?" said the President with a smile.

"I'd do it, sure," Morgenthau said. "Sure, if we can get away with it."

"George Marshall said that if Hitler started shooting our boys as reprisals for our raids, we should announce that for every one shot, we will keep 10,000 German prisoners after the war until they were too old to father children."

"Now that's more like it," said Morgenthau. "Just rub 'em all out."

"Is that your plan? Castration by incarceration?"

"Good phrase, that, Franklin, I like it. No, White and I are still working on something that Ike suggested. I could bring it to Québec for you and Winston to approve."

Morgenthau and his assistant Harry Dexter White set to work to produce a detailed plan for the destruction of German industry and agriculture. He brought the finished outline of this plan to Québec at Roosevelt's invitation.

At Québec, Churchill walked beside Roosevelt as he wheeled his chair along the boardwalk in front of the Château Frontenac, two men isolated on the great promenade, their Mounties and secret service men many yards away.

"Where did Wolfe come up?" he asked, and Churchill replied, "Behind us, upstream a mile or two."

"And Philips tried his hand at this and couldn't make it."

"Philips?" said Churchill.

"Yankee freebooter. About 1665, I think."

"Phipps," said Churchill, who would always brief himself about the history of the locales of his meetings with the President and Stalin.

"You know, it's an extraordinary thing, that we two, I mean Britain and the United States, have managed to stay at peace so long, when there was so much to fight about."

"I trust it will be our legacy Franklin, yours and mine, that we created an alliance in war that became a friendly union in peace. The union of the English-speaking peoples. What a grand idea."

"It is a grand idea," said Roosevelt, looking up at the green-tinted copper roofs of the turreted old hotel. The sun shone down on the few hairs on his head, so he put on his panama hat, and stopped wheeling himself. Behind them, and ahead, the secret service men and the Mounties also stopped, leaving a discreet 30 yards of clear space around the two friends.

"You seem a little tired, Franklin," said Churchill.

"Oh you know, I've had to make a lot of speeches for the election. Not easy to run an election campaign and a war at the same time. I hope you don't have to do it."

"I might," said Churchill, "but not yet, I hope, not this year. Not till we've pushed that devil back into hell."

"We have to talk about that. What to do about Germany. War-crimes trials."

"Here comes Mackenzie," said Roosevelt, "I'm sure he'lll want to have his photograph taken with us, he has an election coming up, I hear."

Mackenzie King posed with them, beaming at the camera, and then took Churchill by the arm to escort him into the hotel for lunch.

At lunch, he asked Roosevelt when Harry Hopkins was coming. Roosevelt said that he was "otherwise occupied." Churchill was amazed because Roosevelt had once doted on Harry, and so had he, for Hopkins' abilities as a fixer/ambassador. Churchill said he was the only man in history who was both his country's ambassador and ambassador to his country. He had often invited him down to Chequers for the weekend, and they had come to depend on each other as much as they enjoyed each other.

As soon as Churchill realized that Morgenthau was subbing for Cordell Hull and for Hopkins, he was on guard, thinking that the Secretary of the Treasury was there to advance the American claim to the remaining resources of the British Empire.

At the beginning of their first plenary session, at a long maple table, Roosevelt asked Churchill to summarize the war situation, which Churchill loved to do. All their meetings so far had begun with a long Churchill paper which surveyed the entire globe from the point of view of the leaders of what he loved to call "the great democracies."

He said that since they had last met at Cairo, their affairs had prospered beyond imagining. Future historians would have the impression of remarkable design and precision of execution. He covered the British campaign in Burma, the attacks on the Japanese navy by both British and American fleets, the American island-hopping campaign in the Pacific.

He said that another of Hitler's allies, Hungary, was trying to surrender to Britain. They would not surrender to the Russians, although the Red Army was at their borders. The war against the U-boats in the Atlantic had been won, the British navy had kept open the supply lines to Archangel, the Russians were advancing towards Germany every day, the bombing campaign had mounted to terrible heights of destruction, the campaigns in Italy and France had been "crowned with success. Everything we have touched has turned to gold," he said. He stuck his unlit cigar in his mouth and chewed on it.

The President thanked him and added a few touches of his own. He was delighted that the British and Americans always cooperated with cordiality and increasing solidarity. The Americans would soon invade the Philippines, and then start mass fire-bombings of Japanese cities. He attacked the Nazis for their suppression of the uprising in Warsaw, which not only proved once more the need to beat them but also their strength in adversity.

The President, having prepared the meeting for this moment, now introduced Secretary Morgenthau, who wanted to discuss his plan for control of Germany after victory. Morgenthau outlined his plan to destroy German industry, ostensibly to prevent rearmament.

"This means the Germans will starve *en masse,*" said Churchill, "while we are occupying the entire country."

"It is essential to reduce their industrial potential to zero," Morgenthau said.

"But we shall occupy it for as long as we like."

"They evaded the restrictions we imposed at Versailles."

"We did not possess the whole country. No, this is too severe. They can not feed themselves as it is. We are being asked to sever their most productive regions in the east to satisfy the hungry Russian bear. And now this plan of devastation masquerading as disarmament."

There was silence round the table.

"I hope this does not mean that you are planning to withdraw from the European mainland, Franklin," Churchill went on.

"Not at all," said Roosevelt. "What makes you think that?"

"This plan presupposes the utter destruction of Germany, which of course would eliminate that threat, but in so doing, abandon Europe to the bear."

Roosevelt said, "Well, we don't want to go that far of course."

"Then just how far do you propose to go?"

Again there was silence.

Morgenthau said, "As far as this plan suggests."

Churchill said, "I hope I have not been brought all this way to discuss a plan which would mean England being chained to a dead body. This is undemocratic, unChristian and unnecessary. No, this will never do."

Morgenthau glanced at Roosevelt for guidance. The President kept a calm face, and suggested that they postpone discussion until the next day.

Walking after lunch on the sunny boardwalk of the Citadel, Morgenthau discussed Churchill with Lord Cherwell, the Prime Minister's chief scientific advisor. Cherwell pointed out that the next day's session was to deal with Britain's post-war finances, so Churchill would want to ingratiate himself with Morgenthau and Roosevelt. "Get your chief to ask Winston at the beginning of the meeting tomorrow to recapitulate today's sessions. Then you'll see, he will change his tune. He knows which side the butter is on. He will not be as harsh against you as he was this morning."

Morgenthau saw the light. He would suggest to the President that American aid should be contingent on British agreement to the Morgenthau plan. He hurried away to get to the President before the afternoon session began.

The next morning, Churchill delivered the recapitulation as Cherwell had said, from memory, in detail, and moderating his opinion of the Morgenthau Plan.

He then raised the subject of postwar American aid to Britain. He pointed out that Britain had sold almost all her foreign assets, and much of her gold. "We have been living off American and Canadian charity for years now. You have been most generous. But if we are to win the peace as we are winning the war, we must have continuity of sharing resources as well as responsibilities." Roosevelt asked Morgenthau to respond.

Morgenthau was excited. He laid out his papers on the table, put on his pince nez and started to read the details. He said that he did not like to differ with the Prime Minister, on whose shoulders rested burdens perhaps greater than on any other Englishman in history, but that the war had cost the Empire most of its foreign assets.

'Which are now lodged in American hands, along with most of our gold,' Churchill thought.

Morgenthau said that it was important to hold Germany down while Britain recovered her world-wide trade. To do this, it would be necessary to abolish German industry. Then Britain would have no serious competition in Europe for her manufactured goods. German militarism would be ended. Russian losses would be compensated by giving her new territory taken from eastern Poland, Poland would take a similar area from Germany. The Germans living in these areas would be expelled to the remainder of Germany.

Churchill was revolted. The details of the plan were more sickening than he had anticipated. He knew that Germany could not feed itself on its own land—the Germans had to export manufactured goods to trade for food. This plan would mean the loss of one quarter of their country, including their best farmland, while millions of impoverished refugees from the lost territories would be imposed on the starving remains of Germany. It would be impossible for Germany to manufacture for export to earn food since most of her factories would be dismantled. The remaining farmland would be less productive because under another section of the plan, the production of most fertilizer would be banned. The conditions that had led to the war in the first place would be reimposed in much harsher form. Churchill thought, 'Morgenthau believes that we would sacrifice human lives in the interests of trade.' Anthony Eden, beside him, stirred in resentment.

Eden exploded. "There will be mass starvation. You can't do this, Winston! After all, you and I have publicly said quite the opposite. Furthermore, we have a lot of things in the works in London which are quite different. Not including mass starvation." He glared at Morgenthau.

Morgenthau said, "But that is what they have done to the rest of Europe."

"Yes," said Eden, "and you don't seem to realize that that is why we are fighting them, because this sort of thing revolts our conscience." Churchill, seeing the languid Eden turning red and glaring round, shook a warning finger at him. "Remember, this will mean that we will get the German trade."

"How do you know what it is or where it is?" said Eden, for he disliked Churchill's dictatorial way of deciding matters of which he knew nothing.

Churchill was shocked. "We will get it whatever it is and wherever it is."

"But they make things we have never made."

Morgenthau was amazed at Eden, who had never talked this way about the postwar when they had met in London. Addressing himself to Eden now, Morgenthau said, "This is by far the best way for you to solve your economic difficulties. You will be independent, as you always have been, until now." Roosevelt looked down at the table, refusing to smile, and thinking, 'Oh, well done, Henry.'

Seeing Roosevelt avoid his eyes, Churchill realized what Morgenthau was saying: 'If you want our financial aid, you must agree to our plan for Germany.'

Furious at this blackmail, he put his hands flat on the table and said, looking not at Morgenthau but straight at Roosevelt, "You know our sacrifices. You know our needs. What do you want me to do, sit up and beg like Fala."

Roosevelt grinned and said, "More likely you will roar like a lion," and stuck his jaw out as Churchill himself often did. He smiled at Churchill, who broke into a grin himself and said, "Ah Franklin, I am going to launch a new ship and name it after you. It will be *HMS Irresistible*."

Roosevelt smiled around the table, and gave a little approving nod of his head. 'Well done, Franklin,' he heard his mother whisper.

Eden touched Churchill's arm as if to draw him aside for a private word, but Churchill shook him off. "Now, Anthony," he said reaching for a new cigar and starting to chew it. "I hope you are not going to do anything about this with the War Cabinet if you see a chance to present it. After all the future of my people is at stake, and when I must choose between my people and the German people, I am going to choose my people. And I dare say that in the end, you will come down on this issue in the same way." He lit the cigar, blew out the match, and puffed out a big cloud of blue smoke in Eden's general direction, who made a point of waving away the smell.

On the final day at Québec, the plan was presented to them in two copies. Roosevelt and Churchill both initialled it.

Halifax, October, 1944

While they were still in the North Atlantic Drift, southwest of Iceland, heading west, Grant leaned on the rail of the bridge at night, brooding and searching for U-boats. Over the dark sea the funnelled freighters smoked their way west, black against the bright horizon.

'If we could light the ships to the same intensity as the horizon against which they are seen by the U-boats, then they'd just disappear.' He made a note in his journal. He remembered the Church of St. George in Halifax, a beautiful old white wooden building, hung about with regimental battle flags. All commemorating victories over the heaps of dead who had stood in the way of British Imperial power. 'And here I am on deck in a windy night thinking out efficiencies against an enemy I never knew.' He watched the long wake covered with the phosphorescent light of the disturbed plankton. By the light of the moon from the south and wide red stain of the sun skidding along the horizon to the west, he began to revise the poem he was writing. But the moon was too dim, so he went into his cabin, and set the portable Olympia typewriter his mother had given him, inside the fiddle of the desk. He reread the poem he had sent to Lord Beaverbrook:

Bomber's Moon

The women of this war must wait and weep
For news of those they love
From sand or clouds or in the deep
Dark ocean where the submarines
Watch for their victims in the sea above.

I saw brave sorrow fill her tired eyes
With news of Rosie's death, as London wailed
Under a bomber's moon, and love's surprise
Was wasted in the blasts that rocked our room.

Oh war, add death to death to death
Till all men vanish from this earthly hell
Leave only children, let only children live
Because they love and keep each other well.

The middle stanza pleased him, but the last stanza seemed incomplete, so he wrote by pen:

Oh war, add death to death to death
For all who led us to this earthly hell
Leave us the children, and all who live
To love and keep each other well.

Four nights later, he was on watch on the open starboard bridge, looking at the tiny light from the Sambro Island lightship to the east, and west to the white haze of Halifax's lights above the dark shore, hoping there might be a letter from Cat waiting for him.

The air was cold and he began to think of new lines for the poem so he went into his sea-cabin and stared at the page, wondering what to do about "*Oh war, add death to death to death*," because he did not like to apostrophize great concepts. He was also worrying about using the word submarines instead of the usual term, U-boats, when he went deaf, was lifted from his seat in the cabin, his papers flung about, the typewriter suspended in midair before his eyes, reddened by light blooming through the burst hatch, then slammed down on his back. He thought he might be a soul migrating from his body on the deck, and then, from the peculiar light and sounds coming through the companionway, thought he must be injured.

He got to his knees, then to his feet and staggered towards the bridge where he saw AS Peavey lying on his back with legs disappearing under him. From far away he heard some screaming. Peavey's mouth was open. He was the one screaming.

Grant rang the siren for action stations, thinking how silly this was, and then, noticing that he still knew what silly was, tried to call the engine room. There was no response. He tried the ship's PA system to tell the Damage Control officer to report to the bridge, but nothing happened.

Grant picked up Peavey, hoping to stop the terrible noise which was growing louder and louder as his hearing returned.

He pulled Peavey to the companionway stairs, which were nearly vertical, and with one hand pulled him down to the open deck, where he laid him down beside the meat locker. Inside the cage, a frozen side of beef defrosting on a hook was turning round and round, dripping red blood in the strange light onto the stinking scraps on the floor of the locker. He ordered two ratings to uncover the lifeboats, then pulled another man whose shoulders were burning out of the twisted hatch on the quarter deck above the engine room. The engine room was afire, black figures were screaming below, with their hands in the air screaming, "Help, help."

He found a rope ladder by the firewall and lowered himself onto the companionway that ran round the upper level of the engine room. Two men walked towards him in a daze, blinded by smoke. He guided them to the ladder. The air was so hot he could not breathe. He followed them up the ladder, his hands blistering on the hot steel.

On the open deck, breathing cooler air, he was flung in the air again, through darkness into outer space where pinwheels of stars bloomed in the dark into vast green light. He slammed down onto the water, sank, holding his breath, then as he came to the surface, ripped open the cord of his life jacket. The jacket inflated and turned him right side up. He bobbed vertically. half-conscious in the water as the ship slid under the sea with bubbles of air bursting out of it.

Able Seaman Art Pipon, his face dark with oil, paddled over in a Carley float. He reached over the side and tried to pull him in, but he and Grant were both covered with oil. Pipon seized Grant by the neck and the crotch and dragged him over the side.

"Sorry," he said as he pulled Grant in, but he just lay there staring up. "Are you all right?" he asked, but Grant said nothing. His face was covered with oil, so Pipon did not recognize him at first.

Pipon looked around and there was no sign of the ship except debris. He found one oar and sat on the central seat paddling towards the sound of voices calling out from the sea around him, but he could not see anyone. When the swell lifted him high, he could see the lights of Halifax. He paddled towards the city. The sea broke open as a gigantic black shape poured upwards. The conning tower of a U-boat rose, canting backwards, then levelled out, and the whole shape hundreds of feet long rested on the surface, rivers of water pouring off its flanks with a roar. It obscured the whole lighted coastline of Nova Scotia, and it rose high in the air above him. On the conning tower was painted a white swordfish.

Steel clanged on steel, and a man's head in a cap appeared silhouetted against the light-haze in the sky. Pipon shouted, "Help." An airplane approached very low, its Leigh light illuminating the water for hundreds of yards ahead. The head disappeared from the conning tower, the hatch clanged, the U-boat crash dived with a roar of escaping air. The light passed over the Carley float and U-boat, and the plane disappeared.

There was no sound in the float except the rustle and drip of his clothing, and Grant's breathing. Pipon paddled towards the light.

Pipon saw lights and heard voices. He could not understand how the shore had come so close to him. He stuck his oar in the water again and pushed. He felt hands and arms picking him up, he saw a face nearby of a man standing on the water, and he tried to speak to tell them to help Grant; from far away he heard a growl, and wondered for a moment what it was. When he stopped trying to speak, the growling stopped. Now his voice would not work. "What next?" he growled.

Grant was in the clouds unable to speak. He tried to shout to the people in the sky around the cloud but they did not hear him. Exhausted by the effort, he lay back on the cloud and slept again.

He woke up in a white cage by a window, where there was blue sky with white clouds in it. A red rose stood beside his bed, and there was Cat sitting beside him, smiling.

"Cat, so glad to see you," he said, "thought I was dead, never see you again." He held out his hand to take her hand but she just sat there looking at him, and he closed his eyes again because he was so tired.

When he woke up again, the vase and rose were still there, and a nurse in a white uniform with curly brown hair was smiling at him. "Welcome back," she said. "Do you know your name?" He twisted his head around looking for Cat, but she was not there. He thought for a moment, then tried to talk, but the words sounded odd, so he stopped, then tried again, and could not do it, and fell asleep.

Some time later, the nurse came back and asked again, while tucking him in. She had to lower the sliding sidebars of the bed, which rose far above him. He had been restless so they had given him this caged bed built for head patients who rolled around in their torment, or stood up and fell out of bed. He was in the dangerous stage marked by the words, "There has been a personality change." The nurses were warned that the patient might grow violent at any moment.

Again she asked his name and he replied, but when the nurse repeated it she said, "Javelli? Was that it?" and he said, "No, no, damn stupid, Giovanelli," and she said "Javelli" again. Then he said, "I want to out." His hand went to his head, feeling the bandage.

"You had a severe concussion. You've been unconscious."

"I am . . ." he paused, searching for the next word, ". . . hossiple?"

"Yes." She smiled. "You're in a hospital."

"Was Cat was here?"

"There's no cat here that I've seen."

He shouted, "Cat. Cat."

"Oh, I don't think so. She's in England, isn't she?" Now she understood, for she had been listening to him talking in his semi-conscious state, often about someone named Cat in England.

"She was a dream. Ship some off?"

"I'm sorry?"

He said, "Ship off? Ship," and his pleading anxious look more than his words told her what he wanted to know.

"There were two survivors. You are going to get a medal."

The nurse left the ward very disturbed. The doctors, who had been ready to release him to a convalescent hospital, now decided to keep him for further observation, although they had little idea what to do except to feed him. In 20 hours in the raft, they estimated he had lost 18 pounds, of 174. So they gave him the best food they could, but he was not hungry and they had to send in a nurse to persuade him to eat.

He could not walk without help, his sight was blurred and his speech incoherent. His hands had been burned, his left thumb was broken, they said. It was wrapped in a tight bandage, and it throbbed.

He awoke from an easy dream of swimming off Sunset Island towards a big white swan, that landed on the water and turned into a sailing ship cruising towards him, to see, standing at the foot of his cage, a young man with a snub-nose and small blue eyes watching him.

"I'm Pipon, sir," said the young man. "Art Pipon. Remember me?"

Grant looked at him. "Were you in ship?"

"The same, sir. You was the captain."

"I remember."

"I heard they all went down."

"I heard. Pipon. You and me."

"They hit us twice. After the first one, I saw youse running around the engine room lifting guys out. One was on fire."

"On fire?"

"His boots, full of oil. But he must have died anyways."

Grant held up his bandaged hand. "Must be I got this," he said. "But how shore?"

"I was in one of them Carling floats, I saw this head in the water in his life jacket, so I hauled him in, and I saw it was you, sir."

"Is that right? Thank Pipon. You saved."

"Yes sir. When I told them what you done on board ship, they said you're going to get a gong."

"Who said?"

"One of the officers at Cornwallis, sir. I think he was a captain."

"No one said me."

"Well, you done it, I only, like, told on you." His face opened a little towards a smile, as if asking Grant's permission to smile, and Grant said, "I'm, thank you, thank you for for . . . . life."

"Anyway, sir, here's my address, just in case."

"Thank you. My address . . ." he paused, trying to remember. "Sorry, can't remember something, oh yes, here is, 40 Moore Park Heights Drive, Toronto. I've been trying, and Hyland 9298, phone number."

"We don't have a phone yet, sir."

"Thanks for memory come back, yes, thanks."

Pipon hesitated at the door. "There was one more thing, sir, just to satisfy my curiosity?" He waited for permission to continue, so Grant said, "Yes?"

"You was always writing something, sir, I saw you in the wardroom some times, before you were made captain, you even had a typewriter. Very neat little piece of work it was, too."

"Oh, yes."

"I always wondered, what was a man writing about, what was there to tell?"

Grant smiled. "Good question. I was a beer . . . something about beer."

"Well, beer is always a good subject, sir."

The forests and white-fenced clapboard towns of Nova Scotia rotated past the train windows, then the river wide as the sea poured by; once, for a few minutes, he saw the backs of white whales spilling green water as they cruised under the speeding window, then they crossed the great bridge to grey Québec, clotted round the Citadel and the green-peaked hotel.

Up the river again, a shunt and bustle in Montreal, and then a long sleeper to Toronto. He awoke, seeing mist from Lake Ontario rising into sunlight that slanted down into dark green cedars beside yellow birch leaves and arbours of red maple, dark brown oak. Flashing by went horses with sun sweating their backs in black fields being planted with winter wheat, drawing wagons loaded with red fruit through the laddered orchards. Little square automobiles, dusted grey, waited beyond the black and white wooden barriers at the crossings; the guard, in his trembling high-legged house by the tracks, waving as they pounded by, whistle roaring.

At Union Station his father Ferdie was standing with a grim expression as the male nurse rolled Grant into the main concourse in a wheelchair. His mother, wearing a mink coat and veiled hat, smiled and leaned down and kissed him with a swirl of Chanel Number 5.

He looked up and shook his father's hand, feeling apologetic for not getting up. Keightley, loaned by Cameron Bannatyne to help on this difficult day, greeted him, shook his hand, then took charge of his small seabag. His father, dressed in homburg and his customary business uniform of midnight blue suit with black pinstripe, rolled the chair.

"How's the noggin?" his father said from behind him. He was trying to be calm but he was pained by the sight of this young man, once so alive, romping through life, coming home pale, head shaved, skinny and bandaged, in a chair.

"All right . . . balance funny, can't see straight yet, but, okay, okay, okay. Getting better, somewhat. Joe here?" He spoke the minimum because he was tired all the time.

"I haven't heard from him."

"Letter?"

"You have piles of mail. But first, let's get you settled."

Keightley and his father helped him into the back seat of the McLaren, then folded up the wheelchair and put it in the trunk.

He was puzzled when Keightley turned the car west along Front Street, not east towards Rosedale.

"Where we going?" he asked.

"Christie Street Hospital."

"Hossiple, what for? Fine now. Don't want hossiple," he shouted, "no hossiple."

His mother put a scented glove on his shoulder. "Dear there's nothing to worry about, it's just for a few tests."

"Had tests, don't want tests, can't do anything, always tired, man gets tired after all, ever so tired. I want home."

"Just a few routine tests, and then you'll be home, safe and sound."

In Christie Street Hospital, Dr. Abe Stern asked him many questions about his childhood, showed him Rohrschach blots, put incomprehensible question-and-answer tests in front of him.

"Why do you eat with your fingers?" said Dr Stern.

Grant shuddered. He had refused to touch the hospital's steel cutlery because the metal made him feel blazing hot steel deck, hands burning on railing, screams on the exploding steel ship. He tried to say, "If you were anything but a pretentious nincompoop, you could guess the answer," but all he could get out was "compoo, compoo," which made him giggle. So the doctor wrote that cutlery amused him.

After three days of this, he said he wanted to be sent home. Dr. Stern said, "We are not ready yet."

"Who are we?"

From his window he could see down to Christie Street. Now and then a wooden-sided streetcar bumbled by with its tall thin glass windows steamed up like a greenhouse, steel wheels and clanging bell like big news coming. Children, old men and women walked the streets. One day he was visited by two men, one a captain and the other a rear-admiral with sleeves covered with wavy stripes in gold, who said, "You have been awarded the Distinguished Service Order. There will be a ceremony at HMCS *York* next week. Will you be well enough to attend, do you think?"

Grant said he did not know what the medal was for, and they described to him the story that Pipon had told him in Halifax.

"Pipon deserves it, not me," he said. "I can't remember any of that."

"In any case," said the captain, "here is the official letter making the announcement, which will be in the paper tomorrow. Bring this along with you to the ceremony if you feel well enough. Otherwise, we can do it here." He got up and said, "Right you are, me boy, well done. You're a hero." He stepped back one pace, they both saluted, turned on their heels and left.

When his mother came in, she picked up the letter and said, "We're so proud of you, my darling boy." She leaned over and kissed him, the fringe of blue veil on her hat tickling his nose, and the usual Chanel.

"If it helps me get out of here," he said, and wriggled down into the sheets, pulling them up over his head, grinning and feeling pleased and foolish. "Don't remember what happened. Say, give it to a ghost."

"Don't say that, dearest. Your father will be so proud."

He kept asking for Cat, and no one could promise she was coming. He asked every day to go home but they told him he was not ready. He asked for a prognosis, but the doctors were vague. He asked if the injury was permanent, but they said he would have to wait and see, that many did recover. They said, "The human brain is remarkably adaptable."

His peripheral vision was reduced and his sense of balance awry, so he staggered walking. He had to look down to see the floor which made him appear more crippled than he was. He was weak. He asked Nurse Whiteford to help him walk for exercise, and he strengthened his legs and arms using weights in the bed. The ringing in his ears and head, the constant headaches, the inability to sleep, were all diminishing. His sense of taste was returning and, with it, his appetite. But there was a gauze curtain before him blurring his field of vision. Along the bottom of his vision there was a cancelled portion of things that ought to be visible and were not, so he had to dip his head forward to see them, making it hard to walk. The gauze also hung within his mind blanking words from his speech, so that after he had spoken a sentence, people had to ask him to repeat himself or explain.

He had decided that since his body was improving with exercise he would try to exercise his mind by writing every day in his diary. He hunched forward over the paper, while he forced his clenched scarred hand over it. He smiled, thinking he was like a kid in Miss Lundy's kindergarten, working with his first crayons. His hand trembled so much the pen blotted the paper. He switched to a pencil. His mind was scattered and his handwriting obscured by his weak and trembling hand. It was such a jumbled mess that he could not read half of it after it was written.

He trained himself to simplify the writing. He set down thoughts, and reread them the following day. Most of his vocabulary returned except for the moments when he could not remember individual words, which might come to mind hours later. He could articulate a little better every week, though he could not make word-plays, jokes, observations and rhymes.

He knew that on the ship he had been writing something, because he had a sense of loss—writing was gone that had been important to him, but he couldn't remember any of the details, except beer. Whenever he tried to remember his earlier ideas, he encountered only blankness.

He borrowed a portable typewriter, but the words would not come. At the end of an hour he would reread the typing—"Grant Bannatyne Giovanelli, Victoria Treloar, 40 Moore Park Heights Drive, Toronto," and then one day, "HMCS *Shenda* was sunk one night off Halifax, those are the facts and the facts and the facts." Then he remembered a seaman in Halifax urging him to write something about beer because "beer is always good, sir." But that was all.

London, October, 1944

Cat came to her father's office in the Strand to lunch with him. He asked her, "Why are you dressed like that?" and she laughed.

"Daddy, it's my Guy's uniform. Don't you remember, your club doesn't permit women at noon unless they are in uniform? This is my uniform when I am nursing."

"The sight of you must be enough to make them want to get better soon. Come along then," and taking his Burberry down from the stand in his crowded office, he went out the door, saying goodbye to kind, white-haired Jessup, his secretary. They had gone down the stairs and were at the main entrance when Jessup came running after them.

"Oh, Dudley, this just came in for you. It's secret and urgent." She handed him a cable form on which words cut out from the incoming telex tape had been pasted. He fumbled for his spectacles, and Cat offered to read it for him. He said, "Mustn't do that. Who knows, these secret cables are sometimes important." He found the spectacles, but could not see well enough in the dim light of the hallway. He stepped out onto the stone verandah outside the building where he read, "REGRET INFORM YOU GRANT SUNK PD SEVERE HEAD INJURIES IN HOSPITAL PD MORE AS AVAILABLE ENDS CAMERON"

Cat, seeing his face grow grave, said, "What is it?"

He handed her the paper.

"Oh my God. Is this the date?" She pointed to numbers at the top right.

Dudley said, "It was sent yesterday at 4 pm our time. It's about 20 hours old."

"What time is it in Canada?"

"Seven hours back."

"Can we telephone?"

"I don't see why not."

"Now? Please, Papa."

"Well, yes of course. I'll ask Jessup to put it through right away."

They went back into his office, and while they waited for the call to be put through, Jessup cancelled their luncheon, and without telling them how she got the food, sacrificed her own lunch—a salmon sandwich, a piece of cheddar cheese and an apple, all originally given her by Dudley, who received food parcels regularly from Bannatyne.

As they sat waiting for the call and eating the sandwich, her father held her hand and they talked about his forthcoming trip to Ottawa and Washington, to organize the flow of new aircraft via Newfoundland, Iceland and the Faeroes.

"Seats to Canada are at an absolute premium," Dudley remarked. "Hallo." He sat up as the phone rang beside him. Normally, Jessup put her head in the door to announce a call, as she would a visitor, but this time, knowing its importance, she had rung straight through.

"Hello, Cameron, can you hear me?" said Dudley. "Yes, very good. Got your cable about young Grant. Wondered how he is?"

He nodded into the receiver, saying, "Yes, I see, I see." and then he said in surprise, "He is? I see. Well perhaps I'd better put her on. She's right here, just a moment, don't ring off."

He handed her the heavy black bakelite receiver. "He's asking for you."

"Hello Mr. Bannatyne, Victoria here," she said, and heard his voice wavering back over the line, "I'm glad you called, Grant's in hospital here, been asking for you."

"Could I talk to him?"

"Oh no, he doesn't articulate very well just yet, if you see what I mean."

"Does he know you?"

"Oh yes, every day there is a slight improvement."

"What do the doctors say?"

"Well, they're somewhat baffled by this type of injury. What they say is we must wait and he must have rest and be peaceful."

"And you say he has been asking for me?"

"Yes, over and over, he says, 'I must see Cat, is she here yet?' He thinks you're coming to see him."

At this her voice started to choke, but she forced out the words over the blockage in a shout, "Well, tell him I am coming."

"Oh well now, can you do that?"

"I can do it, I know I can, my father will help me. After all it's a matter of life . . ." she was about to say "and death," but, not wishing to be melodramatic, amended this to "very important. That's what he wants."

"Well, it's what he has been saying for many days now."

"And when did this happen?"

"Ten days ago, off Halifax. Ship was sunk. He tried to save some crew members. He's getting a medal."

"I'll give you back to Papa now." She handed the receiver to her father and turned away to wipe the tears from her cheeks. She put the telegram in the side pocket of her uniform, with the scissors and aspirin.

Her father was trying to get through to Lord Beaverbrook when she left his office with a little wave of her hand to him, said thank you to Jessup and was on her way back to Guy's. She told her section chief what had happened and asked for compassionate leave. Then she called her father and asked him not to say anything about Grant to Flavia because she knew her mother would immediately try to stop her.

That night in her room, she reread Grant's letters and his poems, and saw the poem entitled "War Song" that Beaverbrook had published in *The Telegraph*, took it out and tucked it into her purse.

She had seen head patients at Guy's and knew that the doctors could do almost nothing for them. So she tried to think of what kind of future she might have with Grant. Did the man she loved still inhabit that damaged body? How much of him was left? If she went to him, would she be just committing herself to a life of nursing him? Would they be able to have children? She unburdened herself to Lady Diana Cooper, who said, "You must go and find out. There was more than enough of him to begin with."

Two days later, Max called to say that he could get a seat for her that night on a York going to Reykjavik, Gander and Montreal, did she want it? Cat said yes, and went home in the middle of the afternoon to pack. She was standing in her slip, packing, when she heard her mother coming up the stairs.

"What are you doing?" Flavia said. "Why aren't you dressed? I thought you were at Guy's."

Cat went on packing. "I have to go away for a few days. Nothing serious."

"What about Guy's?"

"It's a training course they're sending me on."

Flavia was suspicious. Since she had deceived Dudley about France, she had fallen prey to one of the war's minor diseases, mistrust between friends who had to keep secrets from each other. But Victoria was too unimportant to know any military secrets.

She was turning to leave the room, when she saw on the floor the cable which had fallen from Cat's dressing table. She bent over and picked it up. Cat thought, 'Here it comes. I will be calm, I will be calm, I will be calm.'

"What is this?" Flavia demanded.

"I believe it's a cable. Addressed to Papa if you'll notice."

"Don't come the proper little angel with me," said her mother. She had taken in the cable and guessed Cat's plan. "Where do you think you are going? What's this about? You're not leaving." She was asking questions without waiting for answers because she had already guessed the truth and wanted to batter it to death before it could emerge from Cat.

Cat went on packing with her lips closed. For five years, more or less, she had been at odds with her mother. She felt desperate. Nothing was good enough for Flavia's driving ambition. Frustrated in her own designs, Flavia had sublimated them by managing Dudley, with his distant toleration. He had come to believe that he would never make enough of his own potential without Flavia driving him, and pushing others out of his way so that he might succeed. But this system did not work with Cat, who had her mother's energy and youth besides.

"Answer me," said Flavia. "Have you been corresponding with him?"

Cat said nothing.

"How did you get the letters?"

Cat remained silent to protect Lady Cooper.

"You admit you have been deceiving me."

Cat was silent.

"Oh my God, how ungrateful. How could you do such a thing? It's unimaginable. All I have done was for your good."

Cat went on packing but she could feel the anger and the tears rising.

"You're going to Canada. Are you going to Canada? You won't. I forbid it, do you hear? I forbid it."

The more she repeated herself, the more Cat stared at the cable being profaned in her mother's hand. She snatched it away.

"How dare you," said Flavia. She swung at her daughter's face, but Cat held up her arm and Flavia's hand landed on her forearm. "How dare you strike me," Flavia shouted. Cat repeated to herself, 'Keep calm keep calm.'

Flavia panting, her eyes bulging, staring at Cat, looking away then looking back at her again with a desperate look, could not speak.

Cat said, "The man is injured, he is asking for me."

"He is nothing. You're flinging yourself away for nothing."

"If you try to prevent me going, I shall go anyway. But you won't be my mother any more." She was on the edge of laughter because this was so absurd, and she expected Flavia to treat this with contempt.

"You don't know your own heart. You don't know your own mind. You are too young. You mustn't waste yourself on this boy."

"Don't say boy." She knew it was code for 'wild colonial boy,' which to Flavia meant 'unsuitable.' To her, 'suitable' meant a rich young English Jew, with political ambitions, which she and Dudley could gratify.

Cat, seeing her chance while her mother was silenced, said, "The young are fighting this war, the young ones. We are not too young for that. Oh no. Now he is wounded, asking for me." She burst into tears. "And now you want to keep me from him. Mother, how can you be so cruel?"

Flavia was walking around the room, her fists pouncing up and down like a child in rage. She did not understand a word Cat said.

Cat went on, "I have spent a year nursing injured men, I have bent over them and breathed their horrible last breath, no one ever said I was too young for THAT . . ." and she shouted the last word at her horrified mother.

"Don't shout at me," she shouted. "Think what you are doing, Cat. Think. You've been accepted at Girton, you can do anything you like after the war, anything, marry some brilliant young man."

"Those are not my plans," Cat said.

Flavia went on, "He's a colonial, a Canadian, nothing. He has no future outside his country, he can never amount to anything here where it counts. The empire was not built by such people: they are the dross of empire, the ones who could not get ahead here. You have such a bright future here, at the centre of this glorious empire which your father and I have done so much to protect, which this war is to preserve. You can not throw it away for a romantic infatuation."

"He is a poet, he is a soldier, he is good enough to die for us, he is good enough to love. Let the empire crumble, I want none of your hateful snobbery."

"This is blasphemy, this is treason, do you know what you are saying? Everything your father and I have devoted our lives to, oh oh oh, this is too much." She sat down wringing her hands, in tears.

Cat stared at her amazed that she was so deluded. Flavia did not care at all about the British Empire. To her the empire was a worldwide servants' hall catering to her whims in London.

"I forbid you," Flavia raised her voice again. "If you go, it will be your funeral. You will be dead. You will never see this family again."

Cat kept her eyes on the case, averted from her mother, trying not to be angry. Her hands kept repeating the same motions, lifting and setting back down the same blue cardigan.

"How can you repeat your family's mistake?" Saying these words, she knew she was breaking forever with her mother, for the rupture with Max and Cecile was taboo in this house.

Flavia stared at her seeing the final break coming and unable to stop it.

"They hated Daddy without knowing him, out of pure blind prejudice, and see where it got them, and all those years of misery for you and Daddy, and now you do it yourself."

Flavia was gasping for air. She sat down on the bed, her mouth opening and closing, thinking, 'Stop this, I must stop this, the end of everything.' Her ears were roaring, her sight was darkened. She heard bits of what Cat was saying, and she saw her daughter as someone grotesque, far away, speaking words she refused to hear, which she scrambled in her head.

Cat said, "I will not let you destroy my life as they destroyed yours." Flavia, fearing the worst, heard the worst, "as they destroyed yours," knowing her parents were upstairs hearing every word.

Flavia wailed, "You are destroying my life," and began to weep. Cat looked at her, amazed that her mother could be such a hypocrite, and said, "Get over it, Mother, you've used this on me once too often, and I will not be moved again." She walked out of the room.

Max and Cecile, coming down from their rooms on the fourth floor to find out why they were shouting, stopped on the landing above. As Cat started to leave, she saw them looking down and she stopped and said up to them in a trembling voice, "You see?" Cecile Frankfurter wailed and Max looked grim. He started down after her thinking he must do something.

She walked down trembling, hearing her grandfather following her. She thought, 'Father, don't let me down now, don't side with her this time,' and ran along the front hall with her half-packed bag in her hand toward the door, where she hoped her father was waiting with the car.

Flavia leaned against the banister, feeling sick and lost, seeing darkness and vague shapes against the brightness of the front door opening.

Cat looked back, seeing her mother halfway down the stair as the door opened and Caitlin announced Lord Beaverbrook. Cat went towards the door, refusing to say goodbye until she was well out of her mother's reach. The power which had told her before, 'Stay calm, stay calm,' now told her, 'Say goodbye,' so she turned as she reached the doorway and said, "Goodbye, Mother, I'll write soon."

Flavia ran along the hall calling, "Max, Max, stop her." At that, Max Frankfurter walked up to Cat, not sure what to do. Max Beaverbrook stepped forward to intercept Frankfurter, who pushed him away and pulled at Cat's shoulder. His expression was anguish, his hand tightened on her shoulder. Cat, seeing the anguish, feeling the hand, thought he was about to strike her so she twisted away, tripped and fell out the door. Frankfurter reached down towards her, but Beaverbrook stayed his arm, and Cat screamed up at her grandfather, "Don't touch me." Beaverbrook helped her to her feet and she ran down the steps. Frankfurter turned round to Flavia and said with a helpless look, "She's going."

Beaverbrook got her into the Rolls and slammed the door. Flavia ran out and pounded on the door, trying to wrench it open. "No Max, stop," but Beaverbrook told the chauffeur to go ahead and the Rolls drew away.

Flavia sank to her knees on the pavement with her hands over her face. Cecile leaned down beside her in tears and helped her up. Flavia saw, in the darkness of her hands, flashes of light like a thunderstorm. She felt her mother embrace her and say, "Quiet, *liebchen,* I'm here." She trembled and let her mother hug her.

Cat did not look back. She thought, 'If Goma says anything sympathetic, I'll break down.' She sat up tense, trembling, controlled, thinking, 'I'm doing the right thing at last.' Max took her hand and held it in silence until they were past Fulham.

The first time she had been aware of her godfather's looks, she had thought he was ugly. He was squat with too broad a mouth, but now, as his kind enthusiastic spirit smiled in his face, she thought he was beautiful.

"Thank you," she said. "I've never had such a row."

"Your father has Cabinet this afternoon, so I volunteered to come."

"But then you must have Cabinet too?"

"Yes, but I am only Lord Privy Seal now, you know, one that will do, to start a progress, swell a scene or two. And there are very many swells in the Cabinet already. No, I am here not just because you are, my dear Cat"—he squeezed her hand in his warm hand—"but I owe that young man something. I never knew what this war meant, till I read that poem."

"Bomber's Moon?"

"That's the one. He also showed me my own life as I had never seen it before. Despite all my efforts to order my life, and the lives about me, well, I see we all live in mystery; we are always being surprised by life, and he lifted the veil for me, which alas, has dropped again. But for a moment I saw something rare and strange and terrible. My own heart I suppose."

"But Goma, you've mastered life to suit yourself."

"And how would you know what suits me or does not suit me? I don't know myself. When I supported Lloyd George in 1916, I said I did not wish to become Prime Minister myself. Now I am not sure. In 1941, was I awaiting a call from the people, eh? Was I?" Cat was astonished, wondering what was prompting this outburst. As the houses and then the fields rolled by the car window, time was short and she had never talked intimately with him before. Now she wanted to hear all his thoughts before the car got to the airport. "I don't know what I wanted when I was your age. I wanted something, then I committed myself to getting it, and I got it and then I could not remember why I wanted it. I could not even remember wanting it, so I was not sure I had gotten what I wanted." He laughed. "I lived from moment to moment. I wanted to make money, yes I was certain I wanted that, like everyone else around me. Then when I got it, I found I did not want money but the things I thought money could do for me, and the most important of them I found money could not give me, after all. So, you see?"

"Go on."

Beaverbrook sighed, "Friendship. That was it. Not money at all. I give away far more than I spend on myself. What I want to do with money is help my friends, have good times and fun and laughter, build a few things, do some good works. It's very strange to me. It's what my father always preached in his dry old church."

Cat felt disappointed until he said, "What is best in us—love, hope, beauty, honour, courage and humour—can not be commanded. They can only be encouraged. They are already in us, all we have to do is weed the garden."

At the airport he took her to the VIP section, where generals, admirals and air marshals in uniform and moustached men in dark blue suits, ties and waistcoats, wearing homburgs and carrying briefcases, sat in easy chairs smoking and drinking. She was the only person in the room in a dress.

Max said, putting an envelope in her hand, "I was going to save this wee gifty till your 21st, but now seems appropriate."

"But Goma, I'm long past 21."

"Then I owe you some interest."

He embraced her, kissed her cheeks and said, "Don't worry about her, she'll calm down, and if she doesn't, by Jove, I'll make her see reason."

She forgot about the envelope until she was over Iceland circling to land, and she thought she might need the sick bag. She drew out her handkerchief and the envelope fell in her lap. She looked inside. There was a cheque for her on the Bank of Nova Scotia in Fredericton, New Brunswick, for $50,000. The annual bank interest alone would buy a house.

Cat arrived in Montreal, after a long flight from Gander, very tired. She went straight to the hotel Max had arranged, the Ritz, where she put through a call to Mrs. Giovanelli in Toronto. Ferdinand was out west, supervising the renovation of British Commonwealth Air Training bases for pilots, and Eleanor was laid up with a bad ankle, which she had twisted playing golf. But she said that Keightley would meet the plane tomorrow at Malton, the Toronto airport, and bring her to Moore Park Heights Drive.

The next day, Cat walked from the silvery Lockheed Electra to the shed with the wooden letters over the door that said MALTON TORONTO AIRPORT, and saw Keightley awaiting her beyond the arrival barrier. Her luggage was carried in by a black porter with a red cap, whom Keightley tipped.

He said, "Good morning, Miss Victoria, I hope your flight was pleasant."

On the way through the fields round Malton, still shining gold with the autumn stubble, she asked if they might go straight to the hospital, as Mrs. Giovanelli could not join them in any case. He took her there and waited outside as she went up the broad cement steps of the big old building on Christie Street, among factories and small houses.

She was escorted to his floor, and Nurse Whiteford, a kind, grey-haired woman with a Scots accent, took her along the polished linoleum corridor to a door from which an orderly was backing out with a lunch tray.

She went in with her eyes blinded by the brilliance of the light shining through the window right at her, so for a moment she did not see that Grant's head was bandaged and he was lying in a cage. He sat up in amazement and said, "Cat, you're here, nobody tells me things, oh so good to see you." He held out an arm through the bars.

She went towards him but was stopped by the fenced side of the bed. Nurse Whiteford said, "Just in case, sometimes he moves around a lot, you know, head patients." She dropped the side and Cat bent over the bed, appalled by what she was seeing. A thin wasted man, an elemental Grant, substituted for the handsome strong man she had seen rise from the breakfast table at Cherkley and say to her, "Good morning. What brings you here?"

"Here's how we do it, dearie," said Whiteford, as she helped Grant swing his skinny legs over the side of the bed where they dangled. "One two three," said Whiteford, and he leaned forward into her as she thrust her arms under his armpits and lifted him up to stand barefoot and quivering in her arms on the cold floor. 'This isn't Grant any more,' Cat thought. 'I've cast my life away for a shadow. No, I don't want you, bring back Grant.'

"Smooth, eh?" he said with a grin, and held out one arm towards her. She stepped forward, and with Nurse Whiteford's help she took him in her arms. But instead of embracing him, she was struggling to keep him up. She placed one foot backwards to brace herself, and hugged him lest she drop him.

"Don't be scared," he said, "I was way worse than this in Halifax. Out for days. Blind for a while. Babbling day and night. I wish I had a record of it, maybe some good lines?" He grinned sideways at her, because he did not dare lean back. His breath smelled of toothpaste. "I'm coming back, you know. Pretty soon I'll be asking you that same old question again."

'What question,' she thought. 'Will you marry me?' She closed her eyes in pain, and then stared in shock when he said, "Who are you?" and the moment at Sunset Island in the summer of '39 came back like a punch. He was showing her he remembered everything important, and in a moment her whole attitude changed. She was still seeing and holding what she loved most in him, and in life. He was emerging unscathed, but changed, like a person undressed to the bare skin. 'I'm the woman standing here,' she thought.

"You never answered," he said.

"Here's my answer," she whispered, and kissed him.

They sat him up again in bed with the cage open while she held his hand and gave him all her news, omitting the fight with Flavia, even after he had inquired. Then he began to doze off, with her hand in his, so Cat waited for a few minutes to make sure he had gone, then went down to the nursing station to find Whiteford.

Whiteford was coming along the hall, starched whiteness down to her shoes, a smile on her face that said, 'I'm busy and how are you?'

"It is wonderful that you came. He asks for you constantly."

"He seems so feeble."

"He is much better than he was, making progress, more and more, all the time." Cat looked sad, thinking how terrible the injuries must have been. "He lost a lot of weight in the sea, then he was in a coma for days. We had to give him Pablum by hand because we were afraid he would choke. The reports from Halifax said he talked all the time in the coma, poor lamb, and never uttered a foul word once, and asked for you every day. I'm quite sure that now you're here, it will make a wonderful difference."

Cat was silent, feeling the responsibility rise round her.

"You must look to your interests, young lady, if you don't mind my saying so, the nurses are all quite enamoured of him. They positively vie to take care of him. I dare say a few hearts were broken when you walked in the door." Cat made a bleak smile when Whiteford stressed the word 'vie.' She pictured the nurses elbowing each other aside for the honour of the bedpan.

Cat was gone when he awoke, but she had left a note saying she would return that afternoon with his mother. He sat up and began to work on his diary again, to prove to her how well he was doing. He wrote in an unsteady cursive hand, *Cat came today. No warning. Shaky, when she got here. I fear to be seen as I fear that I seem. What a great person, but she seems dismayed by how I look. Must help her get over it.*

For weeks he had imagined her arrival, and feared her dismay, so he had had a strong motive to get better, or at least to appear better. And now she had been sprung on him before he was ready. He was disappointed that she was disappointed. He was afraid she would be so discouraged she might pack up and go home. Then he thought, 'She'll get over this. After all, I did.'

When Cat returned with Mrs. Giovanelli, hobbling on a cane, he tried to reassure her by bringing out the diary entry to show her how well he was doing, and he was struck by the compressed complexity of the third sentence. He read it out—"'I fear to be seen as I fear that I seem,'" and said, "You see how I am getting better, when I can write tricky crap like that?"

He laughed and she was happy, seeing delight return to his face. Mrs. Giovanelli nodded at her, pleased that Victoria was here, bringing joy. This gave her twinges of jealousy: ever since her first visit to his bedside, when he had seemed so averse to her, she had tried to get through to him, to recreate the camaraderie of his youth in summertime at Stone Cottage when the family had gone fishing together, or in winter in the city, when she had baked Christmas cakes together with all the boys. But he had grown away from her, did not share her romantic love of the Empire, disdained her help, grew impatient whenever she tried to remind him of the good times they had once had, and suggested they do again some of the things that had once given them both joy. Now, watching the eager delight in his face, the way his eyes dwelled on Cat, she knew he was gone and would never return to her.

She was getting up to leave the room, feeling unwanted, when he stretched his neck so he could see where she had been and said, "And how are you, Mum?"

She sat down, and smiled at Cat and thought, 'The dear boy,' and all her sadness was gone, and she was restored to the glad feelings that a moment before she had thought were gone forever.

Cat remained with the Giovanellis through Christmas, and visited Grant every day. She applied for admission in the university medical school and was accepted, pending the arrival of her school leaving papers from Roedean. She was admitted to membership in the Tennis and Racquet Club, where she began to meet people of her own age, and saw Grant's name on the prize-winner's board for Junior Badminton in 1935. She walked round his old schools—Whitney Primary School and Upper Canada College—and browsed through his books—Ovid, Joyce, Hemingway, Callaghan, Eliot, Pound, Lampman, Keats. From her mother she heard not a word, but letters from her father gave her the family news.

Flavia's parents never referred to Victoria, Dudley told her in a letter:

> *It seems as if they must relive the days of our own difficulty in 1920 and therefore say nothing. If your name comes up, for instance after I receive your letter, I tell your mother your news, and she listens, without comment. I think, 'least said, soonest mended,' and let it go at that. In any event, I hope you are well, and that your shining presence brings our warrior back to full life. I do approve of your plan to study medicine, but of course if you do that over there, we shall miss you terribly—I do think your mother does miss you and will respond to any gesture of reconciliation. So if you do write a letter, just give her the news pleasantly as if nothing had happened, and I am sure she will read it. Though I can not guarantee that she will answer it right away.*
>
> *Goma sends his best, as I do. Tell me if you need anything. I shall make good all your needs to Ferdie of course. My love to Eleanor and Ferdie. Much love, Papa.*

Tears came to her eyes as she read all this ordinary sweetness, so typical of him, and so precious.

After a brief lonely time at the Giovanellis, she began to feel at home, and also that she was in limbo. She was not engaged to Grant, in fact, neither of them had mentioned the scene in the dining room at Cherkley. She was a sort of friend-nurse, and, unknown to the Giovanellis, she knew she could not go home to Cadogan Square.

The war had eradicated all her desire to study literature and write travel books. The notion seemed trivial now, so she determined on medicine. She had enjoyed much of her time at Guy's, although the work was hard. But as she travelled day by day on the streetcar to Grant, reading to him in bed, writing letters for him, she settled into a routine that suited both her and him. After Christmas, she began to wonder when this time like a trance would be broken by some inconvenient reality, such as Mrs. Giovanelli sitting down with her one day to say, "Now my dear, we have enjoyed having you, and it has been wonderful for Grant I'm sure, but it is time to think about your position. Grant will be coming home soon, and there will be all kinds of therapy, and well, we are wondering what your plans are . . ." Here, Cat's apprehensions trailed off, because she was shocked to think of how much she had given up for Grant, to become a war guest in his house.

Schwandau, November-December, 1944

The world Peter von Metternich had been trained to live in was gone. The expression of his broad face, a mask-like calm towards strangers, alert and pleasant with friends such as Clara, was now very often frozen, as if his personality had withdrawn and even his friends were becoming strangers. He felt lost. It seemed to him there was nothing left for him to do. He grew thin, giving his little food to Helmuth, who at first would not eat it because it was Peter's. But Peter left it on his plate, so Helmuth accepted it, and smacked his lips and patted his stomach and rolled his eyes to make Peter hungry. This gave Peter the first smile he had had since coming to Schwandau months before. He began to eat again. He thought, 'Klaus is gone, but I am here,' and devoted his time to Helmuth. He taught him chess, mathematics, and helped him to carve little birds from basswood.

Clara felt she had a soul-mate in the boy. Since Frau Vogelstein had now admitted her to the kitchen, Clara had access to the shared food supplies so she took food from her own ration to supplement Helmuth's meagre diet. She told herself, 'This is a good investment—it keeps him healthy,' never considering that she herself had lost many kilos. From a healthy 56, which she had weighed when she arrived in Germany in 1938, she had slipped in Berlin to 47 kilos and was now even thinner.

In January, they were informed by Herr Vogelstein, who had seen a copy of the Frankfurt paper, that Klaus' younger sister Caroline, his father and his mother had all been killed in a raid on Frankfurt the previous week. For three days, Tati said nothing and ate nothing. She lay silent in bed, staring up at the ceiling, and only responded a little to Helmuth when he offered her soup or water.

When Clara tried to cheer her up, she responded, "It's no use, you know, life favours the evil and punishes the good." She had been lying in bed that grey mild afternoon wearing Klaus' grey sweater.

"Well, spring is in the air today."

"Life is hell."

"There's no such thing as 'Life.' You're alive, that's all. You decide what you do, that's all. You get the consequences, there is nothing else. There is no one deciding but you. And God, of course," she added as an afterthought.

In this time, when Clara was trying to get documentation so they could leave Schwandau, they heard on the radio that all personal travel was banned. Once more Tati despaired. "Now we're stuck here, no matter what." She forgot that for months now they had been unable to leave because they did not have the new papers from Gisevius.

Peter had followed Gisevius' advice, given at Berlin in June, to write to Allen Dulles at the American Embassy in Berne. Gisevius had already arranged the code sentence so Dulles would know the letter was genuine, "The sun is high in the west." Peter could not write direct to Dulles in Switzerland so he had written via Father Gerstl in Schenkenberg. Years before, Gerstl had christened a boy who was now one of the border guards near Rafz, so he was able to cross as he needed.

But Christmas passed, and New Year's, and there was no answer. As the news of the arrests, trials and executions of their friends came in over radio and newspaper, Peter decided that they would have to move soon. He said, "My pessimism is worse every day, but you don't even notice how bad things are."

Clara thought of everything she and little Helmuth had done since they had arrived here, with no help from Tati and little from Peter. She said, "Damn your pessimism. If you want to feel better, get up and get out and start doing things. You used to walk miles, now you never stir. Why don't you go and help Frau Vogelstein split wood?"

Peter said, "Well, after that little display of temper, I think . . ." he trailed off. "I think I'll chop some wood." He stood before the pile, thinking, 'Be careful, your balance is off and you haven't done this for years.' He was outside for an hour splitting wood, which flew apart because it was frozen. The insides of the logs shone pale brown, scenting the air with resin. 'That was good, no blood on the ground.'

He carried a big armload into the kitchen where Clara was helping Helmuth to sew on buttons. Feeling warmed and satisfied, Peter said, "You still want to get away to Schenkenberg?"He leaned over the oak dining table challenging her, his light brown hair shining in the glow from the window, a bleak little smile on his face.

"Yes, of course."

He went out into the street. Snow had fallen the night before, the streets were shining with the meltwater running over the cobbles. He greeted the grey-haired postman with a scoffing grunt, as if the lack of mail was the mailman's fault, but the deaf old man did not hear him, and smiled back. 'What's he got to be so cheerful about,' he wondered. He turned into the mayor's office, where Herr Vogelstein was leaning towards the fireplace, warming his hands.

"I'm up to 1887," he said, indicating the file boxes he had by his feet, from which he was throwing documents emblazoned with the swastika and the German Imperial Eagle into the smoky fire. Peter was shocked. He opened his mouth to say, "I forbid you to . . ." and stopped.

Vogelstein said, "Orders from the *gauleiter*. We have to destroy all documents to prevent them falling into the hands of the enemy. Bridges, the school, the hydro generators—everything that might help them or us."

Peter felt dizzy. His mental construct of Germany was crashing down leaving nothing. Everything that had formed him was gone. He sat down, stunned. Vogelstein reached into his desk and pulled out a bottle of schnapps. He poured out two glasses and pushed one across the desk towards Peter. He said, "Here's to nothing," and held up his glass. Peter thought, 'I can't drink to that,' and said, "To the phoenix."

Vogelstein shrugged and tossed back the liquor.

Peter said, "I'm very grateful for all you have done. You have risked your life and saved ours. And now we need one last favour."

"Papers."

"Do you remember in the thirties, the Gestapo struggling for power with the SS and the police? They were arresting one another. One Gestapo officer I knew worked out a scheme to protect himself. He issued a warrant for his own arrest and kept it always with him, and of course his sidearm. If an SS officer came with a warrant for his arrest, he planned to pull out his own warrant and say, 'Don't you see, you fool, I've already received it and I'm on my way to surrender right now, get out of my way.' If the other officer was a numbskull, he would get away with it; if not, he would gain a minute or two, time to shoot the other and escape."

Vogelstein smiled. "You need me to issue a warrant for you."

"That's right."

"I would be honoured to issue a warrant for your arrest."

They both laughed. As he handed Peter the order for the warrant to take to the police office, Vogelstein said, "You know, things are in such chaos, you probably won't need this. Just use the fake party papers you came here with—the telephones and telegraph systems are so damaged, I doubt that any policeman will check Berlin."

Peter felt happy walking out of the office. His youthful lightness of being returned—he was free of duty, responsibility, authority. All the unimportant bonds had disappeared, he could concentrate on saving Helmut, Tati and Clara. He was light on his feet now, scarcely limping as he went along the street. 'What about your despair now? And you were so cold to poor Clara. How we treat others depends so much on how we treat ourselves,' he thought, 'Now I am happy, hoping to make Clara happy. But why couldn't I be happy before? All I have now is a little hope I did not have before, but Clara had it with no more reason than I had an hour ago. What a slight thing I am. And the schnapps didn't hurt either.'

The next afternoon he went to the mayor's office and placed a large sum of money before him, saying, "This is part of our family fortune. You have helped to make it. Please accept this as a gift."

The mayor stared at the money and then pushed it back across the desk. "No," he said with a sigh, "I can take the money for the train tickets, that is all. But it will be a lot, because we will have to bribe Pfeiffer at the station to give us the tickets."

∽⧢∾

Dear Alison

Marianne is dead. Do you remember the French girl who came to the St. Andrew's Ball with me? Shot leading an attack on a German division not far from where she was born and brought up (I now find out, too late, but what difference anyway?). I hate this war, so long, so much pain. Who will gain? A few profiteers? Certainly no Germans, unless the ones in prison. The only gain I see for anyone is that it be over, and so it would have been best if it had never been. Banal, maundering thoughts, I am sure, but you can't help them over here. I think of you back there sitting on your tuffet like little Miss Muffet. (What is a tuffet?)

Now you know why you have not had a letter from me for so long which is probably just as well, since you have left the last one which I thought was Very Important unanswered so long or are dolphins reading it.

I can't tell you much about M. because she would never tell me anything about herself, which was—I now find out, too late— because she had left a husband behind in France. Like everything else these days, it is all mysterious but not wonderful.

What counts is that she was brave and very very honourable. Funny too. It has been a very very sad time here because we all lost a good friend and France a hero. Does that sound pompous? Or sort of irrelevant, about the death of someone brave? To see someone young and dead like that, I mean to know, irrevocably, that she is dead is just so saddening I don't know how to cope. It just goes in you and stays there unchangeable, like a rock in the river, round which you must navigate the rest of your life.

God this war is a waste, God how I hate it because it is a waste of time, I can't do anything I want to do, everything we do is wasteful and rotten and horrible and destructive, it has no good result, unless maybe the liberation of people who were free

*before the war anyway, or no worse off than they will be at the
end, in fact probably much worse, all at the cost of the deaths of
millions. I am not able to do any of the things I want to do, such
as take you on a picnic in the islands, get through the Waldstein
without a mistake. Or go on a canoe trip to Hudson's Bay.*

He looked at the letter and thought, 'This isn't it,' and added
in one long rush, *This is just a cry of desperation from a lonely
soldier, I feel I have to unburden to someone and you are the
nearest sympathetic ear. I remember you that day at Wanagami,
and at the St. A. Ball, and wherever else did we go, the Honey
Dew? Isn't it curious, from five thousand miles and years away, I
feel close to you. When did you last write? Please don't think I
am perverse, writing like this so soon after she died, but the
world has changed and so have I. I need a friend. And you're it.*

*I am heartbroken and crushed. Please write—I am lonely as
a beach.*

He could not sign his name—he just added J. And then, on reread-
ing, thinking the letter was too sad, he added a PS to show that he could
still be jaunty: *By the way, you told me at the ball that you liked
Brahms. I went to the* Third *in Wigmore Hall last week, and I must
warn you against him, he will bore you to death. The only interesting
thing about him is that he does so little with so little.*

Wescheren, Holland, October, November, 1944

⁓◕◔⁓

Bernie Hallett was supervising the unloading of the Bren gun carriers from their tank transporters late on the night of October 4, in a muddy field, just south of Boulogne. Rain was dripping down the faces of the tired men, who had travelled all day, eating cold food, and catching only cat-naps in the trucks. Joe Killsbear, recovered from his leg wound, but limping, called Hallett to the radio-phone in his caravan, parked behind one of the transporters, with a portable searchlight blasting light through the window because the caravan's generator had failed again.

Hallett's wet hand slipped on the Bakelite handle of the phone as he settled back on his chair, dropped the phone, picked it up and said, "Hallett."

"Fox," said the wet receiver, "where are you?"

"Just south of Boulogne, I think."

"We want you to get to Antwerp tonight."

"Tonight! It *is* tonight where I am, sir."

"Ike has told Monty he wants us in Antwerp right away to take over from the Belgian resistance. We got a signal today that the Belgians are holding the sluice gates with a thin force. There are no Germans there yet, but there soon will be, because it's Blaskowitz you're up against, and he never quits. Never mind Boulogne, get moving. Those gates control the water level in the port. If they blow the gates, we can't use the port."

"Sir, may I just point out, the men are tired, we have been in the line almost continuously since D-Day except for three days on the beach, under shell-fire, we have advanced a hundred miles since yesterday, no one in this regiment can remember his last hot meal let alone a dry bed."

"I'm sorry, Hallett, this is how it is. Here, listen to this, a signal from Ike, 'Unless we have Antwerp producing by the middle of November, entire operations will come to a standstill. I emphasize that of all our operations on the entire front from Switzerland to the Channel, I consider Antwerp of first importance.' End of quote. All SHAEF new sup-

466

plies including gas and air support are being allocated to us first. Patton and Bradley are hopping mad because we're getting all the goodies. This is our big chance."

"Yes sir."

"Have you enough petrol?"

"I don't know, sir."

"Well, drive until you get there or run out. Advance on the line Lille-Ghent, report to me by radio every hour and we shall have gas air-dropped to you wherever you need it. Now get cracking."

"Yes sir."

"And Bernie, thanks a lot for your helpful attitude all down the line. Bloody good show at Vernières. And more of the same to come, I'm sure."

At hearing his nickname, Hallett felt a spike of happiness, as if the general, often harsh, had put his arm round his shoulders. But when he turned and looked out the smeared window, feeling his wet collar cold on his neck, dreading going out to tell his men they would have to reload and move, he felt so tired he could not move.

General Fox had already arrived by air in Verwoet, outside Antwerp, when the first trucks of the Ossies arrived in the square next morning. Bernie dragged himself across the square to report to the general, who as usual was neat, his fading blond hair combed. He was seated behind his desk eating his breakfast of hot beans from a tin plate set on top of a pile of papers. He pushed the plate aside, and his eyes widened at the sight of Ed Burns coming through the door. Burns, his eyes red with fatigue, a cigarette hanging from his lower lip, was arrayed in a German camouflage cape of orange, white, black and green. A chicken flopped from his arm onto the floor and scuttled under the sofa. Burns lay on the sofa, eyes closed.

Fox burst out laughing, a rare sound. "I swear to God, Burns, you are the craziest soldier in this army. What in God's name do you think that is?"

Burns said, with his eyes closed, "Chicken, sir. Named Mackenzie King."

"What in hell is it doing here?"

"Hiding, sir," said Burns.

Fox raised his eyebrows at Hallett who was hiccuping with laughter, while his eyes were starting to close. The general stuck out his unshaven jaw at Hallett asking for an explanation.

"Burns found it at Vernières, sir," said Hallett. "The men love it."

"You can't call it after the Prime Minister," said Fox. "Why is it called Mackenzie King?"

"Sir, it hides whenever there's incoming. That's why they love it."

Fox did not know what to do. These were two of his best officers, and he felt a strong personal affection for Burns. He frowned, seeing Hallett trying to keep his eyes open, weaving on his feet.

"All right, you got here, well done . . ."

Hallett said, "Sorry, sir" and lay down on the floor in front of him, asleep. Fox stood for a moment staring down. The general and Joe Killsbear got them onto stretchers and had them carried into the officers' mess, the dining room of a big apartment on the square, where they lay stretched out like dead men. The meals were served and eaten with the usual clatter and talk, men stepping over and round them in heavy boots, and neither of them stirred.

After they had clocked 12 hours without moving, Joe awakened them with tea, bacon and eggs. Unshaven, still groggy, their uniforms muddy but now at least dry, they reported to Fox's caravan.

"Well done, you've been moving even faster than George Patton," said Fox, and spread a map in front of them. "Our job is to clear the islands on the north-east side of the river, while the Brits and the rest of the Corps secure the mainland. We have to eliminate the guns here, at the end of this island. We move out tonight, to here." He showed them a village north of the line Antwerp-Turnhout Canal. Their destination was Wescheren Island, along the north-eastern bank and dominating the approaches to the port. Until it was taken, no ship could pass up-river to unload.

Shaped like a tadpole six miles long, the island was fortified on the river side with concrete bunkers, trenches, minefields and machine gun nests. Beyond the far side facing east lay a flooded polder about three feet deep at high tide, and at low tide, an impenetrable mass of reeds and mud. Dutch resistance had found that there were no defences on that side because the Germans knew that no big boats could get through the polder, and no one could march over the soft mud bottom when the tide was out. The only land access was via a road on a causeway 20 metres wide, and a mile long, leading north-west to the island. That road was exposed to massive fire from the southern, tail end of the island. The road from the causeway continuing north, bisected the island lengthways. Halfway along, a village straddled the road.

The Germans had six tanks, a dozen or more 88mm guns, and a dozen or more five-inch guns in the bunkers, plus plenty of ack ack. A "Führer order" had designated the island as a fortress to be held to the deaths of the 2,000 men there.

"One thing is clear," said Fox, "we can't go across the causeway, not even at night. The Poles tried twice to get across the causeway, and got their noses bloody. Then the Brits had a go and though they got on the objective, they were forced back. Jerry is not quite done with us yet, I'm afraid. Anyway, there it is." This commanding man was at a loss. He sucked on his black curved pipe staring down at the map. Burns walked around the room, tugging off his cape and dropping it by the door.

"How long have we got?" he asked.

"Supplies will take a week."

"Landing craft are too noisy," Burns said. "The Germans will hear them coming a mile away. That new sound-ranging gear is very accurate, so they don't even need to see the landing craft to hit them. Besides, the river is mined. We can't get a minesweeper up there until we blow their guns. We may have to wait till we can get the navy and some Lankies up here." He flicked his Zippo lighter and puffed on a Black Cat cigarette.

The general opened the window to a bright calm day. The leaves on the linden trees in the square were a peaceful yellow in the hazy blue light. "We have the gates now, that's the main thing. Let's take our time with the plans, gentlemen. Here at 1400 hours with suggestions. Here are your maps. Thank you."

He handed them their maps, which the British had distributed. They were printed on the reverse side of maps which they had captured from the Germans, marked Operation Sea Lion. The German side, printed in August 1940, showed plans for the German invasion of England.

Hallett's caravan had just arrived, so they went in there to talk. Ed sat back with his arms behind his head thinking about the island with the long thin tail. "The only thing I know is stay off that goddamned causeway until we have a bridgehead." Joe came in and told him the rations had come up, and there was mail. "Super," said Hallett, "distribute it right away."

"And Joe, while you're at it," said Ed Burns, "figure out a way to make a waterborne assault against a fortified coast without being seen or heard."

When Joe came back, he handed a square blue air-letter to Bernie and said, "Canoes, Bernie." He went out. After D-Day, Joe had spent four weeks in No. 24 Hospital in England, but had demanded to return to his unit although he was still limping.

Ed watched the other men reading their mail. He had no desire for a family because his life was plain before him: teach to live, live to reform the country. Capitalists to him were bears in the woods—civilization could not be established until they were tamed. When he had joined up, Ed had expected to find the class system entrenched in the army and had not been disappointed. But he had found out more than he had expected. Marxist theory was fading under the pressure of fighting. The army had burned him clean of a lot of intellectual baggage. The idealized love that as a teenager he had felt for humanity, sublimated at university into Marxism, had never satisfied him, because it had dried into theory.

He thought about politics but he did not care about it. The war had forced him to think only of taking good care of his men, and beating fascism. Here at last was the practical application of communism, within the rigid and ordered community for which he had yearned. He was a huge success in the army, able to apply all his theoretical love for mankind and desire for justice to goals he could see and fulfill every day for people under his command, which was where his Marxist soul had always wanted to have them.

He made notes about this in his diary, then exclaimed, "Canoes."

He got up and went to the door of the caravan. "Joe," he called out.

Joe was kneeling beside a broken-down clutch spread out on a tarpaulin on the cobblestones in front of the steps to the *Palais de Justice*, cleaning away the oil which had ruined the plates. Two Belgian lawyers in their wigs and black swaying court robes walked past the encampment, speaking French to each other, then stopped and said to Joe and the driver with him, "*Bonjour messieurs, nous sommes très reconnaissants de votre aide.*"

The driver-soldier said in a New Brunswick accent, "*de rien mes amis.*"

"Here's the leak," Joe said, and stood up as Ed came up.

"Joe, I think you've hit it, canoes. For the assault on Wescheren. It's brilliant. Let's go see Bernie."

Joe, Bernie and Ed all went to the 1400 hour meeting with Fox. Bernie started by saying, "We've brought my batman, Corporal Joe Killsbear, he's had a brilliant idea, sir. We think it's the solution." He showed the general the situation on the sand table.

Bernie said, "We go where they ain't, round to the north-east side of the island at night and attack at first light."

"You can't get Buffaloes into that polder," Fox said right away.

"We don't go by Buffaloes, sir. We use canoes."

"Canoes? Canoes? I don't understand. You mean canoes you paddle?"

"Yes sir. We could fly them here in two or three days. I know where we can get them. At my camp."

Fox shook his head and then looked up at Joe. "Your idea?" he said.

"It's about like hunting a moose," Joe said. "We got our moose every fall." He glanced at Bernie, who had been his partner on two hunts. "Germans can't hear like a moose."

Fox said, "This is the stupidest thing I've heard all week. Night won't help, they can make it day any time they like with star shells."

"For the star shells we disguise the canoes with reeds and grass, like hunting geese," said Joe. "Stick close to shore. Stay still if they go up."

"Even if they don't see you with their eyes, their radar will pick you up.

Ed said, "Their radar sweep time is about eight seconds, and we're so slow they might not even notice we're moving. If we stick close to shore, they might think we're part of the land."

"I want you to test it," said Fox. He was willing to give this a try because Ed Burns, who was a favourite of his, was supporting the idea.

"We'll do a radar run tonight," said Ed. "If that works, we'll go out on live patrol in a rowboat to see if their radar notices. Then we'll make a live reccy right over to the polder. After that, we go in." He laughed. "It's so goddamned crazy, they'll never think of it. Then we get surprise."

"After you're on the island, you keep 'em busy, so we can send in the Buffaloes," said Fox.

"Yes sir."

When the test patrols had succeeded, they went to Fox again, who said, "My God, what we get up to in this blessed army. All right, let's see it, what are the details, how many men in a canoe, how fast can we move, what's the lift . . ." he paused at the term "lift," which usually meant tons carried in an LCT, or in a four engine transport plane, "what's the lift of a canoe?"

"Two men and a moose," said Joe, and the general scowled at him.

"I'll order them now," said the general. "What kind?"

"Prospectors," said Joe, "and don't forget the paddles. Ash wood."

Five days later, 60 cedar-canvas canoes in wooden crates had arrived by truck from the airport. Joe filled them with water to soak up, and then taught the men the techniques of silent paddling. Most of them knew how to handle a canoe, but few of them could return the paddle-blade silently through the water, edge-first. He emphasized that they must never bump the paddle shaft on the gunwale, or the Germans would hear it. He made them all silence their guns, helmets and ammunition belts in cut-up blankets. When the men got the knack of silence, 180 men could pass 50 feet from a sentry without alarming him.

They would leave just before high tide at 10 pm when fog was predicted. Dawn would be clear. Sixty canoes, each with three men and full battle gear, would paddle north-east, sticking close to the mainland until they crossed the river and reached the causeway connecting Wescheren to the mainland.

About halfway along the causeway, they would pass under a bridge into the flooded polder bordering the eastern shore of Wescheren. The trip would take about an hour and a half: each canoe, crewed by three men, would make four trips, landing two men with gear for three. One man would paddle each empty canoe back for the next lift. They would land a total of 600 men before dawn, complete with two doctors, food, water, stretcher bearers, 60 Bren guns, 200 phosphorous grenades, 12 two-inch trench mortars with 60 rounds each, hand grenades, six radios, 16 portable flame throwers, ten Piat anti-tank launchers, 600 rifles, and thousands of rounds of ammunition.

Once the canoe team was pinning down the Germans in the bunkers, the Buffaloes could land, and the rest of the regiment could sweep in over the causeway, and attack the main force of Germans in the village and beyond.

The regiment's big guns on the mainland had been sighted in individually, the variations in trajectory figured out for each drop of one degree Fahrenheit in temperature at the ammunition dump, and for the loss of firepower in the barrels caused by previous firing. Some of these 25 pounders had been fired over a thousand times, and their barrels had been worn so that the effective range was down over 10 per cent from manufacturer's specifications. All this had been ordered by Fox at Ed's suggestions. In practice, the shells were always landing within ten yards of the aiming point. The creeping barrage would retreat from the pillboxes, while the soldiers attacking from behind, crept up in silence to kill the defenders in the bunkers with flame-throwers and grenades shooting in via the air vents and firing slots.

The weather was as predicted, a thick fog that hung like a ceiling over the buildings, perfect for the attack. On the evening of the attack, a man 50 feet from the base of the stalled Groesbeek windmill vane could see the entry door, but not the hub 20 feet up. Hungry, lousy, tired and frightened, the Germans would not believe that anything could move unheard over the water in this weather, so they would go to sleep, one day closer to the end of the war.

Bernie and Ed went for a walk along the top of a dyke on the edge of the harbour just after sunset. Ed pulled out his leather-bound canteen and handed it to Bernie, who did not even ask what was in it. He swigged, examined it by the pale light of the moon sliding past thin clouds, and said, "I never noticed this before, it's very handy."

"Present from my girlfriend before I left. Full of Johnnie Walker Black."

"A good girl. I'd like to meet her."

"I shot a Kraut on D-Day, padre. Suppose he's one of the good ones and I get my comeuppance tomorrow. Do he and I meet in heaven?"

"I can't believe you said that. I hope you're not getting the wind up."

"Because if I do, I sort of think, what the hell was the point?"

"Point of what? The war? Or killing your Kraut?"

"The war." Ed took a deep drag on his Sweet Cap, flicked it into the canal and allowed the smoke to drift out of his mouth as he looked up at the light-filled clouds.

"I thought you hated the Germans for Spain."

"I do. I did. Maybe that's the point. Hate is not enough."

"But you hate them for the evil they did."

"And they are doing."

"You've answered your own question."

"No, because I started to want to do what I hated them for doing."

"What do you want?"

"Same as you, it's over and we go home."

"Anyway, a Christian doesn't hate."

"Then what in hell are you doing here?"

"Doing here in hell, do you mean?"

Ed yawned. "I'm going to turn in. We've got about three hours."

The first paddles were wet at 8 pm. The canoes moved out in blackness three abreast on silky water, three men in each with blackened faces, reeds and branches sticking up all over the canoe. Once, a star-shell went up, and they froze, faces turned away into the shadows, illuminated as if by the sun, every one of them feeling that he alone was the target of a thousand watchful Germans with machine guns. But no tracers lit the air, the star-shell sank out of sight in a few seconds, and they were dark again.

On the far side of Wescheren, a quarter of a mile behind the German defences, the first canoes hissed through the reeds to the muddy shore. Bernie led number one platoon through the ankle deep water up to firm ground, a long low ridge capped by high poplars silhouetted against the paler fog. To their right, invisible, about half a mile away, stood the shattered windmill at the centre of the German line that ran south from the end of the village. A hundred yards ahead of them, down a slight slope, lay the tents, bunkers and trenches of the south defences commanding the beach and causeway. Nothing stirred, except the swimming fog. The ground all round the defences was cratered with old shell-holes, but they were not deep or wide, since the explosions had been muffled by the sandy earth, which bloomed in the air then fell back mostly where it had been. None of the bunkers had yet been destroyed by the artillery, though several had been tilted out of the vertical by the Lancasters which had bombarded Wescheren last week. The beach sand was stuffed with mines, and in the water stood barbed wire fences placed to herd incoming boats into gaps on which heavy fire was concentrated.

The next flotilla of canoes arrived late, having been lost in the polder. The following arrivals would be late, too, so the last flights could not get over in darkness. Bernie would have half the manpower.

He stood by the canoes with Ed Burns whispering about what to do. Once he heard a man cough by the road, perhaps a German, perhaps one of his own. He whispered an order to the canoe commander to take back to regimental HQ on the mainland. "We have to change the loading order. As soon as the stonk goes in, the rest of you paddle like hell straight across to the north end of the causeway, not in here, make sure everyone understands that. Not to this side, and not straight toward the German lines. They head for beach where the causeway hits the island."

Ed Burns started to object. He was always trying to figure out a safer way to attack, but Bernie knew there was no time to waste—the plan had to be changed, and he did not have enough men to carry out the original attack. "Ed, we're outnumbered five to one, we've got to have reinforcements right away. We can lay down lots of smoke for them, besides we'll be keeping the Germans busy from behind."

Twenty minutes before dawn, half of the planned force—Able and Dog companies—were lying strung out along the road, trying not to cough, or fall asleep and snore. Growing cold, they had curled up with their heads on their arms, warned by their NCOs not to doze off.

The sky grew green in the east and then pale grey above. A few sparrows began to squeak. The top of the sun reddened the soles of their spread-eagled boots. Hallett watched two Germans coming out of the squealing steel side doors of the tilted bunker 50 yards ahead of him, to see the day. At that moment, the incoming shells began to explode along two miles of beach. The two Germans disappeared back into the bunkers. Smoke shells obliterated the calm surface of the river.

For nearly an hour the bombardment continued, not a shell landing among the Canadians behind the German lines, although the shell splinters and fragments of concrete buzzed and sizzled over their heads. All the shells landed on or beside the bunkers. One hour after the bombardment began, it was to cease, and they were to rush the bunkers.

Hallett checked his watch. Eight minutes left. The target area for the shells now moved away from the bunkers toward shore, keeping the Germans in the bunkers, while the infantry crept in safety up to the air-vents and firing slots with grenades and flame-throwers.

Bernie felt light growing around him and looked up: the sky had cleared and sun was slanting in from the blue, while on the river, straight out from the German bunkers, white mist lay over the grey water. In that white fuzz dark shapes began to appear. Canoes. "Oh my God," he whispered. As he lifted his glasses to look again, the Germans in the bunkers began machine-gunning the canoes poking out from the mist. The last minute change in plan had not allowed for the tide which was combining with the current to sweep the canoes downriver ahead of the Buffaloes and right in front of the German bunkers. The Germans were firing straight into the slow-moving canoes.

The wounded in the canoes were screaming, falling over the sides, the canoes were bursting open as the bullets shredded them. Some of the canoes came straight on, firing at the Germans, others turned back, others paddled back upstream to get out of range. The smoky mist kept rising off the water, revealing more and more of the canoes.

Bernie seized the radio and called off the stonk, which lifted right away. He stood up, blew his whistle to start the charge downhill to the bunkers to divert the Germans from the men in the river, but the deafened officers beyond could not hear. They thought there were still five minutes of barrage left and at first they waited, unaware of what Ed was doing, until one by one they saw him screaming and running down on the bunkers from behind, throwing grenades, firing his gun, followed by three other men.

The noise of the machine guns, the incoming fire from the men in the canoes whizzing right past him, the screams of the wounded men made Bernie impervious to everything but stopping the German fire. He jumped up on the sodded cement roof of the first bunker, and threw a grenade into the air-shaft. It rolled back out and lay on the turf on top of the bunker, and he knew there must be a screen in there so he jumped down, and landed on a German. The German fell, shot by Bernie's first platoon sergeant Wickers, and the grenade exploded showering them with turf and bits of concrete.

Bernie screamed at one of the flame-thrower men, weighted down by the huge round tank on his back, "Get up here, hit this thing," and boosted him up onto the roof. The flame-thrower blasted the long tongue into the air shaft. There was a whump from inside the bunker and black smoke blossomed out the shaft and the steel side door blew open and Germans ran out screaming and blinded.

One of the Germans ran with his clothes on fire, then rolled over and over on the beach grass, jumped up and ran towards the sea. Half-way down the beach, he stepped on a mine, and was blown high, his leg dangling behind him as he flew through the air. He landed face down on another mine, which blew him back up in the air, his guts trailing behind him, his leg falling off as he flew. He lay on his back, his guts torn open, and steam rising from them.

Bernie ran round the bunker and shot at one of the emerging Germans. He heard screaming. He reached the open door and fired a burst inside.

A German lying on his back at his feet looked up at Ed and said, "Surrender," and Ed put his foot on the man's neck. The moment he felt his foot on the German, he was aware for the first time that he was hoarse, and had been screaming ever since he had run down the bank. Wickers was standing beside him, six dead Germans were lying all round the opened door, and now screams for help were coming from the Canadians in the canoes who could not land on the shore for fear of mines, could not paddle upriver to the causeway because of the heavy current, and could not retreat because they were now trapped inside the barbed wire.

Bernie found his radio man up on the ridge, ran back up to him and screamed into the radio, "We're on the objective, consolidating now, get the flails up here, we have to save the canoes."

All up and down the beach as far as he could see, Germans were coming out of the torched bunkers coughing and putting their hands behind their heads. Some Schmeisser fire was coming from a house at the far south end of the west-facing beach. His FOO Ben Brown came over, saying to Hallett, "Sir, do you want a stonk down at the far end? This side of the village, they won't quit." He was panting for he had run a half mile with his radio.

"That will be just fine, Ben," said Hallett. "Fire away, I'll warn the men."

The bombardment went in after about three minutes, levelling the house and lifting one corner of the furthest bunker. Hallett saw a small group of Germans running along the road towards him, hands behind their heads. He looked at his watch in amazement: the time was nine o'clock, the firing at this end had stopped, the surviving canoes were hovering off the beach, waiting for the flails to clear the beach of mines, the sun was shining, the beach was in the Ossies hands and he was OK.

Hallett's signalman had been injured in the head, so he could not use his own radio. He borrowed Ben Brown's radio to send the message, "South end secure, send reinforcements on the causeway." A few seconds later, Fox's voice buzzed through the speaker. "Is the causeway secure?"

"Causeway secure. Send the tanks now."

He sat down on a milestone by the edge of the road remembering falling onto the German. He had not even seen the man's face, and he was dead. He remembered feeling nothing.

He lit a cigarette, took a swig of water from his canteen and trained his glasses on the causeway. Small dark shapes moved up the road on top of the causeway towards him, six tanks led by a flail tank. He saw the blur of the chains even now, and a cloud of dust. Then he heard the tremendous slam of the chains on the bricks, followed several times by explosions from detonating mines. 'Well,' he thought, 'if the damned second flight hadn't gotten lost, we would have done this with almost no casualties.' He was starting to get up to see to the wounded, when the shell landed about 20 feet from him, blowing him backwards and rolling him downhill with lights in his head and no sound except a vast ringing, and he thought, 'I'm dying.'

He woke up on his back with white faces above him looking down. Someone was shining a light into his eye. There was strong pressure in his head but no sound. He thought he was alive, but dying. He tried to lift his hand. A hand appeared in front of his face at the right angle and distance to be his own. He told it to move, and the forefinger wiggled. He watched it without feeling it. It was a dirty hand. It was interesting, this hand, it obeyed him, it was his own hand but he could not feel it.

The tanks ground into the scrubby fields on either side of the road and jerked towards the village, firing as they went. Two Wasps accompanied them, sending flame at each house. Then the Germans counter-attacked and two Shermans blew up, the crews burned alive; the flame-throwers were forced back. The Germans fired from every window in every house, their artillery was accurate, and the Ossies were driven back.

When night rose, the Germans still held the village, Bernie had been evacuated to hospital, and the firing died away. The next day, they began to fight their way through the village, mouseholing from room to room. Soon half the village was ablaze. The Germans retreated, and began to surrender, a few at a time. Then dozens ran out of the last few houses, like ants from a burning log, all surrendering.

One prisoner said in passable English that he had been sent to arrange the surrender. Ed Burns, substituting for Hallett, talked to him. The prisoner said that General von Bielenberg was awaiting him in the courtyard of the burgermeister's house at the far end of the village.

Ed considered, then said to the young German, "Go back up there and tell them I accept, but they must come out of the houses into the streets and lay down their weapons where we can see them."

The prisoner walked back up the street and disappeared into the house. As Ed watched with his glasses, a dozen-plus Germans looked from a doorway at the end of the village street, threw out some weapons, and then came out with their hands up. Then several more appeared round the corner of the furthest house, carrying something. A white box. A tall man, with a monocle, in a leather coat, marched towards the box, and stood there. Soldiers began putting things on the box.

Ed told the platoon commander behind him to cover him with automatic fire, and started down the road with Joe beside him, one hand on his sidearm. Ed and Joe walked towards the Germans, their guns at the ready.

As they neared the box, Ed saw that it was a table covered with a white tablecloth on which stood a bottle with glasses.

The German clicked his heels, gave an army salute and read in English from a typed statement, "I am General Heinz von Bielenberg, officer commanding Fortress Wescheren. I surrender this island and my men to you on condition that all my men are treated according to the Geneva Convention." He clicked his heels and saluted.

Burns stared at him without speaking, thinking, 'A general, ye gods, what an operation this is.'

"To save their lives and yours, I have ordered them all to surrender to you. You are Canadians, ja?"

"We're Canadians," Burns said. "And of course we observe the Convention."

The general held out two glasses of champagne.

Joe reached out and said, "*Danke sehr*," and drank. Burns took a glass of champagne.

"To whom have I the duty of surrendering?" said von Bielenberg, this time in German, which was translated by another German officer, smiling with pitiful eagerness beside his General.

Ed gave his name and rank. The general said, "You have canoes. You have Red Indians here, ja? I used to read those stories when I was boy. Please, who did this? I must know the name of the gallant officer who planned this so strange attack."

Ed said, "Here's the man who thought it up," and General Heinz von Bielenberg of the ancient and noble warrior family from Marburg was introduced to the man who had outsmarted him in war, Corporal Joe Killsbear of Bear Island, Wanagami.

Toronto, December, 1944

⁓⳿⳾⁓

Alison de Pencier finished reading Jack's letter about Marianne, wiped her eyes and stared out the window, streaky with rain, past the wet branches to the fog blurring Roxborough Street. 'The poor man. How sad for him. Perhaps I misjudged him. I must write. When was the last time?'

She looked in her correspondence drawer and saw his latest to her beginning, *This long silence of yours reminds me of your mortality.* This struck her at the heart. She had left his letter of May, 1944 unanswered for six months now, because she felt so uneasy about him. But she felt for his sorrow right now. She drew the paper towards herself and began,

Dear Jack

I'm terribly sorry to hear of Marianne. I thought she was so spirited. She had so much life in her. And she was beautiful. Such a waste. I'm sorry.

It is not true that I neglect you because I am basically an indifferent person—it's just that although I know what I want to do, I am often uncertain as to how to go ahead, except at school, where I can usually be certain of most things. Enough, as it appears. Also, very little happens here that would be of interest to you. Jumping out of planes into France, spying on people, blowing up bridges—it is all unimaginable here on safe old Roxborough Street where a car passes about once an hour. The worst thing that has happened here in weeks is that our dog was kicked by a milk-horse, but he is all right now. Paul, my young brother has just come in from school dripping wet, and I am sitting in front of the fire in the living room writing an essay on Piero della Francesca. Brahms' Second symphony is playing on the victrola (I obviously don't agree with you on that) and Mother will bring us in tea soon. Soon she will

*announce dinner, we shall sit down at the table, bow our heads
and Dad will say 'For what we are about to receive may the
Lord make us truly thankful.' There is always good food in the
house except that Mother usually burns the steak. She talks and
talks while we eat and listen in silence. I have often heard her
talk for hours without stopping on the phone to Aunt Marge,
who is a great talker herself, so I wondered how she got Marge
to listen. Then I happened to pick up the extension phone, and I
realized that they talk simultaneously, and apparently they hear
each other, because every now and again they respond to each
other. Quite amazing. So you see, life here is so ordinary, there
is really nothing to say but that, but I am trying for your sake,
poor lonely soldier that you are, although I doubt you will
remain lonely as a beach very long.*

    *It is a good thing Italy is out of the war because we got
back our poor dear Professor Bignani suspected of being a
fascist—people went crazy about the "German" and "Italian"
Canadians and put them in camps though they had been born
here. Anyway, we got back our poor old B. who is very very
knowledgeable. He is tall and skinny with professor hair. Also
a speech impediment, so when he lectures us, he refers to
Gleek and Loman histly, which makes it very hard for all of us.
Also his handliting on the board is impossible to decipher, as it
starts normally but then slants steeply up until he is standing
on his tiptoe putting the last words on. You would think that
glavity alone would pull the words down as it must be hard to
leach so high, and he has bad arthlitis from the camp, poor
dear, but no, he keeps on leaching up, and that makes for a
long class and trouble deciphering the notes. Afterwards we
have to compare what we took down, it is sort of like code-
breaking and even if we do get it into a semblance of sense, we
are still not sure what he was talking about because not all the
terms are known to us yet. Last year, everyone in his class
failed. That has never happened in the university before. He*

was teaching us about Michelangelo painting the Sistine Chapel and a girl from Sudbury asked him what about the other fifteen. Things like that.

I do hope you get home safe and sound.

Yours sincerely

Alison de P.

PS I don't know about Dear, or Distant, but as you have seen, I am not Immovable. I felt very sad about your loss and I hope you will soon get back your usual high spirits.

1945

Northwest Germany, March, 1945

Colonel Bernie Hallett, recovering from his head wound in hospital in
Antwerp, was so fed up with the hospital routine and so eager to get
back together with his friends in the Ossies that he pretended to be better than he was. He was still having nightmares and headaches, but by
smiling and doing all the therapy, by eating all his meals and demanding more, he soon wore down the doctors. They suspected his game,
but let him go anyway because his unit was so short of reinforcements.
The Canadian troops at the front were all volunteers, and the few conscripts in the rear echelons were not volunteering readily any more.

He rejoined the regiment in January in eastern Holland, where
they were driving back the Germans from each village in murderous
slow fighting through blizzards and rain and fog over fields flooded
by order of General Johannes Blaskowitz. Often they were up against
well-trained paratroopers, but now they were also encountering boys
in knickers and armbands who scarcely knew how to reload their
Schmeissers.

Preparing to force the Rhine in March, the Allies concentrated
more guns along the Rhine near Emmerich than had ever been brought
together in war. Operation Plunder assembled more than 3,000 guns
firing day and night in barrages so heavy that everyone in the target

area was dead or wounded or trembling with concussion when the guns stopped.

The air raids destroyed most of the ancient German cities along the river, starting with high explosives that blasted open the buildings. Women and their children buried in cellars and shelters were attempting to get out while the old men of the rescue teams, lit by flames and weeping from the smoke, were tapping and calling into the rubble. Then came scores of thousands of incendiary bombs which ignited the rescuers along with the exposed timbers of the ancient buildings. Steeples and trees on fire emerged from the dark mists that rolled over the cities, then disappeared like swimmers in steep waves. The smell of roasted and decaying bodies was still in the air when the Canadians, British and Americans crossed the river the next day under a plume of smoke so high the pilots saw it from 100 miles away over the English Channel.

Town by town, village by village, even farmhouse by farmhouse, against men now fighting for their own towns and farms and homes, the Canadians fought forward over the flat north German plain. They were no longer liberators, but conquerors, bound for Bremen where, as rumour said, they would make a right turn and then take Berlin.

Joe Killsbear brought Bernie an envelope from General Fox on Sunday, April 8, containing a letter ordering them to take the town of "Forsooth" the next day, then advance on the line Forsooth-Clapburg-Bremen. The letter ended with warm good wishes and "best love to Ed."

Ed Burns had become a favourite of General Fox, who loved his humour, his enormous knowledge, and common sense. The general looked on Ed's poetry as a harmless peculiarity like his freckles which did not impair his usefulness. Fox wanted to appoint Ed to his own staff, but held back because he did not want to offend Hallett.

Bernie called Ed into his caravan and showed him the orders. Ed burst out laughing. "Forsooth," he said, "take Forsooth, but what have we then that we have not now, for forsooth is in truth, but truth, but then of course we shall be in a good position to capture the next position which would be, let's see, forswear, no forestall. By all means let us forestall the fascists, forsooth." He was often manic like this these days, seeing victory so near, hoping to get to it uninjured.

The bull-headed general had once again sent a malapropism instead of an order. Bernie and Ed bent over the German top-sheets, found a small town named Fassoythe five miles ahead on the road to Cloppenburg, and decided that in Fox's mind, Fassoythe was Forsooth, and Cloppenburg was Clapburg. They then discussed what to do. They had already reconnoitred the approaches to the town and discovered that most of the inhabitants had fled, but that there was a unit of paratroopers to the south and east of the town, digging in along the line of a small canal.

Ed said, "I've been thinking about how we do our attacks. Jerry has always been ready for us because we've been going in at first light regular as clockwork, just like him, it's practically one of the rules of war now."

"You want to try tape again?" Bernie was doubtful, but he had to consider every possibility, for his reconnaissance parties had already reported that the road to Forsooth was mined and the Germans had felled most of the roadside trees into the roadway, which was now the aiming point for mortars and machine guns.

Ed pulled out his favourite Black Cats and offered one to Bernie. They stepped out of the caravan into the fresh air loaded with the scent of new grass and blooming trees. Ed's cigarette smoke drifted upwards in tiny swirls and he squinted out over the wet fields. He said, "The problem is that the recce patrol itself doesn't know where it is, so they get the tape all wrong. So tonight I'll go out myself and mark the route."

"We've already had a rocket about senior officers deserting HQ to get up to the sharp end. I can't approve this."

Ed looked at Bernie. He had long ago established his intellectual superiority over his commanding officer, and he knew that Bernie accepted this. He blew smoke and said, "And where the hell were you the afternoon we took Vernières, eh?"

Bernie took a puff of the cigarette and squinted out over the dark ridges of mud, glinting in the new light, growing a faint cloud of steam as the sun grew warmer. He felt he should impose his will on the situation and on Ed, so as not to lose authority. But he also knew that Ed would never change his opinion. Still, he had to try.

"Take Joe with you."

"What for?"

"Cover your back."

Ed leaned forward coughing. He straightened up, red in the face and said, "Too many Black Cats. Tonight I go out. Tomorrow night, around midnight, we attack. Lead man has a masked flashlight, just to find the next tape. The start-line will be 50 yards from their dugouts."

"No stonk?"

"No stonk. We'll have a radio and I'll call one in if I need to."

Bernie was depressed. It was all being taken out of his hands by this officer who was junior to him. He admired Ed, but suffered his arrogance. He should not be taking orders from his junior. Annoyed with himself for getting himself into this situation which led to his criticizing a promising plan, Bernie sighed and diverted Ed. "I was reading a guidebook to this area." He trained his glasses on a tall structure he believed was a steeple. "The church just past the willows was built in the fourteenth century. Anne of Cleves grew up taking communion there. It would be nice to save it." This was his roundabout way of approving Ed's idea, since anything else would involve a frontal assault following an artillery bombardment which would wreck the town.

Ed focussed his field-glasses on dim shapes beside the trees that might be camouflaged tanks or houses, beyond the mist. For a moment their own encampment was silent, there were no planes overhead, and he could hear sparrows in the bushes near the half-destroyed farmhouse in whose forecourt they were parked. The clouds were sliding apart revealing a pale water-blue sky beyond. The Ahe River, brown as gravy with the spring rains and topping its banks here and there to flood into the mucky fields, led east and then turned north, disappearing into a bank of yellow willows agitating with birds.

Bernie held the map ahead of him, tilted so he could see how the river on the paper imitated the river before him. The church spire of the distant town was a faint anomaly on the treeline far away to the left.

Ed took the map, traced his finger up it and said, "The patrol found them here and here." He touched the contour line that showed a slight rise meandering along beside the canal. "They can fire down the road and all along the canal, so Joe shouldn't get any bright ideas about canoes again."

Ed taped the attack route that night and returned as the sky was turning green. There was only one sentinel every 100 metres along a half-mile front south of the town. He told Bernie to maintain sporadic fire all day to keep the Germans in their dugouts. The whole plan would be wrecked if any German came forward and found the tapes.

At midnight, the infantry tied socks over their boots, then stole forward following Ed's tapes. The sleeping paratroopers were surprised and routed, and 98 captured in their dugouts. Another 100 paratroopers, who had been ordered to the north side of town a few hours before the attack, got away from Bernie's net.

One of the captives, the Germans' commanding officer, surrendered the town and said that there were no soldiers left in the town. He had ordered them all away to the east. So far as he knew there were no civilians left—they had taken refuge in Cloppenburg, ten miles to the east.

Bernie phoned General Fox later that morning to report that Ed was on the objective with 150 men, light casualties, and heard the general say, "Well done, again, Bernie, you're up for a gong now, you know, bloody good show, and how is Ed?"

"It was Ed's idea. We attacked at midnight. On the objective at 6 am."

"Midnight. Good God, how'd you see?"

He described Ed's plan, and the general guffawed. "Canoes, attacks by flashlight, I swear, you are the goddamnedest regiment in this man's army, Bernie, but just keep it working. Now clear and secure the town and keep a sharp eye out for traps. The Germans are supposed to be setting up Werewolf contingents for guerilla warfare behind the lines. Then skedaddle on up to Clapburg. Goddamned strange names these places have, eh? And remember me to Ed. You're invited to roast beef here on Saturday night, how's that suit you? Take a day off in Clapburg, but don't get it, get it?"

Bernie suspected that the general talked this way to embarrass him, thinking of him as a sanctimonious God-botherer, but Fox was naturally hearty, beefy, florid. He had been described by one British counterpart as "a beef-tea of arrogance, violence and Sado-sexual bonhomie. Can't stand the bugger. Damn good officer."

Bernie set down the heavy field-phone and ordered the flail tanks up, plus six trucks and Bren gun carriers, and three jeeps. He sat in the front seat of the lead jeep as they followed in the hellish wake of the flails that were slamming the road, kicking up a huge cloud of dust. The road had been bombed and repaired so many times that it was impossible to tell where a mine might be planted in the patched tarmac. They blew up six mines on the way in to town.

Every 100 metres they stopped and his driver edged the jeep close to the side of the road so Bernie could stand steady with his glasses and sweep the motionless town ahead.

The tree-lined road disappeared into dark buildings. No vehicles moved, no horses, no people. No smoke rose from the many chimneys. He was worried about the 100 paratroopers who had gotten away the night before. He thought, 'They might be waiting till we're closer; they might have gone. They sure won't be asleep with this racket.'

The morning was warm and bright, their progress slow, and Ed was beginning to fall asleep in his seat. He was gazing around half-asleep, enjoying the pieces of blue water fallen in the fields, like shards of sky in which he could see white clouds drifting past. 'I'm riding in the clouds,' he was thinking, 'the sky has fallen to pieces in the fields.'

Bernie was in a daze with the warm sun on his shoulders, thinking about Joan's letter, which said she was on her way to Ottawa for "war-work," so she might not be there when he got back. This seemed to him odd, as Ottawa was two hours by car from Kingston. Perhaps she was warning him that she was no longer in love with him. He remembered a photograph of a group of girls at the RMC ball in June, 1941, all in white gowns, all with flowers in their hair, all smiling. He could not remember her face.

Fassoythe was the least damaged town that they had seen in Germany. One casual bomb had burst a well, flooding the road.

The tanks went through first, their guns swivelling from side to side, their treads striking sparks from the cobblestones, leaving a smell of fire-scorched rock in the air. Ed got down from the jeep, where he was an easy target, and walked along thinking how eerie this was, a complete town empty of people. Doors were locked, most of the shutters closed, but through the window of a house beside the sidewalk he saw cutlery laid out on the table.

After the tanks had disappeared around a corner, the sound of sparrows squeaking in the bushes returned, as if the birds had been holding their breath. The men concentrated on every sound—sand crunching under a boot on the red brick, clothes rustling, birdsong. They rounded a corner, Bernie and Ed leading, the rest following spread out. Bernie touched Ed on the shoulder. Standing still, he flicked his eyes ahead to a dark vertical strip of shadow in a doorway. The door, unlike all the others, stood ajar.

Ed tiptoed ahead as Bernie stopped and covered him. Ed stood with his back flat against the outside wall by the hinged side, and reached round to swing the door open. It swung open without a sound, and they waited at least two minutes. Nothing happened.

Ed took off his weird gas-cape and flashed it across the opening. Silence. He dove into the doorway with his sidearm in his hand, rolling along the floor, and lay there feeling ridiculous.

He went upstairs, checking out the whole house, then came back downstairs, and walked toward the narrow front hall past the side window. The paratrooper hidden outside shot through the window. Ed knew what had happened to him so he called out a warning, "Bernie, watch out," and fell forward through the door, leaking blood from his throat with a gurgling sound.

Bernie only heard a gurgling sound. He shouted to the men following him, "By the canal," and sat down, taking Ed's bleeding head in his lap and tying his bandanna round the throat to stem the blood. The stretcher bearers arrived when it was too late. Bernie's trousers were soaked and his battle jacket wet. Ed's blue eyes looking up at the sky were dead.

Bernie laid Ed's head on the brick and got up, staring down. As he looked into the gone eyes, he thought of a line from a poem of Ed's, entitled "To My Lover on My Death," *This empty flesh where once I lived in vain.* He let out a wail that men 50 yards away heard that Ed did not hear.

He sat on the front seat of the jeep staring through the cracked windshield and sent a radio message to Fox telling him what had happened. He was still stunned by the speed of it, the impossibility of saving Ed, the way the German had done it, setting so skilled and simple a trap. And why had the German commander said all his men had retired? Was the surrender an ambush? But Bernie's men had found no more of them.

The message came back from Fox as Bernie sat in the jeep thinking about this and starting to miss Ed, thinking, 'I'll never see him again,' which gave him an irrational desire to go back to the field hospital and see him one more time. He sat for a long time lifeless in the warm sunshine in the front of the jeep, trying to deal with the messages coming in from Fox. But in his mind he kept hearing the shot, the gurgle in Ed's throat.

Fox ordered him to send the tanks through town with a message on the loudhailer, *"Raus, raus, alle hauser mussen evacuieren, stadt wird bombardiert in eine stunde, alle heraus, raus raus."* He got on the field-phone and asked the general for permission to question the purpose of the order, and Fox said, "What do you mean? You were assured the town was surrendered, all the troops were gone, correct?"

"Yes sir, but . . ."

"And now Ed's dead. The best soldier I ever saw, even if he was a pinko. Shot in the back after surrender. Oh no, they're not going to get away with this, this is not war, this is murder. The town was surrendered, guaranteed empty and now it's going to disappear."

Bernie called Lieutenant Taddle over and passed on the orders.

"Why, what's the matter, sir?" said Taddle, seeing tears coming down Bernie's dirty cheeks.

"Just do it, lieutenant," Bernie whispered. He stared down at his hands and thought, 'Not my doing.'

The tanks jerked through, blowing open holes in the walls and windows and doorways of the house, and the Crocodiles poked long drooping red fingers of fire into every opening. Behind them the houses one by one caught fire, pluming smoke then flame up into the sky. The town was dark at noon.

Toronto, Spring, 1945

On a bright warm day in March 1945, Cat Treloar walked four miles across the dreary centre of Toronto to the hospital, flapping her coat open to the warm air, past young people in parks playing tennis. The window was open and spring air billowing through Grant's room.

Grant was dressed in civvies—a Harris tweed sports coat that bagged on him, grey flannels, polished brown brogues, a white shirt and tie, his cheeks shaved shiny, hair brushed, with a big smile.

She kissed him on the cheek, and he sighed, holding her in his arms, whispering in her hair, which was held down by her pinned hat, "You look so nice." He sat down in an easy chair and asked her to pull her chair closer so they could hold hands. "I've been smiling so much since you got here that my cheeks hurt, you'll have to stop being wonderful."

This sort of talk depressed her. For weeks now she felt he had been too grateful, which made it seem that he was going to turn himself into a perennial patient, dependent on others. She hid her disappointment by bending her head to take off her rubbers, then unpinned her hat and shook out her hair.

He sensed that she was upset, so he changed the subject. "Maybe it's time to come clean about your mother."

"It was rather operatic." She hesitated, thinking that if she said that the rupture was irreparable, he would feel responsible. Would he think she was blaming him? She decided to end this limbo she was in. She would leave the Giovanellis' house, take an apartment and go to medical school.

Grant saw the hesitation in her face and leaned forward, holding both her hands, and just as she said, "It was rather operatic," he cut through to what he was thinking. "I meant what I said in London, I want to marry you. I've been waiting to see if I were going to get better, or if what I need in life is a nurse not a wife. But now, I feel better, and I'm sure I can go back to work, and support us, and I love you still, and would you marry me?"

494

She saw him as she had first seen him at Stone Cottage, the young handsome man, looking up at trees, listening to something in the distance. She had wanted him right away, but now that man was gone and in his place, this new Grant with his bent thumb, shaky walk, a certain angry sarcasm looking out of his face. She looked at him thinking, 'No,' and then could not utter the word because of the pain she would see in his face. 'I can't do this to him,' she thought, and with a foreboding of disaster, she said, "Oh, it's so sudden," and stared at him.

He laughed. He fell back laughing, and she blushed, thinking, 'Five years,' and started to laugh herself, and nodded, and said, "Yes." She was smiling but two tears stood in her eyes and fell down her cheeks as she kissed his cheek and stroked his curly brown hair, the soft stubble like baby hair grassing over the red long curving stitched scar.

On a mild grey day, Grant left the hospital in the red Packard driven by his father, who had just returned from supervising renovation of airfields on the west coast. Mrs. Giovanelli in her mink coat sat on one side of Grant in the back seat, Victoria held his hand on the other. The streets glistened with the melt of a light snowfall from the night before, but the day was so warm that flies were buzzing round the snowdrops and crocuses risen above the steaming earth.

Grant got out of the car, refusing to let either his mother or Cat help him. His father held the door open as he manoeuvred himself into position, then stood up and started along the walk, his eyes fixed down on the pavement, helping himself with a cane. Hoover went wild with excitement, lunging towards him. He broke his rope and rushed at Grant, jumping up with his paws on his chest as he had always done.

Grant fell and Hoover stood over him whingeing and licking his face. Grant got to his hands and knees thinking for a moment that something serious might have happened to him. But he got to his feet with his father helping, and his mother holding back the ecstatic dog.

Around the bridal wreath hedge came Joe Shearer in his seaman's uniform. Mrs. Giovanelli, who disapproved of the inept, unambitious Joe, tried to signal him away but he did not notice her, he was so intent on Grant.

Grant said, "Cat, I'd like you to meet my friend, Joe Shearer, Companion of the Company of Gentleman Adventurers into BSS. Joe, Victoria Treloar, Cat for short, my fiancée, from London."

Mrs. Giovanelli was stunned. For months she had been hoping that Grant would be well enough to marry Victoria, but to be informed of this important engagement in such a disrespectful manner, in second place after Joe Shearer, on the front walk, was shock enough to take the pleasure away.

"Grant," she said, "there is a time and place for everything."

"Sorry, Mum. I thought you'd be pleased."

"Of course I'm pleased, I'm delighted," she said irritably. She looked sharply at Shearer, who stood abashed at the sudden hostility.

Mrs. Giovanelli leaned forward and kissed Cat's cheek, who was smiling and looking confused."I'm delighted, of course, my dear, we must start planning right away. Now Joe, if you'll excuse us, Grant is tired. It's his first day back. And he's just had a nasty fall."

"Mother, I'm fine, all the better for seeing this big monkey. Joe, come on in. When did you get back? How long's your leave?"

Joe did not know what to say, because he had been back for almost a week and asking Mrs. Giovanelli every day when he could visit Grant in hospital, and she had been putting him off because she felt Joe was a debilitating influence on Grant. To her he was a great gowk who just dawdled through life without any ambitions. His father, a man of no distinction in Toronto society, was a lowly company lawyer.

They walked in through the front door, which was standing open to bright day for the first time since Christmas. Hoover, understanding that something was wrong with Grant, followed him, wagging his tail and nuzzling his hand. Grant sat in the library with the dog resting his head between his paws by his shoe, looking watchfully up at him with his gold eyebrows twitching.

Cat was charmed by Joe's long-winded stories. Grant had heard vague rumours of HMCS *Hudson* blasting off its rudder with its own depth charges. That the captain was the handsome, dim Smoother Mackie made him weep with laughter. He was able to add that according to the legend in Halifax, Smoother had been given his own destroyer in Montreal and the navy had awarded him a DSO for bringing it alongside in Québec with no self-inflicted damage.

Then Joe added, "I'm married now."

"Joe, amazing! Where is she? I want to meet her."

Joe explained that Yvette was at his house but too shy to come over because she did not yet trust her English. "She learned it in the air force, so every other word is an expletive. She told my mother last night that the soup was unbefuckinglievable."

They had been married a week before, at the registry office in Clinton, near the big RCAF base where Yvette had passed the war, attempting to get a posting to Halifax. Her parents had not been there because they refused to admit that her wedding was legal. Now she and Joe were planning to take a honeymoon in L'Hôtel Traversier in Laurentville, hoping for a reconciliation.

Munich, Spring, 1945

Peter, Clara, Tati and little Helmuth went by night train with many stops to Munich. As the train was arriving early on the morning of Friday March 23, the air-raid sirens sounded. The conductors came through the crowded compartments saying *"Gruss Gott,"* and ordering them off the train. They offered to guide everyone with their masked flashlights, for the station lights were out.

They started down the stairs, dragging their luggage on the broken cement floor. Helmuth, holding Peter's hand, said, "Where's the blue bag?"

Peter, who had been daydreaming of walking between fields of flowers in France, said, "Oh my God." He hobbled for the train, thinking, 'The last capital of the family has been entrusted to me and I have failed my duty.'

When he got back, he said to Helmuth, "Thank you. You've saved us a lot of money. You need a new godfather, and I am volunteering. Would you like that?"

Clara said, "Peter, please, we have to go." Peter swung up a knapsack on his back and as they walked along the littered platform to the end with the whistles shrieking at them, and the sirens growing louder, and the anti-aircraft guns beginning to make the broken glass of the roof shiver and crash around them, Helmuth said, "What's a godfather?"

"It is a wonderful idea," said Tati, out of breath, lugging a heavy suitcase with clothes, sugar and a kilo of carrots, "thank you, Peter, and an honour."

The crowd stopped at the whistled command of a uniformed guard at the top of the stairs down to the shelter. Peter seized Helmuth's square blond head in both hands, bent down and kissed him on top of the head.

Helmuth, who did not like being kissed, said, "What's that for?"

"That's because I am so grateful to you, my godson, for being such a fine protector of the family fortunes."

"Mummy?" said Helmuth. "Can he still be my uncle?"

The whistle went again and the crowd surged as one, down the stairs.

They walked with all their luggage from the station almost a mile to the flat of Bodo, Peter's cousin. Peter used the key Bodo had given him in Russia a year before and they entered to find the place a shambles. Someone had broken in through a window and rifled the apartment for food and clothing. Tati and Clara began clearing up, while Peter and Helmuth went out in search of news and something to eat.

The following morning, they registered with the housing and ration authorities, and within hours, a note from the local *Arbeitsamt* arrived by bicycle courier for Clara, summoning her to report to St. Mark's hospital nearby, for duty as a nurse.

Clara told the head matron that she had volunteered for this work in Berlin in 1941, and had been turned down. "We'll take anything we can get now," said the matron who, despite the shortages of everything, was neat and clean in a pin-stripe uniform with starched cap.

"Go to Nurse Manion downstairs first door on your left, and get a uniform. You can leave your street clothes with her. Then come back up here and fill out the forms."

A doctor came into the room on crutches and sat down with a sigh on the wooden chair by her desk, watching Clara as she left the room. "Does she know anything?" he asked with a yawn.

"Nothing, so far as I can tell, but she's young and strong. She'll do."

"She'll have to do," said the doctor, and put his head back against the pale green wall, where he had rested many times before, making the wall shiny with the oil from his hair. With his eyes closed, he said, "There's another one on the second floor, Sacher, I think. The old man with the head wound."

"Right," said the matron, and marked her chart.

Clara's first job was to help the one-legged orderly to lift Sacher's body onto the stretcher to take him downstairs to the cold room where autopsies had once been performed. No autopsy had been performed in the hospital for over two months now—the deaths were either self-evident, or else no pathologist was available. One pathologist was left in the whole city, who circulated around on a bike trying to visit ten hospitals per day. "We can't go on like this," Matron said every day, and next day, she went on.

Tati was excused from labour service because she was sick and had a child. Clara left at six every day to walk to work because there was no public transport. She came home in late evening, when she began to do the cooking and washing. Peter helped, but Tati spent most of her time in bed. One evening, near midnight, when Clara walked in with a cup of soup, Tati sighed. "If I had your faith, I would be all right."

"You are all right, you just don't believe it. Roll over so I can make your bed." Tati had done nothing all day, so the situation was ridiculous. Tati said, "Oh Clara," in a helpless tone and Clara collapsed on a chair, half-laughing. She closed her eyes and was asleep in a minute. Tati lay looking at her and heard a voice inside saying, 'She is your friend, help her, stop thinking about your sorrows and help her.' She got up, tucked a blanket round Clara and went downstairs for the first time in three days, ready to cope while Clara slept in the chair.

Tati's revival reanimated Peter. The household became cheerful and optimistic again, although nothing in their circumstance had improved. The raids were terrible and the news from the fronts frightening, worse than every dire prediction made by Tati and Peter, yet neither of them was downcast. They were thinking of how to avoid the terrible fate that threatened all of them.

It now seemed that if they stayed together, nothing would go wrong. Tati went to bed at night imagining the turrets and dormers of Schenkenberg, and themselves cheerfully walking through the gothic arch of the front door into its perfect safety. Schenkenberg would be unharmed above the village and they would clean it up and plant a garden, and play music, and work at something.

Heidelberg and Berlin, April, 1945

In March, Albert Speer was in Heidelberg conferring with generals, gauleiters and SS officers about Hitler's order to destroy all factories, mines, bridges, civic records, patents, blueprints, aircraft, food stocks, railway rolling stock, houses, dams, offices, printing plants, canal locks, airports, radio stations, newsprint, generating stations, schools, universities, hospitals, libraries and banks. The invader was to encounter annihilation, hatred and death. Speer made notes of the various opinions which he intended to assemble in one long memo to convince Hitler to relent.

Misty shadows were joining round him when he walked into the parking lot with Colonel Poser, his assistant, wondering if Field Marshal Model would keep his word to preserve the Ruhr installations despite Hitler. He said goodbye to Poser, who would stay here to help frustrate some of Hitler's destructive orders, and got into the back seat of his car behind Kemptka, Hitler's driver, who was at the wheel.

As they drove into night, they stayed tuned to the government radio service that broadcast the positions of enemy fighters and bombers which were strafing the roads. Kemptka could use the headlights only in areas pronounced clear of enemy aircraft by the radio. Whenever a fighter approached the area they were crossing, Kemptka doused the lights and parked. After the plane had flown on, they went roaring down the deserted Autobahn at full speed with all lights on. After dawn, they went by small roads where there was more roadside cover.

In Heidelberg among friends, Speer had known it was reasonable to preserve the nation. But the closer he got to Berlin, the more dangerous it seemed. Hitler had already executed four officers for failing to blow up a bridge. He stared out into the trees thinking the closer he came to Hitler, the farther he was from reality. Hitler knew the war was over, he must now die, and he wanted . . . what did Hitler want?

Speer hesitated to imagine the chaos raging in Hitler's mind. It appeared that Hitler now hated Germans. He refused to imagine the consequences of that: he would avoid vast conclusions and do his duty. But what was his duty? To carry out Hitler's orders. And here he was plotting to frustrate Hitler.

He stared at the papers on his attaché case in his lap, thinking that there was enough here to assure the deaths of dozens of the plotters. Heat crept up his back and down his arms and sweat ran in his armpits. Why had he created these dangerous papers? He must destroy them. But the sight of Kemptka's broad back stopped him: he had just been warned in Heidelberg that Hitler had assigned him his personal chauffeur in order to spy on him.

He began tearing up the papers, occasionally coughing to cover up the sound. He let the bits fall out the window. Kemptka commented on his coughing and suggested that he close the window. Speer assured him he was fine, and kept on until they were all gone.

Hours later, when they pulled into an army refuelling station under a broad camouflage net, he got out of the car to stretch his legs and saw that many of the scraps of paper had lodged in the running board of the car against the rear fender. He bent down to tie his shoe on the board and snatched them all up, then strode off across the parking lot to a tree as if to urinate. There he scuffed a hole in the ground, and covered the papers.

The next morning, he stopped on the Chancellery steps, gazing down the bomb-cratered Wilhelmstrasse at the damage to buildings he had long known, remembering the model in the basement of the Arnim palace. It would never be built, but remain a bit of evidence in a ruin, not the splendour he had designed. 'My life's work turned into dust and ashes, nothing left but ruin and death.'

He walked into the Chancellery, now sandbagged, windows boarded, steps splintered, a great hole in the faux-marble ceiling 16 feet high which he had had such trouble installing on time in 1936. He squared his shoulders and refused to allow himself morbid thoughts of defeat.

He walked along the great hall to the door of the office, which was open, and saw Hitler standing by the big desk giving orders to his adjutant, von Below.

Hitler's left arm was trembling, his uniform hung slack on him so that he looked like an actor in a high drama. It was amazing that he had kept it up as long as this—he did not know diplomacy, generalship, architecture, economics or painting, but he dictated national policy to experts in all of these. He talked of beauty, but he was mainly interested in size. He dreamed of creating, but he set out to conquer, leaving triumph and ruin behind him.

Speer waited in the doorway. Von Below walked past him with a curt nod, and Hitler beckoned him in. Standing up and trembling, Hitler said, "Bormann has given me a report on your conference with the gauleiters in the Ruhr. You pressed them not to carry out my orders and told them that the war was lost. Is this true?"

Speer stared at him awaiting his fate. Hitler's uniform was stained down the front and wrinkled, and his arm shook so much he had to hold it with his right hand.

"Are you aware of what must follow from this?"

Speer nodded.

"If you were not my architect, I would take the measures which have been prescribed in such a case."

He paused.

Speer straightened up as if to face the inevitable firing squad and said, "Take the measures you think are called for, never mind about me as an individual." He was too rebellious and even too tired to argue.

The submissiveness in this self-confident man surprised Hitler. He said, "You are overworked and sick. I have therefore decided that you are to go on sick leave right away. Someone else will run your ministry while you are recovering."

'No," said Speer, "I feel fine. I will not go on leave. If you don't want me as minister, fire me."

"I don't want to dismiss you. The public will be discouraged. But I order you to start your sick leave."

"No. I can't accept the responsibility of a minister while a deputy runs the place."

Hitler said, "No. It is impossible for me to dismiss you. The effect would be serious."

"As long as I am in office, I must conduct the affairs of my ministry. I am not sick." He stressed 'not.'

Hitler looked up, then sat down at his desk. He tapped his right forefinger on the desk and then said, "Tell me, Speer, do you believe that we can win this war?"

Speer was silent.

"If you remain silent I shall take it that your confidence in my leadership conflicts with your belief that we will lose. And I shall be forced to admit finally and irrevocably that you no longer believe."

Still Speer was silent.

Hitler waited.

"My Führer," Speer began, and was surprised at himself for uttering the cant phrase which was so often on the lips of the toadies he despised around Hitler, "I don't know what to say—production stopped months ago, how can we fight on?"

"This is the supreme test," said Hitler, his voice very hoarse now. "If the German people do not pass this test, then they are the weaker and they deserve to die, and they shall die. An honourable death in defeat is worth ten lifetimes of cowardice." He got up and paced around the room. "Speer, if you can convince yourself that the war is not lost, you can continue to run your office."

"You know I can not convince myself of that. The war is lost."

Hitler sighed, and said, "Remember December '41, remember Moscow, remember what we did together to achieve maximum production, doubling it every few months, when everyone said it was impossible, the war was lost . . ." as Speer stared at him, and once again began to feel the effect of that steady gaze accompanied by a flow of implacable argument, armed with facts. He wanted to resist, and once again found his own personality yielding to Hitler's. His sense of responsibility flowed away and was replaced by Hitler, and he felt relief. He would not have to argue, he would have only to obey.

Hitler ended with a plea, "If you could tell me that at least you hope that we have not lost, that would be enough to satisfy me. You must be able to hope," he pleaded.

Speer stared at him, thinking how strange it was that Hitler, who had power of death over him, was begging him. He wanted to give in to Hitler, as he had so often before. But the enormous reality pressing in on this small room stopped him. Hitler said, "You have 24 hours to think about it. Tomorrow come back here and tell me that you hope the war can be won. That is all I need. Faith changes worlds."

Speer, who loved the Berlin Philharmonic, had arranged that the orchestra should give its final performance that afternoon, Thursday, April 12. He had long ago told his friends that when the orchestra played Bruckner's *Romantic Symphony*, the end of the war was very near. The concert was arranged to begin with Brunnhilde's last aria and the finale from the *Gotterdämmerung*, followed by Beethoven's *Violin Concerto*, ending with the Bruckner. The electricity was normally cut off in Berlin in mid-afternoon, but Speer issued orders to leave it on for the concert hours. The auditorium was cold and everyone was dressed in overcoats, hats, gloves and scarves. Some of the younger people could hear the murmur of artillery in the east.

Wagner's sounds frightened many people like an air raid. The crashing and banging of drums were bombs exploding, aeroplane motors sounded in the buzzing of the strings, all this torn open by the horns like sirens howling Siegfried's theme.

Never had he thought that Wagner was realistic—now he thought that everything else is pallid waiting—'This is reality, the rest is a dream. Germany may be destroyed, but we live on in this heroic music. This confrontation with everything is everything. Now I understand Hitler. This is what he is.'

As Brunnhilde sang her final aria, some people were weeping. The stunning power and sadness of the *Gotterdämmerung*, were eerily prescient of the end that they were living through,.

The audience was left in awed silence, feeling that they themselves had been the theme of this tremendous music. Speer and Margarete saw Magda Göbbels in her overcoat waiting for her husband, a patron of the orchestra for years. Speer admired and respected Frau Göbbels, who had—in common with most of the wives of the high party officials—resisted the ridiculous pomposities of their husbands.

The rumour was strong that Göbbels and she were going to kill themselves and their six children if the Russians got into the city. Magda was looking wan and fretful, glancing around, although normally she was a happy and composed person. She kept drawing the coat close round her. He bowed. "Frau Göbbels, is there anything I can do to help you?"

She said, "Dear Herr Speer, Frau Speer, thank you very much, there is nothing I can think of, it is all arranged . . ." and she pulled out her handkerchief and began to weep into it. Margarete moved closer to help mask her face from the crowd, and she dabbed at her eyes and whispered, "It is so dreadful, the children, I can not bear the thought . . . ." She bit her lip and looked around in a panic. "He wants . . . murder, then suicide," she whispered. "I can't do it."

In Margarete's face was a plea to Albert, 'You must save them.'

He said, "I will arrange a boat to come to your dock at the Bogensee tomorrow morning at 6 am."

"Magda," said Joseph Göbbels, hobbling up with a smile brightening his peaked face, "Great news, the turning point—" he was hugging himself, "Roosevelt has just died. It's on the radio, he is dead. He held their whole alliance together, Churchill hates Stalin, now they break up. This is the turning point we have been waiting for . . . I must go to the Chancellery. This is the death of the Tsarina and the miracle of the House of Brandenburg. I'm so glad we held out together. Cheer up, my darling," and he limped away as fast as his club foot would allow, without hearing a word from her or Speer.

"Tomorrow then," said Speer.

"What Tsarina?" Margarete said open-mouthed.

"It's a symbol, from the Seven Years' War," Speer said.

"But what does it mean, can this be the turning point?" Magda said. The hope in her fear-darkened eyes made him angry that she had been so deceived. He said, "It means nothing. It is worse than nothing, it is evil because now we'll keep on fighting with false hopes, while Hitler destroys the whole country. I'm sorry, I can't help that, but I can help save you and the children. At dawn, the boat will be there."

She stood still and said nothing. He went on, "Don't you know your husband is crazy? He's making a film with 10,000 soldiers right now about Frederick the Great thinking that will stop the allies. This is our *Gotterdämmerung*: he is Hagen, Hitler is Siegfried, when he dies, it all comes crashing down on us." He was shaking with a passion he had never felt before. "Forgive me, I can not help it. Such evil never was."

Magda Göbbels said, "I forgive you. You must never speak to me that way again. Goodnight."

"At least accept the boat," he pleaded with her as she walked away. She ignored him.

He watched her walking away thinking of her children, her beauty shot with a bullet. 'Great passion generated by great nonsense. The madness of the Third Reich.'

The next morning Speer went in to Hitler's office in the bunker to give his decision, although he had still not made up his mind. He said to himself, 'I'll know what to say when I see him.'

Hitler said, "Well?" and Speer remembered past triumphs and the hopes of more to come, and felt what he had felt before—Hitler taking over, himself giving in.

He had said no yesterday, and Hitler had forgiven him, he could not do it again. He said, "I stand unreservedly behind you, *mein Führer*." Hitler stared hard at him, and Speer felt like a boy at school called before the headmaster. He waited. Hitler held out his hand and his eyes filled with tears and he said, "Then all is well."

Speer tried to profit from the warm mood. He said, "If I stand behind you, then you must again trust me instead of the gauleiters with the implementation of your decree."

Hitler scowled and agreed.

Speer walked out, planning how to pass on Hitler's orders while making sure they were not obeyed. He no longer cared that he was disloyal, his energy was now confined to a single purpose, to save the country. His conscience was easy, his Hitler vow meant nothing, though he had just renewed it. The theatrics were over. He was in bright air outdoors, and his path was clear. The good of the people, nothing else.

Schenkenberg, Southwest Germany, April-May, 1945

Late in April, Peter heard of a slaughterhouse on the outskirts of Munich where an old horse might be bought. Meat was scarce, but fear of the Russians was so intense that the horses were more valuable as transport than as food. He bought the horse and a landau whose leather hood was spotted with green mould. The horse was swaybacked with streaming eyes and tattered mane, and walked with a dejected air. He was well-trained, for at the lightest touch of the reins his head came up and he threw his weight against the traces, managing a few trots before his head fell again and he plodded once more.

Peter drove the carriage home with a sense of achievement. He was now certain that they would get away. Before dawn, on the 20th of April, they were all ready to move once again. Tati looked out shivering on the cold street layered with mist. She was wearing a darned grey wool dress with Klaus' sweater over it, and a scarf against the cold mist. She settled back on the rear seat with a coat round her knees, Clara beside her wearing plaid slacks and a black sweater, the broken leather hood propped up next to her with a board Helmuth had found in the debris of the street.

Peter said, "Bucephalus is a gallant old warrior who will get us to Schenkenberg." He touched the reins to the horse's flanks. His head came up, his ears pricked up, and he took the traces with energy. With the familiar reins lying in his opened hands, listening to the iron-shod hooves clicking the cobbles as they had in his childhood, Peter felt relieved of the war.

In a couple of hours, they were past the ruined buildings and littered streets among green fields, under a blue sky. The world was good and young again on this bright morning, every hillcrest bristled with dark green pines, or a *Schloss,* in every valley a church steeple marked a village buried in trees.

"We'll have to get out and push up every steep hill," he called back through the yellowed isinglass window, but they were asleep.

Many times that morning, they encountered retreating German soldiers in trucks and on foot, not in formation, but in the long straggling line that had been at first caused by fear of strafing, and now was the disorganized dejection of defeat.

"The Americans are just over those hills," one sergeant said up to him as they plodded by. "Be careful or you'll be thrown in a camp. They're taking all the men."

Helmuth woke up as the sun came round from behind them and warmed his left cheek. Ahead of them a long green valley sloped west. Dust was rising from dark dots on the pale road which he thought might be American trucks. Peter turned up the hill to the left, away from the direct route.

"Where is the war?" said Helmuth. For him war was bombers over his head spilling fire down onto him.

Peter looked at him. "Well, it's past those hills there, and back in Munich, and on the Atlantic."

"Is it very big?"

"Very big. Big as the world."

"Is it big as the sky?"

"Yes, sometimes it fills the sky."

"Then it can come and get us." He looked at the sky.

"Yes. But we can hide."

"Are we going to hide now?"

"Yes, we're trying."

"Where?"

"Schenkenberg."

"I want to live there."

The weather stayed fine and they progressed on the ridges through remote hamlets that looked as if there had never been a war, while below in the valleys they saw the ruins of bridges and towns, and Americans in square little open cars escorting long columns of prisoners moving west.

A week after they had left Munich, they were in familiar hills again, not far from Schenkenberg. The Americans were driving their jeeps and trucks around with little fear of organized German resistance.

On the seventh of May, when the rumours of peace were very strong, but hard to believe after so long a war, Peter reined in Bucephalus by a farmhouse high above the village of Schenkenberg. This farmhouse was the last occupied relic of a hamlet which had been here until the 1930s, when the National Socialists had persuaded most of the people to move down into the village below. As he got down from the landau, two old women who had been cleaning out a chicken coop stopped work and stared at him. Two dogs circled the landau, growling.

He kept his arms by his sides to reassure the dogs and the women. One of the women came towards him. The other stood back. Peter said *"Gruss Gott,"* and asked about the Americans, and the old woman replied, "Get off the road, young man. They are arresting all of you."

"But he's wounded," said Clara, "they won't take him."

"They're taking them out of the hospitals, bandages and all, they spare no one, right into prison camp. And there they starve."

Now the other woman came forward and said, "They took old Richard, 71, out plowing in the fields. The old men are dressing as women now, as you see." He bared his muscular arm and they saw that this was a man, dressed in shawl and skirts.

He said, "I must shave every day. Now I understand Samson and Delilah much better."

Peter said, "Now what shall we do?"

Tati had thought about this moment for days, and she was resolute, because she knew that Peter thought it was his duty to surrender as soon as the country itself had surrendered. He believed that the Geneva Convention would protect him, and he would soon be released. But if he tried to hide, he thought, he would be punished for refusing to surrender.

She said, "You will take some food and stay here. You can find a hay rick, or a nice dry camp-spot, put up your groundsheet for the night, take it down in the day so you won't be seen. And we'll go down into the village and find out what is going on."

"We can do better than that," the old man said. "Come with me." As they walked he explained, "Our troops are still going through, so you must be careful—the Amis are just over there." He pointed downhill, to the west. "But there's a hut up ahead your man could use."

Tati said, "Helmuth, you will be our messenger boy. Remember the way back up here and bring the messages back and forth."

The old farmer in skirts led them along a winding trail through the high woods on a ridge. There were many rocks, and once, a long wet bog which they had to traverse. Peter, despite his bad leg, kept beside Clara. Tati trailed them, trying to keep them in sight, while Helmuth, his short legs unable to keep up, had trouble clambering over the rocks.

Tati hung back slightly to keep an eye on him, staying just far enough ahead that he would not think she was protecting him. Helmuth called out, "Don't worry about me, Mum, I'll catch up, because I never fail."

"There," said the farmer, showing them a forester's hut with one small window. He bent down and picked up a roof-slate which had fallen off. They left Peter seated in the sunshine in the courtyard of the farmhouse, smoking and drinking schnapps with the farmer in his dress.

Tati drove the landau down to the main highway leading to Schenkenberg, where she saw several German soldiers marching along to the east. One of them said, "There's SS just up there," indicating Schenkenberg. "If they catch you, they'll make you dig anti-tank ditches."

So Tati hid their real ID papers and put the fake Nazi papers into the top of her bag. The main square of the village lay about a kilometre ahead past a turn imposed by a spur of the Schenkenberg above them. As Bucephalus brought them around the curve, she saw ahead two Americans in jeeps, with machine guns in their laps, smoking cigarettes. They were parked in the shade of the spur of mossy rock, and they looked so peaceful that Clara went up to them without fear, even waving. She called out, "Hey, what's up, Doc?"

One of the soldiers laughed and said, "Where you from?"

"Canada."

"Canada, jeez, you musta taken a wrong turn somewhere."

"Where's your HQ?"

"Hey, not so fast," the soldier said, getting down. "Papers," he said and snapped his fingers. Tati reached into her bag for the papers, saw the Nazi party papers and quickly stuffed them back in, but the soldier had noticed the swastika. He snapped his fingers and said, "Gimme the bag."

He looked at the swastikas, hoisted his machine gun and said, "Tom, we got a live one here," and motioned her to get down from the landau.

They were led to the *Bierstube* surrounded by US Army trucks and jeeps, their radio aerials flying the lightning-bolt pennant of the division. Inside, with his elbows on one of the long oak tables where the villagers and farmers had met to sing and talk and drink for hundreds of years, sat Captain Ernest F. Fiske of Madison, Wisconsin, Town Major, looking over a line of village women all asking him for information, for favours, permits, food, medicine. They believed they were entitled to such generous treatment because they had refused to help the German soldiers who were fighting on according to Hitler's last-ditch orders.

Fiske, a small, courteous man who spoke Wisconsin German, dealt with each one, but could satisfy almost none of their requests because SHAEF's orders about the treatment of civilians were severe.

Fiske had been ordered by Eisenhower's headquarters to prevent anyone from taking food to the prisoners in the US Army camp nearby. He was to issue a proclamation informing the people of this. Anyone disobeying was liable to be shot. He was also told to seize all food supplies in the area and to issue subsistence rations until the SHAEF cards arrived, which would provide less than 1550 calories per day. Fiske, whose grandparents had emigrated from Braunschweig in

1850, had imagined that he was fighting to liberate his cousins and uncles from the Nazis, so he hated these orders.

They came into the *Bierstube* and stood side by side in front of Fiske's desk, Helmuth holding his mother's hand. The corporal said to Fiske, "This one says she's Canadian, but she's got Party ID." Tati glanced at Clara in despair, asking for forgiveness. Fiske sighed and said in English, "You're under arrest, this is an automatic arrest category."

He motioned to a guard by the door. Clara said loudly, "Those party papers are fake. We are in the resistance. Both of us. Here." She searched through her bag, saying to Fiske, "I *am* a Canadian."

"What are you doing here then?" he asked.

"I married Peter Prince Maria von Metternich in September 1939."

"You lived here all during the war?" He looked at her in amazement. Clara nodded, blinking back tears. He said, "Why weren't you interned?"

"I am a German citizen by my marriage."

Fiske sat back with his hands locked in his lap. "You say you're a Canadian, married to Prince von Metternich but travelling on forged Nazi papers because you were both working for the resistance while also working in the German Foreign Ministry. Have I understood you?" He looked grim.

"That's more or less it, yes," said Clara.

"And where is your husband?" Fiske said to Clara.

She looked him in the eye and told a lie like truth, "I don't know exactly."

She produced her ring, her wedding lines, her Canadian passport, her ration books, a letter in its envelope from her father in London, dated October, 1941, and a brittle yellow clipping from the *Times-Loyalist* front-page story of her wedding, dated September 11, 1939.

The yellowed scrap of newsprint, impossible to fake, convinced Fiske. He passed his hand over his eyes. He had been at this table since 8 am without food and it was now 3 in the afternoon. He took a sip of water and held up his hand to detain the soldier. "Wait a minute," he said to the soldier. He looked at Clara. He believed her. He was forbidden to believe her. He had no idea what to do.

Clara glanced at Tati, who was staring with distaste at this small man whom she took for a paperbound bureaucrat. Clara said, "My friend's husband was Klaus Graf von Zollerndorf who planted the bomb at Rastenburg last summer. I'll translate for her."

"*Ich spreche Deutsch.*" He was wary, for he had encountered so many Germans claiming to be in the resistance that he wondered how the Germans had fought at all. He said to Tati, "Where is your husband?"

"He was shot."

"And you both worked for the Foreign Ministry. I'm sorry, I'll have to lock you up regardless."

"But you don't understand our situation. When terror rules the state, then the normal is fictional," Tati exclaimed.

He stared at her puzzled. "What did you say?"

Clara said, "It means everything is reversed. If you are tortured to make you denounce your friends, you must lie. Everything is perverted. It is a citizen's duty to oppose the state. It takes more courage to lie than tell the truth."

Fiske stared at her in confusion, thinking this was wrong, yet perhaps it was how things had been in Germany.

Tati went on, "The Foreign Ministry was our cover. We couldn't have done it if we had been, oh, I don't know, hairdressers, could we?"

"But what did you do?"

"We worked in the resistance, we helped the men do what they did. We organized everything. Clara took refugees to France."

There was a long silence. He looked down at the table. He thought they must be exaggerating. He could not credit them, the regulations forbade him to assume the innocence of the accused. As the phrase occurred to him, he realized that this was the opposite of the tradition he had been taught to uphold. He too was trapped into doing the opposite of what he believed. He apologized and promised to speed things along as fast as he could.

"What about my son?" said Tati. "Do you think he's a danger to the American army too?"

"It is not a question of your danger to us," said Fiske. "I am bound by the rules governing treatment of possible war criminals."

"War criminals," Tati shrieked. "How dare you! We risked our lives to stop that madman. How dare you?"

"You may keep the little boy with you if you wish."

He picked up an orange from his desk, having noticed Helmuth eyeing it. He held out the orange to the boy, who shook his head. Fiske smiled and handed it to Clara, who took it, and said, "Thank you."

They were placed in the police lockup behind the town hall. Fiske promised to feed Bucephalus.

Tati sat on the wooden bench staring at the stone floor. The window was barred in iron, the cell door was of thick oak with a small Judas window, and one grey blanket lay on the wooden bench. She put her head between her hands and stared down and tried to think of nothing.

The door opened, the grey-haired village policeman in a high-collared uniform from the days of the Kaiser, handed in a jug of water and another orange. Helmuth took it from him and offered it to his mother, who opened her arms to him. He allowed her to hug him while he held the orange up to catch the light coming in from the window.

The Chancellery, Berlin, April, 1945

Stepping up from the bunker into the Winter Garden, Hitler was like a man rising from his grave, grey-haired, grey-faced, cheeks sunken, uniform stained and rumpled. He stared at the heaps of broken glass, charred documents blowing around, the ruins of a collapsed wall of the Chancellery which Speer had designed for him, then straightened his sagging shoulders, and walked resolutely down the line of Hitler Youth boy soldiers. Holding his trembling left hand with his right, he asked, "What is your name, where are you stationed, have you killed your Russian yet, where are you from?" As he spoke, they all heard, and ignored, the distant rumble of Russian guns firing into the city. At the end of the line he stepped back and thrust his arm out in the party salute while his left arm began flapping out of control. The boys returned the salute and said in unison, "Happy birthday, *mein Führer*." He thanked them, dismissed them and walked to the entrance to the bunker and went down the long twisting staircase to the bunker 40 feet underground.

In the map room, von Below floated a street map of Berlin onto the table and Hitler stared down at it puzzled by the scale. Once he had embraced all Europe with his spread arms, now he was planning defence for neighbourhoods. 'Has it all been for nothing?' he thought. 'Can it mean nothing? Will nothing of my work last?'

He turned away from the map without a word, which he had never done before. He said, "Has Steiner begun the attack?" When he was told that nothing had happened, because Steiner had no troops and the Luftwaffe's new jets could not get off the ground for lack of fuel, he shouted, "Then it is finished, nothing can be done. I will die in the Berghof fighting." Göbbels said, "Remain here, *mein Führer*. It is still possible to set a world record by our deaths here."

Eva Braun, who had come to join him here in 'the decisive struggle,' looked at him hoping that once again he would bring off a miracle.

Hitler began a tirade against the generals, the Wehrmacht itself, most of his soldiers, the Jews, the Bolsheviks, the English and Churchill. "I never wanted war with them or the Americans. I underestimated the overpowering influence of the Jews upon the British under Churchill. If only fate had sent them a new Pitt instead of that Yid-ridden half-American souse then all would have been well. But now the English will die of hunger or tuberculosis on their damned island."

Bormann brought in the news that Göring, Hitler's earliest ally in the party, had begun to conspire to take over the government, then to begin negotiations for a surrender. Hitler, at first calm, was enraged when Bormann convinced him that this was not a last-ditch effort to salvage something from the wreckage, but a coup d'état against himself. He began a tirade against the German people, cursing them while the staff stood around abashed at the contempt which they had hitherto seen aimed only at the enemies of Germany. "If the British had quit in 1940, we could have dealt with the Bolsheviks, but no, it was not to be. Now the French and the Italians with their pretence at world power will disappear from the scene, their chance to make friends with Islam destroyed. The Bolshevik Jews are behind all this. They condemned us to make war, and we could only choose the most favourable moment to begin. And once in, we could never back down. What we might have done! But life forgives no weakness."

"They have all betrayed you," said Braun. "Poor, poor Adolf."

"Now nothing remains. I am spared nothing—no loyalty, no honour is left, I am spared no treachery or disappointment."

Early in the morning of Sunday, the 29th of April, he said to Eva, "It is finished," and then said he had decided to marry her. "You deserve at least that." She touched his hand and said, "Thank you, dear Adolf."

A gauleiter with the power to conduct weddings had already arrived. Hitler stood with Eva before him and repeated the responses. Then he turned and kissed her. Several of the officers came forward to congratulate him, and to kiss the bride's cheek. She bent over the marriage register and began signing her name, Eva B . . . then stopped, and crossed out the B, and inserted Hitler. She straightened up and smiled. He inclined his head but he could not smile.

In the main dining room they stood around the table, champagne was poured and a toast was offered. Von Below came in and whispered to Hitler, "I gave it to Blondi." Hitler had ordered him to poison his German shepherd dog Blondi with a cyanide capsule to make certain that it was effective. He followed von Below into the room and looked at the stilled head which had never failed to turn towards him in welcome. Hitler watched for a moment, then turned and walked out.

No effective orders could now come out of the bunker, since communications with most of the armed forces had been cut. Paralysis gripped everyone, hesitation, waiting and wondering were in all their minds. Each person thought of his own fate as depending on the decision of the Führer, who had never failed to decide in time. But now, there was no decision. Once he said, "I will leave the decision to the enemy," and Göbbels, watching him thought, 'This from the leader who never allowed the enemy to decide anything, but pounced when they were dithering. How far we have fallen.'

After the last meeting around the map table, when everyone was waiting once again for a final and irrevocable decision from their leader, he said, "This is the end. I can no longer go on. Death alone remains. I will meet it here in the city." And a few minutes later, as they looked at each other wondering what this meant—would he go into the streets with his pistol in his hand to fight beside the *Volkssturm* boys?—he added, "I will meet it on the steps of the Chancellery." But then he changed his mind again, and said to Eva, "It is time."

He and Eva went into the sitting room. Hitler unbuckled his holster and showed her the pistol, questioning her with his eyes. She shook her head, sat in one of the two overstuffed easy chairs, took out her cyanide pill, put it in her mouth, tried to smile at him, said, "*Auf Wiedersehen*," bit it, swallowed water and waited. In a few seconds, she croaked something, then jerked and was still, her eyes wide open.

Hitler put the pill in his mouth, bit it, swallowed it, then unbuckled the Walther P38 pistol which he had carried into Poland in 1939 and never fired. He set his thumb inside the trigger guard. He put the muzzle to his temple and pulled the trigger.

As ordered, they came in after two minutes. Eva was in the easy chair. Hitler lay back with his arms outspread, his head drooling blood and brains, and blood blown all over the wall behind him. The smell of gunpowder stung their noses.

They wrapped the bodies in two rugs, lugged them up the stairs, soaked them in gasoline, and von Below tossed a lighted paper spill on the soaked rugs. They ignited with a soft explosion. Soon the smell of roasting meat spread through the garden.

The German forces fought for a few more days attempting to wrest concessions from the Allies, who agreed to nothing. Then, on May 8 and 9 Germany surrendered unconditionally, and the shooting stopped.

Now in great cities east and west, people began to celebrate their deliverance. In London, the bells tolled and people kissed each other in the streets; in Paris, soldiers and civilians paraded under the Arc de Triomphe; in Halifax, sailors pent too long in sickening ships rioted in the streets; in New York, ticker tape streamed from the windows of skyscrapers onto dancing people. Winston Churchill urged the people of the west to go "Forward, unflinching, unswerving, indomitable, till the whole task is done and the whole world is safe and clean."

PEACE

Prussia, Spring, 1945

The European war had stopped but it was not finished. In prison camps east and west, in the smashed cities of Italy, Austria, Russia, Poland, Czechoslovakia, Latvia, Lithuania, Estonia, Yugoslavia, Hungary, Rumania, Bulgaria, Greece, France, Belgium, Holland, England, Norway, Denmark and Germany, people went on dying. On the walls of the railway stations of Germany, barefoot refugees read graffiti telling them to, 'Enjoy the war, the peace is going to be terrible.'

All around Dr. Wilhelm von Benzdorf, and ahead as far as he could see on the level road away from Königsberg, refugees were trudging along on bleeding feet. A few people beside them sat nodding on wagons drawn by horses, or tractors running on fuel from charcoal burners mounted on trailers. The wind from the Baltic to the northwest bore the usual salty scent of tidal flats, kelp and fish, now and then mingled with the stinging stink of the charcoal burners. Wilhelm was thinking, 'How will we all eat? We're already hungry and we have hundreds of kilometres to go like this. We're like a plague of locusts going over the fields. And there will be no crops for months.' But he refused to allow misery to depress him: he repeated to himself what he would say to any

Russian who stopped him, "I am Chief of Surgery in St. Luke's hospital of Königsberg on my way to Benzdorf to find my aunt Lil, and then to Berlin to see my uncle Count Nikolai Miloslavsky," and here he stopped, thinking that he dare not admit to the Russians that he was related to an emigré nobleman.

The refugees were too tired to talk as they walked, but when they stopped for a rest or to make camp for the night they would exchange news, names, rumours. On the first night, there were thousands of people milling about the field, calling out names in the dark: "Here is Müller, von Lehndorf, Matthias, Lemberg; I am looking for Schickedanz, Hoffnung, Fischer, Baumann, Danziger." Willy came on a blond very determined-looking young man of about 14, calling out, "Doctor, doctor."

Benzdorf went over to the young man who was holding a swaying oil lantern near his mother and his sister. The younger woman lay unconscious with her bandaged head in her mother's lap. The determined young man said, "She was hit in Königsberg. A hospital orderly dressed her wound."

"What's this?" said Benzdorf. He loosened from the cut scalp behind her ear a gold coin stuck to the bandage with dried blood.

"The orderly put it over her wound. He needed something inert, so we gave him this, and he boiled it and put it over," the boy said.

"Not bad," said Benzdorf.

"He also told us not to let any doctor near the front to touch her; they are all butchers. I should find a man with grey hair," the boy said, peering into his face by the lantern.

"Don't worry, I'm a civilian," said Benzdorf, "and my hair is turning grey tonight, I can tell you. Besides, she needs someone right away. I'm amazed this thing is not septic already."

He could see a piece of grey metal inside the skull, around which the brain in its ruptured meninges was bulging. The brain seemed intact except for the rupture in the meninges. "Jesus help me," he said under his breath. He reached in with tweezers cleaned in alcohol, seized the shrapnel and pulled it out of its bed of brains. It came out without doing any new damage. He stitched the meninges, removed a bone fragment missed by the orderly, closed the flap of scalp over the wound, dusted on a little sulfonamide, shaved away more of the hair and sewed up the scalp. Over the stitches, he taped the incision.

"The coin is for you," said the boy, whose name was Gus. They were farmers and horse-traders from Memelland, on the road for two weeks. The horses had bolted while crossing the freezing river and he had had to swim after them. Dragging, swimming, walking he had ferried his family across the cold river, at that point almost a mile wide. Benzdorf handed them some of his bread.

Gus offered him the coin again, but Benzdorf shook his head. "It is her souvenir."

He tied his boots round his wrist and went to sleep. When he awoke next day, the boy was gone with his mother, brother and sister, and a note with the coin was shoved into the boots. *She was awake this morning and smiling. Thank you, I will pray for you the rest of my life. Gustav.*

In another hand below that, Gus' mother had written, *And I too, Anna.*

Every morning, they were up before dawn and walking, with no breakfast unless a scrap of bread. From time to time, horses pulled wagons past him, their heads hanging in the traces, the drivers strapped on top of piled belongings, children tied asleep on top under blankets, the women nodding beside them. In the ditches were dead horses and human beings. He was sorry for each one. To do nothing seemed to be passing a death sentence on an unknown person who was calling for help. He knew that if he tried to descend into the steep ditch he would fall over, and if he fell, he would be too weak to get up. He noted them in his diary. Days went by like that, the same as the days before. The rain and the light changed. The hunger was always the same.

Nights later—he was measuring time by nights—he was standing in the door of a cattle car in the old station at Rauchen holding on to an abandoned baby carriage. He looked down a long way from the door of the cattle car to the stone platform. He clutched the door frame, afraid to jump. People pushed at him to get out of the way saying, "Go on, go on," but he held fast. A young man in civilian clothes pushed past him, jumped down, then turned and held up his arms. "Come on old fellow," he called up with a smile, and Benzdorf let himself fall into the young man's arms.

'Old fellow,' he thought. 'I'm 35 and already my hair is white.' He watched the young man lifting down his loaded baby carriage, wondering, 'Where do you get the food for such energy?'

Seeing the young man gave him a déjà vu of that first moment when he had arrived here in July, 1934 with four student-friends from Tübingen to work the fields of the estate. The fields around the tracks were a golden shimmer of ripe wheat between dark hedgerows stretching to the horizon. His friends had forecast disaster for Germany under Hitler. 'Now here it is,' he thought. Warm sunlight was quivering in the cool damp air that made the trees seem bleached by humidity, the distant landscape misted over. Grey and brown the stubbled fields stretched away. Nowhere could he see a fresh-turned furrow of black earth glistening with the wet promise of spring. All the farmers had fled.

He pushed his baby carriage off the stone pavement of the platform onto the brick apron, then onto the paved road leading west past a broken-down wagon, a dead, half-butchered horse still in the traces, a steel helmet, brass-cornered suitcases, a framed oil painting of a booted horseman resembling Bismarck, propped up on two red buckets. He started pushing towards Benzdorf, his village, smelling the Baltic in the damp air. He pictured Nikolai seated in the big house in Charlottenburg, smoking his pipe. Farther along, the road sprouted potholes full of water. Cattle walked along in the fields beside the road, accompanying the people.

He limped behind his rattling baby carriage because the sharp gravel was piercing holes in his worn-out soles. He sat down and pulled off his shoes and looked at them, then held them up to the sky. He could see light through the soles. A German officer mounted on a horse walked towards him with two mounted privates beside him carrying rifles. Then something odd about the officer made him stop—the officer's collar was hanging open. The man could not be a German officer. He stood still in amazement as the Russian lieutenant leaned down with his collar hanging open, asking directions in German.

"*Wass ist das?*" said the Russian, indicating the baby carriage, and Benzdorf replied, "Medical supplies, I am a doctor." The officer grunted and continued east. Benzdorf stood there amazed to have seen his first Russians, amazed to have escaped, amazed that he had not been afraid. If there were Russians ahead of him, he was surrounded and flight was hopeless. But there was nothing else to do so he kept walking. Towards noon, under a clearing sky showing patches of pale blue between the black-bellied clouds, Benzdorf heard a motor. The Russian lieutenant braked beside him in a jeep. The Russian reached to the seat beside him and handed out a pair of almost-new boots. With a grim look, he said in German, "Here take these." He put the jeep in gear and continued west.

Benzdorf stared as the jeep drove away, then sat down to pull on the boots. When he stood up, he felt better. His feet were warm and dry, he was for the moment steady on his feet. He thought of Gustav's note, 'Thank you, I will pray for you the rest of my life.'

At that moment he was wearing or carrying all the clothes he owned—three shirts, two pairs of pants, greatcoat, and a cap picked up on the road. When he felt cold, he wore a big red silk handkerchief over his mouth and nose. In his knapsack were a pair of his own old shoes and a Wehrmacht camouflage jacket found on the road. He wore the jacket at night because it might attract Russian fire by day.

In the middle of a broad plain, where there was nothing but unploughed fields and tree-walled road framing the sky ahead, he saw a clump of people. A Russian officer was seated at a wooden desk in the middle of the road. An electric lamp with its plug trailing in the mud stood on one corner of the desk. A queue of people on the verge of the road waited to be interrogated. Two soldiers with rifles stood by the desk. A Studebaker truck was stuck nose down in the ditch. Benzdorf wondered, had the Russians come out here to set up this office in the middle of the fields, or was it a whim, after the truck overturned? Both ideas seemed improbable, yet here they were. One of the soldiers strolled over and lifted a corner of the cover on the baby carriage with the muzzle of his rifle. He peered inside.

"Doctor," said Benzdorf.

"Doctor, come," said the young soldier, a stream of snot trickling from his nose by his lips. He pointed down at the truck and now Benzdorf saw that there was a man inside behind the wheel. The soldier indicated to him to go down there, so Benzdorf slid down the bank and tried to release the young soldier, who was semi-conscious and groaned whenever Benzdorf touched him. He asked the two young men to come down. They dragged their groaning companion up the muddy bank, laughing at his groans, then pulled Wilhelm. He kneeled down beside the wounded man and fainted.

Lying on his back, he felt water pouring over his face. One of the Russians was pouring it over him. He turned aside afraid it was ditch-water. He could not prevent himself from licking his lips though he knew that cholera might lurk in the water. With the help of the Russians he sat up and bent over the wounded man.

He had lost blood but his blood pressure was adequate. Palpation showed that there were no breaks. Benzdorf plucked the gravel and dirt and glass out of the flesh with tweezers, swabbed the edges of the wounds with alcohol, then dabbed iodine right into the cuts while the man yelped as his comrades laughed, and the officer at the desk kept checking the refugees, paying no attention to the yelping driver. Benzdorf bound the cuts on the arm and face in clean bandages and the man looked proud of himself, as if the bandages were decorations, although he had caused the accident.

The Russian major at the desk stared at Benzdorf with hatred, thinking of all the arrogant Germans he had met. The Wehrmacht had torched his village in the north of Crimea just before retreating and he had seen the smouldering pile of ashy ruins that had been his street, his house. He still did not know if any of his family had survived. He began to ask the usual questions—name, papers, party affiliation, and so on. He stared with small blue eyes up at Benzdorf while his rough big hand pressed on the papers. He imagined jumping up and smashing his fist into this German pig's face.

"You doctor?"

"Yes."

"You save German soldiers," the major said.

"I save anyone who needs it. You saw I helped him." He pointed to the wounded driver. The major hissed, "There was gun at you."

Benzdorf said, "There was a gun at my back for five years in Germany," and the major thought, 'Yes, it is the same in Russia.'

"You in Party?"

"No."

"Why Party no good?"

Benzdorf tried to think how to express this in simple German, and sign language. He made the sign of the Christian cross, then pointed at himself, and the interpreter nodded, tapping the side of his forehead to indicate Benzdorf was crazy. The major gazed at him, now seeing a different man, the doctor who had saved his driver, a man who answered him with courtesy and courage. He thought, 'And what about me? Aren't I a decent sort of man too, despite the war? I'll give him a chance.'

He opened his desk drawer and drew out a loaf of fresh black bread from the six he had confiscated from some Poles that morning. He felt warm good feelings towards himself as he handed the bread to Benzdorf with a screwed-on smile and said, "Go."

Benzdorf said "*Danke sehr*" and began to chew fresh bread as he walked.

He felt happy. He began to hum a hymn. He had escaped again, the sky was clearing to hazy blue, the birds were singing, he had cleaned out a wound and saved a life, he had made a Russian smile, his mouth was full of bread and he still had a chance to get to Aunt Lil in Benzdorf, then Uncle Nikolai in Berlin. Despite the bread, which he tried to conserve by eating half a mouthful at a time, he was so tired he could only push his baby carriage by leaning forward on it and half-resting his weight on the edge, which put it in constant danger of toppling backwards.

Later that day he saw an old woman pushing a wheelbarrow. A Russian truck came streaming by and the woman landed in the ditch where she lay still. A thick halo of grey rose from her. Benzdorf blinked, wondering if he was seeing her soul leave her body, but the halo was lice, knocked loose when she fell. He helped her to reassemble the wheel/axle part of the barrow and a galvanized steel tub which had been on it, then they gathered most of the belongings, and dragged the tub along behind, with the wheel tied on top like a little rubber crown.

As Benzdorf walked beside her—neither of them having said a word, they just started walking together—he remembered a story his mother had read to him entitled "The Girl With the Three Walnuts." A young girl walking in the woods meets an old woman hobbling on bleeding feet. The girl tears up her shirt and binds the old woman's feet. Then the old woman gives her three magic walnuts, one containing a ballgown made of moonlight, one a ballet dress made of starlight and one a wedding dress made of sunlight. This was one of the stories in his youth which had made him think that it would be nice to be a doctor who could cure people by tearing up a shirt or piece of gauze. He had called this, when he was young, "gauze magic."

Benzdorf asked to see the old woman's feet. They were bleeding where her overgrown nails had cut into the flesh of the toes. He trimmed her nails with surgical scissors, bound her feet with gauze, and she was able to walk without limping.

They saw a dead woman with her skirt up, lying beside the road. A raven stood on her chest, pecking her face. He remembered houses in Cranz where the bloody mattresses told the story of what had happened to the women and girls of every age. He repeated to himself the names of the villages as he walked: Rauschen. Pobethen. Craam. St. Lorenz. Watsum. Cranz. To him they were an outcry to heaven, and he noted each in his diary.

They marched for another day, sometimes almost alone, sometimes part of a long wavering line that stretched from the horizon ahead to the horizon behind. The wind came cold on their backs from the sea. Russian soldiers marched by singing as they went. Sometimes, seeing Russians ahead, he hid, but sometimes there was nowhere to hide, and they let him pass.

He got to the village of Benzdorf where his aunt lived. About a mile from the Schloss, he saw lying scattered around the street dead bodies. One, two, three, five, six, ten, a dozen. He saw more every time he looked and tried to count. Two old men were standing beside one of the bodies trying to pull it along by the arms. He asked them, "What has happened here?"

"Russians."

There were children, women, old men, all lying around. "But why did they do this? Did they go to the Schloss? Have you seen my Aunt Lil?"

One of the old men pointed to a copse of birches near the next house. He ran over and saw lying there the body of a pastor, his throat cut and the blood turning his shirt black, disappearing down into his black suit. He ran back and said to the second man, "It is Pastor Fischer, not the Countess. My Aunt Lil, Countess von Benzdorf, you know her. I remember you, Jürgen. You were a beater for my father before the war, the other war."

"Yes sir."

"Well, where is she?"

"Sir, they took her."

"Who took her, where?"

"Yesterday, at evensong, sir, Mongols. That way."

Benzdorf set off along the road to Ganzau. As he was entering the village, hoping to find shelter for the night, a young Russian soldier called him over to the stoop of a house where a fire was burning in an oil drum. Two more soldiers stood watching as the young soldier searched Benzdorf and then inspected his papers. The soldier looked at the papers and photos of Benzdorf's family. He resolved to say he was from the west, so they would let him go home.

"Where home?"

"Düsseldorf." He smiled as he said it because he could see ahead the spire of his home church above the trees. He was certain the soldier had no idea where Düsseldorf was.

"Why laugh?"

"Düsseldorf kaputt."

"Gitler kaputt."

The soldier, still holding on to Benzdorf's papers, opened the notebook-diary which Benzdorf had been keeping for over two years.

"What is?"

"My diary."

The soldier thrust it at him. "Read." Benzdorf read aloud in his school-book Russian. The night before he had described the scene at Watsum ending with this passage: "The little Mongol soldiers run around like monkeys almost with their hands on the ground. They have no sense of consequence. They think for the moment. To get an electric wire into the house so they could play a radio they had looted, they shot out the glass of a window, then they were cold so they chopped up furniture for the stove, although there was firewood behind the house. Then they had nowhere to sit, so we had to bring them chairs from the next house. They were drinking vodka and singing, not hearing the radio at all. I decided it is best for me to treat them as if I were an animal trainer in a zoo." The soldier, who himself looked like a Mongol, roared with laughter at the description of his fellow soldiers running around like monkeys, and then said, "Tolstoy kaputt," and threw the diary in the burning drum.

They locked Benzdorf in a freezing cold room in a house with windows barred by wooden slats. As he went, he glanced up at the lintel over the door, and there was the inscription chalked there by Catholic boys making the traditional rounds of hymn-singing at Christmas. The inscription read "1C9M4B5," meaning 1945, with the letters CMB interpolated. These stood for Caspar, Melchior and Balthazar, the three Magi coming to Bethlehem with gifts for the infant Jesus. He sat down with his back against the wall hoping that Catholic magic would work for a Lutheran.

In the evening, he watched through a crack in the boards as a Russian soldier shouted, "*Frau komm*," and dragged a screaming young girl by her long blond hair from the house across the street, flung her on the sandy street, ripped up her smock dress, undid his trousers, and raped her as she screamed and struggled. Her hair lay spread in a pool of dirty water. The Russian boy guarding Benzdorf licked his lips, looked around to see if the coast were clear, and grabbed the girl as she crawled away on her hands and knees. Benzdorf yelled out, "*Nein nein*," and the girl screamed again.

He lay curled up on the floor with the silk handkerchief over his face to conserve heat. He vowed to replace the burnt diary with a diary he would write in his head and memorize by repeating it aloud every day. The first entry was the rape. The girl's hair was in the mud. The animal soldier was on top. She was screaming.

A few nights later, May 9, all the Russians were drunk, celebrating the end of the war. All the prisoners were released to wander round the village, given extra food and even vodka. The Russians set fire to a house in the afternoon, and roasted several pigs in the embers, which the prisoners were invited to share. As this was going on, Wilhelm sneaked away in the dark and was many kilometres west the next morning, when the prisoners were counted. The Russians did not bother searching for him—they arrested the first healthy male they came to and imprisoned him in Wilhelm's place.

Aurich, Rheinberg, June, 1945

Alison de Pencier's letter made Jack Giovanelli feel hope. He wrote her an enthusiastic letter, and she replied quickly, which made him dream of home, and her, and happiness.

He was hoping to be demobilized since he thought he was no longer needed, but his commanding officer Colonel Curran said, "You still have a job to do, young feller me lad."

"What is it, sir?" Jack stood at attention before the colonel's desk.

"At ease, Giovanelli. We need you to interrogate a couple of German prisoners."

Jack tucked his cap under his arm and stood at ease. "Sir, I don't speak German."

"You'll have translators. You're going to observe one of our experts interview General Blaskowitz."

Jack was about to protest when the colonel held up his hand as he gazed down at the paper on his desk and said, "Now don't say it, there's a good fellow. You've got a good record so far, and this is important. We can't let the criminals go home as if nothing had happened, can we? And we don't want to punish any poor innocent saps who were just helpless conscripts, do we?"

"No sir."

"This is more or less the nub of the whole show, isn't it?"

"Sir?"

"The war, Giovanelli. To get rid of the bad 'uns."

"Yes sir."

"Right then."

The colonel sympathized with this young fellow, for he wanted to get back to his wife and children as soon as possible. He dreamed of going sailing with his son on Lake Winnipeg, catching a fish, eating dinner with his family on the verandah on a warm summer evening, so his tone was tired when he began again, "There's a little place in north Germany called Aurich, where we have a prison camp. And in the camp is a Kraut general called Blaskowitz who is accused of some rather nasty bits and pieces, sending some Jewish children away to camps in Poland and a massacre at a place called Oradour. Now, you were in the south of France for months, and we want you to go with our interrogation team, headed by Colonel Bernie Hallett. He'll be your CO on that part of the trip, then you'll have a jeep and driver for the next leg."

"Bernie Hallett? Colonel of the Ontario Scottish?"

"Do you know him?"

"Yes sir. Good man. He was my counsellor at Camp Wanagami."

"Just watch Hallett—he fought against Blaskowitz's boys in Holland, and he has had some experience doing this work—he's a historian, teaches European history at Queen's. Hallett will do all the questioning. You're there to judge if Blaskowitz makes sense according to what you saw in Lyon. You'll be flown over in a Dakota tomorrow, and be met at the airdrome by someone from Crerar's HQ. Here are your orders." He handed Jack a single sheet of paper with the regiment's parachute crest embossed on it, in an envelope.

"They've got very comfortable digs there and the food is very good, I hear. Just a couple of days at Aurich, and then down to interrogate another type in a place called Rheinberg, where the Yanks have a big camp. Commander is Captain Israel Beins. Here's a letter to him from the Berlin Document Centre, people who are researching for the Nuremberg war crimes trials. Now, this chap at Rheinberg is named Overmanns, but we don't know if he's the right one. The one we're after used to be stationed at Lyon where some of these deportations started. But it's a common enough name, so he might not be the right man. That's why you have to go—because the one we are after is the one you saw."

"But what's the evidence that the criminal is the one in Rheinberg?"

"Well, Blaskowitz's chief of staff told us the men from the unit that Overmanns was in, when they were stationed at Lyon, retreated up the Rhone and ended up defending Rheinberg, so we told the Yanks, and they said yes, they had members of that unit there. Overmanns is automatic arrest category, but we don't think the Yanks have been very swift about identifying these types."

"But why me? I spent about six hours in Lyon."

"According to your after-action report, you were accosted in Lyon by a one-legged poof in mufti who tried to pick you up for some fun and games. Right so far?"

"Except he wasn't one-legged, he had a limp."

The colonel made a correction on the paper before him.

"What is he supposed to have done?" Jack asked.

"He rounded up some FFI and had them shot. Standard procedure, we're doing it right now to the Werewolves in Germany, but the French want him, and the Yanks don't want to let him go before he's interrogated in case the French just hang him on general principles. And that's where you come in. You have to decide if the man you find there is the same one you saw in the railway station in Lyon. Then comes the big one, this woman Tatiana von Zollerndorf who claims she is the widow of the man who placed the bomb in Hitler's bunker. She's being held by the Yanks in some place called Schenkenberg south of Stuttgart. She claims she picked up some fuses from one of our johnnies in Annecy in '44. According to our records, that must have been you, so you can tell if she is the one you met."

"Yes sir, I did a drop in Annecy in '44. I remember her, very beautiful."

"Yes, well, that's as may be. Beautiful or no, she was rather high up in Ribbentrop's unsavoury crew. And the Yanks figure she's telling them a fairy story. Then you're home again."

"And now we get to the good part—you're back here, and I hand you a medical certificate stating that you're one of the walking wounded. A nice little blighty in the leg, will that do? Now let's see you limp out of here with a smile on your face and faith in your colonel's good intentions."

Jack was smiling. "I have had fun serving under you, sir, and I admire the way you have handled us all, it has been splendid. Now I know that sounds like a speech straight from Chums, but it's more from the heart."

He snapped up a brilliant salute, and exaggerated his limp as he went out. He turned at the door and said, "Howzat, Colonel?" and limped on out.

"You don't salute without a cap, Giovanelli," the colonel said and laughed.

On his first evening in Aurich in north Germany, Jack met Bernie Hallett in the mess, in the dining room of an ornate red-brick resort hotel on the edge of the city, one of the few intact buildings in the town.

"Hello, sir," said Jack standing by the colonel, who was seated alone at a big round table. German prisoners in white mess jackets were serving them dinner, while a quartet of two violins, cello and viola were playing Schubert's *Death and the Maiden*. Hallett glanced up and, instead of the happy smile of recognition that Jack had anticipated, said nothing.

Jack said, "Very appropriate music, don't you think, sir?"

Hallett looked around vaguely.

"May I sit down?"

Hallett shrugged.

Jack sat beside him, holding a stein of beer he had brought from the bar. He pulled out a package of cigarettes. A waiter-prisoner came forward, snapped open a Zippo lighter for him. Jack lit up and nodded at the prisoner. "So," said Jack, looking around, "how are you, sir?"

"Terrible."

"Why, what's the matter?"

Bernie said nothing.

"I heard that Ed Burns was shot."

"Shot and killed. By a sniper. In some godforsaken little town. Then we destroyed the whole place. Ed was dead anyway."

"I was sorry to hear that. I know you were close."

"We were like left and right. He told me he took you to join up."

"It seems so long ago. I remember we took the train to Camp Borden, and he got me into the paratroops."

Bernie sighed and took out his cigarette case, and the waiter-prisoner leapt forward again, lighter at the ready. Bernie said, "There's a line of his poetry I can't get out of my head. *This empty flesh, where once I lived in vain.*"

Jack completed it for him, *"And loves gone by that can not come again."*

Bernie stared out the window at the wreck-scape.

The next morning Bernie took him to the interrogation room. There, seated in the lobby at a long table flanked by papers and cardboard cartons of files, sat two military lawyers, plus Blaskowitz, an interpreter, stenographer and one SHAEF-approved interrogator.

The interrogator, a major, began the questioning. "Colonel General Johannes Blaskowitz, this is an investigation preliminary to deciding whether or not we should charge you at Nuremberg with war crimes committed by troops under your command in Poland in 1939 and in France in 1944. You are required to answer all our questions to the best of your ability, and evidence given here will be used to decide the question of prosecution, and the use of the evidence here acquired in the event that procedures against you are proceeded with."

He was reading in English from a cyclostyled sheet, on which he made a note now to edit the meaningless language. The translator asked for clarification. The interrogator made a few more notes and improvised another version of the final sentence, which was translated.

The interrogator said, "Do you understand?"

"I understand," said Blaskowitz. His broad face was rigid and he sat erect.

"You will now make an opening statement outlining your responsibilities in a general way, first in Poland."

"I will begin by saying that this camp is a disgrace and a complete contravention of the Geneva Convention, which never occurred under my command. Any officer under my command maintaining a prison camp in this condition would have been relieved of his command and court-martialled. The Markgraf von Baden has already written to *The Times* about the dreadful conditions here, and I have a copy."

He handed the copy across the desk to the major, who pushed it aside.

The major said to the stenographer, "Strike all that. Be it noted that the prisoner, upon being asked for a general outline of his duties in Poland, indulged in a tirade against his imprisonment."

He offered Blaskowitz an icy smile, eyes intent, teeth bared. "And now will you cooperate?"

Blaskowitz sighed. He sketched in what he had been ordered to do in Poland in September, 1939—to guard Tenth Army's northern flank, and if possible, capture Warsaw. "As for crimes, yes, these were committed by the SS, not my troops, and I complained several times in written memoranda up the line directed to the Chief of the General Staff."

"You did?" said the interrogator in surprise. "Where are the memoranda?"

"They should be in the archive of the German General Staff."

"And what other confirmation do you have?"

"What do you mean?"

"Did you keep copies?"

"Not among my personal effects, no, of course not."

"This is a matter of life and death for you, may I remind you."

"My honour is not at stake."

"What does that mean?"

"I acted as a German officer should at all times."

"What does that mean?"

"I obeyed the Geneva Convention, which you are not doing, so you are all hypocrites here, questioning me about crimes I have not committed, while committing crimes yourselves."

"You say we are accusing you, but no one has accused you of anything, General. I think though this shows you have a guilty conscience."

"I did not say accused, it was mistranslated, I said 'questioning.'"

The interrogator said to the stenographer, "The prisoner showed a guilty, quarrelsome and uncooperative demeanor from the very beginning of the interview." The translator said, "Should I translate, sir?"

"By all means," said the major, with a hating smile at Blaskowitz.

Blaskowitz listened and made no comment.

The major started again. "Troops of *Das Reich* division under your command burned 600 French civilians alive in a church in Oradour-sur-Glan in June, 1944."

"They were not under my command."

"What do you mean? You were commander of all German forces in the South of France at the time."

"That division was under the direct control of the Führer at the time."

"We have captured the original of an order you sent to the commander of that division on June 1944, in which you order him . . . where is it?"

He adjusted his spectacles and began to read from the letter in English translation. "You will henceforth obey all the rules of war and the Armistice convention signed in June 1940 with regard to the civilian population. You will not discipline the general population in any way. You will inform this HQ of all guerilla activities, so that they may be dealt with by troops under my command."

"Yes, exactly, you see," said Blaskowitz.

"See what?"

"They were not under my command. That's why I said 'henceforth.'"

"Let me remind you, this is an order given by you to them. Therefore you were in command, therefore you are responsible. You ordered that massacre."

"I did not, that is incorrect. I tried to stop that sort of thing going on. I had no right to give that order, I was risking a discipline from the Führer, which is a very serious matter. I was removed from my command in Poland for just this sort of thing. I was risking being sent home a second time in disgrace."

"Why send an order you did not expect to be obeyed?"

"To save their lives."

"Whose lives?" the interrogator shouted. "The men of *Das Reich*? Yes. You wanted them to get to the front and not dilly-dally around with the Maquis when they were needed in Normandy. Isn't that correct?"

"Yes, that is correct. But it is not why I sent the order."

"Aha," he shouted, "he admits it was an order. Write that down."

"I had no right to send it, it was against orders to send it, but there was a slim chance it would be obeyed, because even in the SS there are men with honour, or at least, so I thought in 1944."

With this sentence, Blaskowitz lowered his voice and looked down.

"You ask us to believe that a German general sent an order that was against a Hitler order, an order which he did not expect to be obeyed?"

"It is so. If it were obeyed, it would save the people in the villages who were not the enemy, at least not openly. Only the Maquis were the enemy."

"A very clever answer, General."

Blaskowitz stared coldly at him, then said, "It is the truth." For a moment the interrogator leaned forward returning the stare and then dropped his eyes to the paper. He said, "We will continue after lunch."

After lunch, the general was questioned about the rounding up of some FFI in Lyon in the month that Jack had been there.

"They were shot on your orders," the interrogator said.

"Not mine," said Blaskowitz. "All over France, the Führer's orders were the same. Guerilla warfare is to be punished by death. It is the same in every army of every occupying force. *Francs tireurs* are liable to be shot even if they surrender, and the FFI were *francs tireurs*. They say so themselves. In any case, I pardoned six of them in Lyon whose case seemed doubtful."

Jack glanced at the interrogator for permission, and receiving a nod in reply, said, "How many of the FFI were arrested in Lyon?"

"I think it was six," said Blaskowitz.

"So all were pardoned?"

"Yes."

"Who was the arresting officer?"

"I don't remember."

"Was his name Overmanns? Henke Overmanns?"

"I can't recall. Perhaps it was."

"Was it he who ordered them shot in the first place?"

"I don't know. Somebody did. Of course, it was all in obedience to the orders from Rastenburg. Disobedience to such orders is punishable by death in the Wehrmacht, so Overmanns or whoever would have been shot."

"So it was his life or theirs?"

Blaskowitz said, "You have understood."

The interrogator now asked Bernie Hallett to take over. "A parachute regiment under your command was defending the town of Fassoythe in March, 1945. Is that correct?"

"I believe so, yes, the 106th, I believe."

"Their commanding officer surrendered the town after an attack by the Ontario Scottish regiment. The surrender took place at about nine Ack-Emma of March 29th, at which time some one hundred men were taken into captivity by the regiment. One of our battalion commanding officers, Edward Burns, accepted the surrender, and then was shot by a sniper." He stopped. Blaskowitz said nothing. Bernie said, "This was against the rules of war, it was against the Geneva Convention for members of a unit which had surrendered to continue to fire on our men. It was a trap set by one of your men."

"Was this sniper in uniform?"

Bernie had dreaded this question. He remained silent. He had vowed a just vengeance but if he lied to get it, it would not be just.

"My point is that one of your men shot one of our men after the surrender."

"I notice that you have not answered the question. If the man was in civilian clothes, he was not one of my men."

"Perhaps he changed his clothes." Bernie was very uncomfortable because he did not know how the German had been dressed.

The general shook his head and smiled. "How ridiculous. Soldiers do not carry mufti into battle, as I am sure you are aware, Colonel Hallett."

"Regardless of his dress, he could have been ordered by you or one of your HQ commanders to keep firing after the surrender."

"That is outrageous. I never issued such an order in my life, nor would I."

The British captain looked at Bernie who was silent, staring down at the table, unable to look at Blaskowitz. "Colonel?" said the captain.

"That's all, I guess," said Bernie. There was no vengeance here. He had the power to kill Blaskowitz by the report he would write, but he was not sure what to say. Hanging Blaskowitz would not bring Ed back.

That night in the mess, Jack asked Bernie why he had stopped questioning Blaskowitz. "If you want to know," said Bernie, "I didn't trust myself." Jack was left wondering if this meant he might take out his sidearm and shoot the German, or that he feared he might weep.

Bernie took a big swallow of beer, and muttered, "Besides, it was pointless."

On his way to Rheinberg to interview Overmanns, Jack rode with Sergeant Duke Campbell by jeep along the shattered roads of northwest Germany, past broken dykes, flooded fields, skeletons of burned houses, animals lying in the fields, legs up. Every Rhine bridge for 100 miles was destroyed, their roadways leading straight down into the mined water.

They saw a team of eight women harnessed like horses pulling a manure wagon on which a woman was standing, hurling liquid manure onto the field with a shovel. The horse-women were bent forward, faces towards the ground, but when they drew near, he saw their agonized looks and the sweat drooling down their cheeks. Small children were weeding vegetables in gardens by ruined houses, where more women were clearing away bricks. There were no men anywhere.

He had worked cutting hay one summer with Jimmy Caughey at the farm at Stone Cottage, so he felt the hot hay-seeds prickling in their clothes, the sweat trickling down the inside of shirts, the harsh tug on the backbone as fork-tines slammed into the bedded mass of timothy in the blazing hot hay-mow, and he wanted to call out to the women. He waved, but no one acknowledged him.

They drove south on the east bank of the Rhine searching for the town of Wesel where there was supposed to be a pontoon bridge leading to the west bank. They stopped for a few minutes to read the map, searching for the spires of Wesel. Ahead, at the far end of a shaky pontoon bridge, stretched a dump where the city ought to be. As they drew nearer they realized that the dump was Wesel. Nothing was standing—not a chimney, not a steeple, not a roof, no wall. There was nothing recognizable as a human construction. There was not a human being in sight—no one scavenging bricks or furniture as there had been in all the other towns. Dust and papers blew over the shallower parts that might have once been streets. They drove along the trail bulldozed through the mess, and emerged on the far side in silence, and drove out into the countryside again.

"Sergeant, there's something dead in this vehicle," Jack said as they drove on a road two metres above the surrounding countryside, which for generations had been sinking into the collapsing coal tunnels far below.

"Yes sir, I smell it too." They stopped the jeep and inspected all around and could find nothing. Jack stepped away from the vehicle and sniffed the air. "It's coming from up there," he said, pointing ahead.

The smell grew more intense as they approached the barbed wire fences and guard towers of Camp Rheinberg. When they turned off the engine, they heard a woman's amplified voice singing "Who's Sorry Now?" through loudspeakers fixed to the roofs of the guard towers. To each side of the entry road, the towers and barbed wire stretched away in a double row 12 feet high enclosing a field streaked with trenches, dotted with mounds and humps. The smell was a stink like rotten meat that made it hard to breathe. A crude sign hanging on the barbed wire by the gate was lettered PWTE A1 Rheinberg.

"Welcome to the perfume factory," said Sergeant Mullins, over the music, as he noticed them waving their hands in front of their faces. He held towards them an open pack of Camels. They all lit up.

Jack asked for Captain Beins, and was told to wait while the sergeant took their ID into the guard tent. They sat in the jeep smoking and looking around. Within the perimeter were the cages behind the inner fences of barbed wire strung on tall poles. Occasionally one of the mounds stirred and a man crawled out. Here and there, skeletal bearded men in rags, with darkened eyes, leaned against each other. "Jesus, sir would you look at that," Campbell whispered, pointing his cigarette. On the other side of the gate about 50 feet away corpses were stacked like kindling, six feet high, six feet wide, maybe 20 feet long, next to a Quonset hut inside the wire. Six prisoners in filthy uniforms walked out of one of the cages, with a German NCO walking ahead. They came to the pile of corpses by the steel hut and began to heave them up onto a truck, with a sloppy sound. A dark fluid began to ooze out from the bottom of the pile and drip over the tailgate of the truck. Jack turned away and vomited.

"The captain will see you now," said the sergeant coming back. He looked at Jack with a smile. "It happens the first day here, but you get used to it," said the sergeant. "Anyway, he's over there in that farm-house, see, past the trees?" He pointed to a copse of stick-like trees next to a two-storey farmhouse half a mile down the road.

"HQ is upwind today," said the sergeant. "You'll be all right."

They drove away into sweeter air up a slight rise to the farmhouse. Jack turned and saw that the camp extended far into the glare of the sun to the south, and at least a mile to the west. Even here, half a mile from the camp's north edge, he could hear dance band music, now playing "Sentimental Journey."

In the big kitchen of the farmhouse where files were piled in a stone sink beside a plywood desk stood Israel Beins, a dark-haired young lieutenant with a cold expression, tamping his pipe. Pink wallpaper hanging in rags from the far wall framed him. As he watched the Canadian jeep approach up the road, Beins remembered Anne-Elisabeth in Reims, two months before. He had thought she was French, but she woke up in his arms one morning and whispered, "*Ich liebe dich.*" He went rigid in her arms, thinking, 'I'm sleeping with the enemy,' pulled on his clothes and left still dressing, as she ran after him to the door.

He burned her letters, he hung up on her phone calls, cursing himself for sleeping with a Kraut. Her cousin Raymond explained that she was an Alsatian, that the province had been annexed by the Germans during the war, all citizens had to speak German, she was neither a spy, nor a Nazi, not even a German, but a decent French girl.

Beins thought he had had a narrow escape until his superior officer Colonel Philip Lauben came into his office one day, closed the door, stood before him with a sheaf of papers in his hand, and said, "I see we have been having some fun with the numbers, Izzy?"

Beins admitted he had been stealing, and was about to say it had been only for Anne-Elisabeth and her family, who were starving, then realized it would make no difference to Lauben. He said, "Everyone's doing it, why pick on me?"

Lauben cut him off and said, "Look, you speak German. We're having trouble getting people to take over the prisoner-of-war camps, so you can have a court martial, or else command of a Prisoner of War Temporary Enclosure in Germany, with no loss of pay."

"What's the matter with the camps?"

"You'll find out when you get there. Court martial or camp?"

Beins, six weeks into the camp now, was standing in his office wondering if he should take the jeep to Strasbourg and make it up with Anne-Elisabeth, when two strangers walked in.

"Who sent you, what do you want?" Beins said.

Jack said, "We've been sent to interview a prisoner we think you have here. Named Overmanns. If he's the one we want, you're to release him to our custody. For war crimes trial." He showed the handcuffs he had been given at Aurich, the letter to Beins from the Berlin Document Centre and the orders.

"Huh," said Beins, lighting a wooden match with a flick of his fingernail. He puffed at his pipe, sucking the sulphurous flame deep into the bowl and puffing out. Then he sat down on an inflatable rubber ring cushion he used for his piles, and said, "Siddown."

He pushed an ashtray and a pack of Old Golds across the desk and caught a splinter of plywood under his fingernail. He said "Shit, this is the worst, meanest most fucked-up place on the face of the suffering globe." He put down his pipe and sighed. "You'll have to stay the night in an old monastery we've fixed up a bit for visiting heroes like you." He laughed. "No women allowed. Do you need to draw rations?"

"Well, yes, I was told I might mess here."

"You Brits?"

"Canadians."

"You sound like Brits."

The phone rang. Beins ignored it. "What about gas?"

"Yes, we used a full tank and five five-gallon jerry cans to get here.'"

"All right, now, what do you want to see this guy for, whaddya *know* about this murderer?" By which Jack understood with a thrill of fear, he meant Overmanns.

"His name is Henke Overmanns, Lieutenant. He's wanted on suspicion of shooting some French FFI prisoners in Lyon last August."

"Well, you know, we don't know who the hell we've got in here."

"Don't you have a list of names?"

"We started out with around 120,000 of these bastards, but there's only 100,000 left. You want us to write out all their names?" Beins was offended. "They'll be lucky to get out of here alive."

"Why don't you feed them?"

"Orders from SHAEF. No food for prisoners, or at least damn little. Anyway, if you want to walk in there and start asking around, feel free."

"Couldn't you just put an announcement on the PA?"

"Now that's zooty. Ask this war criminal to turn himself in."

"We don't have to say why he's wanted. Just order him to report. Germans are obedient."

Beins stared at him, wondering if this guy admired Germans for their discipline.

"After all," said Jack, "he hasn't got much to lose, has he?"

At this reminder of the conditions in the camp, Beins grew nervous. He hated the camp and he approved of it. He called out, "Myers." The sergeant came to the door.

"Get on the PA and order Henke Overmanns to report to the gate."

Overmanns was brought in with an interpreter, a German trusty. Overmanns was gaunt, leaning on the interpreter, his blond beard matted with filth and grey with lice, like his thin hair. He sat on the floor against the wall. He said over and over, "*Wasser, Wasser*," pointing to his mouth, and "*Brot, bitte.*"

Beins came into the room saying, "Not here, Jesus, can't you see, he's covered with lice."

Jack said, "Get him some DDT, you can get typhus from this."

"Out," said Beins, pointing out the door.

The interpreter lifted Overmanns from the floor and hauled him outside to a tree, where he sat down with his back against the trunk. Overmanns kept saying, "*Wasser, Wasser*," pointing to his mouth and, "*Brot, Brot, bitte.*"

The German interpreter, who was fed enough so he could do his job, looked at Jack. He went into the house and asked the sergeant for water. The sergeant brought out a glass of water and a loaf of bread. He walked over to Overmanns and poured the water into the prisoner's lap. He dropped the bread on the ground beside him, stepped on it, turned his heel in it and stalked off.

Jack jumped up, grabbed the sergeant's forearm, twisted his hand up behind his shoulder blade making him scream, and growled, "Get the water."

The sergeant, hunching his shoulders, ran into the house where he collided with Beins coming out. Beins looked at Jack's grim face and went back inside. The sergeant got more bread and another glass of water and handed it to Jack, who now realized that he had his hand on his sidearm. He grunted, "Thanks," and went back to the interpreter, who held the glass to Overmanns' lips.

Overmanns was picking bread out of the ground and stuffing it into his mouth. He grabbed the new bread and ate it like a dog, then sucked on the water glass and said, "*Mehr, mehr.*"

Jack, sitting on a milking-stool in the grass, drew out his interrogation form on a clipboard and began the questions, What is your name, when were you born, where were you born, mother's maiden name, father's name and occupation, your schooling, your unit, rank, serial number.

Overmanns had no *Soldbuch* and no ID disc. These had been confiscated from the prisoners when they had entered the camp, so Jack put down only what he was told. Then he began the serious questioning.

"Were you stationed in Lyon in May, 1944?"

He asked the question in French, and Overmanns replied for himself, in French. From then on the interview was all in French.

"Yes," said Overmanns. Jack went on to establish that Overmanns had been stationed in Lyon in May, 1944. He then began the questions which he had memorized at Aurich.

"In the Gare de Perrache in Lyon, May 19, 1944, you tried to pick me up, you offered me a lift, you said it was dangerous for me to be there with the *Milice* all round, they were looking for young men like me for forced labour."

Overmanns stared at him. "Perhaps it is so, I don't remember you." A nostalgic look came over his gaunt bearded face. "I saw so many people in that station. I was there a year or more."

"Did you order your men to shoot some French prisoners?"

"No," said Overmanns with puzzled shock. "I ordered nobody to be shot."

"But you were in command of the guard troops in the centre of the city round the station, weren't you?"

"Yes."

"And the relatives of the dead men said that those were the troops that shot their husbands and brothers and son, six of them in one day, July 28, 1944. Remember?"

"I think I heard about that, but I did not do it. I was gone by then."

"Aha, so you knew it happened?"

"I heard of it. I did not know of it except by rumour, I was sent north to Colmar. Then later, Rheinberg. Is this place Rheinberg?"

"How did you hear about it?"

"One of the men who had been in Lyon told me, here—is it Rheinberg? They told us it was Büderich."

Now Jack realized Beins had been listening, for he called out from the doorway, "He was at Büderich first."

"Then how did I get here?" Overmanns asked.

"You were marched," Beins called out.

"I don't remember that at all."

After a few minutes, Jack thought that Overmanns was telling the truth—he knew nothing of the shooting of the FFI, except the rumour that had reached him later. One reason to believe him was that Overmanns was so sick and weak that he could not maintain a lie. Another was that his story hung together. Another was Jack's intuition.

Jack said, "Interview's over," thinking he would stay overnight and come back in the morning, to see if Overmanns told the same story.

He got up. Overmanns was listless on the ground, asking for more bread and more water. Jack resisted the impulse to bend down and help him up. The interpreter glanced at Jack as if for permission, then bent down and dragged Overmanns to his feet. The sergeant handed him a cardboard tube filled with DDT powder, and he began to dust Overmanns.

Overmanns was half-standing, leaning against the tree with the interpreter beside him, as Jack turned his back and walked toward his jeep.

Jack had a powerful déjà vu—he was leaving the station at Lyon, Overmanns behind him with a pistol, aiming at him, the shot was coming at any moment, he would be hit in the back, he had to run, at last he reached the streetcar, grabbed the handle, swung himself up. At the moment he put his hand on the door-handle of the jeep, he knew that Overmanns had not killed the prisoners. If he were a killer, he would have shot Jack in the street.

He turned away from the jeep with his head down and walked back to Overmanns still with his head down. He said, "Now listen to this— I'm going to believe you, but maybe nobody else will. I'm going to report that there must be two guys called Overmanns and you are not the man I saw in Lyon. Because that's what they're wondering, understand? Just say you were never in Lyon. You were not there, understand? You're off the hook. You won't be charged."

Overmanns looked puzzled. Jack added, "You're safe, you can stay here."

"Sir," said the translator, "if he stays here he dies."

Jack turned and walked away without meeting Overmanns' eyes. "Go, go, go," he said as they got back into the jeep.

Cecilienhof Palace, Potsdam, July, 1945

Churchill sat at the huge round table in the Cecilienhof glowering at Stalin. The Soviet Premier had stymied him on the subject of Poland. It was for Poland that the British and French had gone to war, Churchill had reminded Truman, with no effect on the President.

Truman had no wish to involve the USA any further in the violent politics of Europe so he wanted to placate Stalin. Truman had avoided Churchill's gaze as the meeting had wound up, then he had hurried into the courtyard alone, when he realized that somehow the Prime Minister had gotten ahead of him and was standing waiting by the red star formed of begonias which Stalin had had planted in the central circular bed of the Cecilienhof courtyard..

"Very symbolic, Mr. President, don't you think?" said Churchill.

"What is, Prime Minister?"

"The red star planted in our midst."

"I guess so."

"And no doubt they plan to propagate it farther into Europe. Would you take a stroll with me round the *Neuer Garten*?" Churchill asked. Truman, seeing no escape without insulting this great man, whom he had met for the first time two days before, agreed, thinking they would just walk the circle because he did not realize that "*Neuer Garten*," or New Garden, referred to the park that spread in lawns, groves of trees and bushes, and the immense Cecilienhof palace out to the *Jungfernsee*.

Churchill led him at a rapid pace. A white jeep patrolled the path bordering the shore, and American, Russian and British soldiers were searching the ground with metal detectors. Churchill and Truman went round the side of the building down towards the blue-brown water 100 metres away, then left up a slight rise, Churchill doing most of the talking as the President listened.

"The Russians are already betraying us in Poland," Churchill said. "Remember that in 1939 they were in league with the devil whom we have just dispatched. And now I am informed that Mikolajczyk and the rest of the London Poles are being held against their will and we shall never see hide nor hair of them again this side the Lubyanka."

"What's the . . ." Truman hesitated. "What was that word again?"

"Lubyanka. A large prison in the centre of Moscow, there the Soviets keep, and I may say, torture their prisoners. I dare say we shall see one day soon, 'confessions' of a sort from those poor Poles."

"Okay. So what's the deal?"

"It means we are letting down the Poles unless we do all that lies in our power to rescue Poland from the claws of the bear. We must stand together, unmoved by their threats and firm against their tyranny."

"Oh sure," he said.

Churchill smiled and said, "Mr. President . . ."

"Harry, please."

"Thank you, Harry. Winston here." He grinned at Truman as he said, "We must be friends, the fate of the free world depends upon us."

"I know that the President . . ." Truman hesitated, aware that once again he had made the same old mistake of referring to "the President" when he meant Roosevelt. He had respected Roosevelt so much that he was reluctant to push his own modest self into the great man's place. Churchill waited. Truman went on, "My great friend was in full agreement with that."

"Our mutual friend," said Churchill.

"Sure," said Truman. "Well, I got it. We gotta see about the Poles."

"But the bear is occupying a significant part of Germany right now," said Churchill. "In effect the Poles have become a fifth occupying power, without any agreement with us."

"I hear there's lots of German refugees coming out now and we're gonna have to feed 'em all."

"At least eight millions have come and, if that old butcher has his way, another ten millions are coming. A million have died on the road already."

Truman, who had served in France in World War One, and knew of Herbert Hoover's relief work in Poland in 1919, sighed. "It's mighty frightening to see the hatreds of our fathers' war coming round again."

"Let us sit here and talk about these matters," said Churchill, and sat down on a cement bench looking through some oaks towards the lake. A team of soldiers with mine detectors came towards them, sweeping the ground.

Churchill began to describe his plans. Until the Polish question was settled, the western Allies must not hand over any more German territory to the Russians. They should withhold all material aid, even what had been promised under Lend-Lease. None of the German ships and other reparations promised to Stalin should be sent. There could be no peace treaty with Germany that left the Polish border question vague.

"If we agree on this, we shall at least have some bargaining counters in our discussions with him," Churchill said, lighting a cigar and settling back. The day had been hot, the slight breeze through the woods was welcome on the back of his neck and he felt expansive.

"That's all peanuts," said Truman, who now sprang his big surprise. "I wouldn't want to make small threats like these when we already have the atomic bomb." He grinned and tilted his straw hat backward.

"This is indeed good news. The test was a success then?"

"Terrific. It was way bigger than their predictions. They told me the one bomb was the equivalent of 20,000 tons of TNT."

"Good Lord. This is indeed the weapon of Armageddon."

"You got it," said Truman.

"Excuse me," said Churchill, "we've got it, and thank God they do not."

"So, you see, when I tell Uncle Joe, I figure he'll be mighty impressed. I hope so, anyway. Then he might be just a little bit more cooperative."

Churchill grinned, thinking this jaunty little man had the right approach. He missed Roosevelt's grand vision, but at the same time he was glad that Truman understood what had escaped Roosevelt—the Russians would never yield to persuasion. Only self-interest would move them, or fear.

Truman was starting to ask about the opinion of the British voters in the election that Churchill was now facing, when he noticed a young

American officer running up the path towards them. He arrived gasping in front of the two men, and said, "Mr. President, you'll have to move, right now, there may be a bomb here, please right now, come with me," and he started down the path beckoning Truman to follow.

Churchill sat for half a second, miffed that he had not been mentioned—only the President. 'Am I not worth a warning from someone?' he was thinking, as he heaved himself up and lumbered after the nimble little President. He had a sudden presentiment that this foreshadowed the election result—he would be cast aside, without a warning.

Now two jeeps came up the path, followed by a squad of men with shovels and mine detectors, spread across the hot dried grass. As Churchill and Truman watched from a safe distance, the men first swept the ground with the metal detectors, then marked off an area with ropes and posts, and began digging.

They sat on a bench farther away, watching the digging as they discussed the effect of the bomb on Anglo-American policy towards Soviet Russia.

After an hour, an American captain hurried up to Truman and saluted. "What is it, Captain?" said Truman.

"Documents, sir, look important. And fuses, one of our experts recognized them, British style, silent fuses, used for assassinations."

"Let us see them when you are ready," said Churchill. "And make sure you keep them safe. You may find our Russian friends will take an undue interest in them. Have them delivered safe to my room first thing, please."

The officer glanced at Truman. Churchill said, "Have them delivered to the President's suite, I meant, of course."

Schenkenberg, July, 1945

Captain Ernest Fiske faced a dilemma. Although he believed Clara and Tati, they had no documents supporting their story, so he had to detain them while awaiting an interrogator from Army HQ in Regensburg.

Fiske was not married but he liked children, and was growing fond of Helmuth, who was cheerful and helpful, running errands around town, helping to wash the jeep, taking things apart to see how they worked. Once he found Helmuth sitting on the floor with the broken lock from the tavern door in pieces before him, figuring it out. He showed Ernie the broken spring, and told him he needed one more small screw to fix it. This Ernie provided, and Helmuth put it back together, and it worked.

They played chess sometimes in the afternoon. He liked to see the boy intent over the chess board, learning with astonishing speed. One night Helmuth, reviewing a game which he had lost, told Ernie where he thought he had gone wrong, and replayed all 14 moves of the game. This was a boy he wanted to help.

Fiske hated to see these young women wasting away in jail with inadequate rations, so he allotted them rations for four adults. He ordered the windows of the second floor of the Gasthaus Schroeder barred and posted a guard downstairs, so he could keep them there instead of in the dank jail. In the hotel, the women had the use of the bedrooms, bath and kitchen. Although Fiske was forbidden to fraternize with Germans, once in a while he even went to the hotel to dine with them on food he brought with him.

Clara asked for permission to telephone to her father in London, but the lines were reserved for the military so Fiske sent a telegram for her. Sir James responded right away, offering to come over to see her, or to supply transport for them all to Switzerland. She replied that she was being held for questioning, and could he send food. The answering telex was forwarded "with approval" by the CO of the Canadian

Army, General HDG. Crerar. Sir James demanded to know the charges against Clara, and where to send food parcels.

Fiske said, "I'm sorry, food parcels are not permitted."

Clara was incredulous. "Not permitted? Why? The people are starving and you will not allow food parcels? Who decided that?" She put the telex under his nose with her finger on the words "with approval."

"I don't know," said Fiske. He was unhappy because he agreed with her, and now he saw he was going to have to do more about her situation.

"I do think you should enter some kind of official protest against this. It's madness. I can't understand it, the Allies are starving us."

Fiske looked at her thinking, 'Exactly.'

Another week went by and no interrogator arrived from Regensburg. A telex came from her father saying that he had run into unexpected roadblocks in attempting to have her released. Lord Beaverbrook was interceding with the Prime Minister, but the situation was difficult because the detaining power was not the UK or Canada, but the USA. The Allied Supreme Command had been dissolved, and each ally was independent now. The war crimes investigators were overwhelmed by Nazis, senior generals, SS, as well as witnesses among refugees.

That night, Fiske remembered having received, on May 1, a top-secret telex telling him to be on the lookout for any German intelligence cryptanalysts who might have knowledge of German decrypting of Russian signals, and he saw his chance. He sent a telex to Frankfurt saying that "we have just discovered in our holding pens" two women who had been working in the Foreign Ministry, who should be debriefed. He told no lies, but let Frankfurt imagine what they might. After several weeks, nothing had happened—the telex had not even been acknowledged—so he repeated. Back came the routine acknowledgement, 'Ack Ur message PD'.

One bright afternoon in June, Fiske was thinking about how hot the rooms in the hotel would be, and what a shame it was that the two women were interned there, when they might be living in cooler air up in Schloss Schenkenberg. He walked up the high street to the hotel entrance and called up. When they came down, he told them he would release them if they gave him their word of honour to live at the Schloss, and report every day to him in the village.

"But is it habitable?"

"I don't know. The mayor told me that the Wehrmacht requisitioned it years ago, but then decided it was too remote, so it has just been standing empty all this time."

Tati said, as they trudged up the hill with Helmuth, "He might have done this weeks ago. He's such a limited little man."

"Don't you see his predicament? He's in the army, he can't disobey."

"You didn't let that argument stand in your way when you risked your life against Hitler, did you?" said Tati.

They paused on the hillside, out of breath, near the spot where Klaus had stopped the Maybach in September 1939 so Tati could pick flowers. She stood saying nothing, staring over the valley.

Helmuth looked up into his mother's face, seeing that something was wrong. "It'll be all right," Clara said.

She took Tati's arm and they started walking again. Helmuth studied the view as his mother had done, down to the village roofs crowded together like heads conversing, and the heat haze of the fields along the river valley. "Do you like it?" Clara asked him.

"I like it up here," said Helmuth. "It's quiet."

"This is where your father and I were married," said Tati.

"And where Peter and I were married," said Clara.

"On the same day," said Helmuth.

Clara smiled. "Using the very same flowers for a bouquet, that we picked right around here."

The embrasured windows of the tall, steep-roofed Schloss were blinded by sheets that had been there since 1940, now turned grey. The ivy had grown right over some of the lower windows, slates had fallen from the roof and shattered on the driveway which was patched with weeds. Roses in bloom fell thickly about the hedges and from the trellises, the hedges were 20 feet tall, and there were no voices but the sparrows chattering in the ivy and cicadas in the deep hot grass where the lawns had been. No one had been in it since Klaus' father had closed it. They walked under the gothic arch of the main gate, just high enough in the centre to admit a man on horseback. In the salon, they saw in the dim light from the sheeted windows the pale blurs of the covered furniture, brown newspapers from 1939 in the rack in the library, two empty champagne bottles standing on the massive deal table in the kitchen.

Helmuth ran upstairs and they heard his footsteps running down the hall to the 12 bedrooms.

Tati stood on the slate floor of the main hall, scarcely breathing, looking at the Stromberg radio and remembering the Hitler broadcast that changed their lives, the music of the Bosendorfer piano at the chapel door, the accordion band in the evening and the dancing that had made her sweat, and the events in the bedroom upstairs afterwards, for which she had yearned, and which had given her Helmuth. She lifted the dust cover from the blue slipper chair and fancied that she could see the impression of someone's body on the cushion. She shivered with the cool gloom of the building, and went back out.

Clara gazed out the open door at the tangled garden shining in the sun, touched her belly and knew that she was pregnant. Her period was three weeks overdue, and she had at first thought this was because she was eating so little, had lost much weight, and had been active from sunrise to sunset every day. But the sensation of sweat that did not break out on her skin, and an apprehension of nausea that did not occur, decided her.

Tati went out the open door dragging her feet as she walked, then stopped, a dark figure haloed in brilliant sunshine. Clara thought how much she had changed since those days. In repose, she was more beautiful than she had been, because suffering had turned her from a lively girl to a pensive woman. Tati called Helmuth back downstairs, and they decided that it was impossible. There was no water, no hydro, and too many memories. "Let's see if there are any clothes left," said Tati, "and get out of here."

Tati was looking out the window of the hotel past the wooden bars Fiske had had nailed to prevent their escape. She heard Clara in the bathroom, vomiting. Clara was kneeling before the toilet, wiping her mouth and wagging her head back and forth and moaning. Tati kneeled beside her, held her head and began stroking her hot forehead.

"What is it, do you think?" she asked.

Clara coughed, vomited again and Tati wiped her mouth.

"I'm pregnant."

"Oh God," said Tati.

"No, Peter," said Clara, and laughed and choked again. Tati brought her a glass of spring water and fed it to her, and mopped her sweating face. She helped Clara to undress, because she knew from her sailing days on the Baltic that to be cold prevented seasickness.

Clara sat on the edge of her bed naked, but not shivering.

"Why didn't you tell me?"

"I haven't told Peter." She thought of him alone at night in the hut. "Tati, I have to get out of here. I need proper food, I need milk, and protein and fresh fruit, the raspberries have been in for days and we haven't had one yet."

"Well, we could ask Fiske," said Tati.

"We could tell him, you mean."

"Tell him you're pregnant?"

"Tell him about the papers."

"What papers?"

"That we buried by the Cecilienhof."

"What for? They'll just confiscate them."

"They'll prove our case. We have to help ourselves now. They've arrested P.G. Wodehouse for treason, and all he did was make a broadcast for Göbbels making fun of his internment. They've arrested Ezra Pound, and they're holding him in a cage saying he's mad. The mayor of Montreal is in jail for sedition, what chance do I have? I've got to do something, or I'll be in jail when the baby comes."

"I don't know any of these people. Who is Pound?"

"You saw Wodehouse in the Adlon the night of that party, remember? Ezra Pound is a poet. They arrest a famous writer for a few broadcasts, and we've been writing propaganda for them. We can't count on Ernie, he says himself he is breaking orders to help us. I have to save myself. And the baby."

Tati was convinced that it was impossible for anyone in the occupying armies to believe what they had been doing. Several of the resistance leaders who had been in Gestapo jails had been interned by the Allies because they had remained members of the Nazi party. It did not matter that they had retained party membership only for cover while working for the resistance. Tati was sure that the Allies would destroy the papers or, at best, impound them in some remote archive, never to be seen by the public. She was determined to have them in the family and then one day to publish the true story of the resistance. In her imagination was burned the scene of her husband's last moment, his back towards the wall in the courtyard of the Bendlerstrasse, eyes open, hearing the rifle-bolts slam home, and then shouting, "Long Live Holy Germany."

"Clara," she said, "this is the last bit of him that I have. What did he die for? He died for German honour. He was *saying* it when they . . . when they . . . ." She stopped to compose herself. "Do you think that anyone in an Allied uniform today believes there is such a thing as German honour?"

Clara decided to let Tati cool down before talking again. Tati rampant gave way to Tati rational in two or three hours. 'Perhaps Fiske will let us go when he knows I am pregnant,' she thought.

Fiske congratulated her and asked after her husband. "Can I help you get the news to him? Do you know where he is?" Clara, imagining Fiske announcing the glad news to Peter in a dress, giggled.

"Sorry," she said, "I thought you said, 'Do you know *who* he is.' I don't know where, I guess in a prison camp."

Fiske took her pregnancy as a compelling reason to ask his family in Wisconsin for vitamins and milk powder parcels. He drove her to see the US Army doctor at regimental HQ in the next village. Peter sent them a note via Helmuth saying he had been robbing farmyards and leaving money on doorsteps. *But I've no idea of prices. Please advise how many* pfennigs *for two eggs warm from the hen. Love, Peter.*

On a hot morning in the middle of July, Clara and Tati were walking down to the village pump with their buckets, when far ahead, Clara saw Fiske come out of his office in the *Bierstube* shading his eyes against the hot sun.

Clara said, "It's time to end this. I'm going to tell him about the trunk."

Tati stopped walking. "No," she said. "I forbid you."

"You know we didn't wrap them very well, they could be rotting away to nothing now. We have to liberate them before another winter."

"Don't give in, Clara, this is all we have left."

Fiske greeted them with a smile. "I'm glad I found you. I have something for you." He handed a paper bag to Clara. She opened it and smelled the ripe raspberries inside.

"You are so kind to us. I haven't tasted one yet this year."

"Shall we go inside, it's so hot here. I have something to say."

He stood by the long oak table. He was in shirt sleeves and the women in light cotton blouses and dirndl skirts they had brought from the Schloss.

He gave Clara his chair, and straddled the bench beside Tati. "I had a call from Regensburg, they have sent someone here to interrogate you."

"Do you know anything about him?"

"You met him in Annecy last year. He is coming by jeep and should be here any minute now." Clara's eye fell on the headline in the *Stars and Stripes* newspaper on his desk, BIG THREE MEET AT POTS-DAM. Churchill, Stalin and Truman were meeting at the Cecilienhof to talk about Germany.

Light filled the room as the door opened and a tall young man in khaki shorts and short-sleeved shirt came in, bending under the low lintel. He smiled and said, "Good morning. Lieutenant Giovanelli, First Canadian Parachute Regiment. I'm looking for Captain Fiske."

Tati recognized Jack right away and smiled happily at him, but he looked at each one of them as if they were all strangers to him.

Fiske shook his hand and said, "What languages do you have?"

"English and French."

"I speak German," said Fiske. "May I present Freifrau Clara von Metternich and Freifrau Tatiana von Zollerndorf." Tati kept smiling hopefully at him. Jack was thinking, 'Why is she looking at me like that?'

She said, "Annecy? Remember me?"

"Oh my God, you're Tatiana. You've changed."

"I'm sorry I forgot my lines."

"I'm sorry I didn't recognize you. Are you all right?" He was shocked to see that the woman he had thought so beautiful was now gaunt and sad.

"A lot has happened. Lieutenant Fiske has put us in a very nice prison." She lifted her chin and looked at Fiske challengingly. He looked down.

Jack sat down and let out his breath. "Yes. Wow. Annecy. I almost didn't speak to you when I saw that German talking to you."

"He wouldn't stop. I was so nervous I forgot what to say."

"Kissing me was an inspired idea."

Tati said, "I'm sure it would be any time." Clara gasped. She had forgotten this flirtatious Tati.

Tati said, "I'm glad you got away all right."

"I walked to the Med. There was a safe house."

"I took the fuses back with me. Too bad they didn't work."

"Really? But a bomb went off."

"The fuses worked," she waved her hand. "But we didn't stop Hitler."

"No. From your name, I guess that it was your husband?"

Tati nodded.

"Fuses?" said Fiske.

"Ten fuses," said Jack. "For the bomb at Rastenburg, as I later found out."

"There were eight," said Tati.

"No, there were ten," said Clara, "We used two for the test, gave Klaus two, and buried six with the documents by the Cecilienhof." Tati did not at first notice this betrayal because she was concentrating on Jack, smiling.

"Wait a minute," said Fiske. "You buried bomb-fuses near the Cecilienhof. Where they're meeting? It's here, in the paper, they've found them." He showed them the story in *Stars and Stripes* about the discovery of a trunk full of fuses. "But there's nothing here about documents."

"They were there. With the fuses."

"What was in them?"

"All the memos and notes for our work. And the new constitution."

"Where did you bury these things?"

He gave her paper and pencil and she drew a map of the grounds.

"Where is north?" said Fiske as soon as she handed it to him, but she could not be sure. So she told him the date, time of night, and the position of the moon. She also oriented the map to the lake side of the Cecilienhof. Fiske picked up the phone. "Now, let's see what we can do."

Jack walked with them up the hot street towards the hotel. Tati took his arm and said, "Well, we'll hope for the best." She smiled up at him. "Now I'm going to do something nice for you," she said to Clara. "Despite your intended treachery."

"Where are we going?" Jack asked. He was surprised when she took his arm holding him close, but all he could feel of her chest was ribs.

At the door to the hotel, Tati looked at him with her most winning smile and said to Clara, "I can't let go of him now that I've found him again. He's the best-looking lieutenant we've seen in a long time, isn't he? Perhaps we can find you something for dinner." Feeling the strange energy between these two women, Jack didn't know what to say.

Clara said, "We have potatoes and some pork fat."

"And raspberries," Tati said. "Raspberries in pork fat, what do you say? Will you dine with us?"

Jack said, "Maybe you'd be interested in ham? They gave me a bunch of tinned hams before I left."

"What a perfect lieutenant you are. Your ham is invited too. Would there be enough for Ernest?"

"Hello, who's this?"

Helmuth rushed in the door behind them and circled round his mother, and stopped, seeing the stranger in the enemy uniform.

"Helmuth, this is Lieutenant Giovanelli. He's come to help us."

"*Draussen sind Jungen in Ihrem Jeep,*" Helmuth said. Tati translated and Jack ran outside and caught two boys in the back seat of the jeep rummaging through his gear. He held one by the arm, two tins fell down, and the other boy ran up the street with Helmuth after him.

"Well, we still have two," said Jack, holding out the tins to Tati.

Tati said, "I have an idea. You don't speak German, so you need a translator."

"Well, I can usually scrounge one," he said.

"Peter," Clara exclaimed.

"You can help a fellow countryman, if you will."

"Who is that?"

Tati glanced at Clara. Jack said, "You're a Canadian?"

"Yes."

"What are you doing in this godawful country, excuse me."

"I was here for the whole war." She began to weep thinking of it, and took out her handkerchief to blow her nose.

Tati said, "Her husband delivered the fuses to Klaus at the Bendlerstrasse. He's hiding up on the mountain, can't come down. He's only got his Wehrmacht uniform now, no papers. He's your new translator."

Clara said, "Just vouch for him, say he was captured by your—*our*—army up north, and came down here with you."

Jack looked at Tati and said impulsively, "Okay."

Next morning, as they were discussing how to present this fable to Fiske, Clara saw him standing silhouetted in the doorway. She looked at Jack in panic, wondering how much Fiske had heard. She said, "Come in, come in, we're having a Canadian reunion."

"I've talked to Regensburg," Fiske said. "You're going to the Berlin Document Centre to help them. I'm to issue you a temporary pass."

"We're free," said Tati. She clasped her hands over her head and pirouetted. "Thank you, Lieutenant Liberator."

"How can we get there?" Clara asked.

"I could drive you," Jack said, his eyes on Tati. Fiske looked annoyed, seeing this newcomer starting to take over his role as their protector.

"Berlin," Tati exclaimed. "My grandfather is there. Perhaps my mother will be back from Ravensbrück. Oh, this is all so wonderful, I am in heaven after hell."

"You'd better ask Captain Fiske for papers for your translator," Clara said firmly to Jack. "He'll have to come too."

"My translator lost his papers. He needs a temporary *laisser passer*."

"Okey-doke," said Fiske, drawing out a fountain pen. He sat down on a stool and opened his notebook. "Where is he?"

"Well," said Jack, "he's German, a prisoner, I, uh, left him in Hemmering at his aunt's house. He was due for a spot of leave."

"Leave? He's a prisoner." He closed his notebook.

"But he's been released. He's a trusty."

Fiske frowned and said, "Well, anyway, I'll need name, birthdate, birthplace, rank, serial number, where he was captured, the usual."

He looked up at Jack but Clara replied, "Peter Maria von Metter-nich, lieutenant, Ninth Infantry, Potsdam, born Bonn, May 19, 1916, brown hair, brown eyes."

Fiske looked at her. "Von Metternich? Do you mean that this is your husband?" he said.

"Yes, isn't it an extraordinary coincidence?" she said. "He was cap-tured by . . . what unit was it, Jack?"

"Uh, oh, well, First Canadian Div. Near Oldenburg, I guess. He never said exactly."

Fiske put the pen down. They were all silent.

"This is an incredible coincidence," he said.

"It is. Incredible," said Clara. She choked back a laugh.

Fiske was baffled. He thought, 'They told me the truth earlier and I didn't believe them, now I know they're lying, but I guess I owe them one.'

"Well," he said, picking up the pen, "you'll have the papers in the morning."

"Mummy," said Helmuth, "are we going to Berlin?"

Tati looked at Fiske who said, "Better not take him. You'll have to go through the Russian zone, and they are very unpredictable. He can stay with me. I'd like to have him."

"No," Helmuth said, "I want to go too."

"No, dear, it's too dangerous."

"Then you can't go."

"I want you to stay here with Captain Fiske, and all your friends."

"No, I want to go with you. Fiskie can come too."

Fiske said, "Well, you know, I've been wanting to see Berlin, and I've got some leave, and you can't all get in the one jeep."

Tati embraced Helmuth, looking up at Jack with a smile. Seeing Tati's smile constricted by sorrow, Jack remembered Alison's com-pletely happy smile, and was stabbed with yearning. Surprised by the force of his feelings, he turned away from her and sought something to say to Clara, but his throat was dry and raspy, so he said in a dry harsh tone, "Where are you from?" Unused to speaking English, she answered, *"Neu Braunschweig,"* and Fiske gave a start, remembering where his ancestors had lived. Then she said, "I mean, New Brunswick."

That night getting ready for bed, Clara said across the room, lit by one candle-stub, "Do you realize you're always touching him?"

"Who? Helmuth?"

"The lieutenant, Giovanelli."

"You're such a prude, aren't you?"

"Tati, you're being so obvious."

"What's obvious?"

"I don't know, what do you feel, are you in love with him? What happened in Annecy anyway?"

"Aha, that's it, is it?"

"No, of course not, I didn't think that you . . . that you would . . . you know . . . anything improper."

"The words just stick to your tongue, don't they?"

"Tati," she complained, and hesitated, feeling like a schoolchild being reprimanded. She had thought she should offer a gentle criticism, how had Tati turned this around so fast?

"If you want to know, I was being bothered by a German soldier, I needed help, and in walks this young god who has flown down from the sky bearing the sword to slay the dragon, and I forgot my password, so I threw my arms around him and kissed him."

Clara was silenced.

"On the mouth."

Now Clara smiled. "Well. He is extremely inviting."

They both giggled. "And that drove the danger away. There is method in my madness."

The next day they drove in Jack's jeep up the narrow track to the road that led along the ridge to the farmer's house. Clara knocked on the door, but there was no answer, so she went in and called. No one came out. She looked into the barn adjoining the house, and no one appeared. She said to Jack, "His hut is along the way, we'll try there."

As they walked past the corner of the barn, she heard a sound behind, and whirled round to see Peter just ducking out of sight behind the jeep. Clara called out as she ran towards him, "It's all right, Peter, it's all right. He's a friend, he's going to help."

Peter stood up looking frightened and skinny, and then just leaned on the back of the jeep. She came up to him and put her hand on his shoulder.

"Peter, this is Lieutenant Jack Giovanelli of the Canadian Army, come to help us."

Peter looked at Jack, who was feeling very strange, torn between his former duty to apprehend this enemy soldier and his promise to help him.

Peter said, "I have to give myself up, I can't stand this any more, Clara."

"It's over, he's going to help us. Jack, my husband, Count Peter von Metternich." Peter held out his hand. He tried to click his heels and bow, but he was so weak that he overbalanced and fell towards Jack, who caught him. Clara put her arm round him and said, "It's all okay, he can give you a paper saying you're his translator, you can wear some of Klaus' clothes from the *Schloss,* we're all going to Berlin, they want to see Tati and me there, oh Peter, darling, I'm pregnant." She began to weep and laugh. He said faintly, "That's wonderful," still leaning against her. She put both arms around him and whispered, "It's over, darling, it's all over and you're safe, we're all safe." She took him in her arms and drew him up close to her and hugged him hard. "It's all over and we're safe and I love you."

"It doesn't seem possible," he said.

She helped him to the door of the jeep like an invalid, explaining the deal they had with Fiske, and Peter looked at Jack, trying to understand this enemy who had returned Clara to him in a jeep.

Jack asked Peter if he would act as his translator.

Peter said, "Well to be honest, my English is rusty."

Jack said, "It sounds fine to me and, besides, for me to say 'my German' would already be an exaggeration."

Peter said, "Well, then, yes, I agree." And then, "You know, the last time my English came in handy was in the spring of 1940, when I was sent on a course in Paris to teach English to our generals who were preparing to set up our military government in London."

Aldershot, July, 1945

Bernie Hallett kept seeing Ed coming out of the house, then lying in his lap bleeding with his blue eyes open not seeing. Every night, he was court-martialled for neglecting his duty in the face of the enemy thereby causing the death of a soldier under his command. He could not sleep, he lost weight, he did not want to talk to anyone.

General Fox sent him to see the padre, Darcy Renison, who asked him if he had prayed recently. Bernie stared at him. Renison suggested that they pray together but when Bernie kneeled, he felt he should be sighting down a gun barrel. The love and praise he had once felt for the world and humanity were completely gone. He recited the Credo with no conviction, forgetting some of the words, and at the end he felt embarrassed for making the good-natured padre assist in this farce.

Renison asked him sympathetically if he had lost his faith, and Bernie replied that during the war he had blown his brains clear of a lot of foggy beliefs. A great clot of something had come away, "Like blowing my nose. It was a great relief. I didn't have to go to church parade and sing hymns and try to believe in a loving God with murder all around. I could just get on with the job without trying to dissemble. And I didn't have to listen to the hypocritical sermons conscripting God to help us kill Germans."

Hearing faith in God compared to a plug of snot, Renison was shocked but he nodded sagely, as he often did.

"So you regret the war?"

"Not victory. Killing. My best friend died in my lap. I killed my German. I slept at night, except when I was afraid."

"What did you fear?"

"The Germans."

"Not God's punishment."

Bernie looked at him wondering if he understood anything at all.

Then Renison said, "Perhaps your punishment is what you're going through now. Life without faith."

He thought about that, and of how happy he had been those days, those years, at camp, when the world had been beautiful, and he had been full of thanks and praise. He sighed. "I don't think I ever had any. Or if I did, it meant nothing, because look what I did. In any case, I look back on myself in those days and think I was, well, an asshole."

"Perhaps you didn't have the courage to live up to your faith."

Bernie looked at him, shaking his head, thinking, 'These padres never had to face a German with a gun.'

Renison went on, "You were born without it. You can get it back."

Bernie said nothing. The faith he had had when he was young seemed simple-minded to him now, and he did not want it back. But he had been happy then and he was miserable now. So he said, "How?" more as a rhetorical question than as a request for guidance.

"First, by wanting it. By wanting it to change you into a better and happier person in God's image. Then by studying faith. And by practicing it. It comes down to, 'Love God, and love your fellow man.'"

"For Christ's sake, padre, think what you're saying. Love the Germans?"

Renison smiled. He sat still for a long time making no comment. Then he got up. "Hate makes you miserable. The way to be happy is not to be miserable."

Bernie felt desperate at seeing his only hope about to leave. He said, to retain him, hoping he might find a formula for retrieving the faith that apparently had once made him happy, "I don't know what to do."

"Bernie, I hope you remember, you were a happy man when you kept to the faith. I'll do anything I can to help you bring it back. Start with praise."

Bernie waited till the padre was gone and tried to say, "Praise the Lord," but he thought, 'For killing Ed?' and could not do it. Then the trial in his head started again.

Berlin, July, 1945

⚜

Tati sat with Jack and Helmuth on the way to Berlin. Helmuth was asleep on Jack's bedroll in the back as they passed the train station at Zossen. They were halted by traffic at the station, and she saw people lying on the platform in the open air. Others came up to them and after inspecting them, either left them alone, or bent down and removed their boots. Tati put her hand to her mouth. "Jack, they're stealing the boots from the dead ones."

A woman shuffled up towards the side of the jeep dressed in rags with her bare thin arms out begging, her dirty, bruised face contorted with hopeless suffering. She closed her eyes and put her hands on the door frame just as Jack put the jeep in gear to move ahead. The woman slumped down the side and Tati screamed as she heard a thump.

Jack slammed on the brakes and Tati jumped out expecting to see a dead body, but the woman was crawling away. Tati bent down to her and she looked up with a malevolent expression, her lips peeled back from her bleeding gums. Tati said, "I'm so sorry, it was an accident." The woman rolled over on her side with her head on her arm as if she had decided to die right there. A tall woman came up to them and kneeled down. "She's one of the ones from the east," she said, and rolled the woman's head onto her knee and gave her water from her canteen. "Have you any food?" she said.

Jack called, "They're honking, we're blocking the road," but Tati paid no attention, taking a can of ham and a loaf of black bread to the tall woman.

While they were driving through the ruins of central Berlin, directed by Russian police wearing white gauntlets, Wilhelm von Benzdorf was limping from Lehrter station towards his grandfather Nikolai Miloslavsky's house in Charlottenburg. He was in a canyon of ruins: rubble rose left and right in hills above his head, ending at walls without roofs, without windows, with door openings but no doors, the cooked skins of houses, insides fluttering wallpaper, outsides blackened with smoke. From parts of the rubble black smoke dribbled up. He had known Berlin before the war but now there was nothing that he recognized. The streets were like animal paths. The people seemed more like ghosts than the living.

If he did not get food and clean water soon, he would faint, and it would be hours before he could walk again. But he managed to keep going, to an American army barracks with a long queue, where he waited. Then, farther off, he noticed a crowd of men flocking like sea-gulls round a huge garbage bin. He went there, shoved in, and got some banana skins which he began chewing as he reached in for more. A shout went up behind him as an army cook in white apron threw out .some paper bags. Wilhelm scrambled over a prostrate man, apologiz-ing as he seized a wet paper bag from another man, and found a half loaf of white bread speckled with coffee grounds. He apologized to the man he had pushed and gave him a piece of the bread, to which the man said, "More," holding out his hand.

The food in his pocket made him feel rich, but he remembered enough of his medical training to avoid eating it all in one gulp. Instead, he parceled it out to himself slowly, over the hours to evening. Now he thought he might be strong enough to risk the long climb towards Charlottenburg. But he stopped after a while, disoriented. Where the Tiergarten forest ought to be was a field of black leafless tree-trunks and stumps. A man in a wide black hat told him he might get shelter at the boathouse, so he limped on through the charcoal ruin to the *Neuersee* and came upon three boys, one sitting on another's shoulders, going through the pockets of a man hanging by his neck from rope strung up to a blackened lamppost, while two more undressed him, pulling off shoes, socks, underwear, until he was stripped.

Benzdorf said, "You can't do that," and one said, "We're doing it."

Benzdorf thought, 'If they get some food for these things, maybe that's good.' "But you must report this to the police." The boys paid no attention. He wanted to ask for the shoes but they ran off with them.

The boathouse on the *Neuersee* had been burned but the canoes had been saved and people were sleeping under the upturned hulls, the luckier ones lying on the brown mouse-holed canvas shrouds that had covered the racing shells on the Spree before the war. For a mouthful of bread, he bought a place for his head under the stern of a racing shell, lay down and went to sleep with the remaining bread in his crotch.

On a still, warm summer morning when the birds in Charlottenburg were singing as if there had never been a war, Count Alexei Nikolai Miloslavsky, asleep on the dining room floor under a car-rug, heard the Poles in the upstairs of his house arguing, then singing, then clattering down the stairs, returning a few minutes later. There was also a refugee Jewish family in the basement—altogether 16 people had been living in the house when Clara and Tati had arrived the day before with Peter and Helmuth. Beside them in the house now were the old count, his daughter the countess, very subdued and nervous after her release from Ravensbrück, the six Jews and the eleven Poles. There were also, although the count did not know this yet, two orphan children sleeping on old feed sacks in the garden shed.

Clara and Tati had solved the food problem for the Miloslavskys, bringing with them bread, canned peaches, pounds of bacon, butter, sausage and maple syrup given Clara by General Maurice Pope of the Canadian Military Mission, to whom she had reported on arrival. The Canadians had no idea what to do with her, since they had not been informed by anyone that she was to report, so they told her to billet herself and come back the following day when General Crerar would have some word from the Military Government. Now she and Tati had been ordered to report to the Berlin Document Centre where the Allies had a huge office collecting evidence for the Nuremberg War Crimes Tribunal.

The Charlottenburg house was, for the moment quiet, and the old count stepped out into the sweet morning air of the garden, run wild like everything in Berlin. The floribunda roses, which he had planted himself in the '20s, were lying beside the brick path that ran round the side of the house to the rear garden, climbing up the trellis he had built for them, and falling into the bridal wreath. So he cut one and put it into his shirt pocket as his morning contribution to tidying the place, and then noticed that someone had left a bundle out by the garden gate the night before. He bent down, saw that the bundle was a human being, and whispered, "Can I help?"

The man opened his eyes and said, "Uncle Nikky?"

"Oh my God, is it you Willy?" said the Count. "What has happened to you?"

"What has not," said Willy.

"You poor boy," said the count helping him to get up. Willy's bare feet printed patches of blood on the brick. Nikolai tried to embrace him, but Willy pushed him back. "I'm covered with lice," he said.

Willy took off all his clothes in the sunshine in the garden. They cut his hair and washed off his skinny body under the garden hose, dabbing at his hairy parts with kerosene Clara had begged from the Canadians. The count gave him clean underwear and trousers and a shirt, though they had no extra shoes, so they improvised sandals with rubber from an old tire, and curtain pulls.

He told his story to them all, and then asked for a table and a typewriter so he could type out his manuscript. He had already managed to write down 40 pages in longhand, but he wanted a typewriter to record the rest, as it was so difficult to remember and to recite it all. Already, some parts at the beginning were melting together in his head like watercolours.

Clara begged a typewriter from General Pope, whose office had six with German keyboards, of no use to them since the Canadians spoke English and French, and only enough German to give orders.

The Berlin Document Centre was in a damaged building on Wasserkäfersteig in Zehlendorf just off the Grunewald in the Russian Zone of southwest Berlin. It had been a depot of the postal service and was surrounded by armed guards patrolling barbed wire hedges. Clara and Tati walked in under scaffolding where tired-looking German labourers were carrying hods of bricks, up plywood steps laid over the broken stones, and in to the main marble-floored hall, echoing with typewriters, voices speaking English, Russian, German, manacled men shuffling by with their heads down. The prisoners slid their shoes along, as the laces had been removed to prevent them from hanging themselves.

"Look," said Tati, "that's Albert Speer," as Speer, with a sad expression on his handsome face, shuffled by in a tattered red sports jacket, looking down at the floor. He was followed by Rudolf Hess with armed soldiers ahead and behind.

They waited an hour in an anteroom for a British colonel to order them in. A brisk young aide, who reminded Tati of Klaus, took them in to the office. The colonel, a quiet, remote man named Ian Badger, looked up at them, told them to sit down without rising himself, and said, "Who are you? Why are you here?" He sipped at his china cup of coffee, a luxury that neither Tati nor Clara had seen for months. Tati started to explain.

"I say," Badger interrupted, "are you the two who worked in the Foreign Ministry?"

"We both did, yes," said Clara.

"We had a telex about that from Frankfurt. Said you have some documents about cyphers. I understand one of you is Russian?"

Tati said, "I was born in Russia, but I left when I was one year old."

"But you speak it?"

"Yes of course, at home with my mother and grandfather."

"I see, very good. Well, what can you tell us?"

"Well, we did no code work at all," Tati began.

"Cypher. Cypher is the word the boffins use," said Badger. He leaned back, tenting his fingers together before his eyes, and smiled at her through the tent. It seemed to Tati that he thought this gesture made them complicit in some spy-like way, but she concluded that he was a bit dim.

"We were translators mainly. At first we did some propaganda, but mainly it was routine paperwork, except of course for our secret work."

"Yes, yes, that's what we want, secret work."

"I meant for the Kernslau Circle."

"Aha," said Badger, with a 'now-we're-getting-somewhere' lift of his thick eyebrows. He picked up a pencil and tapped it.

"The documents you dug up in Potsdam are about the Kernslau Circle."

"Ah yes. What is the Kernslau Circle?" He was alert, scenting spies and secret codes that could be used against the Russians. As she explained, he looked more and more remote. She paused and said, "Could we have a cup of coffee?" Clara smiled but the colonel leaned back assessing Tati, then got up and went to the door. He asked the tall, strong-looking young aide-de-camp to bring two cups of coffee.

"Thanks," said Clara, smiling at the young man. Tati averted her gaze, because he looked so like Klaus. Badger offered them Players cigarettes from the tin on his desk. They lit up and Tati sat back feeling the dizzying rush from the nicotine. She said, "That makes me feel positively civilian."

"Now, tell me about the documents," Badger suggested.

After a minute or so, Badger had the drift of it, and let his mind wander back to England, to his daughter Pippa, now 21. Pippa had grown tall and strong that summer working on the farm in Devon, and now she was at Bristol, studying architecture, which pleased him. She was all he had left, since Brenda had died in an air-raid in 1940. Pippa was like this Clara, with her red-blond curls, and her freckles and her eager look. He held up his hand. "Yes, yes, that's all very well," he said, "but it's not quite the thing."

Clara said, "What thing is it not quite?" and smiled at him. As she felt her smile begin, she also felt her nausea begin. She stubbed out her cigarette and took a deep breath.

"I just remembered, I'm not supposed to smoke till after the baby."

"Oh, congratulations. I'm sure that is a wise policy," said Colonel Badger. As if in sympathy, he put out his own cigarette.

Then, fussing with things on his desk, he said, with many "Do you sees?" and "Don't you sees?" that the "so-called German resistance" was of no interest. "In fact," he concluded, "our policy is that, insofar as it tends to exculpate Germans and restore German honour, we ignore it. Only German crimes concern the centre."

Tati said, "Will you return the papers to us?"

"Good heavens, there is no question of that."

"They are our property."

"Excuse me, they belong to us. Who used to own them is as irrelevant now as the Nazi Party."

"It seems that to you the Party is still extremely relevant."

"Young lady, I won't debate you. Will you or will you not assist us?" Tati glared at him, so he looked at Clara, who said, "To do what?"

"We would like you to catalogue the papers and go through them with one of our experts so that we can check certain statements made by the prisoners. You have knowledge of some of these criminals, I believe?"

He handed a paper across the desk. "I would like you to go into the outer office if you would, and work with Lieutenant Chippin for a bit."

"But that is not what we came here to do," said Tati.

"But it *is* what you *will* do," said Badger.

"It's not why we did this work," said Tati. "We want this story told in public, in a book, not ransacked by lawyers who will miss the whole moral point of it."

"Why you did anything is of small significance," said Badger, but she interrupted, "You don't understand, this is the historical record of the resistance, the record of the bravery and decency of all the Germans who had not lost their souls. We had no thought of vengeance, we were trying to bring down the regime, end the war, and return the country to decency and justice. We were helping you."

He leaned back in his chair and said, "Perhaps you don't understand. What is wanted here is crime, large-scale crime with lots of witnesses, and documents. Germans are beasts. We are here to document that. *Verstanden?*"

Clara looked down at her hands in shame for this man and Germany. Tati sat rigid staring at him thinking of Klaus' last words in the courtyard. She got up, put her hands on the desk, and said, "My husband gave his life for a concept of honour that it will take centuries of education to inculcate in chilly little souls such as you." She turned and walked out.

Colonel Badger waved his hand at Clara, and said, "Take care of her, do. If she speaks like that to anyone else around here, she'll be arrested."

"What could you possibly arrest her for?"

"Don't worry, we'll think of something."

Clara ran out and took Tati by the arm as she went through the door of the outer office. Lieutenant Chippin stood up, seeing her coming, and watched in surprise as she stormed past him to the door with Clara tugging at her arm. In the noisy main hall, Clara whispered to her, "They have the papers, there's nothing else we can do. At least let's look at them, maybe they'll let us take notes."

Tati whirled around and hissed at her, "Let us take them."

Lieutenant Chippin came up and said, "I'm afraid I must ask you to accompany me," and led them to a big quiet room, the office of a former manager. There was a large desk before a tall straight upholstered chair covered in *petit-point*. In the centre of the carpet stood their trunk, on its tattered oilcloth, to which bits of grassy earth still clung.

Tati said, "Where are the fuses?" and the aide said, "They were returned to the British Army. Now, we would like you to catalogue all these documents in English and German with just a brief sentence or two describing origin and purpose, and also to prepare an index of these names, referring to the file folders by number." He handed them a series of green file folders with numbered tabs, and six sharp pencils. He sat with them for half an hour while they worked on long legal-size pads, sorting, defining, writing heads. Then he left them alone.

Clara smelled the earth and mouldy oilcloth, feeling the fear of burying this trunk. She had thought that Tati might break down at the sight of so many documents bearing the impress of Klaus' mind, and even his neat handwriting interpolating corrections in the typescripts, but she sat down and worked with strict efficiency. She said, "Let me sort them out, and you write down the file titles." So they set to work, Tati arranging them in neat stacks as Clara wrote out the headings and inserted them into the folders. They were served a sandwich lunch with coffee, and by mid-afternoon they were nearly done. Chippin asked them if they would like tea, and Tati said yes. As soon as he had left the room, Tati took out one file folder, and handed half the papers to Clara and whispered, "Stick these in your pants," hoisted her skirt, and stuffed a thick wad of documents out of sight. Clara started to protest, but Tati hissed "Shh," as Chippin came to the door.

After tea, they walked out. Clara felt the papers starting to slip out of her torn old underpants, so she bent to stuff them back up while Tati covered for her. The hall was so crowded and the Germans so shabby, that no one paid any attention to them.

Outside, Tati walked to a corner hidden behind a pile of rubble, and they drew out the papers.

"Here's the new constitution, lots of memos, Klaus' whole plan for the seizure in Berlin last year. All the most important stuff."

"What are you going to do with it?"

"Give it to Jack. His family owns a newspaper."

"This is getting worse and worse, Tati. They'll know we stole them."

Tati gestured around, "What have we got to lose?"

"They can put us in jail."

"The whole country is a jail."

Jack was due to return to Aurich early next morning, so Tati asked him to come into the garden of the house that evening. As they went to the stone bench in the side garden, she took him by the hand, holding a package tied with blue ribbons in her other hand. They sat down, side by side. She set the sheaf of papers by her side.

His heart was thumping. She was so warm to him that he felt she was going to say something intimate. He did not know what to say, except that he was very attracted to her, and he was glad she was putting on some weight. Feeling her thin hand warming in his, he wanted to protect her, to take her in his arms and kiss her and fondle her and take her to bed, except that he was afraid that when he saw her scrawny body he would feel guilt, because he ought to be feeding her instead of making love to her bones.

Tati was amused to find herself holding his hand like the flirt she had been. She wanted to talk about the papers, but now that he was so close to her, and the evening so warm and she was starting to feel healthy again, perhaps it might be beautiful to make love with him. Then perhaps they might all go to Canada together, where it would be good for Helmuth to grow up. All this fluttered in her mind like curtains around an open window as she said, "I want you to do something for me and for history."

"Did you say history?"

"These are the most important papers of the Kernslau Circle. I want you to take them home and get them published. Look, the new constitution, names for the top posts in the provisional government, orders for the Replacement Army to seize the radio stations and telephone exchange on July 20, 1944. This is history. This is why you came to meet me in Annecy." She held the papers towards him, but he did not touch them.

"Don't you think they belong here?"

"The Allies will lock them away or destroy them. You know how we are being treated. If it weren't for these papers, it would be illegal for you and me to be here talking like this."

"But to have them is illegal. They're stolen."

"Yes, from us," she hissed. "Our history is being stolen."

"I wouldn't know what to do with them."

"You know us, you can vouch for us, your family owns a newspaper, you can get them published," she said.

He put his elbows on his knees staring down at the long grass in which tiny white daisies were blooming.

"If these are not saved and published, my husband's sacrifice will have been worthless. Someone has to tell the truth."

He looked her in the eyes, thinking that the sorrow he saw there was her own history.

"Tati, I want to say something worthy of you, because I admire you so much. You came to Annecy, and I feel sorry for you and all you have gone through, so I'd like to help, but I can't."

She took his hand and pressed it, and looked up to him. "You must. My husband died for this. For what's in here."

"I'm sorry."

"He was trying to do the right thing in a horrible time."

"So were we all."

She sighed. "What did the war mean to you?"

He shrugged. "Victory. What else?"

"Oh Jack, don't be flippant. It's not worthy of you."

She looked at his lively eyes, the smile-corners of his mouth, and thought, 'He's still just a boy.' She said patiently, "Jack, why did *you* come to Annecy?"

He said, "I was ordered to go," thinking, 'Why hide from her?'

"You joined up for a reason, didn't you?"

"It was expected."

"Who expected it? You?"

"My father. He was wounded in the first one. This was just our fathers' war all over again."

"You volunteered for a specially dangerous service. Was that for your father? Or for the cause?"

"What cause?"

"The cause that brought us together in Annecy. It's the same one now."

"I don't know, Tati," he said. "You're trying to trap me into saying something that, if it was ever true of me, is not true now."

"But you must have believed in something greater than yourself."

He squirmed on the bench. "I'm no hero. The heroes are dead."

"What did you think about what you and I were doing?"

He said nothing. She went on, "Jack, it was universal. At that moment, I was German and you were British, but you and I were on the same side. Humanity. If it didn't mean to you what it meant to me, everything we did, and all the ones who died mean nothing, and I couldn't bear that." She looked at him with panic in her eyes.

He said, "Tati, I wasn't thinking, I was just doing my job. To get the war over. But you have made me think, and I know what I want now. I don't want vengeance, I just want the war to end." He pulled out cigarettes for them both.

She said passionately, "It's not over for us."

He blew smoke rings into the twilight and said, "No, obviously not."

"We want you to help finish it so the world will know these heroes, and why they risked their lives. Among whom I count yourself."

He remembered what she had said at Annecy: 'I can help you, I have immunity.' And he thought, 'You owe her this.'

He sat for a long time saying nothing, then put out his cigarette. "The people at the BDC are going to know what's happened."

"They have no idea what is in the trunk. *Was* in the trunk."

"Neither do I," he said. "I haven't a word of German."

"Look, here, Clara has done you a four-page précis and list of the contents. You can find someone to translate the rest."

She tied the ribbons, put the papers in his hands. "Thank you."

They walked back to the house, Jack carrying the papers, and she said as they went up the steps, "Not a word to anyone, not even to Fiske, until you're home."

But the next morning, Wilhelm came to Jack as he got down from the jeep to say goodbye to everyone. Wilhelm said in a low voice in careful French, "You are going to Canada, please guard my diary, of what is happening to the refugees. I will send it to you."

"I'm not a publisher, I don't know anything about that sort of thing," Jack said, annoyed that Tati had told Wilhelm.

"Please, I beg you," Wilhelm said, as they went up the brick walk to the porch where Tati and Clara were standing looking at him. "I was writing in my head all the time I was walking here, now I can finish on paper, and send to you. They must be helped."

Jack sighed, seeing the hope in Wilhelm's face. "I'll see what I can do, but there's no chance. This is a problem for governments."

"Governments make problems, not solve them," Wilhelm said with such a friendly smile that Jack smiled too.

Jack took the steps two at a time and stood there grinning around at everyone who had come out to say goodbye, including Count Nikolai and the Countess, still silenced.

"I'll help you come to Canada, if you want," he said to Peter, who shook his head.

"Germans are not allowed to emigrate. Germans have not been popular tourists lately."

Jack hugged Clara hating to be parted from them, wanting to get them out of this terrible place.

Then Jack took Tati's head in his hands, kissed her forehead and whispered in her ear, "Please don't tell anyone else what I am doing, all right?" He embraced Tati, and kissed her. She kissed him and held on to him for a long time.

Jack got into the jeep, feeling that if he did not go right away he would not be able to leave her. She watched him go thinking that if her life had not already been torn to pieces, it would be tearing now.

On the way back to Schenkenberg, Clara, Tati and Peter talked about how they might live. Peter said, "Now people will sit around the dinner table talking about whether we should fight the Bolsheviks, like the '30s except the talk will last longer, because even the Russians are tired of war."

Tati said, "I'm tired of Europe. I want to leave. What is Canada like, Clara? Could we possibly go and live there?"

"Some bears live in Canada," said Helmuth.

"I survived," said Clara. She laughed when she saw Tati's face, so bleak at the prospect of Canada, put her arm around her friend and patted her. Tati remained upright and listless as Clara said, "When they lift the ban, we can go there. My father has a farm in New Brunswick, we could have a house and a garden and send the children to school. Peter could teach something at the university, we could live on the farm. It could be wonderful."

Tati thought, 'I could have had Jack, I saw it in his eyes.'

Coming home on the troopship still wearing her zig-zag grey war-paint, Jack stared over the rail into the pale fog like a roll of white fur round the ship under a dome of blue sky. The drunks in the salon behind him were shouting out "We are the D-Day dodgers" as they celebrated their release from Europe with songs and vomit. He looked back over the white wake to the horizon where Marianne was lost.

He felt huge and awkward walking into the booming concourse of Union Station. He hugged his father and mother, both grown smaller. Everything was familiar, but he felt estranged from the boy who had gone away from them. It was as if in returning to civilian life, he was putting on clothes that did not belong to him. He was harsh, tense. The enduring, thoughtful part of him was sad, although the lively, momentary part of him was happy to be home and alive. He marvelled at the people walking round the undamaged streets, unafraid of the sky. Then he shrank away from them, feeling irrelevant. What could he do among these people? How could he live? Could he study composition? Find a girlfriend? Have children? The prospects were bewildering.

He stopped in the shade of the pergola in the garden of his father's house, and saw an old man in a baggy blazer leaning on a cane beside a young woman in a blue dress. There was no one else on the bright grass. It must be Grant, with Cat Treloar. He stayed in the shade of the clematis vine feeling that the scene was surreal: to enter it would make it real.

Grant looked over and called out, "Hi Jock."

Jack said hello to Cat and they stood there in the awkward Canadian fashion, neither kissing nor shaking hands but grinning, waiting for the other to say something. Grant, slurring his words through the new sneering droop on the left side of his mouth, said, "That's mine," pointing at the tweed sports coat Jack was wearing. Jack took it off and handed it over. Grant gave him a bitter smile and handed it back.

"You see how brotherly love survives even years of war," Jack said to Cat, omitting that his mother had given him the coat because his own clothes had been eaten by moths.

Jack said, "I hear you're a hero," and they sat down, Cat on the other side of Grant. She was wearing a broad-brimmed straw hat which shaded her features. Jack longed for someone beautiful and young like this to love.

"They gave me a medal but I don't remember a damn thing." Grant touched his head. "Then they took it back because I went to the German Embassy in Dublin to pick up my binoculars."

"What were they doing there?"

"I was drinking in a pub, and this German diplomat fastened on me—it's a long story. In any case, I was a hero on Monday and a spy on Tuesday. Stupid, stupid people."

"What's the prognosis now?" Jack asked.

Grant sighed. "More therapy. Weights. Don't look so creepy, I'm going to be just fine. Cat and I are getting married."

"I heard, congratulations."

"He's made remarkable progress," Cat said.

"She's a remarkable nurse," Grant said, and looked at her with that new, drooping smile. It seemed to Jack now that his brother's face had been smeared. He could not easily look at him.

"How long have you been here?" Jack looked at Cat.

"Since November."

"Wow, and what do you think of our fair country?"

"I love it so far," taking Grant's hand with her right hand. She held out her left hand to show the engagement ring.

"Well, isn't that nice," said Jack. He saw Alison in a wedding dress. smiling. "I bet I'm looking at your discharge pay and a half."

"McTamney's, my boy, McTamney's, much cheaper than whatsit . . . you know . . . Berth, Eklis . . . with the blue box . . ." Grant said.

"Birks Ellis Ryrie," said Jack.

Cat laughed, surprised at the frank way these Canadians talked about money.

Jack leaned back, smelling the roses, peonies, new-cut grass, and sat up again, feeling restless, that there were things to do, places to go, meetings to attend, duty. "When is the great day?"

Cat said, "August 18," and smiled at Grant. Jack turned away, shocked by his brother's wounds, thinking how sad for her to get only this skinny remnant of the strong handsome man who had been his real brother.

That hot night Jack turned out the lights in his bedroom and undressed by the open window looking through the maple trees to the street. He opened the drawer of the walnut desk which his mother had given him, where he had studied for ten years, and smelled soap, from a small piece he had forgotten. He passed through years of his journal, and letters from John Arnold—all signed "love"—to him at Châteauroux, records of study hours spent on trigonometry, history, French. And then many entries to do with Alison de Pencier. There was a sealed envelope inside those pages, addressed to her in his handwriting, with a King George's face five-cent stamp. He opened it. The date was Friday, October 25, 1940.

He grew dizzy as he read, as if he were teetering on the rim of a hole in time, looking down on emotions of years ago, still living in the tiny black eggs of writing far below. A page of juvenile quips embarrassed him and made him wonder why Alison had ever put up with him, and then he came on a passage that reminded him of the lost feelings of his romantic youth: *You think I am not serious enough—it's true, I am serious about nothing except not being serious, although I might make an exception for you. But you inspire me, I am ready to be quite lost about you, OK, no more fooling around, here is my heart, you make me feel beautiful, here's what I mean, I'm 12, it's the last sad day of summer, I go down to say 'goodbye dear lake, I'll see you next spring' and there's a red leaf floating on blue water, like my heart left behind.' OK, Keats, Donne, and Shakespeare, the way the lines turn as you go through them, and there's the perfect word sitting like joy on a branch, that flies away and takes you with it. And OK, the muskrat swimming across the sunset leaving a wake like God writing his signature under a portrait of beauty, Renata Tebaldi singing "Vissi d'Arte" from* Tosca, *where her voice breaks and your heart breaks with it. Robin rolling his rrs in the trees in the evening. On and on—whatever pleases and is fruitful is beautiful. Beauty makes life worth living. That's what you have. That's what I want.* He saw himself, a skinny kid, happy-natured, romantic, completely ignorant of women, scribbling at this desk, and he thought, 'That's not me, not any more.' But at the same time, his heart was beating faster and he knew those young feelings were alive in him.

He called Alison's house, but no one answered. He asked friends at the club and heard that she had won a scholarship for post-graduate studies in England. Then Gillian telephoned to say that Alison had gone to their island, called Longuissa in Muskoka.

There was no phone on Longuissa, and he could not wait to write to her, so he sent a telegram to their post office, said goodbye to Grant and Cat, to his mother and father and Greg, packed his stained old dunnage bag with civilian clothes smelling of moth balls and flung it up on the rack over his seat on the CPR train to Muskoka Landing.

The taxi-boat delivered him to the dock at her island. He left his bag in the shade of the boathouse and walked up a hot winding path among blueberry bushes, gentians, Indian paintbrush, scented with wild roses and sweet grass. At the top, beyond a fire-hot plain of rock stained orange and blue-grey by lichen, he saw an old green cottage under pine trees hissing in the wind. On the screened verandah a figure in a white shirt was seated at a desk. Jack walked up to the screen door, but Rafe de Pencier did not look up. Jack tapped and de Pencier went on writing. Jack opened the door and said, "Hello," and heard a woman talking in a room beyond.

Rafe squinted into the glare and said, "Good morning," though he had just had lunch. Jack said, "I hope you got my telegram, sir."

Hearing his voice, Patience de Pencier came walking and talking through the screen door from the kitchen, which banged behind her, and said with an anxious pleasant look on her face, "Ah, Lieutenant Giovanelli, home from the wars. How are you? Are these flowers for us? Thank you, how very thoughtful. I'm afraid Alison is not here. Would you like tea? You must be tired after the long trip. How did you come? By train I expect." Everyone reminded her of someone, so her conversation was endless. "I saw your Aunt Lally in the club last week, and she told me you would be coming home next week, and here you are, as advertised. She was with her champion golfer friend from Vancouver, the one who married the Shaughnessies, or was it the Watsons, but that family, who had to go to North Carolina for the tournament, but she couldn't because her clubs were made in Scotland. But her cousin is Ambassador, and she called him on the long distance telephone from Niagara Falls where she was waiting for word in the same suite her parents had been in 1919 on their honeymoon next to the Duke of Cumberland who was a friend of the Ambassador, don't you love it, just arrived from Washington and he was able to let her through the gate when nobody else could. But she came fifth."

Bursting to speak, Jack interrupted Patience during the tournament. Interruptions happened to her so often that she now regarded them as part of normal conversation.

Jack said, "Has she left for England?" as Patience went on about golf, so it would have been reasonable for Patience to think Jack meant the golfer, but she was so conscious of Jack's interest in Alison that without missing a beat she switched from golfer to daughter and replied, "No, no, we rather hope she won't, don't we Rafe?" at which he looked up from his papers and said, "Could you just repeat that, dear?"

Patience had been talking for at least five minutes, so she stopped, getting ready to repeat it all, and wondering if Rafe was teasing her, which gave Jack the chance to ask, "Is she here with you?"

"Oh yes, she's gone up the old moose trail. Sketching. We think she has a career in front of her. I'm quite sure. Don't we Rafe?"

Expecting no answer, she went on, "Are you staying the night?" Rafe looked up in surprise, wondering why she was asking him such an odd question.

Jack, relieved at this generous solution to the delicate problem he had imposed on the family, said, "Yes, thank you very much. I just got back day before yesterday, and . . ." he was about to say that this was the reason he smelled of mothballs, but Mrs. de Pencier flooded on about the bat problem in the boathouse, her way of saying he would sleep there.

The trail led away from the cottage past Ladies' Bay, reserved for the women of the family, who went there for their shiners in the morning. He walked along, listening to the sound of the small waves licking the rocks. The path turned inland. Into the quiet burst the echoing chant of the veery thrush, like a flute in a cathedral. A seagull flew low over the trees, shrieked and glided away.

She was seated with her back to him, in the middle of the trail, on a folding wooden seat, with a large painting on an easel in front of her.

He forced his leg to walk normally despite the stiffness, because he did not want her to think he was damaged goods. He also made a bit of noise when he was still well down the trail, so as not to cause her to make a bad stroke. A few yards away, he snapped a twig with his foot, said, "Hello," then came round beside her.

She was wearing a bug hat which veiled her face, blue cotton trousers clutched at the ankles by socks, and a white shirt closed at her neck. She said, "Hello," and, as far as he could see within the shadowing bug hat, perhaps smiled. "What a surprise. I wasn't expecting you."

"Well, I've been looking forward to you."

She glanced at the canvas and dabbed a bit of green on a pine branch on the right side, then looked at him through the bug netting. "I'm finished," she said, and put on another dab of paint. She bent over to store paints in the box.

"Are you glad to see me?" he asked.

"I'm glad you're safely home." She smiled, remembering his arms waltzing her around at the St. Andrew's Ball. He grinned at her, thinking, 'Yes, you're young and happy, and you're the one I want.'

"I brought you something." He handed her a small box. She laid the brush on the palette, opened the box and saw perfume.

"Thank you," she said. "That was very thoughtful of you." She refrained from adding, "I never wear perfume."

He said, "From Paris."

"I see. Nina Ricci."

He guessed, "Do you ever use it?"

"No." She giggled. "Maybe I could start." He smiled, at a loss, seeing her so cool, but not unwelcoming.

The painting showed the lake shimmering beyond outstretched branches reaching in from either side towards the gesso-ghost of a young woman standing, with her face, hair, shirt and skirt sketched in pencil on the white gesso underpainting. The effect was eerie—a young woman not yet present in the world would soon come to life among tree branches reaching out for her like hands.

"What's she doing?" Jack asked.

Alison had imagined the painting, without thinking much about it. She said, "I don't know, maybe she's thinking about how things grow," and realized it was true.

She lifted the veil and swept off her hat. "How did you find me?"

"I just looked in my heart and there you were." He smiled.

She smiled, as if to say, 'Another one of your silly jokes.'

"How long have you been back?"

They were walking back along the path now, Jack carrying the easel. He told her a little of what he had been doing, and she described the last weeks of her course, and her exams. He said, "I've been thinking about you a lot." She waited. He felt panicky, but rushed on anyway. "When I left here, I meant to write to tell you how I felt about you, how much I valued you, and still do. I went home that night and wrote it all out in a letter, telling you how wonderful I think you are but I never sent it, I don't know why. I left it in a drawer. I meant it, anyway . . ." He paused.

She was looking down and away from him, and walking. "I do value you, I mean . . ." He paused again. "I mean, I don't mean to sound like a mining engineer, assaying you for ore . . . I just think you're beautiful . . . oh God." Her younger brother Paul, his body burned dark brown, his hair bleached white, his manner slow and amiable, was walking up the path towards them, having been sent as chaperone by his mother.

Their dog Kong, a huge, black hairy mutt crossbred from a poodle and a German shepherd, came bounding up the path to meet them, his enormous feet flapping, snuffled their groins, leaped up and licked Alison's face, bounced around, then bounded back down the path, as Alison smiled and called after him. At the cottage verandah, she threw a tennis ball for him, and he bounded back up the steps with the ball in his drooling mouth. Kong dropped it over the side of the verandah, and then bounded down after it, snuffled around and could not find it.

Alison called down encouragement to him, "There it is, right by your nose, you've got your foot on it. Oh no, get the ball, your schnozz is right on it," all in complete unselfconsciousness, as if giving a dog directions in English were a normal thing to do. Then she turned away and said with a happy smile, "He's just a puppy."

She stood close by him, showing the sketches she had done of loons in their nest, geese upended, their heads buried underwater, their tails comically in the air, and Kong, crouched to spring at a ball, staring down puzzled by his own reflection in the water, asleep on his belly, legs splayed out, watching the artist with one eye open. He thought, 'This is the happiness I want, this is the girl I want,' feeling her warmth close beside him. He closed the book wanting her to stay close, thinking of saying, 'You are wonderful, I love you.'

Alison, wondering if he was embarrassed by his outburst on the trail, and wary of being alone with him again because she was unsure of her feelings, suggested that they go sailing with Paul in the dinghy.

Sitting in the boat beside him, she thought, 'He is very handsome, but he doesn't know how to approach a girl.' She wondered what would be the right way for a young man to approach a girl, and decided she was far from ready to be approached for anything, except art college.

After dinner, they played crokinole and then Professor de Pencier turned on the battery-operated radio. The CBC announcer told them of the latest firestorm raid on Tokyo, which had destroyed the rest of the city excluding the Emperor's palace, and also of a threatened rail strike in Canada. If it occurred, they would all be marooned here.

After dinner, as Jack followed Paul to the boathouse by flashlight, he probed the boy for information.

"Does your sister talk about her boyfriends much?" he asked.

"I know she gets lots of phone calls and letters."

"Does she ever say anything about me?"

"Are you Jack Biddell?"

"I'm Jack Giovanelli."

"She says you're funny, but I think she means weird."

Paul went back up the path wondering why people paid so much attention to his sister.

Jack went to bed watching pale northern lights shimmering beyond the black pines. Sometimes Alison looked at him so happily that he was dizzy with answering happiness, but if he took this as encouragement, she shrank away. Her face would be calm again, and he loved this serenity as well. He went to sleep with a whippoorwill chanting nearby and bats flying in the hole of the screen window a few feet over his head. He dreamed he was at table with the de Pencier family. He was dressed in white tie, with bare feet under the table and Mrs. de Pencier was singing, "Whip-poor-will, whip-poor-will," and he stared hard at Rafe willing him to tell her to shut up. He opened his mouth to tell her to shut up, but she had stopped.

The next day at breakfast on the verandah, people seemed to be avoiding talking about their plans for the day. He thought, 'I'll wait and see if she plans anything for us to do together.' She asked him if he wanted to come with her to pick blueberries, and he saw himself on one knee in the blueberry bushes proposing, but then she decided to send him with Paul, while she stayed in the house to help her mother with the housework.

After he and Paul had picked several quarts, Jack was thinking, 'She had her chance, she could have shooed the kid away yesterday and she didn't. She could have suggested this morning that we go alone for the berries, but she didn't. She's doing her best to avoid me, but she's too polite to kick me out even though she doesn't want to hear what I have to say. And that's why I came, to say it, and now I've blown it so now I'd better go.'

He said he would take the noon train to Toronto. Alison said she would paddle him to the landing, but she said nothing to indicate that she was either surprised or disappointed.

The wind was blowing white-caps across their bow, so they paddled hard. Jack, kneeling in the stern, regretting he was leaving, proposed silently to her back.

He set the canoe on the cinder path at the landing, avoiding her eyes, and she said, "You're very quiet all of a sudden."

"I was wondering how to tell you why I'm leaving so soon."

She said, "Why are you?"

He bent forward, hoisting up his knapsack. "Alison, I'd like to stop this dancing around. I've known you for years. I wrote to you all through the war, getting so little in return, pouring out my heart to you in letters, and when I get here, what do you say? 'Hello.'"

"Well, what did you expect me to say? Goodbye?"

"Well, at last a quip, thank you."

"It wasn't a quip," she said, nettled. "That's your specialty, I thought."

"I know, you think I'm not serious, I'm too flippant. Yes, well, I was a kid when I first met you, and I guess part of me still is, but I know one thing. When I was scared to death on that mountain with the Germans coming, and one bad move meant I was dead, well . . . ." He trailed off having intended to say, 'I was thinking about you,' but then said, "Well, I was going to say, 'I was thinking about you the whole time,' but I wasn't. I was scared silly thinking about how to get out of there, and then I got away, and *then* I thought about you, and that made saving my life worthwhile, because it isn't good enough to just live. I want to live for something, someone . . ."

He took a deep breath and faced her squarely.

"When I joined up it was because you made me see the truth about what I wanted to do, and you did it again just now. Because you are the beautiful truth. And when I got back I knew I had to come up here and say, 'I love you, you're what I lived through the war for,' and everything would be wonderful, but now I see it is useless. I did love you but it's been too long, Alison. I can't live on no hope, and I just want you to know before I leave that my feeling for you was beautiful but now it's dead, you killed it in me, and I won't bother you ever again. So goodbye and thanks for the weekend, or whatever it was."

He waited a second or two, just in case, but she said nothing so he walked away and got on the train.

He sat down by a window, lit a cigarette and thought, 'Get that girl out of your head, Jack, you've been thinking about her too much. Forget beauty, and truth, Keats was talking to a jug, for God's sake.' The train pulled him away past old two-storey farmhouses built of clapboards weathered silvery grey, stuck in small fields among knobs of bedrock erupting through the thin sheet of earth. Some had been abandoned, on others exhausted people scarcely lived on land that imprisoned them.

'There's the real world that needs improving, get to reality, do something to improve the world, end the wars, increase wealth, eradicate poverty.' He would be a crusader on behalf not of a single woman or a family, but of poor, beaten-up humanity. Then he thought, 'I don't want to do that, and it's too late now for music, I haven't practiced for five years.' In the back of his mind was also the knowledge that Grant would never write again.

He pulled out his journal and began to write: *Young Jeremy grew wise before his time. In the war, he was a soldier who jumped into*

France with a bomb for Hitler in his knapsack . . . . He was still writing when the train pulled in to Toronto four hours later.

Alison stood on the platform dumbfounded. Her emotions confused her thoughts, which had not happened to her since she was thirteen. She thought, 'Did I misjudge him?' and this brought such a rush of regret, and astonishment, and pity for him standing hurt in front of her smelling of mothballs, that she wanted to shout at the train, 'Wait, I didn't mean it,' but it was steaming away under black explosions of smoke, and she did not know what she did not mean.

She got into the canoe oblivious to the scene around her and began paddling back to the island. The wind pushed her off course to the north and she had to work hard for every yard. She was thinking, 'Could I love him?' and this produced such erotic panic that she could not think of anything but telling herself to calm down, it was all ridiculous, he was just a boy. But at this thought her heart pounded in protest. 'He's not a boy, he's a man home from war who loves me. And very handsome.' She did not believe that his love was dead—she thought that must be romantic rhetoric. But then she thought, 'If it's true he's no longer a boy but a man, then he meant it. It was beautiful and it's over, and I killed it.'

This was so agonizing she stopped paddling. The canoe twisted stern to the wind and began blowing away from the island. She sat for a while, feeling the wind cool the tears in her eyes. She had hurt him, and lost him, and she did not know if she wanted him or not. The canoe blew farther north. She tried to assemble her thoughts but nothing would stay certain in her mind. As soon as she thought she had understood or decided one thing, she realized something was left out, and she had to revise her thoughts. She picked up the paddle and aimed for Longuissa but the wind was too strong. She had to quarter the wind to the lee of the island, then paddle close to shore. She was irritated that he was not there to help. She pulled the canoe up the beach by the boathouse and looked back towards Muskoka Landing, thinking, 'Wait, you'll soon calm down and know what to do,' but her feelings were too powerful, and she began to realize that for once she was not going to be able to decide what was best to do, she was going to have to do what she wanted.

The next morning Patience found Jack's bathing suit, razor and a mothball-smelling sweater in the boathouse, and Alison said, "I'll take them to him. When I go down next week."

"I can't leave Rafe and Paul," said Patience, thinking that because she could not go to the city, Alison could not go either, since the girl could not stay there alone overnight. It was Patience's life to serve others, and if necessary she would impose her services on others to make a place for herself.

Alison knew what her mother was thinking, so she said, "Mother, I'm 23 years old now. And I want to go to the library as well."

"You can't stay at the house. The dustcovers are on. You'll have to go to Aunt Cynthia's." She closed her mouth in the tight line that indicated the matter had been decided.

Alison climbed out of the hot station up the ramp from Union Station, amazed at the heat which was penetrating even here, underground. She took the Yonge Street car up the long hill to St. Clair Avenue and walked, wet with the heat, west to Aunt Cynny's apartment. The door was locked, the edge of the telegram envelope she had sent was visible under the door, and she wondered what to do. She walked in the tree-shade back to the Racquets Club, and phoned Molly, then Honour, then Heather, and found that they were away, or there was no answer.

'Well then,' she thought, 'I have to stay at the house.' She took the streetcar back down the hill and walked under the cooling shade of the great elms arching over the street, to number 93. The key was in the crack in the bricks under the milkbox. She swung the Dutch front door open onto the dim cool interior, where the white cloths blurred the furniture on the wood floors, bare for the summer.

She opened her bedroom window, and tested the bath water, which ran rusty and cold because the coal-fired heater had been turned off. She felt excited and free, to be lying in a cool tub in the middle of a hot summer afternoon alone in the city. She dressed in a print skirt, pale long-sleeved blouse, sandals, and a straw sunhat.

Swinging the paper bag with his sweater and bathing suit inside, she set off on the long climb back up the hill into Moore Park, not thinking of what she would say or do. She would arrive, they would talk and laugh, as they had that night at the St. Andrew's Ball when she had felt so happy and confident in his arms, smiling up at him, with one hand holding up the hem of her twirling skirt, and flirty words coming to her lips.

The house, which she had never seen before, soared up three storeys to many gables and steep red slate roofs, verandahs all about, a conservatory, a two-storey coach house, hedged round with tall oaks and maples shading long lawns and beds of peonies, roses, delphiniums and phlox. It was a house for many children, a dog, maids, and busy gardener. As she walked up the front path, at a diagonal from the corner, she heard a loud party going on in the far end of the garden. The huge front door, four feet wide, was standing wide open, giving onto a front hall in which a grandfather clock was sounding seven.

She called in, "Is anyone home?" A maid came by, carrying a large silver tray on which were canapés, and said that Mr. Jack was in the back garden and that she would call him.

He came with bouncy steps across the dining room into the front hall and then stopped six feet from her and said, "Oh," in a warning tone.

"You forgot these, I brought them down for you." She handed him the bag.

"Thanks. You could have mailed them."

She took this as a reproach, as it was intended, meaning, 'Don't bother me.'

"Anyway, thanks," he said.

Alison smiled and said, "I had to come down anyway."

"Oh," he said. "So, thanks."

Behind him the maid returned with a tray full of empty glasses and plates, the sound of laughter and loud voices from the garden coming in. Now Sarah Bannatyne approached, smiling, silver hair shining. She said, "Jack, do introduce us."

Jack sighed and introduced them, without looking at Alison, and Mrs. Bannatyne said, "Do come in, dear, we're having an engagement party with people here from all over. I know your mother, she was a Mason, I think?"

"Yes, that's right," said Alison, looking up at him hopefully and thinking, 'This is the chance he needs.' But after Mrs. Bannatyne had left, he said, "Well thanks, see you around," looking over her shoulder to the front path. But she stood her ground for a moment, and said, "I wanted to see you."

"What for?" he said.

"Well, do I have to have a special reason?"

Jack thought. 'She still doesn't know what she wants.' She sensed this and looked down, thinking she might say, 'Maybe I misjudged you,' getting ready to say it when along came his brother Greg. Jack introduced him, then Greg went by. She thought, 'This is not the moment,' and then, 'But there will not be another.'

She was perplexed at the coldness that had replaced his eager love and she felt sorry for him and for them both, and wished she could make him understand that she wanted to break free of the bonds that kept her from expressing to him the feelings which all her life she had been so trained to keep hidden that she had never been sure what those feelings were, or would be if she let them grow, or what to do about them, except that she should never let anyone know she was feeling them.

He stood waiting, impressed by her obstinacy.

She said, "Well then, goodbye for now," and went down the front path. He watched her go, feeling vengeful satisfaction at having had the power to reject her and then he thought, 'The one true love of your life is walking down that path.'

She thought, 'I'll give him one more chance' and, although it was the wrong way home, dawdled along the sidewalk bordering the back garden, knowing he could see her over the hedge.

He went back into the house and through the dining room out onto the dining room verandah, ran down the steps, and out the path through the back garden and caught up to her. He said, "We're getting good at parting but no better at being together," and before she could stonewall him, added, "Why don't you come back and have dinner? You could have a shampoo first, if you like."

"That won't be necessary, thank you," she said, and turned round with a pirouette.

The maids brought out a long trestle table to the garden because the house was too hot, and Jack and Greg helped them to set up card tables and bridge chairs. They floated a long tablecloth onto the wood, and because it was fun they lifted and did it again, until the maids, laughing, asked them to stop so they could set the places.

On lawn chairs seated round them, calling out advice and criticism, were all the family, plus A.G. Douglas and his new girlfriend Julie Tarkai, Joe Shearer and Yvette.

Then Greg opened the French doors to the dining room, and Jack played on the old upright piano as they sang,

> *There'll be bluebirds over*
> *The white cliffs of Dover,*
> *Tomorrow, just you wait and see*
> *There'll be love and laughter*
> *And peace ever after*
> *Tomorrow, when the world is free.*

Then they went on to

> *In days of yore*
> *From Britain's shore*
> *Wolfe the dauntless hero came*

And planted firm Britannia's flag
On Canada's fair domain.

That reminded them of

Rule Britannia,
Britannia rule the waves
Britons never never never
Shall be slaves.

After that, Grant, who was drunk, stood up unsteadily and said, "Ah, who needs all that patriotic gore? When we came into port I'll tell you what we sang:

Away away with fife and drum
Here we come, full of rum
A-looking for women to peddle their bum
In the North Atlantic Squadron."

This song provided a moment of embarrassment which their good mood turned into laughter, everyone making allowances for Grant the wounded hero. That he was still here and able to sing reminded them that they had all survived the war, and nothing could now disturb their revels, and everything terrible would be put away in wrappings of forgetfulness, and all the joys empearled in happiness.

Jack walked Alison home later that night. At the door, she did not stop, but opened it and walked in. At that moment, he realized she was in the city alone and was inviting him into the house.

Kingston, Wanagami, August, 1945

Bernie Hallett walked down the gangplank, steadying himself with a hand on each rail. The war was still spinning in his head like a gyroscope. He stood on the pier, in the blood-stained battle dress he had been wearing at Fassoythe, looking for the enemy. Cranes were shrieking round him, locomotives howling, diesel engines roaring, air-brakes exploding. He was penned in between a huge wooden crate stencilled ANTWERP, PORT OF, EXPLOSIVES, FIRST CDN DIV. FOR THE USE OF, and the gigantic side of the *Empress* bearded with rust, towering up like a skyscraper, with the shadow of cranes swinging huge crates on taut cables over his head. A corporal in brown uniform got out of a brown car stencilled CANADIAN ARMY, saluted him and said, "Colonel Hallett?"

"Yes, Corporal."

The corporal handed him a letter. It read, "You are requested to report to the Commanding Officer of the Base Hospital, Major Dr. R.E. Payne immediately on landing. He will hand you your further orders."

Bernie got into the back seat and stared out the window, wondering, 'Why am I like this?' He hated steel. He hated engines. He could not tell the doctor about the trial. He had done nothing wrong. Why was he putting himself on trial all the time? The doctor could not help him. Imagine a doctor called Major Payne. What a stupid doctor he must be. He would say stupid things. The real crime was words. Wars are caused by beliefs. Beliefs are caused by words. The entire war had been caused by words fired out of mouths like bullets aimed with one purpose, kill. The less he spoke, the less he helped to kill Ed.

Major Payne shook his hand, invited him to sit down, and offered him a cup of tea. "How do you feel?" said the doctor.

'Terrible,' he heard in his head, but said nothing.

"What are you going to do now?"

Bernie thought, 'Weep.'

The doctor looked curiously at him. "I was thinking of the next six months, say."

Bernie shook his head. He did not want to be advised to do anything but what he wanted to do, and he did not know what that was.

He did not want advice because it would cause him to argue, and the trial every night cost him endless argument. He did not want psychiatrists bumbling around trying to help because he knew no one could help him. The only thing he could do was to end the trial somehow.

The doctor, who had sent many men home in damaged condition, knew that he could not help this colonel. Damaged men like Bernie Hallett were being discharged from the army and then discharging themselves from society. He thought of them as army vagrants. Many had already disappeared into the bush. Payne had seen the same thing after the Great War, when his father had gone into the bush in northern New Brunswick and built a cabin, one of hundreds that one could see throughout the Maritimes, the tin chimney sending up white smoke, a dog barking at the edge of a clearing where a man with a hoe had his back to the road.

Bernie was given $1200 and a ticket home. That was his discharge, and his thanks.

At home in Kingston his mother, wide and solid in a flowered print dress and tight hair, suggested that he take off his battle dress because it was so warm. He shook his head, and she asked once again, "What is wrong, Bernie, dear?" He heard the judge call the court to order.

"We're only trying to help."

His father Birdie, a thin acute man with a gentle smile, watched him without saying anything more than civilities. He was sensing the enormous change in this young man, formerly so sure of himself, whom he had called "a heaven-gazing Anglican." He understood because he had come home from the Great War feeling helpless and hurt, but had been forced to go to work right away and whatever had been wrong with him was left 'to sort itself out in time,' as they said in those days.

At the table on his first night home, Bernie's young brothers, twins aged 16, were gazing at him in perplexity, making him feel like a big stranger here. 'Who is this?' their wide brown eyes seemed to say. Their questions about the war revealed to him how far the facts were from what they had been told. 'Reality is grief,' he wanted to tell them, but it would involve conversation so he said nothing.

His father invited him onto the verandah to take their coffee. The evening was bright and peaceful, a few people strolling on the sidewalk waved at them. His mother handed him a cup of coffee and said, "There is no easy way to do this, Bernard. I'm sorry to say that Joan has moved to Ottawa and left you a letter. She told me before she left that she wrote to you months ago breaking the engagement, and we said nothing, thinking you would get the letter, but it appears that it must have gone astray. She left a copy here."

He laughed. "Look, it's typed," he said, and put it down.

His mother glanced at Birdie with a worried frown.

Bernie said, "It's so typical. She probably gives reasons." He started to laugh, almost hysterically it seemed to his mother.

Then he sighed and said, "Anyway, she's a nitwit. I don't know how I ever got hooked up with her."

His father smiled, but his mother said sharply, "Bernard, that's not like you."

"Mother, I'm not like me."

She sat back rebuffed, thinking, 'Whatever can he mean?' although he had just agreed with her.

He arrived at Wanagami Station in mid-August 1945. He had his kitbag, a knapsack on his back and $1120 left in his torn battle-jacket with the blood of Ed Burns black on the chest.

The *Wanagami Queen* was tied up smokeless at the town dock, covered with red dust from the iron ore in the train cars that had passed here every day during the war, and were now motionless mirages in the heat. He went into the Hudson Bay Trading Post, searching in his battle-dress pockets for the list of supplies he had made on the train.

The clerk, Darwin Hubbs, a tall bearded man with a huge broad head like a buffalo, said in a low sad tone, as if he had been here too long with the stuffed moose whose head thrust from the log wall over his head, "Welcome home, stranger. I hear you had a hot time in Berlin."

Bernie imagined the rest of the moose on the other side of the wall, kicking to be free. He thrust out the paper on which he had written the list of supplies he would need.

Hubbs looked at it, and then said, "Can't read these pecker-tracks." Bernie looked at the paper, getting ready to read it out, but something had happened to his handwriting. He could not make out a single word. So he said to Hubbs, "Going into the bush. I'll need outfitting."

"Going to winter over?" said Hubbs, as he started to walk around the store.

Behind and above him spread wooden drawers with brass pulls in which were set faded cardboard tickets naming the contents. He began placing items onto the low counter where trappers in the spring would thump down their catch. Grey Owl had traded here in the 1920s; beaver, mink and fox for flour, tea, salt, sugar. As Hubbs measured, weighed, wrapped, suggested, he questioned Bernie subtly, and realized that he was planning to go up into the Gowganda, 50 miles deep, build a cabin and winter over.

"Why don't you go back to your camp and winter over there? I know where you could buy a damn fine team of dogs. Cheap."

"Couldn't feed them."

"Set nets."

"Ice."

"I got an ice jigger here." He pointed up to the long, bowed jigger with the hooks which travelled by spring action under the ice, towing a line. "With dogs, you could come on out any time you like."

"Don't want to come out."

"Rough time over there, eh? Here's some new bully beef from Argentina. Eats up real good." He put in a case of the beef and said, "If you get sick."

Bernie stared at him thinking, 'I'm already sick.'

In an hour it was all there—axe, bow-saw, whetstone, hammer, screwdriver, plane, hand-drill, cooking utensils, cup, plate, bowl, nails, Robertson screws, stove-pipe, baling wire, toque, mackinaw, boots, leather gloves, beaver-backed mittens, green denims, wool shirts, citronella, fishing net, rope, .303 rifle, bullets, salt, kerosene lamp, lampwick, oil, snowshoes, canvas, wool Stanfields, four six-point Hudson Bay blankets, Baker tent, groundsheet, net-jigger, some seed potatoes, enough flour, beef, salt pork, dried peas and beans for three months.

He sat down by the dock in the shade and wrote a postcard to his mother and father. *Everything OK. B.*

Hubbs helped him load the canoe, then said, "Keep your wicks trimmed, eh," and walked back to the store.

Bernie kneeled in the canoe, waiting to feel happy as he had always done when setting out on a canoe trip, everything he needed embraced in those curving gunwales. He dug in the paddle. Keys, engines, money and death disappeared in his wake.

On the fifth morning, he paddled north up the Red Rock River through Diamond to Ghost Lake and began to unload on the shore of the island in the grey warm afternoon. He would keep the tent warm in cold weather by building a fire directly before the opening, with the tent flap poled high above the fire, deflecting the smoke away, so he started to build the green-wood backwall right away.

He was sweating so much in the heat that he was working naked. Once he looked up and saw his bloodstained battle-jacket swinging on a bush where he had just hung it. This was the first time, except when bathing or sleeping, that he had taken it off since England. He remembered putting it on in England, thinking, 'This will show them where I have been and what I have done.' He looked at the battle dress swaying a little in the breeze like a flag he had planted in this country.

The next day while he was cutting logs, the court martial in his head began again, so loud and strong he had to stop working. It always ended up with him being convicted and led away towards a door. Beyond the door was darkness. This was the lump of darkness containing something alive that was going to happen to him, and here the trial always stopped.

He sat in the clearing looking at the branch where the battle-jacket was swinging, and the courtroom door swung open. The door opened onto this place, this clearing. His sentence was to be here.

London, Paris, August, 1945

⚮

Dudley saw a blue airmail envelope lying on the floor inside the front door. No one had picked it up because the only maid-servant left in the house was on holiday. The stamp was Canadian, so he knew it was from Cat. The basement door opened and Flavia emerged, her face flushed, carrying the breakfast tray up from the kitchen. He said, "Good morning, my dear, but you mustn't strain yourself," although if she did not, there would be no kippers this morning. He stepped forward to take the tray, then remembered the envelope in his hand and pushed it in his pocket.

Flavia handed him the tray and said, "Was that the post?"

"Something from the War Office. There's a rumour I'm to get an OBE."

Flavia, who had seen the airmail blue of the envelope, and suspected he was hiding a letter from Cat, nevertheless was distracted by the thought of a medal for her husband. This would mean Buckingham Palace, being presented at Court again, their names appearing in *The Times*. "Well then," she said, as they settled down to the long table in the dining room, where her mother and father were already waiting, Max Frankfurter with *The Times* set before him.

"Good morning, good news. Dudley is to get the OBE," she said, to test him in what she still suspected might be a lie.

"What for?" said Max suspiciously, and Dudley laughed.

"Stands for Other Buggers' Efforts, don't you know."

"Begging from the Canadians and Americans, more likely," said Max. Flavia gasped but Dudley was used to Max by now, and said, "I dare say you've hit on it, Max."

Flavia had been making an extra effort to please Dudley since Cat had left six months before. She was feeling guilty because her mother had never chastised her for the scene with Cat: she thought this was because

Cecile had never shared Max's rejection of herself. Ever since arriving in London, Max Frankfurter had behaved towards Flavia coolly, but without the hatred which he had maintained religiously for 23 years and which was now exhausted.

He could not offer her forgiveness because he could not bring himself to ask her for it. And now, the hatred having taken shape, persisted without any strength in it, like rust that clings to the form that the strength has left, as Dudley said to Flavia, without much hope that she would realize the aptness of Eliot's concluding phrase, *Hard and curled and ready to snap*. It was this poetical streak in him, unsatisfied during his life, that had responded sympathetically to young Grant, and made him see why Cat loved him.

Dudley took the letter to Diana Cooper in Paris where her husband Duff was British Ambassador. She welcomed him in their magnificent drawing room which she had just redecorated at such an amazing cost that even the money-boffins at the FO in London were awed. She handed it back to him and said, "And now I suppose you want Flavia to go to Canada for the wedding." As she said this she realized that she wanted to go too.

"She doesn't know yet."

"She must know right away. You can not hide from a mother the news of her daughter's wedding, now can you?" She was thinking, 'How thick men are.'

"The point is, will she forgive Cat? I mean, I must say, I am rather fed up with it all. I mean, dash it, she goes to Occupied France and saves her dragon's-breath father, who hated her for 20 years and condescends to her every day he is living in her house. And now she treats her own daughter like a pariah, although Cat has been a biddable girl all her life and never caused her mother grief. People astound me."

Diana looked at him in some surprise, thinking she had not seen him so vehement for some time, and decided to skirt this minefield. She said, "These things are not done to gain gratitude, which is in any case always short-lived, but rather because one wants to do them, knowing the alternative is that one's conscience will make one's life intolerable, for a few minutes."

Dudley smiled, and she went on, "We have to come back to London tomorrow. I suggest you make the arrangements for flying over there—by the way, is money a problem—currency is so difficult now, it used to be so easy to skim along on a current of debt . . . ." She trailed off.

"Airplane tickets."

"Oh yes, for three of us—Duff can't leave here, of course, unless for something of crucial international importance, such as Ascot Week. Hush this up until you and I and Flavia are together, with champagne, and all will be well. I shall bring her a wonderful hat from Paris and tell her that she is to come to the wedding with us and to be good about it, and I think she will be—but it must be a *fait accompli*. That way, she will be forced to do what her better nature wishes her to do. And that suicidal pride of hers will be silenced. The art of handling people is to sniff out what it is they want to do and then make them think it is their duty to do it."

Georgian Bay, August, 1945

∽⟡⟿

Cameron Bannatyne turned on the radio in the living room at Stone Cottage to hear the CBC news of the surrender of Japan on Tuesday, August 14. The Emperor of Japan, the first in the long history of the nation to address his people directly, said in a squeaky voice, "We must endure the unendurable."

"Well, that's that," Cameron said, and raised his glass of scotch and soda. "To victory." Everyone in the room and listening through the french doors to the verandah repeated it after him, "To victory," and they gave three cheers.

Unable to bear the noise and heat indoors, Grant glanced at Cat sitting on the fender of the fireplace, and they got up and went outside. The memory of her first day here in 1939 was so strong that she felt a vague sickness heat her stomach. She took his hand and smiled at him, but his brow was anxious. "Are you all right?"

He said, "My dizziness has suddenly stopped." He laughed. "It makes me feel dizzy."

"That sounds like good news." They walked into the rose garden and sat on the cold stone bench in the shade.

Cat said, "Do you remember coming up to me in the garden just about here in '39? It was a hot day just like this."

"Not really."

"There were white butterflies—see, just like those ones— and bees were making the hydrangeas shake just as they are now, and I was thinking about you, and then the gong went for a picnic." She looked at him. "Remember?"

Just then Jack and Alison came out from the house and ran towards them. "Come on swimming," Jack called.

"Just a minute," Cat replied, and looked up at Grant.

"Oh sure," he said quietly. "The lake is still there too, just like in 1939."

For the other wedding guests due on Thursday, Cameron Bannatyne had arranged a private train to run on the CPR tracks to Mindemoya and to leave two sleeping cars there for the young men. The young women slept in the boathouse, in the changing rooms of the bathing platform, aboard *Spindrift*, or the marquee tent in the west garden, where the young men came at night to whisper their messages of love through the canvas walls. A summer kitchen under a tent was set up next to the main kitchen. In all, Cameron provided accommodations for 90 guests.

The weather held hot. Grey-haired men in white flannels played croquet on the north lawn with women in flowered dresses, and young men and women in shorts went sailing in the two dinghies, or picnicked in the islands aboard *Spindrift*. Couples walked the roads and shadowy paths through the woods, holding hands. Young women, glistening with coconut oil, lay for hours in the sun acquiring the tan that would acquire a man. Boys dove off the ten-foot tower, or aquaplaned behind the speedboat, and everyone danced at night to the Victrola on the north verandah overlooking the moon-barred lake. The sexual energy of the young people spread to everyone, like a flooded river in spring fertilizing regions arid for a long time.

As Dudley guided Flavia on their first dance together in six years, he kissed her rouged cheek. He said, "Do you remember, when we were here in '39, I said you could play a chukker or two on the verandah, didn't I, and here we are waltzing, isn't it fine?"

"Indeed I do," she said, thinking he wanted revenge for her resistance to Grant and his family.

"And what you said about Cat and Grant?"

"Yes, I said yes." She had already given in to Diana's advice to come out here, but her teeth were clenched. She hated hearing him crow.

But Dudley had freed himself from her during the war. He had calmed the Cabinet storm that had erupted over her mission to France. He had coped with what he thought of as her "madness" over Cat and Grant. He had settled quarrel after quarrel between her and Max.

He lifted her arm and whirled her round, and she thought, 'Well, and why not?' and then realized that this was the answer to the question, 'Are you glad you came?' And when she realized this, she felt permitted to be happy for the first time in a long time. She danced, surprised to be happy, until everything she had been dreading about this trip faded away with the thought, 'Everything is all right now.'

She said in Dudley's ear, "Thank you, my darling, you are indeed my good angel," and Dudley smiled, and sighed and felt his patience with her was rewarded. At that moment he felt a stirring of ardent interest in her such as he had not felt since far back in the war, perhaps before it, and he pressed her close to him.

Watching them dance by, Sarah thought, 'There is nothing so sexy as a wedding,' and gazed round the floor in satisfaction, for it was she who had arranged the details of this grand gesture made by Cameron.

Next morning, just after breakfast, Jack was seated at the big oak desk in the second-floor landing in front of the fireplace, where he had often sat during the Christmas holidays, doing homework. He was trying to write a witty speech in praise of Cat, before he made the toast to the bride. He stared at what he had just written:

In this family lately, everything that has happened has been subject to the great fact of marriage. That life should be continued into the next generation and that this young man and this young woman should happily and solemnly swear to continue it, in love with each other, has been agreed to be an undertaking so great that although it must be consummated in private, it should be celebrated in public with a ceremony enjoining the young couple to do what they so fervently wish to do that they must be prevented from doing it until the ceremony is over.

He laughed, balled up the paper and hurled it at the fireplace, and jabbed at the next sheet. *You can only succeed at monogamy by the exercise of virtues which make it unnecessary.*

'Cut the bloody quips,' he thought. 'What people want on a wedding day is genial sentimentality.' He lit a cigarette and drank some coffee, wishing he were outside with Alison. He was wearing shorts and his bare thighs were sticking uncomfortably to the cracked leather of the chair. He could smell roses, cut grass, white raspberries, and sweet william drifting through the window, and hear voices of people emerging from the dining room below. Someone passed behind him going to the stairs and said "Good morning," but he only grunted and continued staring out the window, wishing he were out there. He wrote of the bride's beauty, her amiable, delicate nature, and gave up, knowing it was Alison he was praising. Then he remembered something Grandfather Bannatyne had said to him the previous night, after he had told the old man, "I'm thinking of getting married."

"Have you picked the winner?"

"She's here. Alison de Pencier."

"I noticed her. Very sweet-natured girl."

"I'm pretty much in love with her."

"Does she know what you're considering?"

"I don't know myself. I might propose this weekend, but I'm not sure."

"Jack me boy, you mustn't vacillate. In marriage, love is no substitute for determination."

That made up his mind. Rapidly and firmly he wrote what he wanted to say in the speech, folded the paper and stuck it in his pocket.

He found Alison downstairs, and said, "Would you like to see our birchbark canoe?"

She came with him to the gloomy launch house where the white birchbark canoe hung in the rafters. He asked, "Have you been on a canoe trip since you were at camp?'

"No."

"Would you like to go on one?"

"Yes, but it would depend on who was going."

"I wonder what a canoe trip honeymoon would be like."

"It would be wonderful," she said immediately.

"That's what I thought."

Very excited, he went to the door of the launch house which opened onto a mass of huge rocks on which he had often run to the bathing platform 50 feet away, bouncing from the pinnacle of one rock to the next, four or five feet above the shallow water. He now ran lightly across them, reached the wooden walkway round the changing rooms, turned around and saw her hesitating in the dark doorway of the launch house. She started to go back in the launch house to go the long way round through the woods, when he made a chicken cluck sound, taunting her. She looked over towards him and thought, 'If you want him, jump.' She leaped to the first rock, where she stopped, looking at the next, a steep point on which she could not stand. She would have to do as he had, ricochet from rock to rock. He called, "You can do it, just don't stop." She jumped, and kept on dancing till she arrived right beside him. He said, "Great. Will you marry me?" She looked up at him breathless from the run and couldn't speak. Her smile said 'Yes.'

Ferdie, Eleanor, and Grant Giovanelli, Cameron and Sarah Bannatyne, Max Beaverbrook and Diana Cooper, Rafe and Patience de Pencier, Dudley, Flavia and Cat Treloar, in sundresses, sunshorts, white ducks, crested blazers, straw hats and dark glasses that cancelled their eyes, were seated on lawn chairs watching Jack and Alison finish their tennis. At the beginning, Jack condescendingly threw her a lead, 0-3, thinking he would take the last six games in a row, but she was too good for him and won. Jack came off the court with a grim look, having twisted his injured knee. "You've got a nippy style," Max said to Alison, who smiled and wiped her brow with her bandanna.

Jack, who liked this wry old man, so short, wrinkled, and busting with energy, lay down on the grass beside him and said, "Uncle Max, I always follow your advice. What can I do about my backhand?"

"Take lessons," said Max. He sipped his gin and tonic. "I think your father would like to give you some advice about those papers of yours.

The ones you want your father and me to publish. That you got from young Clara Dunsmuir and what's her name, in Germany."

"Clara von Metternich," Jack corrected him, "and the Countess Tatiana von Zollerndorf, née Princess Tatiana Miloslavsky."

Ferdie said, "Jack, we've been talking about all this, and we felt it would be best if you just let the whole thing drop."

Jack got up to sit in a chair and looked at his father who was wearing, as he liked to do in the summer, garish colours, white flannels, white canvas shoes, blue and white striped socks, and a turquoise shirt with a blue and white silk ascot knotted at his neck. Why would a serious man dress so frivolously?

He asked, "Why is that?" hoping that they had good reasons. He did not want to pursue this strange business, but needed a compelling reason to give to Tati.

Cameron spoke up now, his deep voice as usual adding gravitas to his words, "The editor, Henderson, looked at it, and he says it's a lot of nonsense. Quite likely the whole thing is a fake."

"Did he say why?"

"Well, he doesn't read German so he doesn't give chapter and verse," said Ferdie, a close friend of Henderson, "but he can read between the lines."

"He can read between the lines that he can't read?" Jack said. Grant snickered.

"There's no need to be sardonic. Henderson knows our readers' wants, and it isn't this nonsense about 'Good' and 'Bad' Germans."

"But just a few weeks ago, my CO ordered me to go all over Germany to help sort out the good 'uns from the bad, for the Nuremberg people. Those were his exact words."

"I think you've missed the point, dear boy," said Max, who did not realize how condescending his acquired English phrases sounded in Canada. "The point is, that there *are* no good Germans."

"But that is just what these papers show. There were, and that's why you can't reject them without even reading them. After all, no one disputes that a bomb went off in the bunker, do they?"

No one disputed this. He looked around, impatient with these old Empire lovers.

Max coughed, and looked at Cameron and then at Ferdie as if for approval, then cleared his throat. But before he could speak, Alison said, in her light high voice, "May I say something?"

"Of course, my dear," said Max.

"I've read them, and I agree with Jack."

"In German? Do you read Old German?" said Max. "The writing all changed you know in 1941."

"Gothic German, or Old German as you call it, was never used on typewriters, so these are in Roman German, and yes, I read both."

Ferdie said, "Henderson says there is no interest in Toronto, or indeed anywhere in Canada, in finding out about good Germans because everyone for six years has been taught there are only bad ones. The argument about Nuremberg is specious because the difference that they are finding out is between bad Germans and dangerous bad Germans. The ones who have committed crimes against millions of people." He put his hand to his neck fingering the scar of the shrapnel which had wounded him at Ypres.

"I should say so," said Flavia, "including my father and mother."

"These people helped refugees escape from the Nazis, including your father and mother," Alison persisted. Everyone was quiet, seeing not the serene young woman with the happy smile, but a quite different Alison, informed and determined. "They risked their lives every day. When Tati came back to Berlin after meeting Jack in Annecy, all she put in her report that day to Klaus von Zollerndorf, her husband, the man who planted the bomb at Rastenburg, was . . . well here, I'll read it to you." She began reading aloud in German, then said, "Sorry," and translated.

Got off at Zoo Station, badly bombed but operating, 12 hours late, first train blown off tracks by bombers near Frankfurt-am-Main, three killed, I was knocked out, bruised, finished in a goods wagon. No electricity in flat, no water, phone working, Klaus at Zossen, bombers coming.

"This is a young mother who was carrying a suitcase full of bomb fuses to assassinate Hitler. She was almost killed, and that's how she reports it."

"Was that German you were speaking just now, my dear?" said Rafe.

"Yes, Dad."

"Are you studying German, I was under the distinct impression that you were in Art History or something."

"Yes, Dad. German is very useful for Crete and Troy."

"Well, good for you. Useful in the ninth century as well. Carolus Magnus spoke Frankish which had elements of Old German, as well as Latin."

There was a baffled pause after this, as often happened after the professor spoke. His speeches came like oracles from another world which they respected for reasons that they had all forgotten.

Max waited the few seconds that people customarily allowed for the professor's words to evaporate harmlessly, then said, "But Cameron asked me to comment, and I can tell you as a former Minister of His Majesty's government charged with providing the weapons we needed after Dunkirk—well, never mind all that—we had to fight, damme, and my newspapers blasted the Hun morning, noon and night— where was I? Dammit Cameron, you shouldn't fill my glass every chance you get."

"Perhaps you mean you shouldn't empty it every chance you get," said Cameron, and Max burst out laughing. They all roared with laughter, and no one would look at Jack. He was feeling more and more excluded from the general accord, but more and more obstinate.

Alison said, her voice squeaky with tension, "It's a newspaper you publish, I should think you would want to publish this, because it seems to be news to all of you."

This got a round of laughter, and cries of "I say, well done," and *"Touché."*

Jack looked at her with delight. Everyone else was derisive, except for Grant, looking as usual, strained, as if it was all a bit too much for him. Their smug faces said, 'We are right, we don't wish to discuss it.'

Jack said in a vehement low voice, "There were Germans who believed in the things we were fighting for. Tati deserves better than starvation." A hubbub of voices clamoured as if a gauntlet were thrown down, "Not in my lifetime . . . I didn't go to war to help feed those murdering Krauts . . . twice in a generation . . . the Hun is a bad 'un . . ."

Alison said something, but no one paid any attention to her light voice. Max said, "There has already been a good deal of criticism of my Lord Bishop of Chichester for his remarks in *The Times* in favour of the Germans, and I will not sully my hard-won newsprint with such rubbish, and there's an end to it." Max understood the fear, bitterness and loathing that was still burning in all of them.

Jack said, looking right at him, "What these people say is not rubbish."

Everyone was quiet. Jack was breathing hard. His father glared at him, his mother looked anxious. Beaverbrook said in a low voice, "Young man, I admire your ardour and I have no doubt as to your courage, but I can tell you from long and bitter experience with the Hun, there is no saving him. He is a warmonger, there's an end to it, and the few honourable exceptions you may have met do not disprove the generality of that truth."

"I have met them and you have not, Alison has read the papers and no one else here has, so we know that what you are saying is untrue."

Alison looked at him, fearing he had gone too far. His mother patted the air with her hand to say, 'Calm down.' Jack looked at Alison, thinking she was the only person who understood what he was saying.

Ferdie Giovanelli's hand was twitching by the ribboned package of documents on the table beside him as if he were thinking of flinging it away, and Jack imagined his father feeding the papers into the incinerator in the woods, the last record of the devotion of Tati and Clara burned in a forest 4000 miles from Berlin. He felt he was parting irrevocably from his father when he said, "I'll take those, Dad," and picked up the package. He put his hands over the papers in his lap.

Max held the floor for a long while with stories of Churchill, the hero of the day. The topic of Tati's papers was now banned. To most of the people in the garden, peace was nothing but the continuing pleasure of victory.

On Saturday morning, August 18, the wedding party left Stone Cottage by car to drive three miles through farmland and forest to the small white wooden church built at the ancient naval base by the British in the War of 1812. Jack walked with Grant up the wide aisle, and stood beside him as he turned and looked down the aisle at the sound of the wedding march. In the hot white light of the doorway stood Dudley in his morning coat with Cat in white silk and taffeta on his arm, looking composed but stiff. Jack saw Grant's face, a dark glower, with the hint of a bitter smile, and wondered what was going on in his brother's mind. He patted Grant on the shoulder but his brother did not seem to notice. Grant was thinking, 'There she is, dressed in white like a nurse to take care of me for the rest of my life.' For a moment, he felt so bitter that he almost wept with frustration, and then straightened his shoulders as if he were on parade.

Cat looked down, distressed by his bitterness. She feared she was wasting her life with this marriage, but her fists were clenched inside the bouquet of roses. They exchanged the vows enshrined in the holy old words, kissed under the lifted veil. This time Grant smiled at her, and she felt the rush of yearning for him she had felt six years ago when, with his eyes lifted towards the treetops and listening to a bird singing, thinking thoughts she had imagined were prophetic and poetic, he had, without intending anything, taken her life.

Jack made a speech before toasting the bride on the sunny lawn south of Stone Cottage. He made a few jokes and then said, "They met right here at Stone Cottage, six years ago now, almost to the day. Many things have happened to them since then, and we have seen how Grant has made a remarkable recovery, even from winning a medal. This augurs well for them, I think. Grandfather Bannatyne helped me the other day when I was asking for a little advice about some nuptial plans of my own. I had said I was in love and thinking of getting married . . ." He paused and looked straight at Alison standing not far away to his left, looking up and smiling at him. His heart thumped hard, knowing her smile meant 'Yes.' He mouthed the words "I love you" towards her and she blew him a kiss. He lost his train of thought for so long looking at her that people began to cough, and he said with a big smile, "Grandfather Bannatyne told me, when I was asking for advice about love and marriage, 'In marriage, love is no substitute for determination.' And I think today, at the close of this very long lovers' campaign, we are witnessing the wedding of two persons who possess both those great qualities."

Here he turned and smiled at Grant and Cat, then finished with, "Now I can not say, having shared a bathroom and a bedroom and a sports locker with my big brother, that he is a speckless saint, but he has been tried and found not wanting, and as for Cat, well, I ask you to join me in raising a glass to the loving bride." He lifted his glass, looked at Alison, and said loudly, "The bride."

That evening, the single and married, the young and old, friends and strangers, did their hair, put on makeup, and dressed for each other. They danced and ate and walked hand in hand on the lawns and on the dock to admire the rising moon, looked each other in the eyes as they turned around the dance floor, embraced and kissed and undressed each other, and for a while lived without regret or yearning or sorrow or ambition or worries and were happy. This happiness lived on long afterwards so that years later, all those who had been there would say to one another, "You were there, wasn't it wonderful?"

Wanagami, Autumn, 1945

Bernie Hallett was gaunt, bearded, long-haired, when Joe Killsbear came paddling in one warm day in late October and let the tilted canoe sit on its reflection in the ice-calm water. He said, "*Ah neen shoganosh.*"

Bernie knew the reply, '*Ah neen nishnabe,*' but said nothing. He wanted Joe to go away. Joe knew why Ed had died.

The canoe drifted closer, then Joe got out and sat on a log and pulled out papers and tobacco. He rolled and lit. He passed papers and tobacco to Bernie without a word, and Bernie rolled and lit. After a bluejay had called and a red squirrel had run around the clearing and yellow birch leaves had fallen, Joe got up and pulled the pack from the canoe, and put it on the shore. He had come here to ask Bernie to go moose hunting, but now he said, "I don't think you're going to make it here."

Bernie said nothing, thinking, 'You're probably right.'

"Why not winter at the camp?"

Bernie thought, 'Maybe I will.'

Joe paddled away.

In the pack were flour, oranges, lemons, tea, salt, sugar, pork, moose pemmican, fish-hooks, a net and three copies of *Uncanny Tales*.

The next day Bernie packed up his gear. He portaged it all twice, then paddled around the point of Sand Bay to the camp. The air was bright and cold, the wind at his back and he blew down the bay like a sailboat, steering with his paddle in the water, and his breath blossoming out in the sunny air before him.

He waited for winter as they had crouched in the trenches waiting for the attack. He wanted winter because snow would silence the gunfire, bombs, telephone shouts, cries, groans, laughter, screams, tank-roar, rocket whine, sizzle of bullets and dying men whimpering.

Snow would make Ed stop gargling blood.

The grey clouds built and swirled, then came down low at him like fighter planes. Wet snow loaded branches that broke and slumped onto the flimsy roof, tearing loose a strip of metal that hammered like machine guns in the wind, snow blew through the cracks beside the chimney and hissed on the hot stones like bullets hissing past his head, the mercury shrank to a stub, trees exploded like rifle shots, and the whine of the wind was the shriek of Stuka sirens aiming straight down at him in the trench open to the sky with his hands holding each other in his gut so they would not fold up over his steel helmet. Branches groaned all night against tree trunks like wounded men.

Two days later, splitting wood in snow to his knees, the new-iced lake glittering dangerously in the sun, the trestled canoe a long white coffin, he heard a command, 'Down on your knees. Head on the stump.' He kneeled with his head to the cold wood and heard the words surging through his head, 'I will be better, I will be hopeful and not despair, I will be thankful and full of praise.'

'You're too weak.'

'God has given me something stronger than strength. God has given me faith.'

His forehead was cold. He thought, 'It's over.' He stood. His eyes were cold, his feet were humid in the boots, the frozen birch flew apart as he struck. The war had retreated.

When the lake was locked away under three feet of blue ice, he began to cut and haul the blocks for summer. One night, feeling he had accomplished a lot and therefore might be cheerful, which he formerly avoided because it would magnify the sorrow that would come later, he remembered the camp library in the dining room.

He shovelled away the snow by the door and went in. The frozen books in green mouldy covers still stood where they had been left in 1939. They crackled when he touched them, their cold pages opened stiffly, reluctant to part from each other. He pulled out *The Canadian*

Settler's Guide by Catherine Parr Traill and *Roughing It in the Bush* by her sister, Susanna Moodie.

He read the guide book that night after dinner before the fire, and came on the sentence, "In cases of emergency it is folly to fold one's hands and sit down to bewail in abject terror; it is better to be up and doing."

He thought of the conventional little English girl coming out here in 1832 to live in a log cabin in the bush, writing these lines in a room so cold she had to hold the ink bottle between her legs to keep it from freezing, and began to laugh, a little rusty chuckle that was the first since he could not remember, maybe since Ed died.

"Oh Bernie," he said aloud, pronouncing his own name fondly, "'tis folly to bewail, it is better to be up and doing." He was more or less in love with Catherine Parr Traill.

In spring, Bernie climbed Dreamer's Rock cliff and sat on warm granite in the sun, looking west over new pale green in patches among old dark green.

He got up and walked casually to the edge and looked over, 200 feet straight down to the first scree, then water torn open by busted rocks. Treed hills rose away to a blue that seemed to be the sky but was the colour of nothing. 'Everything is nothing,' he thought. 'Why should anyone kill himself? There's been enough killing for a lifetime. It is better to be up and doing.'

A red canoe with two people crawled up the lake.

When he got back, Jack and Alison were sitting on the dock in the sun with their gear piled around them and their canoe pulled up on the beach.

"Glad to see you, sir," said Jack. "I'd like you to meet my wife. Alison, this is Colonel Hallett."

"Just plain Bernie," he corrected. "I hope you'll stay for dinner. I've got spring pickerel."

Alison said, "Thank you. That sounds wonderful."

EPILOGUE

Grant and Cat Giovanelli bought a house in Toronto with the money given by Max Beaverbrook. Grant published a collection of his war poems, which had a small success, but wrote nothing more. He drank too much, depended more on Cat, sold life insurance for a while. Cat graduated in medicine from the University of Toronto, specializing in brain trauma and made several original significant contributions to techniques pioneered by the Montreal Neurological Institute. They had two children, one girl, Victoria Sarah, and one boy, Joe. In 1961 they went to Germany and found Richard Müller, the German diplomat Grant had met in Dublin. Müller helped Grant to find the young sailor Grant had taken prisoner on *Sheguiandah*. They met in Bonn, and Grant asked him why he had joined such a dangerous service. The man said, "Because my father starved to death in 1919." They went to Frankfurt to see Cat's grandparents, who received them indifferently. When Cat left, she remarked, "That was like a school reunion—I hardly recognized them, and we have almost nothing in common any more." The Frankfurts died in 1962, never having seen their two great-grand-children.

Ferdie Giovanelli continued successfully as publisher of *The Times-Loyalist* for many years. Eleanor Giovanelli took piano lessons, thinking she might resume the career as concert pianist that she had once dreamed of. She thought 'Resume my career' although she had given only one performance in 1937 in a hall she rented herself. Mainly she played golf and mah jong.

Cameron Bannatyne died in 1946 of a heart attack brought on by his exertions during the war. After his death, Sarah travelled, stopping off many times at Max's houses in London, the Bahamas and the South of France. Over dinner one evening in April 1954, on the *terrasse* at the Restaurant Bacon at Cap d'Antibes, he told her she was the inspiration for his new book. He lived a long and happy life, giving away millions of dollars, having many friendships and affairs, and died a wealthy man in 1964.

Dudley Treloar was awarded an OBE in 1946 for services to the Empire. He died of cancer in 1971. Despondent after his death, Flavia failed in a suicide attempt in 1972. Cat and Grant visited her several times, and she doted on her grandchildren. She moved to Toronto in 1976 and died in 1984.

Joe Shearer lived at his parents' house with Yvette, whose parents were shocked and grieved at her marriage. But Yvette's mother began to write her daughter, who planned a visit to Québec City, with a side-trip to Laurentville, in hopes of a reconciliation.

Clara had her baby, a healthy boy whom they named Klaus. Captain Ernie Fiske agreed to be his godfather. She and Peter, with the two children, and Tati, stayed in Schenkenberg until 1949 when Germans were allowed to emigrate. They went to Toronto, where Peter opened a riding school, and Tati taught music. Then Peter decided that the climate in Niagara was good for wine grapes, and made a huge success of his winery there, with the help of Clara and Tati and Helmuth. The boy was good-looking and intelligent in every aspect of school. Many times he was called a little Nazi and Hitler lover and the principal would do nothing about it. Clara went to see the guilty boy's father, who called her a Kraut bitch, and slammed the door in her face. At night sometimes Helmuth sighed when he thought of his handsome brave father, and wished his life were over so he could meet his father again.

Bernie Hallett refused to teach history any more, and returned as director to Camp Wanagami in 1947 with Joe Killsbear as program director. They continued for many years to teach white-water canoeing and woodcraft to white and aboriginal children.

Albert Speer was tried at Nuremberg for war crimes and sentenced to 20 years. He was released in 1966 and wrote a notable memoir.

Johannes Blaskowitz was accused of war crimes, and jailed. Awaiting trial, he jumped into a deep stairwell and died.

Henke Overmanns starved to death in the American camp at Rheinberg in autumn 1945.

Raoul Laporterie survived and was awarded the medal for heroism by the Yad Vashem Institute in Israel. Nine years later, the French government awarded him the Légion d'Honneur.

A small stone monument to the memory of the victims of 1944, which did not mention Marianne, was erected by the people of Grenade-sur-l'Adour in 1979.

Nikolai Miloslavsky died of starvation in Berlin in March 1947. His daughter and his nephew Wilhelm von Benzdorf also died that year, of TB brought on by starvation.

Helmuth James von Blücher was arrested by the Gestapo in 1944, imprisoned, tried and executed in April 1945.

Hans Bernd Gisevius escaped to Switzerland, survived and wrote a valuable account of the resistance.

All the other members of the resistance associated with Klaus and Peter were arrested and executed.

Jack Giovanelli entered university in 1945 to study English and music. He woke every morning with the uneasy sense that he had started on a life of pleasure without satisfaction. In the spring of 1946, Jack and Alison were married and took their honeymoon on a three-week canoe trip through Wanagami. Then Jack was asked to contribute music and lyrics to a musical show at Trinity College, which was so popular it was repeated eight times and filmed by the film club. A revised version for the general public succeeded at the Royal Alexandra Theatre in January, 1947. Intent on creative work, he was happy.

Alison finished her Master's degree at the university and painted a show for a small gallery, which sold out in the first month. She was asked to paint the sets for the professional production of Jack's show. She also designed the costumes, which, along with Jack's discharge pay, brought in enough money for them to live. They had three children, Raphael, Marianne-Louise, and Patience. In 1956, Jack and Alison walked, cycled and hitchhiked through France. In Esperacedes, they found the shepherd Becker who had saved Jack, and bought him a drink in le Bar de Georges.

Jack returned Tati's papers to her after she had emigrated to Canada. She wrote an expert and sensitive introduction but 141 publishers in Germany, London, New York, and Toronto turned them down. They had the manuscript of the papers privately printed in English and German, and circulated them to friends and relatives. They offered free copies to university libraries, which refused them. In 1981, sensing a change in political climate in Germany, they offered the book to a big publisher in Berlin, who accepted it. The book was an immediate best seller. The title was *After We Died*.

Endnote

James Bacque's best-selling books have been published in nine languages in eleven countries around the world.

Interviews with eye-witnesses and research through six Western countries gave him authentic background for this fictional retelling of the Second World War.

Bacque was educated at Upper Canada College, and Trinty College, Toronto. He and his wife Elisabeth have four children and nine grandchildren. They live in Toronto, and Georgian Bay, Ontario.

Readers interested in learning more about the author and his books may consult www.jamesbacque.com. They will find material about the creation of the novel, along with source notes, maps, and suggestions for further reading.